DEDICATION TO DR. ABD'EL HAKIM AWYAN

Pay attention to whatever inspires you,
for it is "spirit" trying to communicate with you,
that's why it's called "inspiration" as "in-spirit."
—Abd'el Hakim Awyan

H ello, I am Penelope Torribio, author of *The Ghost of Tomb 11, Tel el Armana Egypt.* I am dedicating this book to Dr. Awyan, an Egyptian Wisdom Keeper who grew up on the Giza Plateau. Dr. Awyan is founder of the School of Khemitology. The School of Khemitology's mission is to bring together researchers from many different disciplines to discover real truths about ancient Egypt's sacred buildings and their possible connection to sacred sites all over the world.

I first learned about Dr. Awyan on my first tour of Egypt in 2007. Regretfully, Hakim passed on a year later, in 2008, before I had an opportunity to meet him in person. However, because of the many videos of Hakim telling his stories and sharing his knowledge, I grew to feel like I actually knew him. Nearly twenty years later—when I started writing my second novel in the Charles Dayton Stratton mystery series located in Egypt—Dr. Awyan just jumped into the novel, contributing his own stories and some of his theories and knowledge.

Thank you, Patricia Awyan Leymanbof Horus Rising Productions, for allowing me to use your photo of Dr. Awyan and for assuring me that Hakim would have been "tickled pink" to be portrayed as a character in *The Ghost of Tomb 11, Tel el Amarna, Egypt*. A surprise ending to this story is that my husband and I joined Patricia on a wonderful tour of Egypt in January and February of 2024. See khemitology.com if you think Egypt might be in your future.

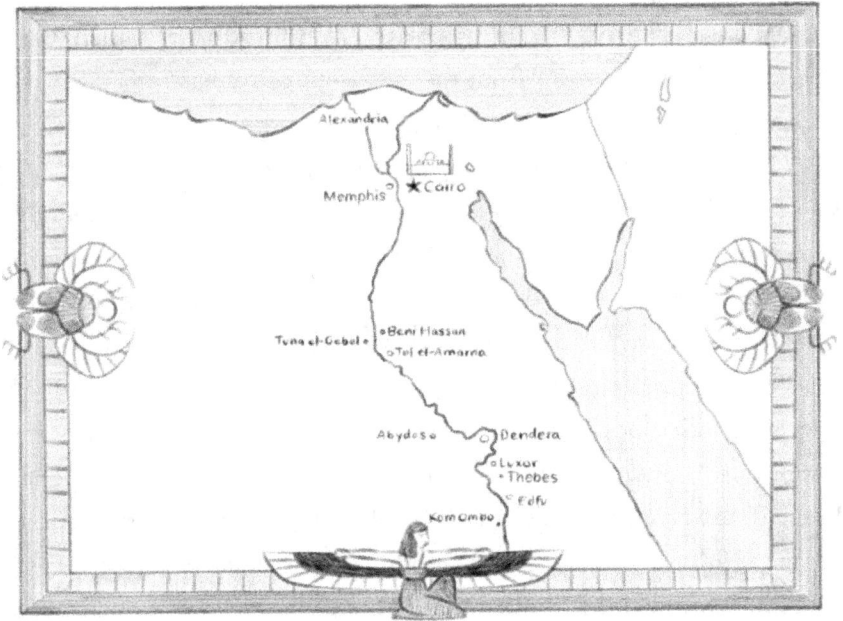

ACKNOWLEDGEMENT

A special thank you to my talented granddaughter, Ava Azarmi, whose illustration for the chapter heading of Tomb 11 has brought a unique and captivating visual element to the book. She completed her illustration just before graduating from high school. Now, at the publication of the *Ghost of Tomb 11, Tel Amarna, Egypt,* she is a student at Cal Arts majoring in animation.

Thank you also to my daughter, Sarah Torribio, a professional editor, talented journalist, songwriter, and screenwriter. Sarah's meticulous editing has not only polished my first novel in the Charles Stratton series, *The Ghost of the Jangling Keys,* but also my second and longer novel, *The Ghost of Tomb 11, Tel el Amarna, Egypt.* I look forward to her continued editing on my third book, which I am just forming in my mind, with the possible title of *Ghost of the Jaguar People,* Palenque, Mexico.

I am deeply grateful to Linda Cook and Ann Broadbent for their invaluable feedback on Tomb 11 from the viewpoint of readers unfamiliar with ancient Egypt, and for Ann's encouraging email:

"Hello Penelope! I just finished your wonderful book...weeping the last 15 pages. A mixture of love for the sheer beaty of the story, the loving and dear characters, the depth of your incite and fascination for all things Egyptian, and a touch of bittersweet as I close the last page! There must be at least two or three more books to follow!!! Thank you for sharing this incredible journey."

When I began writing The Ghost of Tomb 11, I was in a writer's group associated with a local bookstore, The Book Bungalow, in St. George, Utah. I want to acknowledge my friends and fellow writers, Carolyn McDonald, Diane Richardson, and Valerie Paitoon. Thank you for supporting me as I began the journey of writing The Ghost of Tomb 11, Tel el Amarna, Egypt.

I must acknowledge the authors of hundreds of books and articles I have read about Egypt over the last twenty years. I would like to give special recognition to E.A. Wallis Budge's books, where I learned a little about writing hieroglyphics and the early Egyptologist, and Robert Feather's book *The Cooper Scroll, where he posed the idea that the treasures listed in the copper scrolls likely came from Akhenaten's great treasure.*

And finally, a special thanks to Phillip Glasses, a noted American composer, for his opera, *Akhenaten,* based on the translation of Akhenaten's writing. This beautiful opera helped build an emotional bond between Pharaoh Akhenaten and me.

CONTENTS

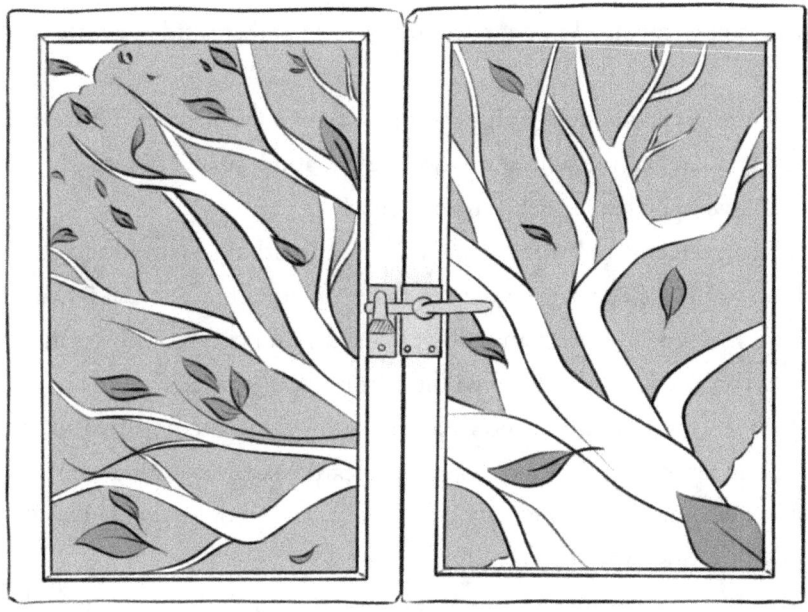

CHAPTER 1

WIND

C harles Dayton Stratton III heard a strange rattling at the casement
window of his third-story room at the Château du Mont, a boys'
school in France. Two windows attached in the middle by a brass latch
moved in and out, in and out like they were breathing. Old Limbs' branches
were waving wildly outside as if the tree were trying to warn Charles about
something like maybe he shouldn't leave for Egypt tomorrow.

What! Why did he think that? Charles had dreamed of seeing the pyramids since he was a little boy. And now, just because there was this strange
wind and things weren't going the way he'd planned, he was thinking he
shouldn't go to Egypt. The brass latch rattled louder. Old Limbs' branches
reached out, tapping on the windowpanes so hard Charles thought the glass
might shatter. Maybe Limbs just wanted to say goodbye. Charles flipped the

1

latch. A strong wind pushed into the room with a whoosh, bringing with it a flurry of leaves and dust. His roommate David's neatly-stacked homework flew up to the ceiling. The pages circled around and around like little paper airplanes.

Charles yelled goodbye to his tree, his very first friend at the Château du Mont, and latched the window. Leaves, dust, and homework settled to the floor. Scowling, Charles picked up the debris.

The dark-haired boy wondered for the hundredth time why David's mom and dad wouldn't let his roommate go to Egypt with him. They said their son was too young to visit such an exotic place without his parents. But Charles' parents didn't think he was too young to travel to Egypt. They had arranged for Jacques, the assistant at the Château du Mont, to accompany the boys. David's parents knew Jacques. They had heard Madame Constance say she couldn't run the school without him. Certainly, he could handle two boys who were almost twelve years old.

But David's parents wouldn't change their minds, not even when Charles' mother had called them from Nigeria to explain the wonderful and educational trip they'd planned for the two boys. A strange moaning sound now joined the rattling of the brass latch. Even the wind seemed to be in sympathy with the boy.

Charles cried out to no one, "It's not right going to Egypt without David!"

The wind moaned and whistled louder, and the brass latch shook.

It was David who'd sent Charles' story about the two ghost children on the fourth floor of the Château du Mont to *Ghost Stories Magazine*. If he hadn't, Charles wouldn't have sold his first story, "The Ghost of the Jangling Keys." He wouldn't have earned his first money from writing, five hundred dollars. The publisher of *Ghost Stories Magazine* had invited Charles to submit more articles. He'd even enclosed a list of *One Thousand Famous Hauntings*.

While Charles was looking at his check, David was reviewing the list. It was his roommate who recognized that Charles' next story should be about *The Ghost of Tomb 11, Tel el Armana, Egypt,* because Charles loved Egypt so much.

David was right. Ever since Charles could remember, he'd loved everything Egyptian, especially learning about the discovery of ancient tombs by Egyptologists like Howard Carter, Margaret Benson, and A.E. Budge. Charles had even taught himself to read and write hieroglyphics from Budge's books, *First Steps in Egyptian Hieroglyphics* and *The Hieroglyphics Dictionary, Volumes 1 and 2.*

Both boys agreed that Charles' next story should be about the Ghost of Tomb 11. There was just one problem. How were they going to get to Egypt? Then, a miracle happened. At least, it seemed like a miracle. Charles received a letter from his mother.

Dear Chucky,

Next month, you will turn twelve years old. I cannot believe you are growing up so fast. Your father and I want so much to be with you on your birthday, but something urgent has come up. We must go to Central America.

We will be out of touch for nearly a month. I probably shouldn't tell you this, but it is a little bit dangerous, or we would take you with us. Don't worry, we will have security.

I know this can't make up for our missing your birthday, but you can have any gift you want, just write back soon.

Love, Mother

At first, Charles was mad. He had so many questions. Why did his parents have to go to Central America? Why couldn't they take him with them? What kind of danger? What security? And what did he really know about his parents, who'd sent him away to school a year and a half ago and had each visited only once and never together?

Then Charles remembered something. He and David needed to get to Egypt. Charles immediately wrote his parents telling them the only thing he wanted for his birthday was a trip to Egypt with his roommate David. He suggested that Jacques, Madame Constance's all-around man at the Château du Mont, would be a great chaperone.

Charles' father wrote back, saying an Egyptian tour sounded very educational and that he'd make all the arrangements for the trip. It was perfect—except David's parents said he was too young to travel to Egypt.

Charles looked towards the window at Old Limbs, who seemed to have calmed down a bit. His branches were now just gently waving back and forth, back and forth. It was too late to change his mind. The plane would leave tomorrow morning. Charles pulled his leather suitcase from the closet and tossed it onto the bed. He hadn't used it since his arrival at the Château du Mont, which felt like a thousand years ago.

He unfastened the gold clasp on his light brown suitcase. As it lay gaping open on his bed, he tossed in clothes, toothpaste, a toothbrush, and a comb. He added an English-to-Arabic dictionary, a traveler's guide to Egypt, and a copy of *The Egyptian Book of the Dead* his father had given him. Finally, Charles placed a book his mother had sent him into the netting on the top side of the suitcase.

The book was a collection of poems by Percy Bysshe Shelley, born in 1792. It was a small book, maybe six or seven inches high, but the maroon leather cover and the softly glowing gilded pages made it look important. Charles' mom had placed a note inside the book, right where it opened to a poem called "Ozymandias."

The poem was about a man who discovered a giant broken statue in the Egyptian sand. His mother said she thought of Charles when she read this poem, not just because he loved Egypt but because she believed one day he'd grow up to be a great writer like Percy Shelley.

Having read the introduction and a couple of long narrative poems, Charles wrote an essay about Shelley for his English class. He wrote in his paper that he particularly liked Shelley's explanation of poetry: '*Poetry lifts the veil from the hidden beauty of the world, and makes familiar objects be as if they were not familiar.*'

Charles didn't know if he could ever learn to write like Shelley, but he thought he understood what the writer meant. A poet should write so people see things differently, even commonplace objects.

Outside the casement window, Limbs stood stock-still, like a statue. The wind had stopped. Charles went to the closet, stood on his tiptoes, and reached for a package in the far corner of the top shelf. It was wrapped in tan mailing paper and tied with a thick white cotton cord. Stamped on top of the package was an image of a purple crown and the words *Royal Teinturier*. What did that mean? Charles reached for his French-English dictionary and looked up the phrase. *Teinturier* meant dry cleaners; he should have guessed that.

His friend Farak gave him this package last Christmas, saying that since Charles loved Egypt so much, he might like to have a real Bedouin outfit. The Egyptian boy told him in a gloomy voice that he'd worn these clothes only once, the day his father brought him to the Château du Mont.

When he arrived at the school in his brand-new Bedouin clothes, Madame Constance told Farak that all of the boys were required to wear uniforms. Farak despised the Château uniform with its short navy-blue trousers, matching navy-blue jacket, white shirt, and short blue-and-white striped tie. The uniform was topped off with a ridiculous blue cap, with a small bill and the school's initials, *CDM,* embroidered in gold thread.

Farak said it was the saddest moment of his entire life. He never wore his Bedouin clothes again. He even remembered the date of the last time he wore them, September 30, 1975, nearly ten years ago. He'd kept the clothes for some reason, even though he'd outgrown them. Farak said he thought it might be a kind of fate, so he could one day pass them on to Charles.

Regarding the uniforms, Charles knew exactly how Farak felt. When he'd arrived at the Château du Mont, Madame Constance told him he had to give up his white tennis shoes, corduroy pants, and colorful polo shirts for that exact same silly-looking uniform.

When Farak gave Charles this package, he'd meant to try the Bedouin clothes on, but the Christmas holiday was filled with events. Then David and all the other boys returned from vacation, and the new classes began. Charles forgot about the Bedouin clothes, but he was thinking about them now.

He tried to break the cotton cord that tightly bound the package, but it was too strong. Pulling open the top drawer of his dresser, Charles found his red multi-purpose Swiss Army knife. He cut the cord with the knife's tiny scissors, then tossed the knife with a little white cross on its handle into his suitcase, thinking you never knew what you might need when traveling through Egypt.

Charles looked at the empty bed across the room. He couldn't even say goodbye to his roommate. David was captain of the Château du Mont's soccer team, and thoroughly devoted to *le football,* as the French call the sport. He and his team were at a three-day tournament in the town of Giverny, outside of Paris. Charles decided to write his roommate a farewell note.

Dear David,

Jacques and I leave tomorrow. I'll keep a journal so that, in a small way, you'll be with me as we travel through Egypt. And when I meet the Ghost of Tomb 11 in Tel el Armana, I'll tell him about my friend David Montgomery, the bravest boy I know. If I ever need courage, I'll think of you. When we are grown, we will go to Egypt together.

Sincerely, Charles Dayton Stratton III

CHAPTER 2

A BAG OF GOLD

S itting on his bed, Charles pulled back the brown paper wrapping from the package Farak had given him last Christmas. At the top of the pile of clothing was a beige-colored *gallabiyah*. He pulled the flowing robe over his head. Its hem fell almost down to the floor, exposing just the toes of his white tennis shoes. Next on the pile was a sleeveless overcoat called a *tob*. Charles slipped the blue-and-white striped cotton tob over his gallabiyah. He walked to his closet, where a mirror was attached to the back of the door. When he saw his reflection, he gasped. The boy in the mirror looked like a real Bedouin.

He gave a little twirl, feeling exactly like Peter O'Toole in "Lawrence of Arabia." That was the movie of the week Jacques had shown the boys in the ballroom of the Château du Mont several months ago. Charles loved that movie. It was about a real person, Thomas Edward Lawrence. Lawrence was an archeologist and British military officer stationed in Arabia and the Sinai Peninsula during WWI. He grew to love the desert and the Bedouin people. He even began dressing like a Bedouin.

Thomas Edward Lawrence was a noted military strategist and leader, but it was his writing—his description of the beauty of the desert and the heart of the Bedouin people—that made him famous all over the world. Jacques introduced the movie, saying "Lawrence of Arabia" was considered by many to be the greatest motion picture ever produced. After seeing the movie, Charles agreed. When watching the film, he actually felt like he was riding a camel deep in the desert with Peter O'Toole beside him.

Now, standing before the mirror, Charles thought he looked almost identical to Lawrence, except for one thing. He was missing a *kufiyah* or head cloth. Walking back to the package on the bed, he found a long cloth matching the color of his gallabiyah. Throwing on the kufiyah, Charles ran back to the mirror.

He looked ridiculous. One side of the cloth was much longer than the other. But when he pulled on that side to make it even, the other side became too short. After quite a few attempts, the kufiyah looked pretty straight. Charles remembered he'd left the *aghal* on the bed. An aghal ties the headscarf onto the top of the head. Keeping his hand on top of the kufiyah, he walked back to the bed. Without looking down, Charles felt for the aghal. Where was it? He knew he'd seen it when he picked up the headcloth. Maybe it fell under the bed. Charles tried to locate it with the toes of his shoes, but no luck. In fact, the effort caused him to trip on the hem of his gallabiyah. To keep himself from falling, he dropped his hand from the kufiyah. The headcloth slipped forward, completely covering his face.

"What is this, a Charlie Chaplin movie?" Charles shouted to no one.

He finally found the aghal. It was under his pillow. He had to start all over. Picking up the aghal, he noticed that it was no ordinary aghal, because Farak was no ordinary Egyptian; he was a Bedouin prince. The inch-wide leather was covered with *lapis lazuli*, red coral, and gold beads. Charles thought it was beautiful.

Returning to the mirror he arranged the kufiyah, fastening the aghal around the top of his head. He studied his reflection and decided that, except for his dark blue eyes, he could truly pass for an Egyptian boy, a Bedouin boy. He thought, you never know when you're going to have to not look like a tourist—when you might need to blend into your surroundings. Then, whispering aloud, Charles said, "This is especially true when looking for ghosts."

All that remained in the package were a large beige shoulder bag and cloth sandals with leather soles. In the shoulder bag, Charles placed a notebook, black, brown, and blue fountain pens, some brown ink, and the large Egyptian map his butler had sent to him from his room back in Newport, Rhode Island.

Charles jumped in surprise when he heard a knock at the door. Who could it be, and how could he explain why he was dressed like an Egyptian? While he was thinking this, there was a second knock, a little louder this time. If it were Madame Constance and she thought he wasn't in his room, she might do what she frequently did, barge right in to make sure Charles and David were "keeping their quarters tidy."

He cracked open the old wooden door. Ciel de Nuit, Madame Constance's black cat, meowed loudly, pushing his way through the narrow opening. Behind the cat was Francis Bacon Bernstein, the eight-year-old mathematical genius who'd taken to following Charles around the school. No one talked to Francis. Charles guessed it was partially because of his bright red hair and freckles and partially because the students found it disconcerting to know a boy so young who understood more about math than the math teachers—and wasn't afraid to point this out.

Charles opened the door to allow the small boy in, but Fran didn't move. He just stood there with eyes open and mouth gaping.

"Come on in, Fran, and hurry," Charles said.

"Wow! You look great, just like an Egyptian *sheikh*," the boy said, his words tumbling over one another. "Where did you get those clothes? Is that what you're going to wear when you get to Egypt? I came to say goodbye. I wish I could go to Egypt with you and wear Egyptian clothes just like you."

"I'm not going to wear Egyptian clothes in Egypt unless I have to—unless there's a need for me to blend in, you know, to not look like a tourist."

Fran nodded, indicating he understood.

"Sorry you can't come to Egypt with Jacques and me, Fran," Charles said. "Madame Constance thinks you're too young to travel without your parents. David's parents won't even let him go to Egypt with us, and he's nearly twelve years old."

Fran held out a white sack. "This is film, black-and-white. My mom sent it to you. She thinks you're a great photographer, and so do I."

"Thanks, I was just going to pack my Leica," Charles said, pulling a silver metal camera from the top drawer of his dresser. "This was my father's camera when he was a boy."

"Wow!" was all eight-year-old Fran could say.

"I promise I'll take interesting photos and tell you all about Egypt, especially anything having to do with mathematics. But for now, I have to get out of these clothes and finish packing."

Fran picked up Ciel de Nuit, whose name meant night sky, and walked out the door. Before Charles could take off his Egyptian clothes, there was another knock on the door.

"What is this, Grand Central Station?" he mumbled to himself.

Opening the door a crack, he saw the Egyptian teen Farak. He opened the door wider. Farak stared at Charles for a few seconds, then said quietly, "You look just like a Bedouin boy, Charles. More than I imagined you would. I came to bring you this notebook with the names and addresses of some of my family members, my tribe. If you are in any trouble, you can contact any of them. Just show them the pyramid replica I gave you during the winter break and they will do anything for you, even lay down their lives."

Charles wondered if Farak was kidding about laying down their lives, but he didn't look like he was joking. Actually, he looked both serious and sad.

"Can't you go home to Luxor before you go off to Brown University?" Charles asked the Egyptian boy.

"No, my parents are sending me with my brothers to tour the United States. They think it will help me to know more about your country. I wish, with all my heart, I could go with you instead, Charles," Farak said, handing him a small black notebook. The Bedouin prince bowed slightly and walked out, shutting the door.

A few moments later, there was another knock.

"What?!" Charles whispered. This time he was certain the person at the door would be Madame Constance, but it wasn't. It was Farak again.

He said, "I was so startled when I saw you looking like a Bedouin, I forgot to give you this."

He handed him a small blue velvet bag. Charles thanked him, and Farak bowed again and walked out the door.

Charles was very curious about what was in the blue bag, but he was determined not to do one more thing until he was out of the Bedouin clothes. Removing each piece, he carefully folded it and placed it into the shoulder bag. Then, sitting next to his leather suitcase, he reached for the pouch and poured the contents into his left hand. There, shining like pirates' doubloons, were eight gold coins, each larger than a quarter.

Examining the coins, Charles discovered they bore the image of a young man wearing a fez. He thought it was probably Farouk, who became an Egyptian king at the age of sixteen during the 1920s. Charles had written a report about King Farouk in his International History class. The ruler's full name was "His Majesty Farouk I, by the Grace of God, King of Egypt and the Sudan." Charles had read that some Egyptians loved this boy king, while others, including world leaders, believed he was a self-centered boy who greatly abused his power. In Charles' report, he had wondered what kind of king he might be at sixteen years old.

Charles' attention went back to the coins. He guessed they must be very valuable. His first thought was he should give them back to Farak. Then he remembered something Farak told him. In the Bedouin culture, one should never return a gift freely given. To do so was some kind of terrible insult. Maybe he could take the bag of gold to Egypt, and then, if he didn't need to spend the coins, he could return the gold to Farak. Examining the shoulder bag, Charles discovered a small pocket sewn inside. He carefully placed the blue velvet pouch into this secret hiding place.

Charles needed to pack one more thing: the replica pyramid. He hadn't planned on taking it with him for fear it might be lost or stolen. But at Farak's suggestion that he might need it, should anything happen, he went to his top drawer and pulled out a white stone pyramid wrapped in red cloth. He tucked the pyramid with its gold capstone into the shoulder bag. At that moment, he heard another knock.

"Who's there?" he asked. Ciel de Nuit meowed, calling for attention. He opened the door. The black cat slipped into the room, his tail held high. Behind the cat stood Madame Constance.

"Good evening, Madame Constance," Charles said, relieved he was no longer wearing the Bedouin attire.

"I just came to check on you, Charles. Jacques says that you will be leaving by taxi at 3 a.m. Do you have your passport?" Madame Constance asked with tight lips. She did not believe this trip to be a good idea. She added, "Remember to stay with Monsieur Gerard. Do not wander off."

"I will, I mean, I won't," Charles assured Madame Constance.

Shaking her head in concern, the headmistress picked up Ciel de Nuit and walked out the door.

CHAPTER 3

THE GIFT OF A PYRAMID

C harles reached for the pyramid inside the Bedouin-style shoulder bag
Farak had given him, removing its red cloth cover.

What did he know about it? According to Farak, it was said to be an exact
replica of the Great Pyramid of Giza, except it was only about five or six inches
tall. On the top of this little pyramid was a capstone covered in gold. If this
replica were accurate, it meant the Great Pyramid also once had a golden
capstone, an idea mocked by many of the so-called experts in Egyptology.

But this pyramid had something on it that Charles had never heard anyone mention or write about. He turned the little pyramid over and over in his hands. If it were an exact replica, the Great Pyramid must have once had some kind of writing on all of its sides, even the base.

Farak told him the relic had been in his family for hundreds of years. But no one in his tribe knew how to read the symbols on its sides. It appeared to be a language, but what language no one in his tribe knew. It was not hieroglyphics, that was for sure, as both Farak and Charles were well-versed in this ancient Egyptian form of writing.

When Farak gave Charles the pyramid replica last Christmas, he'd told him the story of how he acquired it. Afterward, Charles went straight back to his room to capture in writing a story that sounded straight out of *The Arabian Nights*. When Charles was young, his mother used to read to him from her collection of *The Arabian Nights*: fairy tales, poems, fables, parables, and anecdotes from the East and Middle Eastern cultures. Of course, this was before she and Charles' father tired of him and shipped him out to the Château du Mont.

Since he was all packed, it seemed a perfect time to read his journal containing Farak's story. Charles reached up to the top shelf of his closet and pulled out a leather-bound notebook. Thumbing through its pages, he found the title, "The Bedouins of Thebes and the Pyramid Relic."

He'd written the story in brown ink with the gold fountain pen his father had given him. Charles thought the brown ink made it look more ancient and exotic. Sitting down next to his open suitcase, he read Farak's story aloud.

I was seven years old. My mother called me out of my room and told me my grandfather wished to speak to me in the Tarabin Room. I knew I was in big trouble. My grandfather is the Sultan of the Tarabin Tribe. The Tarabin Room is a vast building adjacent to Grandfather's quarters. It is the pride of our tribe and is where all the great business of the Bedouin Nation of Thebes is conducted. Children are never allowed in the Tarabin Room; that is why I knew I was in big trouble.

The reason I was summoned to the Tarabin Room was my refusal to follow the commandments of my parents. To live, to survive, in the harsh desert, the Bedouins have developed strict rules everyone must follow. The people must abide by the decrees of their leaders, and children must follow the dictates of their parents. To fail to do so threatens the survival of everyone in the tribe. Even though Egypt's Bedouins are no longer allowed to live in the desert, the ancient rules still apply.

Charles had wanted to know more about the Bedouin code of conduct, but Farak had waved him away.

"Do not ask me, Charles, what happens if a commandment is broken. Every man, woman, and child has heard terrible stories of the consequences. Everyone agrees that if we are to stay together as a tribe, these commandments must be obeyed."

Charles continued reading the Egyptian teen's story.

I was supposed to accept, without complaint, all of my parents' decisions. However, I was only seven years old, and my father had just told me I was being sent to a boarding school in France. I could not believe it. I could not fathom that my family would abandon me.

I begged my mother to try and change my father's mind, but she would not stand between my father and me. I did not want to leave my parents, my people. I did not want to leave my Egypt, my horse, my camel. So, I said I would not go. I refused to leave my room, refused to eat, and if my parents came in, I would shout at them to get out. I was certain my parents had told my grandfather of my behavior.

Charles couldn't help but remember when his parents had informed him that he was going to the Château du Mont. He was nearly ten years old, and he'd acted the same way Farak had, maybe worse. He continued reading:

My mother escorted me to the Tarabin Room and stood there while I opened the ornately carved wooden door. It led into the cavernous space my cousins and I called the Room of Swords. We called it that because when there was a dispute between tribal members, my grandfather, wearing the Sword of the Sands, would call all those involved in the dispute to the Tarabin Room. He would lock the door, and no one could come out until a resolution was achieved. Sometimes this took several days. As kids, we would put our ears to the door and listen to the thunderous battles from within. Finally, an agreement would be made, and the door unlocked.

I was certain Grandfather was going to lock me inside this room until I agreed to go to the Château du Mont. It is said that once my grandfather takes a position, he never loses. I stepped through the doorway. It took my breath away. This was the most beautiful room I had ever seen. The floor was made of marble: blue, golden-yellow, and white tiles weaved together, forming amazing geometric patterns. As I stared down at the floor, I felt like I was entering another world.

My mother must have shut the door behind me. I stood like a statue, just inside the doorway. I could not move. I could not go forward, and I could not go backward. I lifted my gaze from the floor to the walls. They were covered by intricately designed tapestries in rich reds, blues, browns, greens, and yellows. The ceiling was twenty feet above my head. It is a replica of a night sky, painted indigo blue and sprinkled with white stars, linked together by gold lines. The stars and lines form animals and gods, many looking like they are battling each other.

Finally, I looked ahead to where my grandfather was sitting on a giant gold throne, about sixty feet ahead of me. He was wearing the regalia of a Bedouin king. Beside him was the Sword of the Sands. It's a daunting weapon, curved like a crescent moon well over three feet tall.

The Sword of the Sands belongs to the head of the Bedouin nation, the ruler, my grandfather. However, the man sitting before me didn't look like my kindly grandfather. He didn't look like the gentle-looking man who often came into my bedroom at night to tell me stories of when we were the Tarabin Tribe of the Western Desert.

'Come, come,' my grandfather said, waving me in. He was not smiling, and it took me some moments before I could convince my feet to move forward. As I did, I saw Grandfather was wearing an amulet as big as a dinner plate on his chest. It was made of gold with various colored gems surrounding a figure of

the sun god Ra, portrayed in the form of a falcon with a sun disk on his head. I had never seen Grandfather wearing this amulet before. I thought, I am in huge trouble.

In a deep voice, Grandfather said, 'So, you don't want to go away to France, to the school the Château du Mont? Is this true, Farak?'

'Yes, Grandfather, it is true. I do not want to go away from my family and my Egypt.'

My grandfather reached down and pulled me up onto his lap. I was small then, and he was very large. I sat on his lap, staring at the amulet. He spoke more gently then.

'You were chosen to go to school to become a financier. Do you know what a financier does?'

I said I thought it had something to do with money.

'You have shown, even at your young age, that you are brilliant at mathematics and analysis,' Grandfather said. 'I am going to talk to you like a grownup, Farak, and I want you to listen very carefully. I have told you many times about our history. When I was young, we lived as nomads in our desert. We slept in the sand, moving like a river from oasis to oasis, a separate nation, free. It was our belief that no one and everyone owned the land upon which we lived and traveled.

Then, a decree was passed, a terrible decree. It claimed that the rulers of Egypt owned all the desert land. The decree determined that we could no longer live as free Bedouins of the Western Desert. Many of our young men and women fought this edict, and many lost their lives. The Egyptian government was too powerful; they had too many soldiers and allies from Europe. We moved our people to the city of Luxor, bringing with us our great skill of raising and training camels and Arabian horses.

Unlike many nomadic tribes that were absorbed into the society where they were forced to move, our people have been able to sustain themselves and even thrive with God's gifts to us, camels and Arabian horses. However, the world is changing again. We can't keep our money under our mattresses. We must learn *how to manage our wealth if we are to help our people stay together to preserve our own culture, our own music, and our own laws.*

Unfortunately, we are not prepared. We are not educated in modern economic ways. You have been chosen to help us, to help your people, by going to school and learning the modern ways of finance. Know this, Grandson. As much as you wish to stay here in Egypt, we wish this even more. However, in life, we sometimes have to make hard choices. Great leaders, great men and women, and, in your case, a great child, must put what is best for their people over personal desires. Do you understand this, Farak?'

I nodded. Grandfather smiled, and I was no longer fearful of him.

'Good. Now I have some gifts and a story for you. The first gift is a bag of gold coins. They are very valuable. They symbolize our future, your future. You can't spend this gold in a store, but if you should need currency for a very great cause, you can exchange this gold for money in any country. Be very careful and don't tell others about this gold, for it is said to be a corrupter of souls. It is our secret. Do you understand this?'

I promised I wouldn't tell anyone, not even my father and mother. Grandfather looked pleased.

'Next, I will show you something few people have ever seen. It is called Aten or the Pyramid of Aten. As you know, Aten is the power behind the sun, the power behind all that is.'

Grandfather held out a small pyramid, five or six inches high. On top of the pyramid was a gold capstone. He said this pyramid was a relic that had been passed down from leader to leader of the Tarabin Tribe, for hundreds of years. A story and instructions were passed down with it. The story is that the relic pyramid is an exact replica of the Great Pyramid of Giza.

Examining the relic, I asked if that meant the Great Pyramid once had a capstone made of gold. Grandfather laughed and said, 'Yes, and it is said that when this gold capstone was upon the Great Pyramid, the morning sun would cause it to send out brilliant rays of light in all directions. The sunrise called men in fields and shops, and women in houses and gardens, to come together to celebrate a miracle: humankind's ability to create great beauty.'

'What do these symbols say?' I asked, turning the pyramid around and around in my hands.

'As of yet, no one has identified the language, so we do not know what it says. However, instructions to help discover the pyramid's secret are passed down from leader to leader. Every ten years, several replicas are allowed to be produced. These are to be given to special people who will take on the search for the relic pyramid's messages. I believe you are one of these people, Farak. Today, I am going to give you two replica pyramids.'

Grandfather gave me some directions. He said one pyramid was for me to keep. The other was to be given to someone I believed would help find the secrets of the relic pyramid. He warned me to be very careful who I gave the second replica to because I would be bound to them forever.

I asked him how one could tell the difference between a replica and the real relic. Grandfather said that was a good question. He showed me all four sides of the pyramid, then turned it upside down, revealing its base.

'Everything is the same on the four faces of the pyramid,' he said, 'but on the bottom, these particular symbols are only found on the original pyramid.'

I promised Grandfather I would discover what the writing said. He put me down off his great lap. Our talk was over.

I determined to discover the key to interpreting the Pyramid of Aten. However, the next thing I knew, I was flying to France to become a student at the Château du Mont. I found the school, the change in language, and the change in culture so different and so challenging that the memory of the Pyramid of Aten became fainter and fainter.

When I met you, Charles, that very first time in that little museum in the Egyptian artifact area, it was as if my mission had been dug up from a deep, deep tomb and a golden light shined down upon it. Your love of Egypt, Charles, brought the Aten Pyramid back into my life. And that is why I am giving you one of the replicas my grandfather gave to me.

Charles closed his journal and placed it back in the closet. It seemed to him a miracle that he, who had loved Egypt all his life, would be given such a gift by a real Bedouin prince. Maybe in his travels in Egypt, Charles could discover something that would help unlock the secret of the Pyramid of Aten. He wrapped the replica in its red cloth and placed it in the cotton shoulder bag, then locked the brass clasp of his suitcase. By seven o'clock a.m., Jacques and he would be on a plane headed for Cairo, Egypt.

CHAPTER 4

CHARLES AND MR. SMITH

The plane was sitting on the runway of the Charles de Gaulle International Airport in Paris. Charles was in seat 224C. He stared out the window at an unexpected thunderstorm. Bolts of lightning danced around the plane. He heard someone in front of him say it was the biggest thunderstorm he'd ever seen, and this guy was pretty old. Then, there was this huge crash of thunder. It shook the plane, and the sky opened. It looked like it was pouring the entire Nile River directly on the jet. The only thing Charles could see out the window were some blurry blue runway lights. Suddenly, he had an uncontrollable desire to jump out of his seat and dash out of the plane and into the rain. His old fear of adventure, which Charles thought he'd left behind in Newport, Rhode Island, reared up like a bucking horse.

"Run!" his mind screamed. Charles stood up. Pale and with eyes wide open, he looked to see if he could find Jacques. They'd been sitting together when they got on the plane, but the stewardess had separated them. She'd explained that Jacques was sitting next to an emergency exit, and children were not permitted to sit in these seats. She'd made Charles change places with some guy twelve rows forward. Evidently, he was too young to sit in the emergency row, but not too young to sit by himself as he flew all the way to Cairo, Egypt.

Charles felt cross and tired. He began to think dark thoughts, like nobody in the world really cared about him. He'd just about decided to get off the plane, with a plan to run away and join a circus, when the stewardess started talking about oxygen masks and floating seat cushions. It was too late. His adventure to Egypt was set to begin, ready or not.

The man seated beside Charles asked where he was from.

"Timbuktu," Charles mumbled.

The man smiled and said, "That is very interesting, young man."

Charles tried to remember where Timbuktu was, or if it were even a real place, but his mind was blank. The plane tilted up and up and up until the captain came on the loudspeaker and announced that they'd reached thirty-five thousand feet. Charles began to think about his trip to Egypt. He should have waited until David could go with him. He wasn't even sure he wanted to meet any ghost in Tel el Armana, not without his bold roommate. The ghosts at the Château du Mont weren't that bad, but you could never tell about ghosts.

The pilot came back on the loudspeaker announcing it was alright to move about the plane if necessary. Charles stood up to look for Jacques. Before he could find his chaperone, his eyes met those of a man sitting in 254C. When Charles looked at the man, all he could think of was the color gray. The man wore a gray suit. He had gray hair, expressionless gray eyes, and a gray complexion. Even the hat he held on his lap was gray. Without a break in expression and without blinking, the man stared straight into Charles' eyes. It felt like the guy knew or recognized him.

Charles had a creepy feeling about the man in 254C, but nature called. He got up and walked past the Gray Man toward the restroom at the back of the plane. The man got up, pulled his hat low over his eyes, and followed Charles.

"What is your name, boy?" the man asked Charles in a low, gravelly voice.

"My name is John Smith," Charles answered confidently.

"Are you going to Egypt?" the Gray Man inquired.

Charles wanted to say, "We're on a nonstop flight bound for Cairo. Of course I'm going to Egypt!" Instead, he asked the man his name.

"Robert Smith," the man answered with a tight smile. "Where are you from, Mr. Smith?"

"Paris, France," Charles answered. Looking directly at the man beside him, he returned the question. "Where are you from, Mr. Smith?"

"Chicago. Do you know where that is?"

Before Charles could answer his question, the red light on the bathroom door turned green. The conversation came to an end. Charles entered the miniature bathroom and locked the door. Why was that guy asking him all these questions? Why did the Gray Man sound like he already knew the answers? And why did they have the same last name, even if Charles was made up?

Slipping out the tiny metal door, Charles was relieved to see the Gray Man was no longer waiting there. Returning to his seat, Charles passed Mr. Smith without looking at him. He reached for his backpack, stowed under the seat, then secured his seatbelt.

Pulling out pen and paper, Charles wrote a note to Jacques: '*The man in 254C is acting very suspiciously. We'd better keep an eye on him. P.S. I call him the Gray Man.*'

Jacques came up to ask if Charles was okay. Charles handed him the note, whispering, "Don't read this until you get back to your seat." Then, in a loud voice, Charles said, "Thanks, Uncle Bruno. It will be great meeting my parents at the Cairo Airport, won't it?"

Jacques went back to his seat, confused. Reading the note, he wondered what Charles meant about keeping an eye on the man in 254C. How had the boy met him? Jacques concluded that Charles had a great imagination and was a very suspicious young man. Suddenly, out of the blue, Jacques remembered his meeting with Charles' mother. It was the ten-year-old's first Christmas at the Château du Mont. Mrs. Stratton had shown up unexpectedly. She requested that Jacques join her for tea in the writing room.

When he walked into the small room, a dark-haired woman wearing a maroon suit stood up. Crossing the room, she held out both her hands to greet him. It almost felt like she knew him. Up close, he noticed she had striking deep green eyes surrounded by long eyelashes. Strangely, behind those eyes, he thought, lay secrets and sadness. Jacques' mind turned back to the words she spoke.

"Mr. Gerard, I know my coming is unexpected. Even Charles does not know I am coming. I flew in from Morocco this morning. My husband and I are staying there for a few more days, then we will resume our travels down the coast of Africa in our yacht. Still, I just had to see Charles, even for a few hours. May I ask you to do me a favor?"

"At your service," Jacques responded. *He had no idea why he would say such a ridiculous thing to Charles' mother.*

"I plan to take Charles to Notre Dame de Chartres, the cathedral in the city of Chartres. My mother took me there when I was his age, and I still remember everything: walking the labyrinth following my mother, the rose window, the whole atmosphere like moving inside a giant and most wonderful kaleidoscope. It was so dark, with shards of rich color dancing all around me. I want Charles to see this, too."

"What is it that you would like me to do?" he asked.

"After Charles' and my tour of the cathedral, I must leave for Morocco immediately."

"So fast?"

"It is necessary, Mr. Gerard. We should be done with our tour around four o'clock. I want you to meet us outside the cathedral. I wish for you to come in a

taxi, not in a school vehicle. You are to return Charles to the Château du Mont, but first you must drive by the Eiffel Tower, and maybe stop for a croissant and tea. Meanwhile, I will take another taxi to the airport."

Jacques had wanted to ask why she was making something that could be easy, like him picking up Charles in the school car, so complicated. However, something in her eyes stopped him from asking.

Then she said, "Oh, yes, and Charles is not going to like this arrangement. He will not want me to leave."

Mrs. Stratton was right; Jacques had to drag Charles into the taxicab. Charles was yelling at the top of his lungs that he was being kidnapped. Charles' mother must have warned the taxi driver that the boy was a bit difficult, because he turned around and said, "Your mother told me to tell you that you must behave."

At that Charles began kicking, then opened the door, attempting to jump out of the moving taxi. When Jacques and Charles returned to the Château du Mont, the boy was so angry he didn't talk to anyone for an entire week. Jacques felt Mrs. Stratton's visit made no sense, so he decided not to think about it.

Now, what wasn't making sense was why Jacques was remembering her visit when he was on a 747 heading for Cairo. Since Charles had asked him to keep an eye out for the passenger in seat 254C, Jacques decided he needed to see what the man looked like without raising suspicion. Opening his briefcase, Jacques pulled out the copy of *The Egyptian Book of the Dead* Charles' father had given him. He walked casually past Charles' seat, then turned around so he could get a view of the Gray Man.

"Here is *The Egyptian Book of the Dead* you asked for," Jacques said to Charles.

"Thank you, Uncle Bruno," the boy replied in a loud voice.

Jacques scanned the people behind Charles. He found the man in gray with a gray hat on his lap. Now that he knew what the man looked like, he'd keep an eye out for him when they reached the Cairo Airport. The man looked harmless enough, but for some reason, Jacques, who never had premonitions, felt a sense of foreboding.

CHAPTER 5

THE TAXI DRIVER AND THE MENA HOUSE

Jacques and Charles walked out of the sliding glass door of the Cairo Airport. Immediately, a plain black car pulled up with a homemade cardboard sign taped on its side saying, "Taxi, American Spoken." A sturdy man in a green Hawaiian shirt with white flowers on it jumped out of the taxi and opened the back door.

"Where are you headed, dudes?" the taxi driver in the Hawaiian shirt asked.

Jacques answered, "The Mena House Hotel. How much?"

With a toothy grin, the man answered, "We will both know that when we get there, won't we, dude?" Grabbing their suitcases, he tossed them into the trunk of the car.

Charles looked at Jacques. Jacques shrugged his shoulders, then pointed toward the open door of the black cab. Charles climbed in. Jacques went to the other side of the car and slid into the backseat.

"My name is Samy," the taxi driver said as he pushed a cassette into the tape player. The taxi pulled out of the airport to the squeal of tires and the harmonies of "Surf City."

"It's Jan and Dean," Samy yelled out over the music. "Do you know them?"

Jacques said he wasn't familiar with them. Charles said nothing. Samy sang loudly along with the tape.

Going to Surf City 'cause it's two to one,
Going to Surf City, going to have some fun.
Going to Surf City 'cause it's two to one,
Going to Surf City, going to have some fun.
Two girls to every boy.

The taxi driver in a Hawaiian shirt, the modern airport, and the freeway were not what Charles had expected. It looked like any other airport.

Samy turned down the music and craned his head toward the back seat, asking, "How long are you going to be in Cairo?"

Jacques reached for his itinerary, but Charles answered before he could pull it out of his pocket. "Five days."

Turning his attention back towards the road, the driver said with enthusiasm, "Five days? Five days! You are in luck. It just so happens that my next job is six days away. I will be your driver. No worries. I know this city like the back of my hand. Just yesterday, I was driving this American around and he said to me, 'Samy, you know this city like the back of your hand.' What are you interested in? I know the best place to buy gold and silver jewelry, not cheap stuff like that tourist jewelry, 18 carats."

Jacques said, "We are not interested in jewelry."

"How about real antiques, Egyptian relics?" the driver asked. "Many people in Egypt will cheat the tourist. Not me; I am the real thing. My family has been in the antiquities business for almost a hundred years. We know the real stuff from the fake stuff."

Jacques said, "We are not here to shop."

"We are here to study and to learn," Charles explained. "After visiting the Giza Plateau, we plan to spend four days in the Cairo Museum."

Samy whistled. "Four days in a museum with all that old stuff? Most people can't take more than four hours. I'll take you to some exciting places. Do you like dead people, boy? Look at that area on your left. That's the City of the Dead, with miles and miles of tombs. It was a cemetery, but now it is home to thousands of people, no one knows exactly how many."

"The government came into a poor section of Cairo with bulldozers and pushed over their homes," the driver continued. "Men, women, and children had no place to live. The government didn't think about this, or they didn't care. Anyway, many families had to move in with relatives—dead relatives," Samy said with a chuckle. "What's your name, dude?"

Charles thought about saying his name was John Smith, but Jacques answered first. "This is Charles, and I am Jacques Gerard."

The driver spoke to Charles as if he were an old friend. "Chuckie, I have a cousin who lives in the City of the Dead. I could get you in there."

"You seem to have a lot of relatives here, don't you?" Charles asked. He looked at the hundreds of mostly small buildings, some square and some round. But Charles wasn't interested in modern Egyptian tombs, or anything modern, for that matter. He was only interested in ancient Egypt.

"You are from America?" Samy asked.

Charles answered, "We are from France, but we prefer to practice our English."

Jacques looked at Charles, wondering why the boy was telling their taxi driver he was French. Charles had his own questions.

"I notice that you're playing surf music and are dressed rather unusually for an Egyptian."

"Okay, yeah. My father sent me to America to go to school, UCLA. Everyone in my dorm would go down to Santa Monica Beach and surf," Samy said, smiling at the memory. "I must admit that I, myself, was a pretty good surfer. Then suddenly my father called me back to Egypt. We had a family emergency. I never went back and now, here I am driving the best taxi in Cairo."

"How long have you been driving a taxi in Cairo?" Charles probed.

"About four years, yep, four years," the taxi driver answered.

"Four years? Well, don't you think it would be better if you'd painted a sign on your car saying taxi, like the other taxi drivers? I mean, wouldn't it be better for business?" Charles asked innocently.

Samy looked up at the rearview mirror, catching the reflection of the young boy with a mop of dark hair and deep blue eyes. He said, "I have found that it is often a very good idea to learn to trust people. Do you not agree, Mr. Jacques?"

Jacques didn't know what to say. On the one hand, it seemed like Charles was a very suspicious boy. On the other hand, why did Samy have a handwritten sign on his car when he'd been a taxi driver for four years?

Without waiting for an answer, Samy said, "This is another one of my favorite songs." He cranked up the stereo even louder.

Little GTO, you're really lookin' fine,
Three deuces and a four-speed and a 389.
Listen to her tachin' up now,
Listen to her why-ee-eye-ine.

Samy turned down his music slightly and craned his head toward the back seat again. "What kind of car do you drive, Jacques?"

"I drive a French car, a Citroën."

Samy was impressed. "I love Citroëns! That is the car where you can drive on three wheels. How fast does it go?"

"I don't know. I never tried to find out."

"That's interesting," the driver said. "So you never tried to find out?"

Jacques looked almost embarrassed. Charles figured he didn't want to admit it was the school's car and that he didn't have a car of his own.

The taxi pulled off the freeway. Samy drove down an old, two-lane street. "This is the little town of Giza," he said in his tour guide voice.

Charles stared at the many small businesses lining the road of the town of Giza. "This looks like a one-horse town," he said with a country twang.

"What do you mean by that?" Jacques asked, staring at Charles.

"I heard that in an old cowboy movie. It just means that it's a small town, most likely with only one street."

"Well, that is what it looks like. But maybe we could call it a one-camel town," the taxi driver said with a cowboy twang.

Just then two soldiers on camels, their dark rifles lying over their laps, passed the taxi on the right-hand side.

"It looks like we should call it a two-camel town," Jacques said, laughing at his own joke.

The buildings were crowded together on both sides of the two-lane road. There were cement buildings that looked almost as old as the pyramids and small stores made of wood, some brightly painted in pastel colors, some desperately needing paint. And then there were the *kiosks* or temporary stores, small stalls shaded by canvas awnings that were every color imaginable: red-and-white striped, pink, blue, tan, gray.

Charles saw people in gallabiyah on both sides of the road: men in turbans and women with headscarves, some with veils pulled across their faces, revealing only their dark eyes. A sprinkling of tourists weaved in and out of the shops. A donkey cart with green plant material piled twice as high as the wagon bed passed the taxi on the left side of the road. The sun was at its zenith, sending out blinding heat and light. Jacques was grateful that Samy's taxi had air conditioning.

Now, this is Egypt, Charles thought. If only David were with him, it would be perfect.

The taxi driver pulled up in front of a two-story building, saying, "We'd better go in for a little food and drink."

Jacques protested, saying, "We'd rather go straight to the Mena House."

But Samy was already out of the car, pointing towards what he claimed was the best restaurant in town. The taxi driver in his green Hawaiian shirt entered, calling out that he had brought two very hungry friends. He walked to the back of the establishment, then bounded up a steep and narrow metal staircase that led up to what turned out to be the roof of the building.

A woman in a beige gallabiyah was sitting on the floor next to a square outdoor oven. The metal door was open. Inside its chamber was a combination of black ash and fiery embers.

"This is Rena," Samy said. "She is the best flatbread-maker in town."

Rena smiled shyly, adding, "You say this to all the bakers."

"No, not true. I bring all of my favorite customers here specifically for your flatbread, and the other foods, of course."

Charles watched as Rena patted a ball of dough until it was flat and round. She placed the dough on a wooden paddle with a two-foot-long handle and pushed it into the oven. The bright orange embers popped and glittered. Charles could see the bread puff up like a pillow. The smell of hot bread filled the air. After a moment, Rena pulled the paddle out of the clay oven, flipped the hot flatbread over, and returned it to the embers. When the second side was golden brown, Rena pulled out the paddle again and placed the flatbread on a red plastic plate.

Samy divided the flatbread into three pieces. Up to that moment, Charles hadn't realized he was starving. The flatbread was soft yet chewy, and all Charles could think was it tasted much better than the bread they served at the Château du Mont. Samy pointed to a table shaded by a red umbrella, then disappeared down the stairs. He returned with menus and glasses of water.

A voice on a loudspeaker outside called Muslims in the town of Giza to afternoon prayer. Charles walked to the edge of the roof and looked down to the street. People emerged from stores and businesses. Almost thirty men lay down little prayer rugs on the sidewalk. Soldiers on camels brought their animals to a standstill.

Samy rolled out a blue prayer rug. Kneeling, he dropped his head to the carpet. Then, raising his hands, he said, *"Allahu Akbar,"* which Charles knew meant "God is most great." Samy repeated this four times.

Charles turned from watching Samy back to searching the town, trying to memorize details he could put in his journal. While gazing down, he noticed something strange. While most people had stopped to pray or at least halted in respect, someone was weaving impatiently in and around the worshipers. That person happened to be Mr. Robert Smith, noticeable in his gray suit and gray gangster-style hat. Startled at seeing the Gray Man from the roof, Charles pulled back away from the edge. Samy stood up, scanned the area, and quickly rolled up his rug. He mumbled something about it being a little too hot to be eating on the roof and led Charles and Jacques downstairs to the dining room.

The smiling owner of the restaurant brought them lamb stew, steaming beans, rice, and more flatbread. Charles noted that Jacques ate like there was no tomorrow, a phrase his mother had used on him back in Rhode Island. Their lunch was topped off with a cool, pale orange mango yogurt drink.

Jacques stood up. "I must say that was delicious. Tell your friend upstairs that we enjoyed everything, especially her flatbread. Now, I could use a nap. We left the Château du Mont at 4 o'clock this morning, and my eyes are closing."

Samy got up and walked to the door. Charles watched as he looked up and down the street. "All clear!" the driver shouted with a wide smile.

Charles wondered what Samy meant by that. Did he mean everyone was finished with their prayers, or did the taxi driver suspect someone was following them? No, Charles shook his head. That couldn't be the case, because neither he nor Jacques had mentioned the Gray Man, Mr. Smith, to the taxi driver.

Jacques and Charles climbed back into the taxi, but they could have walked. The Mena House Hotel was only steps away from the restaurant. As the taxi pulled through the ornate gates of the palatial hotel, Samy, quite unnecessarily, pointed out the Great Pyramid. No one could miss it. It loomed above the northern part of the town of Giza and the Mena House. Charles wondered what the Great Pyramid, the only one of the *Seven Wonders of the Ancient World* still standing, was doing in the vicinity of this luxurious hotel House. Charles had imagined walking miles under the hot desert sun just to get a look at the grand, ancient, and famous structure. He imagined suffering great thirst, maybe even a sandstorm. But he never imagined seeing the Great Pyramid visible from their hotel.

As Samy pulled up under the hotel's *porte-cochére*, Jacques got out his wallet to pay the taxi driver. Samy waved him off. "I am your taxi driver while you are here in Cairo. We will work out this money thing later."

"I would suggest you take your money and run," Charles said. He'd heard that line in a movie. What he really wanted to suggest was that Jacques find another driver, one who looked and acted more Egyptian—who didn't play surf music and didn't have a cardboard sign saying, "Taxi, American Spoken."

Without paying, Jacques thanked Samy, informing him they wouldn't need his services tomorrow as they were just going to the Giza Plateau. The boy and his chaperone walked into an elaborately decorated gold lobby. Charles' father had made the hotel arrangements.

As the manager handed Jacques the room key, he said, "You are staying in one of the Mena House rooms with the best view of the Great Pyramid."

Jacques thanked the *commis á la réception* before turning to Charles and saying with enthusiasm, "This is convenient, having the pyramid at our doorstep. We won't even have to leave our room."

"Funny," Charles said peevishly.

Charles was grouchy. He thought it felt more like they were visiting Pyramid Disneyland than the ancient site, deep in the desert, he'd dreamed of all his life. Once in their room, though, as Charles looked out the window at the greatest and most mystifying edifice in the world, its magic overtook him. He wanted to go straight to the pyramids, but Jacques said firmly that they'd planned to go tomorrow morning, so that was when they were going to go.

Charles watched as his traveling companion unpacked his suitcase, placing everything neatly in the top two drawers of a beautifully carved wooden dresser. Charles stared out the window at the great triangular form looming before him. Jacques was lying on his bed with his tour book in hand.

"Did you know that no mummy has ever been found in a pyramid?" Charles asked, turning to look at Jacques.

"No, and I do not know if I believe that. I have seen many movies where the mummy rises out of the sarcophagus to wreak revenge on someone trying to steal his treasure. Why would they put this in the movies if it wasn't real?"

Charles stared at his chaperone, eyebrows pulled down, and lips pinched together in disbelief and disapproval.

"Yeah, then why did they put the flying elephant in 'Dumbo?' That's a movie," Charles responded. "Do you believe in flying elephants? Maybe you should read some books on Egyptology."

"I have a book, Charles. This tour book has it in black-and-white. It says Egyptologists agree the Great Pyramid was the tomb of the builder Pharaoh Khufu. Right here, it says that at some time in its 4,000 years of existence, tomb robbers broke through something called the subterranean chamber, and then emptied the entire pyramid."

"But where is the proof?" Charles asked.

"The proof is in this book," Jacques answered.

Charles disagreed. "From what I've read, a mummy was never found, nor did they find any treasure that would have been buried with the great pharaoh. There are no illustrations showing the pyramid's construction, or his mummy being placed in the Great Pyramid."

Jacques was engrossed by his tour book. "Look, Charles! They say many people believe that at one time the capstone of the Great Pyramid, now missing, was covered in gold. That definitely would have been something to see."

"We'll see it tomorrow," Charles said.

"How?" Jacques responded.

"In our minds," Charles answered with a laugh.

"A swim, that is what I am looking forward to. I never thought I would be staying in a hotel with a pool that reflected the image of the Great Pyramid. We don't even have to go to the archeological zone. We can see everything from here, tonight."

Charles looked at his chaperone, eyes wide open in disbelief, and said accusingly, "Jacques!"

"Just kidding, Charles. We are slated to visit the Giza Plateau tomorrow, and that is where we will be."

"By the way, I saw Mr. Robert Smith in Giza," Charles said nonchalantly.

"When?" Jacques asked, sitting up in his bed, all his attention now on Charles.

"When I heard the call to prayer. We were on the roof of the restaurant. I looked down over the side. Everyone had stopped for prayer–except for Mr. Smith. He was walking down the street, weaving in and out between the worshipers. He seemed to be looking for something or someone. I think the taxi driver noticed him too, because he peeked over the side of the roof, then immediately suggested that we eat downstairs because it was so hot."

Jacques looked at Charles curiously. "What makes you so suspicious of this Gray Man, as you call him?"

"I don't know," Charles said. "When he looked at me on the plane, it was like he knew me. And the questions he asked, I felt like he already knew the answers."

"Did you ever see him before?"

"No, I never saw him before."

"And what concerns you about our taxi driver?" Jacques asked.

"It's just that he has a Hawaiian shirt and a cardboard sign on his taxi, and he looked at me in the rearview mirror."

Jacques looked doubtful. "Personally, Charles, I think Samy has been helpful. However, I will keep an eye out for your Gray Man. Now, I know what we should do. It says in my tour book that no one should miss the opportunity to swim in the temperate water of the Mena House Hotel's pool. It says here that the water of the pool reflects the image of the Great Pyramid, like a mirror."

"Oh, no! I forgot my swim trunks," Charles responded sadly.

"Oh, me too. I did not think we would be swimming in the desert or in the Nile River teeming with hippopotamuses and crocodiles. So I failed to pack my suit. Maybe we can buy swimsuits here."

Jacques and Charles located the gift shop where they bought matching suits with the words Mena House. Arriving at the pool, Charles noticed that the blue water was surrounded by a large grassy area dotted with pink, yellow, purple, and orange flowers. He informed Jacques that he thought this oasis was out of place, being as they were so close to the Sphinx and the pyramids.

Still, the cool water felt refreshing as the man and boy waded into the pool, interrupting the perfect reflection of the Great Pyramid. After the swim, they had the Mena House restaurant's specialty, fried chicken.

Returning to their room, Jacques flopped onto his bed, and his eyes closed. Charles stared out the window. The dark sky showed a few stars over the top of the pyramid.

"Tomorrow morning, before dawn," Charles said to himself, "I'll be standing by the greatest piece of art ever created by humankind: the Sphinx."

CHAPTER 6

GIZA PLATEAU AND THE WISDOM KEEPER

Charles jumped out of bed as if an alarm clock had gone off. Although it was still dark, he could see the hazy form of the Great Pyramid of Giza and the promise of the sunrise to come. It was time to get up.

"Jacques, it's morning," Charles said.

"What time is it? "Jacques asked in a gravelly voice.

"It's 4 o'clock. The sun will be up soon. We need to be on the plateau before it rises," Charles answered.

"You know, Charles, the Great Pyramid has been standing there for over 4,000 years. I do not think it is going anywhere."

Charles gave Jacques a baleful stare. "Don't you know anything about Egypt?"

"I have to admit, not much."

"For the ancient Egyptians, dawn was a magical time, the time when Ra, the creator of all Egyptian gods and goddesses, steps into his Boat of a Million Years. Doesn't that sound great? Boat of a Million Years," Charles said, making his voice sound deep and important. "I read that phrase some-where. I wonder what it means? I'll have to find out when we get to the museum. Anyway, at dawn Ra is supposed to enter his boat and steer it through the day until the boat becomes weak and darkness is allowed back in. We need to be on the Giza Plateau at dawn—when the energy is strongest."

"Yes, but we are not ancient Egyptians, Charles," Jacques said, one eye open, the other shut.

"And I read that we have to be by the Sphinx, not the pyramids, for the best effect," Charles added, taking no note of Jacques' comment.

"All right," Jacques groaned, struggling to sit up.

Together, man and boy walked down the Mena House hallway. Pass-ing up the elevator, Charles led Jacques down the stairs that spilled out onto an even more golden lobby.

"Do you think there might be time for us to have a little tea?" Jacques asked, eyeing the dining room filled with excited tourists gath-ered around tables with white linen tablecloths, shiny silver teapots and little silver vases filled with fresh flowers. Charles kept walking.

They exited the hotel together. It was now 4:15 a.m., predawn. They weren't in France, that was evident. The air was dry, and there was the foretelling of the heat to come. To Charles, it felt just like it was supposed to. Sleepy taxi drivers lined the driveway, waiting for customers. They perked up when they saw the pair come out of the Mena House. "Taxi? Taxi?" they all called. Charles walked brusquely by, followed by Jacques.

"Our plan is to go straight to the Sphinx, which is on the other side of the Great Pyramid. It's farther away, so we have to walk really fast."

Jacques looked doubtful. "Why are we walking? If we took a taxi, we would be there in ten minutes."

"Because we need to know how it felt to be in the desert and to come across the pyramids and the Sphinx for the very first time. We need to feel how it would have been back in the ancient days, when nothing like the pyramid had ever been seen anywhere in the world. When nothing had ever been built that was as tall, as expansive, and as exacting as the Great Pyramid. Imagine how stunned we'd have been! That's what we need to capture."

"Capture how?" Jacques asked.

"Capture in our minds," Charles answered.

"You keep saying that phrase, capture in our minds. What exactly do you mean, Charles?" Jacques asked.

Charles thought a moment. "Because imagination—the ability to create something out of nothing, to put ourselves in a complex scene from the past, or even the future—may be the one thing that distinguishes you from a camel." Charles laughed heartily at his own joke, adding, "We'd better hurry Jacques."

Illuminated by the hotel's floodlights, Charles noted with distain the carefully manicured, unnatural landscape. Quick yellow butterflies fluttered from one flowering bush to another, and brown birds sang soft songs from palms and small feathery bushes, or picked at little bugs in the green, green grass. The guard at the gate saluted Charles as he passed. Then, Jacques and Charles turned right. They didn't need a map. The Great Pyramid towered above the little shops at the end of the town of Giza.

Finally, there were no more little shops, no gardens, and no more grass; there was just a long trail of buses, taxis, small trucks, donkey carts and camels carrying soldiers with dark rifles flung across their laps. All of these were headed for the Great Pyramid. All Charles and Jacques had to do was to follow everyone else.

The Great Pyramid stood at the top of an incline. A sharp triangle, like a child's drawing of a mountain, loomed in the shadowy dawn. Vendors in galabeya ran towards the buses and taxis, selling little replicas of the pyramids, crude paintings of Egyptian gods and goddesses on papyrus, and necklaces and keychains featuring the Eye of Horas or scarabs. There were also cameleers offering camel rides. It was the latter that caught Charles' attention.

Jacques was staring up at the Great Pyramid. Even in the early gloom, or maybe especially in the gloom, he was startled by its enormity. None of the photographs or movies he'd seen had managed to capture the startling magnitude. The smaller pyramids Khafre and Menkaure looked like little children next to the Great Pyramid, although Jacques had read in his tour book that the Khafre Pyramid was twenty stories high, a great feat of building for an ancient culture with only stone and copper tools.

Jacques wondered who'd planned this pyramid. And why had they envisioned such a strange and huge structure? Charles was right--there was something about arriving at this pre-dawn hour, that pulled him into a rapport, a connection, a bond with this ancient pyramid, which at this moment Jacques felt would never be broken.

Breaking into his chaperone's thoughts, Charles said, "I think we should take a camel to the Sphinx. It'll be much faster, and it's getting late."

Jacques shook his head. "I don't think so, Charles. That was not in my job description. I have read how camels are quarrelsome; they spit and, I believe, they bite."

"People have been riding camels for thousands of years, Jacques," Charles said as he caught the eye of a cameleer.

"Would you like to ride to the Sphinx?" the elderly Egyptian asked Jacques as he brought the camel down on its knees.

Jacques answered no and Charles answered yes, both at the exact same time.

"Just try it," the guide urged Jacques with a wide and friendly grin. "Come on. If you no like you can get off, no problem—your money back, guaranteed."

Jacques wasn't sure how it happened, but he found himself straddling the back of a kneeling camel. The guide said something to the dromedary. The camel immediately leaned forward on his front knees, then hopped up to his front hooves. Jacques felt his head jerk forward. His legs lost contact with the sides of the camel, and he desperately grabbed for something to hold onto. He could only find the edge of the camel's blanket, which seemed to serve as its saddle. He held on with both hands, hoping against hope that it would prevent him from falling from his nine-foot perch.

"Charles Dayton Stratton," Jacques yelled.

Jacques' torment wasn't over yet. The camel jumped from its back knees to its back hooves, causing his head to jerk backward. His legs flew out even further from the camel's sides.

"I told you I was not going to ride a camel," Jacques yelled.

The camel guide looked at Charles and smiled broadly, his dark eyes shining from a map of wrinkles carved by the desert sun.

"See, no problem," the cameleer yelled up to Jacques.

Jacques scowled at Charles from his precarious vantage. A second guide approached with another camel. This camel knelt before Charles.

"You are such a beautiful camel," Charles whispered, reaching out to pet him.

He was beautiful, if you didn't look at his funny face. A camel's face has a protruding snout, split upper lip and a flappy lower lip. The lower lip barely covers the bottom teeth, which extend well over the dromedary's upper teeth. The result is that camels look like they are perpetually smiling a very large, toothy, silly smile.

Charles' camel was the color of caramel candy. He had large, dreamy dark eyes with long, cartoon-like eyelashes. Like all dromedaries, the camel had a long neck, a stubby tail, and a single hump. The camel's reins and harness were made of a deep red cloth decorated with a headdress of gold tassels and bells. His saddle was a thick piece of red-and-green plaid fabric.

The driver gave Charles a little shove, and he was up on the hump of the camel. The boy did something he seldom did; he smiled from ear-to-ear. Charles instinctively pulled his legs in close to the camel's sides. His whole body followed the movement of the animal as it hopped from knees to hooves. "I was born to ride a camel," Charles thought to himself.

Charles Dayton Stratton III was in Egypt, on the Giza Plateau, on a camel, looking straight at the Great Pyramid, just as he'd dreamed hundreds of times before. He looked over at Jacques. Now that Jacques' camel was standing, it looked like Jacques, too, was born to ride a camel. Charles reached for his Leica camera, slung over his shoulder by a strap. He set his aperture, held his camera steady, and pointed his lens towards Jacques.

He snapped a photo of Jacques on a camel, right in front of the Great Pyramid. Charles didn't know it then, but he'd captured the exact moment when Jacques discovered he wasn't just the chaperone of a twelve-year-old student. He was in Egypt on his own adventure, maybe the adventure of a lifetime.

Charles looked at the cameleers, one young and one old. They were walking ahead of the camels, holding the reins. Jacques looked perfectly happy being led around the Giza Plateau like a little kid on a pony ride. Charles wanted to ride the camel by himself, like T.E. Lawrence did in the movie "Lawrence of Arabia," but he didn't have a choice.

The two cameleers kept up a conversation in Arabic, punctuated with laughter. This reminded Charles he'd forgotten to teach himself the major language of modern Egypt. He decided when he got to the Cairo Museum, he would buy a book on learning to speak Arabic. He also set a goal to pay attention to the sound of the Arabic language. For now, there was nothing for him to do but observe the awakening of the Giza Plateau.

Sunrise was coming. There was an increasing sound of the engines of trucks, buses and cars mixed with a cacophony of neighing horses, braying donkeys, roaring camels and shouting, galabeya-clad salesmen trying to gain the attention, and business, of tourists. The Giza Plateau wasn't what Charles had expected it to be, not like he'd dreamed it would be. He'd seen thousands of pictures of the Giza Plateau, yet was unaware of the road running alongside the archeological zone. He knew nothing about the town within walking distance of the Sphinx and the pyramids.

It was the photographers' fault, Charles determined. They simply didn't include the road or the town in their shots. Would he do the same? Would he turn his lens away from the things he didn't want to see in his photographs? Charles learned something: photos can tell the truth, or they can lie by omission.

Charles called down to the man holding the reins of his camel, pointing in the direction of a clump of mostly single-story buildings. "What's that place over there?"

"That is Nazlet El-Samman," the cameleer said. "It is my home and the home of many people who live and work here on the Giza Plateau."

"How long has the town been here?" Charles called out.

"It is said it has been in existence since the 7th century, but my family first came here in the 1930s, when the Mena House put out a call out for people to give camel and horseback rides to their guests."

"Does this mean you're a Bedouin?" Charles asked. "I have a friend who's a Bedouin. His family lives in Luxor. His grandfather is the sultan of the Tarabin Tribe. They're caretakers of camels and horses too."

"Yes, we know that family. The sultan is my father's great friend," the cameleer said.

"Wow! What a coincidence. What's your name?"

"My name is Yousef Awyan. My father's name is Dr. Abd'el Hakim Awyan. What is your name, young man?"

Charles had planned to be tightlipped and cautious throughout their journey, but something told him he could trust the English-speaking Egyptian man. "My name is Charles Dayton Stratton III. I can't wait until I tell Farak. He attends the same school I do, the Chateau du Mont in France."

"Yes, I believe I have heard about this boy."

"Your father is a doctor?" Charles asked.

"He is not a medical doctor. He has doctoral degrees in both Egyptology and archeology."

"He does?" Charles said, his blues eyes wide open. "I love Egyptology and archeology."

The Egyptian smiled at Charles' enthusiasm. "What my father is most proud of, however, is being the founder of the School of Khemitology."

"What's the School of Khemitology?" Charles asked, peering down from his camel.

"I can answer that question better when you are not up so much higher than I am," Yousef said with a laugh. "Now, we had better speed up a little so that you are at the Sphinx before sunrise."

Charles fell silent as his eyes focused on their destination, the Sphinx. They traveled over yellowish sand and past strange tunnels and piles of crumbled blocks, maybe from old temples. That was another thing the photographers had avoided. He'd have to ask Yousef about the tunnels.

As they drew nearer to the Sphinx, Charles remembered that the iconic monument was sometimes called "The Terrible One." It didn't look terrible to Charles. It looked like a housecat that was quit pleased with himself and his place on the Giza Plateau. Of course, Charles thought, if the 260-foot-long, 55-foot-tall statue somehow managed to come alive, pulling itself off its limestone base and pouncing in Charles' direction, he might consider it the Terrible One.

Jacques, Charles, and their guides arrived near the Sphinx, where camels waited to take riders back to the pyramids. The camels knelt and the boy and his guardian dismounted. Jacques commented on how much easier it was to get off a camel than to get on a camel. Once on the sandy desert floor, Jacques became strangely talkative. He told Yousef about Charles' love of Egypt, and how the boy had taught himself to read and write hieroglyphics. Jacques explained that Charles' parents had pressing business and had asked him to accompany their son on a well-planned tour of Egypt for the boy's twelfth birthday, which was one week away. Yousef's attention was pulled away from Jacques by a small black car kicking up yellow dust in its wake as it sped down a small dirt sideroad close to the Sphinx.

"You have come at an auspicious time, Charles," Yousef said. "My father, Abd'el Hakim Awyan, Wisdom Keeper, scholar of the ancient mysteries and head of the School of Khemitology, has unexpectedly come home. He's been in Europe speaking to various groups of archeologists. We didn't expect him back for several more days. I would like to invite you to join the group of people standing inside the paws of the Sphinx. When we are through with the sunrise ceremony, I will introduce you to my father."

"Wow, we're so lucky, Jacques!" Charles said as they walked towards the Sphinx.

Jacques agreed. Just then, a tall, thin Egyptian man in a sky-blue galabeya emerged from the back seat of the black car and stepped onto the sand. He waved to the group standing between the Sphinx's paws, a smile taking up most of his face. "I made it." The man, who Charles guessed was Yousef's father, turned towards the east. Everyone grew silent. He raised his arms high above his head. Exactly at that moment, a tiny red glowing spark, as strong as a laser beam, appeared above the dark and rocky horizon.

Charles had thought they were getting up early to see the Sphinx at sunrise. Now he understood they were joining the Sphinx as it welcomed the coming of Ra, the sun god, ruler of the sky, the earth, and the underworld. Ra, the creator of all. Everyone watched in silence as the sun transformed from a tiny dot, raising up to a full and perfect red sphere. Ra painted the scene in its scarlet and gold likeness.

The Egyptian man turned towards the delegation standing in the paws of the Sphinx. "Welcome!" he called out and led the applause that marked the end of the ceremony.

Yousef's father led the people as they slowly circumambulated the great reposed lion's body with the pharaoh's head. He called attention to the carving, the tail and, most particularly, the water erosion along the Sphinx's colossal base.

"Where'd that water erosion come from?" Charles asked.

Yousef, who was in front of Charles, answered, "There are several theories. Both involve the idea that the Sphinx is much much older than most Egyptologists believe. The first theory is that, once, the Nile River ran at the foot of the pyramids and the yearly summer flood caused the water marks on the Sphinx. The second theory is that at one time this entire area was not desert but instead a tropical region, and a great rainfall caused the water damage. We at the School of Khemitology are still studying this mystery. But we know this much: unusual water marks exist in what is now a desert region."

Charles had no idea what the School of Khemitology was, but he liked the name, and he intended to find out as much about it as he could. He and Jacques joined the people sitting on the ground between the paws of the Sphinx. Dr. Abd'el Hakim Awyan, Yousef's father, stood before them.

"I see there are some new people here and some old ones, though not nearly as old as I am," he said. "Some say I am as old as the Sphinx, but I contest this." Everyone laughed.

"By old, I mean the people who have been with us before and who may know something about the Khemit School of Ancient Mysticism. By new, I mean those who may know little or nothing of Khemitology. I must make it clear to our newcomers that, despite the name, it is not a school."

A school that wasn't a school. It sounded like a riddle to Charles.

"We are not teaching known theories to people," Dr. Awyan continued. "Rather, the School of Khemitology is a gathering place for those searching for clues and evidence to put forth supportable theories regarding the history, construction and function of Sphinx and the Egyptian pyramids, and their connection to other sacred sites all over the world. Our members represent all disciplines, talents, and interests."

Charles looked around, wondering if anyone else was interested in ghosts.

"Most traditional Egyptologists, historians and archeologists claim the Great Pyramid was built during Pharoah Khufu's reign," Dr. Awyan said. "They estimate it took 24 years and thousands of slaves, using a stone-to-stone method, to build."

"We disagree," Dr. Awyan said, pointing to the Great Pyramid emerging from the dawn. "Our mathematicians have calculated that to build a pyramid 482 feet high, using 2.3 million stones—some weighting up to 80 tons—would require the builders to place one stone every two minutes. Does this make sense to any of you? "

Charles raised his hand high in the air, as though he were back in a classroom at the Chateau du Mont. "Yes," the old Egyptian said, pointing towards the boy.

"Why does everybody believe the pyramid was built in 24 years, especially since they had no metal tools during Khufu's time?" Charles asked earnestly.

"That, young man, is a very good question. If you get a chance to meet one of these esteemed scholars, you should ask them," Dr. Awyan suggested to Charles.

Charles thought, tomorrow Jacques and I will be at the Cairo Museum, he would try to find someone to answer regarding the watermarks on the Sphinx and the practicality of building the Great Pyramid in twenty-four years.

CHAPTER 7

DR. AWYAN

C harles noticed the dark-haired woman wearing a flowing white dress and sitting cross-legged in the sand next to him.

She spoke up, pointing to Charles. "This boy asked a very good question, Dr. Awyan. Why do most Egyptian scholars refuse to look at the Great Pyramid and the Sphinx with an open mind?"

"I can think of several reasons for scholars to exhibit such an extreme lack of curiosity," Dr. Awyan answered with a smile. "Number one, they would have to rewrite their books and articles, which have declared that absolutely, positively, and most assuredly, the pyramid was nothing else but Khufu's tomb. Number two, they would have to consider whether the ancient builders might have been more intelligent than they are or, to be absolutely truthful, than any of us."

Soft laughter echoed from between the paws of the Sphinx.

"Number three, they might have to recognize that the ancient structures were created with the help of technology more advanced than our own. And number four, these same Egyptian scholars would be forced to apologize profusely to those of us whom they have labeled conspiracy theorists, mad hatters, or just plain loco."

The group sitting around the Sphinx applauded, whooped, and hollered. Dr. Awyan waited a moment until the group grew quiet.

"Allow me to tell you a little about my own story," the old Egyptian said. "In the 1930s, the Mena House decided to provide camel and horseback rides for their guests. They put out a call for experts in the care and breeding of camels and horses. The Awyan Tribe, to which I belong, decided to answer their call. I was three years old when my family came here. And this, my friends, was my playground."

Dr. Awyan spread his long arms out to each side of his body as if engulfing the entire Giza Plateau. The audience clapped in appreciation. Charles' applause was among the loudest.

"To give you an idea of how long ago this was," Dr. Awyan continued, "the Sphinx was still buried up to its neck in sand. At the time, there were no bars on the tunnels that weave in and out and under the Giza Plateau. There were no soldiers with rifles to keep people out of the area. As a child, I had complete freedom. I walked in the Giza tunnels, crawled in these tunnels, and swam in these tunnels. Yes, there was water in the tunnels when I was a child."

Charles wondered what it would be like to swim in an ancient underground tunnel.

"Being a curious boy, I asked my mother endless questions. What were these tunnels? Who built them? What was their purpose? Why did they have water in them? At first my mother didn't answer and simply shrugged her shoulders, but I never stopped asking."

"Eventually, she told me some of the answers to my questions were se-crets, secrets traditionally passed down from mother to daughter, moth-er to daughter, generation after generation. You see, originally Egypt was a matriarchy. It was the women who were the rulers, the scholars, the Keepers of the Secrets. They were called the Wisdom Keepers. I wanted to know these secrets, and I guess I drove my mother crazy with all my questions."

Everyone laughed. Dr. Awyan paused, then held up his finger before resuming his story, indicating the next part was important.

"One day my mother told me that, at her urging, the matriarchs of our tribe had agreed I would be the first boy initiated as a Wisdom Keeper. My mother was my first and greatest teacher. She told me the tunnel system was part of a great energy engine, which empowered the ancient people to do all the magical tasks that have been attributed to them."

Dr. Awyan gestured toward the pyramids.

"The energy allowed them to import, carve, lift, and set stones of amazing weight, with such precision that the process cannot be replicat-ed today. It allowed the ancients to create, store and distribute energy."

"This energy was used not only for building," he continued, "but also for understanding the power of the human mind—its ability to create and heal. If you want to know more about Egyptian energy healing, we have several people in our group who specialize in this area."

At that, Dr. Awyan indicated several members of the tour, includ-ing a man holding a microphone and a tape recorder, the dark-haired woman who'd spoken earlier, and two women carrying harps and rattles. Strangely, the Wisdom Keeper appeared to be also pointing at Jacques. Charles looked questioningly at his chaperone. Jacques, who seemed taken aback at being included, drew back further into the shadow cast by the Sphinx. The Egyptian continued his story.

"As a teenager, I was fascinated with everything Khemit. Khemit is the ancient name for Egypt. It means black land, referring to all land fertilized by the flooding of the River Nile, around which a great civilization arose, seemingly out of nowhere. I was enchanted, enthralled, and determined to learn as much as possible about these ancient people."

Just like me, Charles thought.

"I learned English early on," Dr. Awyan said. "This enabled me to become a tour guide for the British and American guests who stayed at the Mena House. One man made many return visits to the Giza Plateau, always choosing me as his guide. We shared a great love of Khemit."

"This man encouraged me to go to a university," Dr. Awyan continued. "When I told my father I wanted to go to school and study Egyptology and archeology, he said, 'Balderdash, Son! There is no money in this.' Being the fool I am, I went on to pursue traditional degrees in Egyptology and Archeology."

More laughter erupted from the people around the Sphinx.

"Eventually, I discovered something. My father was right, as he nearly always was. There is no money in this."

By this time, the people sitting between the paws of the Sphinx were rocking back and forth with laughter.

"I learned from my teachers at the university that 100 percent of them lacked the great experience of playing in and around the Sphinx and pyramids from the time they were very young. I learned they were declaring things that were not scientifically verified, as if they were set in stone. My biggest issue with Egyptologists is that most of their minds are closed tighter than the Great Pyramid before it was crudely breached."

Charles tried to picture the men who'd first broken into the pyramid, armed with shovels, picks, and crowbars, climbing up its steep sides on long wooden ladders. They must have been very disappointed to find out there was nothing inside the pyramid—no treasure, not even a mummy.

"At the Khemit School, our minds are open, wide open," Dr. Awyan said, mimicking an explosion with his hands. "We reach out to people from all disciplines, encouraging them to share their knowledge, research, and experiences. So, when we break for lunch at the Pizza Hut, I urge you to talk to each other. I will be back in an hour and a half."

Yousef went to his father. Charles saw Dr. Awyan's son pointing to him and Jacques. The tall Egyptian beckoned for them to join him.

The Egyptian scholar looked intently at Charles. "So, despite living far away in the United States, you developed a love of Egypt?"

Charles looked up into the deep brown eyes of the Egyptian and said, "Yes, I love Egypt, ancient Egypt, Khemit."

Dr. Awyan smiled at Charles' use of a term he no doubt had just heard. "Very good. I would like to invite you to lunch at the Pizza Hut across the street. I believe you will find your companions interesting."

"Isn't this great?" Charles said to Jacques as Dr. Awyan walked towards his black car. "Doesn't it seem strange to have a pizza parlor right across the street from the Sphinx? But there it is."

"All I know," Jacques said, picking up his pace, "is that I am starved, so starved I could eat a camel."

Charles looked at his chaperone in shock.

"I am just kidding," Jacques said with a slight smile.

Dodging vehicles as they crossed the street, they entered the blue door of the Pizza Hut. About thirty people were there, sitting on long benches next to long tables covered with red-and-white checkered plastic tablecloths. The people by the front window with the best view of the Sphinx waved Jacques and Charles over to their table. A large bear-like man with shaggy dark hair and a beard welcomed them.

"I believe we have ordered enough food for a small army. You are welcome to join us. In exchange, you must tell us why you came to the Giza Plateau," the man said, looking at Jacques.

The others at the table, especially Charles, waited for him to answer.

"Well, I am here," Jacques began slowly, "to discover how ancient people were able to build these structures when it is believed they only had soft copper tools. I am also looking after a bright if slightly trouble-prone boy."

Trouble-prone, Charles thought crossly. What was Jacques talking about? Then, recalling the perilous events of the past year, Charles didn't protest.

"The mysterious workmanship of the pyramids is also what first pulled me into the study of Khemitology," the woman across from Jacques said. "But now, my focus is sound frequencies and their healing abilities."

Jacques remembered how Dr. Awyan had pointed him out as one of the healers in the group. Or had he just imagined it? The two women, who were also the cooks, began delivering platters of food to the table. There was a lull in the conversation as everyone began eating. Charles heaped his plate with scrambled eggs and a large square of flatbread topped with melted cheese and some kind of ground meat. He hadn't realized that he, like Jacques, was starving.

The dark-haired woman turned to Charles and Jacques. "My name is Sherry Stevenson. My story is that several years ago, I met a man from Switzerland named Hans Jenn. He was experimenting with the power of sound and how it could possibly have been used to levitate the gigantic stones of the pyramids and temples. He also believes the ancients used sound frequencies as a healing tool. I was fascinated. Now, the study of sound and how it can be used for the betterment of humanity has become my life's work."

The bear-like man interjected. "Our friend here is modest. She earned a degree in the physics of sound and has written several best-selling books on the subject." He introduced himself as Rodriguez and said his main interest was exploring the similarities among ancient pyramids and sacred buildings all over the world. Charles thought he looked more like a lumberjack than an archeologist.

"Through years of study, I have discovered there are confounding commonalities among ancient structures and their builders," Rodriguez said. "There are similarities in their stories, building techniques, astronomy, calendars, and energy lines, not just in Egypt but all over the earth. So far, I have published three books on the subject. We have discovered so many new connections since my last book, I believe I could write one hundred more."

Charles was amazed to discover he was sitting at a table with two authors. One of them, Sherry, the woman interested in sound frequencies, turned to him. "What brought you here, young man?"

The room became quiet. Charles wondered what he should say. Should he tell them he'd been published in *Ghost Story Magazine*? No, he thought, these were real authors.

Instead, he said, "Ever since I was a little boy, I've been interested in ancient Egypt. My mother gave me my first Egyptian book on my fourth birthday. The title was *Mummies, Tombs, and Treasures: Secrets of Ancient Egypt*. From that moment on, I read everything I could about Egypt. Every day I dreamed of visiting Egypt, not as a tourist but as a student. Then, a miracle happened."

"A miracle?" the woman repeated, leaning forward.

"Yeah," Charles said. "My parents abandoned me."

The woman looked surprised. "I fail to see how that qualifies as a miracle. If anything, it sounds tragic."

Charles explained there was more to his story.

"You see, I turn twelve in nine days. My parents wrote to me at my school. They said they couldn't come to France to celebrate my birthday. The letter ended with my mom saying I could have anything I wanted as a gift. I guess she felt guilty. At first I was mad, because my parents never visit me."

The dark-haired woman nodded in understanding.

"But then," Charles continued, "I remembered something. I remembered I wanted to see the pyramids and the temples and the Nile. So I wrote my mother, telling her all I wanted was to go to Egypt. My parents planned this trip as a present. They asked Jacques to accompany me, because they think I'm too young to travel by myself."

Everyone in the room agreed it was a good idea for Charles to have an adult with him. Jacques burst into the conversation. He told them Charles knew practically everything about Egypt, and that the boy had even taught himself to read and write hieroglyphics. Charles was surprised. It almost sounded as though Jacques was proud of him.

"I, on the other hand," continued Jacques, "know very little about Egypt and Egyptology. Everything I know, I learned from movies. For instance, I am familiar with how pharaoh mummies can come back to life to take revenge on those who enter their tombs and rob them of their treasures. And I know that inside a pyramid, one may discover bats, snakes, and millions of hungry scarabs."

Everyone at the table laughed heartily, confessing that they too had watched those sensational movies as children.

"I wish I'd taught myself to read and write hieroglyphics at your age, or even at my age," the dark-haired woman said. Everyone in the Pizza Hut talked and laughed between bites of flatbread, scrambled eggs, and slices of mango.

The head of the School of Khemitology walked into the Pizza Hut and over to the front table. He beckoned to Charles and Jacques, asking if they would like to join the group on a little tour of the Great Pyramid.

"Wow, would we ever!" Charles exclaimed. "We'd love to, wouldn't we, Jacques?"

Dr. Awyan looked at Charles with new interest, then turned to the boy's chaperone. "May I have a little chat with this young man, Mr... .?"

"Jacques Gerard. I am Charles' guardian. I bet you won't have to ask him twice."

Charles joined Dr. Awyan at a small table beside the blue door.

"Do you see that building over there, the one behind the Sphinx?" the Egyptian man asked.

"If you mean the Great Pyramid," Charles said with a snort, "of course I do."

"Do you know what I believe about this pyramid?" the old Bedouin asked as he began connecting sugar cubes, creating a rectangular base.

Charles studied the Egyptologist's face, then said, "No, not exactly. I know you don't think it's King Khufu's tomb. What do you think it is?"

"I think—" Dr. Awyan whispered, leaning closer to Charles, "I think it is a gigantic book containing messages from the ancients, to the people of the future."

Dr. Awyan placed a second layer of sugar cubes, making the second layer slightly smaller.

"Are you saying, Dr. Awyan, that the ancient Egyptians were trying to communicate something to the people in the future, to people like us?" Charles asked in amazement plopping a sugar cube in his mouth without thinking.

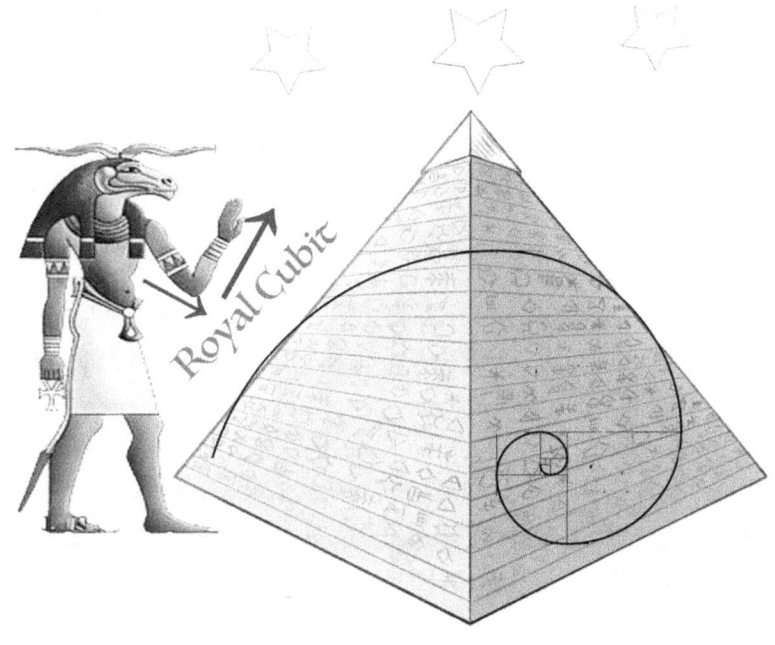

CHAPTER 8

MATHEMATICS AND ANCIENT EGYPT

D r. Awyan placed a third layer of sugar cubes, making this layer slightly smaller.

"How can a pyramid built eons ago contain messages to the people of our time?" Charles asked in amazement.

"The question is, if these ancient people wanted to communicate with people in the far future, what language would they use?"

"Hieroglyphics?" Charles ventured.

"That would limit their communication only to those who could read hieroglyphics. And, as you no doubt know Charles, Egyptologists have yet to discover a complete lexicon of Egyptian hieroglyphics. Even if we had discovered a complete language, no one has found any written messages from the planners or builders of the pyramids or the Sphinx. Can you believe it, Charles? No plans, no notes, and no illustrations in a country with hundreds of tombs and temples teeming with illustrations and messages. Quite strange, isn't it?" Dr. Awyan said, placing a fourth layer of sugar cubes on top of the third layer. This layer was slightly smaller. Obviously, Dr. Awyan was building a sugar cube pyramid.

Charles looked puzzled. "Yes, it does seem weird. But what's the language you're speaking of?"

"Mathematics."

"Mathematics?" Charles echoed.

"Yes, mathematics. It is a language that can be learned by anyone in any era. It doesn't matter if they are Egyptian, African, French, Southeast Asian, Indian, American, German, Mexican, Latin American, Japanese, Russian, or Chinese. And it doesn't matter if they are engineers, teachers, anthropologists, tour guides, students or even Egyptologists," Dr. Awyan said with a laugh. "This language is available to all who care to learn it."

"Where are these mathematical messages written?" Charles asked.

"In the structure of the pyramids themselves. We at the School of Khemitology are reaching out to mathematicians to help us, to teach us how to translate the messages we hypothesize were sent to us by the pyramid builders."

Charles looked deep into the Egyptian's eyes. "Dr. Awyan, I've read a number of books on the Great Pyramid written by mathematicians, and they said nothing about messages from the Pyramid Builders."

"Correct," Dr. Awyan said, his voice slightly ironic. "These mathematicians have measured the Great Pyramid. They have counted and calculated the weight of the stone blocks. Then they added the weight of all of the stones to determine the size and mass of the entire pyramid. They have measured the number of acres covered by the base of the Great Pyramid, and estimated the height of the missing capstone. However, this is just surface mathematics. It does not, and will not, reveal the messages of the ancient builders."

"What do you think the Pyramid Builders were trying to tell us?" Charles asked.

"That is the question. I am sorry to say that in my education, I forgot to become a mathematician. There are so many mathematical questions as to exactly when the pyramids were built, why the pyramids were built, and how they could be built with such primitive tools with such precision. There are questions regarding why there are so many correlations and mathematical coincidences among other ancient structures, and even objects in our solar systems. The Wisdom Keepers have hinted that we humans are not using all of our potential. From this, I conclude the messages are meant to help us discover our true and powerful selves. We just need to find people willing to take on this project of translating mathematics into language that someone like me could understand."

Charles thought he knew someone smart enough to discover the mathematical language of the Great Pyramid. He found himself telling Dr. Awyan about his most eccentric classmate. "At my school, there's this boy. He's only eight years old, but he's a mathematical genius. His name is Francis Bacon Bernstein."

"Nice name," Dr. Awyan nodded in approval. "Francis Bacon: philosopher-scientist, author of *Novum Organum*, the father of inductive reasoning. I must admit, Francis Bacon is one of my favorite philosophers. He believed in opening the mind, casting off limiting thinking, and using experiments to prove or disprove a theory, no matter how fond experts have grown of an idea. With a name like that, your friend's parents must have recognized something special in this boy."

Charles thought about the ginger-haired kid who'd taken to following him around the Château du Mont. He told Dr. Awyan that none of the other kids talked to Fran but David and him.

Charles said, "Fran wanted to come to Egypt, but Madame Constance said he was too young to travel without his parents. Anyway, I told him I'd take photographs and pay particular attention to anything that had to do with mathematics. He'll be so excited to learn the real language of the Great Pyramid is his favorite subject, mathematics."

"Well, now, I feel greatly encouraged to know two boys will soon be looking into the mathematical mysteries of the Great Pyramid," the Egyptian said, placing another row of sugar cubes on top of the last. "Regarding young Francis Bacon, why doesn't anyone talk to him?"

"It might have something to do with him being skinny and having red hair and freckles," Charles speculated, "and the fact his teeth are kind of uneven because his adult teeth haven't all come down yet. But mostly, he stands out because he knows more about math than the teachers at the Château du Mont. He asks too many questions no one can answer."

Dr. Awyan clearly enjoyed hearing about the red-haired child prodigy. "I know exactly how he feels about asking too many questions that no one can answer. It was one of my biggest problems when I was his age," the Egyptian said, placing another layer of sugar cubes. The pyramid was taking form.

"I don't know as much about mathematics as Fran, but I know a lot more about Egypt than he does. When I get back, we can work together to interpret the messages of the Pyramid Builders. Where should we begin, Dr. Awyan?" Charles asked, adding several cubes to the sugar pyramid.

Dr. Awyan smiled at Charles' enthusiasm and the boy's confidence that he and a schoolmate could unlock secrets that had evaded the most earnest seekers for eons.

"My humble suggestion is you start with the study of prime numbers, then move to meters, including how the meter was derived. Next, explore the connection between the Great Pyramid and the Golden Ratio, examining its dimensions in meters as well as in the cubit and Royal Cubit measurement systems. Also, throw in a little study of pi, and the speed of light."

"Is that all?" Charles joked, adding a sugar cube to the pyramid he and Dr. Awyan were building.

Dr. Awyan continued as though the boy hadn't spoken. "Then you may be able to perceive how the ancients used one or more of these constants to build the pyramids and other sacred sites in the Band of Peace."

"What's the Band of Peace?" Charles asked.

"According to my mother, it includes twenty-two pyramids along the Nile River," Dr. Awyan said.

Charles expressed amazement that there were twenty-two pyramids. He only knew about a handful.

"Khemitologists hypothesize that there are many more pyramids yet to be discovered, not only in Egypt but around the world."

Charles took out his moleskin notebook. He spoke aloud as he jotted down a summary of the subjects Dr. Awyan said needed to be studied. "Okay," he repeated, "prime numbers, the Golden Ratio, meters, cubit, Royal Cubit, pi, the speed of light, and how each of these relate to the twenty-two pyramids in the Band of Peace."

"Oh, yes," Dr. Awyan added, "and while you are studying these measurement tools, keep an eye on the stars, particularly Orion in Orion's belt and Polaris, the star closest to the celestial pole. Study their movements, not only in this time frame, but their positions throughout history. Add the study of the Sphinx and the Zodiac, and the distance to the sun and the moon in all forms of measurements. I think that will keep you and your friend busy for a while."

Busy! Charles figured they'd have to move into the library—*le bibliothéque*, as they said in French—at the Château du Mont. He couldn't wait to tell Fran about the language of mathematics and the Great Pyramid.

"Ah, I see the bus has arrived, and we haven't even finished building our pyramid," Dr. Awyan said remorsefully.

Charles looked out the window and saw an old bus pulling up in front of the Pizza Hut. It had a long nose, and the entire bus appeared to be shuddering and rattling. It looked like it had been painted with flat blue house paint.

"Are you ready?" the founder of the School of Khemitology asked.

"Yes, I can't believe I am actually going to go inside the Great Pyramid. Thank you, thank you so much, Dr. Awyan," Charles said, signaling Jacques to follow him.

Hakim Awyan sat in the front seat across from the bus driver. The driver turned out to be the same man who'd held Jacques' camel reins as they rode from the Great Pyramid to the Sphinx. Could it really be only this morning? To Charles, it felt like days ago.

When everyone was seated, the bus driver gave Dr. Awyan a small round microphone connected to the instrument panel via a curly black cord. The microphone crackled as the founder of the School of Khemitology asked, "Is everyone ready?"

"We're ready," the people in the blue bus rejoined in one voice.

"On our way to the Great Pyramid I will tell you a little story. When I was a young boy, maybe eleven, I decided to climb the Great Pyramid all by myself. I forgot to ask my parents' permission. I had no idea how difficult this climb would be. It took me almost all day. When I reached the top where the capstone should have been, I looked down on the Giza Plateau. I had never been up so high in my entire life. My heart began pounding wildly inside of my chest. I was breathing hard and soon became too dizzy to stand. I lay down at the top of the pyramid."

"I realized I would never be able to climb down," he continued. "I was fated to die on top of the Great Pyramid of hunger, thirst, and heat, and no one, even my family, would even know where I was. From my prone position, I noticed something in a crevice a few feet from me. I crawled my way over, still too afraid to stand up. I reached into a narrow hole and pulled out a small black leather notebook. On the first page, written in Arabic, were these instructions: '*To return to the base of the Great Pyramid one must focus on the spaces and not the stones.*' I wondered who had left this message up on the top of the pyramid, but it rather felt like a message from God. I took this advice very seriously. I didn't look at the stones. I didn't look down. I looked only at the spaces. It was nightfall before I got down. As you can all see, I lived to tell the tale."

The people on the blue bus applauded Dr. Awyan's story. Jacques thought he would never consider climbing up the Great Pyramid. Charles wondered if anyone was allowed to climb the Great Pyramid anymore, because if you could, he'd like to try, especially if David was with him.

The blue bus pulled into the Great Pyramid's parking lot, filled with all kinds of vehicles, dust, sand, tourists, and salesmen.

Dr. Awyan said firmly, "This morning, we are going into the Great Pyramid. I ask you all to stay together. Don't talk to anyone outside our group. Don't stop to buy anything. Go up the stairs and through the iron door. Enter quickly."

Charles was surprised at the Egyptologist's warning. Why all the secrecy?

"We will be locked in the Great Pyramid for two or three hours. Some of the pyramid tour guides are not going to be happy about this. However, this visit has been prearranged."

What! Locked inside the Great Pyramid? This wasn't something Jacques had bargained for. He was remembering an old movie he'd shown the boys at the Château du Mont a few months ago. It was called, "The Land of the Pharaohs." Jacques now knew that spectac film was based on the story of Pharaoh Khufu and his pyramid tomb. At the end of the movie, Khufu was dying. His slaves, friends, and even his beautiful wife, played by Joan Collins, gathered inside the King's Chamber to say a last goodbye to Pharaoh. But Khufu, not wanting to spend eternity by himself, had set up a terrible surprise. With one pull of a lever, everyone was trapped, buried alive in the Great Pyramid of Giza. Now he, Jacques Gerard, was about to be locked inside this exact same pyramid. He felt a little queasy as he tried to push away the memory of "The Land of the Pharaohs," to convince himself that it was, after all, just a movie.

Dr. Awyan stepped out of the old blue bus. His tan gallabiyah swirled around his long legs as he dodged souvenir salesmen, tourists, and camels. Charles rushed to catch up with the Egyptologist, attempting to imitate his long strides. He was sorry he hadn't worn the gallabiyah Farak had given him, so he could look like Dr. Awyan and blend in with real Egyptians. But how could Charles have known he'd be invited to join a private tour inside the

Great Pyramid? He reminded himself to take lots of good photos, or David might not believe him. He could hardly believe it himself!

Pulling his camera strap off his shoulder, Charles stopped to let Dr. Awyan walk ahead so he could take a photo of the Egyptologist leading the way to the entrance of the Great Pyramid. Dr. Awyan pointed to a hole about sixty feet up from the base of the pyramid. "That is the entrance. No one quite knows why they chose to put a door up so high."

"I like it," Charles said. "It'll be like climbing the pyramid."

Jacques' cameleer-turned-bus driver stood at the gate of the first entrance.

"How did he get here before us?" Charles asked Dr. Awyan. "We were walking so fast."

"My guess is that he didn't stop every few seconds to take a photograph," Dr. Awyan said, raising an eyebrow and ending in a laugh.

The cameleer-bus driver was blocking the gate, allowing only those who were on the Blue Bus Tour to enter. Dr. Awyan was right, the tour guides weren't happy about the closure of the pyramid. Charles snaked up the sixty-foot stairway to the entrance. Reaching the platform at the top, he decided it was a perfect place to photograph what his art teacher Mademoiselle Fleuret called an establishing shot. Here, he could take a broad photo of the Giza Plateau. Placing a steady finger on the shutter button, he snapped a photo of tour guides, camels, salesmen, tourists and, in the distance, the old blue bus sitting in the sandy parking lot. Afterwards Charles, still thinking about Dr. Awyan's childhood story, asked his guide if he left the notebook on top of the pyramid.

The old Egyptian answered, "I wish I could say that I did leave the notebook up on the top of the Great Pyramid, to help other young people find their way down. Sadly, however, I brought the notebook down with me."

Charles thought he would have done the same thing, so that people would believe him when he told them the story of finding the notebook. He then turned his camera towards Dr. Awyan, framing him as he walked towards the pyramid's metal door. Charles snapped the photograph and then, ducking under Dr. Awyan's arms, entered the Great Pyramid of Giza.

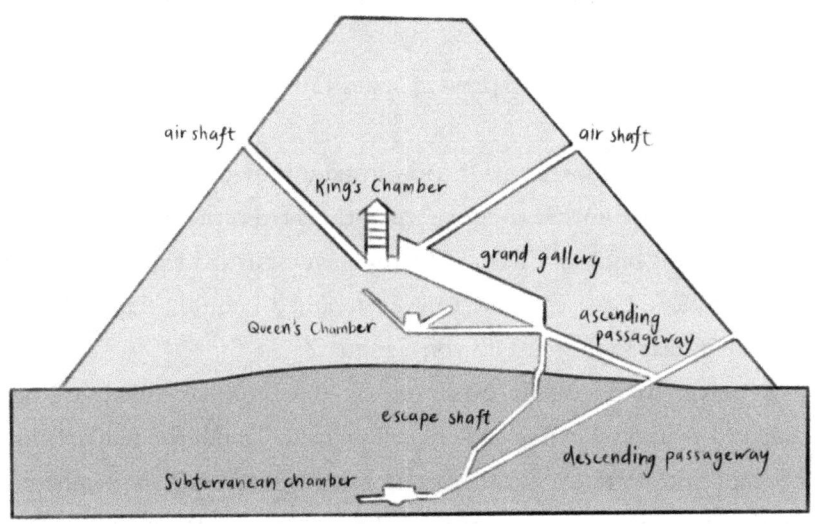

CHAPTER 9

INSIDE THE GREAT PYRAMID

S tanding halfway down a stone ramp leading to the main passageway, Charles knew exactly where he was. He'd studied and studied the interior of the Great Pyramid, trying to figure out why there were only three small rooms in the pyramid with a base covering thirteen acres, and which had originally risen to 481 feet including the capstone. He'd always been convinced there were undiscovered rooms—filled with undiscovered treasures. Charles looked back towards the entrance. Yousef and Jacques were the last to enter the Great Pyramid of Giza. Dr. Awyan's son slammed the heavy iron door shut with a great bang, then slid an iron bar across the entrance. No one was going to get into this pyramid, Charles thought, not unless they blew it up, maybe with TNT.

"Is everybody here?" Dr. Awyan asked. "If you are not, raise your hand." The founder of the School of Khemitology pretended to look around. "I don't see any hands up, so I assume we are all here and ready to go. At this point, we have a choice to go up or down. Which do you choose?"

In unison, the group expressed a desire to go up towards the royal chambers.

"Very good, follow me," Dr. Awyan said, moving to the front of the line. Jacques was allowed to move past others from the Blue Bus Tour so he could stand behind Charles. As the group turned right towards the royal chambers, Charles said, "I never dreamed I could actually be here, inside the Great Pyramid. Did you, Jacques?"

Jacques shook his head. "No, I can say quite emphatically that I never dreamed I would be inside the Great Pyramid. To tell the truth, it looks more like a utility ramp in the back of a storage building than an ancient Egyptian pyramid. Not one movie I have ever seen featuring pyramids or tombs showed anything like this: bare stone walls and a steep, narrow ramp lined by electric lights."

"You know movies are not scholarly tomes, Jacques," Charles said reproachfully. "They're just fiction, entertainment. You have to read books and magazines like *National Geographic* to get a clearer picture of Egypt. Still, I have to agree, electric lights along the ramp are not what I expected. I think oil lamps or even flashlights would be better, more authentic."

The ramp grew steeper. Dr. Awyan called out that if he should fall, he hoped someone would catch him. Those familiar with the Egyptologist laughed. They knew that over the years, their tour guide had climbed up and down these stone ramps thousands of times. Dr. Awyan warned everyone to watch their heads, pointing towards a ceiling that appeared to be closing in on the group.

"Sometimes the ceiling will be three feet high, and then the next thing you know it rises to twenty-seven feet. Either the designers were daft, or they had some reason for the dramatic changes in the ceiling height. If any one of you knows why, I beg you to tell me, especially about the part where I have to bend double to get up to the royal chambers."

People laughed in sympathy. Charles soon understood their sympathy, as even he had to crouch down to get through some parts of the ramp. The climb was even more challenging due to the dramatic 40-degree angle of the three-foot-wide pathway. Jacques was breathing heavily, mumbling something about lack of sleep. Charles, also breathing heavily, answered, "At least it's cool in here."

"It's always 68 degrees," the man in front of Charles volunteered. He stretched both hands out toward the ceiling. "Thank you, Pyramid Builders," the man said dramatically.

"I found it!" Dr. Awyan called excitedly from the front. "I found the Queen's Chamber! Hello, anybody here? Oh, I am sorry, there is no queen in here." Some members of the group laughed. Others groaned as they rushed up the steep ramp to see what Dr. Awyan had discovered.

The Blue Bus Tour group gathered in a room that was almost square, 18 feet by 17 feet. Suddenly, everything went black. Several people brought out flashlights. Jacques chided himself for not putting his flashlight into his backpack. Then again, how was he to know he'd need a flashlight? "What happened to the lights?" he called out. "Maybe it is the circuit breaker?"

"No, no, we requested the lights be turned off when we reached the Queen's Chamber," a woman's voice answered. Charles identified the speaker as Sherry, the lady in the Pizza Hut interested in sound and healing.

"A strange request," Jacques said, sounding slightly nervous.

"We always do this," Sherry said. "It establishes the proper atmosphere. And when it's time, it will help us focus on the frequency work we'll be doing inside the chambers."

"I should have guessed," Jacques mumbled.

"Not to mention," Dr. Awyan added with a chuckle, "we're saving on the cost of electricity." Charles found himself laughing along with the rest of the group.

"Some of you already know this information, but I'll recap for the sake of our newcomers," Dr. Awyan said. "The Great Pyramid is supposedly the tomb of the fourth dynasty pharaoh Khufu, 2556 BCE. As most of you know, there are only three discovered rooms in this pyramid, all three comparatively small. There is the Subterranean Chamber, which is ninety feet below the base of the pyramid; the Queen's Chamber, in which you are now standing; and the King's Chamber, which is higher up and slightly larger than the Queen's Chamber." The Egyptologist continued. "Now, if you are finished examining all the missing furniture, statues, clothes, makeup, perfumes, jewelry, and tapestries a royal queen would require in the afterlife, I think it is time to go up to the King's Chamber."

As Dr. Awyan walked out of the Queen's Chamber, he handed Charles a small flashlight. With everyone gone, Charles was engulfed in nothingness, blackness, silence. "I am Charles Dayton Stratton III," he whispered aloud. "I am in the Great Pyramid alone. I am here not as a tourist, but like a real Egyptologist."

"Hello, Charles. You stayed behind, too?" someone asked.

Fumbling with the switch of the flashlight, he aimed its narrow beam in the direction of the voice. It was Sherry, looking ghostly in her flowing white gown. She was wearing earphones and a stethoscope around her neck. In her hands, she held a black box.

"I thought I was alone," Charles said.

"I thought I was alone, too," Sherry said. "For some reason, this is my favorite place in the Great Pyramid, although the King's Chamber is showier, the Grand Gallery more resonant, and the Pit more mysterious. Anyway, I decided to investigate why I liked this chamber more than the other places in this pyramid."

"You've been here before?" Charles was impressed.

"This is my fifth time with Dr. Awyan," Sherry said. "This time, I brought my stethoscope and my compact audio spectrum frequency analyzer. And here in my backpack I have a rather small gravimeter."

"What's a gravimeter?" Charles asked.

"It measures gravity," she said. "Could you help me remove my pack?"

Charles grabbed the pack. It was heavy. This Sherry must be in great shape, he thought. He'd been panting as he came up the ramp, carrying only a small pack for his camera. He asked the physicist why she wanted to measure gravity.

"A number of members of the School of Khemitology are exploring the idea that the ancient Egyptians may have used sound frequencies to affect gravity, which may have to do with the ability to move heavy objects."

"So you believe different frequencies have the ability to affect gravity?"

"Yes," Sherry said. "We are all left with the question of how immensely heavy stones could have been laid together so precisely, when we could not replicate this even with our heavy machinery today. This led to the idea that either there is such a thing as magic, or the ancient builders used sound frequencies to help raise and place the great stones of sacred buildings, not only in Egypt but all over the world. Would you like to help me conduct an experiment?"

"Yes!" Charles answered excitedly, thinking how lucky he was to be conducting a real experiment inside the Great Pyramid.

"So what you are saying is you believe that sound frequencies might affect gravity?"

"My particular interest is how sound frequencies and gravity may have been used in healing, but those of us interested in gravity and frequencies all work together," Sherry said, pulling a cylinder out of her large backpack.

The cylinder was about four inches in diameter and 12 inches high. It looked like a machine of some kind. Sherry pulled out a small notebook and asked Charles to shine his flashlight on its pages. Turning on the gravimeter and the frequency analyzer, she copied some numbers from each machine. Next, Sherry pulled from her backpack a scale and some small rocks she'd gathered from outside the pyramid. She weighed the rocks and then made more notes in her notebook.

From the side pocket of her backpack, she pulled out what she explained were Tibetan bells and gave them to Charles. The bells consisted of two heavy bronze disks, about three inches in diameter, connected by a seven-inch leather cord.

"Hold the leather cord and click the two metal disks together," Sherry directed.

The disks made a pure tone that rang through the Queen's Chamber, echoing off its walls. "Good," Sherry said. "Now turn off your flashlight, and I'll combine my voice with the Tibetan bells."

Charles flipped off the flashlight. His unusual companion took a deep breath, letting it out with a loud sigh. She breathed in again and then let out a resonant "ohhh" sound. The boy hit the two disks together again. The combination of the sound of the Tibetan bells and Sherry's voice created a relaxing vibration around Charles. The woman took another deep breath and sang out again, this time changing her vowel to "ee." Charles hit the metal disks together once more. This was repeated several times. Finally, Sherry sang different vowels, one right after the other: *Ear earer, ear earer, ear earrer, ear earer.* It was not a beautiful sound, but Charles felt something surging intensely through his body. He didn't know what it was, but it made him feel stronger, more present, and somehow suddenly more grown-up.

After a few minutes of practicing what Sherry called toning, she told Charles he could turn his flashlight back on. She recorded the numbers from the gravimeter and her audio frequency analyzer. Then, she recorded the weight of the rocks.

"What happened?" Charles asked.

"Nothing," Sherry admitted. "There didn't seem to be any difference between before and after toning. But it was my first such experiment and I'll try again. You see, I don't know why but I always come back to this area, this niche where a statue was supposed to have stood. It's as if this place speaks to me. I'll have to spend more time here to discover why, but for now I believe our group is waiting for us. We'd better hurry because we're due at the King's Chamber. The ceremony is about to begin, and I happen to be the leader."

Charles thanked Sherry for letting him be part of her experiment. She told him that he made a great assistant. Charles decided he'd have to look for his own set of Tibetan bells, and a gravimeter. He didn't know where to find a gravimeter, but he seemed to remember seeing a set of Tibetan bells in the key shop that was featured in his first published article, "The Ghost of the Jangling Keys," in *Ghost Story Magazine*. When he got back to the Château du Mont he would look for the Tibetan bells, and he would ask his science teacher to direct him to some science catalogues. Charles followed Sherry up the ramp to the King's Chamber.

When they reached the King's Chamber, Charles found that lanterns had been placed around the room, spreading soft light on the huge, pinkish-red stones. Dr. Awyan welcomed Charles and Sherry as they entered. He walked to the rear of the room and stood by a large stone box, called the *sarcophagus* by many Egyptologists. It was the only object discovered in the Great Pyramid. The box had no lid and appeared to have a corner broken off.

Dr. Awyan stood, casting a giant shadow over the sarcophagus and onto the wall behind him. If Charles could capture this moment, it would be the best photo he had ever taken in his entire life. Charles enlarged the aperture, slowed the shutter speed, held his camera perfectly still, and finally carefully pushed the shutter button.

Dr. Awyan said, in a quiet voice that echoed off the walls, "As you can see, the King's Chamber is a little larger than the Queen's Chamber. Some of these stones weigh 80 tons, which is slightly more than I can lift, actually more than a hundred ancient Egyptians could lift. Don't ask me how they got these stones up that steep, narrow ramp we just climbed, or how they got these reddish stones from the Aswan region to the Giza Plateau. Aswan is 450 miles away from here."

These were the same questions Charles had pondered for years.

"Then," Dr. Awyan said, "I have something else to add to your list of things not to ask me. Why is there no written record of the building of the pyramids on the Giza Plateau, not in the pyramids or anywhere else in Egypt? For such a huge project, involving so many workmen, this doesn't make sense to me. Does it make sense to you?"

Several members of the group mumbled that it made no sense.

Jacques was still wondering how ancient Egyptians, who had no metal tools, could have cut all these coral-colored stones. How had they made them fit together better than any modern masons using the best technology?

Dr. Awyan pretended to search high and low around the King's Chamber. He finally asked, "Does anyone know where the lid to the sarcophagus has gone? I can't see it anywhere."

A few people called back that they didn't know where the lid was. Charles had expected the Egyptologist to provide answers to the mysteries of the Great Pyramid. Instead, the expert seemed to have an endless supply of questions. "Does anyone know how much the sarcophagus' lid might weigh?" No one answered. Dr. Awyan continued. "Does anyone know why the sarcophagus' lid is nowhere to be found, either inside or outside the pyramid? All these questions are why this pyramid is called the world's largest and greatest mystery."

Charles smiled. If there was anything he loved, it was a good mystery. As Charles and Sherry entered the King's Chamber, everyone in the group was clapping. Dr. Awyan acknowledged the applause with a slight bow. Charles deduced that the Egyptologist had just concluded his lecture. What had he missed? He'd have to ask Jacques.

CHAPTER 10

INSIDE THE KING'S CHAMBER

"Now," Dr. Awyan said, "I will turn you over to Dr. Sherry, whose specialty is sound physics."

The Blue Bus Tour Group applauded the dark-haired woman, shimmering in her flowing white dress. Charles remembered the bear-like man saying Sherry was a physicist. He marveled at his luck. He'd just conducted an experiment with a real scientist inside the Great Pyramid! Charles had a basic idea of what a physicist was, but what in the world was a sound physicist? He looked at Sherry standing in front of the sarcophagus with the missing cover. Charles lifted his camera and snapped a photo of the woman in white in front of the pink stone sarcophagus.

Sherry explained that each person would have their time inside the sarcophagus. "I promise it will be an amazing experience," she said. "Who'll be first?"

Dr. Awyan pointed to Charles. He got up from the floor where he had been sitting and walked self-consciously to the sarcophagus. It was approximately three feet tall. Charles' first thought was he wished like anything his friend David could be with him. His second thought, as he lay down inside a six-foot-five-inch-long sarcophagus, was he was glad the cover was lost.

"Close your eyes, Charles, and relax," Sherry said in a soothing voice. That was easy for her to say, Charles thought. He was the one in the coffin.

To the others, she said, "Follow my lead. We'll be singing different vowel tones. In ancient Egypt, vowels were believed to have magical powers. This is a major reason there are no vowels in hieroglyphics. One doesn't want to accidentally cast a magical spell by writing or speaking the wrong vowel sound, does one?"

For some reason, this made many people from the Blue Bus Tour laugh. Charles, on the other hand, wasn't sure he thought this was funny, at least not while he was lying inside the sarcophagus.

The sound physicist continued. "It is interesting to note that—possibly stemming from ancient Egypt—Hebrew, Arabic, Aramaic, Maltese and maybe more languages have what is called a consonantal alphabet, in other words a written language with no vowels. I believe the origin of these consonantal languages is ancient Egypt, where there was a belief vowels had magical powers. Who knows if this is true or not? To be on the safe side, I suggest we all clear our minds and visualize things of beauty or other positive thoughts as we sing these vowels or, more precisely, intone them."

Charles heard Sherry's sweet, pure voice beginning to tone the open vowel sound *Ah*.

All the others joined her. Charles could feel the stones of the sarcophagus vibrating like a massage chair. Meanwhile, the tones of the magical vowels swirled around the pinkish-red stone box. Harmonies enveloped Charles, entering the top of his head. They traveled through his body to his feet, then moved back up to his head. He actually forgot where he was. The toning stopped. Dr. Awyan reached down and helped Charles climb out of the sarcophagus.

"Is it over so soon?" Charles asked.

"You have been in this old coffin for five minutes," the Egyptian said.

"But it felt like only a few seconds!" Charles exclaimed.

"Don't talk now, just try to remember the experience," Sherry said as the next person climbed into the sarcophagus.

Charles walked to the end of one of two lines of people gathered on each side of the stone box. He sat down, feeling confused and disoriented. What had happened to him? He tried to remember, but his mind was blank, yet felt full. Everyone started toning again. It took Charles a few minutes to realize Jacques was missing. He wasn't in the sarcophagus. He wasn't in the two lines leading up to the sarcophagus. Where was his chaperone?

Charles slipped out of the King's Chamber. As soon as he was out of the chamber, away from the lanterns that lit up the red stone walls, he was cast in darkness. He turned on the flashlight Dr. Awyan had given him and walked down the ramp to the Queen's Chamber. Pointing his flashlight into the chamber, Charles was relieved to find Jacques. He was holding a flashlight, flicking its beam around the room. The resonant sound of chanting from the King's Chamber spilled down into the Queen's Chamber.

Jacques jumped when he saw a shadowy figure enter the room. Recognizing Charles, he said, "I did not want to climb into that sarcophagus, even if it is not a true sarcophagus."

"Yeah, but it wasn't that bad. In fact, it was interesting," Charles said, flashing his beam towards the shelf Sherry said should have held a statue.

"I don't know what to make of all this," Jacques said. "This is not the Egyptian trip I imagined."

"Me either. But I think we're very lucky to have met Dr. Abd'el Hakim Awyan, don't you?" Charles asked fervently.

"He is a remarkable person, that I will admit," Charles' guardian answered.

"Where'd you get that flashlight?" Charles asked.

"Dr. Awyan gave it to me," Jacques answered. "It was as though he guessed I was going to leave the group and and come to the Queen's Chamber. However, how could he have known? I didn't even know myself."

"Maybe it had something to do with Dr. Awyan pointing to you when we were sitting between the paws of the Sphinx," Charles said. "Don't you remember? Dr. Awyan said there were several healers in the group, then gestured directly at you."

"I thought I must have imagined it. Maybe Dr. Awyan was really pointing to somebody else."

"It looked like he was pointing directly at you. But how could he? He doesn't know you. He doesn't know about all the frequencies you can make with your violin and organ."

"That's just music, Charles," Jacques said, shaking his head at the thought there might be a connection between his music and healing.

"How do you know? Have you experimented with frequencies? Anyway, I came to find you," Charles replied.

"Thank you, Charles," Jacques said. "I am sorry I took you away from the ceremony."

"I already spent some time in here with Dr. Sherry. She said for some reason it is the Queen's Chamber, and not the King's Chamber, that she is most drawn to. I helped her with an experiment," Charles explained with authority.

"What kind of experiment?"

Charles shrugged. "It's kind of complicated, and anyway it didn't work out."

"I am still interested in what kind of experiment you were doing," Jacques insisted.

"It had to do with toning," Charles said. "I helped by playing the Tibetan bells and Sherry sang some vowels."

"I thought this Sherry said sounds could cast a spell or make magic," Jacques said with slight concern in his voice.

Charles was nonchalant. "Sherry just wrote down some numbers from the frequency analyzer. Then she used a small gravimeter. It measures gravity, as the name implies."

"I don't know about your being in here alone with a machine that measures gravity, Charles," his chaperone said.

"I wasn't alone. I was with Dr. Sherry, and it was nothing," Charles said. "She just placed some rocks she found outside the pyramid on a scale, then looked at the gravimeter and wrote down some numbers. Then she toned and I played the bells. She checked the scale again and wrote down the numbers shown on the gravimeter. The rocks weighed the same, and there was no change on the gravimeter. Dr. Sherry said the experiment showed no difference, but that she'd keep trying, using different frequencies and stuff."

Jacques frowned, then asked, "What was she looking for?"

"She's trying to determine if different sound frequencies can affect gravity. She think this might explain how the Pyramid Builders could move such large and heavy stones. Dr. Sherry also believes that gravity might be connected to frequencies and healing."

"Interesting," Jacques said, determining to keep a closer eye on this adventurous boy.

Charles and Jacques became aware of a deathly quiet. The ceremony must be over. Minutes later, the people in the Blue Bus Tour shuffled silently by the doorway of the Queen's Chamber.

Dr. Awyan broke the silence. "We are going to what we Egyptians call the Pit, or what the more sophisticated and knowledgeable Egyptologists call the Subterranean Chamber. We will be going down ninety feet below the base of the pyramid."

Charles and Jacques joined the end of the line. Jacques decided it was only slightly easier climbing down the ramp than up, as he had to keep from descending too fast while watching out for the height of the ceiling. They went past the ramp that led to the exit and kept on going lower and lower down the steep ramp.

"Ah, here we are," Dr. Awyan announced. "Some people say this is their favorite area. However, if I had any power, I would ask the Minister of Antiquities to get a broom and clean this place up. It is a mess! Look at all the strange and roughly-hewn blocks. What could the ancient builders have been thinking? My mother would not have approved."

Laughter broke the silence that had descended over the group as they inspected different areas of the Pit.

The bear-like man named Rodriguez walked up beside Charles and said, "Hakim is correct. Some people find the Pit the most fascinating; I am one of them. There is much speculation as to the purpose of this chamber. Some believe it was a place for the builders to store supplies and equipment."

Jacques, who was standing by Charles, wondered what equipment that would entail: ropes, stone hammers, soft copper blades?

"Just as in the upper chambers, no equipment has been discovered, or anything else for that matter. Some believe the so-called Pit is the unfinished burial chamber for Khufu's mummy," Rodriguez said. "But I would think if this were going to be the everlasting headquarters for the pharaoh, he would make sure it was finished and decorated. As you can see, there is nothing on any of the walls down here."

Charles looked around at the empty chamber. He felt like a real archeologist, a very puzzled one.

"Some say it is unfinished because Khufu, who supposedly designed the Great Pyramid for his tomb, suddenly had a change of heart," Rodriguez continued. "Their theory is that Khufu decided he didn't want to be buried low in the pyramid, like the pharaohs before him. I am with Dr. Awyan. I don't believe this pyramid was built as a tomb."

Dr. Awyan walked over and joined a small group where Rodriguez was saying, "Some members in our group believe the Giza Plateau was a waterway, and that the Nile River stood right in the pyramid's footprint. This would mean that the Great Pyramid would be much older than 4,500 years, as is generally believed by Egyptian scholars."

"What do you believe, Dr. Awyan?" Charles asked as he ducked out of a tunnel leading nowhere.

"As I said earlier, as a child, I played in the many tunnels around the Giza Plateau. A number of these tunnels had water in them. I am open to the possibility that this pyramid served as a power plant, among other purposes. However, one person's guess is as good as another's. That is what my father always said."

Charles shook his head. "It's strange. I never read about tunnels in any of my books on the Giza Plateau."

"Exactly," Dr. Awyan concluded. "If you cannot explain something, you have a tendency not to think, talk or write about it."

Dr. Awyan turned from Charles and addressed the group. "I believe our time in the Great Pyramid has come to an end. We will start what some call a challenging ascent, back up to the entrance area. As we exit, I suggest we refrain from talking until we are all safely outside with our feet firmly on the ground. After that, you are free to do as you wish."

Charles and Jacques watched as Dr. Awyan and the others walked back towards the bus. Charles had an idea. "Let's circumambulate the Great Pyramid, Jacques."

"Circumambulate?"

"It means…"

"I know what it means," Jacques said. "It is just that I thought we might circumambulate back to our hotel room."

Charles looked imploringly at Jacques. "We only scheduled this one day to be on the plateau. I'd like to walk around the circumference of the Great Pyramid at least once in my life."

"That sounds reasonable," Jacques said to his charge.

He began walking silently beside Charles, who kept his hand on the sides of the pyramid as much as possible. The sun beat down strongly, but Charles didn't seem to be aware of it. Arriving back at the entrance, Jacques wiped the sweat dripping down his face with his handkerchief.

Charles turned to Jacques. "Did you know this pyramid has eight sides, not four?"

"No," Jacques answered.

"It was discovered by a pilot in 1940," Charles said. "To see it, you've got to fly over the Great Pyramid during the equinox, when the sun is shining at a particular angle. Anyway, it's been proven. This pyramid is eight-sided."

Jacques stifled a yawn. "That is very interesting, Charles. We will have to talk about this later, after a swim, our lunch, and a long, long, long nap."

CHAPTER 11

THE HOME OF THE TOMB ROBBERS

J ust as Charles and Jacques reached the edge of the pyramid parking lot, a black car with a handwritten sign saying "Taxi, American Spoken" pulled up beside them. The driver, wearing a Hawaiian shirt, tan pants, and huarache sandals, jumped out and held open the back door of his cab.

"How did you know we'd be here?" Charles asked, climbing into the back seat of the car.

"Elementary, my dear Watson," Samy said. "Yesterday, I dropped you off at the Mena House. The Mena House happens to be next to the most famous place in the entire world, the Giza Plateau. So, I cleverly deduced you'd want to visit this site. I estimated how long it might take you to visit the pyramids and the Sphinx, and here I am. I love Sherlock Holmes, don't you?"

Charles was skeptical. How had Samy figured out exactly when he and Jacques would be ready to leave for the short, if sweltering, walk back to the Mena House? The driver's timing was especially uncanny considering Jacques and his spontaneous camel ride, their unexpected meeting with Dr. Abd'el Hakim Awyan, and the resulting private tour of the Great Pyramid. Charles wanted to ask him more questions, but it was too much to think about when the temperature was 90 degrees and rising.

Traffic was heavy. Charles guessed many of the tourists were heading back to their air-conditioned hotel rooms. Samy turned on his tape player and hummed along with a surf tune, which began with manic laughter and the refrain "Wipe out!" He turned down the volume slightly, craning his head backward to speak to his passengers.

"I love the drums on this song, don't you?" The boy nodded, if just to get Samy to turn around and put his eyes back on the road.

Charles looked over at his chaperone. Jacques was wiping the perspiration from his forehead with a handkerchief embroidered with his initials, J.G. He didn't seem to notice anything disconcerting about this Egyptian-surfer-taxi driver.

"You guys are probably a little tired after a camel ride to the Sphinx and a tour through the Great Pyramid, so I'll pick you up in, say, four hours," the driver said. "That will give you plenty of time for lunch and a rest."

How did Samy know exactly what they'd done this morning? Charles stared at the driver, who looked back at him through the rearview mirror. Samy was wearing a bright red Hawaiian shirt covered in yellow and white hibiscus flowers. It was not quite the dress of some kind of criminal or spy. But then again, maybe he dressed like that to keep people from staring at him. He was so unexpected, so wild-looking. Charles had noticed people tended to look away from someone who looked different. He was definitely going to keep a close eye on this taxi driver.

When Samy pulled into the Mena House driveway, Jacques pulled out his wallet, ready to pay him. But the the driver shook his head and told Jacques, "No worries, dude. It's all in the package."

Neither Jacques nor Charles asked what was included in the package, or how much it would cost, or even where they might be going after lunch. Jacques was too exhausted, and Charles was too deep in thought.

Four hours later, Charles and Jacques walked out of the Mena House to find Samy waiting for them. "Ah, here you are!" he said, holding the taxi door open. "Did you have a nice rest?"

Jacques told him they'd had a great lunch and an even better swim.

"Sounds totally tubular," Samy said, pulling out of the hotel drive at an alarming speed.

"Where did you say we were going?" Jacques asked. Samy, who was now weaving expertly through traffic, craned his head to look at Jacques and Charles.

"Remember when I told you about the houses of the tomb robbers?"

Jacques said yes, adding that it wasn't a name you could easily forget.

"I've got a cousin who lives in one of these houses. I told him you were dying to visit. Get it? Tomb? Dying to visit. Ha! Ha!" Samy laughed at his own joke.

He reached over and fumbled through his glove compartment, then pulled out another of his cassettes.

"Hey, Charlie. I have a surprise for you. See this audio tape? It's ancient Egyptian music. I still prefer surf rock, but I thought you might like some ambient background music for our visit to one of the houses of the tomb robbers."

"Why do they call these abodes the houses of the tomb robbers?" Jacques asked, staring out at the town of Giza, hoping not to see Mr. Smith walking down the sidewalk.

"Because it's against the law for ordinary Egyptians to dig for Egyptian artifacts," Samy said, slipping the tape into the cassette player. "Of course, it's perfectly alright for foreigners to dig up our artifacts and take them back to their own countries."

Charles frowned. "That doesn't seem right," he said. "I read that foreigners even took the bust of Nefertiti. It's in some German museum."

"True," Samy said. "And I agree, the powers that be shouldn't have sold the greatest artifacts of Egypt. Anyway, people like my cousin's family constructed simple houses into the side of a hill, where they could dig without detection by the government. It's a practice that continues to this very day."

Charles was fascinated. Imagine turning your own home into an archeological site!

"Most of us Egyptians believe people should be able to dig on their own property and keep what they find, especially since ancient Egyptians are our ancestors," Samy continued. "Some of these tomb houses have been passed down from generation to generation. My cousin's family has lived in their home for over one hundred years."

The taxi driver stopped talking. The sound of harp, finger cymbals, drums, and rattles swirled around the car. He was right, Charles thought, this music made a much more appropriate soundtrack for driving around the Egyptian countryside.

Out the windows of their taxi, they looked at children on donkeys, men driving bull carts filled to overflowing with hay or branches, teenagers on camels, and long-legged white egrets flying over blue-gray irrigation water. Children waded in the cool water, while women stooped over the water's edge washing clothes.

Charles looked in every direction, soaking in sights he'd dreamed about for years. He wanted to pull his camera from his shoulder to take some shots, but it was no use. Even if Samy stopped his taxi, Charles wouldn't have known where to point his lens. He felt, for the first time, the exasperation shared by all photographers—there wasn't enough time to capture all of the amazing things around him.

A little village came into view. It was guarded by soldiers on camels with rifles resting across their laps. The taxi rode past stalls covered with colorful cloths and filled with produce, poultry, and piles of spices in red, orange, ochre, tan, and brown. Samy stopped to buy some coconuts with little red straws stuck in a hole in the shell. Riding down the road, the three of them enjoyed the sweet, refreshing flavor of coconut milk.

After several hours of travel, Samy pulled to a stop at the foot of a rounded hill. Tucked into the side of the hill were houses painted in pretty pastel colors. Charles thought the colorful houses—blue, green, yellow, pink, coral, and purple—looked like a child's toy set. He knew this much: The inhabitants weren't trying to be invisible. Maybe their houses were like Samy, appearing so outlandish that the authorities didn't pay attention to them.

The three travelers walked up a narrow dirt lane. Halfway up the hill, Samy turned towards a coral-colored house fronted by a white-covered patio. In the shade of the patio, three Egyptian men in pale gallabiyah sat cross-legged on the ground. Each man was creating a statue of an Egyptian god. It appeared to be the same god in different stages. Charles recognized the form. It was the deity Thoth, god of the moon, magic, mathematics, and writing. Thoth was Charles' favorite Egyptian god.

"This is my cousin's main business," Samy said, pointing to the sculptors. "My cousin sells these figurines to the best tourist shops in Cairo. I can promise you that his statues are real. They are carved, not poured into a mold like the fake statues. Let me show you."

He picked up a fourteen-inch-tall Thoth statue. Taking a lighter from his pocket, Samy held the flame under the figure.

"If it were fake," Samy explained, "it would burn like paper. But see, this one doesn't burn. It's the real thing. It's made from alabaster, the stone of kings."

Samy poked his head inside the front door of the small house, then beckoned for Charles and Jacques to come inside, calling out, "We're here!"

The three visitors were greeted by a man who looked a little like Samy, solidly built, wearing a green-and-white striped gallabiyah and a generous smile.

"Let me welcome you into our home," he said. "I am Lateef, meaning mild and kind-natured. I say the name fits, don't you? I am the owner of this tomb robber's home, though I don't see myself as a robber but instead as an Egyptologist."

A young girl about Charles' age came up and stood beside the man. Lateef introduced the girl, who was wearing a blue gallabiyah. She had shiny dark hair arranged in two braids.

"This is my youngest daughter. We call her Doli," the man said.

"This is Charles and Jacques. I told you about them," Samy said.

"Oh, yes," Lateef said, looking at Charles. "Samy said you were interested in tombs." Charles had not actually told Samy he was interested in tombs, but the man was right; he was interested in tombs.

"Doli, take Charles to our tunnel," Lateef said. He signaled to Jacques. "You can come with me."

Doli pulled back a blue curtain in the living room. Behind it was the entrance to a tunnel, shored up by various pieces of wood. Charles asked the girl if it was safe. She just smiled at him. He guessed that she didn't speak English. The two children entered the tomb, standing up. After walking twenty feet, they bent over as the ceiling was only about three feet high. A couple of minutes later, Charles found himself crawling forward on his hands and knees.

The girl shined a flashlight towards the end of the tunnel. She showed Charles a pile of digging instruments. Some of the tools were just stones tied to pieces of wood with leather straps. Doli chose a small pick and hit the dirt at the end of the tunnel. Dust fell from the ceiling.

This was no king's tomb, Charles thought. If it was a tomb at all, it was probably that of a poor or middle-class laborer, meaning if they came across a body it would not be mummified. It would look like a skeleton or, worse, like the living dead. Doli seemed unconcerned. She struck the dirt again with a bang. A clump of soil dropped down on Charles' head. He decided he was ready to go back to the living room. The girl laughed at him as he backed out of the tunnel.

Once back in the living room, Doli pointed to a large basket. It was filled with pieces of jewelry, beads, and shards from clay pots. It even looked like there was some real gold in the basket. It would be fun discovering artifacts, but Charles still didn't like the idea of discovering a body. He had his mind set on finding a royal tomb with a painted sarcophagus and a highly-decorated casket, with perhaps a glimmering gold life mask and, finally, a neatly-wrapped mummy. Dolie gave Charles a turquoise bead. He thanked her. A moment later, Jacques came into the living room carrying two packages wrapped in brown paper. They said goodbye to the tomb robbers and stepped outside. Charles noticed the packages and asked his guardian what he had purchased. Jacques looked slightly confused.

"I was in a room filled with hundreds of statues. The next thing I knew I was paying for not one, but two statues," Jacques said with wonder in his voice. "One is Thoth, the god of writing, the deity you said was your favorite. The other is Ra, whom I was told is the creator of all. I don't know what I am going to do with these statues, or how I am going to carry these around with us on our trip. How do these things happen, Charles?"

Samy heard Jacques' questions and informed him that anything he bought would be shipped straight to the Château du Mont. Jacques assured Samy he was not going to buy one more thing.

"Never make promises you can't keep," Samy counseled with an astute smile.

Charles gave the taxi driver a closer inspection. What was it about him? He just didn't seem normal. Jacques, however, didn't seem to notice, especially since he was already napping in the back seat.

Nothing beside remains. Round the decay
Of that colossal Wreck, boundless and bare
The lone and level sands stretch far away

- OZYMANDIAS -

Percy Shelley

CHAPTER 12

POETRY ON THE GIZA PLATEAU

B ack from the tomb robbers' home, Jacques began thumbing through his Egyptian tour book. Charles picked up the poetry book his mother had given him. He decided since he'd visited the Sphinx in person, he should reread "Ozymandias" which, according to his mother, was Percy Bysshe Shelley's most famous poem.

I met a traveler from an antique land,
Who said—"Two vast and trunkless legs of stone
Stand in the desert. . . Near them, on the sand,
Half-sunk a shattered visage lies, whose frown,
And wrinkled lip, and sneer of cold command,
Tell that its sculptor well those passions read
Which yet survive, stamped on these lifeless things,

The hand that mocked them, and the heart that fed;
And on the pedestal, these words appear:
My name is Ozymandias, King of Kings

Charles began to read the poem aloud in a commanding voice. Jacques looked over, startled.

Look on my Works, ye Mighty, and despair!
Nothing beside remains. Round the decay
Of that colossal Wreck, boundless and bare,
The lone and level sands stretch far away."

"I think Percy Shelley is saying that no matter how important a person thinks he is, even a king or a pharaoh will pass away, will die, and eventually all symbols of his existence will be covered by sand."

"Hmm! Ozymandias," Jacques repeated the title. "I will admit that this short poem does make one think, but at this moment it seems like a light read is in order."

Jacques picked up his tour book and plopped down on his bed.

Charles was still pondering why his mother had written on the front page that she believed someday he, Charles Dayton Stratton III, might become a great writer, a poet like Percy Shelley. He had never written a poem, but he thought he might try to write a poem about his visit to the Great Pyramid. Finished, he handed Jacques his notebook, saying, "This is sort of a poem."

Pyramid Poem
Today I touched the Great Pyramid,
conceived in a stoneless desert.
I touched that geometric granite megalith
that could do nothing less
than proclaim to the gods
that humans had become like them,
grand creators.

As I laid my hands upon
the sun-warmed stones,

I imagined slaves who had
with simple copper tools honed
Pharaoh Khufu's eternal home.
His pyramidal tomb,
safely hidden in secret rooms,
yet to be discovered.
I had never thought that Khufu's tomb
might just be a theory,
passed on by Egyptologists
in picture books, stories, and scholarly tomes
that had filled my dreams with mummies' moans,
and sand-traps that closed my mind,
to theories of any other kind.
But as the smallest crack can down the strongest wall,
a quiet voice from between the old Sphinx's paws
asked questions about time, mathematics, and physical laws,
breaking the hold of tradition's claws.
I looked anew at the Giza plain,
for information that could explain.
What is right?
What is true?
As I began to write,
I became aware of a low, rumbling tone,
something like a mummy's moan.
It said, 'Ye who holds the key,
return that which belongs to me.'
I asked, 'Are you talking to me?'
What do you mean by 'Ye who holds the key?'
And what do you want returned?
If you mean your casing stones,
it is too late.
They have become the floors of ten thousand homes.

Or do you mean, return your golden capstone?
It is too late.
It was melted down long ago
by your evil foes,
formed into coins, necklaces, rings,
and all kinds of beautiful things.
Your casing stones and gold can never be returned to you,
And there is nothing, nothing I can do.
I heard that low growl again. 'Hmmmm!
Listen, boy; it is the revelation of my true form
that must be returned to me.
And you, boy, you and your friend, hold a key,
The key which will set me free.'

Jacques looked at Charles and, without saying a word, walked to the desk and pulled out a pen and paper with a Mena House Hotel letterhead on it. He sat down at the desk and began to write. When he was finished, he handed his paper to Charles, saying, "This is sort of a poem."

The Sphinx
Upon a huge camel I did hop.
Rode to the Sphinx, clippity clop.
The Sphinx roared loudly, then said with a laugh,
'You must answer this riddle if you want to pass.
What walks on four legs, then two, then three?
It is not very hard, I am sure you will agree.'
I thought and I thought, scratched my head, tapped my brain.
'Oh,' I said, 'I know:
a baby, a young man,
and an old man with a cane.'
—Jacques Gerard, the Giza Plateau

Charles stared at his traveling partner. After a pause, Jacques burst out laughing. Charles joined him, laughing so hard he fell on the floor. The sound of their laughter spilled out of their room, down the hall of the Mena House Hotel and, just maybe, onto the Giza Plateau where the great Sphinx joined them in their merriment.

"What was the voice of the pyramid in your poem talking about?" Jacques asked.

"It might have something to do with this," Charles said, walking to the dresser where he brought out something from the third drawer. Charles pulled off the red cover and handed the replica pyramid to Jacques. Jacques turned it over and over in his hands, squinting at the lines carved on its side and touching the deep golden capstone.

"This is beautiful," Jacques said. "Where did you get it?"

"Farak gave it to me. He told me it's a replica of the most valuable heirloom of the Faruq clan. It's kept hidden. Farak told me that few people are allowed to see the heirloom. Every ten years, an artisan is selected to make a few replicas. The artist is selected by the head of the royal family for their talent and loyalty. These replicas must be exact in material, form, and decoration or writing. Farak told me the only difference between the replicas and the heirloom pyramid is in the writing on the bottom of the pyramid."

"What does the writing say?" Jacques asked, handing the pyramid back to Charles.

"I don't know. Even Farak's family doesn't know. But the story that has been passed down for centuries is that the heirloom, and thus this replica pyramid, is an exact copy of the Great Pyramid of Giza."

"It is an exact replica? It does not look like it." Jacques said.

"I think he means the original cover stones of the Great Pyramid looked like this pyramid. In other words, the Great Pyramid had writing on all of its sides and a gold capstone."

"Why did Farak give you this pyramid?" Jacques asked Charles.

"He said it was because I reminded him how much he missed Egypt, and because I love Egypt so much."

"That was very nice of Farak," Jacques said, taking back the pyramid and examining it more closely.

"It's more than nice. The person who is gifted a replica pyramid also accepts the challenge of finding out the significance of the heirloom pyramid. This replica is one of the reasons I wanted to spend so much time in the Cairo Museum. I'm hoping to find a key to what is written on the five sides of the pyramids. Will you help me look, Jacques?"

"Yes, but where do I start?"

"We start by looking for this kind of stick writing," Charles said. "Hey, I just thought of something. Why would Samy want us to meet him at 5 a.m.?"

"He probably has a cousin who runs a shop filled with authentic Egyptian artifacts. Although truthfully, I am not buying one more thing," Jacques promised.

CHAPTER 13

THE STEP PYRAMID AND A DAY LOST

At five o'clock a.m., the black of the night sky was just beginning to be replaced by a dark gray. As Jacques and Charles walked out of the hotel, Samy jumped out of his black taxicab and opened the back door. Charles ran around to the other door, behind the driver's seat. Jacques slid into the backseat.

"Hello, you two, right on time," Samy said as he slowly pulled out of the Mena House driveway.

"Why did you say we were meeting so early?" Jacques asked. "I don't believe the museum opens until 9 a.m."

The taxi driver, dressed in an orange Hawaiian shirt scattered with white plumeria blossoms, stretched and yawned before answering. "Oh, I might have forgotten to mention it. We're going to Saqqarah, believed by many to be the oldest pyramid in Egypt."

"What about the Cairo Museum?" Charles asked. "I told you we planned for four days at the Cairo Museum. This is day one."

"Dude, the Saqqarah Pyramid is only 15 miles away from the Cairo Museum. When we're finished with our tour of this significant historical site, I'll take you to that dusty old museum, quick as a wink," Samy said with a wink. "You don't want to miss Saqqarah, do you, Charles?"

"No, I don't," Charles answered. "And this morning I did put a brand-new roll of black-and-white film in my camera."

"What's wrong with colored film?" Jacques grumbled.

'Black and white are the colors of photography. To me, they symbolize the alternatives of hope and despair to which mankind is forever subjected.'

"Did you make that up?" Jacques gasped, staring at the eleven-year-old sitting next to him.

"No, I didn't make it up. It was in an essay Mademoiselle Fleuret read to us in class. But isn't that a great quote?"

"Don't you ever play, Charles?" Samy asked, shaking his head.

"I believe that play is in the eye of the beholder, or in the hands of the participant," Charles answered. "For me, photography enlarges my view of the world around me. It involves a mixture of observation and imagination and therefore qualifies as a kind of play."

Jacques jumped into the conversation, saying, "Mademoiselle Fleuret, the art teacher at the Château du Mont, says that somehow Charles' photographs are not just a picture of something but contain a narrative."

"I try not to drive and philosophize at the same time, especially before the sun has risen above the horizon," Samy said, turning left onto the two-lane road of the town of Giza.

"You have a point, Samy," Jacques said. "Wake me up when we get to..."

"Saqqarah," Charles filled in their destination. "It's home to the Step Pyramid, dating back more than five thousand years ago. The Step Pyramid doesn't look like the pyramids of Giza. Some people call it the Wedding Cake

Pyramid because it has at least six layers. Also, it has some of the earliest examples of the Pyramid Text."

"Well, young man, you certainly are up on your knowledge of Egyptian archeology," Samy said.

"I'm afraid I forgot to put Saqqarah on our itinerary. Thank you, Samy," Charles said. The driver glanced at Charles through his rearview mirror.

"Anyway, since Saqqarah is so close, we won't miss much of the Cairo Museum, day one," Charles added.

It was still dark when Samy crossed a two-lane bridge, which Charles believed traversed the Nile River.

Less than a mile later, Samy made a sharp turn south. The scenery changed from cityscape to countryside. As the sun rose, it turned the sky a rosy orange. The taxi entered a small town. Samy pulled his cab over to the side of the road. An Egyptian woman was cooking on a wood stove. Next to the woman was a kiosk covered by a bright pink umbrella. Samy and the woman brought over to the taxi three cups of tea, flatbread with vegetables, rice, and a bag of sugar cookies.

"Now, this is touring," Jacques said as he finished a bite of the best sugar cookie he'd ever tasted.

Samy pulled into a gravel parking lot. There were no other vehicles, not even a camel.

"Is it open?" Jacques asked.

"For us it will be," the taxi driver claimed.

"Let me guess," Jacques said with a smile, "the guide is your cousin."

"You are correct," Samy said with a laugh as he opened the back door for Jacques.

The path to the Step Pyramid began at the ruins of an ancient temple. Charles, Jacques, and Samy walked silently through the remains of a once-beautiful temple with graceful stone arches and roofless columns. Charles carefully aimed his camera, hoping to capture the feeling of walking through a temple, not as it looks now but the way it looked four or five thousand years ago.

Near the end of the temple, Samy stopped, pointing towards several great columns around them that looked like they had held up the roof of a large round room.

Samy whispered, "See that area over there, marked by stones in the shape of a cube?"

"Yes," Charles whispered back.

"This is believed to be the most important area in an Egyptian temple. It is the room of the Holy of Holies. Only the highest priests and the king or pharaoh were allowed to enter the Holy of Holies. It is where the ancients believed the gods and goddesses of the temple dwelled. It is also said to have held great treasures and, even more importantly, powerful instruments of magic."

"What kind of magic?" Jacques asked.

"What kind of instruments?" Charles asked.

"Good questions," Samy replied. "Of course, it's in ruins now, and whatever was here is now long gone. Still, it might be a good idea to thank the gods for allowing us to enter their sanctuary, just to be sure."

"Just to be sure of what?" Jacques asked, staring at the platform and trying to imagine what this part of the temple looked like thousands of years ago.

"You know, to be sure we have good luck. One might need luck when entering a necropolis," Samy said.

Samy faced the Holy of Holies and spoke a few words in Arabic. When he finished, Charles snapped a photo of the driver and Jacques standing by the carefully arranged stones.

"The word necropolis refers to a large cemetery adjacent to a city," Samy said. "This area is part of the ancient capital city of Memphis. As you know, Memphis was one of the oldest and most important cities of ancient Egypt."

"Right," said Jacques.

"Right?" Charles echoed, smiling at the man who knew practically nothing about Egypt.

"You might be interested to know, Charles, that this area is not exactly a cemetery. It's a burial place of the sacrificed," Samy said, his voice suddenly low and ominous.

"The burial place of the sacrificed? I don't think I like the sound of this," Jacques said, looking around for possible mummies.

"It was really quite a clever money-making scheme. The ancient priests convinced the royals that if they were mummified after death they'd be better prepared to face the afterworld. However, as you know, Charles, mummification of the human body is complicated and time-consuming," Samy explained.

"Yes, it took seventy days to complete the mummification process," Charles said, looking at his guardian.

"Indeed, the mummification of a human was lengthy and expensive," Samy continued. "The high priests devised an alternative plan. Instead of mummifying the bodies of the poor, they'd mummify a replacement, a stand-in, an animal. The priests somehow convinced the populace that mummifying a substitute corpse would guarantee even the poorest person a better afterlife."

"Personally, I don't care for the whole idea of mummification," Jacques said.

"Then you are in the wrong town, buddy," Samy said, laughing. "Oh, and I'd better tell you that we're now in the presence of millions of mummies."

"Where are they?" Jacques asked, scanning the desert and the Step Pyramid looming in front of him.

"Right under your feet," Samy said. "Although this looks like just desert sand, under this sand are miles and miles of underground tunnels teeming with animal mummies."

"That is just plain eerie," Jacques said, staring at the ground under his feet.

"In Saqqarah, the animal of choice was the raven," Samy continued in his tour guide voice. "The priests raised the animals to be sacrificed. For a price, they would mummify the animal, add a few prayers, and guarantee the family of the deceased that their loved one would have a pleasant afterlife. It was rather brilliant; this way, they got a little money from a lot of people, and it was less work to mummify a bird than a person. This little scheme helped the priestly caste become very rich and powerful, sometimes richer and more powerful than the pharaohs."

Charles looked down at his feet. Somehow, thinking about a mummy or two in a tomb didn't bother him. But the thought of tunnels filled with millions of mummified animals was creepy.

Jacques pulled out his tour book from his backpack. "It says here the Step Pyramid is two hundred and five feet high. And in this area, there are at least three-and-a-half miles of tunnels and chambers. It was built as a tomb by a man called Imhotep, for King Djoser."

Samy said, "Some people call this pyramid the Queens' Pyramid. That's because eleven female mummies were found in several of its rooms."

"That is unsettling," Jacques said, shading his eyes against the sun to get a better look at the pyramid shaped like a wedding cake.

Charles looked up at Jacques with a slight frown. "About the Step Pyramid being older than the Great Pyramid, I'm not sure that Dr. Awyan would agree. He might not even believe the Step Pyramid is a true pyramid. Remember, Jacques, Dr. Awyan told us that no mummies or writing were ever discovered inside a pyramid. This seems more like a tomb than a pyramid."

As they drew closer to the Step Pyramid, a man in a gray gallabiyah emerged from a tunnel dug out below the base of the six layers of the pyramid. The Egyptian gave Samy a friendly wave. He followed the wave by holding up his little finger and thumb while tucking the other fingers into his palm, then twisting his hand right and left several times. Samy returned the gesture.

"What does that sign mean?" Charles asked. He was eager to learn all he could about Egyptian customs.

"It's the shaka sign, which Hawaiians use to signify friendship and the aloha spirit of welcome. It's also a signal used by all the surfers in Southern California. It means just hang loose."

"Just hang loose?" Jacques repeated slowly.

"Yeah, it means relax, man. I'll be glad to teach it to you, Jacques," the Egyptian in the Hawaiian shirt offered. "It might come in handy."

As they approached the entrance to the Step Pyramid, Samy and the guard shook hands.

"Jacques, Charles, this is my cousin Chuma, meaning wealthy. It is a hopeful name, as he is still looking for his treasure."

"Hello, Chuma. Thank you for allowing us an early entrance," Jacques said.

"You are welcome," Chuma replied. "There are many passages in this pyramid. Some lead to rooms, and some lead to dead ends. It is something like a maze. Shall we start in one of several rooms where they discovered the eleven mummified wives of King Djoser?"

"That is a lot of wives," Jacques said.

"Some people speculate that these wives were killed so the king wouldn't be lonely in his afterlife, but I don't think so. What do you think, Charles?" Samy asked.

"I think, wow, we are walking inside the Step Pyramid where they found real mummies. This is great!" Charles said, not exactly answering Samy's question.

Jacques wasn't enjoying himself as much as Charles. He tried to chase away a barrage of terrifying thoughts, like what if they came across some undiscovered mummies? What if tens of thousands of scarab beetles were scrabbling and scuttling around the floor of the very next room they entered? What if they never found their way out of this maze-like pyramid?

As they moved down lower, Jacques turned his concern to oxygen. "Do you know how pyramids provide for air circulation?" he asked the guard.

The man in the tan gallibyah just laughed. Charles took a photo of Jacques scowling in the frame of a stone doorway. As they walked down to the lower rooms of the pyramid they discovered blue-green decorative tiles, as well as paintings and etchings on the walls. Charles carefully examined each and every one of them, occasionally jotting down notes in his journal.

"Considering Dr. Awyan said there were no mummies in the pyramids, and the fact there are no decorations in the Great Pyramid, I have a hypothesis," Charles said as they headed deeper down some roughly-hewn stairs that looked like they could go on forever.

"I think this must be a tomb that just sort of took the shape of a pyramid. What do you think, Jacques?"

Jacques gave out a yell.

"What is it?" Charles called up the stone stairs.

"I believe it is a herd—a flock, a murder, or a troop—of scarabs, or whatever they call them," Jacques said with a slight quaver in his voice.

"Oh, it is just our temple cat," Samy's cousin said reassuringly.

Relieved, Jacques reached down and gave the yellow cat a scratch on its head. The cat, seeing he had no food, left the way he had come. Jacques mumbled something about the museum having been open for several hours, and that he had no interest in seeing the place where eleven young women met their fate.

When Charles failed to answer him, Jacques summoned more authority. "Charles Dayton Stratton III, I am starved and, as your guardian, I believe you are starved, too. It is time to leave."

"Just hang loose, man," Samy said. "If you're hungry, we're in luck! It just so happens that I have a cousin who owns a restaurant nearby."

Charles wondered again exactly how many cousins Samy had. Unsurprisingly, the restaurant turned out to have a shop attached. After lunch, Charles bought a book about ancient astronomy. Jacques bought a book about cruising the Nile, and three silver bookmarks decorated with a filigree image of Bastet, the cat goddess.

"I have no idea why I bought these," Jacques said, surveying his souvenirs with a look of surprise.

Charles pointed the lens of his camera toward Jacques and snapped a picture, adding, "My guess is your small purchase was a way to keep yourself from buying that gold ring with the large scarab on it, the one Samy's cousin got you to try on. Now, let's plan our next move."

Jacques shook his head. "Charles, I just spent hours and hours crawling through a dark tomb filled with mummy dust and thousands of scarabs."

"You know you didn't see any scarabs," Charles said reproachfully.

"And I walked over a million mummified ravens, and who knows what other sort of mummified animals," Jacques continued. "I need to go back to the hotel, take a nap, have a swim, and enjoy a leisurely dinner."

"But the museum!" Charles said.

Jacques waved his hand, dismissing the boy's concerns. "I talked to Samy, and he has promised to get us to the Cairo Museum tomorrow morning, precisely when it opens. With both of us looking through the museum, I think we shall find the answers you are seeking. Three days should be enough."

Charles protested, but Jacques was firm.

That night, Charles had a dream. It seemed so real, like it was a memory. In the dream, he was four or five years old. He was in his bedroom on the third floor of his parents' mansion in Newport, Rhode Island. He could hear the pounding of the ocean waves on the rocky cliffs below. His mother was in his bedroom with him. She looked beautiful in a red velvet dress.

"I'll hold you up, Chucky," his mother said, "and you look into the crack in the stone and tell me what you see."

"I see wondrous things, Mother," Charles said. "I see a chariot covered with gold, and toys and furniture, all gold. I see a sarcophagus and strange carved animals. Now, let me hold you up. What do you see?"

Somehow, in his dream the little Charles of several years ago was able to lift his mother up to peer through the crack. She was light as air.

"I see wonderful things, too," his mother said excitedly. "I see a staff with a gold falcon on top. The falcon has big blue eyes, just like you, Chucky. Oh, and over there I see a beautiful falcon pendant. The falcon has his wings spread wide and in each talon he holds an *ankh*, the symbol of everlasting life. The pendant is decorated with turquoise, coral, and lapis lazuli. It is set in gold."

Young Charles made a promise. "When we enter the tomb, Mother, I'll give you that pendant. It will look so pretty with your dress."

"Thank you, Chucky," his mother said, reaching out to hug him.

When Charles woke up, it was still dark. He felt sad and lonely. The dream had made him realize more keenly how much he missed his mother. He was filled with questions. Why had his mother and father sent him away to the Château du Mont? Why didn't they ever come to see him? What did he do to cause all this? Unable to come up with adequate answers, Charles shifted his thoughts. He didn't want to think about his parents anymore.

Tomorrow, Charles and Jacques would be at the Cairo Museum. He intended to learn more about the city of Tel el Amarna and, hopefully, discover something about the pyramid replica. Finally, Charles fell into a dreamless sleep.

CHAPTER 14

THE TOUR GUIDE AT THE CAIRO MUSEUM

J acques felt dizzy as he gazed upon thousands of Egyptian artifacts. There were statues of pharaohs, gods and goddesses; sarcophagi, pieces of pottery, papyrus, jewelry, and furniture; small and life-sized boats, remnants of clothing, cosmetics, medicines, musical instruments; and real mummies, both human and animal.

All these were thrown together, regardless of category, age, excavation date, or location. Most were unlabeled and touchable by visitors. This place, with its jumbled display of priceless objects, didn't look like any museum Jacques had visited before. Other museums kept their valued Egyptian artifacts in sealed glass cases, perfectly displayed, honored, each accompanied by a description printed on a carefully-placed plaque. Visitors could know at a glance what each object was, the estimated date of its creation, and when and where it was discovered. In other words, you could pass through such an exhibit without thinking.

Not true here. It was the museum-goer who had to make sense of it all. Jacques scanned the room for Charles. He discovered him leaning over a sarcophagus, his lips moving as he read the inscribed hieroglyphics. Not for the first time, Jacques found himself puzzled by this boy, now standing on tiptoe in his white sneakers to get a closer look at an ancient script. Why did he love Egypt so much? What was the magic behind the pyramid replica, and what was driving Charles to pore through this huge and cluttered museum? More to the point for Jacques, how long was this search going to take? He decided he'd better ask Charles.

Jacques took a decisive step towards the stairs but was pushed back by a tour guide with a dozen visitors in his wake. The tall man was dressed in a flowing tan gallabiyah. His light blue turban matched his blazing blue eyes. A brown scarf with beads and embroidery on its bottom edges was draped over his shoulders. It fluttered as he stalked by, stealing Jacques' attention from Charles.

With a wide sweep of his arms, the tour guide said, "Gather around, everyone. Keep close. Keep close. We are walking towards the north wall, where we will find a giant statue of the Pharaoh Akhenaten, and a few artifacts from his ruined capital city of Tel el Armana."

Jacques' ears perked up. Had the man just said Tel el Armana? That was the very city Charles was determined to visit! The tour guide was now a dozen feet ahead and traveling fast. Jacques glanced around the room but didn't see his young charge. There was no time to find him. He wondered what to do. The next thing Jacques knew, he was following the people in the tour, attempting to look nonchalant behind the paying tourists.

The tour guide swirled around to face his audience. His gallabiyah twisted around his lithe body, then fell in graceful folds with a soft swish. Jacques was nearly hypnotized.

110

"This, my dear friends, is one of three large statues of the Pharaoh Akhenaten, the most mysterious pharaoh of all time and, in my belief, the most maligned." The tour guide ended his spiel in a loud whisper.

What did he mean by saying most maligned, Jacques wondered.

"Like the two other effigies," the guide said, "this statue was cut up into pieces and buried beneath the sands in the capital city of Karnak, the temple region of Thebes. Dismembering these statues and burying them was part of a deliberate plot to erase the existence of the Pharaoh Akhenaten from all of history."

Jacques looked up at the twenty-eight-foot-tall statue. It depicted an unattractive man with a protruding stomach, wide hips, thin arms, a long face, a flabby chin, and thick lips. No wonder this statue was buried under the sands, Jacques thought. It was probably Akhenaten himself who ordered the destruction of these unflattering statues. The sculptor was probably condemned to a tomb-like prison for the rest of his life, however long that might be. Jacques chided himself for his flight of fancy. He was beginning to sound like Charles. He forced his attention back to the tour guide.

"Akhenaten's enemies not only destroyed and buried these large statues. They also traveled the length of Egypt, hammering off every mention of Akhenaten's name, and every image of him they could find."

This is a terrible story, Jacques thought.

"And that's not all," the charismatic guide continued, pointing a finger at the statue. "At the end of Akhenaten's seventeen-year reign, the high priests of Egypt and their soldiers destroyed his capital city of Tel el Armana, said to be the most beautiful city ever built. They leveled it to the ground, and then they murdered Akhenaten."

Everyone on the tour was hanging on the guide's words. He lowered his voice. "For more than two thousand years, no one spoke about or knew of this pharaoh. The high priests had successfully erased Akhenaten's name from all of history—or so they thought. Some things, however, refuse to be buried."

It was true, Jacques thought, remembering the deaths of his own parents and grandmother. He felt the familiar dull ache in the pit of his stomach, then wondered what had caused him to make such a personal connection. What did the death of an Egyptian pharaoh have to do with World War II and the murder of his own family?

The guide continued, his voice Shakespeare-dramatic. "In 1798, members of Napoleon's army—which was invading Egypt—discovered evidence of the ruined city. They explored some of the tombs, but as they were not Egyptologists, they discovered little about Tel el Amarna and its people. It was almost a hundred years later that an Egyptian woman, looking for kindling to make a fire, made the amazing discovery of *The Amarna Letters.*"

"The Amarna Letters," Jacques repeated in a low voice.

The guide held up what looked like a thin, reddish brick. "This is a replica of one of over 300 letters written, not on papyrus, but on clay tablets covered in a wedge-like writing. This writing is called Cuneiform."

Jacques felt almost light-headed. This was it! He realized with a thrill that the writing on Charles' replica pyramid was Cuneiform. He couldn't believe it. While Charles was hunting all over the museum looking for clues, he, who knew so little about Egypt, had found the answer. Charles was going to be dumbfounded, that was certain.

The first thing Jacques learned was that Cuneiform is not a spoken language. Instead, it's like a code between people who speak different languages. Secondly, he learned Cuneiform became obsolete not long after Akhenaten's capital city, Tel el Armana, was razed to the ground by the high priests' army.

The guide continued. "Some people call Cuneiform the red language, as it was generally etched on red clay. Others call it the wedge-language, because the symbols are wedge-shaped. Still others consider Cuneiform to be the most difficult and stupidest script in the entire world."

What? Jacques looked in surprise at the man in the blue turban.

The tour guide paused for effect. "Oh, yes. That was me when I was young," he said with a laugh. "I found out about the *Amarna Letters* in college and was fascinated. I vowed to learn Cuneiform, so I could read the letters myself. It only took me twenty years of study."

The tour group laughed. Meanwhile, Jacques' mind was racing. He was sure the writing on the replica pyramid was Cuneiform. Perhaps this guide could be the one to translate the messages.

The man was on the move again, his enraptured audience following close behind. He stopped in front of a bust, a statue depicting only the graceful head, neck, and shoulders of a woman. Jacques recognized her. It was Nefertiti, rumored to be the most beautiful woman who ever lived. He had to admit she was attractive, except for the missing eyeball.

"I'm sorry to say, this is not the authentic bust," the tour guide apologized. "The real bust resides in the Berlin Museum. You may ask why. It was discovered as part of an archaeological dig led by German archaeologist Ludwig Borchardt on December 6, 1912, to be exact. They found it in a long-buried workshop of the sculptor Thutmose, along with other unfinished busts of Nefertiti. Naturally, Borchardt and his colleagues decided it belonged to Germany. At least we have a good replica of the bust of Nefertiti, whom Akhenaten declared was not only his wife, but co-ruler and co-pharaoh of Upper and Lower Egypt."

Jacques stared at Nefertiti, trying to imagine her with both eyes intact. The guide moved them to the next place on his well-planned tour.

"Here is one of the few engravings of Akhenaten with his family. It's the very picture of familial affection. Akhenaten is kissing one of his daughters. Nefertiti is holding two other children. They had six daughters in all. Above them is the sun shooting out rays, each ending in a tiny hand, representing Aten, the power behind the sun and all there is. Although it has been disputed, I call Akhenaten the first monotheist."

Much maligned monotheist, married to Nefertiti. For Charles' sake, Jacques hoped he would remember the substance of the tour guide's presentation.

"It was not only the high priests who considered Akhenaten a threat," the guide continued. "It was also the kings and rulers surrounding Egypt.

Akhenaten refused to send his soldiers to fight battles for nearby royalty, as was the convention at the time. Akhenaten told neighboring leaders that the one god, Aten, created all people and loved all of them regardless of the language they spoke, the color of their skin, or even what gods they worshiped. Akhenaten reasoned that Aten created all, and thus all people are related. Why would he send soldiers to kill his own relatives? This innovative pharaoh might be one of the first pacifists."

The world could use more leaders like Akhenaten, Jacques thought.

"Alas," the guide said with passion, putting the back of his palm to his forehead. "How I long to tell you more about Akhenaten and his capital city. However, all good things must come to an end. I will leave it to you, each of you, to discover for yourself what this mysterious man contributed to Egypt and beyond. For those of a scholarly bent, allow me to suggest a few areas of exploration: the Amarna Letters, Cuneiform, Aten—the power behind everything—monotheism, the *talatats*, and the relationship between Akhenaten, Nefertiti, Meriaten, and Tutankhamun."

Jacques repeated the suggestions in a whisper to himself, hoping it would help him remember the advice of the guide, who was now headed toward the stairs. The man stopped, flipped his scarf around his neck theatrically, and looked at the tour group with eyes the color of his turban.

"I have one more area of research for you," he said. "With good reason, some people believe Pharaoh Akhenaten and his co-ruler Pharaoh Nefertiti possessed more gold, silver, copper, jewels, and valued writings than any other rulers in Egypt's history. The question is, where did this treasure go? I bid you all *hazana saeidan*, meaning good luck."

The guide floated downstairs, his gallabiyah flowing around him as he moved. Jacques located Charles. The boy's face was pale, his eyes dark and a little unfocused.

"It looks to me like it is time for cookies and tea," his chaperone said, an unnatural smile making him look like the Cheshire Cat.

Charles eyed Jacques dubiously but followed him out the museum door and across the busy street to a shop, where they seated themselves under a green-and-orange umbrella.

CHAPTER 15

DR. MCALLISTER AND CUNEIFORM

J acques and Charles nibbled on sugar cookies and sipped golden-colored tea, shaded from the afternoon sun by the umbrella, surrounded by shopkeepers and tourists. Charles looked rested.

Jacques asked his charge, "Could you remind me exactly what we are looking for in this overstuffed museum?"

"We have two main areas of focus," Charles said with exaggerated patience. "The first is to find clues regarding the pyramid relic Farak gave me. The second is to find anything we can about Tel el Armana."

"I see. May I borrow your pen and notebook for a moment?" Jacques asked with a sly smile.

Charles slid pen and paper across the tabletop to Jacques, who scribbled furiously for some time.

"There, I am done. Please allow me to read this to you," Jacques said. "Obviously, the writing on the relic pyramid is not hieroglyphics, or Farak and you would have been able to translate the symbols. Nor is it written in any known language of today, or someone would have deciphered the markings by now."

"It is my guess it was written in Cuneiform, the system of communication invented by the Sumerians some five to ten thousand years ago," Jacques continued. "It is said that Cuneiform was developed as a tool to enable financial agreements and trade between people who spoke different languages."

Charles was amazed. He couldn't have been more surprised if his chaperone had suddenly begun tap dancing on the plastic table.

"Several thousand years later, the people of the Middle East expanded this writing system," Jacques said. "It was used to express more complicated material, like mathematics, astronomy, and literature. Cuneiform, of course, means wedge. This is because the scribes used a stick to create the wedge or stick-like writing, primarily on red clay tablets."

"Where did you learn all this?" Charles demanded.

"Allow me to continue," Jacques said. "We might discover more information by studying what is known as the *Amarna Tablets*, first discovered in the Place of the Letters of the Pharaoh, buried in the sand in Tel el Armana."

Charles stared into the smiling, dark eyes of his traveling companion. "Jacques," he exclaimed, "I can't believe this is you speaking! The *Amarna Letters or Tablets?* The Place of the Letters of the Pharaoh?"

"Who else could be speaking, my dear boy? I see no one else around."

Charles was confused. How had Jacques managed to discover the very information he'd been searching for?

"I have made a list of areas of research for you, Charles," Jacques said. "You should look into the following: the *Amarna Letters*, the Pharaoh Nefertiti, the talatats, or bricks, from Tel el Armana, Tombs 11 and ..."

"Tomb 11?" Charles repeated, flabbergasted.

"Yes, Tomb 11 and Tomb 25," Jacques said, certain those were the numbers the tour guide had cited.

Charles was more than amazed. He'd never mentioned the Ghost of Tomb 11 to Jacques.

His chaperone continued. "You might also examine the relationship between Akhenaten, Nefertiti, Meriaten and Tutankhaten, and give special attention to Aten, the power behind all there is. There is one final question of interest. What actually happened to Akhenaten's great treasure?"

"Akhenaten's treasure?" Charles repeated, eyes boring into Jacques' dark brown eyes.

Jacques patted the boy on the head. "While you were reading hieroglyphics, written thousands of years ago, I was researching the most up-to-date information on Egyptology, especially Egyptology in Tel el Armana."

"Really? You have to tell me where you learned all this information," Charles said, squinting at Jacques in suspicion.

"I got it from good authority," Jacques answered innocently.

Charles was becoming exasperated. "What good authority?"

"I heard it from a tour guide," Jacques answered. "He apparently knows quite a bit about the Pharaoh Akhenaten and Tel el Armana."

"A tour guide? How do I meet him?" Charles' heart was racing. Meanwhile, Jacques was calmly cleaning up the leftovers from their snack.

"Elementary, my dear Watson, as Samy would say. He works here at the Cairo Museum as a tour guide."

Charles sprang to his feet. "We have to find him, right now!"

"Charles, be careful crossing the street!" Jacques yelled as the boy stepped onto the vehicle-filled road, heading back to the Cairo Museum.

Charles showed the guard his hand-stamp and ran up to the woman at the tour counter.

"We want to go on a tour," he said, breathing hard.

"You're in luck," the woman said, smiling at his eagerness. "A tour is just about to begin."

Jacques, who'd caught up with Charles, looked over toward a group of people encircling a man in a white shirt, black tie, and dark gray pants. He shook his head and said, "That's not him."

Jacques turned to the woman at the counter. "Do you have a tour guide who is wearing a gallabiyah? He is tall and has blue eyes."

"Oh, yes, you must mean Dr. McAllister. He is one of the most popular guides. However, he left for a conference a few minutes ago. He is due back the day after tomorrow."

"The day after tomorrow!" Charles said, throwing his hands up in frustration. "Can we get his phone number?"

"I'm afraid we don't give out personal information about our employees," the woman said sweetly.

Jacques took over, thanking the woman and leading Charles away. "According to our schedule, Charles—actually your schedule—we will still be at the Cairo Museum, searching through thousands of artifacts, the day after tomorrow. In the meantime, I suggest we visit the gift shop."

"You want to go shopping at a time like this?" Charles asked incredulously.

"Charles, it is evident I need a notebook and a pen," Jacques said. "In addition, we should check out the books to see if there is anything about Tel el Armana, this ruined city causing so much excitement. In fact, I consider Dr. McAllister's departure for a conference to be a blessing in disguise, as Madame Constance frequently suggests."

"Why is that?" Charles asked crossly.

"It will give you time to form the questions you wish to ask this Egyptologist, who may be the one person who can read the markings on your pyramid," Jacques said sagely.

Charles mulled this over. "You're right, Jacques," he said. "I do need to write down my questions. I don't even know where to start."

The gift shop was crammed full of jewelry, statues of gods and goddesses, paintings on papyrus, Egyptian rugs, pyramid replicas of all sizes, books, bookends, and bookmarks. Jacques found what he was looking for, a black notebook with Tutankhamen's gold funerary mask on the front, and a pen with a removable mummy on top.

Charles came up scowling. "Jacques, I couldn't find a single book on Tel el Armana."

"It is probably because most of the books here are photographic books, and the people who destroyed Tel el Amarna didn't leave much to photograph," Jacques said. "I suggest we look for a book on the *Amarna Letters*. Some of those tablets contain Akhenaten's own words."

Jacques and Charles searched through the books lining the back wall but found nothing. Charles walked up to the counter and asked the cashier, a dark-eyed youth with a friendly smile, if they carried any books on the *Amarna Letters*.

"Sorry, we are cleared out. We have had quite a run on the Amarna books since Dr. McAllister joined our staff a couple of weeks ago," the gift shop attendant said. "However, we do have one copy of a book actually written by Dr. Donald McAllister. It is called *Cuneiform*. I don't know what it's about, as I haven't read it yet."

"We will take it," Jacques said. "And Charles, I am dead on my feet. As your caretaker and mine, I insist we go back to the Mena House where I can take a swim and you can start brushing up on your Cuneiform."

As they walked out of the museum, several hours ahead of schedule, Charles wasn't surprised to see a black taxi with a handwritten sign idling in the parking lot. The surf music from its tape player joined the cacophony of sounds outside the Cairo Museum.

CHAPTER 16

BEHIND THE STATUE OF HATHOR

The next day Charles and Jacques, with the help of Samy, arrived at the Cairo Museum exactly when it opened. Jacques glanced down the stairs to where Charles had been standing when the boy suggested they split up so they could cover more ground. Charles had moved from the sarcophagus to a large stone tablet. He was intently writing notes.

Before Jacques could join him, something caught his attention. He thought—or imagined—he saw someone with a gray hat crouching behind the statue of a woman or goddess, who seemed to be looking in Charles' direction. Jacques was immediately on alert but, when he looked again, there was no one there. Scanning the museum, Jacques saw no one with a fedora hat. Being suspicious was catching. Why was he so nervous? If he saw Mr. Smith, he would simply go up and talk to him. No big deal, as Charles would say. He would ask the Gray Man what he was doing in Egypt. Yes, that was exactly what he planned to do. Jacques walked swiftly down the stairs, not towards Charles but to the rear of the statue where he might have seen the gray hat of Mr. Smith.

Jacques walked slowly around the statue. It was about eight feet tall, on a stand about five feet wide, large enough to conceal a man. But there was no one there. Still, Jacques could not shake the feeling that someone was following Charles. Jacques examined the statue in front of him. She looked attractive, except for her rather strange ears. What kind of ears were they, Jacques wondered, leaning closer. As he moved forward, Jacques tripped over some metal signage. It explained this was a statue of Hathor, the cow goddess.

"Oh, yes, the cow goddess," Jacques whispered, wondering why this goddess chose to have cow ears. The sign said that Hathor emerged during the Old Kingdom. Jacques had been studying about these kingdoms. First, there was the pre-pharaonic period, meaning before pharaohs, and then there was the Old Kingdom, which began five thousand years ago.

"That makes you pretty old, Hathor," Jacques said in a whisper.

He continued reading. Hathor was the goddess of beauty, music, dance, love, laughter, pleasure, and fertility. No wonder she was so popular, Jacques thought. He looked at the foot of the statue. It was strewn with coins, flowers, and messages, some written on papyrus. Although Hathor was five thousand years old, evidently some people were still praying or making offerings to this goddess.

Jacques thought about what Samy had said at the ruins of the Holy of Holies in the sanctuary of the Step Pyramid. The driver had suggested they make a prayer, just in case. "In case of what?" he'd asked Samy. The taxi driver had answered offhandedly, "In case the gods are watching."

Without thinking, Jacques reached into his pocket and brought out a handful of coins. Checking to see that no one was watching, he placed the coins at the foot of Hathor, heeding Samy's warning that, "One can never be too careful when it comes to the gods and goddesses."

Jacques walked towards Charles, his eyes sweeping around the museum. He assured himself that he'd only imagined spotting Mr. Smith. Turning back to his charge, Jacques asked, "How about a little lunch? I'm famished."

"Okay, but we have to come right back here. There's so much to see." The boy spread his arms straight out to include all that was around him, then added, "What were you saying to Hathor?"

If Jacques had the tendency to blush, his cheeks would have been red. Had he really spoken aloud to a stone statue of the cow goddess Hathor? He and Charles got their hands stamped for re-entry by the Egyptian guard. They stepped outside under the scorching sun. It seemed to Jacques that there were more people in front of the museum than inside of it. Across the very busy main street, vendors stood beneath colorful red, pink, green, and orange umbrellas. They were selling food, jewelry, curios, rugs, papyrus, statues, and "true Egyptian artifacts."

As they crossed the road, Charles noticed the sky was gray, filled with smoke, gases, and chemicals. "I read somewhere that Cairo has a pollution problem," he told Jacques. "It's not good for people, and it's definitely not good for antiquities."

Looking at the multitude of cars, motor scooters, taxis, buses and trucks, Charles groused to Jacques that the Egyptians should have stuck with camels as their main form of transportation. A small rust-colored truck overflowing with bales of golden hay stopped in front of Charles and Jacques. The truck pulled forward. Behind the truck emerged a man wearing a yellow Hawaiian shirt with bright red hibiscus flowers springing from sprigs of dark green leaves. In his right hand, he held a bulging cloth bag with a smiling bear and the words UCLA Bruins on it.

Charles groaned. Adding to the man's incongruous dress, he had rolled up his tan pants almost to his knees and was sporting neon-green flip-flops.

Not one other person Charles had seen since setting foot on Egyptian soil looked like this questionable taxi driver.

"I brought lunch," Samy called out through the throng of people and vehicles.

Jacques yelled back, "Thanks, we are starving!"

"All tourists are starving after a couple of hours in that dusty crypt," Samy said, pointing at the museum and then to an area with tables shaded by brightly-colored umbrellas.

"How did you know we'd be here?" Charles asked slyly.

"Elementary, my dear Watson," Samy replied. "I dropped you off at the Cairo Museum at 10 o'clock. It's now 1 o'clock, lunchtime. Generally people get hungry and thirsty at lunchtime. There's no food court inside the museum, so I figured you'd emerge looking for something to eat. Clever, aren't I?"

Charles didn't answer. He was getting tired of this Sherlock Holmes act.

"How does anyone make any sense of all the Egyptian artifacts inside this famous museum?" Jacques asked Samy. "Everything is thrown together, disorganized and unlabeled."

"I've asked myself that same question so many times," Samy said before taking a large bite of a flatbread and lamb sandwich. "Shall we go shopping?"

Charles scowled at the taxi driver.

"Thanks, Samy, but Charles appears to be frantically looking for something in particular," Jacques said.

"What might that be, Charles?" Samy asked. Both men looked at Charles. He didn't want to answer in front of the man in the Hawaiian shirt, the one who unexpectedly showed up, even when plans had not been made.

"Mainly, I'm practicing my ability to read hieroglyphics," Charles said. "And as I told you, Jacques and I are interested in anything about the area of Tel el Armana."

Samy shook his head. "There's nothing in the city of Tel el Armana. It was destroyed thousands of years ago, returned to the sands on which it was built. Its secrets, if any, were buried forever."

"How do you know?" Charles demanded.

Samy shrugged. "Everybody knows this."

The taxi driver poured hot tea from a red-and-black plaid thermos bottle into three blue plastic cups. They watched the tourists in saris, safari outfits, business suits, robes, and headscarves walking around the small open-air booths. None of these people stood out like Samy. If the guy missed surfing so much, Charles thought, why didn't he return to Southern California?

When they'd finished eating, Jacques thanked Samy for lunch and reminded Charles of his manners. "Thank you, Samy," Charles said. "The food was good. See you at five o'clock, closing time."

For Jacques, it was a long two-and-a-half hours. He followed Charles around the museum like a mother hen, checking to see if anyone in a gray hat was lurking behind a statue, all the time thinking about the need for someone to tidy up this disheveled museum.

As man and boy staggered out of the Cairo Museum, they spied Samy parked across the street. Approaching them, Samy suggested a visit to the earliest surviving mosque or Islamic house of worship, Al-Azhar Mosque, which dated back to 988 CE. Jacques, however, said he needed to declutter his mind. He added that the idea of swimming in the reflection of the Great Pyramid trumped visiting mosques and tombs.

After dinner, Charles wrote in his journal while Jacques thumbed through his Egyptian tour book. After some minutes, Jacques looked up. "I forgot to mention, I may have seen Mr. Smith in the museum today."

"Where? When?" Charles asked, brow furrowed.

"This morning," Jacques said, deliberately casual.

"Why didn't you tell me?" Charles demanded.

"First, I am not quite sure I saw him," Jacques said, closing his book. "Second, the Cairo Museum jumbles my thinking. The only way to reset my overstimulated mind is to sleep. I suggest you put aside your writing and do the same."

Charles flopped on his bed and lay there with his arms across his chest, like a small mummy. After a moment, he sat up, irritated. "Jacques, I can't sleep and it's all your fault, bringing up Mr. Smith at a time like this."

"I told you, I was not sure it was him. It was probably a shadow or something. It's your fault I've become suspicious," Jacques said accusingly.

"You should have found out for sure before telling me," the boy grumbled.

"I apologize, Charles. It was most likely an illusion, caused by spending so many hours in a place so unorganized and confusing," Jacques said. "I will be happy when we meet Dr. McAllister, and then head for the overnight train to Luxor. I tell you, Charles, I am looking forward to getting on a train and watching the scenery from a comfortable seat. After a nice night's sleep, we will be in Luxor."

CHAPTER 17

KING TUT AND THE TRAIN TICKET

Charles and Jacques were standing in front of the Mena House watching cars wheel in and out of the gate, but Samy's taxi was not among them. Charles had specifically told the driver they needed to be at the Cairo Museum the moment it opened today. Tomorrow, they'd be on the train to Luxor. Today was Charles' only chance to speak with Dr. McAllister.

He had some questions memorized. Could the writing on the pyramid relic be Cuneiform? If so, would Dr. McAllister be willing to translate the inscription? Did the Egyptologist know anything about Tomb 11, Tel el Armana? And did he have any more information regarding Akhenaten's treasure?

"What time is it?" Charles asked for the third time.

Jacques glanced at his wristwatch. "It is 8:45 a.m. And knowing what time it is will not get Samy here any faster."

Charles was growing more impatient by the minute. "I told Samy it was important that he get here exactly at 8 o'clock, or we might miss Dr. McAllister."

"I do not think we will miss Dr. McAllister," Jacques said. "Anyway, I see Samy pulling into the driveway as we speak."

Jacques glanced at Charles, who had his hands on his hips and a scowl on his face. He knew from experience that his young charge was about to blow up.

"Charles, listen to me," Jacques reasoned. "Yelling at our taxi driver will not help."

Samy, wearing a pink Hawaiian shirt covered in palm trees and coconuts, held up a green rectangular piece of paper that looked remarkably like a ticket. He jumped out of his black cab with its handwritten sign, "Taxi, American spoken." He opened the back door for Jacques and Charles to get in.

"Hey, dudes, I have a surprise for you," Samy said before Charles could admonish him. "You know how we've been getting along so well? A friend of mine owns a taxi in Luxor. He's offered to lend me his vehicle, as he is traveling to visit his brother in the UK. Can you believe it?"

"You're late and we don't need a driver in Luxor," Charles informed him.

"Of course, you need a taxi driver in Luxor. You can't walk everywhere," Samy said. "And I know Luxor like the back of my hand. My family lived there for ten years, and I took some college courses at South Valley University of Fine Arts in Luxor. I focused on the artistic heritage of Thebes, so I'll be your driver and your tour guide."

"We're going by train," Charles said flatly.

"I know, dude," the Egyptian in the pink Hawaiian shirt said. "That's why I'm a tiny bit late. I stopped off to get my train ticket."

Samy waved the ticket towards the back seat. Charles said nothing. He looked at Jacques, but his guardian's eyes were closed. He was either deep in thought or "resting his eyes," as his chaperone liked to say. Samy pulled his taxi out onto the main road.

"It's a good day for the Beach Boys, don't you think?" Samy asked, looking into the rearview mirror, then turning his head around and giving his passengers a grin.

Charles nodded in agreement, just to get the man to turn around and keep his eyes on the road ahead. Samy turned on his tape player and turned up the volume. It was not a cheery song. It was a slow song about some guy mooning over a surfer girl. Samy joined the singers, harmonizing in a high-pitched voice.

Little surfer, little one,
Made my heart come all undone.
Do you love me? Do you, surfer girl?
(surfer girl, my little surfer girl)
I have watched you on the shore,
Standing by the ocean's roar.
Do you love me, do you, surfer girl?

"Charming song," Jacques called out sarcastically over the chorus.

Charles glared at the singer behind the wheel. He wasn't in the mood for sentimental surfer music; his mind was on ancient Egypt. And anyway, he was suspicious about this taxi driver who showed up unexpectedly, and got a ticket to Luxor without asking if they wanted a driver.

"What did you say you studied at UCLA—besides surfing?" Charles asked Samy sardonically.

"I believe my answer would have to be girls," Samy replied with a laugh.

Charles shook his head, wondering why this supposed taxi driver never gave a direct answer to questions about his history. Samy stopped in front of the museum. His passengers jumped out.

As soon as they were out of the cab, Charles confronted Jacques. "Why didn't you tell Samy we don't want him to be our driver in Luxor?"

"Charles, Samy was trying to be nice and helpful," Jacques said. "He speaks English, and he speaks Arabic. He knows the sites in Luxor, he studied the artistic heritage of Thebes, and his friend is lending him a taxi. It does not seem like a bad idea to me. Now let us find Dr. McAllister."

Entering the Cairo Museum, Jacques and Charles got their hands stamped and walked swiftly towards the tour area.

"There he is," Jacques said, pointing to a tall man in a gray gallabiyah. He wore a blue turban and a long white scarf that dangled down to his waist. Gathered around him was a group of about twenty people. He was motioning everyone to stay close. Charles had hoped they could just blend in with the tour group, like Jacques had done earlier. But the tour guide was speaking German. Neither Jacques nor Charles spoke German.

Charles looked at Jacques and whispered, "What should we do?"

"Do you have his book with you?" Jacques asked.

"Yes, it's here."

"Hold it up high in the air, and tell Dr. McAllister that you purchased his book and would greatly appreciate it if he would autograph it for you. That is what authors do, they sign their books," Jacques explained.

Holding up the black book with the gold-embossed word *Cuneiform* on it, Charles yelled out, "I bought your book. Will you sign it for me, sir?"

The tour guide stopped abruptly, his flowing gallabiyah wrapped around his legs like it had the first time Jacques had seen him. After speaking a few German words to his tour group, Dr. McAllister walked in quick steps towards Charles.

"So you bought my book. Did you read it?" asked the man with sparkling eyes, the color of the blue sky.

"I skimmed through it, as I'm on vacation and I don't have much time to read," Charles explained. "So far, I've found it very enlightening."

"Enlightening?" the tour guide said, raising his eyebrows.

"Yes, enlightening," Charles said. "I would be grateful if you would autograph your book for me. Also, I'd like to ask you a few questions."

"Hmmm," Dr. McAllister said, rubbing his chin.

"Yes, I would be happy to autograph my book and answer your questions. In return, I would like to know why a young man like you would find my book on Cuneiform enlightening. My tour ends at 12:30. I have a lunch break before my next tour. We could talk over lunch."

"Great," Charles said. "We'll be here at 12:30 sharp."

Dr. McAllister gathered his German-speaking group and headed for the stairs leading to the second floor of the museum.

"See, Charles, everything is working out nicely," Jacques said, looking pleased. "Now, we have about three hours before meeting our Dr. McAllister. I think this might be a perfect time to visit the Treasures of Tutankhamun exhibit. Remember, Dr. McAllister said that to understand Akhenaten one needs to explore the relationship between the pharaoh of Tel el Amarna and the boy pharaoh of Thebes, Tutankhamun."

"Good," Charles said. "The theme for this morning will be the connection between Akhenaten and Tutankhamun."

"The theme for this morning?" Jacques said, shaking his head in bewilderment. "Charles, what kind of boy are you, anyway?"

"Just a regular boy who loves Egypt."

"We're here, but I don't see a sign for Tutankhamun. All I see is a sign saying, Entrance to the King Tut Exhibit.

"Tut is short for Tutankhamun. It seems some people have difficulty remembering words with more than three syllables," Charles said.

"Personally, I don't blame them," Jacques replied. "There appear to be a lot of new names to remember in Egypt."

Jacques paid the entrance fee for the King Tut exhibit. Charles read a plaque aloud, explaining to Jacques that the exhibit would begin with an exact replica of the tomb of the boy pharaoh, Tutankhamun, exactly how it was when Howard Carter discovered it.

"Did you know, Jacques, that Howard Carter started working in Egypt when he was only seventeen years old? I'm almost seventeen."

"From my calculations, you are not exactly twelve yet," Jacques said.

"I'll be twelve in a few more days," Charles informed his guardian.

Charles related that it took Carter thirty-one years before he made this amazing discovery, a tomb untouched by tomb robbers.

Jacques stared at the treasures of the boy king, many covered in layers of shimmering gold. He was mesmerized, entranced, spellbound, almost unable to move. Jacques couldn't take his eyes off that radiant gold, hammered into such beautiful objects.

As he stared at the gold, Jacques had a sudden inclination to return to the shop of Samy's cousin and buy the gold scarab ring their taxi driver had convinced him to try on. Maybe he should buy it. Not out of vanity or love of gold, he tried to convince himself, but as a constant reminder of this moment, this first time seeing Tutankhamun's wondrous treasures. He was beginning to understand Charles' obsession with ancient Egypt.

Meanwhile, Charles spent the first hour not looking at King Tut's tomb but examining dozens of photographs taken of the excavation of his tomb by Harry Burton, Howard Carter's photographer. How did Harry Burton manage to pull his viewing audience into his black-and-white photographs, taken over sixty years ago? Charles thought that Burton somehow made his viewers feel like they were actually there, in person.

He recalled something Mademoiselle Fleuret had told her students back at the Château du Mont: "There is one thing the photograph must contain: the humanity of the moment."

That is what Burton did. He not only documented the greatest discovery of all time, but he also managed to capture the humanity behind the discovery. His camera lens and film did not just capture Carter and King Tut's treasures. They captured the Egyptian workers toiling in horrendous heat, digging in the hot sand, climbing down dangerous tunnels, all to make Carter's great discovery possible. That was the kind of photographer Charles wanted to be.

Jacques pulled his eyes from the store of golden treasures to find Charles. "Did you find anything about Akhenaten and Tutankhamun?" he asked the young Egyptologist.

"Yes, in this photograph here." Charles showed Jacques a photograph taken inside the tomb of King Tut. "See this throne? I believe I can see the symbol of the power behind the sun, not Ra but Aten."

"Charles, if you don't mind my suggestion, why look at this black-and-white photograph when we could look at the exact reproduction of the boy pharaoh's throne?" Jacques gestured towards a gold chair with colorful characters carved into the backrest.

"Good idea, Jacques," Charles said, rushing to the exhibit of the tomb.

"Tutankhamun was eight years old when he was crowned pharaoh," Charles said. "This was after the destruction of Tel el Amarna and probably the death of Akhenaten. When King Tut became pharaoh, Egyptologists claim, he brought back the old religion, the old gods and goddesses, putting the high priests back into power."

"But why," Charles mused, "would Tutankhamun allow a carving on the backrest of his throne of a symbol of Aten and figures which, I am sure, are Akhenaten and Nefertiti?"

"That is a good question, Charles," his guardian said.

"Look, Jacques, this sign says Tutankhamun was originally called Tutankhaten. King Tut's birth name had the name Aten in it. His name was changed when he became pharaoh."

"Maybe Akhenaten was Tutankhamun's father," Jacques suggested.

"The only problem with that theory, Jacques, is that there are a number of references to Akhenaten's six daughters, but no references to a son," Charles said.

"That is confounding. How can we explain this?" Jacques said, staring at the golden chair.

Looking at his watch, Jacques announced it was time to head towards the tourist counter where they were to meet Dr. McAllister. "Maybe he has a theory about the chair's backrest and the parentage of Tutankhamun," he suggested.

"That would be great. I hope he'll be willing to translate the writing on the relic pyramid," Charles said, crossing his fingers.

"I, too, have written down several questions for our Dr. McAllister," Jacques said.

Seeing Jacques' black notebook, decorated with a golden funeral mask of King Tut, made Charles laugh.

CHAPTER 18

AKHENATEN'S POEM

D r. McAllister was just finishing his tour. Guests gathered around him, laughing and talking. When he finally turned to Jacques and Charles, Jacques asked him to join them for lunch. They left the museum and walked to the edge of the road. It was busy as always, teeming with cars, trucks, bicycles, and rickshaws, all zooming down a street with no apparent lanes.

Dr. McAllister stepped off the curb, undaunted. The Egyptologist lifted his arms above his head and, miraculously, the traffic parted long enough for him to make his way to a booth across from the museum, with Charles and Jacques scrambling after him. Jacques was reminded of the old Hollywood movie "The Ten Commandments," where the biblical prophet Moses, played by Charlton Heston, made a similar gesture before parting the Red Sea.

The trio found a table with pink plastic lawn chairs shaded by a faded green umbrella. Jacques went to buy refreshments from a nearby vendor. He returned with three lunches, consisting of the ever-present flatbread and ice-cold bottles of Coca-Cola. Charles looked at his drink, so familiar and yet so different. The label was printed in Arabic. Water condensed on the sides of the bottle from the heat, and there was no cup brimming with ice cubes.

After a moment, Dr. McAllister turned to Charles. "So, you found my book, *Cuneiform*, enlightening. I find the subject enlightening myself, but I'm wondering why it is of interest to a boy of..."

"Twelve," Charles answered.

"Nearly twelve," Jacques said, correcting him.

"Because I need something transcribed," Charles said. "It's a mystery and a secret. We're hoping you can help us."

Dr. McAllister looked at Charles with new interest and then, scratching his chin, said, "Hmm! A mystery? A secret? I believe you have caught my attention."

As quickly as he could, Charles told Dr. McAllister about Farak Faruq and his family's heirloom pyramid. He related how Farak had presented him with a replica, adding that after he had leafed through Dr. McAllister's book on Cuneiform, he and Jacques had decided the Egyptologist might be able to translate the writing.

Jacques noticed that Dr. McAllister looked all around before replying. Apparently, everyone around here was suspicious. "Do you know what I think, Charles and Mr...?"

"Gerard, Jacques Gerard," Charles' chaperone said.

"I think it was wise that you and Mr. Gerard did not bring the pyramid into the museum, especially if the capstone is truly made of pure gold," Dr. McAllister said. "How can I see this pyramid?"

Charles looked all around before answering, taking a cue from the Egyptologist. "You can see it tonight. It is back at the Mena House."

"Tonight? Oh, my," the Egyptologist said, shaking his head. "I am speaking this very evening at a conference of German Egyptologists and anthropologists."

"But we're leaving for Luxor tomorrow on the train. You must come tonight. Can't you cancel?" Charles pleaded. "This is important, very important."

"I agree it is important. If I had not given my word, I would be at the Mena House as soon as I concluded my work at the museum," Dr. McAllister said. "It just so happens, however, that I am the main speaker. Then, after my talk I'll be guiding conference attendees through the Step Pyramid. I will not be back until very late."

Jacques noticed that Charles was nearly in tears. The trip had involved a lot of waiting for a boy who was very nearly twelve.

"Are you are coming back to Cairo?" Dr. McAllister asked in a kind tone.

"Yes, we'll return in two weeks," Charles said. "We'll be in Cairo for several days before leaving for France. Our plan is to tour Tel el Armana."

"Tel el Armana!" the Egyptologist exclaimed. "That's one of my favorite spots. What is your interest in Tel el Armana?"

Charles wondered if he should mention the Ghost of Tomb 11 but decided against it.

"I've been interested in tombs and Egyptian treasures ever since I was a child," Charles said. Dr. McAllister and Jacques smiled at Charles' words indicating he'd left childhood far behind.

Charles continued. "I heard that even though most of Tel el Amarna has been destroyed, there are several interesting tombs up on the hillside."

"If it is treasure you are looking for, there is none in these tombs," the Egyptologist said. "There are only riches to be found for those of us interested in the writing and illustrations on the tomb walls. This being said, what are your questions?"

Charles opened his notebook. "I guess my first question is, what do you think about Akhenaten?"

Dr. McAllister rose from his pink plastic chair. He held both arms out to his sides, as if to summon all the people around him. He began to recite some words, speaking in a tone that was melodious and, Jacques thought, too loud. Despite being on this strange adventure, Charles' chaperone still preferred to be inconspicuous.

You arise beauteous in the horizon of the heavens,
oh, living Aten who creates life.
When you shine forth in the Eastern horizon,
you fill every land with your beauty.

Bystanders, both tourists and Egyptians, turned to listen to the man in the tan gallabiyah and blue turban. Sweeping his hand across the sky, Dr. McAllister continued his recitation.

Oh, Aten. You are so beautiful: you are great,
gleaming and high over every land.
Your rays embrace the lands and all you have created.
You are Ra and reach out to all your creations,
and hold them for your beloved son.

More and more people had gathered around Dr. McAllister. Meanwhile, Charles was scribbling things down in his notebook.

You are afar, but your rays touch the earth.
Men see you but know not your ways.
How manifold are your works: they are secret from our sight.
Oh, unique God, no other is like you.

Dr. McAllister lowered his voice, and his audience drew even closer, captivated by the man's commanding presence.

You made the earth after your own heart when you were all alone,
all men, herds and flocks, all on the earth that goes on its feet,
and all that is in the sky and flies with its wings,
the land of Egypt, the foreign lands of Syria and Nubia, too.
You put every man in his place and fulfill his needs,
each one with his sustenance and the days of his life counted.
Their language is different, and they look different.

Their complexions are different, for you have distinguished the nations.
You make the seasons to bring into being all your creatures,
winter to cool them, and the heat of summer to come from you.
You have made the sky afar off,
so when you rise you can see all you have made.

Dr. McAllister's voice rose, as did the excitement of the crowd. Jacques decided the man must have studied theatre before deciding on Egyptology.

You alone rise in the form of the living Aten.
Shining afar, yet close at hand,
You make millions of forms out of you alone,
towns and villages, fields, roads, and river.
All eyes see you before them,
for you are the Aten of the day,
over all the earth.

"These, my friends, are the words of the greatest pharaoh who ever lived, Akhenaten," Dr. McAllister said. Having concluded his speech, he let his arms fall to his sides and dropped his head. There was a moment of silence. Then, the audience of strangers erupted in loud applause. Charles was up on his feet, clapping the loudest.

Dr. McAllister bowed slightly, returning to his chair. The three ate in silence. When they were finished eating, Jacques asked, "What is it that you were quoting?"

"I was quoting from the Prayer of Akhenaten, discovered on the walls of Tomb 25, Tel el Armana, Egypt."

"Tomb 25! Is that Akhenaten's tomb?" Charles asked.

"No," Dr. McAllister said. "It was designed for Ayes, Nefertiti's father."

Charles looked up at the Egyptologist and said, "That is the greatest poem I have ever read—I mean ever heard. Why do you think so many Egyptologists call Akhenaten 'nefarious'? Couldn't they tell by the words of his poem that he had a great heart?"

"Many Egyptologists are unfamiliar with Akhenaten. His existence has been almost totally erased, buried in the sands of Tel el Armana," Dr. McAllister said, looking despondent. "If they do know of him but are entranced by the stories of the ancient gods and goddesses, they fear him. They fear Akhenaten, the killer of the gods."

"What are they so afraid of?" Jacques asked.

"They are afraid of the very thing Akhenaten held to be most true: There is only one god. And I have to admit that at, one time, I was no different than most Egyptologists."

Charles looked at him questioningly.

"When I was a boy and young man, I loved all the stories of the gods and goddesses of Egypt," Dr. McAllister said. "I loved reading about tombs, mummies, and ceremonies meant to ensure a happy afterlife. I did not look kindly upon this strange pharaoh who declared there was only one true God. It was hard to like a man who had ordered the names of the ancient gods and goddesses to be chipped off the walls of temples and public buildings."

Jacques wondered if there was some justice in the fact that this pharaoh, who had sought to eradicate the memory of the old gods, eventually found himself banished and his name eradicated.

"I thought Akhenaten was a mad king," Dr. McAllister continued. "I figured he wanted immense power and thought he could achieve it by declaring himself the favorite son of Aten. However, as I began to study Akhenaten through his own words, I changed my mind. Most Egyptologists do not read Akhenaten's original writings, and so they just pass around the idea that he was nefarious. That is why I call him the most maligned of all of Egypt's rulers."

Dr. McAllister gulped the last of his tea and wrapped up the remainder of his sandwich. "I have to get back to work. When you return from Upper Egypt, contact me," he said, pressing a business card into Jacques' hand. "I will keep my calendar clear and, if you wish, will join you on your tour of Tel el Armana."

Charles was amazed at their good fortune. "Wow! That would be great. One more question. Could Tutankhamen have been Akhenaten's son?"

"That is a very good question. I hope you discover a definitive answer."

The guide turned to the road, lifted both hands in the air, and the traffic parted.

CHAPTER 19

THE TRAIN AND CHARLES' GRAVE MISTAKE

Hiking, clambering, and poring through the Great Pyramid, the Step Pyramid, and the Cairo Museum—all in the unrelenting desert heat—had taken its toll on Jacques. Once seated on the train, ensconced with Charles in a private compartment, he had just enough energy to open the map showing their route south towards Luxor. Charles, of course, was full of energy.

When Samy's cousin dropped them off at the Ramses Railway Station, Charles was enthusiastic about the the station's exotic name. Jacques, by contrast, had felt wary as well as weary. He half-expected Samy's relative to produce a store of souvenirs, looking for a quick sale.

Charles' father had reserved first-class seating, which included a sleeper car for the two travelers. Samy had purchased a general class ticket and thus was seated elsewhere on the train.

Jacques knew his young charge wasn't happy about Samy coming with them to Luxor. Charles had pleaded with Jacques to tell their taxi driver they didn't need him anymore. However, Jacques knew next to nothing about Luxor. Samy had not only lived there, but had studied the history of the world's largest outdoor museum. Jacques had read this nickname in his tour book. He felt relieved having a known driver. Charles didn't trust Samy, but that wasn't so unusual. Jacques' traveling companion was proving to be a very suspicious young man. Anyway, it was all too late now. Samy had boarded the train.

The taxi driver was in high spirits, announcing, "If you need me, I'll be sitting only six cars up."

Charles took a seat by the window. He'd never been on an overnight train in his life. Jacques, buried under the pages of his tour book and map of Egypt, looked up and announced the train wasn't scheduled to depart for fifteen minutes. Charles had a great idea. He'd surprise his chaperone by demonstrating how much he could look like an Egyptian boy. Jacques would be so surprised by his transformation.

Charles brought the cotton sack out of his suitcase and headed for the restroom at the front of the car. He removed his shirt and pants. Then he slipped on the gallibyah and tob Farak had given him and tied on the headdress with the agil. He added the shoulder bag, which contained his pyramid and writing material. Charles glanced in the mirror, and smiled at his reflection. He looked just like an Egyptian kid, a Bedouin boy. Jacques might faint, Charles thought with a laugh as he stepped out of the bathroom.

Just as he walked out the door, the conductor entered the car calling, "Ticket! Tickets!"

The conductor took one look at Charles and began yelling at him in Arabic. Charles looked around to see why the conductor was so upset. The train whistle blew, and the train jolted and moved forward. Before he knew it, the conductor had grabbed Charles by his shoulders, dragged him to the car's door, and shoved him, not so gently, off the train and onto the platform.

"I'm an American! I'm an American citizen," Charles yelled to the conductor, but he must not have understood.

The train began moving. Charles waved frantically, calling out, "Jacques! Jacques!"

The train sped up. Charles ran south alongside his car until he could no longer keep up. The train moved faster and faster, becoming one giant blur as it left the station. Charles was breathing so hard, he thought he might pass out. Once he caught his breath, he knew the train would not be coming back. What should he do?

Charles walked in a stupor towards the ticket counter inside the station building. He had to stand in line behind five people. When he got to the front of the line, he tried to explain how the conductor had put him off the train. The station master stared at the boy in a gallibyah and head cloth, and asked for his ticket. Charles told him he'd been on the train and that he didn't have the ticket. The man at the ticket window didn't seem to understand a word he was saying. Behind Charles, the line was growing longer. The man at the window motioned for him to move aside. Charles began yelling at the top of his lungs at the station master. In fact, he yelled at everyone in the railroad station. He informed anyone within hearing that they would be in a lot of trouble if they didn't help him. He demanded they call the American Embassy. The people in the line were getting agitated. The man at the window called for a military policeman.

"I have to get on that train!" Charles yelled desperately. Then the policeman dragged him through the train station and pushed him out the door towards the street.

"You are going to be in so much trouble," he warned. "I'm an American and my father is on that train!"

The train was no longer in the station, and no one would listen to him. Tears began running down Charles' cheeks. Yelling and crying, however, wasn't helping. He needed to calm down and decide what to do. He figured when Jacques became aware that Charles wasn't on the train, he'd get off the train at the next stop. Maybe he should hang around the station until the train from the south arrived. But what if Jacques couldn't get a ticket on the train heading back to Cairo? What if the policeman wouldn't let him hang around the station? He'd better devise a backup plan.

Let's see, Charles said to himself, what do I have with me? He had eight gold coins, a pyramid, a book of poems, a pen, ink, a large map of Egypt, and a few Egyptian pounds. He didn't have a train ticket or a passport, nor did he have any idea where he and Jacques were headed once they got to Luxor. He also didn't have his camera, jeans, shirt, tennis shoes or, most importantly, Jacques.

If Jacques didn't show up within an hour or two, Charles decided, he'd look for the American Embassy. They were supposed to help all Americans. Jacques would surely know this, and they'd soon be reunited and headed for Luxor.

***

Back on the train, Jacques awoke from a sound sleep. He wondered how long he had slept. Checking his watch, he saw it was at least forty-five minutes. He needed some tea. Charles wasn't in his seat. Jacques surmised he was probably in the restroom, which was at the front of the car. Jacques waited a few minutes.

When Charles didn't come out, Jacques knocked on the restroom door, calling out, "Charles? Charles, are you in there?"

There was no answer. Maybe Charles got bored and decided to go up six cars and talk to Samy. Jacques staggered through the train. He found Samy in the crowded general class car. He was seated with a portable tape player on his lap, wearing earphones and mouthing the words to a song. Jacques put his hand on Samy's shoulder. He jumped, then removed his earphones.

"Have you seen Charles?" Jacques asked.

Samy shook his head. "No, I thought he was with you."

Jacques felt sheepish. "I fell asleep. When I awoke, Charles wasn't in the car or the bathroom."

Samy jumped up from his seat, eyes searching the train car.

"You go back to your car," he advised Jacques. "I'll search forward. Knowing boys, Charles is probably in the dining car. I'll check there first."

Jacques nodded. He could picture Charles trying to order a flatbread hamburger. "I bet that is where we will find him," he agreed.

He was relieved that Samy was on the train. Charles had to be on the train somewhere. There was nothing to worry about. Jacques was feeling calmer—until the name Mr. Smith popped unbidden into his head.

A few minutes later, Samy and the conductor came into Jacques' car. "He wasn't in the dining car," the taxi driver reported.

Jacques knocked on the bathroom door again. Getting no answer, he walked in. By the sink was a stack of neatly-folded clothes, but no Charles. He called Samy and the conductor into the restroom. Samy picked up Charles' clothes. What could have happened to him? Samy asked the conductor more questions in Arabic.

He turned to Jacques and said, "We have an answer, but it isn't good. The conductor says when he came into this car to stamp your tickets, he discovered a Bedouin boy trying to get a free ride on the train. The boy was dressed in a gallibyah, a tob, and a headdress. The conductor says he picked up the stowaway and placed him gently on the station platform."

Jacques had a sick feeling in his stomach. Charles must have somehow found some Egyptian clothes. Then, in a case of mistaken identity, the conductor put him off the train. Jacques was carrying Charles' train ticket, his passport and all the money. Jacques admonished himself. He should never have undertaken this trip with a twelve-year-old. What had he been thinking? Now, he'd lost Charles.

Samy and the conductor went to the front of the train to talk with the engineer. The engineer said he'd contact the Cairo station, instructing them to look for an unaccompanied boy dressed as an Egyptian.

"Did you tell him the boy has blue eyes?" Jacques asked Samy. The taxi driver said he had.

Since their bags had been checked in through to Luxor, Jacques and Samy had to arrange for the luggage to be sent back to the Cairo station. They were able to get on the next train north. Jumping off the train, Samy and Jacques searched the entire train station—no Charles. Jacques was sick to his stomach.

***

Back in Cairo, Charles was feeling like the unluckiest boy in the world. The policeman who'd thrown him out of the station blocked his way every time he tried to reenter. A train had come from the south, but apparently Jacques wasn't on it. The only people to exit the station were an elderly Egyptian couple. They shooed Charles away when he tried to talk to them. Jacques had given him strict instructions that if they got separated, he was to go to the American Embassy. That was what he should do.

Charles asked people on the sidewalk where the American Embassy was located. They just hurried past the boy in the gallabiyah. Charles raised his hand to call a taxi, but no taxi would stop. He'd learned one thing from his misadventure. It wasn't easy being a Bedouin boy in Cairo. What could he do? Money, money would make a taxi stop.

Charles waved a handful of Egyptian pounds in the air. "Taxi! Taxi!" he called.

It worked; a taxi driver pulled to the curb. At the same moment, a man in an apron pushing a handcart came up on the other side of Charles. The man's cart was piled high with large metal boxes. The box on the very top, which was even with Charles' head, began to slip. The man pushed the cart forward, trying to stop the box from falling on Charles, but it didn't work. In slow motion, Charles saw the box coming toward him. The last thing Charles remembered was a terrible pain as the corner of a metal box fell hard against his right temple. After that, everything went black.

CHAPTER 20

BRIDGE OVER TROUBLED WATER

After an hour of looking for Charles, Samy said to the increasingly anxious Jacques, "Don't worry, I am sure Charles must have gone to the American Embassy, just like you told him to do. Let's take one of those taxis waiting outside the station. It will be faster than calling my cousin to pick us up."

Arriving at the American Embassy, Samy spoke in Arabic to the woman in a brown gallabiyah and headscarf at the front desk. She rushed off, then returned to the front office with a man in a tan suit named Nelson. Agent Nelson escorted Jacques into a little office with a glass window in the door. He pointed to a wooden chair. Jacques sat down and began his story. He told the agent that the boy he was in charge of was missing. Before Jacques said one more thing, the agent asked to see his passport. Then he asked for Charles' birth certificate. Jacques gave him the certificate and a letter from Charles' father permitting Jacques Gerard to authorize any medical procedures his son might need on the trip.

Thinking about medical procedures made Jacques feel queasy. What could have happened to his charge? Why was this man taking so long to get through the paperwork? And where was Charles? Jacques nervously wiped his mouth with the back of his hand, then insisted he had to talk to Madame Constance, headmistress of the Château du Mont, the boys' school Charles attended and where he was employed.

The agent lifted his hand, stopping Jacques from talking, and picked up the telephone on his desk. "This is the American Embassy in Cairo. I need to talk to someone about a lost American boy, nearly twelve years old."

While Agent Nelson was waiting, he informed Jacques that he was calling the CIA in the United States. Agent Nelson told the agent on the other end of the phone about the missing boy, and how he'd disguised himself in Bedouin attire.

The man behind the large wooden desk said, "Agent Nelson is checking on the whereabouts of Charles Dayton Stratton III's parents. He will call back soon."

Jacques checked his watch. He'd been at the American Embassy for forty minutes. He told the agent that Charles' parents were out of the country. The phone rang. The agent picked up the black telephone. After listening for a few minutes, Agent Nelson put the phone back in its cradle.

"You are correct, Mr. Gerard. The secretary employed by Charles' parents reported that he has not heard from Mr. and Mrs. Stratton for more than a week, and that he expected they would be 'out of touch' for several more weeks. The agent asked the man to call him as soon as he heard from them. He gave the butler his private number."

Picking up the phone again, the agent dialed another number, that of the Château du Mont. Nelson calmly explained to Madame Constance that one of her students was lost in Egypt, a Charles Dayton Stratton III. He handed Jacques the phone.

What could he say? He told Madame Constance the story of Charles' going into the restroom and changing into Egyptian clothes and how the conductor, mistaking the boy for a freeloader, put him off the train.

"I assumed since we were on the train we were safe," Jacques said. "I am afraid, Madame Constance, that I opened up a map of Luxor and the next thing I knew I fell asleep."

"Samy, my taxi driver, and I looked all through the train, but he wasn't on board. Then Samy asked the conductor in Arabic, which I do not speak, if he had seen a boy. The conductor told Samy that he thought the boy was a stowaway and had gently removed him from the train, just as the train was leaving the station."

"Samy, the taxi driver? It is a long story, but he agreed to come to Luxor because he knows this ancient city like the back of his hand." Jacques was aware that he was rambling incoherently.

The headmistress let Jacques tell his story uninterrupted. For Jacques, this felt worse than if she had begun yelling, like any normal person would. Jacques ended the conversation by saying that Samy and he were going back to the train station to look for Charles. He added that he was certain he would find him. Exactly how he was going to find him, Jacques was not sure.

The agent took the phone back and informed Madame Constance that the American Embassy was on the case and would find her student. He vowed that he personally would notify the military police, the newspapers, and the French Embassy. He gave Madame Constance his personal phone number, then hung up.

When Jacques left the building, he found that Samy had been reunited with his taxi. He was now wearing a tasteful white Hawaiian shirt dotted with small palm trees. Samy jumped out of his cab, opening the back door for Jacques. Jacques sat down in a daze.

Samy jumped in the front seat and announced he'd already gone back and talked to ticket salesmen, station superintendents, porters, janitors, and train assistants. No one remembered seeing a boy with deep blue eyes in a gallibyah. As Samy pulled out of his parking space, Jacques just grunted in response.

Once on the road, the taxi driver swiveled his head around and looked at Jacques. His white shirt was wrinkled, his face gray with stress and taut with worry.

Jacques ran his hands through his neatly plastered black hair, causing it to stand up in sharp points. He reproached himself for the hundredth time. He should have kept an eye on Charles, at least until the train pulled out of the station. No matter how hard he wished for time to go backwards, however, it would not. What could he do? What should he do? He knew only one thing for sure. He would not leave Egypt without Charles Dayton Stratton III.

More questions arose. Where should he go? Where could he stay? The image of an Egyptian man who claimed to be older than the Sphinx popped into his head. In his mind's eye, Jacques could see Dr. Awyan standing right in front of him wearing a gray gallibyah, a blue turban, and a wide smile.

Samy asked, "Where do you want to go, boss? I have a cousin..."

"I would like to go to the train station again."

They had no luck. Charles was not there. It was late, and there were few people in the station.

Samy asked, "Now, where should we...?"

Before Samy could finish his sentence, Jacques said, "I need to go back to the Giza Plateau. I must talk to Dr. Awyan."

"Good idea, boss. I will take you there, as soon as we have dinner," Samy said, driving away from the train station.

This time, Samy did not put a tape in the car's cassette player. He drove to the same restaurant in Giza where he'd taken Jacques and Charles on that very first day. Samy whispered to the owner, and soon a light supper was placed in front of Charles' distressed guardian. When dinner was over, Samy and Jacques drove up the road to the plateau, now closed to tourists. Several soldiers stood beside a wooden barrier that barred access to the archeological zone.

When Samy told them their destination, the barrier was raised. Jacques stared at the huge, shadowy triangular shape of the Great Pyramid, which loomed to his right. It was lit up by a boat-shaped moon and crowned by a sprinkle of stars. Charles was somewhere under this same sky. Was he injured, lost, kidnapped? Jacques' stomach churned at the possibilities.

There were no other vehicles on the road, only Samy's black car moving silently through the black night. He drove past the School of Khemitology, and Jacques was relieved to see a light gleaming from the window of the old cement building. At least someone was still there. Samy made a U-turn and pulled up in front of the school's office. Jacques knocked on the door.

Dr. Awyan's son Yousef answered. He stared at the two men at the door, then asked, "Where is Charles?"

"That is why we are here," Jacques said. "We were supposed to be in Luxor by now, but Charles was put off the train by a confused conductor before we left the Cairo station. I didn't notice his absence until the train was well out of Cairo."

"Before you say more, I will get my father," Yousef said, pointing to some straight-backed chairs as he walked out a door behind the front office. A few minutes later, Yousef and then Dr. Awyan entered the room.

Dr. Awyan's gray turban was tilted a bit to the right. He was not smiling. "Charles is missing?" he asked.

Jacques explained what had happened, ending with, "I must find him. I have to find him."

Dr. Awyan looked at Jacques. He saw a trembling man with desperation in his eyes. Yousef brought in two more chairs. The four sat in a tight circle as Jacques told his full story, Samy contributing missing details like their trip to the American Embassy.

Dr. Awyan said, "Fortunately, Charles is a very level-headed young man. He must have gotten lost somehow on his way to the embassy. I will send a message out to all of our people to look out for the boy. I assure you, our communication system travels faster than wildfire, maybe faster than the speed of light," the Wisdom Keeper said with a slight smile.

"Thank you," Jacques whispered hoarsely.

"If you don't mind my saying so, you look terrible, Jacques," Dr. Awyan said.

155

"He's right, you do look terrible," Samy agreed.

"How long has it been since you slept?" the older Egyptian asked.

"I don't know," Jacques answered, plopping down in a chair.

"Yousef will walk you over to the Khemitology Guest House. You can stay there tonight. I'll send someone over with water and some food. There is nothing more for you to do tonight, Jacques, but to eat and get some rest."

Samy and Yousef carried Jacques' and Charles' luggage into the Khemitology Guest House. Yousef suggested Jacques take the third-floor room, which faced the Sphinx. He promised that when the sun rose, Jacques would have a spectacular view of the entire Giza Plateau. Jacques dragged himself upstairs.

"I'll be back in the morning," Samy called as he walked down the creaky old wooden stairs.

Within twenty minutes, a young man in a brown gallabiyah brought up a platter of cheese, fruit, and flatbread, along with a pot of hot tea, and placed it on a small table next to the window. Jacques had only eaten a few bites of soup at the restaurant. He ate, brushed his teeth, washed his face, put on his blue-and-white striped pajamas, and fell into bed.

In what felt like only moments later, the sun shone through the window, causing Jacques to reluctantly open his eyes. He'd awakened hoping yesterday was a bad dream. Yet here he was in a room on the Giza Plateau, with no Charles. He stumbled towards the window and looked out at the Sphinx. He, no she, didn't look happy. Dr. Awyan was adamant that the Sphinx was female, not male, claiming that predynastic Egypt was matriarchal. The Sphinx looked anxious, careworn, and weighed-down, reflecting Jacques' own feelings.

As he looked at the Sphinx, Jacques recalled the silly poem he'd written about his first camel ride and an imaginary talk with the enormous statue. In it, he'd solved the famous riddle of the Sphinx. He also remembered Charles' serious poem in which he talked to the spirit of the Great Pyramid. Charles was a remarkable boy, Jacques thought ruefully. Charles *is* a remarkable boy, he corrected himself. Where could he be?

As Jacques dressed, he caught sight of his image in the closet mirror. He looked exhausted. He felt exhausted. But that wasn't going to do. Jacques brought his shoulder blades back, raised his head, stood straight, and took several deep breaths. He was going to find Charles, and of this he had no doubt.

Hearing a knock at the door, Jacques took several steps to open it. In the doorway was a different young man from last night. He carried a tray with flatbread, scrambled eggs, rice, fruit, and orange juice and placed it on the table with the view of the Sphinx. The young man greeted Jacques in English with a cheery good morning.

Bowing slightly, the young man said, "It looks like it is going to be a beautiful day. Goodbye. I hope you have a good day, sir."

The young man sounded like he was practicing his English. Jacques gave him a smile and thanked him, repeating that he hoped the young man would have a good day, too. Sitting at the small wooden table, Jacques watched the orange sun rise in the eastern sky. Its path painted the sky a rosy pink. Jacques' eyes settled back on the Sphinx, marveling at how her expression had changed. She no longer looked anxious. She had taken on the role of sentinel, guardian, lookout, protector. It was the same role Jacques intended to take.

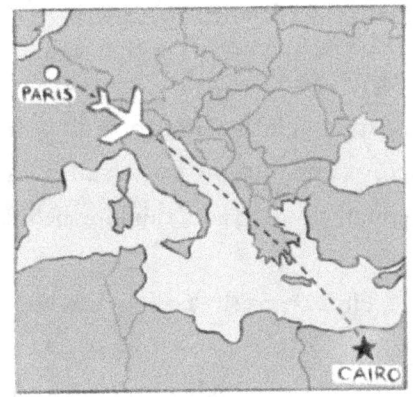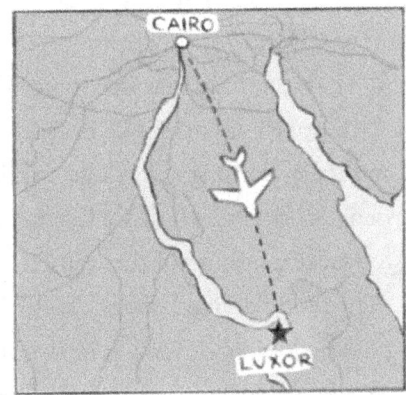

CHAPTER 21

FARAK AND DAVID HEAD FOR EGYPT

F arak knocked on the door of David's and Charles' room on the third floor of the Château du Mont.

"Come on in, Farak. It's a little lonely here without Charles," David said, ushering the teenager into his room.

With no greeting, Farak said, "I received a message from one of the students. He said Madame Constance requests that you and I come to her office immediately."

"Both of us?" David asked with a frown.

"Yes, both of us," Farak answered, his forehead furrowed.

"It must have something to do with Charles and Egypt," David said, his lips in a tight line.

"I believe so, too," Farak said.

David grabbed his uniform jacket, pushing his arms into the sleeves as both boys ran down the three flights of stairs. Turning towards Madame Constance's office, they slowed down a bit. The door was open. Madame Constance was standing in front of her desk, hands clasped in front of her. Deep wrinkles showed on her brow.

"What is it?" Farak asked.

"Close the door and sit down. I have something to tell you. But I do not want to tell you."

"What is it, Madame Constance?" David asked.

"It appears Charles put on some Egyptian clothes after boarding the train at the Cairo station. The conductor came into the car to stamp the passengers' tickets. He saw a boy in Egyptian clothing and, thinking he was a stowaway, put him off the train."

The blood drained out of Farak's face. He was positive Charles was wearing the Bedouin clothes that he'd outgrown.

Madame Constance continued her story. "Jacques didn't notice Charles was gone until the train was on its way to Luxor. It took him half a day to get back to Cairo. Charles was nowhere to be found. Jacques was sure he would be at the American Embassy, as planned beforehand. Unfortunately, he was not."

"How long has he been missing?" David asked.

"I'm not sure exactly, due to time differences. Jacques assures me that they will find Charles. They have put up flyers around the station, and the local newspapers will soon be running stories about the disappearance of an American boy."

"Yes, an American boy that looks like an Egyptian boy," Farak mumbled to himself.

"Where is Jacques at this moment?" David asked.

"Jacques says he is staying with friends near the Giza Plateau," Madame Constance said, opening up the map drawer on her desk and pointing to a symbol of the Sphinx. "Of course, I cannot get in touch with Charles' parents. They are always off traveling somewhere. I just thought you two should know, as you are close to him."

"How could Jacques have friends in Cairo when he's never been there?" Farak asked.

Madame Constance answered, "Jacques said something about the School of Khemitology. He says he will stay there until Charles is found or..."

"Or what?" David asked, now looking even more worried.

One of the cooks knocked on the door. "I am sorry, there is something I must attend to," Madame Constance told the boys. "There always is."

"Thank you for informing us," Farak called out. "May I use the phone? I believe my family can help locate Charles."

"Yes, yes, that would be good," Madame Constance said as she hurried out the door.

Turning to David, Farak said, "I am afraid this is all my fault."

"How can it be your fault?" David asked. "You weren't even there."

"I gave Charles the Egyptian clothes, the ones I wore when I came to the Château du Mont. If I had not given them to him, he would never have been put off the train."

David shook his head. "I still don't think it's your fault."

Farak reached for the phone sitting on Madame Constance's desk.

"Hello. When is the next plane leaving for Cairo?" The Egyptian boy reached for a pen and paper and began scribbling. "Egyptian Air. Seven-thirty. Okay, I would like to make a reservation." Farak reached into his wallet for the information requested. Then, he made another call to Cairo.

"Please connect me to Nile Air," he said. "Yes, I would like to make a reservation from Cairo to Luxor, 2 a.m. tomorrow. I will be flying in from Paris on Egyptian Air Flight 367. I will arrive at 1:30 a.m. Thank you. Here is my information..."

The older boy made another call, this time requesting that a taxi pick him up at the Château du Mont at 4:30 p.m.

"Why are you going to Luxor when Madame Constance said Charles was put off the train in Cairo?" David asked.

"Because my family lives in Luxor, and they know many people all over Egypt," Farak said. "My father and grandfather can put out a call for everyone they know to look for Charles."

David looked at the phone on Madame Constance's desk. He needed to go to Egypt too. He couldn't call home. His parents claimed he was too young to travel so far. The only people he knew who might agree to take him were his grandparents. He picked up the phone. David was relieved to hear his grandmother's voice on the other end of the line. He knew she'd understand how important it was for him to go to Egypt. He told her what had happened to Charles, insisting Jacques would need support. His grandmother said she'd make the arrangements. They'd leave the day after tomorrow.

"But Grandmother," David cajoled, "I need to leave now."

"If he's discovered within two days, we won't need to go," she said reasonably. "If not, Jacques really will need our help and support. I'll contact Madame Constance with the particulars. I'll also help your grandfather, not to mention your parents, understand why we must go. Goodbye, David. Pack!"

***

Madame Constance decided she must tell Mademoiselle Fleuret. The art instructor was the most unconventional teacher at the Château du Mont. The headmistress wasn't sure she approved of the woman's teaching methods, nor her excessive familiarity with students, though she certainly got remarkable results. However, the professor had a special rapport with Charles. Also, though she hated to admit it, the headmistress felt the need for support. It wasn't every day one of her charges went missing.

Madame Constance entered the arts building, where she found Mademoiselle Fleuret teetering on a stool. She was on her tiptoes, attaching one of her students' charcoal drawings up onto the art board. The headmistress could see that under Mademoiselle Fleuret's mandatory black teachers' robe, she was wearing a rainbow-colored skirt and that her black shoes had pink shoelaces. It was completely unacceptable, but there were more important things to worry about at present. Once the art teacher was safely on the ground, Madame Constance asked if she could speak to her a minute.

"Yes, of course," the art teacher answered.

Madame Constance clasped her hands once again. "To get down to it, you probably heard that Charles' parents arranged for Jacques to take him to Egypt for an educational vacation. I expressed my belief that Jacques, who has never had children, might not be up to the task. Mr. Stratton believed he was. It turns out I was correct. Jacques has lost Charles."

"What do you mean, Jacques has lost Charles?" the art teacher asked.

"Well, not exactly lost him," Madame Constance said. "It seems that while waiting for the train to leave for Luxor, Charles went into the bathroom and changed into Egyptian clothes. Heavens knows why!"

"Mon dieu!" Mademoiselle Fleuret exclaimed.

"When he emerged in his costume, the conductor mistook him for an Egyptian boy and a stowaway. Just before the train pulled out of the station, he put Charles off the train and onto the platform," Madame Constance continued. "Meanwhile, Jacques was taking a well-deserved nap behind a map of Luxor. When he awoke, he assumed Charles was in the restroom or the dining car. By the time he discovered the boy was no longer on the train, the train was several hours out of Cairo."

"Charles is missing? Where is he?" the art teacher asked. "And where is Jacques? He must be frantic."

"Jacques and his taxi driver, Samy, returned to the station. Charles, however, was nowhere to be found. Jacques had instructed Charles to go to the American Embassy should they become separated, but Charles never arrived. Now everyone is looking for the boy, even the military police. Oh, my, I think I had better sit down."

Clearly feeling faint, she squeezed herself into a desk better suited for a young student. The art teacher looked concerned.

"I am sorry, Madame Constance. This must be very difficult for you. Let me give you a drink of water," she said, rushing to the sink.

Madame Constance gulped water from a glass that looked like it had recently been used to mix paint. She thanked Professor Fleuret—the headmistress refused to call her Mademoiselle Fleuret, believing the too-casual name bred excessive familiarity with students.

Madame Constance reminded herself of one of her favorite sayings, "You must lead by example." She had to collect herself.

"This is shocking news, and I feel so sorry for poor Jacques. I want you to find someone else to take my classes, immediately. I am going to Egypt," the art teacher said firmly.

"You are not," Madame Constance said, her eyes wide with shock.

"Yes, I am. This is very serious, Madame Constance. You cannot go, although I am sure you wish you could, but I can," Mademoiselle Fleuret said resolutely.

Resigned, Madame Constance left without saying another word. Returning to her office, she found Farak waiting for her.

"Madame Constance," the Egyptian teen said, "I am leaving for Egypt immediately. My taxi will arrive soon. I must pack."

"But Farak, your classes," the stunned headmistress said.

"I am through with all my tests and even if I were not, Charles is more important than classes," Farak said unwaveringly. "My family knows many people throughout Egypt. With my help, I am sure we can find him."

As he left the room, Madame Constance collapsed into her chair. She had just poured some headache powder into a glass of water when the phone rang.

"Hello," she said. "Oh, yes, Mrs. Montgomery. No, I really don't think that would be advisable to take your grandson to Egypt. Farak has made arrangements to return to his family in Egypt. Farak says his family knows many people in Egypt, and they will put out the word that an American boy is lost."

"Furthermore," Madame Constance continued, "our art teacher Professor Fleuret—an exceedingly competent woman—also insists on traveling to Cairo to lend support to Jacques in his search for Charles. So, as you can see, you do not need to go. Besides, taking David out of school is out of the question."

Madame Constance listened for a few minutes. "Very well," she said, sounding defeated. "I will see that he is ready, but really..."

Evidently, the speaker on the other end of the phone had hung up. With her left elbow leaning on the desktop, Madame Constance held her heavy head. What was happening? Was everyone in the entire school going to Cairo to find a missing boy? At any rate, Professor Fleuret was correct. Madame Constance did wish with all her heart she could go to Egypt. Charles was her responsibility. But what should she do? What could she do?

Whatever you do or dream you can, begin it;
Boldness has genius, power, and magic in it.
- Goethe

CHAPTER 22

GOETHE AND THE FBI

A gray-haired man sitting at his mahogany desk sipped hot tea as he read from an ancient-looking book. The book was *Faust, Part II* by Johann Wolfgang Von Goethe, a 19th-century German writer, scientist, and philosopher.

He'd read Faust many times before, but the words seemed to change as one got older. In the background, there was a rumbling noise. Through his office window, he could see a flash of lightning illuminating the billowing dark clouds. He'd recently read that lightning can be five times as hot as the surface of the sun, amazing news. He'd always found the loud clash and crash and bang of thunder that followed a lightning strike more unsettling than the lightning itself. At any rate, he thought, Faust reads better during a thunderstorm.

Taking another sip from his cup filled with finely-brewed tea, Dr. Charles Dayton Stratton thought about his life. He'd endured his share of tragedies. He'd lost his only son and, a few years ago, his wife of forty years had passed on. Everyone, however, faced tragedies. He knew he was fortunate. He was chair of the Philosophy Department at the prestigious Harvard University. He enjoyed opening the minds of students to the greatest thinkers throughout history. His occasional talks and articles were appreciated by his peers. He had a comfortable, if old, home within walking distance of his office at the university. And he enjoyed the company of his friend and confidant Alfred, even though the man had confounded him by adopting the role of his butler for some unaccountable reason.

The professor's life was pleasant and predictable. Then again, as a practically unknown philosopher once wrote, "It is exactly when you are comfortable that life tends to show its sense of humor, bringing abrupt and dramatic change."

There was a polite knock on his office door, which stood slightly ajar. "Yes, Alfred," Dr. Stratton said, smiling at his old friend.

Alfred P. Hart walked into Dr. Stratton's office wearing his too-formal black jacket and pants, a gray vest, and a wide gray tie. Dr. Stratton often asked why he didn't wear something more casual, but Alfred insisted he was quite comfortable. Dr. Stratton felt slightly embarrassed to be in the company of such an old-fashioned-looking butler, considering he rejected class systems of every sort. He believed any man or woman with courage and sense was equal to a king.

"Excuse me, Professor," Alfred announced, "but there are two men at the door. They say they are from the FBI."

The professor raised an eyebrow. "The FBI? I think we'd better let them in, don't you?"

"Yes, Dr. Stratton," Alfred said, adopting the formal tone he always employed when guests entered their home.

Alfred returned with two men dressed in dark suits, white shirts, and narrow black ties. The older man was wearing a fedora hat. Yes, thought

Dr. Stratton—who was wearing the unofficial academic uniform of a forest-green corduroy jacket with leather elbow patches and gray slacks—they certainly looked like FBI agents.

"Sir," said the younger of the two men, "Charles Dayton Stratton is lost in Egypt."

"Well, that's very interesting, considering I am Charles Dayton Stratton and, as you can see, I am not lost in Egypt. I am, however, lost in this book," he said, holding up the ancient volume. "Are you familiar with Goethe?"

"I'm afraid not, Sir," said the young man.

"Hmmm," Dr. Stratton replied with slight disapproval.

The older FBI agent interjected. "What my colleague meant to say is that a twelve-year-old boy, Charles Dayton Stratton III, has gone missing in Egypt. The American Embassy asked us to contact you, to see if you know anything about his disappearance."

"I think you gentlemen had better sit down," Professor Charles Dayton Stratton said, wondering if he'd nodded off while reading Faust and was inside his dream.

The agents settled on straight-backed leather chairs facing the professor's desk.

"You'd better take a seat too, Alfred," Dr. Stratton said to the man hovering near the door.

"What you are saying is that there is a twelve-year-old-boy who appears to be in my lineage," Dr. Stratton said, "and this boy has somehow disappeared in Egypt. First, I must tell you that not only do I know nothing about Charles Dayton Stratton III's disappearance, but up until this very moment I knew nothing about his existence."

"Are you saying you are not related to the boy?" asked the older agent.

The professor sighed. "No, I didn't say that. You see, nearly twenty years ago my only son disappeared. He said something about needing to be realistic about the world and having to make difficult choices. Then he just walked out the door and out of my life. My wife and I never saw or heard of him again. His name is, of course, Charles Dayton Stratton II. It is entirely possible, although surprising, that he could have a son. It's also possible that he would have named his son, my unknown grandson, Charles Dayton Stratton III. Is the boy's father in Egypt?"

Consternation showed on the older agent's face. "No. We were told the boy was in Egypt with a Jacques Gerard, an employee of the Château du Mont, a French boys' school in France."

"So this boy, Charles Dayton Stratton III, was attending school in France and for some reason he was sent to Egypt with this Mr. Gerard," Professor Stratton summarized. "And then, somehow the boy disappeared."

The older agent glanced at a yellow tablet on which he'd scribbled some notes. "Yes, sir," he said.

The younger agent took over. "You see, Dr. Stratton, the man and Charles had boarded a train in Cairo bound for Luxor. The boy apparently stepped into the car's bathroom and slipped on some kind of Bedouin costume. As he stepped out of the bathroom, the conductor entered the first-class car and mistook the boy for a young Egyptian stowaway. According to the conductor, he carefully removed the boy from the car, placing him on the platform, after which the train sped off."

Dr. Stratton shook his head. "Grandson or not, this is a confounding story, sounding more like a child's adventure tale than a true-life story. At any rate, it is very concerning, isn't it, Alfred?"

"Yes, very concerning, Professor. Where was Mr. Gerard during this escapade?" Alfred asked, leaning on the edge of his chair.

"It is reported that Mr. Gerard was studying a map of Luxor, Egypt. He closed his eyes for a moment. When he awoke, the train was many miles out of Cairo. He made a thorough search of the train, but the boy was nowhere to be found. A Mr. Samy, a taxi driver or tour guide, questioned the conductor and learned of the mistaken identity."

"Mr. Gerard disembarked at the next station to return to Cairo," the younger agent continued. "He asserts that it took four or five hours before he was able to return to the Cairo station. Charles was no longer there. They had prearranged that, should there be any mishap, they were to meet at the

American Embassy, but the boy never showed up. I believe that was three or four days ago and he is still missing."

Leaning forward, Dr. Stratton asked, "What has been done to find this boy?"

"The military police have been alerted," the older agent said. "The American Embassy has placed flyers throughout the Cairo station. The *Watani News*, an English and Arabic paper, will run a front-page story about the missing boy today. A reward for information about his whereabouts will be mentioned in the article."

"Where are the boy's parents?" the man who looked like a butler asked the agents.

"Yes, where are his parents?" Charles Dayton Stratton asked, placing his hands on his desk and leaning forward.

"His parents are, quote-unquote, out of touch," answered the older man with the yellow notepad.

"Out of touch? What does that mean?" demanded Dr. Stratton. "I'm sorry, but if this is my son's child, I'd like to know where his father is."

"It appears the parents have a mansion in Newport, Rhode Island."

Dr. Stratton scratched his head. "Rhode Island? So near? Alfred, this doesn't seem possible, does it?"

"No, Dr. Stratton," Alfred agreed. "It doesn't seem possible or plausible. Newport is only a couple of hours' drive from here. Surely..."

"But they say the boy's name is Charles Dayton Stratton III?" the professor interrupted Alfred.

The younger of the two agents handed Dr. Stratton a page from his yellow notepad.

"We've got some information for you," he said in a business-like manner.

"I see this has some phone numbers," Dr. Stratton said, squinting at the writing. "We've got the American Embassy; a French boys' school called the Château du Mont, headed by a woman named Madame Constance; and a number where Mr. Jacques Gerard is staying in Cairo. The School of

Khemitology? I never heard of the School of Khemitology. What seems to be missing is the phone number of Charles' parents."

"I am afraid his parents' number is classified," said the younger man.

"Classified?" Dr. Stratton erupted. "What the blazes! Did you hear that, Alfred? His parents' phone number is classified. What does that mean?"

Dr. Stratton turned to the older agent. "Do you know what it means?"

"No, sir. I don't," he replied.

Dr. Stratton picked up a long, curved pipe lying on his desk. Without lighting it, he put the pipe in his mouth. He shook his head. "It appears, gentlemen, that I have some decisions to make. Thank you for this information. I am glad, for your sake, the thunderstorm outside seems to have abated."

Alfred showed the two FBI agents out and returned to the office. He looked nearly as shaken as the professor. "Do you think this could really be Charlie's son?"

"I am not sure but, what I know is, I must leave for Egypt as soon as possible."

"This is rather sudden, so unexpected," Alfred said to his employer and friend.

Dr. Stratton nodded in agreement. "As Goethe wrote, '*Life belongs to the living, and he who lives must be prepared for change.*' Do you wish to come with me, Alfred?"

"No, I think I'll stay home and hold down the fort, so to speak."

For the first time since the FBI agents entered his door, Dr. Stratton had time to think. He wondered, as he had countless times before, why his son left the way he did. The professor liked to imagine he could bear anything, but the loss had been so very hard on Charlie's mother. This was all too painful to think about, so Dr. Stratton pondered the journey ahead instead.

He'd always dreamed of going to Egypt but had never taken the time. Now he was going. He thought of an appropriate line of poetry from *Faust, Part II.*

Oh, came a magic cloak into my hands
To carry me to distant lands.

I should not trade it for
The choicest gown,
Nor for the cloak and garments of the crown.

He was going to Egypt to find his grandson. There was no question of whether his choice was logical or whether it was a good time to go. The eldest Charles Dayton Stratton had no idea how he was going to locate a boy in Cairo, considering he spoke no Arabic and knew nothing about the area. Still, if there was even a small chance of this boy being his grandchild, he was going. He reached again for words written by his most constant companion, Goethe.

Whatever you can do or dream you can do,
Begin it.
Boldness has genius, power, and magic in it.
Begin it now.

CHAPTER 23

THE KHEMITOLOGY GUEST HOUSE

Jacques walked next door to the School of Khemitology. Both Dr. Awyan and Yousef were behind the counter. They waved him in. Dr. Awyan told him he looked much better.

"We have sent out notices to all our people describing Charles' age, size, blue eyes, and curly black hair," Dr. Awyan said. "Meanwhile, Jacques, you are welcome to stay in the guest house for as long as necessary."

Jacques was overwhelmed by the Egyptologist's kindness. "Thank you. Thank you, Dr. Awyan," was all he could say.

"What are you going to do today?" asked Yousef.

"First, I will return to the American Embassy and see if they have heard anything," Jacques replied.

"Do you need transportation?"

Jacques shook his head. "No, Samy said he would be here this morning. In fact," he said, glancing out the window, "I see his taxi driving up right now."

As Jacques walked out of the School of Khemitology, Samy jumped out of the car. He was wearing a sky-blue Hawaiian shirt embellished with images of surfboards stuck straight up in the sand. "Where are we headed, boss?"

"To the American Embassy," Jacques answered.

Jacques had been assigned a caseworker, Mr. Allen Flores. He was a pleasant-looking man with light brown eyes and a light brown suit. Mr. Flores said he'd contacted the local newspapers and received assurances that they would run stories about Charles. When Jacques asked if he could call Madame Constance, Mr. Flores showed him to a small room with a few chairs and a black phone.

The operator connected Jacques to Madame Constance's phone at the Château du Mont. Madame Constance picked up her provincial-style phone on the first ring. "Jacques, is this you? Have you heard anything, anything, about Charles?"

"No, not yet. Dr. Awyan says he is sure we will locate him soon. Dr. Awyan is the founder of the School of Khemitology, which is right across the road from the Sphinx. He knows lots of people in Cairo. The American Embassy is going to run articles in the newspapers today."

"Jacques," Madame Constance confessed, "I am afraid I made a terrible mistake. I told David and Farak about Charles. Farak has already left for his family in Luxor, claiming they can find Charles. I am looking at the map of Egypt. They live 800 kilometers from Cairo. What can they do?"

"I do not know, Madame Constance," Jacques said. He tried to imagine how Farak's family, five hundred miles away, could find Charles, who should be in Cairo—somewhere.

"That's not all," Madame Constance said. "I also got a call from Mrs. Montgomery, David's grandmother. She and her husband plan to take David out of school and fly to Cairo to help find Charles. I told her you were taking care of things, that such a journey was completely unnecessary, but she wouldn't listen. She said the plans had been made. They will come into the Cairo airport tonight."

"Tonight?" Jacques echoed.

"Wait, there is more," Madame Constance said. "When I told Mademoiselle Fleuret about Charles, she insisted I get a substitute art teacher immediately. She plans on flying to Cairo as well. She said you needed her support. I couldn't talk sense into anyone."

"I have noticed that when you spend much time with Charles, good sense seems to go out the window. I do not know what we are to do with all these people," Jacques said, overwhelmed.

"I was wondering, do you think I should come?" Madame Constance asked plaintively.

Her offer shocked Jacques. He wanted to say absolutely not, but instead he calmly said, "I do not think that will be necessary, Madame Constance. I will keep you apprised of all that is happening."

"All four of them are flying into Cairo, arriving at 8 p.m. tonight," Madame Constance said. "I don't know what they are planning."

"So the plane hasn't left yet? Can you tell them a taxi driver named Samy will pick them up at the airport? He'll be wearing a Hawaiian shirt."

"A Hawaiian shirt?" Madame Constance sounded puzzled.

"Forget the shirt," Jacques said. "I will have him hold up a sign so they can identify him."

"Very good, Jacques. Call me with any news. I feel I should be with you, but who would run the school? Oh, dear," the headmistress fretted. "I feel as though I have lost all control."

"I felt the same way last night, but today is a new day. I will find Charles," Jacques said with resolve.

He had just set the black phone back in its cradle when Mr. Flores burst into the room, calling out breathlessly, "The FBI has just contacted me. They've discovered a Charles Dayton Stratton!"

Jacques' eyes lit up with hope. "Where is he? Where is Charles?"

"I should have been more specific," Mr. Flores said. "They have discovered a grown man named Charles Dayton Stratton. He will arrive in Cairo at the airport at 9 p.m. tonight."

So, at least the FBI had been able to locate Charles' father. Thank heavens, Jacques thought, breathing a sigh of relief.

Mr. Flores said, "He is Dr. Charles Dayton Stratton, and he might be Charles' grandfather."

"I do not think so," Jacques said. "Charles told me he has no grandparents."

"Well, the FBI believes he might be the boy's grandfather."

***

That night, Samy arrived at the Cairo Airport wearing a bright blue Hawaiian shirt with scenes of crashing waves against a sandy shore, with palm trees and a brilliant full moon. Holding several name cards, the taxi driver stationed himself near the customs office.

The door opened and the first to walk out was a boy about Charles' age. He was followed by two older people and the most colorful-looking woman Samy had ever seen. The woman was wearing a full skirt with every shade of the rainbow on it. The skirt reached almost down to her pink tennis shoes, which were tied with yellow shoelaces. She wore a blue blouse with rainbow fringe around the bottom, and over her red hair was tied a scarf the color of her shoelaces.

Samy held up a sign with Mademoiselle Fleuret's name on it, though he doubted the colorfully dressed woman could be a teacher from the Château du Mont. When she spied Samy and the sign, she skipped towards him.

"Oh, Samy, right? Could you hold up my name card again? It would make such a great photograph. David, could you take the photo?" She handed her camera to the boy, saying, "Just push this button right here."

Samy took a dramatic stance, smiling his best smile and holding up the placard with Mademoiselle Fleuret's name on it. The woman pretended to be running towards Samy. After retrieving her camera from David, she threw her arms around the surprised taxi driver.

"Madame Constance told me about how you are helping Jacques," she said breathlessly. "*Merci beaucoup!* He is such a sweet, dear man."

"Are you sure you're talking about Jacques?" Samy asked.

David ran up to Samy, calling out, "Have you found Charles yet?"

"No, dude, not yet," the driver admitted.

"These are my grandparents, Mr. and Mrs. Montgomery," the boy said, pointing to a man standing next to a woman in a large straw hat with a purple flower in its brim.

"So, there is no news about Charles?" Mrs. Montgomery asked.

"Nothing yet. The only news I have is that a Professor Charles Dayton Stratton is flying in from the United States tonight. The rumor is he might be Charles' grandfather."

"Charles doesn't have a grandfather," David said, folding his arms in front of his chest. "He doesn't have any family, except his parents. If this man says he's Charles' grandfather, I don't think we should trust him."

Samy looked at the blond boy with freckles standing beside him and thought for a moment how much like Charles he was.

"Well, the American FBI thinks he might be related. The man is a professor of philosophy at Harvard University. Have you ever heard of Harvard, young man?" Samy asked David.

"Yes, I've heard of Harvard," David answered, wariness in his voice.

"Jacques received a message from the American Embassy stating that, while Dr. Stratton isn't certain Charles is his grandson, he's flying to Cairo to find out," Samy said. "I'm going to drop you off at the School of Khemitology Guest House, then come back to the airport to pick up Dr. Stratton."

"Oh, our suitcases," Mademoiselle Fleuret said, looking around. "There is the conveyor belt, number 2 from Paris."

"Mine are the lavender suitcases," Mrs. Montgomery called out. "I believe there are five of them."

"Five lavender suitcases," Samy echoed, scratching his head and wondering how he was going to get all the luggage into his taxi.

"I like to come prepared," said the woman in the straw hat with the purple flower in its brim. "George prefers a single gray suitcase and, of course, Mademoiselle Fleuret's suitcases are those two red ones. Red suitcases are so easy to find on the conveyor belt, don't you think, Samy?"

Actually, Samy didn't know what to think. He was still captivated by the art teacher.

"Hey, Grandmother, you forgot to describe my suitcase," David reminded her. "It's blue and it has a soccer ball logo on it. Grandfather bought it for me."

Surrounded by suitcases, Samy decided they should call a ramper to bring a cart. It took several minutes to figure out how to get all the luggage into the taxi's trunk and in the back seat.

"If you do not mind, Samy, I will sit up front with you," Mademoiselle Fleuret said. "It must be fascinating being a taxi driver in one of the most famous cities in the world. I always wanted to come to Egypt, but I never dreamed it would be so soon, and under such alarming circumstances. What do you think happened to Charles?"

Before Samy could answer, David addressed the taxi driver, saying, "So, you know Charles?"

"Yes. I was at the airport and they, Charles and Jacques, asked me to be their taxi driver while they were in Cairo," Samy answered. "Dr. Awyan told me to tell you we've been invited to the Pizza Hut for breakfast tomorrow morning."

"Pizza for breakfast!" David said. "Now this is a country that knows how to eat. I love pizza. I could eat some right now."

Mrs. Montgomery opened her large purple purse and pulled out a sandwich wrapped in wax paper. She also handed David a small carton of orange juice. "That should hold you until tomorrow, young man. Would anyone else like a turkey sandwich?"

Both Samy and Mr. Montgomery accepted. The redheaded art teacher produced a grain and fruit bar, while Mrs. Montgomery nibbled on one of her homemade cookies. It was late. There was very little traffic on the freeway, and soon the taxi was pulling into the archeological zone. Samy told the soldiers at the gate their destination.

Once at the Khemitology Guest House, they all piled out of the taxi. Samy carried Mrs. Montgomery's strangely heavy suitcases, the color of grapes, into the guest house. She thanked him and tried to pay him. Samy refused, but Mrs. Montgomery insisted, adding that the money should cover Dr. Stratton's taxi ride as well. Then, she said with a sweet smile, "I understand you were on the train headed for Luxor when Charles disappeared."

"That's right, Mrs. Montgomery," Samy said, staring at her sharp blue eyes.

"You were not in the cabin with Charles and Jacques?"

"No," Samy shook his head. "I always travel third class, and they were in first class."

"Interesting, Mr. Samy," she said. "We look forward to seeing you tomorrow morning."

Jacques was waiting for them in the sitting room. He shook hands with Mr. and Mrs. Montgomery and greeted David. Then to his disconcertment, Jacques found himself enveloped in the arms of Mademoiselle Fleuret. She patted him on the back, saying how sorry she was, how difficult it must be for him, and how glad she was to be there to help him through this ordeal. She assured Jacques that they would find Charles soon.

After the effusive greeting, Jacques found himself ensconced in one of the overstuffed green chairs in the sitting room, with one of Mrs. Montgomery's turkey sandwiches in his hand. Samy left to get Dr. Stratton. After finishing his sandwich, Jacques said, "If it is alright with you, Mrs. Montgomery, I will assign Dr. Stratton the downstairs room."

"Mr. Montgomery, I thought you and your wife would like to have David nearby, so I put you on the second floor, left side. That room has two beds and a bunk bed. Mademoiselle Fleuret, I have placed you across the way from the Montgomerys on the second floor."

"Where are you staying, Jacques?" Mademoiselle Fleuret asked.

"I am on the third floor, next to the dorm. Down here is a kitchen, and there are restrooms with showers on all floors."

"*Trés bien*," Mademoiselle Fleuret said. "We are so fortunate that you have made friends with Dr. Awyan, and he has allowed us to stay at his guest house. I look forward to meeting him."

Jacques took several trips to the second floor, helping Mrs. Montgomery with her luggage. Once upstairs, David said to his grandmother, "Jacques doesn't look very good, does he, Grandmother?"

"No, he doesn't. Jacques looks like a man who has surrendered to fear," she said. "And it is my belief that surrendering to fear creates a fog that may obscure the very path one seeks."

"In other words, David, your grandmother thinks it was a good idea for us to come," Mr. Montgomery explained.

"I'm sure I do not need an interpreter, George," Mrs. Montgomery said as she left the room dressed in her purple bathrobe and matching feathered slippers.

David placed his clothes in one of the chests in the room, then ran to the window and stared out at the shadow of the Sphinx under a sky sprinkled with stars. "Where are you, Charles?" he demanded aloud.

"I hope he is asleep, like we should be," David's grandmother said.

The next morning, Mrs. Montgomery decided to explore the downstairs. She found the kitchen equipped with a propane stove and a supply of pots, pans, dishes and, most importantly, teabags. She poured water into a red tea kettle and put it on the stove to boil.

Mrs. Montgomery walked through a swinging door to the sitting room. She hadn't paid much attention to the space last night. It had been such a long day. The room was small. It could comfortably hold ten people, but only three would gain possession of an olive-green overstuffed chair. She headed for a small table closest to the the front window. The table had two straight-backed wooden chairs. On the northern wall was a glass case filled with what looked to be ancient Egyptian artifacts. She made a mental note to meticulously examine its contents at another time.

"This will do," Mrs. Montgomery said briskly.

The kettle alerted her with a whistle, more like a piercing scream, that the hot water was ready. Mrs. Montgomery poured the boiling water into a small ceramic teapot decorated with a painted gold Sphinx. She added several bags of jasmine tea and set the teapot on a wooden tray to steep. She then filled a saucer with sugar cubes. Opening the small refrigerator, she located a glass bottle of cream and poured it into a small pitcher.

Replacing the cream, Mrs. Montgomery noticed a bag with three sugar cookies. She added these to the tray and then, using her hip, nudged open the swinging door that led to the sitting room and headed for the table.

At home, waking up early and having tea was her private ritual in a house almost always filled with children and grandchildren. With a cup of steaming tea, she could think about the coming day. This morning, once everyone was up and about, she intended to call a meeting to gather clues to Charles' disappearance.

Spying a small library table near the entrance of the guest house, she found a neat stack of stationary with the logo of the School of Khemitology. As usual, she carried a pen in the pocket of her robe. Between sips of jasmine tea, she wrote down questions and things to be considered.

Halfway through her process, she glanced out the window and was shocked at what greeted her. It was the Sphinx! She'd traveled all over the world but, for some reason, she'd never traveled to Egypt. This may have been fate. Perhaps she had to wait for this exact moment, when coming to Egypt was not just a trip but a necessity.

Charles was David's roommate. From all David had told her, their friendship had a very rocky beginning. For one thing, they were as different as different can be. Her grandson was blond with light blue eyes and a delightfully impish smile. He was responsible, loving, and the light of her heart, though she sometimes worried he was a little too serious. To hear David's account, in the early days, Charles was self-centered, stubborn, cantankerous, spoiled, unsociable and, worst of all, didn't like sports.

David was very athletic and especially fond of football. The sport, popular all over the world, is called soccer in America, *le football* by the French, and affectionately referred to as "footy" by fans in the United Kingdom. Whatever it was called, David loved the game. He'd been chosen soccer captain at the Château du Mont, and all the boys at the school liked and admired him.

After three months of the roommates not speaking, David came home on a visit declaring to his grandmother that Charles was adventuresome, courageous, creative, and maybe the smartest person he'd ever met. He never mentioned what brought about this change of thinking, but she'd been quite relieved. Now, however, it appeared that Charles' adventuresome nature had led to a situation where he was lost in a country where he didn't speak the language and, for some reason, couldn't find his way to the American Embassy.

What would she do if it were David lost in a foreign city, in Egypt? Would she panic, or would she take control, as was her habit? She'd always been a firm believer in the power of positive thinking. Charles had to be somewhere. Maybe he was sick, or maybe he decided to travel somewhere else. In either case, Charles would come back, of this she was certain.

The Sphinx, which had been a mere shadow last night, was now shining gold in the morning sunlight. Mrs. Montgomery whispered, "Help us find this lost boy, Sphinx."

She turned to see a sturdy man with gray hair wearing a red-and-gray plaid bathrobe approaching her table. "Oh, hello," she said. "You must be Professor Charles Dayton Stratton. I am Dorothy Montgomery, the grandmother of Charles' roommate David."

"You are the woman with many lavender suitcases. Samy told me you flew in from France last night, just before I came in from the United States," Dr. Stratton said.

"I am happy to meet you, Dr. Stratton. Would you care for some tea?"

"Yes, thank you. So, you are requesting help from the Sphinx?" he asked.

"I close no doors when it comes to finding a lost child," Mrs. Montgomery said, pouring tea into a cup and handing it to the man in the plaid bathrobe.

Mademoiselle Fleuret came down the stairs artfully dressed in a full skirt with multi-colored panels and a green blouse that matched the color of her large eyes. Over her curly red hair, she'd tied a white scarf covered in orange flowers. She was holding a camera.

"*Bonjour,*" she said "I have been up on the roof looking for Charles and taking photos of the Giza Plateau, particularly our good luck charm, the Great Sphinx of Giza."

"Dr. Stratton, let me introduce you to the art teacher at the Château du Mont, Mademoiselle Fleuret," Mrs. Montgomery said. "She has identified your possible grandson as a very talented photographer."

Standing up, Dr. Stratton gave a slight bow towards the colorful woman. Sounding a little self-conscious, he said, "I am pleased to meet you Mademoiselle. I think I had better dress for breakfast." With that, he slipped into his room on the first floor.

Looking after the man in the plaid robe, Mrs. Montgomery said, "David claims that Charles does not have a grandfather, but I hope he is wrong. Dr. Stratton seems so nice, and just what Charles needs in his life. Now, I must dress for breakfast and prepare for our first meeting to gather clues and information about our missing young man."

The art teacher exchanged places with Mrs. Montgomery. Staring out the window, she spoke to her good luck charm, the beautiful and ancient Sphinx.

"Could you employ your magnetic powers to bring our Charles back from wherever he is? I would also request that you speed up this process, as I would love for Charles and me to have some time together to photo-document our trip to Cairo before we have to return to the Château du Mont."

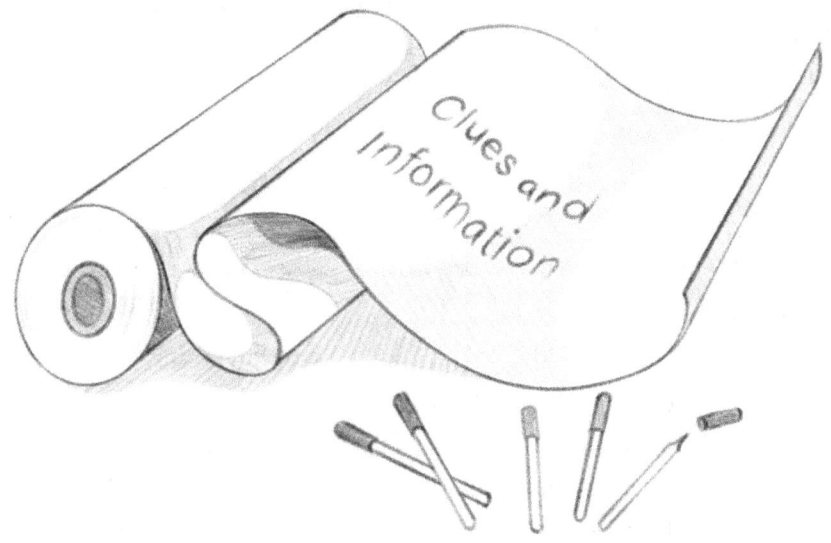

CHAPTER 24

CLUES AND INFORMATION

At Mrs. Montgomery's request, the guest house group gathered in the Pizza Hut across from the Sphinx. David looked at his grandmother. She looked different. She was wearing a tan jacket and a split kind of pant-skirt like she was going on a safari. Her blondish hair was pulled back into a ponytail. Her freckles, which David had inherited, were more pronounced.

Everyone was sitting on benches beside a long table except his grandmother, who was stationed at a table in the back of the room. A man burst in the door of the Pizza Hut, his cream-colored gallabiyah whipping around what some would tactfully call a robust figure.

"George?" Mrs. Montgomery said, sounding shocked.

David looked at his grandfather. "Wow, you look official!"

"Dr. Awyan told me I would be more comfortable in this robe. He said the hot, dry weather of Egypt is unsuitable for suits. But he was wrong. I don't feel one bit more comfortable, Dorothy. I've worn suits all my life and..."

"I think you look adorable, George," Mrs. Montgomery said, interrupting his rant.

"This is serious, Dorothy," Mr. Montgomery said. "We have a lost boy here."

"And that's exactly why we are here, to gather clues and information," his wife assured him.

Ten seconds later another man entered the room, letting the door slam behind him. He was wearing a navy blue Hawaiian shirt with a red hibiscus print. "Sorry I'm late, and I'm completely innocent," Samy blurted out.

"So you're here, Mr. Samy," David's grandmother said. "At this point, it's not a matter of guilt or innocence. It is a matter of information. I've asked the nice woman behind the counter, Mandisa—a rather poetic name—for a large sheet of butcher paper and I've brought some writing implements."

She held up eight pens of various colors. "Each of us has a little bit of information. Together, we might discover clues to help us locate Charles."

Mr. Montgomery interrupted. "Dorothy, I think we should call the police."

His wife shook her head indulgently. "George, you know the police have been called. I'm sure they are working on Charles' case."

"Case! Listen to how you're talking, Dorothy," Mr. Montgomery sputtered.

"I'm sure they are working on Charles' mysterious disappearance," Mrs. Montgomery said. "Is that better, George? However, you know the police in cities as large as Cairo have many demands on their time, while we are here for only one reason. I suggest we all work together to find leads that might help the authorities find Charles. Do you all agree?"

Jacques, David, Dr. Stratton, Samy, and Mademoiselle Fleuret looked around at each other, then nodded. George stared in wonderment.

"Let's start with the youngest," Mrs. Montgomery said. "That would be my grandson, David. What do you know?"

"I don't know much except Charles has loved Egypt since he was a little kid," David said. "He even taught himself how to read and write hieroglyphics. He knows the history and geography of Egypt, and the names of all the gods and goddesses."

"I don't think he would have felt afraid when he was put off the train. He'd see it as a kind of an adventure," the boy continued. "He'd find his way to the American Embassy. But something must have happened to him. What do you think it could be, Grandmother?"

"This isn't the time to speculate," Mrs. Montgomery said. "It's time to put our heads together and form a clearer picture. Please continue, David."

"Back at the school Madame Constance called Farak, an Egyptian student and friend of Charles, and me into her office. She told us Charles was lost. Farak said he was going to fly straight to Luxor. He made travel arrangements right in Madame Constance's office. I called you, Grandmother."

"Thank you, David," Mrs. Montgomery said.

She jotted down notes in blue ink, then circled something in red. Mr. Montgomery surveyed the room. Everyone was looking at Dorothy, his Dorothy, as if she were some kind of authority on missing persons.

"May I ask a question? Actually, the question is for David," Dr. Stratton said, looking at Charles' roommate earnestly. "Why would this Egyptian boy decide to fly to Luxor?"

"Because that's where Farak's family lives," David said. "I should mention, Farak is a Bedouin prince. His grandfather is a sultan, the head of a large Bedouin group called the Tarabin Tribe. They're experts in raising and training camels and Arabian horses."

"I love Arabian horses," Mademoiselle Fleuret said dreamily.

By this time, David's words were tumbling over one another. "Farak said there are thousands of Tarabins all over Egypt. He was sure if his grandfather put out a call, they'd find Charles. And he told me something else. He said Charles' disappearance was all his fault."

Everyone in the room had their eyes on David.

"Why would he say that?" his grandmother asked, purple pen in hand.

"Farak told me that last Christmas he gave Charles some presents from Egypt, including the Bedouin clothes he wore when he arrived at the Château du Mont. Madame Constance told Farak he had to put them away and wear a uniform like the rest of the boys, but he kept his Egyptian clothes, even though he outgrew them."

"The night Charles left for Egypt, Farak came to our room to give him some addresses. I wasn't there. I was at a game. When Charles came to the door, he was wearing the clothes Farak had given him. Farak was shocked because Charles looked just like a Bedouin boy, except for his blue eyes."

Mrs. Montgomery nodded appreciatively. "That must have been surprising."

"Farak said if he hadn't given Charles his hand-me-down clothes, he wouldn't have been mistaken for a stowaway, kicked off the train, and somehow made to disappear."

"Did Farak mention what the clothing looked like?" Mrs. Montgomery asked.

"No, but another student, Fran went to Charles' room the night before he left," David answered. "He said Charles looked like Lawrence of Arabia or an Egyptian prince. He even had something around his head that was almost like a crown. Fran asked Charles if this was how he planned to dress in Egypt. Charles said no, not unless he needed to blend in."

"How did Fran find out about Charles' disappearance?" Jacques asked.

David shrugged. "You know how rumors fly around the Château du Mont. Everyone knows."

Mademoiselle Fleuret nodded her head in agreement.

"Farak gave Charles the clothing that led to him being mistaken for an Egyptian stowaway," Mrs. Montgomery said. "As Helen Keller once declared, '*Alone we can do so little; together we can do so much.*' And see? Together, we've managed to solve at least one mystery."

Mrs. Montgomery paused, drumming her nails on the desk. "If Charles looked like a prince and not a pauper, why do you think the conductor removed him from the train?"

"The conductor probably thought the stowaway was in disguise," David speculated. "That's why he put him off the train."

Jacques shifted uncomfortably on the bench, his mind going back to the mishap on the train. Farak was wrong. It was not the Egyptian teen's fault but his own. He silently scolded himself. His one task was to watch this boy. Instead, he'd napped behind a map. He should have at least waited until the train left the station before becoming so preoccupied.

Jacques felt an enormous weight on his chest, specifically near the left breast pocket where he kept his fountain pen. He was a bachelor. What did he know about children? Charles' parents should never have chosen him to accompany their son to Egypt. When Jacques turned his attention back to the conversation, Mrs. Montgomery was asking David to describe the color of Charles' gallabiyah and accessories.

"We're going to have to ask Farak," David answered. "I was at a soccer tournament, as you know, Grandmother."

Mrs. Montgomery gave him a sympathetic look. "Do you have anything else to add, my dear?"

"Let's see," David said thoughtfully. "Charles showed me the letter his parents sent him. They were sad they couldn't be with him when he turned the important age of twelve. They said he could have anything he wanted for his birthday. At first Charles was mad, but then he decided the letter was a miracle. He wrote back, saying the only thing he wanted was for him and me to go to Egypt together."

"As you know, Grandmother, my parents wouldn't let me go on the trip," David continued. "They insisted I was too young to travel so far without family, even though I'd already turned the important age of twelve. If they'd let me go, I'd have been with Charles, and he wouldn't be lost in Egypt today."

"It is not your fault, nor is it Farak's fault," Jacques called out from the bench. "I am to blame. I was the one asked to chaperone Charles."

"Mr. Gerard, we're not casting blame here," Mrs. Montgomery said. "We are still in the fact-finding phase. Do you have anything else to add, David?"

David wondered if he should mention that Charles needed to come to Egypt so he could find the Ghost of Tomb 11 in Tel el Amarna and write another story for *Famous Ghost Stories Magazine*. He decided that information was probably unimportant.

"Mademoiselle Fleuret," Mrs. Montgomery said, addressing her next subject.

The art professor walked to the front of the room and stared for a second at Mrs. Montgomery's colorful writing on the butcher paper spread on the back table.

"What I know is that Charles is an exceptional photographer. He brought the camera his father gave him for Christmas to Egypt, promising to take the best photos he could. He uses a classic Leica."

A classic Leica? A shock ran through Professor Stratton's body. He stared at the teacher in the colorful attire, a scarf holding back her curly red hair, her wide smile accentuated by carefully-applied red lipstick.

Why did he feel as though he were in a play? So far, the discussion had included words like prince, sultan, stowaway and disguise, not to mention the terrible disappearance of someone who might be his grandson. Now, a woman who looked like a Gypsy had mentioned a classic Leica.

Dr. Stratton felt like he was traveling back in time. It was his son's twelfth birthday. Charlie wanted a camera. He and his wife splurged to buy him a classic Leica. Charlie was a talented photographer from day-one. Mrs. Montgomery had managed to unravel another mystery. Dr. Stratton may not have learned where Charles was, but he was now certain who he was: a grandson, his grandson, lost in Egypt.

"There is something that concerns me," Mademoiselle Fleuret said. "Jacques told me Charles left his camera on the train seat next to him. The boy always keeps his camera with him. For this reason, I believe Charles must have been kidnapped."

Charles' teacher had spoken the unspeakable. There was total silence in the Pizza Hut.

"I want to thank you, Mademoiselle Fleuret," Mrs. Montgomery said. "However, I suggest we keep dire theories to ourselves for the present. Hasty conclusions may lead to great mistakes when delving into the mysterious."

"Really, Dorothy? Delving into the mysterious?" George awkwardly removed himself from between the table and the bench. "Normal people, especially grandmothers, don't speak the way you've been going on, as if you were a detective in a crime novel."

George looked around the room beseechingly as if to find an ally, but no one spoke. Mrs. Montgomery was unperturbed. "Unusual times demand unusual language, George. Now, Dr. Stratton, it's your turn to speak."

Dr. Stratton walked to the table and cleared his throat.

"As I explained, I had no idea I had a grandson until the FBI showed up at my door two days ago. I haven't seen or heard from my son for almost twenty years. We didn't even have a falling out," he said. "One day he told me that some people have to be realistic, that we can't just put our heads in the sand. He added that some people have to make difficult decisions, and that was it. That was the last we ever heard from our son."

Dr. Stratton sighed. "When the police gave up on Charlie's case, we hired a detective, one of the most noted private investigators in the eastern United States. Unfortunately, he couldn't find a trace of our son. He had just disappeared."

Mademoiselle Fleuret moved to Dr. Stratton and rested her hand on his shoulder. "Professor Stratton, that must have been so painful for you and your wife."

"Thank you, my dear," Dr. Stratton said. "Your mention of the camera is an important bit of information. It's led me to conclude that this boy with my name truly is my grandson. I gave my son the exact Leia you described when he turned twelve. For the first time in years, I believe my son is alive, and that he married and had a son."

Dr. Stratton's voice became gruff, and he blinked away tears. "It's heartening to learn all this, but this situation opens old wounds. Why did my son never come home, and why didn't he tell me I had a grandson?"

"It appears to me there are several mysteries revolving around Charles," Mrs. Montgomery said thoughtfully. "From what David tells me, each of Charles' parents visited his school only once in a year-and-a-half, and they didn't come at the same time."

"True. And each time they stayed only a few hours," David added. "I felt sorry for Charles."

"You've always been a sensitive boy, David," Mrs. Montgomery said. She jotted a note with a purple pen: *'Charles had a mysterious relationship with his parents.'*

It was time for her next interview. "Okay, Mr. Samy," Mrs. Montgomery said, giving his Hawaiian shirt a once-over.

Samy launched into his story before Mrs. Montgomery could ask him any questions.

"I picked Charles and Jacques up at the airport in my taxi. I took them to the Mena House Hotel. Charles told me he wanted to spend four days at the Cairo Museum. No ordinary tourist wants to spend four days in a museum. I insisted they visit a couple of other places. I think it's safe to say we bonded."

He looked at Jacques, who shrugged in agreement.

"Jacques and Charles said they were going to Luxor on the train," Sammy continued. "A friend of mine in Luxor offered to lend me his taxi, so I decided to go with Jacques and Charles on the train. My ticket was in general class, not first class. The next thing I knew, Jacques was screaming that Charles was missing."

"I do not recall screaming, though I was certainly alarmed," Jacques said. "But the rest of Samy's story is true."

"Thank you, Jacques," Mrs. Montgomery said, writing the words "screamed" and "alarmed" next to his name.

She turned her attention back to Samy. "So, you are just a taxi driver? Is it usual for a taxi driver to borrow a taxi in a city 500 miles away, so he could be a driver for customers he barely knows?"

Mrs. Montgomery wrote down Samy's name and profession, followed by a question mark in red.

"I have lots of friends in Luxor," Samy said. "My family had a taxi company there for ten years. I thought it would be a good chance for me to visit old friends and make a little money."

"A good response, Samy," Mrs. Montgomery said. Then, turning to her husband, she asked, "George, have you anything to add?"

"You know I don't know anything," Mr. Montgomery said. "What I want to know is why you are acting like this. I tell you, Dorothy, it is darn disconcerting."

"We will talk about that later, George," Mrs. Montgomery said, turning her attention to Jacques.

Everyone noticed the dark circles under Jacques' eyes. He straightened up, ready to answer Mrs. Montgomery's questions. He walked very slowly toward her table, as though approaching a gallows.

"Jacques, try to remember as much as possible, even if you don't think something is pertinent. Don't worry, Jacques, no one blames you. Together we will find Charles Dayton Stratton III, of this I am sure," Mrs. Montgomery pronounced, waving her purple pen in the air.

"How can you be so sure, Dorothy?" her husband asked. "Dorothy, you are giving everyone false hope."

"Hope, George, is never false," his wife replied with a reassuring smile.

Jacques told them about Charles' father arranging for him to take Charles to Egypt. The boy's father made all the plans, purchased tickets, and made the hotel reservations. Mr. Charles Stratton II wrote Jacques a note informing him that he and his wife would be "out of contact" while he and Charles were in Egypt.

"He didn't mention where they were going?" Mrs. Montgomery asked.

"No, but I did not find it unusual. Charles' parents apparently travel a great deal," Jacques answered. "As David said, each parent visited Charles only once during his enrollment at the Château du Mont. They visited separately and each stayed just a few hours. I do not know if this is significant, but when Mrs. Stratton visited Charles, she insisted I pick him up at the Cathedral at Chartres after their visit there. I was not to drive the school's vehicle, but she did not tell me why. She told me to hire a taxi."

Dorothy, using a purple pen, jotted down something about Charles' mother, then underlined it in red.

"Anything else, Jacques?" Mrs. Montgomery asked.

"I have to say this about Samy, thought I doubt it is important. When we got off the plane, Samy drove up. Charles wondered why his taxi was the only one with a handwritten sign. It said 'Taxi, American Spoken.' We had no reason to be suspicious, except that Charles is always suspicious."

"Oh, is that so?" Dorothy said, narrowing her eyes and looking at Samy. The taxi driver, who was looking around the room, didn't respond.

"Oh, yes," Jacques remembered. "Charles met a stranger on the airplane from Paris to Cairo. The man asked Charles several questions, including what his name was. For some reason, Charles replied that his name was John Smith. Then, Charles asked the man his name. He told Charles his name was Robert Smith."

"Charles thought this so-called Mr. Smith was unnaturally interested in him," Jacques continued. "I felt Charles was being overly suspicious. He named the stranger the Gray Man, because he was dressed in a gray suit and hat and he had gray eyes and gray hair. I believe we saw this man two other times."

"Mr. Smith, the Gray Man?" Mrs. Montgomery said. "And you say you saw him on the plane and two additional times?"

Jacques nodded. "The first time was just before we arrived at our destination at the Mena House. Samy wanted to take us to his favorite local restaurant. While we were on the roof eating lunch, Charles looked down and saw Robert Smith walking down the street. I believe I saw our driver, Samy, peek over the roof also. He immediately suggested that perhaps we should eat downstairs."

Samy said, "You know that it was very hot on that roof."

"Samy's right," Jacques agreed. "It was very hot on the roof. The next time I thought I saw the Gray Man was in the Cairo Museum. I spotted, or imagined I spotted, Mr. Smith in a gray gangster hat, standing behind a statue of a woman with cow ears."

"A woman with cow ears?" Mrs. Montgomery repeated.

"Yes, Hathor, a popular ancient goddess of happiness and prosperity," Jacques explained. "The statue was close to where Charles was standing, reading hieroglyphics on a sarcophagus. Later, I asked Charles if he'd noticed Mr. Smith at the museum. He said he hadn't."

"Hmm, interesting," Mrs. Montgomery said, scribbling more notes on the butcher paper. "Jacques, you don't need to repeat the story about Charles being put off of the train by that conductor, but do you have anything else to add?"

"No, nothing," Jacques answered, deciding he didn't need to mention the relic pyramid and Charles' objective of finding Tomb 11 in Tel el Armana.

"Oh, we did meet one other person," Jacques called out. "He is a guide at the Cairo Museum. He wrote a book called *Cuneiform*. We bought the book and had lunch with him the day before we left. However, I am sure this has nothing to do with Charles' disappearance."

"His name, please?" Mrs. Montgomery asked.

"Dr. McAllister," Jacques said. David's grandmother finished writing and looked at her chart.

"At this point, we're not sure what is important, and what is not. You have all done an excellent job. If you don't mind," Mrs. Montgomery added amiably, "I have some suggestions. Professor Stratton, would you go to the American Embassy and see if they have heard anything more about Charles, or your son?"

"George, would you and Jacques go to the police department and ask them to give you a list of the hospitals and...other important places? Check to see that the boy Charles is not in any of these, although I am sure he is not. Mademoiselle Fleuret and Samy, would you go to the newspapers and TV stations and urge them to carry the story?"

"I'd be happy to go with Samy," Mademoiselle Fleuret said. "I brought this photo of Charles, a portrait taken by one of my students."

Dr. Stratton asked the art teacher if he could see the photograph of Charles. He looked deeply at the 5 x 7 image of a boy with dark curly hair. He didn't look like his son, Charlie. Charlie's hair was lighter, and his eyes were green like his mother's. Dr. Stratton was, however, reminded of his own boyhood photographs. Their facial characteristics were not identical but the expression was the same, strangely serious for a child. His mother used to tell him he was born old. This boy, too, looked like he was born old. Dr. Stratton thanked Mademoiselle Fleuret and handed her back the photo.

"I will have a copy made," Mademoiselle Fleuret said. "He is your double—something around the mouth and chin and the same dark blue eyes."

Everyone except Mrs. Montgomery and David filed out of the Pizza Hut. David's grandmother breathed a sigh of relief as she rolled up the butcher paper and tucked the colorful pens in her large purple purse.

"What should I do, Grandmother?" David asked.

"You and I are going to sit right here, in sight of the Sphinx, and think."

Grandmother and grandson watched people come and go, some in buses, some in taxis, some in donkey carts, some on horseback and some on camels. After a few minutes, the woman in the safari outfit said, "David, it just occurred to me that you and I might think better on the back of a camel. Do you agree?"

"Oh, yes, I do agree, Grandmother."

CHAPTER 25

SOCCER BY THE SPHINX

After an exhilarating ride around the Giza Plateau on tan camels
with brightly-colored cloth saddles, grandson and grandmother
returned to the School of Khemitology Guest House. They sat in the
front room and snacked on cookies in the shape of pyramids, washed
down with glasses of milk. Mrs. Montgomery reached for her notes,
spreading out the butcher paper on the library table. With her reading
glasses on and pens at the ready, she looked like she was in her element.
David watched his grandmother and wondered what he should do.

Finally, he said, "Grandmother, can I step outside for a minute?"

Mrs. Montgomery waved distractedly at David, which he took to mean
yes. As he walked out the door, he was startled by a noise coming from the

other side of the School of Khemitology. It was the unmistakable sound of a soccer game.

No other game sounds quite like it. In soccer, there's no silence as spectators wait for someone to throw or hit a ball. The chatter among players is as much a part of the game as the movement up and down the field. As captain of the Château du Mont's soccer team, David made his team practice this chatter. The chatter, he told his teammates, was to create misdirection, like a magician's sleight of hand. Whistleblowing, verbal cues, yelling, and even purposely giving incorrect advice creates an environment of confusion and, in David's mind, an excitement unparalleled by any other game. This was what he was hearing.

The soccer field was a vacant area between two simple cement homes. It didn't look like the carefully-groomed fields on which the boys of the Château du Mont played. Their fields were made of grass or artificial turf. Boundary lines were carefully chalked. The goal was marked by a strong net, held firmly by a large metal frame.

This field was covered with the same light yellowish sand on which the Sphinx and the pyramids sat. Darker sand had been brought in from someplace, and carefully poured in almost straight lines to mark the boundaries. The netting for the goals was lightweight, maybe borrowed from a badminton set, and stretched between two poles.

Looking at the makeshift field and the players, wearing clothes ranging from shorts and T-shirts to full gallabiyah, reminded David of a conversation with his grandfather. His grandfather, once a near-famous soccer player, told him the great thing about soccer was it could be played by anyone, anywhere, on any surface: grass, artificial turf, sand, dirt, roads, cement, snow, ice, and even mud. He said soccer was a game that belonged to everyone.

David had written a paper about soccer in his English class. He'd quoted a French soccer journalist, Jean Eskenazi. Eskenazi wrote that soccer was a universal language. He declared it to be "the only denominator common to all people, the only universal Esperanto...a world language, whose grammar is unchanging from the North Pole to the equator."

In the Montgomery family, everyone was a soccer fanatic. David had loved the sport for as long as he could remember. His mother claimed he came out of the womb a soccer player. It was embarrassing, but almost true. David had begun playing soccer when he was two years old; his mother had photographs to prove it. His brothers, two of his sisters, and his grandmother had all played soccer in college.

His grandfather had been a professional player for the UK team, the Wolverhampton Wanderers. They'd even earned their way into the World Cup. He told David, with exaggerated sadness, that the World Cup was the end of his soccer career. The competition was so fierce and the level of athleticism so high, he'd told the news reporters, he'd felt like they were playing against men from outer space.

"The point being," his grandfather told David, "the real goal of soccer is to have fun, develop skills, be a great communicator, be a great team member, entertain your audience and...win the World Cup." David's grandfather had laughed out loud as he added the last part.

The soccer ball rolled out of bounds, right to where David was standing. He couldn't help himself; he did a little footwork to show he could control the ball, then kicked it to the boy who'd punted it out of bounds. All the boys on the soccer field stopped playing and stared at him. Then, one boy ran off the field and the other boys waved David in.

It didn't take them long to discover he was an accomplished player. In the end, David used his head, sending the ball past the goalie. His team won. David was cheered on, not just by his team—the ones with the blue armbands—but by all the players. For the first time since Madame Constance informed him Charles had disappeared, he lost that sick feeling in his stomach.

When Charles talked about Egypt, he described pyramids, temples, gods, goddesses, hieroglyphics, and mummies. David had gotten the idea this was what modern Egypt was like. When he got here, though, he'd found kind, friendly people. And now he'd discovered a bunch of Egyptian kids who loved soccer, just like he did. David concluded that if Charles needed help, someone would help him. For the first time he believed, as his grandmother believed, that Charles would soon be found.

After an hour's play, David thought he'd better go back to the Pizza Hut and check on his grandmother. But when he looked in that direction, he saw his grandmother and Dr. Awyan walking toward the soccer field. Dr. Awyan held a brand-new soccer ball in his large brown hands, still in its box.

Dr. Awyan and Mrs. Montgomery were in deep conversation, the Egyptian in a gallabiyah, his grandmother in tan pants and a lavender blouse. Dr. Awyan was explaining to Mrs. Montgomery how the School of Khemitology came about.

"Using the word school is a misnomer. I have no remembrance of how we started connecting school with Khemitology. As you no doubt know, the definition of school is an organization providing instruction. We do not provide instruction. We do not tell our members what to believe and then test them to find out how well they have learned what we taught them."

"That is very interesting," Mrs. Montgomery said. "I believe I would like this kind of school."

"In the School of Khemitology," the old Egyptian said, "we are all on the path of discovery. I'm reminded of a quote by French author Marcel Proust. *'The real voyage of discovery consists not in seeing new sights, but in looking with new eyes.'* By bringing people of all disciplines and interests together—sharing our views, experiences and thoughts—we can give each other new eyes."

"That's quite profound, Dr. Awyan," Mrs. Montgomery said. "Proust is also one of my favorite authors."

As Dr. Awyan approached, all of the soccer team members gathered around him. He handed the captain of the team the new ball. The players shouted in celebration. David noticed his grandmother was carrying a large package. "What have you got there?" he asked her.

"I thought you and your friends might need a pick-me-up, so I asked Mandisa to prepare a little repast."

The pizza was appreciated almost as much as the new soccer ball. After they'd consumed every bit of pizza, Mrs. Montgomery passed out little wet towelettes she'd brought from England. The boys took the wrappers over to a sack she'd provided for trash, and the game commenced.

Within seconds, the new ball went out of bounds in front of David's grandmother. She couldn't help but perform her "inside-of-the-foot curl shot" she'd been famous for in college. The ball flew up in the air, landing in front of the goalkeeper's penalty area. The goalkeeper attempted to grab the ball, but it was kicked to the side by a red team member. Then, in one beautiful move after another, the ball reached the goalkeeper wearing orange. He attempted to stop the ball but failed. The blue team went wild. Everyone was ecstatic, no matter which team they were on.

"That was a great move, Mrs. Montgomery," Dr. Awyan said. "Where did you learn to play soccer?"

"As Agatha Christie said, '*Never tell all you know—not even to the person you know best.*' I believe it is a quote from her novel Secret Adversary."

Dr. Awyan replied, "Conversations are always dangerous—if you have something to hide."

"Oh, I see you are familiar with one of my favorite Agatha Christie characters, Miss Marple," Mrs. Montgomery said. "You are full of surprises, Dr. Awyan."

"As are you, Mrs. Montgomery. I think we will get along quite well. Now, what do you think has happened to our young Charles?"

"I don't know, but I can't rid myself of the belief that he has chosen to go on an adventure. And you, Dr. Awyan?"

The old Egyptian answered, "I never question a woman who wears purple and trusts her instincts."

CHAPTER 26

A MYSTERY WRITER'S REVEAL

M ademoiselle Fleuret entered the Khemitology Guest House, Jacques in tow. She greeted the woman sitting at the wooden table.

"Oh, hello, Mrs. Montgomery. Jacques and I made copies of Charles' photo and dropped them off at several newspapers. Each of the papers agreed to print the photo and will announce a hefty reward for anyone providing information leading to the discovery of our Charles."

Dr. Stratton entered the guesthouse. Sighing, he plopped down in one of the overstuffed green chairs.

"My trip was an utter failure," he said. "I talked to the people at the American Embassy, and they said there was no further news regarding Charles. I asked about Charles' parents. Mr. Flores reports that neither the mother or father have been located. Then, I tried to call my friend Alfred, who is at my home in Cambridge, Massachusetts, and he did not answer the telephone."

Just then Mr. Montgomery, Jacques, and Samy walked in the front door.

"It was a grueling day, Dorothy. We visited all the hospitals and the other places you suggested," Mr. Montgomery said, glancing at the two boys. "No one matching Charles' description has been admitted."

"Good job, everyone," Mrs. Montgomery said. "Tomorrow is another day."

Everyone left for the Pizza Hut except Mrs. Montgomery. An Egyptian youth entered the guest house with a note for her husband. She directed him to the second floor. A few minutes later, the young man and George emerged from the stairway. The youth went out the door. Mr. Montgomery entered the front room, where his wife was writing notes on her butcher paper.

"I have just received a note from our son, John," he said briskly. "He says I am needed back at the corporate office immediately. You and David must pack. We leave tonight."

"But I am needed here, George," Mrs. Montgomery replied.

"Dorothy, the French and American embassies, the Egyptian police, Dr. Stratton, Jacques, Mademoiselle Fleuret, and Dr. Awyan—not to mention Farak and his family—are all here looking for Charles. Believe me, they can do this without you."

"I disagree, George," Mrs. Montgomery said, standing up and looking at her husband eye-to-eye. "The more parties involved, the more confusion. This calls for someone with an organized mind."

"Please sit down, Dorothy," Mr. Montgomery said, seating himself across from his wife. "It appears to me that this trip to Cairo and the extreme desert heat have been a little too much for you. You're not acting like the woman I married."

"I should hope not," Mrs. Montgomery said. "I was twenty-one at our wedding and I've learned a few things since then. As for me being unbalanced by the heat, except for my profound sorrow that Charles has not yet been found, I have never felt better in my life."

She patted her husband's hand. "If you must go home, George, then you must. David and I, however, are staying."

"I don't believe this is advisable, Dorothy."

"We'll be perfectly safe here," Mrs. Montgomery said. "David has sworn he won't leave Egypt until we've found Charles. And as you may have noticed, my particular skills and talents are necessary for the success of this mission."

"Success of this mission!" Mr. Montgomery spluttered. "What do you mean, talking like this? These are not the words of a grandmother of ten."

"How do grandmothers talk, George?" his wife inquired. "I'd be interested to know."

"They don't stand up in front of a bunch of people with butcher paper and colored pens, gathering clues and assigning jobs."

"How can a woman be expected to be happy with a man who insists on treating her as if she were a perfectly normal human being?"

George frowned. "Are you saying you're not happy with me? We've been married for forty years, Dorothy."

"Oh, George, that is a quote by Oscar Wilde, one of our favorite English writers," Mrs. Montgomery said with a titter. "It has been a good forty years. However, '*It is a wonderful fact to reflect upon, that every human creature is constituted to be a profound secret and mystery to every other,*' as Charles Dickens wrote."

"And exactly what profound secret or mystery do you have, Mrs. Montgomery?" George asked.

"I'm so glad you inquired," Dorothy said, leaning towards her husband. "As you know, reading has been my lifelong passion. A few years ago, it began to seem as though the books I read were speaking to me, encouraging me to start writing. Victor Hugo wrote, '*A writer is a world trapped in a person.*' I was starting to feel more and more trapped, so I began to write."

"Why would you feel trapped? You have a family that loves you, a beautiful home."

"I don't mean I was trapped but that my mind was entrapping me, demanding I put pen to paper," Mrs. Montgomery said. "As William Faulkner once said, *'If there is a story in you, it has to come out.'* That's how I was feeling, like there were stories in me that needed to come out."

"So, you needed to write stories," George said. "That's very nice, Dorothy, but what has this got to do with anything?"

"It has to do with my becoming a different person. You see, George, I have become a mystery writer."

Mr. Montgomery stared at his wife, stunned.

"This might help explain things," Dorothy said. She reached into her purse, pulled out an envelope, and handed it to her husband.

"A check for fifty-thousand dollars? You...you are carrying around a check for fifty-thousand dollars in your purse, in Egypt! Have you lost your mind, Dorothy?"

"I received a letter from my publisher just before we left for the airport," his wife explained calmly. "I shoved the envelope into my purse without looking at it. When I opened the envelope, I found this check."

"You got a fifty-thousand-dollar check from your publisher?" Mr. Montgomery held his hands at his sides, palms up, as if asking the universe to help him understand.

"It's actually an advance for my author's tour. I meant to tell you about it, as the U.S. Coast to Coast Author's Tour for Mystery Writers is coming up soon. However, things got a little complicated. Once here in Cairo, I naturally started using my skill as a mystery writer to help find Charles."

"Writing detective stories doesn't make you a detective. And you're not going on a U.S. author's tour by yourself," he said staunchly.

"Do you mean you intend on going with me on the author's tour?" Mrs. Montgomery asked, smiling broadly. "That would be so wonderful, George."

"I don't know what I meant, but I know one thing. I'm telling our children about this, and they're going to be very upset."

"Mothers are used to upsetting their children," Mrs. Montgomery said. "Sometimes I think this might be one of our primary functions."

"You did all of this without telling me?" George said, waving his hands in the air.

"At first I thought you wouldn't be interested. You were always so busy with the shipping company. And when I started writing, I had no idea anyone would be interested in reading one of my stories. I was just following the Persian mystic Rumi, who said, *'Let yourself be drawn by the strange pull of what you love, it will not lead you astray.'* I was being pulled, George, pulled to write."

"Pulled to write mystery books?"

Ignoring his comment, his wife said, "After writing my first book, *The Mystery of the Woman in the Red Hat*, I read a quote by Mark Twain. He said, *'Write without pay until someone offers you pay. If nobody offers within three years, the candidate may look upon this as a sign that sawing wood is what he was intended for.'*"

"I could not help myself," Mrs. Montgomery continued. "I sent my manuscript to a publishing company. My intent was to find out if I should be content with sawing wood, or if writing was what I was intended for."

"I know what you're thinking," she continued. "Anybody with proper, sensitive feelings would rather scrub floors for a living. But I should scrub floors very badly, and I write detective stories rather well. I don't see why proper feelings should prevent me from doing my proper job."

"Now see here, Dorothy," Mr. Montgomery exclaimed, "I never wanted you to scrub floors!"

"Oh, George, that's a quote by another suspense writer, Dorothy L. Sayers. The point being that, as it turns out, I too write detective stories rather well. The next thing I knew I was published, and my publisher was asking for another book which, thankfully, I had already begun."

"Wouldn't it be better to write things you know about, like the history of women in soccer, or gardening? You love gardening."

Mrs. Montgomery corrected him. "I used to love gardening, but I have little time for gardening now."

"You've given up gardening!"

"See how busy you are, George? The flowers failed to come up, and you didn't even notice."

"I'm sorry, Dorothy," Mr. Montgomery said.

"And what's wrong with mysteries?" his wife asked. "A newer author, Donna Tartt, asserts it's a moral duty for a novelist to entertain and distract. She said, '*People who read your books are sick, sad, traveling, in the hospital waiting room while someone is dying.*' I understood exactly what she meant."

Dorothy reached out, clasping both of George's hands. "Throughout my life, mystery books helped me through moments of great stress, like when one of our children was in the hospital. They helped me through times of boredom. They allowed for great moments of relaxation, which is very hard to come by if you have five children and ten grandchildren."

"I have read hundreds of mystery books by authors like Agatha Christie, Arthur Conan Doyle, Dorothy Gilman, Elizabeth Peters, Raymond Chandler, Dashiell Hammett," Mrs. Montgomery continued. "From reading these mystery books, stories began to form in my mind."

"I just think you might have told me about this sooner, Dorothy," Mr. Montgomery said.

"Since the cat is out of the bag, so to speak, let me tell you about my ongoing series. Each book is called *The Mystery of the Woman in the Red Hat*, followed by a colon and the name of a city. The one I'm working on now is *The Mystery of the Woman in the Red Hat: Mandalay, Myanmar*. The great thing is that I can go on forever, since there are thousands of cities around the world."

"Look here, Dorothy, you're taking our perfectly good vacations and turning them into mysteries. I consider that an invasion of our privacy."

"Our trips are lovely, but they hardly make for thrilling reading," Mrs. Montgomery said. "They simply serve as the backdrop for my stories, which generally include murder, mysterious disappearances, and all kinds of intrigue. I don't even use my real name as the author. I use the *nom de plume* Alice Carroll Lewis."

"After Lewis Carroll, author of *Alice in Wonderland*," Mr. Montgomery said dryly.

"Now you're getting it! A mystery writer—or a real-life sleuth—must be prepared to go down the rabbit hole, and sometimes it is very dark down there."

Mr. Montgomery was quiet a moment. "So you're not leaving with me?"

"David and I are staying," his wife said firmly.

"I must go to our room and pack," Mr. Montgomery said, resigned. "Would you like me to take your check back to the house?"

"Oh, would you, George? That would be a weight off my shoulders. And do say hello to everyone."

George's eyebrows furrowed again as a shadow of doubt fell over his face. Then he kissed his wife and patted her shoulder.

"Just one moment, George," Mrs. Montgomery said, fishing in her handbag. She retrieved a paperback novel, *The Woman in the Red Hat: Glasgow, Scotland,* and handed it to her husband. "In case you want some light reading for the plane ride."

George took the book wordlessly, then left to pack.

Dorothy let out a sigh, then returned to her butcher paper notes. "That's done," she said aloud. "Now, I must concentrate on finding Charles."

CHAPTER 27

CHARLES FOUND AND LOST

Madame Constance sat at her white gilded desk, rumored to be from the palace of King Louis XVI, who was executed by guillotine in Paris in 1793. Her left elbow rested on the desk's glass cover. Her hands held up what felt like her increasingly heavy head. She'd just received another call from the American Embassy in Cairo. The woman on the phone said Charles hadn't yet been found, though they were still looking and they had hope.

Hope? They had hope? She needed air. The headmistress walked to the double French doors opening to her garden, which Jacques had planted at the end of winter. She took a deep breath, not noticing the purple, red, yellow, and orange blossoms that had burst into bloom. Nor did she notice the beautiful songs of the small grayish-yellow birds covering the branches of a nearby cherry tree. She felt unsteady. Her focus was on oxygen.

Taking another breath, she walked back to her desk and plopped down in the chair. A strand of iron-gray hair pulled out of her tightly-wound bun and fell in front of her troubled blue eyes. She tried to push the errant wisp of hair back where it belonged, but it refused to stay. To her, it was just another symbol of a life out of control.

If you asked anyone about Madame Constance and her role as head-mistress of the Château du Mont, they'd say she ran a tight ship. They might add she was a great regulator, that she brought order to an unruly world by anticipating problems before they occurred, taking the proper steps to forestall chaos. Madame Constance knew some people thought her cold. Over the years, she'd found drawings showing her baring fang-like teeth, brandishing a stick at her students, and placing a cone-shaped dunce hat on a boy who'd failed to solve a math equation that would have puzzled Einstein.

In truth, she'd never harm a student. If her students really knew her, if they could get inside her head and her heart, they'd know she considered each of them to be her own child. But there was so much that needed to be done to keep this old ship afloat. She didn't have time to show how much she cared.

Although he would never have guessed it, Charles was a favored child. Perhaps the special feeling Madame Constance had for him stemmed from the way his parents had dropped him off at the Château du Mont and then seemed to forget about him. Or maybe it was because he came to the school so angry, so scared, and so vulnerable that her heart could not help but reach out to him.

There was no doubt he was a difficult child. He'd tried to run away, jumping out of a moving car. He'd thrown his breakfast on the dining room floor, saying French food was "weird" and he'd never eat it. In front of other students, he'd said the Château du Mont's uniforms made the students look silly, and he'd never wear anything so ridiculous. Eventually, though, he had to. And, of course, he'd been adamant he would never have a roommate.

Madame Constance laughed a bit, thinking back on the day she asked David Montgomery, her most congenial student and captain of the Château du Mont's famous soccer team, to be Charles' roommate. David didn't have

214

an easy row to hoe. Charles had hidden the poor boy's underwear, and thrown both his and David's possessions and bedding all over the room. The worst thing was, they didn't talk to each other for three months. Eventually, however, they'd become friends, as she'd hoped and believed they would.

Madame Constance felt she'd played a large part in helping Charles become a happier boy. Seeing his near-miraculous transformation made him even more special to her. Now, he was lost in Egypt. She'd never approved of this trip. She'd known it was a bad idea from the very beginning. When Mr. Stratton asked if Jacques were a trustworthy person, she had to say yes. She'd told Charles' father she had known Jacques for several years and that he was a good man. Then, he asked if Jacques had any vacation time coming. She had to tell him the truth, that her hardworking assistant had accrued more than six weeks of time off.

The next thing Madame Constance knew, she'd received a letter from Mr. Stratton with an itinerary for a seventeen-day trip through Egypt for Jacques and Charles. No one had asked her permission. Now, one of her students was lost, ill, kidnapped or ... she didn't want to think about any other options. If this weren't bad enough, one of her teachers and two of her students were currently in Cairo looking for Charles.

Madame Constance pulled out a shallow drawer running along the top of the desk, which had been specially designed to hold maps. Considering the desk's age and supposed history, it was quite possible it had held some of the maps that affected events during the French Revolution. Now, the drawer held a map of Egypt. Madame Constance had purchased it even before Charles had disappeared. She'd intended on following the itinerary of Jacques and Charles as they traveled through Egypt, a place she'd always wanted to visit. Now, there were so many people over there looking for Charles she needed a map to keep track of them.

Madame Constance generally disapproved of writing in books or on maps. Running a school that was housed in such a historic building had made her acutely aware of the importance of preserving things. Just this once, though, she felt compelled to write down the names of those who were in Egypt and where they were staying.

Madame Constance found a large blank space under the word Suez, and there she wrote her list. Jacques. Mademoiselle Fleuret. David Montgomery. George and Dorothy Montgomery. Professor Charles Dayton Stratton, a man the FBI believed might be Charles' grandfather. Dr. Abd'El Hakim Awyan, head of something called the School of Khemitology. At the bottom of the list, she added the French and American embassies.

Madame Constance used a magnifying glass to locate the town of Giza, near the Archeological Zone where the pyramids and Sphinx were situated. She moved her index finger to the shape of the Sphinx. Although it wasn't named on the map, Jacques insisted that right across the road, near the Sphinx, was a village called Nazlet El-Semman. Nazlet was the site of the Khemitology Guest House, where Jacques and the others were staying. Jacques claimed Charles had so impressed Dr. Awyan, founder of the School of Khemitology and an Egyptologist, that he had invited them on a tour of the Great Pyramid. Madame Constance's mind drifted from Charles as she remembered she'd always wanted to go inside the Great Pyramid. She brought herself back to reality by reminding herself why she so rarely traveled. She worked to build sturdy, intelligent, resilient boys who would go on to have their own adventures. Madame Constance liked to think they took a piece of the Château du Mont and its reliable headmistress with them wherever they went.

Jacques had tried to explain that the School of Khemitology was not a school but instead "an association of people who looked past preconceived notions and asked big questions." It made little sense to her, but at least the organization seemed hospitable. Dr. Awyan had vowed to help find Charles, and he'd offered to let Jacques stay in one of the Khemitology rooms during the search. As more and more people arrived to look for Charles, Dr. Awyan opened more and more rooms.

But the people in Nazlet weren't the only ones she had to keep her eyes on. Returning to the map, Madame Constance traced her finger along the

Nile River, heading south to Luxor. Luxor was where Farak's family lived. The Egyptian boy was another of Madame Constance's favorites because he was unerringly polite and, like Charles, stranded far from home. Farak was convinced he and his family could help find Charles, even though Luxor was five hundred miles away from Cairo, where Charles had disappeared. Everything seemed so confusing.

Madame Constance wondered again if she should go to Egypt. It would be a simple matter to call one of her colleagues and ask them to take over the school for a week or so. No, she scoffed; that would be ridiculous. What could she do? She'd never been to Egypt before, and there were already so many people there looking for Charles. She'd be of no help at all. And yet, the impulse to go to Egypt continued to nag at her. The headmistress was still arguing with herself when she heard a knock on the door.

"Come in," Madame Constance called out.

It was Fran who, despite being only eight, was the Château du Mont's resident mathematical genius. He entered the office with his mother, followed by Madame Constance's cat, De Nuit

The ginger-haired boy wished her good afternoon. "*Bon après-midi,* Madame Constance," he said, showing off a phrase he'd just learned in his French class. "*Ma mère, elle est venue me voire.*"

"I am happy you have come to visit your son, Dr. Bernstein. I heard from Fran that you are teaching physics at the University of Paris this summer."

"Actually, I haven't started my classes," she said modestly. "That will be in two weeks. I am very excited."

She turned to her son. "Fran, say goodbye to Madame Constance. I need to talk to her about something."

"*Bonne journée, Madame,*" Fran said in his best French accent. The boy started to walk out the door, but he and Ciel De Nuit were lured to the French doors by the songs of the birds in Madame Constance's garden.

"Are those ortolan buntings?" he asked.

"Yes, they are," Madame Constance said, wondering how Fran's parents kept up with their son's insatiable curiosity.

"Ortolan buntings summer in Western Europe and spend the winter in Africa, the continent where Charles is currently lost," Fran said. "I read they're now an endangered species because the French love to eat them. Who'd want to eat such a tiny little bird? And wouldn't we miss their beautiful singing if they went extinct?"

"Fran," his mother said.

"Alright, Mom. I'm going." Fran knelt down, stroking the coat of the black cat. The cat had struck a hunting pose. "Come on, De Nuit," he said. "I'll ask Marie in the kitchen to give you some nice milk." He picked up the black cat and walked out the door.

"It's strange, Dr. Bernstein," Madame Constance observed. "Ciel De Nuit never lets anyone touch him except for Jacques, Charles, and me, of course. Now he's taken a liking to your son. How do cats decide on who they allow near them?"

"My hypothesis is they can sense a person's intentions," Fran's mother said. "They can tell when someone is kindly-disposed toward them. However, while the social instincts of house cats is a fascinating subject, I think we should skip the small talk. I know you must be extremely anxious about Charles, as we all are. Have you heard anything new?"

Madame Constance sighed heavily. "I just received a call from the American Embassy, and they say they are still looking for him."

"It is just as I feared," Dr. Bernstein said. "I came here, Madame Constance, because I've decided to take Fran to Egypt."

Madame Constance was alarmed. She didn't know how many more names she could fit on the map or in her head. "I do not advise this, Dr. Bernstein. We are in the middle of summer school."

"I'm aware of that but, as you know, Fran could teach his math classes," Dr. Bernstein said. "And because Charles taught Fran how to read and, more than that, to love reading, he's excelling in all his other classes."

"He is a fine student," Madame Constance agreed.

"Fran's very upset about Charles, and I believe he'll benefit more from a trip to Egypt than he will suffer from missing a week or so of school."

Madame Constance tried to dissuade Fran's mother again. "You know, there are already many people looking for Charles in Egypt. It might be too confusing to add two more."

"I've already contacted David's grandmother, Mrs. Montgomery," Dr. Bernstein said. "She told me her husband left Egypt yesterday on some kind of business matter. She has invited Fran and me to stay in her room at the School of Khemitology Guest House, along with David. She and I are like-minded about the situation. We believe the more people who are thinking of and searching for Charles, the more likely it is that he will be found."

Madame Constance was taken aback. "Really, Dr. Bernstein, do you, considering your scientific mind, believe this to be true?"

"Yes. In fact, my students and I will be experimenting with this exact concept," she answered. "There is a growing number of physicists theorizing that there is a connection available to living beings that involves non-direct communication. Some identify this as a vibratory field. It would seem possible that the more people focusing on a single goal, the more likely the goal will be attained."

"I hope this is so, Dr. Bernstein," Madame Constance replied.

"Have you talked to Charles' parents?" Dr. Bernstein asked.

"Unfortunately, they're unavailable at the moment. Their butler reports that they are supposed to be on a boat off the coast of Central America, and that they had informed him they would be 'out of touch' for three or four weeks." Madame Constance shook her head. "Imagine sending your child off to Egypt and then being, 'out of touch.' It is most unbelievable."

"Fran told me Charles was almost like an orphan," Dr. Bernstein said. "I understand what he means now."

Madame Constance shook her head and frowned. "I have urged the butler to contact me as soon as he hears from Mr. and Mrs. Stratton. It would be easier if we could contact them through this vibratory field you are speaking of, though I'm not sure that I entirely believe in it."

Dr. Bernstein turned and looked at the bookcases covering most of the walls in the office. "I just wanted to say, Madame Constance, I think you and I have a lot in common."

"Really? How so?" the headmistress asked, looking more closely at this small birdlike woman, a scientist with sharp green eyes and curly dark hair.

"I've been examining your bookshelves. I see we've read many of the same books. You have books by French explorer Alexandra David-Néel; Gertrude Bell, the so-called Queen of the Desert; the great explorer-journalist Rosita Forbes; the Scottish explorer Dr. David Livingston; and the legendary aviator Amelia Earhart. I believe that you are an adventurer, Madame Constance, as I am."

"Well," the headmistress blushed, "yes, I do love great adventure books, though I have no adventures to speak of in my own life, except now, it appears, I have lost a student in Egypt."

"We will find him, Madame Constance," Dr. Bernstein said.

The phone rang as Dr. Bernstein exited the door. Madame Constance picked up her white-and-gold phone. She recognized Jacques' voice. He asked if she was sitting down.

"Yes, I'm at my desk. Why?" she asked. "Charles has been found in the City of the Dead? He is alive? Oh, Jacques, I am so relieved. What do you mean, he disappeared again? This is unbelievable, Jacques. Do you think I should come to Cairo? Alright, I will wait for your call."

Ciel De Nuit slipped through the side door and jumped up into Madame Constance's lap. She picked him up and walked out the side door to her garden. This time, she observed the wild array of colorful flowers that Jacques had planted at the end of winter. How could Charles have disappeared again, she wondered? Jacques understandably sounded shaken. That meant she had to remain strong. Returning to her desk, she gave Ciel De Nuit a final stroke on his shiny black coat and placed him on the floor. Then, she pulled out the secret map drawer, scratched off the name of Mr. Montgomery, David's grandfather, and added the names of Fran and Dr. Carolyn Bernstein.

CHAPTER 28

WAKING UP IN THE CITY OF THE DEAD

Charles could only open one eye. Wherever he was, it was dark. It was so dark, he might as well have not opened his eye at all. Where could he be? He raised his head to find out, causing a sharp pain to shoot out from his right temple. He felt a thick bandage had been wrapped around his entire skull. What had happened to him? Bits of thoughts and memories danced around his brain but, try as he might, Charles couldn't put them in any logical order. Nothing made sense. His felt his eye closing. He struggled to stay awake. He needed to ...The boy couldn't finish his thought. He was asleep again.

Hours or days later, Charles struggled to open his eyes. He wasn't in a hospital room. It was too dark and there was a smell of old dust, the way it smelled on the fourth floor of the Château du Mont, where the Ghosts of the Jangling Keys had resided for all those years. How long had he been in this room? Before he could figure it out, he was asleep again.

Charles felt someone sit on the edge of his bed. He groaned a little and tried to sit up. Someone placed a cool cloth on his hot face. He opened his eyes to find a woman dressed in a black gallabiyah and headscarf, but it wasn't her dress he looked at in the dim, dim light. It was her kindly eyes and sweet smile.

When she noticed he was awake, she patted his arm and said a few words to him. She was speaking Arabic. Where was his English-to-Arabic dictionary? Charles answered himself; it was back on the train with Jacques. How long ago was that? How long had he been here? Where was Jacques? He had to find him. He tried to sit up. The woman gently pushed him back down on the firm pillow. She began to sing in a soft voice. She rose from his bed, walked to the stove, and returned with a bowl and spoon. Holding Charles' head up slightly, she fed him broth. It was warm and comforting. He'd have to think about Jacques later. He fell back into a dreamless sleep.

This time, Charles woke up rested. The pain in his head was gone. But where was he? It was dark in this room, but it must be daytime because a narrow beam of bright white light spilled in from outside through the bottom of the wooden door. The light was filled with dancing dust particles. There was also a burning lantern in the middle of a large table. There was no one else in the room but Charles. He inspected the walls, the ceiling, and the floor. All were made from cement. Not the bright cement of Boston's sidewalks, but the dark and grainy cement of—he didn't want to think about it, but he couldn't help himself—the dark, grainy cement of cemetery headstones.

Maybe Charles was still asleep and dreaming. He sincerely hoped so, because the room he'd been sleeping in looked exactly like a tomb, a mausoleum. A mausoleum is a free-standing building constructed as a monument enclosing the interment space or burial chamber of a deceased person or people. He remembered this word from his last vocabulary test at the Château du Mont, one thousand years ago.

Thinking about his boarding school reminded Charles of Jacques. Where was he? Was he alright? He pulled up on his elbows. At the side of the room were several piles of mats and straw baskets filled with what looked like bedding or clothing. There was a cupboard with visible dishes and, by the door, a small wood stove with steam rising from the top of several dark pots. Charles looked away from the light of the lantern and doorway and stared towards the other end of the room. What he saw sent a chill through him. It was a casket, an ornate cement casket. Tears flew out of his eyes and his voice choked as he cried for his mother, though he knew she was nowhere near Egypt. It was all too much. He allowed himself to sob in self-pity.

A few minutes later, the woman in the black gallabiyah rushed in through the sunlit entry. Four children of various ages followed her. She knelt and stroked Charles' head, making soft sounds of comfort. The children gathered around her, looking at Charles with great curiosity. The biggest boy said, "English." The younger children chanted, "English, English."

Charles whispered, "American."

The children then chanted, "American, American."

The mother walked to the stove and poured broth from a pan into a cup. She brought it back to Charles. He drank some of the broth, then laid back and fell asleep again.

At first, he dreamed he was back in his home in Newport, Rhode Island. He was in his room by the window, looking out over the crashing Atlantic Ocean. Then, the dream changed. This time, he was inside a mausoleum and ghosts were walking around him, whispering words he could not understand. He had to make himself wake up, but it was like being in the ocean and finding you had dived too deep. You kick as hard as you can, pushing your arms against the water, struggling, struggling to reach the top. Your sides hurt, your head hurts. Finally, you break through to the surface of the water and breathe in the air you need so badly.

Charles sat up and looked around, but he might as well have stayed asleep because he was still in a tomb. He was in a tomb in Egypt. Not the kind of tomb filled with treasures and mummies but the kind of tomb you see in

223

black-and-white movies, with coffins lying around and gravediggers lurking about. His eyes focused through the dim light, and he saw six mats scattered this way and that on the cement floor. On each mat was a different-sized body. These people were not gravediggers. Charles figured it was a father, a mother and four children, a family, and they were living in a tomb. His mind was no longer clouded by the terrible headache and irresistible desire to sleep. He was awake, and Charles knew where he was. He was in the City of the Dead.

Samy, the taxi driver, had pointed out this tomb city on the first hour of the first day he and Jacques had arrived in Egypt. He told Charles he had a cousin who could get him inside the tomb city if he wanted, but he wasn't interested. He told the taxi driver he was only interested in ancient tombs, temples, and pyramids—not modern ones. But he ended up here anyway, without Samy's help.

Charles was feeling better. The one thing he needed to do, for sure, was get to the American Embassy. For now, though, he had a more immediate problem. He had to go to the bathroom, and he couldn't wait. In his foggy state, he'd seen people disappearing behind a blanket at the end of the rectangular room. He guessed this must be where this family went to do what everyone has to do. Charles would have run for the curtain, but he had a few problems. He wasn't sure how to get up from a bed, considering he hadn't walked for what he surmised was a long time. Once on his feet, he'd have to talk himself into moving toward the cement coffin that stood in the middle of the tomb. He was also leery about what he'd find behind the curtain.

The first issue wasn't that hard. He got on his hands and knees, put his feet on the floor and rocked up to a standing position. He felt a little unsteady, but he could walk. The second issue was harder. Charles told himself that he shouldn't be frightened of a coffin. After all, he'd just spent nearly six months thinking about and communicating with two resident ghosts at the Château du Mont. He shouldn't be afraid of ghosts. But he'd been separated from the two ghost children—victims of the French Revolution—by large iron bars. Charles started wondering exactly how the gate had kept the ghosts from stepping through the gate to the third floor. He, David, and Jacques would have to discuss that when he got back to school.

Anyway, Charles told himself, there probably weren't any real ghosts in this tomb, just skeletons. Somehow, thinking about skeletons didn't give him the nerve to walk by the five-foot-high cement coffin. What did help was, he really had to go. Keeping his eye on the hanging blanket in the back of the tomb, he quickly passed the coffin. He pulled aside the blanket. There was a a tiny oil lamp, casting shadowy light on a large pot. This was it, no question about it. He hated the thought of it, but he no choice. As quick as he could, Charles did his business. He returned to his bed. He didn't lie down. He just sat on the edge of the bed. He had to think.

It was nearing morning. Charles could tell by the tiny bit of sunlight trying to get in under the bottom of the old wooden door. He heard a voice coming from a loudspeaker outside the tomb. He recognized it as a call to prayer. The mother stirred. She looked in Charles' direction. By the dim light of the lantern, Charles saw the sweetest smile he'd ever seen, even sweeter than his own mother's. The woman moved towards him, her arms spread out. She held his head against her body, looking up, speaking what he knew must be a prayer of thankfulness. He allowed this to happen. She had cared for him when he couldn't care for himself.

The mother called out to her sleepy family. They smiled at Charles, happy about the American boy's return from the dead. They couldn't pay attention to him for long, though. The voice on the loudspeaker was calling. Each family member picked up a little rug from a large straw basket. The ancient wooden door creaked loudly as they pushed it open. The soft gray light of early-morning pooled at the entry of the tomb door. The family walked out, father and boys to the right, mother and girls to the left.

Charles walked to the door and looked out. There were men, women, and children as far as he could see, all kneeling and facing east. He'd learned from his social studies teacher that they were facing the holy city of Mecca in Saudi Arabia, where the Islamic prophet Muhammad was said to have been born. Charles was interested in watching this early-morning prayer but suddenly felt dizzy. He staggered back to his bed thinking, if only I could get my strength back. He needed to get to the American Embassy. Jacques would be terribly worried. Charles lay down on his mat and closed his eyes.

When he awoke, his head was clear. He wondered how long he'd been here at the City of the Dead and where Jacques was. He was sure that his chaperone would still be here in Cairo looking for him. Just then, one of the boys from the family, a child about Fran's age, entered the tomb, tan gallabiyah fluttering. He'd been very interested in Charles and had spent many hours sitting on the end of his bed, trying to talk to him. But Charles had been too ill and, besides, the boy didn't speak English and Charles didn't speak Arabic.

Fortunately, the whole family spoke a universal language, one that anyone could understand. It was the language of kindness. The boy seemed very excited. He ran straight to Charles and handed him a note. Charles squinted at the paper, trying to read the tiny but perfect writing. Realizing it was too dark in the tomb to read, he staggered to the door. The note was lit up by the mid-morning sun. It was written on stationary from the Osiris Hotel in Cairo. Charles was relieved to see the note was in English.

It said, '*I am Aamen Halabi. I attend the University of Cairo. My major is English. As you can see, I write English very well, and people say that I speak it well too. I heard about your plight and have volunteered to escort you to the American Embassy. Coincidently, it is my goal to work at the American Embassy as an interpreter. I will be out of my last class at 5 o'clock. I shall be able to visit you around 7 o'clock tonight. We shall then go together to the American Embassy. I hope to practice my English with you. Sending my most deep respect. Humbly, Aamen Halabi.*'

So, he was going to the American Embassy in just a few hours. Charles returned to his bed in his tomb in the City of the Dead. He lay down feeling depressed and exhausted. His Egyptian vacation was over, that was for sure. No doubt Madame Constance would insist that Jacques bring him straight back to the Château du Mont. He would not get to travel up the Nile, explore ancient temples, or discover the ghost of Tomb 11. Never, ever was there such an unlucky boy as he.

CHAPTER 29

THE TRANSLATER AND THE DISAPPEARANCE

A young man dressed in Western attire stood at the doorway of the Wasims' home in the Western Cemetery of the City of the Dead.

"Hello," the youth called out in English, leaning his head inside the one-room tomb-home. "Can you tell me if this is where I can find the American boy?"

Mrs. Wasim waved the young man in and pointed to where four boys and one girl were standing by a cement casket. The casket loomed above their heads, casting shadows in a room lit only by an open wooden door. Each of the children had tousled dark curly hair, and each was wearing a rumpled gallabiyah. The teen said something in Arabic. The children laughed and pointed to the tallest of the boys.

Smiling, the young man strode to where Charles was standing. He spoke English with an Egyptian accent. "I am sorry that I did not recognize you, Sir. I am your translator, Aamen Halabi."

The youth held out his right hand for a traditional handshake. Charles felt awkward being greeted like a grown man, but he reached out his hand. The translator gave it a firm and enthusiastic shake. Charles looked at the Egyptian youth dressed in tan pants and a white dress shirt. He thought he looked pretty young to be a translator.

But Charles said, "I am pleased to meet you, Aamen Halabi. My name is Charles Dayton Stratton III, from the United States of America. You didn't recognize me because I'm not dressed like an American. I have a story as to why."

"You have a story? I love stories more than anything. This is perfect. You know what I am thinking, Sir?"

"No, what?" Charles asked, pulling his hand back from Aamen's powerful handshake.

The interpreter replied enthusiastically, "I am thinking that since I am nearly a professional interpreter, we ought to tell your story to all your new friends: the Wasims, who saved your life, and all the neighbors who prayed to Allah for your swift recovery from your most terrible and life-threatening injury."

Charles reached up and touched the cloth bandage tied around his head, a reminder that he was still recovering from a terrible head injury.

"I—I thought you were here to escort me to the American Embassy," Charles stammered.

"Yes, the American Embassy! I apologize, Sir. As it turns out, the embassy closes at 7 p.m. I had no idea that the American Embassy closed so early. If I had, I would have come sooner. But then I would have missed my very important class on Customs and Common Practices of American Politicians. But do not worry, Sir. I spoke with Mr. Wasim, the taxi driver who found you nearly dead outside the train station. Of course, he is the owner of this tomb-home, husband of Mrs. Wasim, and father to these delightful children," Aamen said, smiling and pointing to the mother and the children beside her.

He then spoke in Arabic, evidently translating what he had just said to Charles. The mother and her children laughed heartily.

Aamen switched back to speaking English. He told Charles that Mr. Wasim had agreed to drive them to the embassy early the next morning, adding, "So you see, Sir, you have plenty of time to tell your story."

Charles looked at the kind mother who'd fed him and nursed him back to health. Then, he glanced at the Wasim children jumping up and down beside him, filled with anticipation and excitement. He decided that they did deserve to hear his story.

"Okay," he said to Aamen. "But I don't know what I am supposed to do. I don't know how to start."

"It will be very easy," Aamen said persuasively. "You tell your story in English, and I will excellently translate what you say from English to Arabic. Is this agreeable to you, Sir?"

Charles felt strange being addressed so formally. He told the translater he agreed to tell his story but preferred to be called Charles rather than Sir.

Aamen grinned, which made him look younger, even younger than Farak.

"Follow me," the teen interpreter said. "I know just the place for you to tell your story!"

Charles grabbed the cloth shoulder bag that held all his worldly possessions and followed Aamen out the door. The young man weaved through the narrow alleyways. It was almost nightfall. Braziers, with their yellowish-orange flames, leaped out of the large black pots that provided light in the City of the Dead, as well as functioning as cookstoves where meals were prepared and shared with neighbors.

As Aamen walked, he called out something in Arabic. Men, women, and children followed him like he was the Pied Piper. There was excitement in the air. A story was coming.

The young man stopped before an ornate tomb. It was taller and larger than any of the other tombs in the City of the Dead. It had a big lock on the double door. The door and the lock were made of bronze. It didn't appear that anyone lived in this burial chamber. While most tomb-homes were made of cement, this mausoleum was made from white marble, with light gray lines running through the smooth and glossy surface.

Aamen, with his arms spread out in a grand gesture, said to Charles, "This is perfect, is it not? From up those stairs, we can be seen and heard by everyone."

Charles counted the steps. The sacred seven, he whispered to himself. He knew from his studies of ancient Egypt that the number seven meant completion. It could also mean the end of one's earthly life, in other words, death.

But it was not the steps, nor the size of the building, nor the marble stone that captured Charles' attention. It was what was carved on the brass double doors and the protective eaves of this building.

In the Egyptian tour book Charles' father had given him, it said that the City of the Dead was established for the Muslim population. It was built in 642 CE, the Common Era, and was still in use today. The tombs in the City of the Dead were decorated in geometric patterns or in Arabic writing—except for this tomb.

Whoever designed it had to be a follower of the gods of ancient Egypt, a religion believed to have gone extinct nearly two thousand years ago.

Charles stared at the double brass door, held together by a large brass lock. On each side of the brass doors was a carved figure of Anubis, the jackal-headed god, the god of funeral rites, and the protector of graves. The two figures of Anubis faced each other, guarding whatever lay inside this marble tomb.

Above the door, Charles recognized a carved and painted story of Anubis in his role as a guide through the underworld for the recently deceased. He led the dead until they reached a golden scale. On one side of the scale, Anubis placed the heart of the deceased. On the other side, he placed one of Ma'at's feathers. Ma'at is a goddess with wings. She is the goddess of balance and law. Anubis would then ask the deceased about the choices he or she had made in life. If the deceased made good choices, the heart would be light as a feather, and the recent dead would be guided to a happy afterlife. However, if the person made bad choices, Ammit, Devourer of the Dead—with the forequarters of a lion, the hindquarters of a hippopotamus, and the head of a crocodile—would devour the heart, leaving the dead forever soulless.

Aamen skipped up the seven steps. Charles followed him slowly, sincerely hoping that the lock would not only keep people from entering the tomb but would prevent anything inside the tomb from getting out. He shivered, then scolded himself for being afraid of a mummy. After all, he had been interested in mummification since he was a kid. He guessed he was probably still weak from his head injury.

Charles looked out at the people gathering at the foot of this tomb. He wondered if anyone here knew about Anubis.

Aamen began his introduction, then turned to Charles and asked, "Are you ready, Sir?"

Charles looked once more at the intricately-carved doors, then faced the crowd. His eyes found Mrs. Wasim; she was smiling. She looked proud of Charles, as if he were her own son. She waved. He waved back.

At first, Charles felt nervous, wondering if he could speak in front of so many people. But then he began to recognize the neighbors, many of whom had brought food, and had prayed for his recovery. Maybe it would not be so difficult to tell these people his story.

As Charles looked over their audience, he noticed a stranger standing straight and tall in the very last row of the crowd. It was a woman dressed in black with a black veil or headscarf covering her nose, mouth, and much of her forehead, allowing only space for her large dark eyes, eyes that seemed to look directly into Charles' eyes.

"Just tell your story from the beginning," Aamen instructed. "People in the City of the Dead love long stories."

Charles took a deep breath, telling himself that storytelling was just like writing, only without a pen.

"I grew up in the United States of America, in the state of Rhode Island," he said. "I lived with my parents in a home on a cliff that looks down on the crashing Atlantic Ocean. From my room I could hear the ocean waves, and I loved watching the light of the sun and moon on the water. I also loved Egypt since I was a little boy. I read hundreds of books and articles about Egypt, and even taught myself how to read and write hieroglyphics."

Charles paused while Aamen repeated what he'd said. The translater added great hand gestures and sound effects. When he mentioned that Charles could read Egyptian hieroglyphics, the audience showed surprise and appreciation.

"One day," Charles continued, "my mother and father told me they were sending me away to a boys' school in France. I didn't want to leave home. I didn't want to leave my parents. But they said I didn't have a choice. I was very sad."

Aamen relayed Charles' story, miming a little crying to demonstrate Charles' distress at being sent from his home. The people in the audience looked at the American boy. Some of them glanced over towards their own children, thinking they would never send them away.

Charles was learning something from Aamen. When you write, you don't have to worry about how your voice sounds or what gestures you use. When you speak, however, the sound of your voice, its speed and force, and your body gestures are like details in a painting; they are an important part of storytelling. Charles tried to be a little more dramatic as he described meeting Farak in an Egyptian museum outside of Paris. The audience was delighted by the tale of the unlikely friendship between an American boy and a Bedouin prince. Charles told them about his birthday present from his parents, a trip to Egypt.

The Egyptian audience laughed at the part where Charles decided to surprise Jacques by dressing up as a Bedouin boy. They were agitated when they learned the conductor tossed Charles off the train car just as it was leaving the station. And they grumbled loudly when they heard that the military policeman kicked Charles out of the railroad station, with no justification, just because the man thought he was a poor Egyptian boy.

When Aamen got to the part where Charles was hit on the head by a metal box from the workman's cart, Aamen dramatically fell down the steps and just lay there.

Charles asked the translater if he was all right. Aamen said that he was fine. It crossed Charles' mind that this translater would make a great actor.

As Aamen arose from his place on the stairs, Charles went crazy or something. He reached into his bag and pulled out the pyramid wrapped in its red cloth. He showed everyone the small pyramid with the gold capstone. Charles looked towards the back row. The woman in black broke her eye contact and then rushed off to the right. Charles wished like anything he could take back that impulsive action, but the deed was done. He had betrayed the confidence of a friend. Charles rewrapped the pyramid in its red cloth and returned it to his bag.

Aamen evidently did not notice anything was amiss. He finished the story about Mr. Wasim tying his turban around the boy's bleeding head and bringing him to the City of the Dead. Aamen then whispered to Charles that it was time for him to thank the Wasims and the people of the Western Cemetery, who prayed for his survival.

Charles gave each person in the Wasim family a direct look and a smile. Then he turned and bowed deeply to the crowd. The crowd clapped as if it were the end of a grand play. Charles noticed that the woman in black had returned, bringing with her two other women also dressed from head-to-toe in black. They were not clapping. Instead, each of the three women placed their thumbs and fingers together, forming a pyramid. Charles understood that this had to do with his betrayal of Farak. Why had he shown strangers the pyramid replica? And why were these women in black giving him this sign of a pyramid?

As he considered these questions, the three women moved swiftly, exiting to Charles' right.

Charles thanked Aamen, then grabbed his shoulder bag and skipped down the seven steps. He called out to his interpreter, "I'll be right back."

The sun was just going down, but the narrow pathway between the tombs was cast in darkness. Fortunately, much of the pathway was lit up by the braziers. While Charles appreciated the lights from these small fires, he was disturbed by the shadows they cast. Sometimes, the shadows were orange and tall, sometimes gray and small, but most of the time, the shadows took the forms of dancing animals on tomb walls.

In the absence of the braziers, the three women and their shadows disappeared altogether, causing Charles to hurry to keep up with their dark forms. Should he call out to them? Could they speak English? Should he go back to Aamen and the Wasims? He asked himself questions, but he just kept following the women. He needed to know what the sign of the pyramid meant and, for some reason, he wanted to tell them he was sorry he had shown the people of the Western Cemetery the replica pyramid.

Charles' head began to ache. How long had he been following these women, he wondered? Suddenly, the pathway and the tombs ended. The three women stepped out into a barren desert. Charles stopped in the shadow of the last tomb. What should he do? He watched as one of the women, the shortest of the three, turned and walked south. The other two women kept walking east. The longer he stood there, the further away the women got. He wished David was with him; he'd learned that adventures are better when shared. But David wasn't with him, and he had come this far. Charles took off running, tripping over the rough and rocky sand.

As he drew closer to the women, he noticed that they were moving towards the shadowy figure of a man and three camels. As they approached the man, two of the camels knelt. The man helped the women mount, first the taller woman and then the shorter woman. Once the camels were on their feet, the tall woman leaned down and gave the man something, probably money, Charles thought. The cameleer gave their camels a light slap and the two women took off, riding north at a rapid pace.

Charles knew it was too late to catch up with the women in black. He needed to get back to Aamen and the Wasim family. At this thought, Charles was immersed in sadness. It was his last night in Egypt. He would never get to see Luxor or visit Farak's family. He would not get to tour the famed Valley of the Kings or the many temples on the banks of the Nile River, and he would definitely not discover the Ghost of Tomb 11, Tel el Armana, Egypt. As Charles was feeling sorry for himself, the three-quarter moon rose in an inky sky. It lit up the desert. He could even see the small forms of the women on camels as they traveled north. Charles slowly turned 360 degrees, drinking in the desert. He ended up looking at the cameleer, who appeared to be waving at him. Charles waved back.

The man continued waving. It finally dawned on Charles that the man was not greeting him but beckoning him. Charles' head told him he should go back to the City of the Dead, but his feet and heart moved him in the other direction, toward the man and his camel. The Egyptian man's white gallabiyah seemed to glow in the moonlight. Charles greeted him with one of the few Arabic phrases he'd learned, *Salaam 'alykum,* meaning, "Peace be with you."

The man bowed low to Charles, then looked at him, giving the boy a great smile, his white teeth illuminated by the light of the moon. The man pointed to his camel, obviously asking Charles if he wanted a camel ride.

Tomorrow, he'd go to the American Embassy, and then he and Jacques would fly immediately back to the Château du Mont. Madame Constance would never allow them to continue their vacation. What would it hurt if he took one short camel ride?

The man folded his hands together, forming a step. Charles used this human stirrup to pull himself up on the camel's hump. The camel jumped up off its knees. Charles found himself nine feet off the ground. He reached into the wallet he'd placed in his shoulder bag and handed the man one of the gold coins Farak had given him. He knew this was way more than a camel ride cost, but he was leaving Egypt anyway. Who would need Egyptian gold coins back at the Château du Mont?

The cameleer examined the coin, smiling even more broadly, saying something in Arabic. Then, pointing to the caramel-colored dromedary, he pronounced the name Sahara. The cameleer gave Sahara a little swat, and off the two went.

It was like he was riding through the night sky, Charles thought, as he looked at thousands of planets and stars set in a black sky. It was breathtaking. He felt like a real Bedouin. Charles was able to pick out constellations: the three stars of the Belt of Orion, the Pleiades—seven stars clumped together—the Big Dipper and, beside it, the Little Dipper or Ursa Minor. He followed the pan made of the stars of Ursa Minor, and identified the brightest star, Polaris, the North Star. It was pointing to the direction Charles and his camel Sahara were heading. That was all Charles could identify, but the sky gave him a final gift. A large falling star, a meteorite, swept across the entire sky, east to west, and he was here to see it. Charles thought this was an amazing experience, but now he needed to get back to the Wasim family.

Twisting his body around, Charles attempted to locate the cameleer. The Egyptian in the white gallibyah was walking south, the opposite direction from the one the camel and Charles were headed. Charles was cold, hungry, exhausted, and his headache had returned. He attempted to turn the camel around by pulling the reins as hard as he could to the right. The camel would not change course. Charles tried leaning back firmly, pulling on the reins while calling out, "Whoa, there!"

He had heard this command used on horses in western movies on his television, back in Newport, Rhode Island. But the camel, evidently, had not seen any of these western movies. He did not stop.

What did Lawrence of Arabia do when he wanted his camel to stop or go in different directions? Try as he might, he could not remember. Finally, Charles concluded that there were only two thing for him to do: stay on Stubborn Sahara and go to who knows where, or throw himself off his nine-foot perch, hoping to land safely on the rock-strewn, sandy ground. But, Charles reasoned, even if he managed to land uninjured, he would still have to walk many miles back to the Western Cemetery.

"What should I do?" he asked his camel.

Stubborn Sahara gave a loud snort, and kept walking north under a star-filled sky.

CHAPTER 30

MRS. MONTGOMERY MEETS DR. BERNSTEIN

Dorothy Montgomery, David's grandmother, was standing among the crowds of people at the Cairo Airport waiting for the passengers of Flight 444 to exit customs. Wearing a large black hat with purple flowers around the brim and a matching purple skirt, she didn't exactly blend in. In the latest installment of Mrs. Montgomery's Woman in the Red Hat mystery series, set in Vienna, Austria, her protagonist suggested there were two ways to become invisible. The first was to blend in, to look like everyone else. The second was to look "'uncomfortably different." The theory was that most people were so overwhelmed by their usual day-to-day existence, they didn't like to be confronted with anything strange. Politeness contributed further to the phenomenon. Few people want to be caught staring at someone just because they're different. If Mrs. Montgomery's hypothesis were correct, in just a few hours, no one would be able to describe her, even if directly asked by a journalist or a policeman. She'd be completely forgotten despite, or perhaps because of, her flamboyant attire. One never knows when one needs anonymity, she thought to herself.

Furthermore, the clothes of international travelers vary greatly. Here in the Cairo airport were people in business attire, Indian saris and dhotis, Egyptian gallabiyah, khaki adventure wear, and blue jeans and T-shirts. The mystery writer felt delightfully invisible as she indulged in her favorite pastime of people-watching.

As Fran and his mother walked out the double doors, Mrs. Montgomery reached out a white-gloved hand to the dark-haired physicist. "Welcome, Dr. Bernstein," she said. "And welcome to you, Francis."

"Hey! How'd you know it was us?" Fran asked.

"It's your hair, such a wonderful color of red."

"Oh, yeah," said the boy.

"I met you at the spring science festival at the Château du Mont," Mrs. Montgomery said. "Who could forget your project determining the size of a balloon and the amount of helium needed to lift various objects? If I remember correctly, a mouse was among these objects. Did you ever find that poor creature, Francis?"

"Yes. The balloon was caught in the branches of a tree. Jacques helped us get it down. I think the mouse enjoyed its ride, don't you, Mom?"

"Absolutely, Fran, who would not?" his mother answered, patting him on the head.

"Did you two have a nice flight?" Mrs. Montgomery inquired.

"Yes, and I want to thank you so much for inviting Fran and me to stay with you here in Cairo at the…"

Fran interrupted his mother. "Boy, are we lucky! Usually, Mom teaches physics during the summer at the California School of Technology in Pasadena, California, better known as Caltech. It's one of the colleges I'm considering attending."

"It's never too soon to think about the future," Mrs. Montgomery said approvingly.

"But this summer is different," Fran said. "She'll be teaching classes at the University of Paris, something about frequencies. Isn't that right, Mom? She'll be able to visit me whenever she likes. Mom has a two-week break between classes and, because I've been so upset about Charles, she's brought me to Egypt to help find him. So here we are."

"And I'm glad that you're here, Fran," said Mrs. Montgomery. "The more heads, the better when solving a mystery, that's what I always say."

"Has there been any more news about Charles?" Dr. Bernstein asked.

"No," Mrs. Montgomery said. "The good news is there's no indication the boy has been injured. Or anything else," she added, looking directly at Dr. Bernstein. "We are working with the American and French embassies and the Egyptian police. We can talk about it later."

Mrs. Montgomery smiled at the child standing beside her. "How old are you now?"

Eight-year-old Fran still had a couple of months before his birthday, but he figured that was a technicality. "Nine," he answered with his fingers crossed. That way, it couldn't be construed as a lie.

"You're just the right age to help find your schoolmate, Francis. I'm sure David will be happy to see you."

"Why are you wearing that hat?" Fran asked.

His mother scowled at her son. "Francis Bacon Bernstein, we do not ask questions like that."

"We don't? Can I ask her if this is the kind of hat people wear in Egypt?"

"Fran!"

"That's all right, Dr. Bernstein. The answer is no, Fran. They don't wear this kind of hat in Egypt." Mrs. Montgomery lowered her voice. "I am in disguise."

"Oh, right," whispered the boy.

Mrs. Montgomery pointed to the far-left door. "Our taxi driver is out front waiting for us. Oh, yes, we need to retrieve your suitcases. Porter!"

A thin, elderly Egyptian man in a well-worn cream-colored gallabiyah followed them to the carousel where people from their flight were waiting for their luggage. With Fran's help, the porter located their silver-colored suitcases. The old Egyptian insisted on carrying both bags, Dr. Bernstein's heavy carryon and Fran's backpack.

Walking out of the air-conditioned building, they were hit by the blazing heat of the noonday sun. "We're in Egypt!" Fran shouted.

Mrs. Montgomery waved in the direction of a man wearing a dark blue shirt covered with bright yellow pineapples. He had a string of puka shells around his neck and was standing by a black taxi with a handmade sign saying, "Occupied." While Dr. Bernstein tipped the porter, the taxi driver took the suitcases and placed them in the trunk.

He introduced himself to the newcomers. "I am Samy, the personal tour guide for Charles and Jacques. I was, that is, until Charles tragically, not to mention improbably, disappeared."

Mrs. Montgomery gave Samy a long, sharp look but said nothing.

The driver smiled at Fran. "Hey, dude. I hear you're one of Charles' best friends."

"He saved me from a lifetime of illiteracy," Fran said.

"Fran has a mathematical mind and a touch of dyslexia," Dr. Bernstein explained.

"That means I sometimes see words and letters backwards and stuff like that," Fran said. "Charles taught me to read. Next, he's going to teach me to read hieroglyphics."

"That's radical!" Samy said. "I don't even know how to read hieroglyphics, and I'm Egyptian."

"Do people wear Hawaiian shirts in Egypt?" Fran asked Samy.

"I'm setting the trend," the taxi driver answered.

"Yes, but I don't see any of the other taxi drivers wearing Hawaiian shirts."

"Forgive my son," Dr. Bernstein said. "We are working on our manners."

Samy laughed. "Me too, Fran."

"I'm from America," Fran informed him. "I go to school with Charles at the Château du Mont. It's in France, about three hours south of Paris. Charles is in year six and I'm in year three, but I think I might skip a grade next year. This is my mother, Dr. Carolyn Bernstein. She's a physicist."

"Nice to meet you, Dr. Bernstein," Samy said.

"How did you meet Jacques and Charles?" Dr. Bernstein asked.

"I was their first choice as a taxi driver when they stepped out of this very airport."

"Do you have a last name, Samy?" inquired Mrs. Montgomery.

"Of course, but most people just call me Samy."

"Are you Egyptian? You speak pretty good English," Fran asked.

"I was born in Luxor, Egypt, about five hundred miles south of here. When I was a teenager, my family moved to Cairo. As for my pretty good English, I attended UCLA in Los Angeles, California for a few years."

Fran jumped up and down in his seat. "UCLA? I love UCLA! It's one of the colleges I'm considering attending. My dad, he's an aerospace engineer. He's lectured at UCLA many times about the building of a rocket ship that can travel to Mars. We go with him sometimes, not to Mars but to UCLA."

"What was your course of study?" Mrs. Montgomery asked their taxi driver.

"Surfing, mostly."

"Did you study any other subject?"

"I specialized in International Relations."

"That is very interesting," Mrs. Montgomery said, looking very interested indeed. "And now you drive a cab?"

"Yes, I'm helping my father with his taxi business here in Cairo."

Samy helped Mrs. Montgomery and her large hat into the backseat of the taxi. Fran jumped into the front passenger side seat. His mother began to protest, then decided it wouldn't hurt. Samy opened the left-hand door, and Dr. Bernstein entered the black taxi.

"Everybody ready?" the taxi driver asked.

"I'm ready!" Fran answered.

As Samy pulled out of his parking spot, he slipped a cassette into the cab's tape player. "This is one of my favorite songs," he said, looking towards the back seat, 'It's Surf City' by Jan and Dean." Then he burst into song, trying to harmonize along with the vocalists.

And when I get to surf city I'll be shootin' the curl
And checkin' out the parties for a surfer girl.
And we're going to surf city, 'cause it's two to one.
And we're going to surf city, gonna have some fun, now.
Two girls for every boy.

Sitting beside Samy, Fran was rocking back and forth to the music. Then, recognizing the refrain, he sang out, "Two girls for every boy!"

Dr. Bernstein leaned over to Mrs. Montgomery. "This wasn't quite the introduction to Egypt I had expected," she whispered.

"Well, '*To expect the unexpected shows a thoroughly modern intellect,*' as Oscar Wilde observed," Mrs. Montgomery whispered back.

"I do want to have a thoroughly modern intellect, Mrs. Montgomery," Dr. Bernstein said with a laugh.

The surf song soundtrack continued as they drove past modern and not-so-modern sections of Cairo. "How long is the drive to this School of Khemitology?" the physicist called out over Samy's singing.

He turned down the music and craned his head to look at Dr. Bernstein. "It will take only about an hour unless, like many of my passengers, you'd like me to give you a little tour on the way. Or maybe you'd like to buy something. I have a cousin who owns a shop, real antiquities."

"Thank you, Samy, but not at this time," Mrs. Montgomery said, holding onto her hat as they hit a bump in the road.

Samy pointed out the City of the Dead, telling Fran about the living people who'd turned tombs into homes.

"I want to go there," Fran said.

His mother smiled at him, giving him a light swat on the head with her hat. "Perhaps another time."

Samy drove into a small town where most of the people were wearing Egyptian robes, veils, and turbans. "This is the little town of Giza, located on the outskirts of the Giza Plateau," Samy said over the beat of "Wipe Out."

"Now we're really in Egypt!" Fran called out. "I like this music too."

"This is one of my favorite songs," Samy said. "In my next life, I think I'd like to play the drums."

"Do you believe in reincarnation?" Mrs. Montgomery asked.

"That's a subject I am still thinking about. How about you, Mrs. Montgomery?"

Fran broke into the conversation. "Do all Egyptian soldiers ride camels, and are those real guns they carry over their laps?"

"Yes, they are real rifles and no, not all Egyptian military personnel ride camels," Samy answered. "See that sign? We're about to enter the Archeological Zone. On the plateau, traveling by camel is the most efficient way to move around."

"I want to ride a camel," Fran said.

"You know we came here to help find Charles," Dr. Bernstein reminded her son.

"That's true." said Mrs. Montgomery. "I'm sure, however, that a camel ride can be arranged for you, as Dr. Awyan comes from the people who provide camel rides for tourists. David and I have already had the delicious pleasure of riding on a dromedary, a one-humped camel. While I found this to be a once-in-a-lifetime experience, I'm sure David would be happy to join you and your mother on a little camel ride."

Samy continued pointing out various landmarks. "On the right, we are passing the famous Mena House Hotel."

"You won't believe this," Mrs. Montgomery interjected, "but I was nearly as excited to lay eyes on the Mena House as I was to see the Great Pyramid. The historic hotel was featured in Agatha Christie's classic mystery novel *Death on the Nile*."

"I love Agatha Christie!" Dr. Bernstein said.

Mrs. Montgomery was beginning to see where Fran got his enthusiasm.

"The Mena House is where Charles and Jacques stayed for their first five days in Cairo," Samy said. "The Mena House boasts Egypt's very first swimming pool. At certain times during the day, the Great Pyramid is reflected in its water."

"Did Charles really swim in that swimming pool?" Fran marveled.

"Yes, he and Jacques did take dips in the Mena House pool."

"I want to take a dip in the Mena House pool!" Fran exclaimed excitedly. "I packed my swim trunks, just in case."

The road suddenly narrowed. Clouds of dust and sand billowed around hordes of cars, trucks, taxis, vans, buses, camels, donkey carts, and pedestrians, accompanied by a cacophony of sounds. They had reached the Giza Plateau.

"Look at that!" Fran's mother said, pointing to the Great Pyramid. "It takes my breath away. I've read about the Giza Plateau, but I had no idea how I would feel actually being here. It's like a wish come true."

"It may surprise you to learn that our room is situated directly across the street from the Sphinx, thanks to Dr. Awyan," Mrs. Montgomery said.

"I want to visit the Sphinx, and who is Dr. Awyan?" Fran asked.

"His full name is Dr. Abd'el Hakim Awyan," Mrs. Montgomery explained. "He grew up here on the Giza Plateau, playing in the shadow of the pyramids and swimming in the tunnels beneath them."

"I want to swim in the tunnels beneath the pyramids!"

"As a teenager, Hakim was trained to be a tour guide," Mrs. Montgomery continued. "He discovered that some of the 'facts' he was supposed to convey made little sense, considering his own firsthand knowledge of the buildings and artifacts around the Giza Plateau."

"That's just like my math classes," Fran exclaimed. "The professors make it so difficult to solve problems that are really easy. What did Dr. Awyan do?"

"Hakim began to integrate questions and some of his own theories into tours. Some people found his ideas fascinating and encouraged him to go to school to become an Egyptologist. He earned not one but two degrees, one in Egyptology and the other in archeology."

"What a fascinating and impressive story," Dr. Bernstein said. "I can't wait to meet Dr. Awyan."

"How do you spell Khemitology?" Fran asked Mrs. Montgomery.

"Khemit was the original name of Egypt. It means black soil, *Khemit*, K-h-e-m-i-t. The black soil is the silt brought to the Nile's green area during the yearly flood. This flooding fertilizes the soil, allowing food to grow. It makes life possible in this desert land. Then, of course, the word contains 'ology,' meaning science or branch of knowledge. So it is spelled K-h-e-m-i-t-o-l-o-g-y."

"K-h-e-m-i-t-o-l-o-g-y," Fran repeated the spelling.

"Dr. Awyan became what one might call an official Egyptologist. Instead of presenting popular theories or his own hypotheses, however, he wanted to search for the truth about these great archeological buildings and artifacts. He founded the discipline of Khemitology, the open-minded study of ancient Egypt. Khemitology brings together people from various disciplines—archeology, geology, geography, metallurgy, astronomy, astrology, meteorology, medicine, healing, and physics, as well as people who are just interested in ancient Egypt—to share their speculations and their research."

"I'm intrigued," Dr. Bernstein said. "I hope to find some time to speak with Dr. Awyan."

"Dr. Awyan is in great demand as a speaker, but has assured me he'll do all he can to help find Charles," Mrs. Montgomery said. "He met Charles and Jacques on their second day in Egypt. He was introduced to the pair by his son, Yousef Awyan, who sometimes acts as a cameleer. That's a person who leads the camels that tourists ride."

Out the window, Fran could see a number of people riding camels from Sphinx to pyramid or from pyramid to Sphinx. "I'd love to grow up to be a cameleer."

"Fran, you're interrupting again," his mother said.

"Jacques discovered that Yousef, their cameleer, spoke English," Mrs. Montgomery continued. "Jacques told Yousef they'd come to Cairo because of Charles' love of Egypt, and described how the boy had taught himself to read hieroglyphics. Yousef Awyan shared this information with his father, who was about to take a small group of people into the Great Pyramid. Dr. Awyan was so impressed, he asked Charles and Jacques to join them."

"Charles has so many admirers," Dr. Bernstein said. "Apparently, to know him is to love him."

Fran shook his head. "Actually, David says Charles was mean when he first came to the Château du Mont."

Dr. Bernstein automatically corrected him. "Fran!"

"It's true. And I want to go inside the Great Pyramid, too."

"Few tourists get to experience being inside the Great Pyramid, let alone guided by a Wisdom Keeper like Dr. Hakim Awyan," Samy said.

"What's a Wisdom Keeper?" asked Fran.

The man in the Hawaiian shirt shook his head. "I'm not exactly sure, little dude. I guess you'd better ask him."

"So, you didn't know Dr. Awyan before Charles and Jacques met him?" Mrs. Montgomery had begun jotting notes down in a little notebook.

"I'd never even heard of him."

"One more little question, Samy. How did you find out that Charles was put off the train by that wicked conductor? Hadn't your position as a tour guide ended?"

"I never consider my relationship with those who've chosen my services to have ended. As far as finding out about Charles, Mrs. Montgomery, I heard it through the grapevine."

Samy began singing again.

I heard it through the grapevine,
Not much longer will you be mine.
I heard it through the grapevine,
I'm just about to lose my mind.

"Sung by Marvin Gaye, 1966, I believe. I love American rock music."

Mrs. Montgomery was starting to believe this eccentric taxi driver shared her theory—that he was using his "uncomfortably different" persona as camouflage. She wondered what he was hiding.

"As you may have heard," Samy said, "I was actually on the train when Charles disappeared, only in a different compartment."

"Oh yes, I will be interested to learn more about your experience, Mr. Samy," Mrs. Montgomery said sweetly. "Look, here's the Sphinx."

"I see it! I see the Sphinx!" Dr. Bernstein exclaimed. "Isn't it amazing? I can't believe I didn't bring you here sooner, Fran." The physicist sounded as animated as her son.

"It's bigger than it looks in photographs," Fran said.

"Fran, do you remember the riddle the Sphinx posed in the play *Oedipus the King* by Sophocles?" his mother asked.

Samy burst into the conversation, intoning the famous verses with a voice like a Shakespearean actor.

A thing there is whose voice is one;
Whose feet are four and two and three.
So mutable a thing is none
That moves in earth or sky or sea.
When on most feet this thing doth go,
Its strength is weakest and its pace most slow.

Mrs. Montgomery clapped her white-gloved hands. "That was quite good, Samy. Maybe you should go into acting. Or perhaps you already have," she added pointedly.

"I know the answer to the riddle," Fran interrupted.

"Francis, you may get your chance to share your answer tomorrow," Mrs. Montgomery said. "Dr. Awyan plans to escort us to the Sphinx at 4 o'clock in the morning, just before sunrise."

"We can't search for Charles before sunup, so that sounds just lovely," the physicist exclaimed.

Samy made a U-turn at the Sphinx and pulled up in front of a small building made of cement. It was tucked between many buildings of varying sizes and levels and states of repair. It looked like a Lego city, built by a six-year-old; at least that's what Fran thought. Then he read the sign Pizza Hut and exclaimed, "I love pizza!"

David must have been watching for them. As soon as Samy pulled up in front of the restaurant, he ran out the blue door.

"Hello, Grandmother," he said. "Hello, Fran, and hello, Fran's mother. We've been waiting for you. Jacques has ordered lunch, but it will be another twenty minutes. Can I show Fran around?"

"I think that should be fine. Just stay on this side of the road," Mrs. Montgomery said. "Wait, I should ask if this excursion is alright with you, Dr. Bernstein."

"Yes, if you think it is. David, I can't wait for you to show us around the Giza Plateau," Dr. Bernstein said.

"Me too, and I'm ready for a camel ride," Fran exclaimed, jumping up and down in excitement."

"Don't forget, Fran," David reminded his schoolmate in a serious voice. "Our mission is to find Charles."

CHAPTER 31

THE BUTLER ARRIVES

M rs. Montgomery entered the Pizza Hut, led by David and Fran. The trio was followed by Dr. Stratton and Jacques, both wearing looks of concern. Last came Samy, clad in a bright red Hawaiian shirt with a scene of an erupting volcano. Dr. Awyan was behind the counter, chatting in Arabic with Mandisa.

Before Mrs. Montgomery could take a seat, she noticed her husband sitting at the front table. "George! What are you doing here?"

"I just had to sign some papers at the main office," Mr. Montgomery said, beaming at his wife. "Now I am back, ready to throw myself into the task of finding young Charles."

Mrs. Montgomery planted a kiss on her husband's forehead. Then she remembered something. "George, I'm afraid I gave away your bed."

"What!"

"You weren't here, so I offered your bed to Fran and his mother," she explained. "Remember, there are two beds and a bunk bed. It's perfect for the boys."

"It will be alright, Mr. Montgomery," Jacques said. "I have an extra bed in my room. You can stay with me on the third floor."

"Thank you, Jacques," Mrs. Montgomery said. "That settles things."

"Do you have any other news for me, Dorothy," her husband wondered, "besides the fact I'll now be sharing my quarters with Jacques?"

Mrs. Montgomery shook her head. "Unfortunately, we haven't heard anything else regarding Charles."

"I can't imagine where the boy could be," Dr. Stratton said, rubbing his forehead.

"David has an idea," Fran volunteered.

"Well, I'm certainly glad someone has an idea, David," Mrs. Montgomery said, back in sleuth mode. "What's this theory of yours?"

"It's just a guess, but I think I may be onto something," the blond boy said. "Like everyone else, I thought Charles would go to the American Embassy for help. But we know he didn't show up there, which leaves the question, where else might he go?"

"We've been looking at the geography of Egypt," Fran said, pointing to a map taped up on the back wall. "That's where David got his idea."

"On the plane to Cairo, Farak told me something," David said. "I'd forgotten, but I think it's important. Farak promised Charles that if he ever needed help, his Bedouin family would come to his aid. So it makes sense that Charles would try to get to Luxor where Farak's family lives."

"Tell them how you think he'd get there," Fran said, jumping up and down.

"I'm getting there," David said, waving the younger boy aside. "Charles didn't have his passport, so it's unlikely he could travel by plane, even if he had money. And I don't think he'd attempt the train again. This leaves only one way to get to Luxor, by boat."

David used his finger to trace the blue line representing the famous Nile River, which runs from Cairo to Luxor. "It's my guess that Charles either befriended a fisherman, gaining passage by offering to help on one of the river boats, or became a stowaway on a cruise ship."

Dr. Stratton leaned forward. "David, what makes you think Charles would travel down river? It looks to be a five hundred-mile journey."

"Charles is an adventurer, fearless, and a creative thinker," David said. "He knows how to make plans and implement them. He wouldn't be intimidated by the thought of traveling to a far-off city to find Farak's family. With a plane and the train eliminated, I believe he'd take to the Nile, otherwise known as the African highway."

David smiled, thinking of his friend. "You've got to know Charles to understand how he draws you into things he cares about. He's so enthusiastic and makes everything seem like a wild mystery."

"It is true," Jacques said, nodding. "Why else would a chauffeur and handyman like myself—who speaks no Arabic and has traveled very little—agree to accompany a boy to Egypt? And a trouble-prone boy, at that. You are right, David. Charles has a huge imagination and a gift for persuasion."

"When I came to the Château du Mont, my favorite subject was soccer," David said. "Because of Charles, I'm now fascinated by Egypt and its life's blood, the Nile. He described this great blue river bound on both sides by desert. He told me how the river travels north instead of south, how it's filled with hippos and crocodiles, and how it allowed for the rise of the most wonderful civilization in history. Without the Nile there'd be no pyramids, no Sphinx, and no great ancient Egyptian cities. He told me the Nile is the life's breath of Egypt."

"I guess that boy can be kind of poetic," Samy said, looking at the map of Egypt. "There are many boats traveling south. Getting on one of them might be difficult, but it could be done, especially by Charles."

"It's my suggestion that we go to the local docks and ask if anyone has seen a twelve-year-old American boy hanging around," Dr. Stratton said. "We've learned that when in native costume, he's all too able to pass for a local boy. If no one remembers seeing an American child, we can also ask if they've encountered an Egyptian boy who seems to be on his own."

"Yeah, and don't forget to mention he has blue eyes," Fran said. "In fact, I think David and I had better go with you. I'll go ask my mom."

Jacques was sitting in the corner, listening to the conversation. "I do not know," he said. "I have this feeling that Charles would not leave Cairo."

"It sounds to me like performing this errand is better than just sitting here," Samy said. "I'll meet you at the taxi."

Dr. Bernstein entered the Pizza Hut. Fran ran up and hugged his mother, nearly knocking her over. "Mom, can I go with Dr. Stratton, Jacques, Samy, and David to the docks? David thinks Charles probably stowed away on a boat to get up to Luxor and Farak's family."

"I gather a lot of things have happened while I was taking a shower," Dr. Bernstein said, her curly hair still damp.

"It's just a hunch, Dr. Bernstein, but we think it's worth exploring," David said. "We can keep an eye on Fran."

"What do you think, Mrs. Montgomery?" Fran's mother asked.

"I think it's a great opportunity for the boys to see the Nile, and they may just discover something." Mrs. Montgomery turned to David and Fran. "Stick close to Dr. Stratton, Jacques, and Mr. Samy—one lost boy is enough."

Through the window, David noticed a strangely-dressed man wearing an old-fashioned hat, a black coat that reached nearly to his knees, and a white shirt topped off by a dark bow tie. He was carrying a black suitcase, a black cane, and a piece of paper.

"Look, Fran," David said.

The ginger-haired boy tapped Dr. Bernstein's arm. "Mom, there's a man outside who looks like an actor from an old-timey movie. He is staring at a paper and walking around. I think he's lost or something."

"Okay, boys, go out and ask the gentleman if he needs help," Fran's mother said.

Jacques glanced out the window to make sure the visitor wasn't Mr. Smith. He definitely wasn't. Fran was right, however. The man was an unusual-looking character. He looked as though he'd stepped out of a black-and-white movie. Meanwhile, Fran and David rushed out the door.

Dr. Stratton was still examining the map. When he heard the Pizza Hut door open and then close, the professor turned and looked out the window. He gasped, then exclaimed, "My heavens, it's Alfred P. Hart!"

Fran ran back in, trailed by the strangely overdressed gentleman. David followed, carrying the man's large black suitcase. "Here he is, the old-timey man," Fran said.

"Fran," his mother said, with warning in her voice.

"Sorry, Mom," Fran said. "What I meant was the man who looks like a butler is here. He was looking for the Khemitology Guest House."

"Alfred, you came," Dr. Stratton said, his voice filled with emotion. "Thank heavens! I could use a little support. I tried to call you yesterday when I was at the American Embassy, but I see now that you were preparing to fly out from Massachusetts."

The man in the black hat and waistcoat glanced around the Pizza Hut. "As ever, I am here to assist you in any way, Dr. Stratton."

"Everyone, this is Alfred P. Hart. He is our butler. I mean," Professor Stratton corrected himself, "he was the butler to my wife and me."

Fran grinned. "I said he looked like a butler, didn't I, Mom?"

"Oh, listen to me!" Dr. Stratton continued. "I'm making mincemeat of this introduction. Let me start over. Alfred is my old friend. He knew and loved my late wife and doted on Charles."

"You know Charles?" Fran asked, his eyes wide with surprise.

"I am talking about my son Charles, the man believed to be the father of your Charles," Professor Stratton answered. "Charles Dayton Stratton II. We called him Charlie when he was a boy."

Dr. Stratton reached out to shake his friend's hand. "Ah, how good it feels! The hand of an old friend."

"I see you're quoting Henry Wadsworth Longfellow!" Mrs. Montgomery said, looking pleased.

"Yes, he's one of my favorite American poets," Dr. Stratton said. He introduced Alfred to Mr. and Mrs. Montgomery, Jacques, David, Fran, and Dr. Bernstein, including a brief description of how each was connected to the missing boy.

"I feared Dr. Stratton would be alone," Alfred said. "It is my extreme pleasure to meet you all. Is there any news about this boy, Charles?"

"None whatsoever," Dr. Stratton said. "We have not, however, given up. We are working with the French and American embassies, the Egyptian police, and several of the newspapers. We also have a few amateur sleuths in our midst. In fact, this boy here, David, Charles' roommate from the Château du Mont, has just suggested that his missing friend may have taken a boat to Luxor, which lies some five hundred miles to the south."

"That seems rather strange, doesn't it?" Alfred asked. "Why would he do such a thing?"

"One of Charles' friends from school, a Bedouin boy, has family in Luxor," Dr. Stratton explained. "According to David, this young man told Charles that if he were ever in trouble, his family would help him."

"Yeah, and if you ask me, Charles is definitely in trouble," Fran said. He returned to the map on the wall and traced the blue ribbon from Cairo to Luxor. "We think he stowed away on a boat in order to get to Farak's family."

"And here's the great thing," David added. "When he gets there, Farak will be there."

"A young boy becoming a stowaway. This is a strange story," Alfred said, sitting down next to Dr. Stratton.

"You are absolutely correct, Alfred P. Hart," Mrs. Montgomery said, retrieving her roll of butcher paper and set of colored pens from her oversized purse. "It is a strange story, and it just keeps getting stranger."

Mandisa brought the newcomer a glass and a carafe of water. Dr. Stratton thanked her and ordered one of her flatbread pizzas. He promised Alfred he was in for a delicious treat.

"I must say," Alfred said, smiling up at Mandisa, "I have not been in many pizza parlors, but this one smells delicious."

Dr. Stratton waited as his friend sipped some of his water, then asked the question that was on everyone's mind. "Alfred, why did you come dressed like this when you know Egypt is mostly a desert?"

"I didn't want to get my suit wrinkled, so I decided to wear it as I traveled on the 747 to Cairo."

"Do you really think you'll need such a suit in Egypt?" Dr. Stratton queried.

"As the English writer Oscar Wilde said, '*You can never be overdressed or overeducated.*' And here I find myself, in my best suit and at a school," Alfred said. "What is this School of Khemitology, anyway?"

"The founder, Dr. Awyan, has kindly allowed those of us searching for Charles to stay in his guest house," Dr. Stratton said. "I have an extra bed in my room."

"This was very good of you, Mr. Hart, to fly out to support your friend in his search for a possible grandson," Mrs. Montgomery said, adding the name Alfred P. Hart to the list of people searching for Charles.

"There is more at stake than finding a grandson, though that is certainly momentous," Alfred said. "I assumed that his parents, including his father—whom we believe is our missing Charlie—will have rushed to Egypt to aid in the search for their son. I couldn't let Dr. Stratton meet his long-lost son alone." Alfred took another sip of water, and turned to his friend. "Where is he, Dr. Stratton? Where is Charlie?"

"I am afraid that's another mystery," Mrs. Montgomery said. "Charles' parents are what is being called 'out of touch.'"

Alfred looked at Dr. Stratton in wonder. "So Charles' parents do not know that he is missing?"

"As Mrs. Montgomery said, no one knows where this boy's parents are. To tell you the truth, Alfred, I don't know what I'd say to my possible son if he did come to Egypt," Dr. Stratton admitted. "The more convinced I become that this boy could be my grandson, the more confused and hopeless I feel."

Alfred patted Dr. Stratton on the back. "Do not give up, Sir. '*When today fails to offer the justification for hope, tomorrow becomes the only grail worth pursuing.*' It's a thought that has often kept me going."

Mrs. Montgomery clasped her hands together in pleasure. "Oh, my! What an apt quote, Mr. Hart. I was fortunate enough to see Arthur Miller's 'Death of a Salesman' at the National Theatre of London. It certainly contained a lot of lessons."

Mrs. Montgomery gave the butler a closer look. Now, here was an interesting man. Taking another sip of water, Alfred P. Hart removed his hat. Fran picked it up and placed it on his head, where it fell over his ears and eyes. There was great laughter at the sight of the little boy in the too-large hat. Dr. Bernstein gestured for Fran to return the hat to its owner.

Mrs. Montgomery stuffed her butcher paper and pens into her purse, advising the boys to get ready for their trip to the Nile.

"Dr. Bernstein, I well remember when my children were Fran's age," Mrs. Montgomery said. "How I treasured the occasional break from their welcome but constant company! Why don't you and I have a cup of tea and a little talk? Would you care to join us, Alfred?"

"If Dr. Stratton is headed for the docks, I believe I will join him," Alfred said.

"Not until you change into something more suitable," Dr. Stratton insisted. "I don't want to have to carry you back to the car if you succumb to heat prostration."

Mr. Montgomery smiled. "Mr. Hart," he said. "I have just the outfit for you. It will help you feel truly at home in this glorious, mysterious, fiery country. It will also help you blend in."

"Ah, a disguise," Alfred said, heading out the door.

"Your taxi is leaving for the Cairo docks in fifteen minutes," Samy called out.

Several hours later Samy dropped Fran, David, Dr. Stratton, and Alfred off at the guest house. They were disappointed and exhausted, and Fran's freckled cheeks were sunburned.

"It was a bust, Grandmother," David said. "There were hundreds of unaccompanied boys working around the docks. Who would notice a boy dressed in a gallabiyah, even if he did have blue eyes? I was so certain I had the answer. I guess I should leave the detective work to you."

"Nonsense, a sleuth must be tireless, looking into every possibility. And it will take more than one person to solve this puzzle," Mrs. Montgomery said, looking at her butcher paper notes. In the right-hand corner, she'd listed and then crossed out possible places where Charles might be, including the train station, the Cairo Museum, the American Embassy, the Mena House and the docks, leaving only Luxor as a possibility.

Mrs. Montgomery then snapped back into grandmother mode, quick enough to give someone whiplash. She called everyone to the table and served them egg salad sandwiches, iced tea, and freshly-baked sugar cookies. Dr. Bernstein reminded everyone they would be meeting Dr. Awyan at the Sphinx for the sunrise ceremony the next day. One and all of the searchers were showered and in bed by eight o'clock. Even the boys didn't protest. They had walked far and gotten a lot of sun.

David asked from the top bunk, "Grandmother, do you think we'll find Charles? Seeing all the unaccompanied boys at the ports made it feel so hopeless."

Mrs. Montgomery, poised on the edge of her bed in her purple robe and lavender feathered slippers, was quiet a moment. Then she said, "I heard a quote by Elvis Presley, a singer so talented he was called the King of Rock 'n Roll. *'If things seem to be going wrong, don't go with them.'* What good advice! David, I have found that holding positive thoughts most often brings positive ends."

"Thank you, Grandmother. Goodnight."

"Goodnight, David."

CHAPTER 32

RA AND LANGSTON HUGHES AT DAYBREAK

By four a.m., the waning moon had set, leaving only a few pale stars sprinkled across an inky sky. David, Fran, Dr. Bernstein, and Dr. Stratton were standing outside the closed Pizza Hut. Dr. Awyan approached the group, his gallabiyah lit up by the kerosene lantern he was carrying.

"Is Mrs. Montgomery coming?" Dr. Awyan asked.

"No," said Dr. Bernstein. "Very late last night, someone rang the bell. It was a messenger from the American Embassy with a note requesting that Mrs. Montgomery and Jacques come to the embassy this morning. I offered to go with them, but Mrs. Montgomery insisted Fran and I couldn't miss the magical sunrise at the Sphinx. I believe Dr. Stratton's friend is going with them."

"Very well, follow me," Dr. Awyan said, raising his lantern high above his turbaned head. Dr. Bernstein, Dr. Stratton, Fran, and David followed the founder of the School of Khemitology as he seemed to float across the road. When the small group reached the other side of the road, they encountered nearly a hundred other people gathered to witness what Dr. Awyan called "the greatest show on earth."

"Can David and I go to the Sphinx faster?" Fran asked Dr. Awyan.

The Egyptologist chuckled. "Am I walking a little too slow for you boys?" He handed the lantern to David, who sped off, calling for Fran to follow him.

"Don't worry about the loss of our lantern," Dr. Awyan said. "I have traveled this path so many times, I could walk it blindfolded."

"I just hope we don't arrive to find Fran climbing up the Sphinx," Dr. Bernstein said.

In the few minutes it took the adults to reach the Sphinx, the sky underwent a transformation. It turned from charcoal to dark slate, and a slight halo appeared on the eastern horizon, promising another sunrise. People gathered at the foot of the sleepy Sphinx. They waved excitedly at Dr. Awyan. As the Egyptologist approached, everyone on the Giza Plateau faced east. A hush fell over the desert. Only the irreverent camels sent out their loud brays to welcome Ra, the sun god.

"Why isn't anyone talking?" Fran asked in a loud whisper.

"Shhh!" David responded, putting his finger to his lips.

"This is the moment," Dr. Awyan said in a commanding voice, "when the sun steps out of the boat that carried it through the dark waters of the *duat*, the realm of the underworld. The sun god Ra experienced death as he struggled through the long night and is now ready to take up life again. Ra is ready for a new day, a new beginning. And as Ra rises out of the horizon, the sun god offers each of us here the exact same opportunity. The past is erased."

A red light, bright as a laser beam, peeked out of its rocky bed. Finally free, it rose higher and higher until it took the form of a brilliant red ball. With an almost audible sigh, the sun announced it had once again escaped death.

Applause broke out all over the Giza Plateau. From between the paws of the Sphinx, the chanting of various syllables could be heard.

"You know, Fran," David said solemnly, "I've seen many sunrises in my life. I wonder why it feels more magical here? I only wish Charles was with us."

"Me, too," Fran said in a whisper.

The boys joined the celebrants, who were now slowly circling the largest statue ever made by human hands. David told Fran everything he'd learned about the Sphinx from Dr. Awyan, especially the belief that there was treasure buried under the Sphinx in a secret tunnel.

Fran was puzzled. "Why don't they just dig it out?"

"Number one, because traditional Egyptologists don't believe it exists. Number two, because they're afraid digging under the Sphinx might damage it. And number three, Dr. Awyan believes Egyptologists are petrified as to what else they might find."

"Mummies?" Fran asked.

"I think they're used to mummies by now. Dr. Awyan says they might unearth the truth, and it's different from what most Egyptologists and archeologists are comfortable believing."

Fran nodded his head sagely. "I guess I'm different. I like learning new things."

"Me, too," David agreed.

Dr. Bernstein scanned the crowd until she spotted Fran following David, who was circumambulating the Sphinx. Satisfied, she turned to Dr. Stratton. "So you did not know you had a grandson?"

The older man shrugged. "How could I know anything about him? My own son, Charles Dayton Stratton II, walked out of our house many years ago, mumbling something about having to make hard decisions. My late wife and I never heard from him again. We thought he must have passed away. The FBI at my door changed everything."

"That must have been quite a shock," Dr. Bernstein said sympathetically.

Dr. Stratton was silent a moment, watching Fran and David. The boys were competing to see who could take the longest steps as they circled the Sphinx. "I have been forced to remember the pain I tried to bury for twenty years," he said. "But pain should not be buried. Now I'm here looking for my grandson, my son, and possibly a new life."

Dr. Awyan returned from between the paws of the Sphinx, smiling at Dr. Stratton and Dr. Bernstein. "I always feel more energetic after watching the sunrise on the Giza Plateau. How did you like our little show?"

"It was spectacular," Dr. Bernstein said earnestly.

"I only wish I had the words to describe this experience," Dr. Stratton said. "What I need is a poet, like Langston Hughes, to describe this sunrise. Have you heard Langston Hughes' poem, 'Daybreak in Alabama,' Dr. Awyan?"

"No, I never heard of this Langston Hughes, though I do know where Alabama is. I visited it for a conference," Dr. Awyan said, recalling the hot, humid summer, so different from the dry heat of the Giza Plateau. "I would like to hear this poem, 'Daybreak in Alabama.'"

The professor glanced at the sun, which had just broken the day. He paused a moment, then spoke the words of Langston Hughes he had memorized by heart. His voice took on the cadence of a man describing the sunrise, not in Egypt, but in the southeast of America.

When I get to be a colored composer
I'm gonna write me some music about Daybreak in Alabama.
And I'm gonna put the purtiest songs in it
Rising out of the ground like a swamp mist
And falling out of heaven like soft dew
I'm gonna put some tall tall trees in it
And the scent of pine needles
And the smell of red clay after rain
And long red necks
And poppy colored faces
And big brown arms

And the field daisy eyes
Of black and white black white black people
And I'm gonna put white hands
And black hands and brown and yellow hands
And red clay earth hands in it
Touching everybody with kind fingers
Touching each other natural as dew
In that dawn of music when I
get to be a colored composer
And write about daybreak
in Alabama.

Professor Stratton ended the poem with a request, "Come, great poet, whisper in my ears the words to describe this very moment." Then he lowered his head, in reverence to this amazing writer who could capture the beauty of daybreak.

"My heavens, that was breathtaking," Dr. Bernstein said, "Mr. Hughes' poetry so beautifully brings an even an deeper meaning to an experience. Thank you, Dr. Stratton."

"Yes, thank you, Professor Stratton," Dr. Awyan said, "for reminding me of the power of poetry."

The trio walked toward the Pizza Hut, thinking about daybreak. Before they reached the road, Fran ran up to Dr. Awyan. "Excuse me, Sir. David told me there are water tunnels around the pyramids, and that you've been swimming in them."

"That was a long, long time ago, Fran," the old Egyptian answered.

"I want to swim in the tunnels! I packed my swim trunks."

"Unfortunately, that is impossible," Dr. Awyan said. "The powers that be have placed bars on all the tunnels in this area. No one can go into them anymore, not even me."

"It's strange," Dr. Bernstein said. "None of the books I've read about the Giza Plateau mention these tunnels. And the photographers always make it look as though the Sphinx, and pyramids, are in the middle of a deserted desert."

"It's true. I never knew that the village of Nazlet El-Semman was right across the road from the Sphinx. It's quite surprising," Dr. Stratton said.

"I am afraid that many Egyptologists, journalists and even tourists have a specific belief of what the pyramids and the Sphinx and the land around them should look like," Dr. Awyan said. "For such people, no facts, even those before their very eyes, can ever affect the way they portray this archeological site to the world."

Dr. Awyan gestured across the road to the town where fifty-thousand people lived in a jumble of cement apartments, most in various stages of disrepair and all needing paint. "The government calls the housing of Nazlet El-Semman unplanned. This is because they have their own plans, for expensive hotels, fancy restaurants, green area—meaning golf courses—museums, theaters, and shops. All they have to do in order to build their dream is one thing: get rid of the people of Nazlet El-Semman."

"I don't think they should get rid of the people," Fran said seriously.

"Neither do I. Neither do I," the Egyptian agreed. "For almost one hundred years, our people were needed. We were allowed to build here so archeologists could have cheap labor for their excavations. We were allowed to settle here so people in the so-called hospitality industry could have hotel workers. And then they could have we Bedouins at the ready to provide camel and horse rides for tourists. Now, they think they can get along without us. But what do you do with fifty-thousand people? How can these people survive away from the Giza Plateau, where they have lived and worked their entire lives?"

"I don't like that," Fran said, frowning.

Dr. Bernstein reached out and hugged her son. Dr. Awyan smiled at the boy, then told him to go and drag David away from the camel area. As Fran jogged towards the Sphinx, a young boy in a gallabiyah ran up to Dr. Awyan and handed him a cloth sack. David and Fran ran up beside Dr. Stratton and Dr. Bernstein, announcing that they were starving.

"And rightly you should be," said Dr. Awyan. "I have ordered breakfast. It should be ready."

Holding the now-extinguished lantern high above his head, Dr. Hakim Awyan stepped into the road teeming with vans, trucks, taxis, and donkey carts. The physicist grabbed for Fran's hand as they followed in his wake.

"You don't have to hold my hand, Mom," Fran said. "Dr. Awyan controls the traffic."

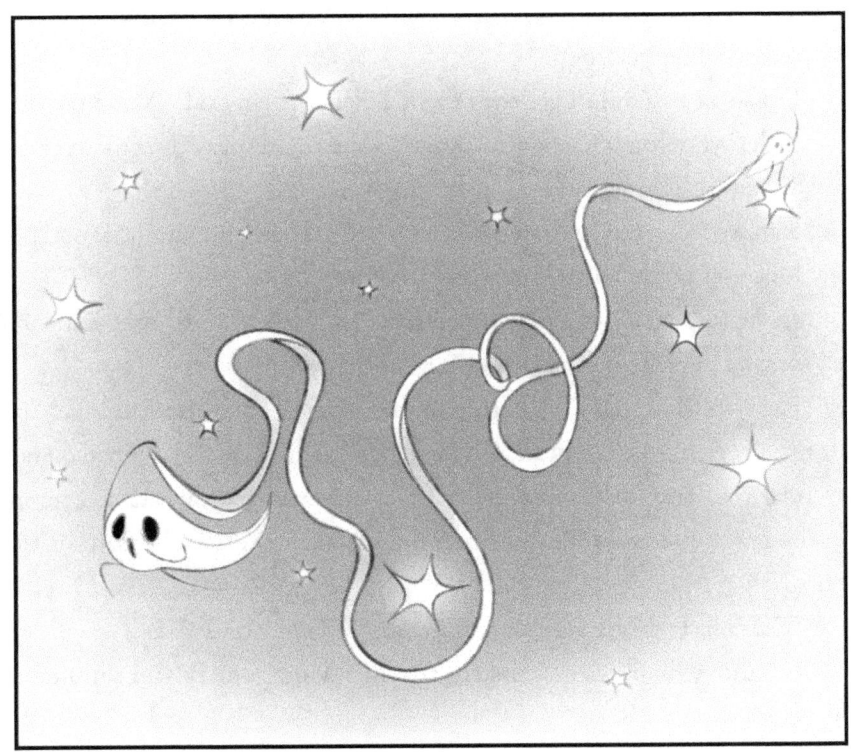

CHAPTER 33

SPOOKY PARTICLES AT A DISTANCE

Mr. Montgomery looked out the window of the Pizza Hut, anxiously awaiting the return of doctors Bernstein, Stratton, and Awyan, as well as the two boys. As they walked in the door, he burst out, "I kissed Dorothy goodnight, and this morning she's missing!"

David looked startled. "What? Now Grandmother's missing?"

"Well, she's not exactly missing," Mr. Montgomery said apologetically. "While you were at the Sphinx, a young man delivered a note from your grandmother saying she was at the American Embassy."

George looked around the Pizza Hut and said, "Has anyone seen Mademoiselle Fleuret, Dr. Stratton's butler, and Jacques? It's confounding the way people keep disappearing."

"I'm sorry you didn't get the news," Dr. Bernstein said. "Mademoiselle Fleuret left yesterday. She flew to Luxor so she could speak directly to Farak and his family."

"Can we fly to Luxor to speak directly to Farak and his family, Mom?"

"Not now, Fran," his mother said.

Mr. Montgomery looked exasperated. "Excuse me, but could someone tell me why my wife is at the American Embassy?"

"Here's all I know," Dr. Bernstein said. "Very early this morning, Mrs. Montgomery and I were awakened by the doorbell. Your wife slipped on her lavender robe and purple feathered slippers and rushed downstairs. I threw on my gray robe and followed. Jacques was already at the bottom of the stairs."

"What kind of robe was Jacques wearing?" Fran wondered.

"Not now, Fran," Dr. Bernstein and Mr. Montgomery said simultaneously.

"We found Mrs. Montgomery standing at the door reading a note from the American Embassy," Dr. Bernstein continued. "She told Jacques that an Agent Flores had requested that she and Mr. Gerard meet him at the embassy as soon as possible. I offered to accompany them, but Mrs. Montgomery insisted Fran and I shouldn't miss an opportunity to see the sunrise at the Sphinx."

"Just then Alfred P. Hart came out completely dressed—and I mean completely—and insisted he was going with them so he could report back to you, Dr. Stratton. The three of them left in a taxi that had just dropped off some tourists for the sunrise ceremony."

"I thought Alfred was so exhausted that he slept in this morning. I didn't even check his bed," Dr. Stratton said remorsefully. "He was wearing his three-piece suit when he left, wasn't he? It's supposed to be even hotter today than it was yesterday."

"Can we discuss something besides clothing for the moment?" Mr. Montgomery pleaded. He glanced at the note again. "Dorothy says Charles was found safe, but there are complications."

"Complications!" Dr. Stratton exclaimed. "What kind of complications? Can't anyone be direct?"

"Dorothy promises to tell us more when she, Jacques, Samy, and Mr. Hart return, which should be sometime around noon." Mr. Montgomery pulled out his gold pocket watch. "It's eight o'clock now. What could they be doing at the embassy all that time?"

"They'll be gone for four more hours! What should we do until then, Grandfather?" David asked.

"There's nothing we can do except sit here and worry," Mr. Montgomery grumbled.

David's grandfather was staring out the window at a grumpy-looking Sphinx when Mandisa entered and began to prepare breakfast. The aroma of freshly baked flatbread filled the restaurant. With the help of Dr. Bernstein, platters of breakfast food were placed on the red-and-white checkered plastic tablecloth at the front table. The slightly stout Mr. Montgomery mumbled something about being so upset he wasn't sure he could eat a bite. "However," he added, "one must keep up one's strength, mustn't one?"

He proceeded to help himself to eggs, fruit, and two pieces of flatbread slathered with butter. Mr. Montgomery cleared his plate but was still frowning anxiously. "Why don't they have a telephone in this restaurant? This isn't the turn of the century, you know."

"Dr. Awyan told me the phone service on the Giza Plateau is irregular. Isn't that right, Dr. Awyan?" Fran asked, his mouth full of scrambled eggs.

"That might be an understatement," the Egyptian said. "But yes, it is irregular."

"I should have woken up and gone with Grandmother," David said, pushing away his untouched plate. "I heard her get up, but I just went back to sleep. Now, it feels like someone, or something, is keeping us from finding Charles."

"David, I was advised by a very wise woman—my mother, in fact—that in life, especially in difficult situations, you must focus on what you want, not what you do not want," Dr. Awyan said. "She would say, your attitude may be the only factor that can turn things around."

"What your mother taught you, Dr. Awyan—this matter of focusing on a positive outcome—has a connection to what my students and I will be researching in my summer classes," Dr. Bernstein said.

"My dear physicist friend," Dr. Awyan responded, his eyes glinting with interest, "we have some time before our delegation to the embassy returns. I would be interested in hearing about the courses you will be teaching at the University of Paris."

"I'd love to discuss it. It might help me better formulate my ideas," Dr. Bernstein said. "Would this change of topic be okay with you gentlemen?"

"It would certainly be better than sitting here staring at each other, worrying about Charles," David said.

"You're right, David," Mr. Montgomery said, putting his arm around his grandson's shoulders. "My, I think you've grown two inches since we got here. It must be Mandisa's excellent cooking."

Mandisa, who was clearing away plates, gave Mr. Montgomery a pleased smile.

"Very well," Dr. Bernstein said. "Fran and David, would you help Mandisa clear the table?"

When the Pizza Hut was tidy once more, the physicist moved to the center bench, facing the group of men and boys as if they were in a classroom. Dr. Stratton removed a small leather notebook and a mechanical pencil from the pocket of his green plaid coat with leather elbow patches. "We are ready, Dr. Bernstein."

Fran's mother ran her hand through her dark curls and began. "I'll start with a brief description of quantum entanglement."

"Mom, call it 'spooky particles at a distance.' It sounds cooler," her son called out.

"As you no doubt know," Dr. Bernstein said, "Einstein's theory of relativity determined that the speed of light is always the same. In other words, his theory determined it a constant and declared that nothing in the known world or even the universe could go faster."

Fran popped into the conversation again. "The speed of light equals 186,282 miles per second. That's pretty fast, isn't it, Mom?"

Dr. Bernstein gave her son a brief nod, took a breath, and continued. "The reason Einstein called the concept of quantum entanglement 'spooky' is that it appeared to challenge his theory, at least on the quantum level."

"The quantum level means things that can't be seen by the naked eye," Fran explained, moving to sit next to his mother.

"That is correct, Fran. Einstein's theory applied to mechanical physics or visible matter, but there seemed to be anomalies when employing his hypothesis in the realm of quantum mechanics or invisible matter. Simply put, the theory of quantum entanglement proposes that when a particle—an electron or proton, for example—is divided, the two halves remained entangled or in contact with one another."

"Yeah, even if one half of the entangled particle is on Earth and the other half is on the moon or even Mars!" Fran added breathlessly. "And when one part is stimulated, the other responds—instantaneously. Isn't that spooky, David?"

"That doesn't just seem spooky, it seems impossible," his schoolmate answered.

"Einstein shared your skepticism, David," Dr. Bernstein said. "However, experiment after experiment seemed to substantiate the idea that split particles could communicate with each other faster than the speed of light. Einstein searched for a unified field theory that would be consistent across mechanical and and quantum physics."

"He kept looking, even on his deathbed, even until his very last breath," Fran said dramatically. "He didn't find the answer but, as Dad says, the good thing is he never gave up."

"Your father is right, that is a good thing. And since then, the theory of quantum entanglement has gained the interest of more and more physicists."

"That's all quite fascinating," Dr. Stratton said. "I can see I've had my head too much into philosophy and literature to keep up on what has been going on in physics these days."

"I've never even heard of quantum entanglement," Mr. Montgomery admitted. "I've been too preoccupied with business in recent years. Perhaps Dorothy is right. She said I need to take my head off my shoulders and dust it off every once in a while."

"She told me that too, Grandfather," David said, laughing.

"Every mind needs a good cleaning now and then," Dr. Awyan said. "So, Dr. Bernstein, you are teaching classes in quantum entanglement?"

"Not exactly," Dr. Bernstein said. "I intend for my course to create an atmosphere similar to that of your School of Khemitology. I won't be teaching entanglement, as such. I will instead give an overview of research in related areas of quantum physics, where so many mysteries lie, not just that of quantum entanglement."

"What kind of mysteries?" David asked.

"For instance, it's been documented that particles can transform into a wave and return back to particle form. The strange thing is these particles sometimes disappear and reappear somewhere else."

"That is pretty spooky. It seems that particles can act like ghosts," David said seriously.

"Like ghosts. I like that, David," Fran said. "Particles do sometime disappear and reappear like ghosts. I know a lot about ghosts because I've seen so many episodes of 'Scooby Doo.' It's my favorite cartoon!"

"I plan to ask students to create their own hypotheses and conduct their own experiments connecting quantum mechanics with what could be termed non-local communication," Dr. Bernstein said.

"If you don't mind my asking," Dr. Stratton said, "how is it that you were asked to teach this unusual course?"

Dr. Bernstein brightened. "I've always loved nature. I became intrigued by the idea that plants, birds, and insects mysteriously communicate with their own kind. For example, how do hundreds of birds fly in tight configuration without bumping into each other?"

"In Massachusetts, where I live and teach, we have these flocks of tiny birds zigzagging through the sky," Dr. Stratton said. "They seem to move as one unit."

Dr. Bernstein nodded vigorously. "Exactly. They change directions in a fraction of a second, with no obvious leader and no detectable audio communication. I began to think that even large organisms, which by definition do not fit into quantum physics, appeared to behave like entangled particles. I wrote a paper on this very premise, which was published in the noted scientific journal *Physics Today*."

"I used the phrase 'clump particles' to connect mechanical and quantum physics," she continued, "hypothesizing that the entanglement in quantum theory might be enlarged to explain the unexplainable in plant and animal species. I got so many letters from physicists and students all over the world that *Physics Today* asked me to write a follow-up article."

"This is quite fascinating, Dr. Bernstein," the head of the School of Khemitology said. "Did you expand further on your premise that animals benefit from some form of entanglement?"

"In my second article, I expanded my thinking into areas of human abilities not generally accepted in scientific circles. These included topics like non-local communication, remote viewing, remote healing, and even time travel. My interest in non-local communication began when I read about the phenomenon of the so-called bush telegraph, in which news seems to travel from one indigenous tribe to the next without any technological explanation."

"My grandmother was Irish, and shared many stories like this," Dr. Stratton said. "When my father was a boy, he was injured at school. My grandmother felt he was in trouble and showed up at the school before they could even contact her. She said this clairvoyance was a gift from her Celtic ancestors, and that it came from living in 'thin places.' She said Ireland is a place where the material and spiritual worlds mingle, and the past and future live alongside the present."

"Thin places," Dr. Awyan said, staring out the window at the Sphinx. "That phrase aptly describes the Giza Plateau, and many sacred sites all over the world. These are the sites that members of the School of Khemitology are researching today."

"In my second paper, I decided to concentrate on people who appear to have an ability to communicate or view areas in a non-local manner," Dr. Bernstein continued. "I didn't get into whether geography, magnetism or the presence of potentially conductive ancient ruins play a part. This concept of 'thin places' may prove to be an area of inquiry for my students."

"What did you use for evidence, other than stories like the one about Dr. Stratton's grandmother?" Mr. Montgomery wondered.

"There is, indeed, lots of anecdotal evidence supporting the concept of what might be called psychic ability. There have also, however, been many studies on the subject," Dr. Bernstein said. "I was in part inspired by a physics conference where a representative from the CIA spoke. He said the agency has conducted many experiments that document cases of remote viewing and non-local communication. Some of these studies have been made public. At the conference, the CIA agents said they knew that non-local communication existed, but they could not find a scientific explanation for how it could exist. They asked us, the scientists at the conference, to find the science behind the phenomena."

Fran's mouth fell open. "Are you working for the CIA, Mom?"

"No, Fran," his mother said. "In my second article, I asked readers to pre-suppose, for the sake of experimentation, that non-local communication is an established fact. The CIA data gives weight to this presupposition. I then posed a question: Could physics, in particular quantum physics, explain how this was possible? I suggested that those pondering my question consider areas such as the quantum vacuum, wormholes, string theory, entanglement, and wave and particle duality. Upon publication of my second article, I expected to receive criticism for mentioning areas many physicists do not accept as suitable for serious study. However, I received many more positive letters than negative from young physicists and students."

"I helped Mom read the letters," Fran said proudly. "I was the one who opened the letter inviting Mom to teach classes in Paris. That's how I ended up at the Château du Mont, so Mom could visit me on her teaching breaks."

"The letter from the University of Paris asked if I would design a class to explore theories of entanglement and other strange behavior among spooky particles. The physics department made it clear that we were not to simply focus on whether non-local communication exists, but to conduct experiments to shed light on various quantum theories that might explain how it could exist. It's a very unorthodox course, but it's been greeted enthusiastically by students and faculty. My four classes filled up almost as soon as they were announced."

"Earlier, you mentioned remote healing. Could that be an area of study?" Dr. Awyan asked.

Mandisa left her place behind the counter and sat down next to Dr. Awyan, her eyes on Dr. Bernstein.

"Yes," Dr. Bernstein said. "Remote healing might fit under the area of quantum mechanics called biophysics. I will be offering this area of study and research to my students."

"We have many members of the School of Khemitology who are adept at bringing balance to individuals without having to touch or even see them. Our associates who are gifted in the manipulation of energy would love to hear your students' ideas in this area."

"When we have Charles safe and sound by our side and my summer classes have concluded, I'd be delighted to share whatever insights we discover," Dr. Bernstein said, smiling.

"Yes, and when I have this boy by my side, I believe I should sign up for one of your classes," Dr. Stratton said.

Dr. Bernstein leaned towards him. "In a way, I think you've already signed up, Dr. Stratton."

"How is that?" the man asked, removing his glasses, dabbing his eyes, then cleaning his wire-rimmed lenses with his handkerchief.

"When Fran learned about Charles' disappearance, he begged me to bring him to Cairo. He was so insistent, I agreed. Madame Constance pointed out that we didn't know the language or geography of Cairo and that there were many people looking for Charles. Without thinking, I suggested to Madame Constance that the more people who gather in Cairo to find Charles, the more likely that he would be found."

"So we are all part of your experiment, Dr. Bernstein?" Dr. Awyan asked, his eyebrows raising toward his blue turban.

She shook her head. "I don't consider Charles an experiment. However, talking to Madame Constance prompted a hypothesis. I couldn't help thinking that non-local communication might play a part in our search for Charles. On my arrival, I talked to Jacques. I could feel his connection to Charles and the strong guilt he carried about losing the boy he brought to Egypt. I have this feeling that Jacques and Charles have become entangled. And as far-fetched as it may sound, I suspect it will be Jacques who will be the one to find Charles."

"So we're here to support Jacques in his objective of finding my grandson?" Dr. Stratton summed up the conversation.

"Yes, I believe that's why we're here," Dr. Bernstein said. "It wouldn't hurt for us to visualize finding Charles safe. And it might prove helpful for us to encourage Jacques to open his mind to the possibility that he has the power of non-direct communication."

"I felt Mr. Gerard's potential the first time I met him," Dr. Awyan said. "He is closed off, due to whatever has beset him in life, but when I shook his hand I felt power—untapped power, like that of a coiled snake."

"Are you sure you're talking about Jacques?" David asked.

"I'll be happy to join this experiment," Dr. Stratton said. "Any course of action is better than feeling helpless."

"Now, Dr. Stratton," Dr. Awyan said with a toothy grin, "you are starting to sound like my mother."

"Mom! I think I see something in my mind," Fran shouted. "My mind says we will find Charles if we all get on camels and go looking for him. I think we should go right now."

David explained to Fran that they had to wait for his grandmother, Jacques, Samy, and Alfred to return.

Fran agreed but insisted he was quite serious, adding, "I can picture it in my mind, like a glimpse of the future: all of us on camels, searching for Charles."

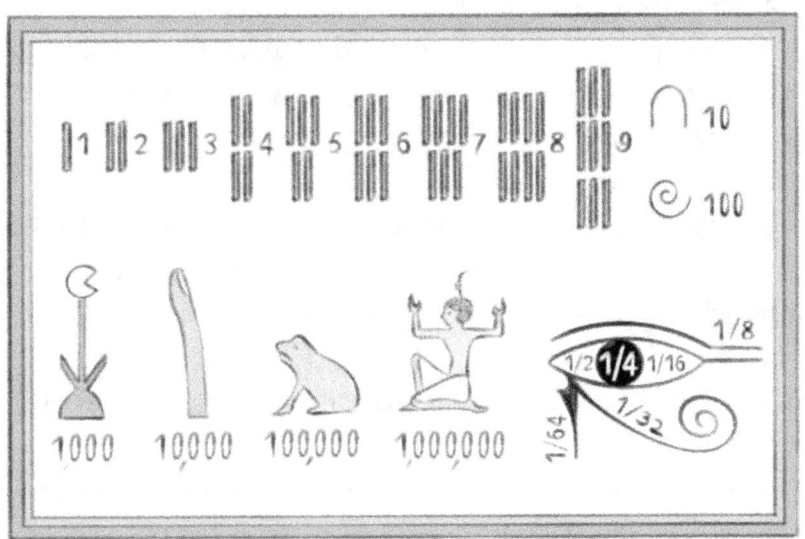

CHAPTER 34

EGYPTIAN MATHEMATICS

A half-dozen tourists entered the Pizza Hut, gave their order at the counter, and sat down at one of the long tables. A few minutes later, there was wild applause coming from the group. Dr. Bernstein turned to see Fran with both arms above his head, obviously preparing to perform a second cartwheel.

"Francis Bacon Bernstein, we do not undertake cartwheels in restaurants!"

"Sorry, Mom. You know Charles and I are in gymnastics. I was just demonstrating to David the concept of momentum, and the ability to energize the human body through concentrated thought."

"Come here, Fran." Dr. Bernstein gave the boy a soft shake, ordering him to apologize to Mandisa.

Fran ran behind the counter and threw his arms around Mandisa's ample waist. He said, "I'm sorry I treated you and your restaurant with disrespect."

Mandisa gave the boy a little hug, and Fran returned to his mother's side.

"Fran, an apology doesn't have to be accompanied by a hug, although I don't believe Mandisa minded a bit," his mother said. "From now on, I want you to think before you act."

Fran promised he'd try his best.

Dr. Awyan handed Fran the bag the Egyptian boy had given him as they were returning from the Sphinx. Everyone in the Pizza Hut watched as the boy pulled out a tan gallabiyah. He immediately pulled the robe over his clothes.

"This is just what I need! Thank you, Dr. Awyan. Now, I'm really ready to help find Charles."

"Why does wearing a gallibyah make you more ready to find Charles?" David asked his schoolmate.

"Because the day before Charles left for Egypt, I went to his room to say goodbye. He was dressed like an Egyptian boy. I asked him if he was going to wear those clothes during his trip. He said only if he needed to blend in, to avoid looking like a tourist. That's what I want to do, blend in."

"Look where that got him," David said matter-of-factly. "Charles blended in so much he disappeared, and now we can't find him."

"I think feeling like Charles might help us imagine what happened to him. What do you think, Mom?"

"I think that it's a possibility, Fran."

The red-headed boy looked closely at Dr. Awyan. Not only was he wearing a gallibyah nearly identical to his own, but he had on a grayish-blue turban. Fran decided that if he had a turban, he'd truly blend in. "I'm wondering, Dr. Awyan, if you might have a spare turban lying around."

Everyone in the Pizza Hut laughed, including the Egyptologist. "Usually, the young ones do not wear turbans or headscarves."

"Yes, but look at me," the boy said, touching his bright red curls. "How can I blend in with this kind of hair?"

"You have a point, young man. I will look around and see what I can find."

The Egyptian boy who'd given Dr. Awyan the cream-colored bag ran into the Pizza Hut, and handed the founder of the School of Khemitology an envelope. Dr. Awyan announced the note was from Mrs. Montgomery, and that she and Jacques would be back in about an hour.

"This waiting is nerve-wracking." Dr. Stratton said.

The Egyptian gestured for Fran to come closer. Fran flushed bright red, certain he was in trouble.

"I'm sorry, Sir, for doing cartwheels in the Pizza Hut."

"That is not what I wanted to talk to you about," Dr. Awyan said, leaning forward. "Your mother tells me you are quite advanced in the area of mathematics."

"I've always been good with numbers, even when I was a little kid."

Dr. Awyan smiled broadly, and a map of laugh lines appeared on his face. "Now that you are so much older, may I ask you, what is your knowledge regarding ancient Egyptian mathematics?"

"I don't know anything about it. Mom, do you know anything about ancient Egyptian mathematics?"

"No, nothing outside of geometry and pi," Dr. Bernstein answered. "Is there a different system, Dr. Awyan?"

"Indeed, there is," the founder of the School of Khemitology said. "Some say the ancient Egyptian system of mathematics had the poetry of logic, the music of reason, and the practicality of a sledgehammer. And, if that is not enough to convince anyone to learn something about ancient Egyptian mathematics, ancient Egyptian mathematics and geometry were said to be gifts from the gods."

"Which gods?" Fran wondered.

"Osiris, Isis, Horus, Set, Seshat, and the great Thoth, the god of science, numbers, mathematics, and geometry."

Fran looked ready to turn another cartwheel. "Wow! I want to learn about Egyptian mathematics."

"Personally," Dr. Awyan said, "I believe everyone should know a little about ancient Egyptian mathematics."

"Why?" David asked.

"To answer this, let me begin with a little story. When I was a small child, I roamed among the greatest megaliths ever built. My playground was the Giza Plateau, with its pyramids, Sphinx, temples, and the ruins of great cities. As I grew older and became a tour guide, I realized the importance of these great structures, not only to Egypt but to the entire world. I was proud to be an Egyptian, descended from such gifted builders. Then I went to university. I was in for a shock," Dr. Awyan said. "I was told the Babylonians invented mathematics and geometry, not the Egyptians. It made no sense to me. How, I wondered, could the Egyptians have built such amazing structures and created such great cities without mathematics?"

"Is it possible they adopted the Babylonian system?" Dr. Bernstein asked.

"No, they had their own distinct system. Furthermore, many Khemitologists, including myself, believe the Sphinx, the pyramids, and other ancient structures in Giza and beyond predate the edifices and cities of the Babylonians. In addition, there is no sign the Babylonians ever built pyramids, structures I sometimes call 'math made visible.' If a decision had to be made on which country produced the first great builders, we believe it would be Egypt."

"Having seen their handiwork firsthand, I'm ready to give your ancestors a great deal of credit," Dr. Stratton said.

Dr. Awyan nodded his thanks. "However, even if one believes Babylonian mathematics predates Egyptian mathematics, it is useful to explore both systems. This teaches students a powerful lesson, that there are alternative methods for achieving similar goals."

"Why haven't I been told anything about ancient Egyptian mathematics?" David asked.

"That is a good question," the Egyptian said, walking towards the back of the Pizza Hut, trailed by Fran in his matching gallibyah. He pointed to a large map taped up on the back wall.

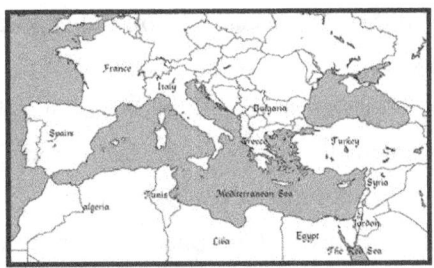

"This is the Mediterranean Sea. This is a modern map, but you can imagine that from 2000-1600 BCE—long before the advent of trains, automobiles, or airplanes—the fastest way to travel throughout the Mediterranean territories was via the waterways. At this time, the Babylonian Empire was the center of the trade route. Accordingly, the Babylonians taught their mathematical system to all the traders, and the traders shared this system throughout the Mediterranean regions."

Mr. Montgomery, who'd joined the group at the back of the Pizza Hut, used his finger to trace the course of the Mediterranean on the map. "That makes sense. From a business perspective," he added confidently. "Just think of that, David. The importing and exporting of goods is both the past and the future. You could do worse than to pursue a career in trade, David."

"I'll consider it, Grandfather," David said. "Go ahead, Dr. Awyan."

"For many years, Egypt had minimal contact with traders from other countries," Dr. Awyan said. "Then, the country's leaders decided they wanted more products. They enlarged their contact with Mediterranean traders. This forced Egyptians to learn the Babylonian system of math. Over time, ancient Egyptian mathematics, the system that was used to build the pyramids, became extinct."

"That's sad," Fran said, frowning.

"As a university student, I became fascinated with ancient Egyptian mathematics. However, to decipher this long-dead system was like finding a bunch of scattered dinosaur bones in a paleontological dig and piecing them together to see what the dinosaur looked like."

"That would be difficult, especially if you didn't know what dinosaurs looked like," David said.

"That is correct. When we started, we didn't know what Egyptian math looked like. There remained only scraps of information. Those interested in rediscovering the ancient discipline have had to cobble the subject together from an array of different sources. Complicating matters, the primary repositories of Egyptian mathematics were taken out of Egypt by other countries. It is ironic that I have had to travel far from home to read what material exists."

"What kind of material?" Dr. Bernstein wondered.

"There's the Rhind Mathematical Papyrus, which was discovered in Thebes by a Scottish archeologist in 1858 and currently resides in the British Museum," Dr. Awyan said. "Then there's the so-called Berlin Papyrus 6619, named to differentiate it from three other important papyrus documents held by the Egyptian Museum of Berlin."

"Is there no record of the ancient system in Egypt?" Dr. Bernstein asked.

"There are some wall engravings but, sadly, our knowledge of ancient Egyptian mathematics remains incomplete. Nevertheless, I know something about my ancestors' system. We have about an hour before Mrs. Montgomery and Jacques return from the American Embassy. Would you be interested in a lesson?"

Fran, David, Dr. Stratton, Dr. Bernstein, Mr. Montgomery, and even the half-dozen tourists who'd crossed the road to eat at a restaurant with the most fantastic view in the world, said yes in unison.

Dr. Awyan went behind the counter and retrieved pieces of butcher paper and pencils. Fran passed out the pencils and paper while the old Egyptian erased the blackboard displaying the special of the day. Dr. Awyan drew seven symbols on the board with white chalk.

"For fun," he said, "let's begin with how the ancient Egyptians expressed numbers. The short line represents one. Nine short lines represents the number 9. The figure representing ten is called a heel bone, or we might call it a tremendous upside-down smile," Dr. Awyan said with a tremendous right-side-up smile.

"The next figure is a partial spiral called a coil or rope, symbolizing the number one hundred. The lotus plant represents one thousand. The crooked finger, like mine," the old Egyptian man said, holding up his slightly crooked index finger, "represents ten thousand. The frog represents one hundred thousand, and a million is represented by a kneeling god with both hands up in the air. By using those seven symbols, a scribe, merchant, master craftsman, priest or pharaoh could write numbers well into the millions."

Fran raised his right hand in the air. "I would like to try and write a large number."

"All right," Dr. Awyan agreed. "Let us all write 1,322,228. Just a little suggestion: I draw a tadpole instead of a frog. For me, it's easier."

"That's a good idea, Dr. Awyan," Fran said.

All the people in the Pizza Hut bent over their papers and drew the figures for the number 1,322,228. Dr. Awyan walked around like a teacher, checking each participant's work.

"Congratulations, you all did an excellent job. However, let me tell you something about ancient Egyptian numbers and words. They are written and read right to left, not left to right."

"Oh, no! Why didn't you tell me?" Fran asked with an upside-down smile.

Dr. Awyan laughed heartily, joined by others in the Pizza Hut. "One more hint. Since each figure represents a number, they can be inscribed in any order. Instead of taking up a long line of space, the Egyptians compressed the figures."

"You mean like this?" David asked as he drew the figures representing the number 1,322,228.

"Yes, very good, David," Dr. Awyan said. "Now, let me ask you. What is 5 X 7."

"Thirty-five," everyone answered, pleased to be back in familiar territory.

"I can see you are all excellent students of Babylonian-based mathematics. The Babylonians invented the times tables that, evidently, you, have all memorized. Egyptians, however, did not have times tables. Now, I am going to ask you all to do something very difficult. Forget you know your multiplication tables."

"That's like asking me to forget how to walk," Fran said.

"Before you walk, you must first learn to crawl," Dr. Awyan said. "How would you figure out 5 x 7 without knowing your times tables?"

"You would write five lines seven times, and then you'd count them," Fran answered.

Dr. Awyan nodded. "Your answer would be correct. However, if it were a larger equation, with bigger numbers, solving the problem that way would be time-consuming and subject to errors. Shall we learn the Egyptian way?"

"Yes," everyone agreed enthusiastically.

"Let me give you three problems: 5 x 7, 8 x 8, and 17 x 246. The first two equations are easy so as to help you learn the form. The final problem is more difficult. Let's start with 5 x 7."

This is the form that we will use: a horizontal line with a vertical line going down in the middle. This forms two columns.

Place the multipliers on the horizontal line on each side. (Always place the lesser number on the left-hand side. For example, 400 x 56 should be written 56 x 400.)

```
   5  |  7
_____|_____
      |
   1  |
   2  |
   4  |
      |
      |
```

Step 1-Underneath the left-hand number is a column. This column is always calculated in the same way. Under the horizontal line, double the number starting with 1. For example, 1, double one=2, double 2=4, etc. You stop doubling when the next number is greater than the number on the top left. In this first problem, the number is 5. If you double 4, it is 8, which is greater than five, so you stop doubling at number 4. Is this clear?"

"That's clear, Dr. Awyan," Fran called out. "One doubled is 2, two doubled is 4, 4 doubled is 8, but that is too large, so you stop doubling at 4. Is that right?"

"That is correct," the teacher in the gray gallabiyah answered.

```
   5  |  7
_____|_____
      |
  √1  |
   2  |
  √4  |
      |
      |
```

Step 2-Under 5, put a check by the numbers in the left-hand column that equal 5. In this case it is 1 and 4.

291

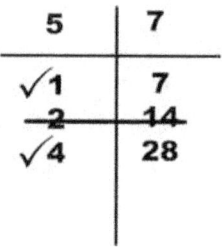

```
     5  |  7
  ────────────
    √1  |  7
     2  |  14
    √4  |  28
              |
```

Step 3-Go to the number above the horizon line, right column. Write this number under the horizon line. In this case, it is 7. Double the numbers: 7 + 7 =14, 14 + 14 = 28. Stop at the same level as the numbers on the left column, which is 3 levels down. Draw a line through the unchecked number or numbers on the left side and continue this line through to the right column. In this problem, that would be 2, so draw through the number 14.

```
     5   |   7
  ──────────────
    √1   |   7
  ──2──────14──
    √4   |   28
               |
```

Step 4-Add the numbers in the right column that have not been crossed out. Add the numbers together: 7+ 28 = 35.

"Is that the same answer we get from your times tables, Fran?"

"Yes. And I like learning this. It's fun."

"I think this system is much longer and more complicated than using the times tables," David said with a grimace.

"I suspect many of you will agree with David," Dr. Awyan said. "I must ask you a question, however. How long did it take you to learn your times tables, 1 through 12? To answer my own question, if I remember correctly, it took me nearly nine months. Egyptian multiplication can be learned in just a few minutes without memorizing the times tables."

"You have a point," David said.

"Let's try another problem: 8 x 8," Dr. Awyan said, "David, what should we do first?"

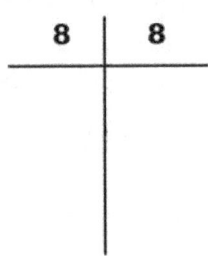

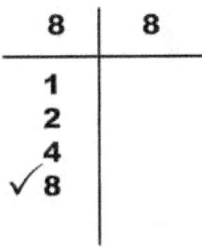

Put a 1 in the left column and then double the numbers until you get to 8 or below. Next, you find the number or numbers that add up to 8. There is only 1 number that adds up to 8, and that is 8. Put a check by that number.

	8	8
	1	8
	2	16
	4	32
✓	8	(64)

Bring down the number on the right column, in this case 8. Then double the numbers in the right column: 8 +8=16, 16+16=32, 32+32=64. Make sure the two sides are even. Cross off the numbers that you did not use to make 8. Draw lines through to the right column, and the answer is 8 x 8 = 64.

"That is very good, David. I think you could be a great teacher of Egyptian math."

"Me, too. I want to teach Egyptian math, too!" Fran said, jumping up and down in his seat.

"Yes, you, too," Dr. Awyan assured the red-headed boy. "Why don't you try a more difficult equation. The problem is 17 x 246."

Fran took on the teacher's role.

Place 17 on the top left column, and 246 on the right column.

$$
\begin{array}{c|c}
17 & 246 \\
\hline
1 & 246 \\
2 & \\
4 & \\
8 & \\
16 & \\
\end{array}
$$

On the left column, write the number 1. Double the numbers on the right until the next double would be higher than 17, meaning stop at 16. Bring down 246 on the right column. Double the numbers until you get to the number even with the left side.

"This is so easy, I can do it in my head," the boy teacher said.

$$
\begin{array}{c|c}
17 & 246 \\
\hline
1 & 246 \\
2 & 492 \\
4 & 984 \\
8 & 1968 \\
16 & 3936 \\
\end{array}
\qquad
\begin{array}{r}
3936 \\
+246 \\
\hline
4182 \\
\end{array}
$$

Now draw a line through the numbers on the left that do not make 17. Draw through the columns on the right side. This leaves only two numbers remaining. Add them together.

David, Dr. Stratton, Dr. Bernstein and the six Pizza Hut guests followed Fran's instructions to the letter, then looked up at their red-headed teacher.

"The answer is 4,182," Fran called out. "I know this is right because I cross-checked it with the ordinary multiplication! Isn't this cool, Mom? I bet Dad will be interested in multiplying like an Egyptian. Don't you think so?"

"Yes, I do, Fran. He will be very interested."

"Samy's taxi is pulling up in front of the Pizza Hut!" David exclaimed. He extricated himself from the bench and the table and ran out the door, Fran in tow. Samy opened the doors, and Mrs. Montgomery, Jacques and Alfred emerged from the taxi.

"Where is Charles?" David yelled.

"Wait until we show you how the ancient Egyptians could multiply!" Fran called out.

David frowned at his schoolmate. "Charles is our first concern."

"I'm sorry, David," Fran said, running up to Jacques, who looked pale and concerned.

The boy asked, "Where is he, Mr. Gerard?"

"Let's go inside," Mrs. Montgomery said, putting her arms around both boys.

CHAPTER 35

LIMO RIDE TO THE EMBASSY

M r. and Mrs. Montgomery, Dr. Bernstein, Jacques, Dr. Stratton, Alfred, and the two boys gathered inside the Pizza Hut. They were not your typical group, happily anticipating a tour of the Giza Plateau. There was an atmosphere of being on edge, of restlessness, and dread. All were waiting for Samy to drive them to the American Embassy, where they were to find out what had happened to Charles Dayton Stratton III.

In a quiet voice, David said to his grandmother, "It's crossed my mind that we won't all fit in Samy's taxi."

"You are an intelligent boy, David. That thought crossed my mind, too. I asked the so-called taxi driver if he could find a more spacious vehicle, one which would accommodate us all."

"Why did you call him a so-called taxi driver, Grandmother?"

"I'm reminded of a quote from *The Man in the Mist* by mystery writer Agatha Christie. She writes, '*Very few of us are what we seem.*' It has been my habit to look for the story behind the story."

David looked confused. "What story?"

"Samy says that as a young man he dreamed of attending college in the United States. He was bright, bright enough to be accepted by the prestigious University of California at Los Angeles."

"That's one of the colleges I'm considering!" exclaimed Fran, joining the conversation.

Mrs. Montgomery smiled at the red-headed boy and continued. "Samy attended UCLA long enough to become an accomplished surfer. Then he gets a note from his father, who says he needs help running his taxi cab business in Egypt. Samy returns to Cairo and happily becomes a taxi driver, whose only customers appear to be Charles and Jacques."

"And us, Grandmother," David added.

"Yes, and us. Does he seem like just a taxi driver to you, David?"

"Are you trying to make our grandson suspicious?" Mr. Montgomery asked.

"Don't worry, Grandfather. Charles has already made me more aware or, in other words, more suspicious of people in my surroundings. But back to Samy, Grandmother. Do you think he might somehow be involved in Charles' disappearance?"

"No way. I like Samy. He says he is going to teach me to surf if we meet in Southern California," Fran said. Fran pretended he was standing on a surfboard, one foot in front of the other, and arms out to the side. "He's a good guy."

"You are probably right, Fran," Mrs. Montgomery said. "However, it never hurts to keep your eyes and ears open. Why don't you boys go and watch for Samy and see what kind of vehicle he's dug up?"

David and Fran looked out the window. It was 3 o'clock, the hottest time of the day. There were fewer tour buses and less traffic. Fran pointed out a rickety open-air truck puffing up the road, but David didn't believe that could be their ride. The truck only had one bench seat in the cargo bed, with no cover for shade. Then Fran spotted a fancy limousine, sleek and black with darkened windows. David shook his head. Following the limo was a donkey cart fitted with seats and a tan canopy. It was perfect for tourists who wanted a more authentic Giza tour than they could find riding in a van. But David didn't believe it could get to the American Embassy in a timely manner. Following the donkey cart was the bus of the School of Khemitology. Fran noted it was an old-timey bus with a long nose. David added that someone had painted the bus with house paint, a flat sky-blue color. The hood of the bus shuddered up and down as it pulled up in front of the Pizza Hut. Dr. Awyan and his son, Yousef, disembarked. They waved to Fran and David as they walked towards the Khemitology office.

David frowned as the bus pulled away. "Where's that so-called taxi driver?" he mumbled, examining all the vehicles driving past the Pizza Hut.

Just then, a man wearing a black tuxedo and a red turban burst into the blue door of the Pizza Hut. He called out, "Montgomery wedding party!"

It took a few seconds for the boys to recognize this formally dressed man as the so-called taxi driver.

"Why are you dressed so funny?" Fran called out.

"Fran!" his mother said with warning in her calm voice.

"I meant why are you dressed so interestingly, Samy?" Fran asked, smiling broadly at his mother.

"I'm driving a limousine that caters to wedding parties," Samy said. "The company belongs to one of my cousins. I asked him if I could borrow one of his limos. He agreed on the condition that I dress like all of his limousine drivers. He claims it is better for advertising than a driver dressed in a Hawaiian shirt."

"Your turban! It certainly is a magnificent color," Mrs. Montgomery exclaimed. "Would you describe it as crimson, scarlet, blood-red?"

"Me, I'd call it lipstick-red," Samy suggested as the group ducked into the air-conditioned limousine. "Lipstick-red, like in the song sung by Connie Francis."

Lipstick on your collar, told a tale on you.
Lipstick on your collar, it says you were untrue.
Bet your bottom dollar, you and I are through.
'Cause lipstick on your collar, told a tale on you, yeah.

"You sure know a lot of songs. I hope I get to know that many songs when I'm your age," Fran said.

"I know twice as many in Arabic. Music is the universal—and maybe the most important—language in all the world."

"Why?" Fran asked.

"Because all cultures have music, therefore it has the potential to bring people together in peace and harmony. It sets a mood. It can even change a mood, and you can dance to it," Samy said, twisting the upper part of his body.

"Very nicely put," Mrs. Montgomery said, looking over the limo with the bow on the hood and a sign saying "Wedding Limo Rentals."

Removing her straw hat with a sprig of dark purple flowers on its brim, she moved to the backseat. George climbed in beside her.

"Perfect," Fran called out to Samy as he and David clambered into the limo. "It has exactly eight seats."

Dr. Stratton came next, then Alfred P. Hart. Alfred was wearing a striped navy blue and gray suit, a gray fedora, and a white shirt with a Westminster collar that wrapped high around the neck, with just the tip of the collar folded down. Jacques was the last to enter the limousine. Lines of strain showed on his clean-shaven face.

When they were seated, Dr. Stratton admonished his friend. "Really, Alfred. You and I are dressed like we are going to get married."

"I believe my cousin who owns this company would approve of your dress," Samy said, jumping into the driver's seat. Turning onto the frontage road, he pushed a button on the cassette player. As the song began, Samy called out, "This is a group called the Dixie Cups, singing 'Chapel of Love.'" As usual, Samy sang along.

We're goin' to the chapel

And we're gonna get married.
Goin' to the chapel
And we're gonna get married.
Gee, I really love you
And we're gonna get married.
Goin' to the chapel of love.

But they were not going to the chapel. They were headed for the American Embassy to learn what had happened to Charles Dayton Stratton III. No one joined Samy in his rendition; all seemed lost in their thoughts.

Reaching the American Embassy, the limousine passengers were directed to a small room on the first floor. Samy stood in the back of the room, his manners as formal as his attire. Alfred, even more formal, stood beside him. The room was crowded with representatives from both the American and French embassies, two officers from the Egyptian National Police, and two journalists from the *Cairo Times*.

No one spoke as they awaited the arrival of the young man who was said to have last seen Charles before his second disappearance. Fran's mother kept her hand on her son's knee as a warning not to ask questions. Another Egyptian officer dressed in an olive-green uniform, with a pistol in his black leather holster, entered the room. Dr. Bernstein anticipated Fran's question of why the man was wearing a pistol and placed her index finger on her lips. Following the officer was a young Egyptian dressed in a blue jacket, white shirt, and a red tie. On his lapel were two small pins. One featured the tricolored Egyptian flag: red, white, and black with an eagle in the middle. The other was an American flag with red and white stripes and, on the upper left corner, a field of stars on a dark blue background. David noted that the young man looked even younger than Farak. He was barely taller than David, yet the youth projected an air of confidence. The young man's posture was erect but relaxed. He glanced around the room, meeting everyone's eyes, one by one. The corners of his lips gently tilted up in a friendly and sincere manner as he was introduced.

"I wish we could deliver the young Charles to you today," said the police officer beside the young Egyptian. "However, as you have heard, young Stratton was found and then lost again. It is very distressing to us all. Allow me to introduce you to Mr. Aamen Halabi, a student at the Cairo University. He was the last to see Charles before his second disappearance. I will let him tell you what he knows."

"Ladies and gentlemen," Aamen said with a broad gesture, his arms held out from his body, hands palms-up. "To begin with, I want you to know that I am extremely sorry for your great loss. I hope that I can be of some small service in recovering Charles from...wherever he might be. Let me begin by informing you that I have nearly finished my university education. More accurately, I have finished my first semester at the Cairo University. My studies are in the area of social and political interpretation and translation, specializing in, but not limited to, the English and Arabic languages."

Dorothy Montgomery took out her notebook and pens from her backpack and began taking notes.

"Some say I am such a talented translater that I should immediately begin working for the American Embassy. Still, I would not ask for such a thing at this time," Aamen said, looking at the representatives from the American Embassy. "Instead, we are here to discuss the distressing disappearance of Charles Dayton Stratton III. Because I am almost a noted interpreter, I was asked to travel to the City of the Dead to meet a boy, a boy who spoke English."

Fran raised his hand. "Why was Charles at the City of the Dead when he wasn't dead?"

"That is a very good question," the handsome young Egyptian replied. "The City of the Dead is where many poor people live. They moved there after the government tore down their homes so big businesses could build expensive high-rise apartments, to gain more tax money. I hope the journalists in this room will write something about this, because this was not a kindful thing to do."

"And some journalists, though I am sure not these journalists," Aamen said, looking towards the two Egyptian women with notepads and pens in hand, "fail to cover the challenge of thousands and thousands of people forced to live in tombs. They never even mention how these people, Egyptian citizens, have greatly suffered and continue to suffer as they tore down their homes, forcing them to take shelter in the City of the Dead. Anyway, Mr. Wasim, the man who saved Charles' life, and his family are among those forced to take shelter in their ancestors' tombs."

"How did this Mr. Wasim manage to save our Charles?" Mrs. Montgomery asked.

"Mr. Wasim is a taxi driver. He noticed a boy standing on the sidewalk not far from the railroad station. He seemed to be trying to summon a taxi. Just as Mr. Wasim pulled over to the side of the road, a delivery man with a cart piled high with large metal boxes rolled up beside the boy. A huge box fell from the top of the pile, hitting the boy in the head."

Jacques gasped and looked back at Samy.

"Mr. Wasim thanked Allah that the boy was not dead. However, he was knocked out cold, completely unconscious and bleeding profusely from a head wound. Mr. Wasim took off his own headscarf and wrapped it around the boy's head. He could find no identification, so he decided to take him to his own home, in the City of the Dead."

David raised his hand. "Why didn't Mr. Wasim take Charles to the hospital?"

"Because hospitals cost a great deal of money. Poor Egyptians cannot even afford to go to the doctor let alone the hospital. This boy was dressed as an Egyptian child. Mr. Wasim had no idea who he was, where he came from, or even where he wanted to go. The taxi driver's wife, Mrs. Wasim, is recognized throughout the City of the Dead as a talented healer. He decided to bring the child to his tomb-home. Mrs. Wasim and her four children cared for the boy as he lay unconscious for nearly a week."

"It is no wonder we were unable to find any trace of Charles!" Jacques called out to Samy.

"Yes, Sir, this explains it. One day the boy, Charles, woke up. When he did, it was clear he did not speak Arabic. He finally made the family understand that he was from the United States. My reputation as an excellent translater of English had spread around the City of the Dead. I had just completed a challenging course, Interpretation for Government Officials, Arabic to English, as this seemed like a very desirable class for someone who hopes to be a member of the American Embassy someday," Aamen said as he looked towards the representatives of the embassy, smiling a very handsome smile. "Naturally, when the American citizen, who did not speak Arabic, awoke, they thought of me."

"As soon as I heard about this boy," Aamen continued, "I procured a ride to the City of the Dead in my friend's *tuk tuk*."

Fran put up his hand. "What's a tuk tuk?"

"It is the three-wheeled vehicle you see on our roads, sometimes called an auto rickshaw."

"Can we please get back to Charles?" David asked, scowling at Fran.

"Yes, Sir. When I discovered that Charles was American, I suggested that we go straight to the American Embassy. This is because of the embassy's excellent reputation and for its tremendous caring for its American citizens. However, it was late, past seven o'clock. The embassy was closed. I assured Charles I would bring him to the American Embassy the very next morning. Mr. Wasim agreed to drive us."

"What in God's name happened to Charles after this?" Dr. Stratton burst out impatiently.

"This is the difficult and strange part of the story," Aamen said. "That very night, on a night where stars filled the black sky, Charles ran away. No one knows where he went."

"He ran away?" Dr. Stratton asked, even more impatiently.

Dorothy raised her hand. "Young man, can you tell us exactly what happened just before Charles disappeared? Please tell us in as much detail as possible. You never know what information is important and what is not when you are approaching a mystery."

Mr. Montgomery looked at his wife questioningly. How, he wondered, can you live with someone nearly all your life and then find out you don't know anything about them?

"When I arrived at the Wasims' tomb-home, Charles told me his very interesting and traumatic story of how he got to Egypt and finally his accident that brought him to the City of the Dead. Since it was too late to go to the embassy, I advised Charles to tell his story to the people who had helped him survive his terrible ordeal."

"Egyptians, especially people who live in the City of the Dead, love stories, and it seemed like the proper thing to do. Fortunately, I, as an almost professional interpreter, was there to assist Charles in telling his story. It is very difficult to find a good interpreter in Cairo," the young Egyptian said with a winning smile directed toward the representatives of the American Embassy.

"Before you start," Dr. Stratton asked, "what condition was this boy in? I mean, had he recovered from his injury?"

"Mrs. Wasim is quite a famous healer. By the time I met Charles, he had almost completely recovered. He only had a small wrapping covering his head. I told Charles that I knew a perfect place for him to tell his story. As we walked, more and more people followed us. We came to a strange tomb, not like the other tombs in the Western Cemetery. It was made of marble with interestingly carved doors and gables. The images seemed to come from ancient Egypt. No one knows who is buried in this tomb. It has a large lock. As far as I know, no one has entered this tomb for many years. I selected it because it has seven steps leading up to a platform in front of the door. This area allowed Charles and I to be more visible. Also, this area makes an echoing sound, so we could be heard better."

"Is that when Charles ran away?" Fran called out.

"No, not yet, young man," the translater said.

David scowled at his schoolmate.

"I noticed a very tall woman in a black gallabiyah. She had a black veil that covered her face except for her eyes. I didn't think much about her at the time, as I had the challenging task of translating for Charles. At my insistence, Charles told his story from the very beginning. Charles told his audience that he came from the United States of America. I expertly explained that the United States was across the Atlantic Ocean. I added a few sound effects, like the jet plane coming from America to France. They felt sorry that Charles had been sent away from his home to go to a school he did not want to attend. He told them about his birthday and his wish to visit Egypt, the country he loved since he was a child. I explained how he had traveled on a plane from France to Cairo, adding great sound effects."

"Finally, Charles told him about getting on the train to go to Luxor," the translater continued. "They loved hearing that Charles dressed up as a Bedouin to show his caretaker how Egyptian he could look. They were shocked at the conductor putting him off the train, although they enjoyed the sound effects of the train and its whistle I added to his story. Then, the entire audience was angry at the policeman who kicked Charles out of the train station when he was doing nothing wrong and was only asking for help."

Mrs. Montgomery, who was scribbling notes, interjected. "So first he was put off the train by the conductor. This, we already knew. Then he was removed from the railroad station by that horrid policeman. Humph! You are certainly right, Mr. Halabi. That policeman should have tried to help the boy, rather than kick him out of the station."

"Everyone in the City of the Dead agreed," Aamen said. "Sometimes the military police—certainly no policemen present—do not get proper training as to how to treat their fellow Egyptians, especially if they do not look prosperous. Back to my story, I interpreted exactly what Charles said. When Charles and I finished telling his story, people were clapping and cheering."

Hearing the anecdote, David missed Charles more than ever. Leave it to Charles to find himself in the middle of nowhere and, instead of panicking, standing up and engaging with the crowd.

But Aamen wasn't finished speaking. "Suddenly, Charles turned to me and said he would be right back. He ran down the seven stairs and turned to the passageway that led to the Wasims' tomb-home. Oh, I forgot to mention that he showed a small pyramid, maybe five or six inches tall, to the crowd before that. Charles seemed to be looking at the back row, where now there were three women, dressed in black with black veils pulled across their faces. Hurriedly, Charles put the pyramid away in a sack."

"Let me get this straight, young man. Charles showed the audience a pyramid. Why did he do this, Mr. Halibi?" Mrs. Montgomery asked.

"I am not quite sure, something about it being a gift of some kind," Aamen said. "It all happened so fast. He showed the small pyramid, then wrapped it in a red cloth. He looked upset. I believe that he had his eyes on the three women in the back row. Then Charles left, saying he would be right back. At first, I thought that he might have needed to go to the bathroom. But why did he not return?"

"Can you remember anything else?" asked Mrs. Montgomery, looking up from her notepad.

"I did notice that about the time Charles disappeared, the three women were no longer in the back row. Do you think this might be important, Madam?"

"Perhaps," the mystery writer answered.

"To end this story, it was getting late. I had in my mind that Charles had gone back to the Wasims to prepare for going to the American Embassy the next morning. A friend of mine drove me home in his tuk tuk. Meanwhile, Mr. Wasim thought Charles had gone with me, because his belongings had been removed from their tomb-home. It wasn't until the next morning that we discovered Charles was neither with the Wasim family or with me. That is when we came to the terrible truth that Charles was missing. I immediately contacted the American Embassy, reporting to this great organization that an American was missing."

Dorothy raised her hand again. "What exactly did these women look like?"

"To tell you the truth, Madam, I didn't pay too much attention. I was taking my translating quite seriously, as I always do," Aamen said, smiling over toward the representative from the American Embassy. "I seem to remember that all three women were dressed in black. However, black is not an unusual color of dress for the women in the City of the Dead. They drew my attention because they stood together in the very back row, were dressed alike, and they all had veils draped over their faces, except for their eyes."

Dr. Stratton frowned and said, "So, as far as you know, no one at the City of the Dead ever saw Charles again?"

"That is correct, Sir," the interpreter answered.

Mrs. Montgomery stood up and looked at the delegation from the Khemitology Guest House. "It is obvious we have to go to the City of the Dead as soon as possible."

"Dorothy, dear," George said. "I believe we should leave this investigation to Egyptian police and the agents from the embassies."

"I mean no disrespect, Mr. Montgomery," Dr. Stratton said, "but the police and the people from the embassies have a lot to do. We are here with only one task, to find Charles. We have a better chance if we all work together. I, for one, agree with Mrs. Montgomery. Our next step is to visit the City of the Dead."

"Sir and Madam, I will arrange a visit with Mr. Wasim and his family for tomorrow morning," Aamen said. "I will also inform my professors that I cannot attend my classes tomorrow, as I will be in the service of the American Embassy and the friends of the American boy, Charles."

The meeting was over. The journalists ran over to talk to Aamen. Dorothy stood close so she could hear their questions and the translater's response. A representative of the American Embassy led the group outside, raising his eyebrows a bit as he watched them enter a limousine with a white bow on its hood. No one said anything; all were buried in deep thought.

After a moment, David scratched his head. "I don't think this story sounds normal, do you, Grandmother?"

"No, I don't think it sounds one bit normal," Mrs. Montgomery agreed. "Who loses an almost twelve-year-old boy, not once but twice?"

"I think Charles turned twelve in the City of the Dead," David said gloomily.

Jacques was pale as he stared out the window at the streets of Cairo. He wondered where Charles could have gone. Why had he agreed to bring a boy to Egypt? Why couldn't life be simple? And where in the world were Charles' parents?

"What do you think of this translater, Aamen Halabi?" Dr. Stratton asked Mrs. Montgomery.

"Personally, I think Aamen is adorable. More than that, the fact that some of his family lives in the City of Dead, and that his shoes need replacing, indicates that he is not from a well-to-do family. Yet somehow he got into college and is taking his studies seriously. His English is remarkably good, don't you agree?"

"Yes, I agree," the professor said.

"He is also enterprising," Mrs. Montgomery continued. "When he got this chance to be in the American Embassy, he left no stone unturned. He wore red, white, and blue and pinned both an American and Egyptian flag on his lapel. He also made sure to express how much he appreciates the American Embassy. I found him a most amazing boy."

"You are so right, Mrs. Montgomery!" Dr. Stratton called out. "Although I do not have your powers of observation and attention to detail, I noticed this boy was exceptional. He showed a great heart for the people who lost their homes. And despite the risk of jeopardizing his deSired employment at the American Embassy, he was courageous. He was not afraid to criticize the government for the way they treat their poor."

"Yes, and I noticed," Alfred said, "this young man looked the journalists straight in their eyes and schooled them as to what reporters should be writing regarding the people of the City of the Dead."

"I would say this young man has a great future ahead of him, and we intend to be a part of it, don't we, Alfred?" Dr. Stratton asked.

"Yes," Alfred agreed.

"Well, I think we should keep our minds on finding Charles first," David said.

"I suggest we keep our minds on our very next step, tomorrow's visit to the City of the Dead," Mrs. Montgomery said, clutching her hat as the limo hit a deep pothole in the road. "I must say, we are in a better position than we were after Charles' first disappearance."

"Yeah, at least we know Charles isn't dead," Fran said.

"Fran, you're too young to be suggesting what has happened to Charles," his mother scolded.

"How old do you have to be, Mom?"

Mrs. Montgomery put her finger to her lips, shushing Fran. "I agree with your mother. It is not the time to speculate about what has happened to Charles."

"Home, James," Dr. Stratton called out to Samy.

Samy nodded as he slipped an audio tape into the player. "One more love song for the wedding party," he said.

Soon, Elvis Presley and Samy were singing in harmony.

Wise men say
Only fools rush in
But I can't help falling in love with you.
Shall I say?
Would it be a sin,
If I can't help falling in love with you.
Like a river flows
Surely to the sea,
Darling, so it goes,
Some things are meant to be
Take my hand,
Take my whole life, too,
For I can't help falling in love with you.

"How can you keep singing when Charles is missing?" David asked the taxi driver.

"If I thought refraining from singing would put Charles next to you in this limo, I wouldn't sing. But my years of experience have brought me to the conclusion that singing, even when facing great difficulties, can clear the mind. What do you think, Mrs. Montgomery?"

"I think, now that you mention it, singing may be a kind of emptying of the mind so that new thoughts can come in."

"I want to empty my mind!" Fran said, and soon, his childish voice was harmonizing with the taxi driver and the King of Rock 'n Roll.

CHAPTER 36

THE BUTLER AND A FEELING OF FAMILIARITY

A lfred leaned slightly on his black cane, capped with a golden lion's head. He didn't need the cane. His legs had healed fine, but he'd gotten used to it, and somehow it had become a part of him like his vests, hats, and bow ties. Thinking about this, he turned to stare at the lion-like statue looming in the growing gloom directly across the street. As he studied the Sphinx's fading visage, he wasn't trying to solve the great mysteries surrounding this ancient sculpture. Instead, he was trying to solve the mysteries of his own self, his own life.

Alfred P. Hart watched the sunset in the east. As it reached the horizon, the Great Pyramid and its smaller companions cast purple shadows over the Giza Plateau. Straggling tourists turned away from these great edifices to climb into taxis and tour buses, heading for hotels where they would study their itineraries to see what tomorrow held for them.

But Alfred wasn't a tourist. His only itinerary was to visit a place called the City of the Dead with the other Khemitology guests. And they wouldn't be going there on a tour. They were going to search for clues as to what had happened to Charles Dayton Stratton III, thought to be the child of Dr. Stratton's son Charlie.

This whole thing was one great mystery. Why had he let his great friend Dr. Stratton travel alone to Egypt to find or not find a boy who might or might not be his grandson? He should have jumped at the invitation to accompany the professor to Egypt. Instead, he'd hidden behind responsibilities that could be given to others. Why? There was only one conclusion: Alfred P. Hart had a character flaw, maybe more than one.

David came out of the guest house door. "Are you still lost?" the boy asked.

"I guess you could say that. I seem to be lost in thought," Alfred answered.

"What are you thinking about?" David asked.

"I guess I was thinking about Charles," Alfred answered, "and also how life can take you on surprising turns, just when you think things are ordinary and comfortable."

"I know what you mean," David said. "That's exactly what happened to me when Charles became my roommate. At first, we didn't get along. I thought we were so different, and I couldn't believe he didn't like soccer. Then I learned something. If everyone was the same, life would be predictable."

"Yes, predictable and comfortable," Alfred agreed.

"Well, I learned that to be Charles' friend, you have to throw predictability out the third-story window, literally," David said with a grin.

Alfred thought that was a rather odd remark. "So your room was on the third floor of your boy's school, the Château du Mont?"

"Uh huh. The fourth floor is locked behind a huge iron gate," David said mysteriously. "Charles made friends with a tree. He called him Old Limbs. I didn't believe that a tree could be a friend, but Charles did."

"So I conclude that somehow you climbed down the tree together," Alfred said, placing his hat back on his head and rubbing his chin.

"Wow!" the boy said, impressed. "You're almost as good as my grandmother at guessing things."

"I am guessing today was very upsetting for you, David."

"Yes, I truly believed we'd find Charles," David said. "I was certain he'd stowed away on a boat and managed to get up to Luxor and Farak's family. But today I found out I was wrong. Now he's disappeared again. Where could he have gone?"

"I cannot guess where Charles may have gone, but I listened to the translator's story and it seems clear he left the gathering willingly," Alfred said. "Now that you explain a little more about Charles' character, I think he may have gone in search of adventure."

"I should have thought of that. Thank you, Mr. Hart," David said, color returning to his face.

"With this in mind," Alfred advised, "I suggest that tomorrow we not only look for clues about Charles' disappearance, but also signs indicating what adventure he might be headed for."

"Thank you, thank you, Mr. Hart. I'll tell Fran that we must look for where Charles might go to find adventure."

Dr. Stratton's butler watched the boy run off. "Time for a drink and a think," he said aloud, twirling his cane as he headed for the Pizza Hut.

Mandisa handed him a cup of water. Alfred seated himself at the small table beside the blue door. Retrieving a newspaper from his suit coat pocket, he folded it to a section revealing a blank crossword puzzle. Pulling a mechanical pencil from his shirt pocket, he began filling in the tiny boxes, muttering to himself as he experimented with different words.

"Mr. Hart," Mrs. Montgomery said.

Alfred looked up, startled. "Oh, excuse me, Mrs. Montgomery. I thought I was alone. I thought everyone had left the building, so to speak."

"Do you mind if I sit down, Mr. Hart?" she asked.

"Please do," he replied. "However, I should be more comfortable if you would call me Alfred."

"Very well, Alfred. I do feel as though I know you well enough to call you by your given name," Mrs. Montgomery said. "From the moment I saw you, I've had this strong feeling you and I have met before. However, for the life of me, I cannot see how our paths would have crossed, you being from the United States and me being from the United Kingdom."

"It does seem very unlikely that we would have crossed paths, as you say," Alfred agreed.

"Still, I cannot shake this feeling of familiarity," Mrs. Montgomery said.

"That is quite peculiar, Madam," Alfred P. Hart remarked.

"May I ask you a question?" Mrs. Montgomery inquired. "Are you at all acquainted with one of my favorite writers of the detective genre, Dorothy Leigh Sayers?"

Alfred placed his crossword puzzle on the red-and-white plastic table-cloth. He looked more closely at the woman peering at him with her deep blue eyes and soft smile. Hers was a lucky face, Alfred thought. At one moment she could appear like a caring wife, mother, and grandmother. The next moment, she could appear shrewd, observant, focused, and perhaps even hard-boiled. This was a woman who would seldom need a disguise, he thought, or maybe this was her disguise.

"Yes, Mrs. Montgomery," he answered. "I am acquainted with Dorothy Leigh Sayers."

"Then you are familiar with her protagonists Lord Peter Wimsey and his man, as he calls him, Mr. Mervyn Bunter?"

"Yes, I am familiar with her literary characters."

"Could it be that my feeling of familiarity comes from you and Mr. Bunter sharing similar qualities?" Mrs. Montgomery wondered.

"Yes, quite so," Alfred said with a chuckle of appreciation.

"Many modern readers of Ms. Sayers complain that her stories are, shall we say, antiquated," Mrs. Montgomery said.

"Do you find this so, Madam?"

"Delightfully so, although I long ago rejected the class system so apparent in Sayers' mysteries," Mrs. Montgomery said. "May I ask if you are a photographer, Alfred?"

"Yes, you may ask, and the answer is in the affirmative."

Mrs. Montgomery nodded. "Of course. Bunter is recognized by all readers as a noted photographer. You have, I am certain, Mr. Hart, a good—more likely great—camera, perhaps gifted to you by your employer."

"Jolly good, Mrs. Montgomery," Alfred P. Hart said. "Yes, this is all true."

"In your front shirt pocket is a Minox spy camera, like the one Bunter himself might wear when working on a case. Are you working on a case, Mr. Hart?"

"No, I am just carrying it should there be a need for some clandestine photography," he answered. "I see now, however, that I must place a handkerchief in my front shirt pocket to assure that no one else with a sharp eye like yours can spy my secret."

"Right. I see also that you are a cruciverbalist, as is the character of Mr. Bunter," Mrs. Montgomery observed.

"Before reading Dorothy Sayers' books, I had never engaged in crossword puzzles. After meeting Ms. Sayers while in hospital—through her stories, of course—I became addicted to the dashed things," Alfred P. Hart confessed.

Mrs. Montgomery continued her line of questioning. "So, you were in the hospital as a patient?"

"Yes, for nearly three months."

"I surmise then that you were in the military?"

"That is correct," he answered.

"I intuit that Dr. Stratton was your commanding officer," Mrs. Montgomery continued.

Alfred raised his eyebrows. "My heavens! You are a clever woman."

"I have a few other guesses," she speculated. "You were injured in battle, taking the bullet intended for Charles Dayton Stratton. You probably saved his life."

"War is war," Alfred said. "Although there may be some differences between the Korean and World War I, I did my duty to protect my commanding officer."

"May I?" Mrs. Montgomery asked, indicating the crossword puzzle.

"Of course, Madam. I could use some assistance."

"After your long stay at the hospital, you were invited to the home of Dr. Stratton to continue your recovery," Mrs. Montgomery said, using one of her colored pens to plug a missing word into the sprawling grid.

"I didn't expect the Strattons to invite me to convalesce in their home, but both Charles and his wife insisted," Alfred said, penciling in another word.

Mrs. Montgomery wasn't done with her inquiry. "You continued to read Dorothy Sayers mysteries and, quite naturally, identified with the character of Bunter, who also took a bullet for his commanding officer, Lord Peter Wimsey."

"I could not help but recognize the parallels between Bunter's life and my own," Alfred confirmed, picking up his mechanical pencil and hitting it softly against the table.

"Yes, I can see how you would. To return to your story, in Dr. Stratton's home—unlike the home of the solitary Lord Wimsey—there was a boy, Charlie. As you became stronger, you began to help around the house, placing special focus on the well-being of young Charles II while his father focused on earning his doctorate." Mrs. Montgomery ventured further.

"It was a comfortable arrangement," she speculated. "You were allowed to practice your art of photography and so forth. Then, as I know only so well myself, life seized you, and years passed. Charlie disappeared, and Mrs. Stratton took ill. This is all as clear as glass."

"You are, indeed, uncannily perceptive," Alfred said.

Mrs. Montgomery scrutinized her companion. "What I have not been able to figure out, however, is why you would take on Bunter's attributes, so strongly that I feel I know you, though we never met."

Alfred handily jotted two more words on the crossword puzzle.

"Allow me to further un-fog the glass," he said. "One evening, a year after Charlie's disappearance, I became quite melancholy. I began to think I really had made nothing of myself, that I was just a servant. I should have gone to a university or apprenticed myself as a cameraman in the movie industry. But it was ten or twelve years too late."

"One night, in the midst of my depression, I picked up Ms. Sayers' *Unnatural Death* for a reread," Alfred continued. "I began to think deeply about Bunter. He was not melancholy. He did his work better than he was asked to do, and he found pleasure in his relationship with Lord Peter Wimsey. That's when I got the idea that Bunter might become my inspiration, my coach, my teacher. I decided I would view my position with the Stratton family as a great gift from the universe. I would do my duties precisely and with great pride. I had only one problem."

"And what was that, Alfred?"

"Dr. Stratton refused to become my Lord Peter Wimsey, insisting on treating me like one of the family," Alfred explained. "This became particularly true after Mrs. Stratton's sad passing. I had to find an appropriate suit for her funeral. It was then I decided to make the small step of dressing like my literary hero, Mr. Bunter. Dr. Stratton tried to get me back to my old ways of dressing. However, I felt so comfortable in my role and my attire that I did what I seldom have done."

"What did you do, Mr. Hart?" asked the woman in purple.

"I stood up to Dr. Stratton, insisting that how I chose to dress was my own business. And so, in my mind, the subject was closed."

"There is a moment where all of us must stand our ground," Mrs. Montgomery said. "Our conversation has been particularly enlightening, Alfred. I expect you've picked up some of the deductive and inductive skills attributed to Mr. Bunter?"

"I believe so, Madam, thought I may not be as perceptive as you," Alfred said.

"That is left to be seen, Alfred," Mrs. Montgomery replied. "We may be needing your abilities as we seek the whereabouts of young Charles. Oh, see, Dr. Stratton is looking for you. Shall we walk back to the guest house? I am still making plans for tomorrow's visit to the necropolis."

"Necropolis?" Alfred repeated.

"Yes, the City of the Dead," Mrs. Montgomery said. "Don't forget your camera, Alfred."

CHAPTER 37

MYSTERY WRITERS' LOVE OF CHESS

After her late afternoon rest, Mrs. Montgomery slipped on her purple feathered slippers and, carrying her purple notebook, shuffled down the bare wooden stairs to the first floor of the Khemitology Guest House. She made a left turn into the small community kitchen, with its multicolored, flowered linoleum floor and small sky-blue cabinets.

She recognized the man standing in front of the old black stove. He was still in the suit he'd worn to the American Embassy, minus the hat. His salt-and-pepper gray hair was perfectly combed, parted, and patted down with some kind of pomade. Mrs. Montgomery absentmindedly touched her own blondish hair. Yes, it was acceptably pulled back in a neat ponytail, secured with a purple rubber band.

"Hello, Alfred," she said. "I see you are making some tea. I discovered quite a while ago that a cold case requires a large pot of hot tea."

"Yes, Madam," Alfred said.

"Although I don't consider Charles' disappearance simply a case, it does appear to be a rather cold case at the moment—doesn't it?" she asked.

Alfred P. Hart looked thoughtful. "Yes. If we are to believe the young interpreter, which I do, Charles was not kidnapped. Rather, he left Aamen Halibi's side willingly for some reason, possibly to follow someone. Who and why are not obvious at the moment."

He turned back to the kettle whistling on the stove.

"Tomorrow, at the City of the Dead, I sincerely hope we will discover Charles' whereabouts, but we cannot be sure," Mrs. Montgomery said. "So, with the help of some strong Earl Grey, I want to mull over all of the clues we have gathered so far."

"Would you like me to bring you a pot of tea when it has completed its steep, Mrs. Montgomery?"

"Would you, Alfred P. Hart?" she answered gratefully. "I will be next door in the sitting room."

Mrs. Montgomery sat down at the table by the window. Somehow, the sight of the Sphinx, crouching cat-like, almost invisible at this shadowy end of twilight, felt comforting. Where was Charles Stratton at this very moment? Was he alone? Was he ill? Was he scared? No, she scolded herself. That kind of fearful and emotional thinking generally lead nowhere. A rational person must keep her mind on the clues and information.

Alfred pushed through the swinging door from the kitchen to the sitting room with a pot of tea, a teacup, a saucer, and a plate of shortcake cookies arranged neatly on a small wooden tray, which he placed in front of Mrs. Montgomery.

"Thank you, Alfred," she said. "Before you take tea to Dr. Stratton, I would like to ask you some questions."

Alfred pulled a chair closer to Mrs. Montgomery and sat down.

"Are you planning on bringing your spy camera to the City of the Dead tomorrow?" she asked.

"I thought it might be less intrusive than my Canon," Alfred answered.

Mrs. Montgomery sipped her tea. "I agree, it would be less intrusive. Now, I am thinking that you doubtless packed at least two decks of cards and a chess set."

"So I did, Mrs. Montgomery," Alfred said.

"Would you mind bringing the chess set up to the third floor, to the room where my husband George and Jacques are staying?"

"You wish to play chess?" he asked, puzzled.

"I used to play a bit," she replied. "I belonged to the chess club at university. However, now I play with only one purpose."

"What might that be, Mrs. Montgomery?"

"To keep my opponent within close range for as long as possible and, in the process, discover whom he or she really is," she answered. "Finally, like a good chess coach, I attempt to pass on a little advice to help my opponent move forward in life."

"And who are you planning to advise?"

Mrs. Montgomery took another sip of tea. "I have become aware that Jacques is suffering from a bad case of guilt regarding the loss of young Charles."

"My experience is that extreme guilt surrounds a person like an eggshell, allowing nothing in and nothing out," Mrs. Montgomery said. "The poor cowering being inside—filled with blame, fear, and feelings of unworthiness—becomes a self-pitying, inert mass of possibilities. I intend to make a little crack in that shell of Jacques with the help of your chessmen, Alfred."

"Yes, Madam," he said, nodding in assent. "I'm sure you're aware that Mrs. Sayers, as revealed through her Lord Peter Wimsey character, also found chess and cards to have a revelatory function."

"Let's see if this is the case with Jacques."

"Very good. I will meet you upstairs in a few minutes."

***

George Montgomery was in his room on the third floor of the Khemitology Guest House when he heard a knock. As he opened the door, he was greeted

323

by two boys in sleeping attire. One wore striped pajamas, while the other had dark blue pajamas covered in planets and rocket ships.

"Surprise!" Fran called out.

"We have visitors, Jacques," George hollered to his roommate.

Jacques, who'd been thumbing through his Egyptian guidebook, greeted the boys. "Did you come to say goodnight?"

"Not yet," David answered. "Grandmother says there is going to be a chess game here."

"Oh, did she now?" Mr. Montgomery said, looking around. "I don't see a chessboard in here. Do you, Jacques?"

Examining the bare room with its three beds, three chairs, three lamps, two wooden tables, and a floor fan, Jacques shook his head. "I see no games here." He walked over and checked the small closet. "Nothing here, either."

Dr. Bernstein came to the doorway in her gray robe. "May I come in?"

Mr. Montgomery waved her in with exaggerated politeness. "Please do, Dr. Bernstein. I suppose you've come to say goodnight, too."

"No," the physicist answered. "Mrs. Montgomery said there's going to be a chess game here and that we wouldn't want to miss it."

Fran wriggled with excitement. "I want to play!"

"Do you even know how to play chess?" David asked.

"No, but I know how to play checkers," Fran said.

"Chess and checkers are not one bit alike," the blond-haired boy said, shaking his head.

Mrs. Montgomery burst into the room in her purple robe and feather slippers.

"We're having a pajama party!" Fran exclaimed.

"Yes, and we have more guests than there are places to sit." Mrs. Montgomery asked the boys to go to the large dorm room and bring more chairs.

George closed one eye to get a better look at his wife. "Dorothy Montgomery, what are you up to?"

Before she could answer, Dr. Stratton came to the door wearing a maroon bathrobe and carrying a teacup. "I heard this is the place to be at 8 o'clock."

George Montgomery checked his watch. It was exactly 8 p.m. "Come in, Dr. Stratton. Everybody else is here, except, where is Alfred?"

The boys returned, dragging two straight-backed chairs into the room. Seeing Dr. Stratton, David said, "I'll get another chair."

Mrs. Montgomery watched as David left and Alfred entered. He was carrying a tray with a large pot of tea, a plate full of cookies and a stack of cups and saucers. Under the tray was a wooden chessboard. Under his right armpit he clutched a red velvet box, which obviously held the chess pieces.

"You, sir, are amazing," Mrs. Montgomery said. "Tea, cookies, decks of cards, a spy camera, a pressing iron, a shaving kit, and a chess set. What else do you have in that black bag of yours, Alfred P. Hart?"

As Alfred moved towards the table by the window, he replied in a soft voice, "That would be telling, would it not, Mrs. Montgomery?"

"I cannot help but be reminded of that character in P.L. Travers' story *Mary Poppins*, with her never-ending carpet bag. Have you read it, Alfred?"

"No, Mrs. Montgomery, but I shall place it on my list of stories yet to be read."

The woman in the purple robe turned to Jacques. "Now, Mr. Gerard, I thought it a bit too early for us to turn in. How about a nice game of chess?"

"I fear I am not much of a chess player, Mrs. Montgomery," Jacques said. "I have on occasion been talked into a game by some of the boys at the Château du Mont, but I am not good at it and seldom win."

"There are many reasons for playing chess, Mr. Gerard, winning being the least important."

"What genius are you quoting now?" George asked.

"Myself," his wife quipped with a laugh.

CHAPTER 38

CHECKMATE

Jacques looked at George and then back at Mrs. Montgomery. "To tell you the truth, I do not feel like playing chess," he said gloomily. "It does not seem like the right thing to do at this time."

"What do you think would be the right thing to do, Mr. Gerard?" Mrs. Montgomery posed.

"Charles is lost, alone somewhere, and you think we should play chess. Does this make any sense?"

"Refusing to play chess when asked by a lady is like refusing an invitation to dance," Alfred interjected. "It's just bad form."

"Why does everyone in this group insist on communicating through metaphors and literary quotes? Why can't people talk in plain ordinary language? In my business, we go straight to the point," George said emphatically.

"I like all the quotes," Fran said. "It's like figuring out a puzzle. Is it alright if I say that, Mom?"

Dr. Bernstein patted the top of Fran's red curls. "Yes, and I agree, Fran."

"When I find a great quote, it's like finding a partner in crime, so to speak," Mrs. Montgomery said. "This partner expresses my own beliefs or arguments more concisely, more cleverly, more persuasively and with more eloquence than I can manage. With a good quote, I am never alone."

"Well put, and I completely agree!" Dr. Stratton called out.

"Yes, Dorothy, and if you happen to change your thinking or your belief, you can always blame the error on your partner in crime, who sadly cannot defend him or herself," George said, laughing at his own little joke.

"Back to our discussion, Mr. Gerard. Would you rather think about a chess game tonight or ruminate about all the mistakes you think you have made—the first of these being that you even agreed to come to Egypt at all?" Mrs. Montgomery said with a sly smile.

Jacques wondered if the woman in the purple robe could see into his mind. It was an uncomfortable feeling.

"Personally, I don't see any sense in this self-punishment," Mrs. Montgomery continued. "Thinking about errors never changes anything. And what if chess is more than just a game? What if its lessons can be directly applied to life, to your life, Mr. Gerard, right this minute?"

"I do not see how they could," Jacques answered sullenly.

"In my youth, I earned a sports scholarship to Cambridge University," Mrs. Montgomery related. "In my second year, I was selected to be captain of the women's soccer team. I got the notion that if I learned to play chess, I would be a better soccer captain, so I joined the chess club. Others on my soccer team expressed disapproval, believing I was wasting time playing chess when I could be practicing soccer."

"In the end, my hunch proved correct," she continued. "Through chess I learned problem-solving skills, critical thinking, and pattern recognition. I learned to look for the strengths in each of my players, and not to be overly dependent upon those I believed to be the best athletes. I became more inventive and could more quickly visualize alternative plays. By the end of the second year, the Cambridge Women's Soccer team went to the International Games."

George stood up, his chest puffed with pride. "Dorothy's name has gone down in the history of Cambridge University as the greatest woman soccer captain of all time."

"Oh, George," Mrs. Montgomery said with a sweet smile. "Anyway, to a great degree I attribute my success in soccer, not to mention mystery writing, to the chess club."

Jacques looked astonished. "You are a mystery writer?"

"We can talk about that later," Mrs. Montgomery said, moving towards the chess board. George ventured closer to the table where his wife was arranging black chess pieces on her side of the board. Jacques was still standing, watching Mrs. Montgomery station her chessmen.

"If you want my advice, Jacques, just play the game," George advised. "Dorothy doesn't give up. She never gives up."

Jacques mumbled something about the entire world coming in to see him lose.

"No, Jacques, they are not coming to see you lose," Mrs. Montgomery said. "However, there is a chance they might be coming to see how you lose. In chess as in life, when you choose to play, you agree to stay in the game, win or lose. If you lose, you shake hands with the winner and vow to play again—this time to win."

Jacques looked at George and then Alfred. "I cannot make any sense of this conversation."

"Recognizing confusion is the first step to finding one's course," Mrs. Montgomery said, as she finished placing the black pawns on the second row of the chess board. "Shall we play, Mr. Gerard?"

"I want to play next," Fran announced.

"You said you didn't know how to play chess. Chess is a completely different game than checkers," David said disdainfully.

"David, perhaps you can explain something about chess. Begin with the set-up, dear," his grandmother said.

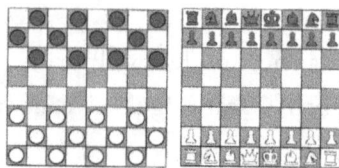

"In checkers," David explained, "all the pieces look the same and move in one direction, with the exception of when a checker is crowned king. That happens when one of the checkers reaches the opposition's side and the player says, 'King me.' That player then earns back one of their lost checkers, which is placed on the king checker like a crown."

"I know all that," Fran said.

David continued. "In checkers, you win pieces by jumping over the other player's checkers. But that's not how chess is played. Really, only the board is similar."

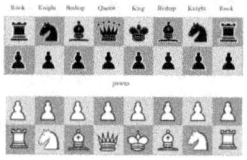

"In chess, you have a dark side and a light side," David noted. "Each player has eight pawns, abbreviated as the letter P by those keeping track of the game. Each player also has one king or K; one queen or Q; two bishops or B; two knights or N; and two castles or rooks, abbreviated R. The queen always begins on her color, so if she's light, she is placed on a light square in the first row. The light color always begins the play. Since Grandmother is setting up with the dark-colored chess pieces, Jacques will start the game."

"I suppose I have no choice in the matter," Jacques said.

David ignored his comment. "On the first move, a player may choose to move their pawn one or two steps forward. After that, a pawn can only move one step forward. A pawn can only capture a chess piece by moving diagonally into the opponent's space."

"You mean like this?" Fran pointed to the board, moving his finger diagonally from one square to another.

"By George, I think you've got it, Fran," Alfred said, taking a sip of tea.

"That's just the beginning, Fran," David said. "In chess, each kind of royal piece moves in a distinct pattern. These must be memorized. The king can move one square in any direction. The queen can move forward, backwards, or diagonally any number of spaces. The rook or castle can move forward, backwards, or sidewards any number of spaces, but not diagonally. The bishop can move diagonally forward or backwards any number of spaces. The knight moves in an L-shape, forward or backwards, either two up and one over, or one up and two over."

"How do you know so much about chess?" Fran asked. "I thought you spent all your time playing soccer."

"You can't spend much time with my grandmother without learning chess." David continued his explanation. "The objective of the game is to capture the opponent's king. Check means the king is in danger of being captured. The king must move. Checkmate means the king cannot move out of danger and so he's captured."

"That is a good brief description, David," his grandmother said with pride.

"Wow! I love this game," Fran said, chomping on a cookie. "It doesn't seem too difficult to me."

"Right," David responded, with all the sarcasm a twelve-year-old could muster.

"Let the game begin," Alfred said in an announcer's voice.

Jacques picked up a pawn on the far-left side of the board. He was still holding the light-colored piece in his right hand when Alfred interjected. "You know, Mr. Gerard, they say that how you begin your game reflects how you conduct your life. Additionally, some claim that if a person changes his or her approach to the game of chess, their life changes."

"I never heard that before, Alfred," Jacques said. "It is interesting, but it does not seem believable to me."

331

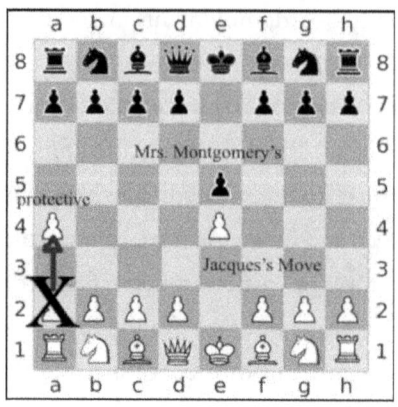

"It appears you plan to start with the move p-a2 to p-a4," Alfred said. "This, my good fellow, is what is called a protective move. May I advise that this is not a time for protection but a time to move boldly forward, straight up the middle, ready for combat? May I suggest a better first move would be p-e2 to p-e4?"

Jacques placed the pawn back on the board and followed Alfred's suggestion.

"That's it," Dr. Stratton's butler said encouragingly.

Mrs. Montgomery nodded in approval.

"Why does this board have letters and numbers on it?" Fran asked.

"It's so people can analyze, learn and teach various chess moves," David answered with authority.

"That is correct," his grandmother said. "Not to mention that in professional chess tournaments, keeping a record of one's moves is mandatory."

Mrs. Montgomery moved her dark pawn, p-e7 to p-e5. Jacques and Mrs. Montgomery's pawns faced each other. She recorded their first moves in her little purple notebook.

They played on quietly. Then, when it was Mrs. Montgomery's fifth turn, she looked at Jacques. "Mr. Gerard, this is a perfect time to look around and discover who is cheering you on, who believes in you, who wants you to win, and even if you do not win will still be your friend. This is the lesson of our chess game tonight. And so, my dear Jacques, I forfeit the game."

"You cannot forfeit the game!" Jacques exclaimed, astonished at her declaration. "It is not over."

"I always laugh when I think about a story I read in *Chess Monthly*," Mrs. Montgomery said. "As you probably all know, in professional tournaments the players are timed so they don't take a week to play one game. In 1935, at the Warsaw Chess Olympiad, Isaias Pleci of Argentina claimed his game on time forfeit against Miguel Najdorf. Najdorf made his move just before the time limit, but before he could press the button on the official clock that tracks the playing time, Pleci picked up the clock and ran away with it."

Mrs. Montgomery ended her story with a great laugh. "That is just what I'm doing. I am picking up the time clock and walking away with it. Come to think of it, we may all be running out of time. Goodnight, see you tomorrow."

On her way out the door, Mrs. Montgomery padded up to George in her purple feathered slippers and planted a kiss on his broad forehead. "Goodnight, my dear."

"I do not understand," Jacques said.

"It's alright, Jacques," David said. "Grandmother's knight was going to take your queen anyway, and then you'd have been a goner."

"Mom, did you pack a chess set?" Fran asked. "I want to practice."

"You know I didn't, Francis Bacon Bernstein. Now say goodnight. We must all get up early in the morning."

Jacques turned to George Montgomery. "How have you endured that kind of conversation for all these years?"

"Believe me when I tell you, Jacques, I don't know," Mr. Montgomery said, shaking his head in amazement. "I guess it's because Dorothy is unpredictable, exciting, entertaining, electrifying, and confounding."

"Not to mention quite mysterious," Alfred added, placing the teapot, saucers, and cups on the wooden tray.

"Tomorrow, we'll be at the City of the Dead," Dr. Stratton said to Jacques. "What if we don't find any clues about Charles' whereabouts? Then what?"

"If you want my opinion," Alfred said, jumping into the conversation, "tonight Mrs. Montgomery reminded each of us that we must play the game. We must move forth boldly, straight up the middle, not allowing fear to stop us or confuse our actions. Now I must return these things to the kitchen. Goodnight."

CHAPTER 39

THE TOUR BUS OF THE GRATEFUL DEAD

Things don't change much in the Giza Plateau, but on this morning the Sphinx seemed to take on an expression of consternation. It was accustomed to being the center of attention, with everyone gazing upon its cat-like form, admiring its immensity and singular place in the history of civilization. Its very existence was recognized as proof of the power of humankind to dream and to manifest.

This morning, however, something happened to disturb the colossal statue. The tour bus of the famous musical group The Grateful Dead chugged past its form, made a U-turn, and pulled up in front of the Pizza Hut across the street. Hearing its motor, scholars and meditators turned away from the Sphinx's silent visage to watch in amazement how the sun brought out the wild and brilliant colors covering every inch of this old bus. The softness of the morning light could not dampen or mute the vivid reds, purples, yellows, oranges, and blues that swirled together in a kaleidoscope of patterns. The crowd walking around the Sphinx stopped and stared across the Archeological Road. They seemed captivated by this movable piece of psychedelic art, purporting to represent an expanded state of human consciousness.

The fact was this distinctive vehicle stole the attention away from the Sphinx. The long-nosed bus pulled and pulled like a giant magnet. More and more of the stone giant's visitors ran across the road and began to circumambulate the remains, not of an ancient civilization, but of the legendary rock band's 1978 visit to Cairo.

At first, the Sphinx took on a greenish shade as she glared jealously at this outrageous vehicle. Then, she thought and thought until it came to her; in a few years, this tour bus would find its way to a Cairo junkyard, while she would still be guarding the Giza Plateau. At this realization, the Sphinx settled down, resuming her imperious expression. The burnt-red sun rose higher on the horizon, turning everything a hazy orange. An array of sounds—braying camels, clip-clopping donkey carts, rattling small-engine cars and trucks, and the whistles of souvenir sellers calling to one another—joined with the sun to announce a new day, a new beginning. Women in gallabiyah greeted each other. Soon, they were creating a harmonious rhythm as they wielded short-handled brooms. With a series of brisk whisks, they swept away sand, litter, and small rocks from the hard-packed dirt sidewalks running along both sides of the road. Boys gathered at the soccer field to get in a game or two before the sun traveled to its crown position, making the soccer ball too hot to handle.

Mrs. Montgomery was dressed in a flowing white pantsuit. On her head was a broad-brimmed straw hat with a sprig of lavender flowers tucked in its purple hatband. She tossed a large purple bag over her shoulder, filled with—who knows what, her husband thought as he stared at the bag.

"What do you think we are going to find today, Dorothy?" George asked.

"Clues, George. Clues."

George's neck, which was already sunburnt, turned a deeper shade of red. "Dorothy, can I ask you something? Why do you think we can locate clues that professionals from the top investigative organizations in the world can't find?"

"What did you think of the first book in my 'Woman in the Red Hat' series?"

"It was fine, gripping actually. I read it in one sitting," George said. "This, however, is real life we're talking about. I don't mean to criticize, but we're not inside of a mystery novel. We're trying to locate a real boy!"

"I understand what you're trying to say, my dear," his wife said patiently. "I agree this is serious. And I firmly believe a matter this grave requires a collaborative effort, employing everyone's gifts. I bring the qualities of a good mystery writer. Mystery writing demands a precise approach, a careful fastidiousness that I believe no amount of training by law enforcement agencies can develop in a person."

"Is this what you believe, Mrs. Montgomery?" Mr. Montgomery said with some skepticism.

"A mystery writer looks at a conundrum that may at first appear incomprehensible, inexplicable, and unsolvable," she continued. "But the writer is dauntless. She moves forward fearlessly, step by step, clue by clue. She connects things, disconnects them, and sometimes reconnects them. The literary sleuth never gives up and in the end, voilà, the mystery is solved."

George looked only partly placated. "So you consider the disappearance of David's roommate a mystery?"

"Charles has been lost two times," Dorothy pointed out. "The first disappearance is explainable, the result of a strange but logical series of events. For him to go missing a second time, though? You have to admit, it is mysterious."

"Granted," George said, bamboozled by his own wife. "But surely there are countless officers and agents hard at work looking for the boy."

"That may be so," his wife allowed. "We, however, stand a greater chance of finding him. To these professional investigators, Charles is just another sad case. For us, he is a boy we know, and the best friend of our beloved grandson. We have the advantage."

George sighed. "An advantage over the professionals?"

"Yes, George. Remember Aamen's description of how the authorities have mistreated the people of the City of the Dead? I believe the residents will be more likely to speak freely to us than to those same officials they believe have contributed to their difficulty living in the *Qarafat*."

George looked puzzled. "Qarafat?"

"It is an Arab word that describes an area where people live in tombs."

"In regard to this Qarafat, wouldn't it be better if just you and I go. It would be simpler, and it could be a date of sorts," George said with a laugh, quite proud of his joke.

Dorothy joined in with his laughter, then asked, "What kind of thank-you party would it be if just you and I went to the Wasims' home? And besides, we can't leave the others here with nothing to do but eat pizza, play cards, or move chess pieces around on a small board."

"Alright, Dorothy." Mr. Montgomery suddenly looked uncertain. "Just out of curiosity," he asked, "what gift do I bring to this search for a missing boy?"

"You remind the searchers to be cautious, George. Not because you are circumspect, but because you really care. David, Fran, and Jacques, not to mention me, need your steadiness, your compassion. This is a very important role, George."

"Well, if you put it that way, Dorothy, I'll carry forth," George said, giving his wife a bear hug. "I believe it's time for breakfast."

When George and Dorothy Montgomery walked into the pizza parlor, they found David, Fran, Dr. Bernstein, and Jacques seated at the picnic table closest to the front window, the best view in the house. The table was teeming with plates of cheese, apples, grapes, baked flatbread, and pots of black tea turned cream-colored with milk.

Mrs. Montgomery greeted the cook cheerfully. "Hello, Mandisa! Everything smells wonderful. May I speak to you a minute?"

"What's all that stuff for?" Fran asked, untangling his legs from between the bench and the table and running to a collection of bags and bottles stationed at the back of the Pizza Hut.

"It is lunch, a small thank-you gift for the Wasims and their neighbors who took care of our Charles," Mrs. Montgomery said, inspecting the bags.

Fran looked doubtful. "Yeah, but they lost him, didn't they?"

"No, Fran, they didn't lose Charles," Mrs. Montgomery corrected him. "I believe that Charles lost himself."

"What does that mean, Grandmother, that Charles lost himself?" David asked.

"If we are to believe our young interpreter, Charles walked off on his own," she explained. "That's one of the main reasons we're going to the City of the Dead today. In order to discover where Charles went, we need to discover why he would leave the City of the Dead when he knew he was going to the American Embassy the next morning."

After breakfast, Dr. Bernstein pulled Fran close to her. "We need to have a little talk. In our family, we have seldom discussed death because, fortunately, we haven't had to. But now, you must come with us to the City of The Dead, which is a very large ceme…"

"I know all about cemeteries, Mom," Fran said, interrupting his mother. "When I'm at home, I watch 'Scooby-Doo' every Saturday morning. The theme of the cartoon is always the supernatural. Shaggy and Scooby—Scooby is a big, floppy-eared Great Dane—are always scared, but I never am."

"Francis, we're not talking about cartoons here," his mother said.

"I know," Fran said. "I'm just saying that I'm quite familiar with cemeteries. For example, I know when a person dies they're often buried in the ground with a headstone that reads RIP. RIP means rest in peace, Mom. Sometimes, though, they place the body in an underground place called a crypt, and sometimes in a place called a mausoleum, which is like a little house for the dead. That's what I think this City of the Dead is, a bunch of little houses built for the dead to sleep in. But their living relatives got thrown out of their homes, so their dead ancestors had to let them move in."

Fran ended his explanation with a big grin, showing an uneven smile composed of baby teeth, empty spaces, and some adult teeth emerging at various distances from his gums. David thought he looked a little like a Jack-o-lantern when he smiled like that, but he didn't tell Fran.

"You certainly do know a lot about the subject, Fran," his mother said, "but you've never actually visited a real cemetery."

"Don't worry, Mom," he assured her. "I'm not one bit afraid."

"To tell you the truth, Francis Bacon Bernstein, I'm less concerned with how afraid you might be, and more concerned about what you might say to the people who live in a necropolis."

"What's a necropolis?" Fran asked.

"It's a large and elaborate cemetery attached to a city, like Cairo. Now, back to the subject," Mrs. Bernstein said, raising a warning finger. "I don't want you to ask questions like, 'Is there a dead body in here?' Or, 'Have you ever seen any ghosts around here?' Also, from what I read, there is a sanitation problem in the City of the Dead. There's no place to put trash, and water is limited. So, I don't want you to say something like, 'Why does it smell so funny in the City of the Dead?' In fact, Fran, I don't want you to ask any questions at all. Just be friendly, smile your beautiful smile, and that's it."

"But, Mom..."

Dr. Bernstein cut him off with a gesture. "That's it. Now, why don't you and David look for Samy and whatever vehicle he might be driving today?"

Dr. Awyan entered the Pizza Hut, looking particularly sharp in a light blue gallabiyah.

"Hello, Dr. Awyan," Fran yelled out. "We're about to visit the necropolis."

The Egyptologist smiled at the boy's enthusiasm. "Yes, I heard about your excursion. I am hoping you will find clues that will lead you to your friend."

Dr. Awyan poured himself some tea in a large blue mug. He walked over to where Jacques was sitting and slid in beside him. "It appears that you and I have become quite popular with the ladies."

Jacques stopped eating his apple slice and stared intently at the Egyptian. "What do you mean?"

"Early this morning, I received a call from Mademoiselle Fleuret," he answered. "She asked me to tell you she is flying from Luxor back to Cairo tonight. She said she had some interesting information for you about Farak and his mother. She also mentioned she was worried about you."

Mrs. Montgomery moved from the counter and stood behind Jacques and Dr. Awyan. "What kind of information?"

"I am afraid our call was interrupted, so I do not know anything more," he said. "Now, Jacques, back to the other lady. After Mademoiselle Fleuret and I were disconnected, I immediately received another call from a woman named Bernadette. She said Madame Constance had given her my number."

"Bernadette? Madame Constance?" Jacques repeated the words as if he didn't understand what Dr. Awyan was saying.

"Yes, Bernadette," the Egyptologist said. "I didn't catch her last name. She said she was flying into Cairo tonight and wondered if I had a suggestion of where she might stay. She told me to tell you she had already bought her ticket and that she would not change her mind."

Jacques' generally inscrutable face transformed. His dark eyebrows raised toward his hairline in dual arches. His deep brown eyes popped wide open. The effect gave Jacques a comical look. Mrs. Montgomery decided this Bernadette had just put a serious crack in Jacques' protective shell, and in a much more effective way than any game of chess.

"I told Ms. Bernadette that if she were a friend of yours, she was welcome to stay at the Khemitology Guest House," Dr. Awyan said. "Now, who is our mystery woman, Jacques?"

"She is a cook, or rather she is a temporary cook. Actually, she is more than just a cook," he said, color rising into his cheeks. "For the last two years, she has been hired by Madame Constance to relieve the kitchen staff at Christmas break so they can be with their families during the holidays. This year, there was only Charles, Farak, and me at the Château. We helped Bernadette decorate cookies, then made up food baskets to take to the orphanage near the school. We went sledding down Snowman's Hill during a snowstorm, and we dined together."

"Where is Bernadette when she is not at the Château du Mont?" Dr. Awyan asked, sipping his tea, and looking over his cup straight at Jacques.

"She attends a university somewhere in France," Jacques answered.

"Somewhere in France?" Dr. Awyan repeated, skepticism in his voice. "What is she studying?"

"I think literature or sociology or something," the Château du Mont's all-around man said, looking uncomfortable.

"I must say, Mr. Gerard," the older man remarked, "you have either an extreme lack of curiosity, or you need some serious assistance in communicating with women."

Mrs. Montgomery, who was listening closely to this conversation, thought this might be the understatement of the century.

"If I had time, Mr. Gerard, I would give you a little coaching, as I have quite a reputation with the ladies," Dr. Awyan said with a great laugh.

"Hey, Mom, what does the Grateful Dead mean?" Fran called out from his vantage at the window.

Everyone inside the Pizza Hut looked towards the window. There it was, the most colorful bus ever created. Every inch of the vehicle was painted in brilliant, swirling colors. It was plastered with sprawling depictions of roses, hearts, music notes, skulls, teddy bears, the head of a man with a lot of hair, and peace symbols. On the side of the bus were the words, *The Grateful Dead*. In smaller letters, it said, *Cairo, Egypt Tour, 1978*.

Dr. Bernstein gasped. When her son looked at her questioningly, she explained. "Fran, the Grateful Dead was about the most popular band on earth when I was in college. I guess I was too busy studying to know they were going to perform at the Sphinx. If I'd known, I would have done almost anything to get here."

"I was here when they came," Dr. Awyan said. "Thousands of people gathered directly across the road, right in front of the Sphinx. It was the band's Rocking the Cradle tour. They held three concerts here on three different nights. Between shows, the band and the crew would cross the road for pizza and conversation."

"You talked to the members of the Grateful Dead?" Dr. Bernstein asked, her voice filled with awe.

"They were all very nice and very interested in Khemitology, especially the band manager, Rock Robert Scully, and his wife Nicki. In fact, Nicki and I have remained friends after all this time. She usually visits at least once a year, often bringing a tour group with her."

Samy entered the Pizza Hut wearing a T-shirt tie-dyed in rainbow colors and a huge smile, followed by a grinning Aamen.

"Can you believe it? One of my cousins loaned me the Grateful Dead touring bus!" Samy exclaimed. "I was out of the country in 1978. It was a real bummer. I missed the Grateful Dead's concert held right here at the Sphinx."

"Dr. Awyan was here then!" Fran said, jumping up and down.

"Well, I didn't exactly attend the concerts, but I did enjoy meeting the band members," the Egyptian replied.

Samy gave the head of the School of Khemitology a deep bow. Mandisa signaled that Mrs. Montgomery's order was ready. She directed Jacques, Samy, and Aamen to carry five-gallon jugs of water to the bus. Meanwhile, Fran and David helped carry out baskets filled with Egyptian pizza, cheese, and fruit.

Dr. Stratton entered the Pizza Hut, asking, "Did anybody notice a rather colorful bus in front of the Pizza Hut?"

"It is our ride to the City of the Dead," Mrs. Montgomery informed the professor. "One of Samy's cousins lent him this vehicle so we can travel comfortably, especially considering we'll be bringing all these bottles and bags with us."

"What is all this?" Dr. Stratton asked.

"Food!" Fran exclaimed. "We're going to have a picnic at the City of the Dead and invite all of the people, at least all the living ones."

"Hmm. I heard there are tens of thousands of people living in the City of the Dead," Dr. Stratton said doubtfully.

"Fran is exaggerating, Dr. Stratton. Grandmother's plan is to invite the Wasims and their neighbors," David said.

"Hello, Aamen. How did you get here?" Alfred asked as he entered the blue door.

"Samy picked me up in that colorful bus. It caused a lot of commotion on the road. People were honking and waving. Samy honked his horn back at them. I waved at everybody. I almost felt like the president of Egypt," Aamen joked.

Dr. Stratton and Alfred sat down at the table. David returned from carrying a load to the bus.

"Hello, David. I was just going to ask Alfred if he recognized this," Dr. Stratton said, holding up a small silver camera.

"To answer your question, Dr. Stratton, I recognize that Leica," Alfred said softly. "It is the camera you gave Charlie on his twelfth birthday."

"Charlie?" David responded.

"We called Charles' father Charlie," Alfred said. "Charlie and I went on many photographic adventures with this camera. We had a competition going about which of us could take the best photos. Due to my work in the army, I was the more experienced photographer. However, Charlie had an eye and heart that leaped out of his photos. I learned a lot from him."

"Mademoiselle Fleuret tells everyone Charles has an eye for photography. She says he knows how to capture a story in a picture," David said. "He must have inherited this talent from his father."

"Alfred," Mr. Stratton said, "I notice you are wearing your spy camera."

"You're wearing a spy camera, Mr. Hart?" David asked in amazement.

"Now see here, Stratton, we should not be telling secrets to every Tom, Dick and Harry."

"I'm not just any Tom, Dick and Harry," David said indignantly. "I'm Charles' roommate and his best friend."

"I am sorry, David. You are correct," Alfred agreed. "You are not just anybody. It's just that, in general, one does not announce the use of a spy camera."

"What I want to say to you, Alfred," Mr. Stratton said, "is that if a quality photograph is required on our expedition, you might want to use this Leica with its famous German lens."

"I will do that, Sir," Alfred said, reaching for the camera covered in fine scratches, indicating its age and use. He secured it in the pocket of his safari jacket.

"I don't know why, but I keep remembering something Charlie said to me when he was twelve. 'When I grow up, I want to help make the world a better place.' Do you think that is what he is doing now, Dr. Stratton?"

The professor shook his head wearily. "I don't know, Alfred. Charlie's leaving was such a shock. When he left, he took only a few clothes and this camera. As you know, we thought he was dead. However, this silver camera and the boy named Charles Dayton Stratton III proves he did not die, and that I have a grandson."

"I'm sorry you feel sad, Dr. Stratton," David said sympathetically.

Alfred patted Dr. Stratton on the back, saying, "I wish you did not have to go through this."

"Me, too," David agreed. "I wish the conductor wouldn't have pushed Charles off the train."

"At first, I wished this, too, David," the professor said. "But if the conductor hadn't put Charles off the train, I wouldn't have learned that my son, Charlie, is alive, and that I have a grandson. Do you believe in fate, Alfred P. Hart?"

"I think each person must decide for him or herself whether something is coincidence or fate," Alfred answered.

"That was such an Alfredian thing to say, don't you think, David?" Dr. Stratton asked with a chuckle.

Before he could answer, Mrs. Montgomery rushed into the blue door of the Pizza Hut. "Alfred, could you take our photographs as we step into the tour bus? Without a photo, I am sure our children will never believe their parents traveled to the City of the Dead in the tour bus of the Grateful Dead."

"I would be happy to," Alfred said, pulling the small silver camera from his bush jacket.

CHAPTER 40

DANCING IN THE STREET

Please send me your last pair of shoes,
worn out with dancing
as you mentioned in your letter,
so that I might have something
to press against my heart.
Johann Wolfgang Von Goethe

A lfred was taking photos of the Grateful Dead bus. Dr. Bernstein walked outside just in time for the next shot. "Your father is going to love this picture, Fran," the physicist said, wrapping her arms around her son's shoulders. Fran stood proudly on his tiptoes in his gray gallabiyah.

After the photo of Dr. Bernstein and her son, Alfred took pictures inside the bus. Its interior was painted even more wildly than the exterior. There were peace symbols, flowers, unicorns, neon-bright teddy bears, dragons, and guitars. The autographs of the band members were integrated among these paintings. David read a name, scrawled near a window at the back of the bus, aloud: "Jerry Garcia."

"That's the lead singer of the Grateful Dead!" Dr. Bernstein said in a hushed tone.

David resumed his self-guided tour of the psychedelic bus. After a moment, he shouted to his grandmother that he'd discovered a photo and autograph of Abd'el Hakim Awyan right behind the driver's seat.

"Wow, Dr. Awyan must be famous!" Fran yelled from the backseat.

"Ready?" Samy called as he pulled the bus onto the road, motoring slowly through the Archeological Zone. Vehicles honked and tourists turned away from the pyramids, waving wildly at the famous bus. The taxi driver pushed a cassette into the player and spoke into a small round microphone attached to the instrument panel by a curly black cord.

"Ladies and gentlemen, this is one of my favorite Grateful Dead songs," Samy said in his radio announcer voice. "It's a cover of 'Dancing in the Street,' co-written by soul legend Marvin Gaye and first popularized by Martha and the Vandellas in 1964."

Callin' out around the world, are you ready for a brand-new beat?
Summer's here and the time is right for dancin' in the street.
Dancin' in Chicago (dancin' in the street).

The song went on to name a bunch of American cities where people were celebrating. Dr. Bernstein began singing along with the refrain, "dancin' in the street." Aamen, the interpreter, joined her. Alfred looked over at Dr.

Stratton and was shocked to see him moving to the beat of the music, his arms waving in the air, fingers pointing left and right.

"What are you doing?" he asked.

"Me? I'm doing what I call seat dancing," Dr. Stratton said, moving his shoulders to the rhythm. "Would you care to dance, Alfred?"

"I don't think so. This doesn't seem like the time or place," Alfred replied, staring in shock at his friend and employer, thinking the heat had gone to his head.

Dr. Stratton had rarely felt better.

"Alfred, there is something about this desert that clears my head. I would say this desert, in its simplicity, leads one to questions of what is important in life and what is not," the professor mused. "I'm not just talking about the Sphinx and the pyramids, but the Egyptians themselves. These people have so little and yet seem to live so large, working in the hot sun, then going back to family to share food and stories. It's like everything is brought down to its very essence."

"That is a good observation, Dr. Stratton," Jacques said thoughtfully.

"I've been thinking, Mr. Gerard. I've lived much of my life buried in books, in the written word, especially the words of Goethe," Dr. Stratton remarked. "I thought Goethe and I agreed that one of the most frustrating aspects of life is '*not being able to understand other people's behavior.*' However, when it comes to this moment, I'm not faced with difficulty understanding other people's behavior."

"Instead," the professor continued, "I'm confronted by the startling realization that I've failed to turn the magnifying glass towards myself, thus believing I was separate from others, even you, my dear Alfred."

"I disagree, Dr. Stratton. You have always been kind," Alfred said.

The professor ignored Alfred's protest. "I've lived my life through the words of Goethe, but I am afraid I've been selective in which of his words of wisdom I've chosen to embrace. Last night, I read this."

Dr. Stratton took out a small black notebook and began to read. *'What is more dangerous is not recognizing that you have placed yourself in solitary confinement, content to surround yourself with books, rather than breaking out to see who you can find.'*

"You have dedicated your life to your students, Dr. Stratton, introducing them to the great thinkers," Alfred said, defending his employer and friend.

Dr. Stratton shook his head. "Charlie Chaplin once said, *'We think too much and feel too little.'* As I ponder that quote, I fear I am guilty."

Alfred shook his head sympathetically. "You have endured a lot of suffering."

"It's no excuse," Mr. Stratton said. "Goethe wrote, *'There is no past we can bring back by longing for it. There is only an eternal now that builds and creates out of the past something new and better.'*

"This is what I have to do," Dr. Stratton declared. "This is what I want to do. And Goethe's quote for today is, *'Life belongs to the living, and he who lives must be prepared for changes.'* Change is what I intend to do. Then I'll be ready to become the grandfather Charles Dayton Stratton III deserves."

"Yes, Sir," Alfred responded, studying Dr. Stratton with an uneasy feeling. He wondered, if his employer and friend changed, would it be possible for him to remain the same?

At Fran's request, Samy had rewound his cassette tape and was playing "Dancing in the Street" again. In the back of the bus, David joined Dr. Bernstein and Aamen, singing the refrain "dancin' in the street." Fran was rocking back and forth, rolling his arms in front of him and singing loudly, changing the words to "dancing in my seat."

Down in New Orleans (dancin' in the street).
In New York City (dancin' in the street).
All we need is music, sweet music.
There'll be music everywhere.
There'll be swingin', swayin', and records playin'
And dancin' in the street.

The bus danced up and down as Samy pulled into a parking lot riddled with potholes. He turned off the music, and everyone stopped singing. They all stared out at a crowded jumble of tombs. They had arrived at the City of the Dead.

Samy handed Mrs. Montgomery the bus microphone.

"I thought I would make a few comments about our visit to the City of the Dead," she began. "I have to admit that, at first, I thought it would be shocking to arrive at this necropolis on a bus with the words Grateful Dead painted on its side. However, after deeper thought, I concluded that nothing could be more appropriate."

Fran raised his hand and, at the same time, yelled out, "Why would nothing be more appropriate, Mrs. Montgomery?"

"Well, Fran," Mrs. Montgomery explained, "I began to imagine that those interred in the tombs of the City of the Dead would be grateful that their very last act on earth would be to provide housing for their kinsmen—their children, their grandchildren, and other descendants. I imagined they would feel that by sharing their burial chambers, they would be remembered and appreciated for providing a place to raise families, making them indeed the grateful dead. So we should all be grateful that Samy found us such an appropriate vehicle."

The passengers on the bus clapped for their driver.

"As Fran surmised, we are going to have a picnic, a gratefulness picnic for the Wasims and their neighbors," Mrs. Montgomery said. "I cannot imagine what might have happened to Charles if these people had not helped him."

"This was an excellent idea, Dorothy," George said to his wife, and everyone on the bus agreed.

Fran said, "I love picnics, especially a picnic in a cemetery."

David looked at his young schoolmate and said, "Fran, this is serious business, not a picnic."

"But your grandmother said it was a gratefulness picnic," the younger boy protested.

Aamen walked to the front of the bus and informed Mrs. Montgomery that he'd be right back. Mrs. Montgomery told the translator they'd remain on the bus until he returned.

Holding up a large purple bag, she said, "Besides food and drink, I brought notebooks and writing supplies to give out to the children. In my travels, I have found children need and want writing supplies. So I ask all of you to help me distribute these. However, if you don't have a notebook with you, keep one for yourself to write down all thoughts you might have or clues you might discover on our visit to the City of the Dead. Now, I will turn the mic over to Dr. Bernstein."

The physicist tapped the mic. "Hello, can you hear me?"

"I can hear you, Mom," Fran said from the back of the bus.

"I just wanted to remind you. While we're having a picnic and looking for clues, take some time to see if you can communicate with Charles, or see if you can visualize where he might be," Dr. Bernstein advised. "When I use visualization as a tool for remembering or thinking about something, I find it helpful to take several deep breaths. Then I close my eyes and focus on what I want to discover, see, or hear."

"I think I see something, Mom," Fran said, eyes squeezed tightly shut.

Before Fran could expand on what he was seeing, Aamen walked up the steps of the bus. Behind him was an excited group of teens, ready and willing to carry the picnic supplies back to the Wasims' tomb-home.

"Fran, do not forget what you just saw," Mrs. Montgomery called out. "Maybe you could write it in a notebook. Tonight, after Jacques, Samy and Alfred pick up Bernadette and Mademoiselle Fleuret at the Cairo Airport, we'll have dinner and a meeting to share clues and information."

Fran exited the tour bus of the Grateful Dead just behind Jacques. "Did you see anything, Jacques, when Mrs. Montgomery asked us to visualize?"

"No, I didn't see anything, Fran," Jacques said.

"Mom says you're the person with the strongest connection to Charles, so you'll most likely be the one that finds him. Maybe you should visualize harder," Fran advised with a huge grin.

CHAPTER 41

LIVING IN THE CITY OF THE DEAD

The passengers of the Grateful Dead bus followed Aamen and eight local teens proudly carrying bags and baskets. The parade greeted elders gathered in doorways or sitting on metal chairs at the edge of the pathway. They passed by kids playing soccer between the headstones of the less fortunate dead, those who could not afford a building in which to transition from worldly life to the afterlife. Some of the mausoleums were crumbling away, shored up with wood planks. Some were painted bright colors, while others were what Fran called "grave-color gray." They could hear women talking and babies crying or laughing.

"Mom," Fran said in a loud voice, "This doesn't look like the City of the Dead. It looks more like the City of the Living."

His mother smiled down at her son and said quietly, "I didn't expect the City of the Dead to look like this either, Fran. These small houses are teeming with people doing ordinary things, like drinking tea and sweeping the walkways, and extraordinary things like making and selling artwork to visitors. Last night, I read that many Egyptians treat the citizens of this necropolis like pariahs. I'm certain those who feel that way never set one foot here."

"What does pariah mean?" Fran asked.

His mother whispered, "Pariah means outcast or an undesirable person."

"I think I see one," Fran whispered back.

An old man sitting in the doorway of a crumbling tomb-home signaled to Fran, smiling a nearly toothless grin. He laughed at the sight of the red-headed boy wearing a tan gallabiyah, while most of the children in the City of the Dead were in T-shirts and shorts.

Fran broke away from his mother and approached the old Egyptian, who was also wearing a tan gallabiya. Alfred used Charles' Leica to snap a photo of the unlikely pair in matching garb. The man shook hands with the boy, then reached into a side pocket in his robe. He gave Fran a pendant that was about two inches long and eighteen inches in diameter. It was silver and cut in a beautiful pattern of curved lines weaving in and out of each other. Behind the filigree design, the artist had placed an iridescent abalone shell. The blue, lavender, and pink colors of the shell seemed to move as Fran held the pendant up to the sun. The boy smiled at the old man, showing his own jagged teeth. He tried to give the pendant back, but the Egyptian shook his head, signaling that it was a gift. Fran bowed his head a little, thanked him, and ran back to his mother.

"Mom, I was wrong," Fran said, holding up the pendant by its chain. "That wasn't a pariah. It was a very kind man, and he gave me this."

Dr. Bernstein examined the stunning silver pendant, then waved at the man still smiling his toothless smile. Fran's mother slipped the pendant over his head. It lay against his gallabiya, glinting in the soft morning light.

"What a wonderful gift," Dr. Bernstein said. "I don't just mean this pendant, Fran, but also the lesson we must never forget. Never judge a book by it cover."

"What do you mean, Mom?"

"That's an old saying that means one shouldn't judge people by how they look or where they live," she said. "Come on, Fran. Let's catch up with the others."

As the teens hurried on to the Wasims' house, Aamen became the guest house visitors' tour guide. "Today we are visiting the Al Qarafat, or the Grand Cemetery, founded in 642 CE. This cemetery has grown and grown until there are now four square miles of tombs, set very close together as you can all observe."

Everyone took a moment to look around. Dr. Stratton used a pair of old-fashioned field glasses to take in the bustling and panoramic scene.

"The Northern Cemetery includes the Mosque of Qaitbey, completed in 1474 CE," Aamen continued. "It is said to be the pinnacle of Islamic architecture in Cairo. For many, it is considered one of the most artful and sacred buildings in the city. Many people have declare that to fail to visit this wonderful site would be a grave mistake."

Fran burst out laughing. "I get it, a grave mistake."

Dr. Bernstein gave Fran a slight frown.

Aamen continued. "In fact, to earn my way through college, I myself have led many tours to the Mosque of Qaitbey. But now, as you know, I am focused on becoming a translator for the American Embassy. I do not have as much time to pursue my touring business."

"As soon as we find Charles, we'd love to have a tour of this mosque, wouldn't we, Grandfather?" David said. Mr. Montgomery agreed.

"Mom and I want to tour the Mosque of Qaitbey, too. As soon as we find Charles, of course," Fran said, looking at David.

Aamen continued his talk. "The Wasims live here in the Western Cemetery. You can recognize this area by those hills over there, the Mokkattam Hills. We call them Cairo's Mountains."

"I don't see any mountains, just those hills over there," Fran said.

"Myself, I have not seen what is called a real mountain like Mt. Everest, but I hope to do so someday. Meanwhile, those hills are our mountains," Aamen replied. "To continue, there is another small cemetery, north of the area near Bab al Nasr, that many tourists like to visit. It is near one of three ancient military gates built to protect the old city. As I am still paying my way through university, I offer my services to tour groups at a very reasonable price." The young interpreter smiled broadly.

Fran raised his hand. "Do people still get buried here? I mean, the newly dead?"

"Yes, this is a living cemetery, an expanding cemetery," Aamen said. "The ordinary people of Cairo and even the old families, the royal families, choose to be placed here when they leave their worldly life. There are funerals in the different cemeteries every day."

"I hope we get to see a funeral before we have to leave," Fran said. Dr. Bernstein bopped her son softly on the head, frowning at him.

"When we debarked from that wild bus, I saw a number of policemen as well as representatives from several embassies," Mr. Montgomery said. "Where are they now?"

"Oh, George, I suggested they stay at the parking area, at least until we first greet the Wasim family and their neighbors," his wife answered. "I thought everyone would be more comfortable and talkative without officials around."

"That was thoughtful of you, Dorothy," George said to the woman in the straw helmet with the purple flower on its rim.

As the group neared their destination, men, women, and children from the Western Cemetery gathered behind the visitors, talking excitedly among themselves. Aamen, dressed in his western clothes, abandoned his tour guide voice, taking on a more personal tone.

"I have asked Mrs. Montgomery if she would like to speak to Mr. and Mrs. Wasim inside their house," Aamen said. "As it is a very compact home, we cannot all fit inside. I have selected Mrs. Montgomery as our representative, because she seems quite good at asking questions. Do you not agree?"

Everyone agreed. Mrs. Montgomery asked if there was room for one more, expressing the belief that Jacques should also speak with the Wasims. "After all," she pointed out, "he is Charles' guardian for this trip."

A twenty-minute hike brought the guest house group to the spot where the teens had put down the baskets. Aamen knocked at a blue door on the right side of the path. The door opened a crack and the young interpreter disappeared inside. The four Wasim children came out smiling, as Aamen must have told them about the gratitude picnic.

"I will direct the neighbors to set up for a grand picnic, and then I will introduce you to Mr. and Mrs. Wasim," the interpreter said. "They were relieved to learn you did not blame them for Charles' disappearance and, in fact, wish to express your gratefulness that they had cared for young Charles."

Looking around, Dr. Stratton said to Alfred, "Since we stepped foot in this cemetery, I keep thinking about one of Goethe's quotes. He said, *'Music is liquid architecture; architecture is frozen music.'* Isn't that beautiful, Alfred? However, being here, I can't help but think that architecture is frozen history. It's not just empty buildings or a place to bury the dead, but rather a place filled with thousands and thousands of stories."

"I understand what you are saying, professor," Alfred said. "You know, Mrs. Montgomery has asked me to take some photos."

"Yes, with your spy camera," Dr. Stratton replied. "It's an excellent idea."

"I'll use the spy camera when I need to be discreet. When I want to capture a moment like any tourist, I'll use the Leica you have loaned me. With any luck, I'll come away with some good images suggesting life in the City of the Dead," Alfred said.

"More importantly, I hope to find and photograph clues as to where Charles might have gone," he continued. "Like you, I cannot stop thinking about our Charlie. I feel as though I need him here, to help me capture the souls of these people who live their lives in tombs. It is quite shocking and quite inspiring, isn't it?"

"Yes, it is, Alfred," Dr. Stratton said, wiping some dust out of his eyes with a green handkerchief.

A handful of boys approached David and Fran, carrying a decrepit-looking soccer ball. With no need for an interpreter, a game was afoot. The boys were kicking the ball in and around the various headstones.

"Grandpa, my teammates at the Château du Mont aren't going to believe I actually played soccer in Egypt, in a cemetery," David said, kicking the ball around an eight-foot-tall headstone.

"I must say, David, considering the condition of their equipment and the constraints of their playing fields, these youngsters are quite accomplished," Mr. Montgomery said, kicking at the ball that bounced in front of him.

Before setting off on his mission, Alfred snapped some photos of the game and the neighbors as they brought out tables and chairs and set them up in the middle of the path. Walking away from the commotion, Alfred soon found himself gratefully alone. Since he'd arrived in Cairo, things had been hectic, to say the least. Maybe he could think, imagine, what could have happened to Charlie's son.

Alfred was convinced Charles had traveled this same route the night he disappeared. The path between the tomb-homes may have once been smooth, but it was now rough-going, full of missing and crumbling stones. This required the photographer to carefully watch his step, all the while looking for clues. But what kind of clues, he asked himself?

Since there was no one around, Alfred took out the Leica to capture some quality photographs of this deserted part of the Western Cemetery. He felt a pang of sorrow as he recalled the many adventures he and young Charlie had photographed over the years, sorrow he'd thought was successfully buried. As young Charlie grew older, the boy became a friend. Alfred should have guessed that Charlie was unhappy and was likely to do something drastic, something incomprehensible. Now, Charlie's son seemed to be following in his father's footsteps, doing something incomprehensible.

Out of the corner of his eye, Alfred thought he saw something move. He slipped the silver camera back into his jacket pocket and prepared his spy camera. He could swear he saw a shadowy form in front of him. It was indistinct, but seemed to dart from one side of the tomb-homes to the other. Alfred felt as though he were being encouraged to follow.

At one point, the shadow appeared to take the shape of an arm pointing to someone or something. Alfred snapped as many photos as he could with his spy camera while walking swiftly as possible on uneven ground.

The sun had climbed to its apex in the sky, and its rays pounded down on Alfred's hat. What he'd thought was a human figure disappeared, if it had existed at all. He stopped to catch his breath. Looking forward, Alfred realized he'd reached the end of the cemetery. A few hundred feet ahead, there was nothing but yellowish sand mixed in with dirt and rocks of various sizes. There were no plants, no people, no shadows, and no tombs.

Alfred glanced at the sky again. The scorching sun seemed to have stolen the color from the sky, leaving it a bland grayish-white. Alfred took out the Leica again, but he couldn't see anything he wanted to photograph, and anyway he was beginning to feel woozy. Why hadn't he brought water? He needed to get back to the gratitude picnic. Snapping a few photos as he left, Alfred headed west. This time, he didn't encounter any shadowy forms.

***

Back at the Wasims' tomb-home, Jacques and Mrs. Montgomery—with the help of Aamen—thanked Mr. Wasim for saving Charles' life and Mrs. Wasim for taking such good care of him during his recuperation. Before they walked outside, Aamen told Jacques and Mrs. Montgomery that Charles had carried a shoulder bag with him, but he'd left nothing behind. He reiterated that he'd assumed Charles was with the Wasims, and the Wasims had assumed Charles was with him. No one in the neighborhood had any idea where Charles had gone.

The talk was over. Leaving the tomb-home, Mrs. Montgomery smiled as she saw tables filled with flatbread pizza and fruit. Something wasn't right, however. It was as though a miracle had occurred. There was much more food and drink on the tables than they'd brought on the bus this morning. Looking around, Mrs. Montgomery spied a tall Egyptian. It was the founder of the School of Khemitology and his son Yousef. Evidently, they'd brought even more pizza, fruit and water from the Pizza Hut.

The policemen and agents from the embassies accepted Dr. Awyan's invitation to the gratefulness picnic. They'd helped carry the bundles the Awyans had brought with them to the Wasims' home. There was a clamor of happiness in the City of the Dead, with kids playing, the adults laughing, and everyone eating. Alfred joined the picnic. He caught the attention of Mrs. Montgomery and explained that, while he'd taken photos with both his spy camera and Charles' Leica, he doubted he'd been able to capture any clues or anything of interest.

"That may or may not be so, Mr. Hart," Mrs. Montgomery replied. "However, please allow me to take your film to Dr. Awyan. I am sure he knows how we can get the film developed."

As she headed towards Dr. Awyan, Mrs. Montgomery was filled with gratefulness. For some reason, she felt they were close, very close, to discovering the whereabouts of Charles Dayton Stratton III.

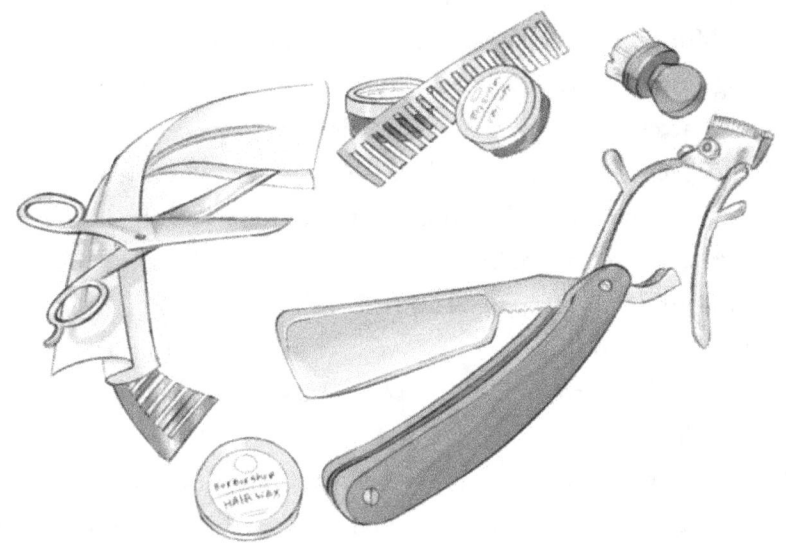

CHAPTER 42

CUT-THROAT SHAVE AND A HAIRCUT

As Jacques emerged from his quarters, Fran asked him, "What happened to your hair?"

"Francis Bacon!" his mother snapped. "You don't say things like that."

"Sorry, Mom," Fran said, still staring at Jacques. "What if I say, 'Mr. Gerard, you look different?' Would that be better?"

"I look different, Fran, because Alfred cut my hair and gave me my very first straight-edge shave," the Chateau's all-around man said.

Fran studied Jacques, musing. "Yeah, but why does your hair look longer than it did before it was cut, like it's puffed up or something?"

"Alfred suggested I give hair gel a try rather than my usual pomade," he answered casually.

"You look handsome, Jacques," Dr. Bernstein said with an encouraging smile.

"Yeah, you look younger," Fran added.

Mrs. Montgomery came down the stairs wearing tan slacks and a matching bush jacket. She wore no hat, her blondish hair instead held back by a barrette with a large lavender flower attached.

"Hello, Jacques. I see you've had a little visit with Alfred," she said with a bright smile. "I read somewhere that, 'To make a fine gentleman, several trades are required, but chiefly a barber.' You look ready."

Jacques appeared puzzled. "Ready for what?"

"I have arranged for Samy to drive you and Alfred to the airport to pick up Ms. Bernadette from Air France and Mademoiselle Fleuret from Egyptian Air."

"You are not coming?" Jacques asked with raised eyebrows.

"I believe you two boys can handle things, and I have quite a lot to do here," Mrs. Montgomery said.

Alfred walked into the small living room where everyone had gathered. He was dressed in a pressed white shirt, black tie, a pinstripe jacket, black pants, and black shoes with a mirror-shine.

The butler-turned-barber said, "We can certainly handle this mission on our own, don't you think, Jacques, old boy?"

Mrs. Montgomery greeted him warmly. "Hello, Alfred P. Hart. It appears you have taken to cleaning up the gentlemen of the guest house in preparation for the arrival of our young women. You use a straight-edge razor, I presume?"

"What's a straight-edge razor?" Fran asked.

Alfred answered, "The straight-edge has been around since the days of the Old West. It has a long sharp blade that can fold into its handle. It's called an open razor or a cut-throat razor. Few people use it nowadays."

"A cut-throat razor," Fran repeated. "Wow! What a great name. I am going to ask Dad if he can get one."

"I read somewhere that a straight-edge razor gives you a clean-shaven mug the ladies love, so you look perfect for picking up your girl," Mrs. Montgomery said, looking at Jacques.

Jacques frowned. "She is not my girl. She is just a friend."

"Yes, a girl who is just a friend and is flying from France to Egypt to support you," Mrs. Montgomery scoffed. "I believe those were her exact words."

Jacques looked uncomfortable. Alfred cleared his throat.

"Back to the subject of the cut-throat razor. I learned the use of the straight-edge razor in the army, and I haven't since resorted to those so-called safety razors," he expounded. "And please don't speak to me about electric razors. They require two shaves a day, minimum."

Jacques adopted a country drawl—choppy and slow—and rubbed his chin. "I've never had a closer shave in my entire life, not even during a high-noon standoff with a local gunslinger. I'm mighty appreciative to you, Alfred."

The room erupted in applause.

"You sound like a real cowboy!" Fran exclaimed, delighted. "You should talk that way all the time. It makes you more interesting!"

"Fran!" his mother said with a frown.

Jacques flushed and grew quiet. His face returned to its usual impassive expression.

"As I was saying," Mrs. Montgomery said, straightening her barrette, "I've arranged for Samy to pick you gentlemen up and drive to the airport, where you will meet the young women. I am so anxious to hear what Mademoiselle Fleuret has to say about her visit with Farak's family."

"I have more news for you, Alfred P. Hart," she continued. "Dr. Awyan says the film you took in the City of the Dead should be developed by the time you return. He has promised to have the prints delivered here to the guest house. Considering the cramped dimensions of this charming sitting room, I have arranged for the Pizza Hut to stay open after dinner for a meeting tonight."

Alfred straightened his wine-colored handkerchief, which had been folded into a crisp triangle and placed in his jacket pocket. "I wonder what kind of vehicle Samy will be driving tonight? I must say, he is a very interesting character."

"Yes, he's definitely a character. Quite unexpected." Mrs. Montgomery sat down in one of the green overstuffed chairs, staring through the window at the tourist-mobbed Sphinx.

"I am afraid Charles was immediately suspicious of this Egyptian man in a Hawaiian shirt, driving a new-model Cadillac with a handwritten sign saying, 'Taxi, American spoken.' But then," Jacques said, "Charles seemed to be suspicious about almost everyone he met on this trip. And Samy has been very helpful since, since ..."

Jacques' voice faded out.

"Being suspicious is kind of Charles' character," David offered. "I think it's because he doesn't really have a family. No offense, Dr. Stratton. Charles doesn't even know you exist. His parents are always traveling somewhere: North Africa, South Africa, Central America, you name it."

Dr. Bernstein shook her head. "I find that sad."

"Charles doesn't know why they go on these trips," David continued. "His parents have visited only once since he came to the Château du Mont a year-and-a-half ago. They came separately, and didn't even stay the night. Charles says someday he's going to run away and join a circus. That's why Fran and Charles are taking gymnastics with Coach Endres at the Château du Mont."

Fran looked astounded. "Really? We're going to join a circus? Charles never told me. Mom, I'm going to join a circus as soon as I get better at gymnastics."

"We'll see, Fran," his mother said.

"You have to admit, Grandmother, that you also have a tendency towards suspicion. I think Samy's been quite helpful," David said.

"Yes, David, Samy has proven to be very helpful," Mrs. Montgomery said. "On this, we can all agree."

"I think Samy is super-cool," Fran said. "He's going to teach me how to surf."

David looked skeptical. "How? I don't see any ocean near here."

"Oh, we plan on meeting back in California, near Santa Monica—once Charles is found, of course," the ginger-haired boy explained. "That would be okay, wouldn't it, Mom?"

"It would be quite a coincidence for us to meet up with Samy in Santa Monica, considering he lives here in Egypt," the dark-haired physicist said. "However, it is not beyond the realm of possibility. Samy claims he went to UCLA, one of the universities your father speaks at for various events."

David held both hands out to his side in amazement. "Claimed? Dr. Bernstein, you're beginning to sound as suspicious as my grandmother."

"Maybe your parents would let you come to California, David. Charles could come, too. Samy could teach us all how to surf," Fran said, crouched down, arms out to his sides, pretending he was balancing on a surfboard.

"Fran and David, why don't you go look for Samy?" Mrs. Montgomery suggested. "Heaven knows what he might be driving this time."

"Oh, Mrs. Montgomery," Fran yelled out, "I believe this time Samy is driving a donkey cart."

"What!" Mrs. Montgomery and Dr. Bernstein called in unison, running towards the window.

"Just kidding," the redheaded imp said. "He's still in the Grateful Dead touring bus."

George came downstairs, doing a double-take when he spotted Alfred and Jacques. "Well, sirs, you seem to be all dolled up. Where are you going, Alfred? I thought it was my turn for the straight-edge razor."

Fran corrected him. "You mean the cut-throat razor, Mr. Montgomery, and they're picking up their girls at the airport."

Jacques looked startled.

"Do you think the two young women can manage Alfred and Jacques?" asked George, giving his wife a little hug.

"I'd give a lot to be a fly on the wall, just to observe this rendezvous," Mrs. Montgomery answered, watching as the two men saluted Samy and boarded the touring bus.

"Hey, dudes. Boys' night out?" Samy asked. He was wearing a tie-dyed Grateful Dead shirt evoking the hippie era.

"We are picking up two women at the airport," Alfred said.

"Just two?" Samy asked with a toothy smile.

CHAPTER 43

HERE COMES THE SUN

Jacques took a seat behind Samy. Alfred slid into the front passenger seat. As the bus passed the Great Pyramid, Jacques was jolted back to the first time he and Charles visited the Giza Plateau. He recalled his terrifying ascent onto the back of a camel, their meeting with Dr. Awyan, and how happy Charles was to be invited inside the Great Pyramid of Giza.

How could Jacques have guessed he would soon lose the boy he'd agreed to guard, to keep safe? Madame Constance was right. He wasn't prepared to take care of a child in a place as exotic as Egypt, especially a boy like Charles.

It was too late now. He'd lost him not once but twice, and everyone knew it. Now, they were picking up Bernadette at the airport. Bernadette! The woman he'd failed to contact after she left her Christmas holiday position at the Château du Mont. And now, she was coming to help him find the boy he'd lost.

Jacques' attention turned back to the bus, where Alfred was questioning their driver.

"May I ask you, Mr. Samy, how you became involved in the disappearance of young Charles Stratton?"

"I met Jacques and Charles in front of the Cairo Airport as they were looking for a ride to the Mena House," Samy answered, dodging a rickety donkey wagon.

"I must say, your costume is rather unusual for an Egyptian taxi driver," Alfred remarked. "You are Egyptian, are you not, Mr. Samy?"

"I would prefer if you just called me Samy, Mr. Hart. Yes, I'm Egyptian," he answered. "I don't generally wear this admittedly showy Grateful Dead shirt."

Jacques considered mentioning that Samy's array of Hawaiian shirts was even more flamboyant, but he didn't.

"I thought the shirt was appropriate, considering I'm driving the Grateful Dead's famous tour bus," Samy said, returning a honk from a van beside the bus. "I feel my getup helps me blend in with this colorful vehicle."

"Yes, I can see that," Alfred agreed. "You blend in like a chameleon, if anyone can be said to blend into this amazing piece of movable art. It's certainly kind of you to stop your work as a taxi driver to help all of us looking for Charles. I heard you were traveling on the same train as Charles and Jacques when the boy was put off the train by that conductor. It was the night train to Luxor, I believe."

Jacques wondered what Alfred was hinting at. Or was he doing more than hinting? Samy had been six cars ahead of their first-class cabin. He couldn't have had anything to do with the conductor putting his young charge off the train. Furthermore, everyone at the Khemitology Guest House agreed that from the moment Charles went missing, Samy had shown genuine concern and been helpful to everyone searching for him. Jacques concluded that some people were just born suspicious, like Charles, Mrs. Montgomery and, now, Mr. Alfred P. Hart.

Jacques recalled some words Mrs. Montgomery had uttered the day before. It was another of her quotes, this one by someone named Mason Cooley. *'Suspicion is the beginning of wisdom and of madness.'*

Who could forget such a statement? And who would want to be suspicious if there were a chance it might lead to madness?

Jacques wondered if Mrs. Montgomery was hinting that he should become more perceptive, more aware of the people and things around him. Then again, Jacques was a loner, as he was beginning to perceive. Loners don't generally need to be suspicious, because they make sure they're usually alone.

Jacques wasn't alone anymore, though. Now there was the complication of Bernadette. This line of thought was very confusing, so Jacques turned his attention to the scenery.

As the tour bus entered the freeway, it attracted more and more attention. Samy ended his conversation with several honks, then reached over and pushed a cassette into the player. He called out, "This song was written by George Harrison of the Beatles. It's one of my favorite songs, simple enough that even I can sing along."

Between the ancient sound system and Samy's loud vocalizing, the Fab Four's optimistic hit filled the bus.

Little darling, it's been a long cold lonely winter.
Little darling, it feels like years since it's been here.
Here comes the sun, doo-dun-doo-doo.
Here comes the sun, and I say,
It's all right.
Little darling, the smile's returning to their faces.
Little darling, it seems like years since it's been here.
Sun, Sun, Sun, here it comes.

Sun, Sun, Sun, here it comes.

As he sang, Samy honked back at people who recognized the touring bus of the Grateful Dead. At the end of the song, he turned off the music and craned his head to look at Alfred.

"Did you discover anything that could lead us to Charles in the City of the Dead this afternoon?" he asked.

Glad Samy's eyes were back on the road, Alfred described how he'd been trying to take photos with his spy camera while walking in unfamiliar and uneven territory. He was quiet a moment and then made an admission. He told Samy and Jacques that he'd seen—or thought he had seen—a faint vision of a woman dressed in black from head-to-toe through his camera lens.

"She seemed to be trying to point out someone or something, but I couldn't be sure she was even real," Alfred said. "I am hoping I was able to capture something on film. Dr. Awyan says the film should be developed and back at the Khemitology Guest House by the time we return from the airport."

"I've heard a few ghost stories about the Western Cemetery over the years," Samy said. "I'll be interested to see what you captured on film. And now, gentlemen, I must take the Grateful Dead touring bus back to my friend. After that, I'll come back to the Pizza Hut. I'd like to take a look at these photos, if that's alright with you. I am familiar with the City of the Dead, as one of my cousins lives there. One can always use an extra set of eyes, right?"

"It is alright with me," Jacques responded. He wondered again just how many cousins their taxi driver had.

Samy drove up to the front entrance of the Cairo International Airport. As Jacques and Alfred left the bus, people began circling the color-fully-painted vehicle. There were people in saris, business suits, torn jeans, gallabiyah, and even a man in a kilt. Samy was in his element, sharing trivia about the long-nosed bus and telling the travelers about the Grateful Dead's concerts at the Sphinx in 1978. Jacques and Alfred walked inside the airport. Bernadette's plane was due to land first. The two men watched people come and go through the door to Customs. Shining like the sun, a tall young woman in sunglasses and a bright yellow dress emerged.

"I believe this is Bernadette," Jacques said to Alfred.

"You didn't tell me she was a movie star," Alfred said, staring at the woman with hair the color of rich coffee with a touch of golden cream, her hair in soft, loose curls.

"Believe me, she did not look like that last Christmas," Jacques said. "She looked more—natural, more sensible."

"Natural? Sensible?" Alfred scoffed. "That is how you describe this beautiful woman walking straight towards you?"

The woman recognized Jacques and called out to him from fifteen feet away. "Jacques, I came as soon as I heard about Charles. You must be worried sick."

Alfred could see that Bernadette was going to hug Jacques, who was in the process of stepping away from her embrace. Thinking quickly, he stepped behind Jacques, pressing his shoulder against the younger man's back, making it impossible for him to escape the comforting embrace.

Peeking from behind Jacques, Alfred said, "I am a friend of Dr. Stratton, Charles' grandfather. My name is Alfred P. Hart."

"Hello, Mr. Hart. I had no idea that Charles had a grandfather. He never mentioned him. Did he mention him to you, Jacques?"

"No, he did not. Dr. Stratton informed us that he did not even know he had a grandson until the FBI came and told him Charles was lost in Cairo."

"The FBI? How odd," Bernadette said, shaking her head in disbelief, adding, "Pleased to meet you, Mr. Hart."

"Have you ever met Mademoiselle Fleuret?" Jacques asked the woman in yellow.

"Yes, I did meet her once or twice. I found her delightful. And I liked her even more when Mademoiselle Fleuret told me she considered Charles a great photographer. Any friend of Charles is a friend of mine." Bernadette flashed a smile that made Jacques look harder for her luggage, which she'd informed him had yellow ribbons tied on their handles.

"Mademoiselle Fleuret is coming in from Luxor. Her plane will land on the other side of the airport," Alfred explained, helping load Bernadette's luggage onto a cart.

Bernadette, Jacques, and Alfred crossed over to the right side of the busy airport where the local flights landed their prop planes. They found Mademoiselle Fleuret standing beside her red suitcase wearing her pink tennis shoes with yellow shoestrings, a full circle floral skirt, a red artist's smock, and a yellow scarf that held back her auburn hair. She was also wearing a rather large necklace made of turquoise and coral in the shape of an Egyptian scarab.

Mademoiselle Fleuret waved at Jacques. Alfred could not help but notice the five rings on her right hand. Her round, black-rimmed glasses accented her large green eyes. Her mouth, with its tastefully applied red lipstick, was turned up in a tremendous smile. Alfred had never seen anyone who looked like her in his entire life.

"Are you sure she is a teacher at the Château du Mont? She doesn't look like a teacher to me," Alfred whispered to Jacques.

Still waving at Jacques, the art teacher picked up her red suitcase and walked towards the two men standing by the woman in yellow. When she reached the group, Mademoiselle Fleuret turned and said, "I've met you before. You work during Christmas break at the Château du Mont, don't you? I spoke to you a couple of times. If I remember correctly, you attend college during most of the year, but for the last couple of years you filled in for the kitchen staff on winter break, allowing them to be home with their families for the holidays. That is so nice of you. Your name is Bernadette, isn't it? I don't remember your last name. As some of my friends do, you may call me Antoinette or Nettie. I am happy you have come to help find Charles."

"I think he is a dear boy. Last Christmas, there were only the four of us at the Château du Mont: Charles, Farak, Jacques, and me. We made baskets for the orphans, decorated holiday cookies, and played in the snow. We had a lot of fun, and we all became very good friends," Bernadettet said, looking directly at Jacques.

"Bernadette is a great cook," Jacques said, examining Mademoiselle Fleuret's pink shoes with yellow shoestrings.

Alfred wanted to kick Jacques for his stupid response, but restrained himself. The all-around man changed the subject, speaking formally to the newcomers.

"I would like to introduce you to Mr. Alfred P. Hart," Jacques said. "He is a friend of Dr. Stratton, Charles' grandfather. Mademoiselle Fleuret, you met the professor before leaving for Luxor."

"Oh, yes, Dr. Stratton is a charming man. I am happy to meet you, Mr. Hart."

Jacques, obviously more comfortable when he wasn't the subject of a conversation, continued his introduction. "Alfred flew in from the United States to support Dr. Stratton. He knew Charles' father as a boy."

"We could all use a little support, could we not, Mr. Hart?" Mademoiselle Fleuret said. She grasped Alfred's right hand with both of her own, and shook it with great enthusiasm.

"Nice to meet you, Mademoiselle Fleuret," Alfred said with a slight bow. "Our transportation is out front."

When they walked out the terminal's door, they saw the colorful bus was surrounded by more than twenty travelers. Mademoiselle Fleuret stared at the Grateful Dead bus in amazement, then joined the throng walking around the vehicle, adorned with hundreds of colorful designs and symbols.

When the art teacher reached the door, she looked inside, exclaiming, "You must be kidding! Samy, are you really driving this Grateful Dead touring bus? I absolutely love it!"

She jumped up the three steps and sat behind Samy, saying, "Now tell me everything you know about this bus. Obviously, it belonged to the band the Grateful Dead."

Samy never looked happier as he explained the particulars of the old bus. He told her about the artist who'd painted the vehicle inside and out, pointing out Dr. Awyan's photo on the back of the driver's seat. Then Samy described the Grateful Dead's three performances at the Sphinx. He ended with, "Unfortunately, I was in the United States attending classes at UCLA. I missed the greatest event ever held on the Giza Plateau, at least in modern times."

"Wow! I am sorry you missed it. I missed it too," the art teacher said mournfully.

Samy turned the key, then leaned over and pushed a tape of the Grateful Dead into the player. Mademoiselle Fleuret, her voice amplified by the microphone and the speakers, joined Samy in singing "Dancing in the Streets."

The two sang with gusto, over and over, until they reached the Archeological Zone. Samy drove to the Pizza Hut and made a U-turn.

Mademoiselle Fleuret jumped out of the bus and ran to the blue door. Seeing Mrs. Montgomery inside, she called out, "Have you heard anything about Charles yet?"

Mrs. Montgomery turned towards the art teacher. Bernadette, followed by Jacques and Alfred, entered the restaurant.

Turning back towards Bernadette, the art teacher said apologetically, "I should have introduced you first. Bernadette, this is Mrs. Montgomery, David's grandmother and professional sleuth."

"I am happy to meet you, Ms. Bernadette. Hello, Mademoiselle Fleuret, that was quite an introduction." Turning back to the woman in yellow, she said, "You look like the afternoon sun. Don't you agree, Jacques?"

But as Mrs. Montgomery turned to look closer at the man with the new haircut and cut-throat shave, she found him exiting the blue door of the Pizza Hut.

"Oh, I see, Samy and Jacques are now intently carrying your suitcases into the guest house. To answer your question, Mademoiselle Fleuret, unfortunately we have not had any news. However, we will soon have Alfred's photographs from today's visit to the the City of the Dead. That was the last place where Charles was seen."

"I wish I could have been with you," the art teacher said sincerely.

"You were doing important work, Mademoiselle Fleuret. I am anxious to hear your report. We will have a brief meeting before dinner."

"You and I are going to be sharing a room across from Mrs. Montgomery and Dr. Bernstein's room, second floor. I will show it to you, Bernadette. We will back soon, Mrs. Montgomery."

Alfred, Bernadette, and the art teacher stepped out the door. It was strangely quiet. A few bats darted around the Pizza Hut sign, catching mosquitoes and moths. There was a half-moon surrounded by a sprinkle of stars.

"I can't believe I am here, Alfred," Bernadette confided. "Everything happened so fast. Marie, one of the cooks at the Château du Mont, called me and said she couldn't believe that Jacques lost Charles. I immediately called Madame Constance to get the details, and now here I am on Giza Plateau, across the street from the Sphinx. Alfred, where do you think Charles Dayton Stratton III is right this moment?"

"I don't know, but I have this feeling that he is on an adventure of his own choosing."

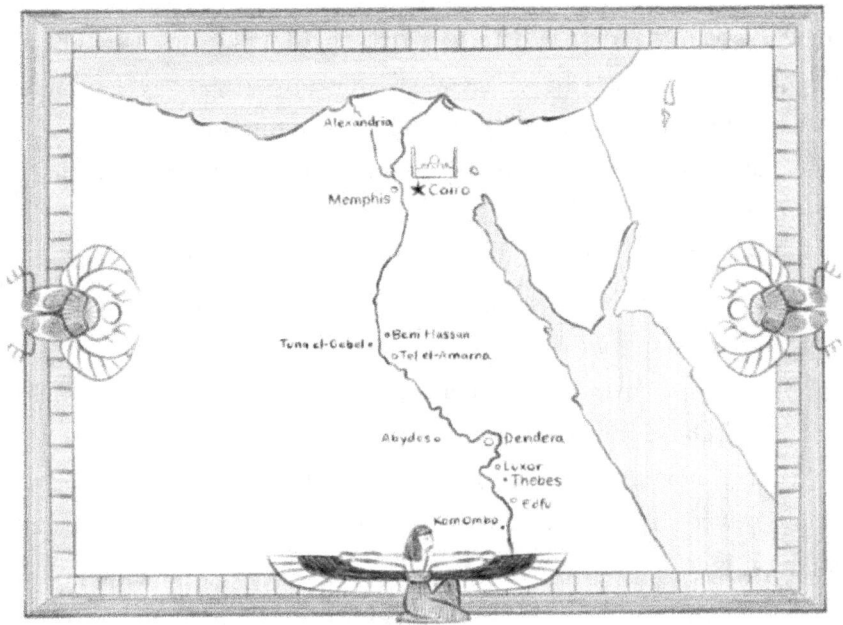

CHAPTER 44

THE ART TEACHER'S STORY AND THE EXPERIMENT

Dr. Bernstein walked into the Pizza Hut. She greeted Mrs. Montgomery, who was sitting at a back table looking at her notes. A few minutes later, George Montgomery and Dr. Stratton walked into the restaurant, each carrying two large paper bags, looking quite pleased with themselves.

"What have you got there?" Mrs. Montgomery asked.

"Chinese food, my dear woman," George said jovially. "A brand-new Chinese restaurant has opened in the town of Giza, and we thought a little variation in the meal department was called for."

Mrs. Montgomery looked at Mandisa, standing behind the counter.

"Don't worry," George said. "I asked Dr. Awyan to tell Mandisa she doesn't have to cook for us tonight; instead, we want her to join us for dinner. When Dr. Awyan told her we were bringing in Chinese food, she was delighted. Mandisa says she's never tasted Chinese food before. If I know her, she'll be adding chop suey to the Pizza Hut menu tomorrow."

"That was very sweet of you and Dr. Stratton," his wife said, beaming. "I expect everyone is starving."

Fran and David slammed open the Pizza Hut door. "You should have seen David on the soccer field this afternoon, Mom!" Fran exclaimed. "I think he's going to be famous someday."

"My grandparents were both famous soccer players, so it kind of runs in the family," David said, looking at his grandfather.

"I don't know about my being famous, but David's grandmother is a very famous soccer player," Mr. Montgomery said, standing a bit straighter and smiling at Fran.

"I didn't realize that you could play soccer when you're old," Fran said.

"Francis Bacon Bernstein, we don't say things like that. It's rude," his mother said, pursing her lips.

"Sorry. I should have asked, 'What team do you belong to, Mrs. Montgomery?' How's that?" Fran looked at his mother.

Mr. Montgomery answered, "She is not on a team right now, young man, but to this very day, there's a huge gold trophy cup in the main office of Cambridge University with her name on it."

"What did she do to earn such distinction?" the boy asked.

"She was captain of the Cambridge women's soccer team. Her team won so many games, and they had so many interesting moves, many created by none other than David's grandmother and my wife: the Step-Over, Rabona, Fake Shot, Cruyff Turn, Roulette, Elastico, Cut, and Rainbow. Their games were so popular that the team attracted attention all over England and beyond."

As Mr. Montgomery told his story, his body gyrated like he was making the moves in his mind. "I recently read in the *Cambridge Newsletter* that

Dorothy had opened the field of women in sports; they are even considering allowing women to participate in professional soccer."

"Oh, George, you know it was just luck that I had such a hard-working
and talented team of women for those three years," Mrs. Montgomery said.

"It is your name on the trophy, dear, and all of your team members
agreed that it was you, your plays, your coaching, that had made them
great."

"Enough of this talk," Mrs. Montgomery said, adding, "Boys, could
you set out the plates and the boxes of food? There will be twelve of us for
dinner tonight."

"An even dozen," Fran said, looking through the packages George and
Dr. Stratton had placed on one of the red-and-white checkered tablecloths.

"When you're finished," Mrs. Montgomery asked, "could you go to the
guest house kitchen and bring the plate of cookies I made this afternoon?"

Fran and David pulled out white boxes of different sizes, each with
a slender wire holder. In the last bag, Fran discovered a large bundle of
chopsticks wrapped in long, narrow white envelopes with Chinese writing
on them. "David, we won't have to put out any silverware; we have plenty
of chopsticks."

"And we don't even need Grandma's cookies, either. Look at this bag
of fortune cookies!" David exclaimed.

Eleven of the twelve dinner guests arrived at the Pizza Hut and were
each greeted by Mrs. Montgomery.

"We are missing one. Where is Samy?" David's grandmother asked.

As if on cue, Samy entered. He'd exchanged his tie-dyed T-shirt for a
dramatic blue Hawaiian shirt. This shirt was covered with women wearing
grass skirts and leis, each woman playing a ukulele.

"There you are, Samy. Ladies and gentlemen, I am sure you are all ready
for dinner. I thought we should have a brief meeting to sum up our very
complex day," Mrs. Montgomery announced. "The first thing I want to do is
give our thanks to the people of Egypt. The children of the Giza Plateau have
welcomed two non-Egyptian boys, inviting Fran and David to play soccer

with them. They helped teach the young, inexperienced athlete, Fran, and cheered on our excellent player, David."

"We have been treated with respect and regard by the residents of the City of the Dead, and all the people who live in the Giza Plateau," Mrs. Montgomery continued. "I have learned lessons about friendship from people of different nationalities, religions, and economic levels. It is a lesson I will never forget, and I will remember to treat visitors to my own country as kindly as we have been treated here."

The people in the Pizza Hut applauded the inspirational speech. After the noise died down, Mrs. Montgomery beckoned toward the art professor. "We will start our meeting with Mademoiselle Fleuret. Please, tell us about your visit with Farak's father and his grandfather, Sultan Faruq."

Mademoiselle Fleuret stood up, her collar necklace with the large blue scarab in the center and her many rings shimmering in the restaurant's lights.

"Before I begin my story, I want to thank Mrs. Montgomery for reminding us of the kindness of the people of Egypt," Mademoiselle Fleuret said. "Farak's family was no exception. Even though the father, grandfather and workers around the house were concerned about the shocking disappearance of Farak and his mother, they treated me with respect and kindness."

"Now Farak and his mother are missing?" Dr. Stratton exclaimed. "You'd think we were in the middle of the Bermuda Triangle."

"The Sultan even insisted on giving me this beautiful scarab necklace, though I made it perfectly clear I was not Farak's teacher but rather Charles' instructor," Mademoiselle Fleuret continued. "He explained that the scarab represented the solar system and also symbolized good fortune. The Sultan said he believed that when we located his grandson and daughter-in-law, we would also find the boy we were looking for."

Fran raised his hand and then, without being recognized, ran up to the art teacher.

"Look, Mademoiselle Fleuret," he said. "I was given a necklace by a man in the City of the Dead. It also has a scarab on it. Now I know it means good luck. We sure are lucky, Mademoiselle Fleuret, aren't we?"

"Yes, we are Fran," Mademoiselle Fleuret agreed.

Dr. Bernstein motioned Fran back to his seat. As Mademoiselle Fleuret continued to recount the story of her visit to Luxor, Mrs. Montgomery took notes on her butcher paper with her collection of colored pens.

"I decided I needed to meet Farak's family, in person, to ask them how we could best go about finding Charles. Luxor is about a five-hour flight in a prop plane," Mademoiselle Fleuret noted. "I was met at the airport by a tall, slender Egyptian man in a white robe and turban. I thought he might be Farak's father, but it turned out to be the family's chauffeur, Baahar. The following information is for Samy. Baahar was driving a 1947 Rolls Royce limousine. It was two-tone, silver and black, with huge headlights over the fenders. The hood of the car was capped with an ornament, a silver-winged woman looking like she was about to fly off on an adventure."

"I would love to drive a Rolls Royce Limousine, 1947," Samy said dreamily.

"I'd like to ride in that kind of car, too, Samy," Fran called out.

Mademoiselle Fleuret resumed her story. "As we drove to the compound, which was several hours from the airport, Baahar gave a running description of the sites we were passing. Thebes, now a part of Luxor, was the largest city in ancient Egypt. Baahar and I drove past miles and miles of roads lined by larger-than-life stone rams. I believe he said there were 1,200 rams."

"Wow, that's a lot of rams!" Fran said, hitting the heel of his hand on his forehead.

"Fran, we're never going to eat dinner if you don't stop interrupting," David said.

"The rams line the road called the Path of God. The Path of God: I thought that was a thrilling name," Mademoiselle Fleuret said. "Baahar told me Thebes is home to two-thirds of the ancient monuments in the entire world. Two-thirds in the entire world! Can you imagine this?"

Albert smiled appreciatively at her description.

"Anyway, I hope sometime you will all get to visit Luxor. Personally, I am determined to go back," Mademoiselle Fleuret said emphatically.

"I can attest to the beauty of Luxor," Samy interjected, "as it is the city of my birth and my boyhood home. My family lived there until I was 18. Then we moved to Cairo, where my father thought our taxi business would be more successful. I still miss Luxor."

"I can see how you would miss it, Samy," the woman in the flowered skirt said. "To continue, as we approached the compound, Baahar stopped being a tour guide. He asked if I knew Farak. I told him I was a teacher at the school Farak attended in France. In that case, he said, he would tell me about the Great Upset."

Mademoiselle Fleuret had the attention of everyone in the Pizza Hut, especially the eyes and ears of Alfred P. Hart. Mademoiselle Fleuret—with her expressive face framed by a hot pink scarf, unsuccessfully restraining her curly auburn hair—was the most amazing woman he'd ever seen.

"The Great Upset, he told me, had to do with Farak's mother. She is beloved by all her people," the art professor related. "She's called Her Highness or *Sit Shahena*, meaning Royal White Falcon, although never to her face. She prefers to be called Mama Mafraq, because she sees herself as the mother of all Bedouins. She is known for her wisdom, and her calm and kindly disposition."

"Baahar said Sit Shahena changed the moment Farak came home from his school in France," Mademoiselle Fleuret continued. "She took one look at the young man, who was a mere child when last she saw him, and it was as though a dam burst. Farak's mother accused her husband and her father-in-law, the Sultan, of stealing her son from her. She laughed one minute and cried the next. This was reported to Baahar by the women who take care of the royal home. They also said Farak's mother became like a pet cat, following her son around, never leaving his side."

"If I had to go 10 years without seeing my Fran, I'd be hysterical too," Dr. Bernstein said, hugging the boy beside her.

Dr. Stratton nodded sympathetically. "The loss of a child is something that is always with you. You forget for a moment and then, with a stabbing feeling in your heart, the memory comes flooding back."

"I can just imagine," Mademoiselle Fleuret said. "It is hard enough for me when my students graduate, moving on to new endeavors. To return to my story, a day ago both Sit Shahena and Farak just disappeared. This was thought to be impossible, as there are so many people around the compound. No one saw them leave. They left no note. Baahar thinks they must have ventured out in some kind of disguise."

Fran raised his hand. "What kind of disguise?"

"He did not say," Mademoiselle Fleuret answered. "He was just guessing, Fran."

"I bet they wore clothes that allowed them to blend in, just like Charles," the red-headed detective mused.

"Maybe you are right, Fran," Mademoiselle Fleuret said. "Sit Fahad Faruk, Farak's father, who will one day be Sultan, spent hours searching in the scorching desert for his wife and son. This, Baahar explained, was why no family member came to meet me at the airport, though I was a highly honored guest. Imagine that! Baahar said I was a highly honored guest!"

Alfred was hanging onto the art teacher's every word. Mrs. Montgomery scribbled notes as the teacher's story unfolded.

"When I arrived at the compound, I was taken to a place called the Room of Swords. *Oh lá lá!*" Mademoiselle Fleuret exclaimed. "It could have been straight out of *The Arabian Nights*, with tall ceilings, walls covered with tapestries, and an amazing tile floor. It had blocks of yellow, blue, and gold forming a large, multi-dimensional maze. It almost made me dizzy. It would take my whole life to try and capture the beauty of that place in a painting."

Alfred P. Hart found himself wondering about Mademoiselle Fleuret's artwork. He'd heard she was a photographer, but apparently she could paint as well. He wondered if he were too old to take an art class at the Château du Mont, then laughed at his own wondering. Mademoiselle Fleuret continued her talk.

"I was led to a table covered with food arranged so beautifully that it, too, looked like a work of art. The most accomplished chefs in France might learn something from the Bedouin chefs. They had fruit: dates, mangos, Valencia oranges, grapefruit, and lemons all arranged like flowers," Mademoiselle Fleuret said, eyes shining at the memory. "The stew was presented in a silver tureen covered in patterns of the constellations. The bread was braided, and the butter molded into the form of perfect little pyramids. I am sorry. I am getting carried away."

"I wish I'd gone with you, Mademoiselle Fleuret. It sounds like a fairy-tale," Fran said.

"As we ate, father and grandfather asked me about Farak. Was he happy? What kind of student was he? Did the other boys like him?" the art professor related. "I answered their questions, but I could not help but add my opinion on the matter. I told them I thought it extremely cruel to take a boy from his family, his people, and his country, and not even bring him home for a visit! I told them this was no way to treat a child."

Alfred considered Mademoiselle Fleuret a heroine, unafraid to speak her mind.

David interjected. "I think it was quite brave of you, Mademoiselle Fleuret, to say that to a Bedouin Sultan."

"I am afraid the words just flew from my mouth like wild birds," Mademoiselle Fleuret said, her description drawing laughter from Fran and Alfred.

"And though they didn't say so," she continued, "I thought they recognized the error of their ways. Then, the subject turned to where Farak and his mother might have gone. I told them that I could not be sure, but I was almost certain that Farak learned where Charles was staying, and left the compound determined to find him. And from what I had heard, Farak's mother had no intention of being separated from her son, so she must have insisted that she go with him."

Mrs. Montgomery reviewed her notes. Bedouin society's strict ideas of a woman's role. Mrs. Faruk's release of pent-up pain from the forced separation from her son. Farak possibly contacted by someone claiming to know where Charles was. Mother determined to follow son. Mother and son left the compound, most likely in disguise.

"Thank you, Mademoiselle Fleuret," Mrs. Montgomery said. "This is very good news."

Mr. Montgomery stood up, his forehead wrinkled with concern. "Dorothy, how can you say this is good news when there are now three people lost in Egypt?"

"Don't you see, George?" his wife responded. "By all accounts, Farak is an intelligent boy, responsible and reliable. He wouldn't leave without a plan. It's obvious he got a lead on where he could find Charles. He decided to go, and his very upset mother insisted on joining him. The good news is Charles will no longer be alone."

"But Grandmother, why didn't Farak call the police or contact us?" David asked.

"David, I believe you have put your finger on another mystery. There is some kind of secret involved here, something being covered up, and it is not just about Charles. Jacques, you were in the tomb-home of the Wasims with me. What do you think we learned?"

"We learned the Wasim family was very kind to Charles and that they saved his life. We learned that Charles thought he was going with Aamen to the United States Embassy the next morning, and that he told his story to the Wasims and their neighbors. We learned that Charles was extremely upset knowing he would have to go straight back to the Château du Mont, and that his dream of touring Egypt had come to an end, even before it started."

"He definitely wouldn't have liked that," David said. "He would make plans to stay in Egypt. But he's a kid, how could he do this without Jacques?"

"That is exactly what I want to know, David. I am his guardian, and he should not go anywhere without me."

"That is true, Jacques, but he didn't choose to go to the City of the Dead," Mrs. Montgomery reminded him. "He believed he was going to go to the American Embassy. What changed his mind? Whatever it was, it is clear that Charles did not like the idea of going back to the Château du Mont without seeing Egypt. This, of course, made him susceptible to a change of plans."

"What change of plans, Mrs. Montgomery?" Dr. Stratton asked, looking distraught.

"That question bring us to our next activity before dinner. Dr. Bernstein and I thought it would be interesting to conduct a quick experiment. As most of you know, Dr. Bernstein is teaching classes in physics this summer based on the postulate that extrasensory perception (ESP), including remote viewing, telecommunication, and remote healing actually exist. How might modern physics explain these abilities? Are you all willing to try an experiment?" Mrs. Montgomery asked.

The guest house members agreed. Mrs. Montgomery asked Fran and David to pass out pens and paper, then called up Dr. Bernstein, announcing that the physicist had the floor.

Dr. Bernstein said quietly, "I suggest you take two deep breaths and attempt to center yourself."

"What do you mean center yourself, Mom?" Fran asked seriously.

"It means that instead of being aware of your surroundings or other people, you are really aware of only yourself."

"Okay, Mom," the red-headed boy said, squeezing his eyes tightly shut.

"Think how you are connected to Charles. See him in your mind's eye."

The room became silent.

"Alright," Dr. Bernstein continued. "Charles was in the City of the Dead. He left the City of the Dead willingly. Just relax and imagine where you think Charles might have gone. Don't worry if you are right or wrong, just let your intuition work and write down your answer."

After a moment, Mrs. Montgomery said, "David, here is my hat. Please collect everyone's paper."

The mystery writer pulled the papers out of her hat and looked through them. "Interesting. It appears that out of eleven people, four indicated they thought Charles is on his way to Tel el Armana. Jacques, could you say a few words about this city?"

Jacques was glad he'd listened closely during Dr. McAllister's tour at the Cairo Museum. "Three thousand years ago, Akhenaten was pharaoh of both Northern and Southern Egypt. He decided to build a new capital city on barren land between Memphis, now known as Cairo, and Thebes, near Luxor. He dedicated the city to the god Aten. As I understand it, he did this because he wanted to move his people from believing in many gods to believing in one god, the power behind the sun and all there is. However, the powerful high priests did not like this idea. They sent their soldiers to destroy what has been called the most beautiful city in the ancient world. Subsequently, all knowledge of Tel el Amarna was erased from history. Tel el Amarna lay buried for thousands of years. No one knew it had ever existed. Charles has a particular interest in Akhenaten's capital city. He made sure it was on our itinerary. Our plan was to go there on our second-to-last day in Egypt."

"Thank you, Jacques," Mrs. Montgomery said. "Our little experiment, and the fact that Charles was so interested in Akhenaten's capital city, leads naturally to the conclusion that our next outing must be to Tel el Armana."

Samy raised his hand.

"Yes, Samy."

"I have to warn you that there is nothing at Tel el Armana, nothing. Everything was leveled to the ground three thousand years ago. A couple of things were discovered, mostly in the end of the 19th century. But presently, there are only a few primitive digs," the man in the Hawaiian shirt concluded. "I told Charles there was no use going there, but he insisted he had to go."

"You may be right, Samy, there may not be anything there—except for the boy we are all searching for."

"I will contact Dr. McAllister," Jacques said. "He is an Egyptologist, author, and the tour guide Charles and I met at the Cairo Museum. He has a particular interest in this Pharaoh Akhenaten. Dr. McAllister had already agreed to accompany us to on our excursion to Tel el Amarna."

"You are right, Jacques. We should contact this Dr. McAllister," Mrs. Montgomery said. "Alone we can do so little, together we can do so much."

As the meeting seemed to be adjourned, Samy, George and Dr. Stratton slipped out the Pizza Hut door. Mrs. Montgomery asked the others to return to the guest house and dress for dinner.

As they walked out the door and into the Egyptian night, David asked Fran what he'd written on his paper.

"I drew a camel."

"A camel isn't a place," David said.

"I know, but that's what I saw. In fact, I saw many camels. What did you write on your paper, David?"

"I wrote Tel el Armana, Egypt, Tomb 11."

CHAPTER 45

FORTUNE COOKIES ON THE GIZA PLATEAU

As everyone entered the Pizza Hut, they saw that a feast had been set on the table: wonton soup, chow mein, kung pao chicken, Peking duck, broccoli beef, noodles, and white rice, not to mention pots of tea. Excitement was in the air. Fran, who was sitting by David, noticed Mandisa didn't know how to use chopsticks. Considering himself an expert, he moved next to her, demonstrating how one eats with chopsticks. The Egyptian woman was giggling so hard, she could barely get one bite into her mouth.

"Just do what I'm doing," Fran said as he expertly picked up a piece of chicken.

At the end of the dinner, David passed out the fortune cookies. Fran read his fortune out loud: *'To avoid criticism, do nothing, say nothing, be nothing.'*

"What does that mean?" he asked, looking at his mother.

"I think it means you need to choose another fortune cookie, Fran," she said, handing him a golden cookie.

Cracking open the cookie, Fran read his new fortune: *'The sun will always shine on you. You will be very successful.'*

"I believe it, Francis," his mother said.

Fran handed a cookie to their taxi driver. "How about you, Samy?"

Samy cracked open his cookie and retrieved the strip of white paper inside.

"You're not going to believe this," the driver said. It reads, *'A new car or a new life, you choose.'* This is an especially difficult decision after hearing Mademoiselle Fleuret's wonderful description of the 1947 Rolls Royce."

"How about yours, David?" Fran asked.

David snapped open his cookie and read the strip of paper inside: *'A good friend is your most valuable possession.'*

The room fell silent. Just then, Dr. Awyan's son Yousef walked in the door carrying a small package.

"Ah, this is what we have been waiting for," Mrs. Montgomery said. "Alfred's photographs."

Mrs. Montgomery reached into her purple bag and pulled out a magnifying glass, while Alfred spread the photographs on the back table.

"Some of these photos are of the people who live in tomb-homes and the surrounding areas," he said.

"Oh, Alfred, these are wonderful photos!" Mademoiselle Fleuret exclaimed. "They could be published in travel magazines, maybe even the *National Geographic*. I am sure of this."

Alfred smiled at the woman in the pink tennis shoes. Then, pointing to a separate pile of photographs, he said, "These photos over here I took as the gratitude picnic was being set out. This third set was shot when I decided to go farther east, past the Wasims' house. The path seemed to run out of people, and the further I walked, the larger the pieces of broken cement and tile I encountered. I was forced to look down at my feet much of the time, just to keep from tripping. I saw no one, but I had the feeling someone was watching me."

"Who?" Fran asked.

"I don't know. It was just a feeling," Alfred replied. "I kept walking, taking as many pictures as I could with my spy camera. I must have walked a mile before I reached the end of the cemetery. At the western end of the cemetery the narrow, tomb-lined path opens to a barren desert. This photograph shows that strange, rocky cliff jutting out of the flat land to the north."

"Oh, yeah, that was Aamen's mountain," David said.

The photographer continued. "To the east and south there was nothing, just vacant land."

Jacques was staring hard at one of the pictures taken via Alfred's spy camera. "I do not know for sure, but see?" he pointed at the picture. "This looks like an arm, a shadowy arm, and a shape that appears like part of a fedora hat."

Alfred handed Jacques a purple pen and asked him to circle his findings so the others would know where to look. Fran was examining each photograph as carefully as any grownup, picking up the magnifying glass as soon as someone else put it down. Finally, he yelled out, "I found something! I found something!"

"What, Fran?" his mother asked.

"Camel poop."

The group gathered inside the Pizza Hut laughed, but Fran looked serious.

"It's important, isn't it?" the boy asked. "Camel poop means Charles may have left the City of the Dead on a camel."

"You have got a keen eye, Fran," Mrs. Montgomery said. "You may be onto something."

Peering at another photograph, Alfred said he thought he saw the shadow of someone looking towards him.

"And look here," Charles' chaperone said, pointing to another spot on the print. "This indentation might possibly be Charles' footprint, still visible in the dry, sandy soil."

"So," David concluded, "it's likely that Charles left the City of the Dead in the dead of night, on a camel. And it's possible that Mr. Smith may have been following him."

"This does not sound a bit good," Dr. Stratton said. "Who could this Mr. Smith be?"

"We can't be sure about Mr. Smith," Dr. Bernstein said, picking up one of the photographs. "This could be just a smudge or a shadow in the shape of a hat."

"But where did Charles go?" David asked sorrowfully.

Mrs. Montgomery said, "I think Fran might be right, and that Charles is on a camel, and on an adventure."

"Dorothy, this is not one of your Red Hat mysteries. This is serious," George said, placing his arm around his grandson's shoulder.

"George, I know it is serious," his wife replied. "We all know it is serious."

Samy bid the people in the Pizza Hut goodnight. A few minutes later, Jacques walked out the door without saying a word.

After a while, Bernadette asked, "Where is Jacques? He has been gone a long time."

"I think he went to the bathroom," Fran said.

"He has been gone too long for that," Bernadette insisted.

"I say we send out a search party," Mrs. Montgomery said, taking control of the situation. "Fran, check the bathrooms. David, you look in all the rooms on the third floor, including Jacques' and your grandfather's quarters. Dr. Stratton and Alfred, could you look outside? And George, could you go to the office of the School of Khemitology and check if Jacques is there?"

One by one, members of the search party returned to the restaurant with no news of the missing Jacques.

"Where could he be at this hour?" Mr. Montgomery asked his wife, adding, "It's past my bedtime."

"I am sure Jacques is just taking a walk to try and figure things out," Mrs. Montgomery said.

"I want to go on a walk and figure things out, Mom," Fran announced.

"It's way past your bedtime, too, Fran. No walk tonight," Dr. Bernstein said firmly.

"Yes, I think it is time for everyone to go to bed," Mrs. Montgomery advised. "It has been a long day."

As they all filed out of the Pizza Hut, the mystery writer examined her colorful notes. Then, speaking aloud, she said, "I believe Jacques has taken a walk—a midnight walk—through the tomb-lined path in the City of the Dead."

Mrs. Montgomery jumped when she heard a voice ask, "What makes you think Jacques has gone to the City of the Dead at this time of night?" The words were spoken by the woman in yellow.

"Several reasons, my dear," the mystery writer explained. "Some come from the clues on this butcher paper, some from the photos, and one from this slip of paper. I found it where Jacques was sitting."

"His fortune? What does it say?" Bernadette asked.

Mrs. Montgomery read the words aloud: '*A ship in the harbor is safe, but that is not why it was built.*'

CHAPTER 46

A POT OF TEA, A MAP, AND A MESSAGE

Mrs. Montgomery dressed without turning on the lights, so as not to wake the boys or Dr. Carolyn Bernstein. She could see a dark pink sky behind the shadowy Sphinx. The sun would be rising soon, but she wasn't going to the sunrise meditation. This morning she needed to think, for there had been another disappearance. Last night, Jacques Gerard had walked out of the Pizza Hut door without saying anything to anyone, and never returned. At least, she didn't think he'd come back. She decided she'd better find out before she went downstairs for a cup of tea.

Picking up her straw hat with violets on the rim and her purple basket purse, Mrs. Montgomery moved quietly towards the door. She padded up to the third floor and knocked on the door of the room shared by Jacques and her husband. George, wearing plaid pajamas, welcomed her.

Dorothy looked around the room. "As I expected, Jacques did not return."

"If he had returned," Mr. Montgomery said, "I'd have come down and informed you. I am sure you didn't get much sleep last night."

"Regarding sleep, you have no idea," his wife answered. "It was nearly midnight. I was just about to lay my weary head down on my pillow when Bernadette and Mademoiselle Fleuret knocked at the door, both in night-gowns, robes, and slippers. They announced that they couldn't sleep because they were concerned about Jacques."

"Who isn't concerned about Jacques? I could barely sleep myself," Mr. Montgomery confessed. "What happened?"

"Of course, our grandson heard the girls come in. He climbed down from the top bunk and plopped down on the side of my bed," his wife said, smiling at the memory. "He told me he couldn't sleep either. Naturally Fran, hearing the commotion, joined David on the edge of my bed. Dr. Bernstein got up, tossed on her gray chenille robe, and joined the others. It was a real pajama party."

"You should have invited me down. I used to enjoy the kids' sleepovers."

"Yes, George. You always loved telling our children and their friends those spooky ghost stories you made up, scaring them half to death," Mrs. Montgomery said, half-frowning.

"They loved them, and you know that, Dorothy," George said with determination.

"Back to my story, George. Fran, in his space pajamas, suggested we all get dressed, find camels, and go looking for Jacques. David agreed. He said Charles was his best friend and he needed to go looking for him like Jacques had. He said roommates look after one another, and he was tired of hanging around the Sphinx doing nothing."

"I hope you warned him not to go off by himself," George said.

"You know I did, George. Next, Bernadette said she didn't fly all the way from France to Cairo for Jacques to disappear," Mrs. Montgomery continued. "Mademoiselle Fleuret was upset, too. She said Jacques was indispensable at the Château du Mont and everything would collapse if he weren't there and, besides that, he was her friend. I let them talk, then told them I was sure Jacques would return in the morning. If not, I predicted, he would definitely contact us. In a chorus, they asked how I knew this."

"Well, how do you know?" George asked.

"It's quite simple. Jacques walked out the Pizza Hut door of his own accord," Dorothy answered. "He must have thought of something, or decided he needed time to think. Speaking of thinking, I need some tea."

Mr. Montgomery opened the door for his wife. "I'll dress, and meet you in the front room," he said with a slight bow.

***

Soon, George was sitting at the little table by the window, staring at a rather grumpy-looking Sphinx. Mrs. Montgomery pushed through the swinging door between the kitchen and the front room. She was balancing a tray with biscuits, teacups, and a steaming pot of tea.

"Allow me to serve, my dear," George said, pouring the golden liquid into a cup decorated with a golden pyramid.

They sat without talking. The only noise was the sound of Mrs. Montgomery's spoon clinking against her cup as she stirred some sugar into the brew.

After a moment, George burst out, "Where could that young man be? Why didn't he take someone with him?"

Mrs. Montgomery, as was so often her habit, answered with a quotation. "Some of my favorite words, ones that have often helped me do things out of my comfort zone, were written by Nietzsche: '*No one can build you the bridge on which you, and only you, must cross the river with.*' Isn't that beautiful?"

"Dorothy," George sputtered. "Jacques is missing, and you're quoting an old German philosopher."

"Nietzsche was more than a philosopher, George," his wife answered with feeling. "He was a collector of words and their etymologies. He wrote prose, poetry, music..."

"The truth is," George said, "I feel half to blame. I knew Jacques was in a dejected state of mind. I should have followed him when he left the Pizza Hut. I should have offered to join him in whatever endeavor he had in mind."

"It wasn't your fault, George. You had no idea he was leaving."

"All I know is I agree with my grandson, roommates look after one another. We can't just sit here, Montgomery."

Mrs. Montgomery smiled. "You haven't called me Montgomery in a long time, George. I fully intend to contact the police and notify the American Embassy, as soon as I finish my tea."

Before she could finish her second cup, Dr. Awyan entered the guest house. He lit up the front room with his white gallabiyah and matching white turban.

"Hello, Dr. Awyan," the couple chimed, standing up to greet him.

"I just received a message from Jacques," Dr. Awyan announced. "It was sent to me by way of a Dr. McAllister from the Cairo Museum."

Mrs. Montgomery breathed a sigh of relief. "Oh, thank heavens! What did he say?"

The founder of the School of Khemitology handed her a folded paper.

"He wrote his message on this map," Dr. Awayan explained. "I would love to stay and talk about its contents, but I am otherwise engaged. They are holding the closing ceremony of the conference on Ley Lines, Sacred Sites, and the Great Connections, and it appears I am the keynote speaker."

Mrs. Montgomery shook her head in wonder. "It sounds positively fascinating, Dr. Awyan."

"In the past days, we have had so many tours and meetings," the Egyptologist said. "I am afraid I have not been available for any of you during this perplexing second disappearance of Charles. That being said, Jacques' message indicates Charles will soon be returned to you. I will return here when the conference is over. This Dr. McAllister says he will arrive here this afternoon, after his final tour."

Their tall Egyptian benefactor bid them goodbye and moved towards the door, gallabiyah swinging around his sandaled feet.

"Thank you, Dr. Awyan. We are relieved," Mrs. Montgomery called, waving after him. Turning to her husband, she added, "My, he looks distinguished in his white robe, doesn't he, George?"

"Yes, he looks good wearing the clothing of his land. When wearing a gallabiyah, I, on the other hand, looked like that portly comedian, Costello, in that ridiculous movie 'Abbott and Costello Meet the Mummy.' You may remember it from one of our first dates."

"I thought you looked quite handsome in that gallabiyah, George," his wife assured him.

"Hmmph," George scoffed. "You were right about Jacques contacting us, just as you guessed he would."

"It wasn't exactly a guess," Mrs. Montgomery said. "I have been studying Jacques, and he is a very responsible person."

"Quite," George said as he turned and walked toward the stairs.

"Where are you going? What about the message?"

"I have to get my reading glasses."

"I can read it to you," his wife protested.

"I think better with my glasses on," George said, disappearing up the stairs.

A few minutes later George returned, looking like the Pied Piper. He was followed by Fran, who was followed by a serious-looking David. Next came Mademoiselle Fleuret, wearing a blue artist's smock and flowing flowered skirt, followed by Bernadette in a turquoise pantsuit. At the rear of the line were Albert and Dr. Stratton, both wearing perfectly pressed pants and white shirts. Albert had added a jaunty dark green vest and a pale green jacket. The parade ended with Dr. Bernstein, ready for a safari in her tailored tan pants and short-sleeved jacket.

"I feel like I'm in the middle of a parade!" Mrs. Montgomery exclaimed.

"I thought that we'd better all gather for the reading of the message," her husband replied. "You read, Dorothy."

Everyone crowded into the small room, some on chairs and others remaining standing. The boys threw themselves down on a red Egyptian rug that covered the old wooden floor. Before Mrs. Montgomery could begin reading, there was a knock on the door. Fran and David ran to see who it was and returned with Samy. He was back in surfer-mode, wearing a dark blue Hawaiian shirt covered in huge pineapples with spiky green stems. It was a colorful gathering for what appeared to be a dark subject.

"Everybody's up. What's happening?" Samy asked.

"Jacques left last night after dinner and never came back," David said. "My grandmother is about to read a message he sent us this morning. You can read now, Grandmother."

Mrs. Montgomery, ensconced in a green overstuffed chair, pulled out the map and unfolded it.

"There is a note on this map," she explained. "Dr. Awyan brought us this map earlier this morning. It was sent to him by a Dr. McAllister, a tour guide at the Cairo Museum. Jacques spoke about him last night."

"What did Jacques' message say?" Fran called out, unable to restrain himself.

"Okay, all. The message seems to have been written in a hurried script."

Greetings, Dr. McAllister. I am Jacques Gerard. Charles and I met you at the museum. I am certain you will remember the 12-year-old who has a great fascination for Egypt. You kindly agreed to accompany us to Tel el Amarna the day before we returned to France. I am sorry to report that Charles has gone missing. It is a complicated story but, at present, I am joining two women who say they know Charles' location. Please get this message to Dr. Awyan at the School of Khemitology at the Giza Plateau. It is across from the Sphinx and just left of the Pizza Hut. I would be most grateful.

"Jacques addressed the following section of the note," Mrs. Montgomery continued, "to Dr. Awyan and all of us at the Khemitology Guest House."

My dear friends,

I am sorry I did not tell anyone where I was going last night. The truth is, I did not know where I was going myself. After our Chinese dinner, I suddenly felt as though a giant magnet was pulling me out of the Pizza Hut. Once outside, I saw a taxi cab—different from the vehicle belonging to Samy—sitting in front of the Sphinx.

"A taxi at night, after the archeology area is closed. That's very strange," Samy mumbled.

When I approached the cab, the driver opened the back door. As I sat down in the backseat, I still did not know where I was going, at least not consciously. But out of my mouth popped the words, 'I need to go to the City of the Dead.'

"What on earth did Jacques think he'd find at the City of the Dead at that time of night?" Dr. Stratton wondered aloud.

"Yes, and why didn't he take me with him?" David said crossly.

"Because he knows your grandmother and I would never allow you to venture out at a time when children should be sleeping," Mr. Montgomery said. "Continue, Dorothy."

The taxi driver dropped me off in the parking lot of the Western Cemetery. I still had no idea what I was doing there, or where I should go. I decided to follow the path we had taken that very afternoon.

"Was it just yesterday?" George asked. "It seems like days ago."

Fran answered, "Yep, it was just yesterday, Mr. Montgomery. Wasn't it, Mom?"

"Yes, Fran. Let's allow Mrs. Montgomery to finish," his mother said, placing her index finger over her lips.

For some time, I saw nothing except a white cow and a black raven.

"Wow, Jacques is lucky!" Fran exclaimed. "I want to meet a white cow and black raven at the City of the Dead."

"Let my grandmother read, Fran," David said impatiently.

Then, something happened. Do you remember the three women dressed in black that Aamen told us about? I met two of them in the area where Charles told his story to the Wasims and their neighbors. They seemed to be waiting for me. They said they knew where Charles was and would take me to him.

"I don't like the sound of this. It sounds like a trap to me," Dr. Stratton said, his lips in a tight line.

At the time of my writing this note, we are in front of the Cairo Museum, which will not open for a few more hours. I hope to get one of the local vendors, some of whom are already setting up their stalls, to deliver this message to Dr. McAllister. If you are reading this, my plan worked. We are traveling by camel.

"I was right!" the red-headed boy yelled in celebration. "Remember last night? I told you we all need to get on camels and go looking for Jacques." His mother shushed him and pulled him closer.

"Fran, I appreciate your dedication to finding Jacques," Mrs. Montgomery said. "Perhaps, however, we should finish his note before we go trotting off into the desert on camels."

The women tell me they believe Farak and his mother may be with Charles. We are leaving in a few minutes. I am writing this note in secret. I must request that you do not call the authorities at this time. I will explain later. Also, I don't know how, but the women know about Mr. Smith.

Regards, Jacques Gerard.

"The women know about Mr. Smith? That is yet another mystery," Mrs. Montgomery concluded.

"If Jacques didn't tell the women he was contacting Dr. McAllister, he must not fully trust them," Dr. Stratton said. "Why shouldn't we contact the authorities?"

He stood up, looking ready to walk out the door. Albert moved to his right side. Mademoiselle Fleuret moved to his left, floral skirt twirling, and placed her arm around the distraught man.

"I understand how you feel, Dr. Stratton," the art teacher said calmly. "How traumatic it must be to learn you have a grandson, only to have him disappear not once but twice. Still, the fact remains that Jacques asked us not to contact the authorities, and he must have a good reason. I suggest we wait. Meanwhile, I will contact Farak's father and grandfather to learn if they have heard anything else about Farak and his mother."

Dr. Stratton remained standing a moment, unconvinced.

"I think Mademoiselle Fleuret is correct," Mrs. Montgomery said. "We should wait to contact the authorities. Anyway, I am not sure what we could actually tell them. Jacques is an adult who left us of his own accord. Furthermore, he sent word of his whereabouts this very morning. He does not meet the criteria for a missing person. Even if he did, how would the police know where to search? Jacques gave no hint as to where he and the two women were headed."

"Maybe there's a clue on the map," David suggested.

Mrs. Montgomery handed her grandson the map. He draped it over a long table in the back of the room. "Grandfather, could you bring me one of your pens?"

As usual, Mr. Montgomery carried an assortment of writing implements in his shirt pocket: a mechanical pencil, red, blue, and black pens, a fountain pen, and a yellow highlighter.

"Be prepared for anything, that's my motto," George said. He handed the highlighter to David, who leaned over the map.

"Jacques was here at the Pizza Hut. Here it is, by the Sphinx," the boy said, placing a yellow dot next to the legendary statue. "He traveled east and then south to the City of the Dead, more precisely the Western Cemetery."

David placed a yellow dot at the Western Cemetery and then connected the two dots.

"In my opinion, there are several mysteries here," Mrs. Montgomery said, rubbing her chin. "Jacques got up from our Chinese dinner and went to the City of the Dead at midnight. He met two women who seemed to expect him. Why would they expect him?"

"Don't forget, the white cow and the black raven," Fran reminded the group. "How would a cow and a raven know Jacques would come to the City of the Dead at midnight?"

"Really, Fran, stop joking!" David commanded.

"I am not joking. My mother says that animals have a sixth sense. So the cow and raven might have guessed that Jacques would visit them at midnight. Isn't that right, Mom?

"Okay, let's move on. Jacques wrote that he followed the same path we took that morning," David continued. "From Albert's photograph, we know there was a large undeveloped area just at the east of the Western Cemetery. Fran noticed there was camel poop in the photo. I believe this is where they went to get on their camels."

"Good thinking, my boy," his grandfather said encouragingly.

"It's a good thing I noticed the camel poop, isn't it?" Fran asked.

"Yes, you are quite an observer, Fran," Mr. Montgomery said, patting him on the back.

"Now, Jacques and the women in black could travel north or south. But in either case, they would end up here," David said, placing a yellow dot at the Cairo Museum.

Everyone congratulated David on his clever thinking.

"No wonder you won the geography bee at the Château du Mont!" Fran exclaimed. "But where did they go from there?"

Mrs. Montgomery looked at the taxi driver and said, "Samy, where do you think they went?"

"My belief is they must have gone to the Western Desert, which is this vacant area west of the Cairo Museum and the green belt. But don't ask me why. The Western Desert is part of the Sahara, the largest, hottest desert in the world. There is little water, few plants, and no shade. And yet, for some reason, it is the home of cobras, saw-horned vipers, poisonous lizards, and dangerous wild dogs. I wouldn't go there, and I'm Egyptian."

Mrs. Montgomery said, "As to going to the Western Desert, Samy, the only thing I can think is, the women in black needed to keep something secret. The Western Desert, a place where no one wants to go, might be a good place to hide a secret. David, do you have any ideas?"

It was Fran who answered Mrs. Montgomery's question. "Remember last night, when we put our intuitions on paper and thew them into the hat? David, you predicted the next destination would be Tel el Armana. And remember, David, I told you I drew a camel? I think this means we should all get on camels and ride to Tel el Armana!" the young boy suggested enthusiastically, adding, "Where is it? Where is Tel el Armana, David?"

"It appears to be slightly on the east side of the Nile. Let me look at the mileage scale. It appears to be 250 miles south from here. I am not sure we can get there in a timely manner by camel, Fran.c

"Well, I am sure Samy can arrange transportation," Mrs. Montgomery said. "David and Fran are correct; our next destination is Tel el Armana."

Dr. Bernstein had moved to the glass bookshelf and was stared at the ancient Egyptian artifacts.

She turned to face the group and said, "I believe I may be responsible for Jacques' departure last night. It was something I said to him yesterday morning at the Sphinx meditation."

"Nonsense, my girl," Dr. Stratton said. "I think it was those fortune cookies I bought for our Chinese dinner. Jacques opened his cookie just before he left. I saw his fortune on the table. It said something like, don't be a boat that stays in the harbor. He read it, then got up and left."

"The actual quote is '*A boat is safe in the harbor, but that is not why it was built,*' if memory serves me," Mrs. Montgomery said.

"See what I mean? It was my buying that bag of fortune cookies that caused Jacques to walk out last night," Mr. Montgmery confessed.

"I do not think so," Bernadette said quietly, brushing a strand of dark hair back from her forehead. "Last night, I treated Jacques as though he were a stranger, not a friend. I must have hurt his feelings terribly. I am afraid that I am responsible for his leaving."

"You think that's bad?" David said. "I asked Jacques just yesterday afternoon how he could stand being here in the Giza Plateau doing nothing, when Charles was lost and alone somewhere in Egypt."

"I was with David," Fran added. "And I told Jacques he needed to get a camel and go looking for Charles, immediately."

"I don't know about all of these things," Samy said seriously. "What I do know is, if I hadn't left so early after dinner, I would have taken Jacques to the City of the Dead or talked him out of going. Then we wouldn't be here wondering where he could be."

"It appears to me that there are many of us willing to be malefactors in Jacques' disappearance," Mrs. Montgomery observed. "It even crossed my mind that my chess game which, truth be told, I was using as a counseling tool—encouraging Jacques to step out, to be bold, to be assertive—might have goaded him into leaving last night."

"I doubt that game could have been responsible, Dorothy," Mr. Montgomery said.

"Thank you, George. However, what I was going to say is that, rather than taking responsibility and feeling guilty for Jacques' departure, we should applaud him for his initiative, courage, and determination. He will find Charles. Of this, we can be assured."

"Thank you, Mrs. Montgomery. That puts a proper spin on Jacques and his actions," Dr. Stratton said, sitting back in his chair.

There was a soft knock on the door. A slim Egyptian woman in blue jeans, a pink long-sleeved blouse, and a white headscarf walked into the room.

"Hello," she said. "My name is Tiye. I am Mandisa's daughter. My mother went out on an errand and could not make it back to the Pizza Hut. I sent her a message that I would prepare breakfast for you. Are you ready?"

"I'm ready," Fran called out.

"I believe we can continue our discussion after breakfast," Mrs. Montgomery said as Tiye led the group out of the guest house.

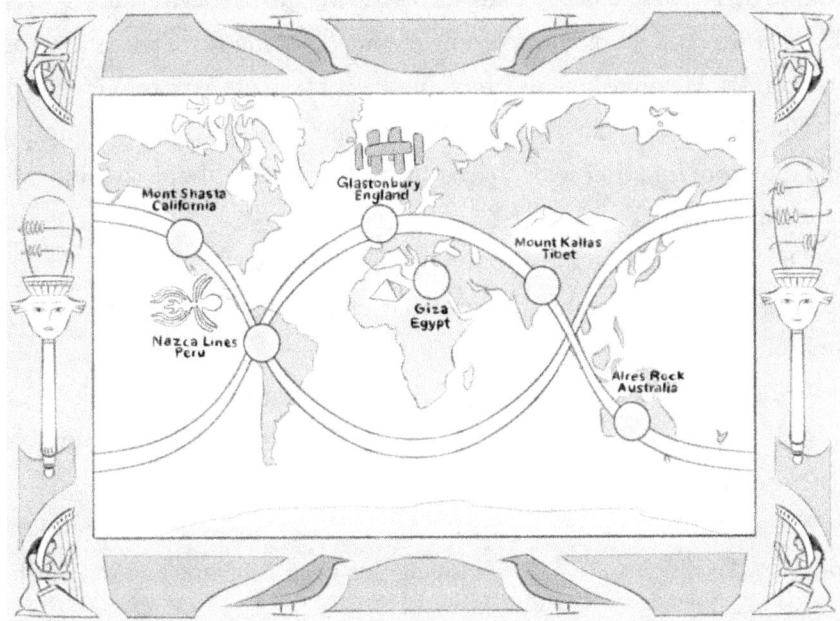

CHAPTER 47

TIYE, EGYPTIAN HEALING, AND LEY LINES

M andisa's daughter unlocked the blue door, calling out, "I brought my toaster and an electric frying pan to make you breakfast."

Fran ran to her side and said, "I love toast!"

"Great. I even brought my mother's homemade mango jelly to put on the toast," the young woman said, holding up a glass jar filled with golden-colored preserves.

"I love jelly," Fran said. "Can I help you make the toast?"

"That would be helpful," the girl said, slipping a bag of bread from behind the counter. "My mother doesn't approve of store-bought bread, but as a college student I don't have much time for baking."

The redheaded boy took to the young woman as if she were a long-lost friend.

"My name is Fran, Francis Bacon Bernstein. That's my mother," he said, pointing. "Her name is Dr. Carolyn Bernstein. That's David, a boy I go to school with, and all of these people are here looking for Charles Dayton Stratton III. He came here to Egypt, but he got lost. He's twelve."

The girl handed Fran the bag of store-bought bread and said, "My mother told me about him. I'm sorry to hear that he is missing. I hope you find him soon. My name is Tiye."

Dr. Stratton greeted the young woman warmly. "Hello, Tiye. Thank you for making us breakfast. I am Charles' grandfather, Charles Dayton Stratton."

"And I am Dr. Stratton's butler," Alfred said with a slight bow.

"He is not! He's a family friend. Stop that, Alfred," Dr. Stratton said vehemently.

"You do look like one of the butlers I've seen in some old American movies," Tiye replied. "We don't usually see people in suits and ties on the Giza Plateau."

"I am Mademoiselle Fleuret," the woman in the blue painter's smock said. "I am the art teacher at the Château du Mont, the boarding school attended by Charles, David, and Fran."

Fran continued the introductions, gesturing.

"That's Mrs. Montgomery and that's Mr. Montgomery," Fran said breathlessly. "They're David's grandparents. David is Charles' roommate. And that's Samy. He's our taxi driver. He likes wearing Hawaiian shirts." Fran grinned his jack o'lantern smile.

"I'm happy to meet all of you," the girl said, placing a large metal bowl on the countertop.

"By the way, Samy, exactly how many Hawaiian shirts do you own?" Alfred asked, the corners of his mouth tipping up in a sly smile.

"Oh, Alfred, hello," the driver said. "I see you're wearing a forest green vest today. Yesterday, you wore a lovely sky-blue vest, and the day before a red vest with some kind of geometric pattern. To answer your question, I'd say I have as many Hawaiian shirts as you have vests."

"Touché!" the self-proclaimed butler said, chuckling. He turned to the young woman cracking eggs into a bowl. "Tiye is a lovely name."

"Thank you," she said, whisking the eggs. "I'm named for the mother of Akhenaten, the great pharaoh of the 18th dynasty. My mother loves that time in Egyptian history. She talks about Akhenaten and his wife Nefertiti as though they were still alive, even though they lived three thousand years ago."

"Is Akhenaten the pharaoh who built the capital city of Tel el Armana?" Mrs. Montgomery asked. "There appears to be a great deal of interest in a city Samy claims no longer exists. It was a site our Charles very much wanted to visit. I believe I should do a little research on this area."

"My mother says it was a very important period in history, and is even important today," Tiye said, tending the frying pan. "Tiye was the wife of Pharaoh Amenhotep III, and the mother of Akhenaten. My mother says Tiye was a great leader."

"I shall have to look into this city of Tel el Amarna as well, Mrs. Montgomery," Dr. Stratton said. "What are you studying in school, young lady?"

"I'm taking classes in physiology as well as other subjects, like tennis," she said, placing a platter piled high with scrambled eggs on the table. Alfred and Fran brought out several plates of toast, and Bernadette filled everyone's cup with water.

"Physiology," Dr. Stratton mused. "Are you thinking of becoming a doctor?"

Tiye sat down at the table, helping herself to some eggs. "I'm more interested in alternative healing," she answered.

"I didn't realize alternative health was popular in Egypt," Mademoiselle Fleuret said, spreading jelly the color of the setting sun on her toast.

"Oh, yes!" Tiye said. "From the most ancient times, natural remedies have been used to treat health issues. My mother and I are particularly interested in oils, vibrations, frequencies, and music as well as dance or body movement as a part of healing. These practices are recorded on many temple walls and papyruses.

"I am just at the beginning of my studies. I wish I could have attended Dr. Awyan's conference this week. Over a hundred people traveled to Cairo to share ideas about Ley Lines, Sacred Sites, and the Great Connections," she marveled.

"What's a ley line?" Fran asked, stacking up piles of toast.

"I am just a student in that area," Tiye answered. "However, Dr. Awyan told me ley lines are straight alignments between various sacred structures like the pyramids, the Olmec and Mayan temples, and Stonehenge."

"Your father and I took you to Stonehenge, remember?" Dr. Bernstein asked her son.

"Yeah, I remember. There were a bunch of tall stones in a circle. I wasn't allowed to climb on the rocks," Fran said.

Tiye laughed, then resumed her explanation. "There are thousands of sacred sites all over the world. Many of them are geometrically connected, creating a worldwide grid. People who map ley lines say the ancient people chose specific locations on which to build their sacred sites, because the ley lines have increased energy frequency, which could aid in healing."

Albert began clearing plates off the table. "So does this mean hanging around the Giza Plateau makes people healthier?" he asked.

"I don't know if that's true, Mr. Hart. It does seem to be a good area for research, don't you agree?" Tiye asked, smiling at the man in the green vest.

George finished his third piece of toast and pushed his plate away, saying, "My compliments to the chef, and to her mother for making such delicious mango jelly."

"I don't mean to change the subject," he added, "but my roommate Jacques is missing. Dr. Bernstein, you said earlier that you may have contributed to Jacques' disappearance. Why do you believe this?"

"Yes, well, yesterday morning, before we went to the City of the Dead, Jacques and I met at the Sphinx," the dark-haired scientist replied. "We had a long conversation as we walked around the Giza Plateau. During our talk, I suggested that he might make an excellent research subject for the classes I'm teaching this summer."

"You mean the class where you'll be teaching about spooky particles at a distance, Mom?" Fran asked.

"Sort of," she said. "I plan on proposing to my students that, for the duration of our class, we put aside skepticism and doubt. For a short time, we will presuppose that some pretty out-there phenomena are not only possible but indisputable. We'll use theoretical physics to explain remote viewing, non-local communication, remote healing, prophesy and even time travel."

"Wow!" Tiye exclaimed, using a term picked up from her favorite radio station. "What a class!"

"I hope others will agree, Tiye," Dr. Bernstein continued. "The point is not to prove or disprove the existence of non-local communication but to investigate how research in quantum physics might explain it. Areas of focus might include quantum entanglement, dark matter, the quantum vacuum, zero-point energy, the holographic universe, wormholes, multi-dimensionality, string theory, and the nature of consciousness."

Dr. Stratton shook his head, impressed. "This is quite amazing, Dr. Bernstein. Alfred, I think we may have buried our heads too deeply inside our books to keep up with such fascinating concepts. I wish—after we find Charles and Jacques, of course—that we could attend one of your classes, Dr. Bernstein."

"That would be quite interesting, indeed," Alfred agreed.

"All this stuff is very interesting, Dr. Bernstein," David said as politely as possible. "But what does any of this have to do with Jacques' disappearance?"

"That's a good question, isn't it, Mom?" Fran asked, smiling up at his mother.

"Yes, it's a good question. On our walk, I asked Jacques if he found it a bit strange that so many people ended up in Egypt looking for Charles," Dr. Bernstein related. "He said he didn't think it was strange at all. Jacques explained that these people knew Charles and would naturally want to help find him."

"That makes sense to me, Mom," Fran interrupted. "I know Charles, and I want to help find him."

Dr. Bernstein pushed her glasses up on her nose. "This sizable group of people, which makes for quite a large search party, began gathering the moment Jacques made a single phone call to Madame Constance. From that one call, all of us came to Egypt, ostensibly to find Charles."

"I wonder what made each of us so bold and so presumptuous?" Dr. Bernstein posed. "How did we think we could find a boy in a country we're totally unfamiliar with, and where none of us speaks the primary language? Considering this, I suggested to Jacques that he had tapped into some quiescent powers. I told him I thought there was a chance that, in some non-local way, he called all of us to Cairo to support him in his search for Charles."

"What did Jacques say?" David asked.

"He suggested that, assuming non-local communication exists, Charles would make a better subject for my students," Dr. Bernstein answered. "He said maybe Charles had called everyone together to find him. I told Jacques his hypothesis was unlikely, because Charles didn't seem to have an overriding desire to be found."

"He didn't want to be found, Mom?" Fran asked, raising his eyebrows nearly to his hairline.

"If he had, he wouldn't have followed the women in black," Dr. Bernstein said. "There was something else that was more important to him than being found. For Jacques, however, nothing was more important than finding Charles."

"From what I've deduced, Jacques is a practical man," Mr. Montgomery said. "I expect he would have found your conversation strange, to say the least."

"You're right," Dr. Bernstein said. "Jacques insisted he didn't believe in extrasensory perception or anything of that sort, though, interestingly, he said he'd come to believe in the possibility of ghosts. Then, I told him about a scientific conference I attended in 1983, at the University of California in Berkeley. There were hundreds of scientists from a variety of fields, and yet the opening speakers were from the Central Intelligence Agency."

"The CIA? Now that is strange!" Dr. Stratton exclaimed.

"The representatives from the CIA said they'd conducted thousands of experiments in the area of extrasensory perception, focusing on remote communication and remote viewing," Dr. Bernstein continued. "They believed these experiments proved without a doubt that there are people who have these powers. The CIA said they'd proven the existence of ESP, but they had no idea why some people seem to have it and some people do not, or what allows for this strange ability."

"I knew you were going to say that, Mom. Just kidding," Fran said, cracking his jagged smile. His joke drew laughter from the room.

"Apparently, my son is a comedian as well as a math prodigy," Dr. Bernstein said with an indulgent smile. "Anyhow, the representatives from the CIA concluded their talk by asking the scientific audience to attempt to find a scientific explanation for extra-sensory perception."

"What does this have to do with Jacques, Dr. Bernstein?" Mrs. Montgomery asked.

"I had this feeling Jacques might be an example of how a strong desire to find someone—someone he felt responsible for—would lead to an opening up in the area of non-local communication. I suggested to Jacques that if he stayed open to the possibility of non-local communication, he might use this phenomenon to find Charles. When Mrs. Montgomery read Jacques' message, I noticed he wrote about an unexplainable compulsion."

"A compulsion?" Fran echoed.

Dr. Bernstein continued. "He said he felt like a magnet was pulling him out of the Pizza Hut. Then, remember, he said he didn't know where he was going. And yet, when he encountered the strange taxi driver, he said he needed to go to the City of the Dead. The words just popped out of his mouth."

"Like wild birds, like Mademoiselle Fleuret said. Do you remember that, Mom?"

"I remember, an apt description. To continue, Jacques' hunch seems to have borne fruit," Dr. Bernstein said. "He arrived just in time to meet the women in black."

"And don't forget the white cow and the black crow," Fran said.

"To conclude, it has dawned on me that our talk may have led to Jacques leaving without a word to anyone."

"Personally, I do not excuse him," Bernadette said with a pout. "But I thank you for sharing this, Dr. Bernstein. I have never thought much about ESP, but at this particular moment I cannot think of another explanation for Jacques' sudden departure last night—or for the other strange things that happened after he left the Pizza Hut."

"I'm going to try and communicate non-locally, Mom," Fran said, squinting his eyes. "Where are you, Charles? Where are you, Jacques?" The ginger-haired boy started spinning around in the center of the restaurant. He ended up so dizzy he fell, sprawling on the restaurant's tile floor.

"Why can't I do this kind of communication, Mom?" Fran demanded in frustration.

"We don't know why some people seem to have the ability to connect with others, however far away, while others do not," Dr. Bernstein said. "We don't know if ESP is inherited or developed. However, I speculate that if we can explain the physics behind ESP, more people will accept its existence. And, the more people accepting its existence, the more people may discover this ability in themselves. This alone could lead to an evolutionary jump for all humanity."

Mrs. Montgomery shook her head wonderingly. "Dr. Bernstein, it appears that there might be more mysteries in quantum physics than in literature. If I had understood this, perhaps I would have become a physicist rather than a mystery writer," she said with a great laugh.

Dr. Stratton cradled his forehead in his hands. "My head is spinning like our young Francis Bacon Bernstein," he admitted. "What I am concluding from this rather wild conversation is that Jacques is on a camel, traveling to meet up with Charles, Farak, and Farak's mother. All indications point to the fact that I will soon be meeting my grandson. I want to thank all of you. I came here to find a boy, but I feel like I found a family."

Mrs. Montgomery walked over and threw her arms around Dr. Stratton.

"One of my favorite mystery writers, Agatha Christie, wrote something profound," she said. "She observed that, '*One does not recognize the really important moments in one's life until it's too late.*' You, however, Dr. Stratton, seem to have the great fortune of recognizing this moment for what it is. I agree. You have found more than a boy; you have found a family, a very large family."

"Thank you, Mrs. Montgomery," Dr. Stratton said. He retrieved a white handkerchief out of his pocket, using it to blow his nose or wipe his eyes; one could not tell.

"I think I will take the boys to the soccer field before Dr. McAllister's arrival," Mrs. Montgomery said. "Fran's spinning reminded me that the boys have not taken any exercise during this long talk. Is that alright with you, Dr. Bernstein?"

"That would be perfect," she said, pulling her son up from the floor and giving him a huge hug.

"I'll go get my soccer ball, Grandmother," David said, running out the Pizza Hut door.

"I'll help him," Fran said, following his schoolmate.

"I think I'll go with you, Dorothy. It's been a little while since I practiced my Cuffy Turn. I don't want to get rusty," Mr. Montgomery said with an impish smile.

Bernadette, Mademoiselle Fleuret, and Dr. Bernstein stayed to help Tiye clean up after breakfast. As they worked, the young woman told them about her grandmother, who was a healer, famous for using oils, sound, and dance to cure ailments. She told the three women that her grandmother had passed these same skills and techniques down to her mother, and that Mandisa was also a well-known healer.

"Mandisa appears to prove the axiom that one should never judge a book by its cover. I'd thought her an excellent cook with a sweet smile. Now, I learn that she is also a noted healer. You're lucky to have such a mother," Dr. Bernstein said, drying a dish.

"I didn't always think so," Tiye said. "When I was a young teen, I had no desire to learn about what I considered to be old-fashioned healing. I only believed in modern medicine. Then, one day, when I was about to graduate from high school, Dr. Awyan took me into the Great Pyramid. He locked the steel door. There were just the two of us inside this ancient monument."

"What happened?" Bernadette asked, breathless with curiosity.

"We climbed up the steep ramp of the pyramid without speaking," Tiye recounted. "My godfather turned into the Queen's Chamber and I followed him. He began chanting in a high-pitched tone, one I'd never heard him use before. I suddenly felt this strange vibration surrounding my body. Meanwhile, a golden light seemed to illuminate the chamber."

"My goodness," Mrs. Montgomery said.

"Then," Tiye continued, "the light felt as though it moved from outside of my body to the inside. It felt like all the systems of my body were pulling together, becoming one. I felt light, like I was floating. Then my godfather said, 'This is just a small sample of the knowledge and techniques your mother possesses as a Wisdom Keeper. It is your decision whether you wish to accept or reject her great gifts.' He told me that if I, and other young people, refused to accept this knowledge, it would likely be lost forever."

"That would be terrible!" Mademoiselle Fleuret exclaimed.

"I was already half-convinced, but my godfather continued with his appeal," Tiye said. "He asked me if I was certain that several thousand years of healing—passed down from Wisdom Keeper to Wisdom Keeper, from mother to daughter—had no place in the modern world."

"How did you answer him?" Mademoiselle Fleuret posed.

"I said nothing at first, and simply followed Dr. Awyan out of the Queen's Chamber," Tiye recalled. "We climbed up the ramp to the King's Chamber. This time, my godfather filled the chamber with a deep resonant chanting. At the sound, I was filled with a great tranquility. I felt like I could see the future, my future. I saw myself helping people understand the ancient healing techniques, not only in Egypt, but all over the world. It was like a dream, but it felt true."

"What did you do next?" Mrs. Montgomery asked.

"I went to my mother and asked her if she would be my teacher in the ancient healing arts. I was surprised when my godfather insisted I go to Cairo University and take classes in pre-med. I was reluctant, because I wanted to learn more about the sound frequencies and the natural remedies my mother had always used whenever I was ill. Dr. Awyan insisted, though. He told me that at the university I'd learn the vocabulary needed to spread ancient Egyptian healing arts throughout the world."

Mademoiselle Fleuret said, "That is a beautiful story, Tiye."

As they exited the Pizza Hut, Dr. Bernstein and Bernadette told Tiye they were eager to learn about ancient Egyptian healing arts. Mrs. Montgomery agreed, saying she hoped the young woman would one day write a book.

"You honor me, ladies," Tiye said, locking the blue door. "Perhaps some-day I will. For now, however, I'd better head to the university for my next class."

The remaining three women walked silently back to the guest house, each wondering where Charles and Jacques could be—right at that moment.

CHAPTER 48

STUBBORN SAHARA

It was not the rising sun that woke Charles from a deep sleep but the strong, pungent aroma of the pack animal on which he was reclining. Charles jumped up, startling the kneeling camel. It gave a growl that built up to a yell, ending in a shriek.

Charles placed his hand on Stubborn Sahara's soft, furry neck and said, "It's alright. We're alright."

The camel closed her large eyes and fell back asleep, but Charles was awake—at least, he thought so. He reached out and ran the rocky sand through his fingers, then inspected the surrounding desert and decided, yes, he was definitely awake. The last thing he remembered, he was on a camel eight feet off the ground.

He recalled asking his camel, "Do you know what I am going to call you? Stubborn Sahara. Where are you going, Stubborn Sahara?"

The camel plodded forward. Charles thought he caught a faraway glimpse of the two women riders and their dromedaries.

"You're following those women, aren't you, girl?"

Stubborn Sahara made a honking noise that Charles decided meant yes. He tried to reason with his camel, but no amount of coaxing could make her turn back. He recalled calling for help as they crossed over a bridge but no one helped him. He remembered fading in and out of wakefulness as the dromedary walked steadily forward in the dark desert. And, now, he was here, on the ground, next to the odorous camel. Charles could see a faint orange halo on the eastern horizon. The sun was rising. Where was he, and what should he do? Could he convince Sahara to return to the City of the Dead? Or should he go forward?

Charles looked west. He saw what looked like an apparition riding towards him. He waved, calling out, "I am here. I'm here."

As the apparition drew closer, he recognized the rider as one of the women dressed in black. He was saved!

"Hello! I couldn't get this camel to go back to the City of the Dead," he yelled, pointing first to Stubborn Sahara and next to the direction from which they'd come. "She just kept following you. I'm supposed to be at the American Embassy in a few hours. They're going to send me home."

He'd thought both women in black were young, the way they rode through the night. But in the light of day, this woman looked a few years older than his mother. She rode her camel past where Charles was standing to where Stubborn Sahara was kneeling. Sahara gave a happy greeting noise to the woman's camel. Apparently, they were friends.

Charles noticed the woman was taller than most Egyptian women he'd seen. She had large dark eyes that seemed to have a light in them. She pulled her headscarf from her face, revealing a gentle smile. Charles was certain his troubles were over—that is, until the woman's hand signals indicated she was going to leave, and he was supposed to stay.

"What? I can't stay in a desert alone!" Charles shrieked.

The woman in black retrieved a canvas water bag and a paper-wrapped package from a cloth bag tied to her camel's saddle. She unwrapped the package and handed Charles a slab of thick, dark bread. It had a sweet, nutty taste. Charles, who hadn't eaten in what seemed like days, thought this was the most delicious food he'd eaten in his entire life. He followed the cakey bread with several long gulps of water that tasted like canvas. He didn't complain. He'd learned that when you were on an adventure, there were certain things you should not take for granted; water was one of these.

"Thank you!" he exclaimed. "Thank you for coming back for me. This is my camel. I call her Stubborn Sahara. I named her that because she wouldn't follow any of my instructions, verbal or physical. She wouldn't stop for anything. I got so sleepy, I think I fell off my camel. I'm due at the American Embassy this morning. They'll probably send me back to France and my school at the Château du Mont. You don't speak English, do you?"

Charles knew he was rambling and that there was obviously a language barrier. Charles wondered why he was talking so much; desperation, he guessed. He continued his plea.

"I really need to go back to Cairo. I have to go to the American Embassy," he said more loudly, hoping it would help the woman in black understand his urgency.

She indicated that she would return. She pulled herself up on her camel and rode west. Sahara complained loudly about the other camel's departure but remained kneeling.

Charles ran after the woman calling, "Wait!"

The woman in the black gallabiyah pointed him back to his camel. Charles watched her disappear over the edge of the dirt path. Where was she going, and why would she leave without him?

A pinhead ball of orange was emerging from the east, promising the beginning of a new day and the approach of the desert heat that scorched plants and threatened lives. Right now, though, it was still cold, and he was so tired. Dropping to his knees, he crawled over to Stubborn Sahara. "I'm freezing," he told the animal. "Can I rest next to you?"

The camel said nothing, just closed her eyes. Charles closed his eyes, too. The next thing he knew, the sun had risen fully, a great orange disk. He was now awake and wondering how long the woman in black would be gone. What should he do until she returned? Taking his shoulder bag off, he pulled out the map of Egypt that his butler had sent him. It had been on his bedroom wall since he was four years old. It was rolled up tight and bound with a rubber band.

He opened the map and spread it out on the ground. It immediately rolled back up. He rolled it out again, this time placing his hands on the top corners and his knees on the bottom. But this made it impossible to read the map. Charles let the map roll back up again, with the plan to look for some large rocks to hold the map open. The sand was mixed with rocks, mostly small. He managed to find four medium-sized rocks. He unrolled his map and placed a stone on each corner.

Charles was very familiar with this map of Egypt. Over the years, he'd placed green X's where Egyptian tombs had been discovered and red X's where he believed there were tombs yet to be found.

"Okay," Charles explained to Stubborn Sahara. "Here's Cairo, and here's the City of the Dead. I followed the three women west. Two of the women mounted camels and headed north. That's when you and I met. I thought I was just going to take a short ride, when you began following the two women in black."

The camel yawned, showing her large, jutting teeth.

"We came to a bridge. I yelled out, 'I need to go to the American Embassy.' No one listened to me. Once over the bridge, Sahara, there were fewer and fewer people, until there were just the two of us. You kept walking and walking. Every once in a while, I could glimpse the two women far, far ahead of us."

Stubborn Sahara looked out over the desert and gave a loud bawling sound.

"Pay attention, Sahara! This is important. Camels can walk fifty to seventy miles a day, or in this case a night. I figure that would put us somewhere near here: Crocodilopolis!"

Charles placed his finger on a red X. He knew a lot about this area. His mother had given him a book called *Crocodilopolis* on his fifth birthday. He had read it over and over again. On the map next to his finger was a drawing he'd made of a crocodile. Charles told his camel that it wasn't a good picture because he was only five or six years old when he drew it.

"Still," he said, "you can tell it's a crocodile, Sahara. It has a long body and snout and many very sharp teeth. Back in the 12th and 13th dynasties, the people of this area worshipped the crocodile god, Sobek. They believed Sobek rose from the dark waters and created order in the world. But the crocodile god was unpredictable. My book said that Sobek sometimes made an alliance with chaos, raining trouble down upon the people of Egypt. I believe that Sobek must have rained some trouble down on me."

He resumed telling his story to the camel, who was swinging her large neck from side-to-side.

"I always liked this part. Sobek's followers worshiped the crocodile god, not just in the form of a man's body with a crocodile head, but as a real live crocodile. The priests selected a crocodile for its beauty and strength. You know, Sahara, I never thought of a crocodile as being beautiful, did you?"

Stubborn Sahara got up and hovered over Charles, who was on his hands and knees looking at the map.

"So you are interested, are you, Sahara?" the boy asked. "They built the crocodiles grand temples with a large pond inside. The priests and the people who worshipped Sobek called the real crocodile the Son of Sobek. Special priests were assigned to care for him. They fed him the best cuts of meat and specially made honey cakes, and sang songs to him. My book said the crocodile would become so tame, the priests were able to decorate the crocodile with a crown of gold and necklaces made of various gems. What do you think, Sahara? Would you like a crown of gold and necklaces made of various gems?"

Charles continued speaking to his camel, the only living thing in sight. "When the Son of Sobek died, as all living things do, it was mummified and given a special burial. Then another crocodile was chosen to take his place. As a little kid, I thought that was the best story ever."

Charles looked around. He noticed the woman in black had left the water bag next to him on the ground. He took a long drink, then apologized to Sahara.

"I read that camels can go a week to ten days without water. There isn't much left in this bag, so I can't share the water. But as soon as we find water, you can drink all you want."

Sahara reached down and gave Charles a soft knock on his back. Charles continued his commentary.

"Now see here, Sahara, I put a number of red X's in this area, meaning that undiscovered tombs would likely be found in the region of Crocodilopolis. What do you think?"

The camel said nothing. Charles rolled up the map and put the rubber band around it. He placed it back into his shoulder bag, then resumed his conversation with the tawny camel.

"We were supposed to stay here, but I think it would be okay if I walked to where we last saw the woman in black and her camel disappear over that edge over there. You stay here. I'll be right back."

The camel knelt back down and closed its eyes. Charles walked down the five or six-foot-wide path. He thought it must be an ancient road, used by travelers for thousands of years. Probably some of them were the exact same people who worshiped Sobek. The desert floor was not made of the fine-grained sand Charles had dreamed of when he thought of exploring Egypt. It was a disappointing sand, yellowish dirt mixed with small rocks, the same kind of sand surrounding the Sphinx and pyramids of Giza. Thinking about Giza made him think about Jacques. What was Jacques doing right now? Was he searching for him? Was he worried? Or was he on a jet plane headed back to the Château du Mont? Had Jacques forgotten about him? Did anybody care? Taking a long breath, Charles decided there was no use spending any more time thinking about this. Somehow he had to find the American Embassy.

CHAPTER 49

THE DESERT FAMILY

Charles glanced up at the sun, which was already a large reddish-orange ball hanging straight above his head. The cold desert was turning hot, and there was no shade in sight. He ran to the place where he'd seen the camel and the woman in black disappearing over an edge. It turned out to be the beginning of a long, steep, descending path leading to a large valley. A green band of land and a blue band of water snaked through the landscape.

In the distance, Charles could see a lake the color of lapis lazuli. His first thought was the canal or the lake would be a great place to take a swim. His second thought was crocodiles probably lived in the canal and the lake. Charles had read that these giant reptiles killed over a thousand people a year. It crossed his mind that perhaps these Sons of Sobek were angry because people weren't building Sobek temples anymore. It seemed that Sobek had gone out of style. Charles decided it was the heat that was making him think this way. In fact, he reminded himself, he shouldn't be thinking about crocodiles at all. He should be thinking that he was not going to die. He was not going to become a pile of bleached bones to be discovered by future travelers. At the end of the path there was water, and where there is water there must be people.

Looking down at the base of the steep trail, Charles' eyes caught movement. Soon he could identify two camels and two people ascending the steep, snake-like path. As they got closer, Charles ran back to his camel. Stubborn Sahara made a sniffing sound as she smelled the air. She followed this by several high-pitched bleats. Both camel and boy watched as two camels and their riders emerged from the top of the ridge. Stubborn Sahara slowly rose to her feet and welcomed the dromedaries with a low-pitched, friendly greeting.

"Hello," Charles called out, running towards the two women.

"Hello, Charles. My name is Subira, and this is Rehima, the Compassionate One."

"Thank you for coming back for me. I guess I got kind of lost," Charles admitted.

"Let's get you on your camel," Subira said.

Rehima made some kind of secret sound, and Sahara immediately knelt on the ground.

"How'd you do that?" Charles asked the Compassionate One as she helped him climb up to the cloth saddle on the hump of Stubborn Sahara.

The woman who had introduced herself as Subira said, "The temperature is rising rapidly. There is shade down by the irrigation canal, where we can talk more comfortably. Let us proceed."

Charles, on Stubborn Sahara, followed the other camels to the edge of the ridge. Charles found that the path looked completely different from his eight-foot perch on his undependable camel. He decided to tell Subira he preferred to walk down the steep path.

"Excuse me," Charles said.

It was too late. Stubborn Sahara was already following the other two camels down the trail. No one was happier than Charles when the three camels reached flat ground. Rehima pointed towards a palm tree-lined canal about a half-mile ahead. As they reached the canal, the Compasionate One helped Charles dismount. The three camels walked towards the sparkling blue water, bending their long necks down to drink. Charles ran to the water's edge to drink from the canal, too, before he remembered the crocodiles.

Rehima and Subira were sitting down in the shade of a palm tree's jagged leaves. Subira called Charles over, handing him two empty canteens. Charles gathered he was to fill them from the canal. With his eyes scanning the blue water for any movement, he placed the canvas canteens in the tepid water. When both containers were filled, he joined the women in the shade of the palm tree.

Subira said, "Last night, in the City of the Dead, you showed the Wasims and their neighbors a distinctive pyramid. How did you come to be in possession of this pyramid?"

Charles thought for a moment about what he should tell these women. There was no use lying. They already knew the pyramid existed. He had betrayed Farak. He had shown the people of the City of the Dead the replica pyramid. The cat was out of the bag, and it couldn't be put back in. He told the women in black about Farak gifting him with an imitation of the real pyramid, the relic pyramid.

"The relic pyramid," Charles explained, "is held and protected by the Tarabin Tribe. The pyramid Farak gave me is called the replica pyramid."

"Why did the Egyptian boy give you this pyramid?" Subira asked.

Charles was quiet a moment, remembering. "He said my love of Egypt helped him get in touch with his own roots. It helped Farak remember his love for his family, his people, his desert. He said he'd almost forgotten after being at the boarding school, the Château du Mont, for so many years."

"Do you know where Farak's family might be found?" Subira inquired.

"Yes, I have their address in here," Charles said, patting his shoulder bag.

"Will you entrust me with their address?" Subira requested.

Charles agreed. Pulling the bag off his shoulder and reaching inside, he handed Subira a small notebook. It had the addresses of the family and friends of his Bedouin schoolmate. "Farak told me that if I showed the pyramid to anyone whose name was in this book, they'd do anything for me, even lay down their lives," he said.

"Hmm," was all Subira said as she brought out her own notebook, copying addresses. She handed Charles his notebook. "I must leave you, but I'll meet you and Rehima later," she told the boy. Rehima helped Subira mount her tawny-colored camel.

"You aren't taking me to the American Embassy today?" Charles asked.

"No, you will not go today," she answered. "There are more important things to do."

"What more important things?" Charles asked the woman sitting high on her camel.

Subira didn't answer his question. Instead, she said, "Rehima will lead you to our friends. You can trust her. She is the mother of a boy just your age. She will take good care of you, Charles. Oh, yes, and although Rehima does not speak English, she understands it perfectly."

Charles turned towards the taller of the two women. "So you can understand me, Rehima, the Compassionate One? But I can't understand you. Believe me, I'm going to learn Arabic as soon as I get back to the Château du Mont. That's where I go to school."

Rehima gave him a reassuring smile.

"I wonder where Subira is going?" Charles wondered.

Rehima didn't answer. Instead, she continued north on her white camel. Stubborn Sahara considered whether she should follow Subira or Rehima. Rehima grabed her reins and led her north. Soon both camels were walking side-by-side. Charles looked at Rehima's camel. It had a noble-looking face. It didn't look a bit like Stubborn Sahara, who had a cartoon-like face. Sahara was a funny-looking camel.

"Why can't I have a noble-looking camel?" Charles mumbled under his breath.

As they walked along the ribbon of blue, Charles watched white long-necked cranes dart above the water. Periodically, the cranes dove straight down, piercing the surface of the water, occasionally emerging with a silver fish in their long beaks. It was hot and getting hotter. Charles looked longingly at the water. If Jacques were here, they would definitely take a dip in the canal.

Rehima and her camel turned and crossed an arched, wooden bridge. They were heading west again. With a loud shriek, Sahara refused to cross the bridge. Rehima returned to Charles' camel, who was crying like a baby, and grabbed her reins.

"Hey," he said to his vociferous mount, "I don't like riding under the burning sun any better than you do. And anyway, camels are used to the desert. I come from Rhode Island, on the edge of the Atlantic Ocean. I'm not used to this kind of heat, so stop grumbling."

Charles laughed at himself for talking to a dromedary. But Stubborn Sahara was falling further and further behind Rehima's camel. There was nothing to do but ride and think. Why hadn't he asked Subira to get a message to the American Embassy? Jacques must have gone to the embassy, as that had been their agreement. Jacques had no doubt contacted Madame Constance. Boy, would she be upset!

How long had it been since Charles was put off the train by that conductor? It must be at least a week. Did his parents know he was missing? Probably not. His parents had told Jacques they'd be "out of touch" while he and Jacques toured Egypt. Where were his parents going, and why would they be out of touch? The sun was beating down on his head. Why hadn't he put on his keffiyeh? Reaching into his shoulder bag, Charles pulled out his headscarf and placed it over his uncombed hair.

Sahara had fallen behind. Rehima returned and grabbed Sahara's reins, again attempting to speed up the camel. But Sahara, refusing to speed up, only slowed down Rehima's camel. When Charles thought he couldn't ride one more second, the woman in black pointed to something ahead. There was a small building breaking the horizon. A half-hour later, they reached a modest stone home. A woman came out of the house's azure door, carrying a baby on her hip. Rehima greeted her, then made some kind of sound. The white camel, hearing this, knelt down. Rehima dismounted, then turned and made the same sound, bringing Sahara down on her knees. Charles would have to ask her what those magic words were.

The woman with the baby led Rehima and Charles to the blue door. Once inside, the young-looking woman placed her baby on a mat and brought out a pot of hot tea. It seemed strange to be drinking hot tea in a hot desert, but it made Charles feel relaxed and sleepy. The woman left Rehima, the baby, and Charles and walked outside. Several minutes later, she returned with a stack of warm flatbread. After Charles had finished the tea and flatbread, the woman rolled out a mat and pointed to it.

Exhausted from his long camel ride, Charles fell into a deep sleep. He dreamed he met two gods, Sobek and Anubis, the god of death, guide to the underworld, with the head of a dog and a man's body. Anubis told Charles he could choose his form of death: mummification or becoming food for the Son of Sobek. Charles didn't like either option, so he forced himself awake.

Rehima was sitting on the floor, talking to the younger woman as she fed her baby. When the mother was finished, she plopped the baby into Charles' lap. He tried to tell her he knew nothing about babies, but she didn't understand him. Rehima handed Charles a rattle made from some kind of bones. Charles shook the rattle; it made a clicking noise. The baby laughed and reached for the bone rattle. Charles pulled the rattle away, then brought it closer, making another rattling noise. When the baby reached for the rattle, Charles pulled it away again. The baby thought this was so funny, he laughed and laughed. After a few minutes, the baby reached for his mother.

There was a knock on the door. Subira entered. Smiling at Charles, she said, "I've got news for you. Your friend Farak Faruq will be joining us at the Temple of Sobek."

"But Farak is in France at the Château du Mont," Charles said.

"He is here in Egypt. I spoke with him," Subira said with a wide smile. "I called the number you gave me. Farak answered the telephone. He said when he learned you were missing, he flew straight to Luxor. He was sure that either you would find him or he would find you. I told him you were safe and that we wished to invite him to the Temple of Sobek, but that its location was to be kept a secret. I promised we would send someone to escort him. We set a place for him to meet his escort."

"Where is this Temple of Sobek?" Charles asked.

"It is not near here," Subira answered. "We still have quite a ride in front of us. We will be leaving soon."

"At night?" Charles asked.

"We always enter the Temple of Sobek at night, so that others will not discover its location," the woman in black explained.

It was as though Charles' favorite childhood book had come to life! He was going to the Temple of Sobek. Charles was trying to imagine what the temple might look like today when a man burst into the house. Picking up the baby, he swung him high over his head. The baby laughed and laughed.

Noticing Charles, the man said, "I am Ammon; I work at the Osiris Hotel." Pointing to the length and breadth of his tiny one-room abode, he said, "I welcome you to our home."

Ammon went back to playing with the baby, whom Charles surmised was his son. He thought the father didn't look much older than Farak. Subira, the baby's mother, and Rehima went outside. When they returned, each was carrying several bags of food. The three women talked and laughed as they prepared dishes of rice, vegetables, beans, and flatbread. The festive atmosphere poured out of the doors and windows of the little stone home and spread out into the darkening desert, lighting it up like a flood light.

Charles wondered why everyone in Egypt seemed so happy. They had nothing: no furniture, no electricity, no running water, no refrigerator. They were poor, very poor. The mother handed Charles his plate like he was one of the family members. Not like his own family—with a butler, maids, and a huge dining room table—but like a real family, those he'd occasionally glimpsed on TV and read about in books. Families he'd thought that he just might like to live with. Charles felt comfortable and surprised. He'd loved

Egypt all his life, but his only thoughts of the country were connected to its ancient past: pyramids, temples, tombs, hieroglyphics, gods, goddesses, pharaohs, mummies, and treasures. He'd never thought about the real people of Egypt, the Egyptians living at this moment in time.

After dinner, the baby crawled from one person to another, and finally crawled into Charles' lap. The baby laid his head on the boy's chest and closed his eyes. Soon, the baby was fast asleep. Charles looked up at Rehima. He didn't know what he was supposed to do. The father, mother and the two women in black laughed, until Charles joined the hilarity. Smiling at Charles, the mother picked up her child and put him on a mat, covering him with a blue cotton blanket.

Ammon led everyone outside. The sun had set; the moon had not yet risen. No one spoke as they stared at the dome of stars surrounding them. The father pointed to Orion's belt. Charles pointed to the Big and Little dippers and the North Star. The boy wondered why it was that you could see the night sky a thousand times and still be stunned by its splendor and its stories.

"We will be leaving in a few minutes," Subira said, attaching a bag to her camel's saddle.

"Are we going to the Temple of Sobek?" Charles asked.

"Yes. You will spend the night there," Subira said matter-of-factly. "To-morrow, your friend Farak will arrive. Oh, good. Look! The moon is coming up and will soon light our pathway."

The mother went into the stone home and brought the baby out, giving him to her husband to hold. The family waved as Rehima, Subira and Charles left for their night walk. Charles felt sad that he wouldn't see this family again, and a little alarmed at the idea of spending the night at the Temple of Sobek.

CHAPTER 50

CHARLES AT THE TEMPLE OF SOBEK

C harles rode between the stars and the land, up gentle sandy slopes
and down. The three-quarter moon—craters visible in the thin, clear
air—illuminated the desert floor, creating sharp shadows of the three riders
on camels.

Charles became aware of a strange calmness inside. No, it was more than that. He felt a kind of completeness. He'd walked inside one of his own dreams, and it seemed more real than his life at home in Newport, Rhode Island, or his room at the Château du Mont in France. He realized the fear he'd felt in the pit of his stomach in the City of the Dead was dread, dread that his trip to Egypt had ended before it had begun. Now, he'd been accepted into an Egyptian family and played with an Egyptian baby. He'd learned a home could be a room, and a kitchen could be an outdoor stone fire pit. He'd discovered people could love and laugh when they seemed to own nothing. He found friendship with a woman who spoke no English and with a camel who was often stubborn and yet great company. Then there was Subira and Rehima, who'd saved his life and made him feel like he was part of something greater than himself.

How, Charles wondered, how could he capture this day and night in writing? After all, it wasn't just a story of events, because most of the action happened within him. Was this true of the greatest writers? Did they write stories to capture what was really going on inside of themselves—to express what they were thinking? What they were observing about others? Did they put these things in story form to keep from boring their readers, or to study themselves more extensively? He would have to think about this.

Tomorrow, Farak would arrive. He would no longer be needed for what-ever mission the relic pyramid was to play in this story. But it was too late to take this day and this night back from him. It was his forever. He petted Stubborn Sahara, studied the constellation of Orion, and wondered what would happen next.

After riding for several hours, Charles and Sahara became aware of a low, rocky mountain looming from the desert floor in front of them. Sahara gave the change in scenery a bellowing greeting, then picked up her pace. An hour's ride brought them to the foot of the small but steep mountain. Subira, Rehima, and their camels had disappeared. Evidently, there was a path some-where. Sahara sped up until finally, the three camels were climbing a steep dirt path in single-file. When they reached the summit and were standing on its ridge, Subira pointed to an even steeper path down the southern side of the mountain. It was bad enough riding down a steep path in the daytime, but riding down a steep path at night seemed like a bad idea. Charles suggested to Subira that they walk the camels.

Subira laughed. "Our camels have taken this path many times before, so it will be fine."

"At night?"

"We try not to come here by day," Subira said.

Yeah, thought Charles, it was a secret. But why? The path down to the other side of the mountain was invisible. With Rehima leading them, Charles found that the hard dirt path wound gently around and around like a giant snake, making their course feel less steep. Once they reached the bottom of the path, Charles found no sign of a temple or tomb, only the flames in a fire pit. He was freezing despite the shawl Rehima had given him for the night ride through the desert. Rehima helped Charles off Stubborn Sahara. Charles ran to the fire to warm his hands. The three camels clopped towards a small pond shimmering in the moonlight. He watched the shadowy forms of the camels, bending down their furry necks and slurping up water. He wished he had his Leica camera with him, but he'd left it on the train on the seat next to Jacques. Thinking about Jacques made Charles wondered if Jacques knew where he was. Had Farak told him?

Subira broke into his thoughts. "Your friend Farak will be here tomorrow, and you will be with your family soon."

Her words made Charles feel melancholy. He answered, "I don't have a family, not really. My parents don't care about me. They're on a boat somewhere on the west coast of Central Africa or Central America. They're always on a trip. I have no brothers, sisters, aunts, uncles, or grandparents. Nobody."

"Maybe so," Subira said. "However, you do have people who care for you. Farak told me there are several people looking for you here in Egypt right now. Your roommate, your roommate's grandparents, and a teacher."

Charles was astounded. "Really? David's here? His grandparents? A teacher? That must be Mademoiselle Fleuret. She's the only one who'd come."

"I heard a French woman's name," Subira replied. "Farak also told me a man came from America who might be your grandfather. He's looking for you, too."

"I don't have a grandfather."

"Everyone has a grandfather, Charles," the woman in the black gallabiyah said earnestly.

Charles was confused, as he always was when he thought about his family. Why didn't his parents ever tell him about a grandfather? Out loud, he said, "My parents never mentioned any grandparents."

"I don't know," Subira said gently. "But I do know there are people who care for you and will celebrate your return."

Charles didn't know what to think about all this. They had arrived in this strange area, lit up by the moon. Many tumbled boulders lay this way and that, some as tall as fifty feet. Where did these rocks come from? Charles was pondering this as he watched Rehima walk to the edge of the water where the camels were drinking. She filled her leather canteen, stroking the side of her camel. When she returned, Charles saw she was holding the reins of two of the three camels. Stubborn Sahara was still at the water's edge. Rehima directed her camels to kneel.

"Hey!" Charles exclaimed, alarmed. "Where are you going?"

"Our task was to bring you here to the Tomb of a Thousand Names," Subira said, preparing to mount her camel. "Now, we must return to our families and our employment."

Charles couldn't believe he was being abandoned yet again. "Tonight? You can't leave me here alone out in the desert."

"If we do not leave now, we will not get home before morning."

Charles was too upset to notice Subira had called this place the Tomb of a Thousand Names, not the Temple of Sobek.

He looked up at the two women seated on their camels and said, "But I don't want you to go."

"You are a charming and courageous young man," Subira said. "We hope we will see you again before you leave for France."

Charles shook his head. "You're wrong, I'm not courageous." He had a sudden thought. "Wait! If you stay with me, my father will pay you a lot of money."

Subira said something in Arabic, and both women laughed. This made Charles angry.

He said, "I demand that you stay here with me," his voice echoing off the boulders.

He slid back to his old self, declaring that nobody cared about him. Rehima's and Subira's camels had started up the trail.

Charles called out, "If you leave me here alone, I'll die, and it will be all your fault."

"We wouldn't leave you alone in the desert," Subira called back to Charles. "Someone will be coming for you very soon. Warm yourself by the fire."

The two women headed back towards the mountain path. Charles ran after them, but they were already up the trail. Walking to the fire, Charles dropped to his knees on the sandy ground. He felt a firm knock on the back of his upper shoulders; it practically knocked him into the fire. Turning around, he found himself staring at Sahara's yellowish buck teeth. Charles could smell her sour breath. Sahara brushed her lips softly against his forehead. She seemed to be telling him she understood.

He petted her furry neck, then spontaneously said, "Kneel down, Sahara."

To his surprise, Stubborn Sahara did exactly that. She knelt. Now, he was in a quandary. Should he get on his camel and follow Subira and Rehima back to Cairo? Or should he stay and spend the night in the—what had Subira called it? Charles remembered that she'd called this place the Tomb of a Thousand Names. Had Subira made a mistake? Where was the Tomb of a Thousand Names? And where was the Temple of Sobek? Charles stared up at the shadow of the two women weaving their way up the mountain trail. Rehima was pointing to something high up on the boulders behind him.

A few minutes later, a man emerged from a hidden path behind the tall, strangely-leaning boulders. He was dressed all in white and was carrying a lantern. The man gave Charles a slight bow, pointed up towards the tower of boulders, and then walked back from where he'd come. Charles could think of nothing to do but follow him. As they moved away from the oasis, Charles heard Stubborn Sahara bawling loudly. He wondered if he should run to his camel, jump up on her cloth saddle, and follow Rehima and Subira up the mountain path. Then again, Farak would be here tomorrow. Charles turned away from his camel and followed the man, stepping behind one of the large boulders blocking the night sky from sight. Charles was exhausted; all he could do was follow the lantern light. Man and boy wound this way and that, climbing higher and higher on a surprisingly smooth, yet hidden path.

At one point, Charles found himself on the top of a boulder with a wide view of the mountain and the valley below. He and his guide had traveled at least sixty feet from the desert floor. From his vantage, Charles could see Sahara standing near the light of the fire. She was looking in his direction. Seeing her made him feel that Stubborn Sahara was his only friend in the entire world. Now, he was leaving her behind, abandoning her.

The man was waiting for him under two large boulders lying over each other, making a bridge. Charles was so fatigued, he wanted nothing more than to sleep. As he thought this, Charles found his legs could no longer hold him up. He slipped to the ground, determined to stay there until morning. The man in the white gallabiyah came back to him. Pointing to a nearby boulder, he gently lifted Charles back up on his feet. The stranger supported him as they walked another ten feet. They had reached a dead end. The guide pushed on a section of stone, and it opened. The man stepped aside and allowed Charles to enter. His guide pulled on a metal handle and the doorway shut. Charles was sure that, day or night, this entrance would be invisible to any travelers passing by.

Charles stood on the top of a stone stairway. He didn't have to count them. It would be seven steps. For the ancients, seven meant the end of something—or death. As he descended the steps, Charles hoped fervently that he was not walking toward his own end, his own death. After all, he'd never even seen the Nile River.

At the bottom of the steps were seven lanterns, softly illuminating a room that was about sixteen by fourteen feet. The chamber was completely bare. There was nothing written or carved on the ceilings, walls, or floor. Maybe this was really a pyramid. It was deathly quiet. Charles decided he should say something to the man he was following. He'd start by introducing himself.

"Hello, my name is Charles Dayton Stratton III. I am from the United States of America, Rhode Island, to be exact."

Charles' speech broke the silence, like the dropping of a glass on a cement floor. The man he was following kept walking.

"I'm here to meet my friend, Farak. His family lives in Luxor," Charles said, faking cheeriness.

The stranger led Charles through another stone door. On the other side of the door was another metal bar. The man pulled the bar across the door and fastened it to a large metal latch. Now, he was sure that no one could get in and no one could get out.

Charles decided to try and talk to the man again. "Subira and Rehima brought me here."

The Egyptian, still holding his lantern, turned and smiled at Charles.

"Okay, we're friends then. Right?" the boy asked.

From that point on, the path they traveled turned this way and that, frequently in dramatic angles, for the most part going deeper and deeper underground. Sometimes, there were two passageways to choose from, sometimes three. Charles wished he'd brought a giant ball of string or breadcrumbs to help him find his way out.

The man in the white gallabiyah stopped walking. He held up his lantern, and Charles caught his breath. The walls were no longer smooth and blank. The large room was covered with reliefs and colorful paintings, mostly of

Sobek, the crocodile god. But there were other figures too. He recognized, these figures, since he'd memorized the forms and attributes of most of the major gods and goddesses of ancient Egypt.

In several carvings, Sobek was standing by Renenutet, Sobek's consort. Sobek's girlfriend, Renenutet, was one of Charles' least favorite goddesses. She was the cobra goddess, whose mighty gaze destroyed her enemies with a glance; she had a woman's body and a snake head. She wore a crown. On another wall, standing by Sobek was Set, another of his least favorite deities. Set had a man's body, and the head of several desert animals. Set was the master of storms, thunder, chaos, and violence, and then there were numerous illustrations of the Sons of Sobek.

In the center of the cavernous room was a large dark pond. The lantern shined on these terrible forms, causing the dark water to appear like it was teeming with crocodiles and snakes. Charles shivered. He looked toward his guide and found him holding a towel and pointing towards the pond.

"You want me to go in the pond?" Charles asked.

The man nodded his head in the affirmative. The boy stood on the edge of the water, looking for any signs of life. Glancing back at his guide, Charles saw he was laughing. Subira claimed Charles was courageous but, right now, he didn't feel courageous. Charles took a deep breath, then stepped into the dark water. It was not hot, nor cold. It was a perfect temperature. Charles swam around the pond, examining each relief and painting. The flickering lanterns lining the large room made the paintings look as if they were moving, like they were alive. This was definitely the scariest and yet the most exciting pool Charles had ever seen or imagined.

The guide held up the towel. It was time to get out. Charles found a pure white gallabiyah on a stone bench. His own clothes were nowhere to be seen. He was relieved to discover his shoulder bag was under a stone bench. He dressed and picked up his shoulder bag.

Now that he was bathed and dressed, exhaustion overtook him. He could barely keep his eyes open as he followed his guide up and down various pathways. The man stopped in front of a dark curtain, holding it open for

Charles to enter. Behind the curtain was a small room with a bed and a desk. When Charles turned around, he found he was alone. He looked at the bed. He hadn't slept in a bed in he didn't know how many nights. He thought he would just lay down for a minute, when he heard a soft knock outside the door of the room.

"You can come in," Charles said, too tired to be alarmed.

A woman walked into the room. She was dressed in a white gallabiyah, too. She also had on a long white head scarf that covered her head and shoulders. Her face was perfectly smooth, despite the fact that a few gray strands of hair escaped her head cloth. Charles couldn't tell how old she was, but he thought she was beautiful.

"Hello, you must be Charles," the woman said in perfect English. "Welcome to the House of Life. I am the Holder of the Keys to the Right and Left Path. I am the servant and keeper of the records of the great creator-teachers Seshat and Thoth, daughter of Akhenaten, devotee of Aten, and High Priestess of the Tomb of a Thousand Names."

"Hello, I am the Seeker of Tomb 11. I greet you," Charles answered.

Where'd that come from, he wondeed. He didn't remember forming these words in his head.

"Seldom do we allow strangers, or one so young, to enter our temple. Yet I have been advised to lift this ban because you are said to be a keyholder. Therefore, if you are pure of heart and understand the importance of keeping a secret, for the good of all earthly elements, you will be allowed to stay."

Charles told the woman in white, "I never told my parents about the Ghosts of the Jangling Keys, or that I am searching for the Ghost of Tomb 11, Tel el Armana, Egypt. I can definitely keep secrets, but I must tell you that I'm not really a keyholder. The pyramid that I showed Subira and Rehima in the City of the Dead is just a replica. Subira told me that tomorrow my friend Farak will be here. He and his family are the real keyholders, or at least the holders of the relic pyramid. As for that part about me being pure of heart, I'm not quite sure."

The woman laughed a joyful and bell-like laugh, sounding almost like the Good Witch of the North in "The Wizard of Oz."

"With such truthful answers, I am sure that you are worthy of entering the Tomb of Secrets. We welcome you."

"Thank you," Charles said. "What is your real name?"

"People call me SeShat, but my name is Meketaten," she answered.

"You mean you're named after the second-born of Akhenaten and Nefertiti, the princess who died as a young girl?"

"Yes, that girl."

"That's sad," Charles responded.

"Yes, it can be looked at as so. However, her early death led to a great jump in the science of health and wellbeing in ancient Egypt. Many lives were saved, and pain and suffering were lessened. So it turns out something that looks bad can, in fact, be a great gift. You must be tired and hungry. I will send you a plate of food and we will talk tomorrow."

Charles knew if he lay down on the bed, he would fall into a deep sleep, missing food and perhaps the chance to see this woman with a bunch of names. What could he do while waiting for dinner? He looked at the desk, which held a lantern. He found a pen in his bag and a stack of paper in the top drawer. He decided to write something to David about the Temple of Sobek.

He tried several narratives, but the words didn't sound right. He remembered that Percy Shelley said the sole purpose for the existence of poetry was to use meaning, sound, and rhymical language to evoke an emotional response. Emotional response: that's what he wanted. He would try to write a poem about the Temple of Sobek.

The Temple of Sobek,
for David Montgomery

I walked down the seven stone steps, entering the Temple of Sobek.
In a white gallabiyah, my guide led me to the sacred central room.
Lifting his lantern, he revealed the dreadful forms of Sobek,
The god with the crocodile head and human body.

It was Sobek, the god of the old kingdom,
Star of the Pyramid Text.
Sobek, who first raised his arms towards heaven,
Commanding the Universe to take form and order.

In front of me was Sobek, standing beside his consort,
Renenutet, her body that of a beautiful woman,
Her head that of a writhing snake, the Egyptian cobra.
She wears a crown of gold and jewels.
Her power? It is to destroy all with her cobra-glance.
It is a terrible visage, David.

On the wall across the dark water, Sobek stands by Set.
Set, the master of storms, the god of chaos and disorder,
The brother and murderer of Osiris.
Why were they standing side-by-side, order and disorder?
I don't know, David.
I just know that both gods
Share the same characteristic:
Unpredictability.
Thus, it was deemed by the ancient Egyptians,
it was best to keep Sobek happy, contented.

As the story goes, one day Sobek formed the real crocodiles.
He declared them his agents, his representatives.
The chosen ones, the most beautiful crocodiles,
He called the Sons of Sobek.
Sobek commanded humans to build temples
For his chosen ones.
They were to be given ponds,
So they would feel comfortable.

They were to be fed the finest of food
So they would feel contented.
They were to be decorated with gold and jewels,
So they would feel venerated.
And they would be assigned their own priests
To praise them, and sing them songs,
So they would feel blissful.

Sobek demanded these rituals,
Not because of his own hubris,
Not because he needed to be worshiped,
Through the Sons of Sobek,
But lest anyone forget what it was like before Sobek—
A universe in disarray, in chaos.
***

Inside the Temple of Sobek,
Holding a towel, my guide pointed to the pool.
I stared at Sobek's reflection in the dark waters.
I wondered, was I to be the food for this Son of Sobek?

Then I heard a voice say,
'This pond no longer belongs to Sobek.
There is but one god, Aten.'
Can you believe it, David?
Akhenaten, Pharaoh of Tel el Armana,
Where the Ghost of Tomb 11 resides,
Spoke these words to me.
Why aren't you here, David?
Aren't we braver together?
I thought of you,
Then I walked into the dark water.

Charles Dayton Stratton III
Temple of Sobek, July 1987
P.S. I think I might have turned 12 years old.

CHAPTER 51

FARAK'S MOTHER AT THE TEMPLE OF SOBEK

C harles awoke. He was in the tiny room with the desk and bed. On
the desk was a flickering lantern and a tray of food. He had no idea
what time it was. When you're in a temple or a tomb where there's no sun
or moon, time doesn't seem to exist. At least, that's what Charles thought.
Still, he knew Farak was due to arrive sometime today. He was starved. He ate
everything on the tray. He peered out the door to see if anyone was coming,
sat on the bed, peeked outside again, and finally fell back asleep. Charles
was dreaming he and Stubborn Sahara were traveling together towards Tel
el Armana, crossing back over the Nile, when he heard a sort of giggle. His
eyes popped open. A woman in a dark gallabiyah was holding the curtain
door open. When Charles' and her eyes met, he stood up. Throwing her arms
over her head, she ran to him and picked him up in her ample arms, saying

something over and over again in Arabic. He looked back at the door and was relieved to see Farak entering the room. His schoolmate was dressed in a white gallabiyah and keffiyeh, just like him.

"Hello, Charles," Farak said quietly. "I would like to introduce you to my mother. I need to warn you that she understands English, but refuses to speak it. She says she has an ineloquent accent."

"Oh, this is your mother? It's a pleasure to meet you," Charles said.

The woman let go of him. He found his feet firmly on the ground again. Farak's mother was smiling widely; even her cheeks and eyes were smiling.

"What's she saying?" Charles asked Farak.

"She's calling you the Bringer of the Jewel. I am sorry to say that the jewel she's referring to is me. She thinks that I would not have come home if it weren't for you."

"Greetings, mother of Farak and Queen of the Bedouin nation," Charles said with a slight bow.

Farak's mother laughed a great hearty laugh, then said something in Arabic.

"She says she's not a queen," Farak translated. "She prefers to be called the Mother of the Tarabin Tribe."

"Should I call her that?" Charles asked.

"She would be honored if you would, because she's welcoming you into the Tarabin Tribe. She says you are now a member of her tribe, our tribe."

"Wow! She's accepting me into your tribe? Can she do that?" Charles' eyes were wide with surprise, his heart beating wildly.

"Yes, she has this power," Farak said.

"Thank you, thank you, Mother of the Tarabin Tribe," Charles said. "This is the best thing that ever happened to me in my entire life."

There was a knock outside the curtained door.

"Come on in. Everybody is here," Charles said.

It was the High Priestess again. Charles gave her a slight bow, as did Farak and his mother.

"Good morning," she said. "I am glad to see that you are all together."

The High Priestess said something in Arabic to Farak's mother. The Mother of the Tarabin Tribe left smiling and waving, almost skipping out the door.

"I think she's headed for the crocodile pond," Farak said. Both boys burst out laughing.

"About my becoming part of the Tarabin Tribe," Charles said, sorrow written across his face. "I cannot accept."

"Why not?" Farak looked puzzled.

"Because I don't deserve such an honor. I've betrayed you, Farak."

"Why do you say such a thing?" the Egyptian boy asked.

Charles gathered his courage, saying, "I don't know how much you know about my story."

"I know you were put off the train in Cairo, as you were mistaken for a stowaway," Farak said.

"Yes. Then I collided with a man carrying a bunch of large metal boxes," Charles explained. "More specifically, I collided with one of his boxes. I was badly injured and was taken to the City of the Dead by a taxi driver named Mr. Wasim."

"That's how you managed to disappear so completely," Farak observed.

"Yeah, I'd suffered a head injury and was unconscious for many days," Charles said. "When I woke up, they called for an interpreter. His name is Aamen. He was going to take me to the American Embassy the next day. That night we met, Aamen encouraged me to tell my story to the Wasims and their neighbors. They had all been so kind to me, and prayed for my survival. I was grateful, but I reminded Aamen that I didn't speak a word of Arabic. Aamen said that was no problem. I'd just tell my story and he'd translate it. He told me to share my adventure, as he called it, in great detail, because the people of the City of the Dead love long stories."

"That is something they share in common with the Tarabin Tribe," Farak said. "When I was young, I sometime feared their stories would never end."

"Aamen and I stood on the stairs of a tomb, seven steps up," Charles continued. "Forty or fifty people gathered to hear my story. At the end, something terrible happened. I don't know why I did it, Farak. I brought out the replica pyramid and showed everyone. I immediately realized my betrayal, but it was too late. The rest of the story is rather long," Charles continued. "There were three women in the back row dressed in black. They were interested in the relic pyramid. They gave me a signal, Farak. They each held their thumbs and fingers in a pyramid shape. I became curious and followed them on a camel. That's how I ended up here at the Temple of Sobek or the Tomb of a Thousand Names—I don't know which one is correct, maybe both, Anyway, Farak, I broke my promise to you. I can't be a member of the Tarabin Tribe."

"That is funny," Farak said.

"What's funny?" Charles demanded.

"I was going to beg your forgiveness. If I hadn't given you my gallibyah and keffiyeh, none of this would have happened."

"Yes, but I'm the one who decided to surprise Jacques about how much I could look like a Bedouin boy," Charles pointed out.

"Listen, Charles," Farak said earnestly. "Bedouins have a strong belief in fate. We believe some things are meant to happen. When something falls under fate, there's nothing anyone can do to stop it from happening. If you hadn't been put off that train, I'd be on my way to tour the United States with my two brothers. After that, I would have gone straight to Brown University."

"Falling under fate? You mean that this wasn't my fault, that fate decided all of this?" Charles said.

"Yes," Farak answered. "In fact, it was probably all my fault. I wanted to come back to Egypt, to see my mother, my father, my grandfather, my people, and my desert. I must have wished so hard that fate decided to intervene. In order for me to be strong enough to come to Egypt, you had to get lost. It makes sense, doesn't it?"

"I guess so. When I get back to the Château du Mont, I'll have to study up on the subject of fate," Charles said.

"You were selected to show these people the replica pyramid so I could come home. Now you are a member of the Tarabin Tribe," Farak insisted. "This is your gift for following the direction of fate. You are now an Egyptian, a Bedouin. I welcome you, my brother."

"Thank you, Farak," Charles said solemnly.

"While we wait for my mother's return, I'll tell you my story. A week and a half ago, Madame Constance brought David and me into her office. She informed us that you'd been put off the train in Cairo and had subsequently vanished. When Madame Constance told us you were missing, David and I were both determined to come to Egypt to find you. I knew I must go to my home in Luxor, even though it's over five hundred miles from where you were put off the train," Farak related. "My tribe knows thousands of people all over Egypt. As soon as Madame Constance left her office, I made my travel arrangements. Then, David called his grandmother. David told her it was imperative that he go to Cairo, where Jacques was staying, accompanied by his grandparents, of course."

"Where are they staying?" Charles asked

"Jacques made arrangements for everyone to stay at the Khemitology Guest House," Farak said.

"I know that place," Charles said. "It's right across from the Sphinx. Jacques and I made friends with the founder of the School of Khemitology, Dr. Hakim Abd'el Awyan."

"I have to be honest," Farak said. "I do not truly understand this place that's called a school, and yet is said not to be a school."

"According to Dr. Awyan, the School of Khemitology is an organization dedicated to discovering the true purpose of the Great Pyramid and other sacred sites in Egypt and beyond," Charles explained. "He allowed Jacques and me to go with his tour inside the Great Pyramid. He is a Wisdom Keeper. I told him about your family, and he said he was friends with your grandfather."

"I know the Awyan family," Farak confirmed. "My parents took me to visit them just before I was sent away to the Château du Mont. Dr. Awyan

453

took us inside the Great Pyramid too. Even though I was young, I still remember traveling those steep ramps."

Charles shook his head, bemused. "It's amazing how the threads of our stories come together. And now, David, his grandparents and Jacques are at the Khemitology Guest House."

"More fate, I guess," Farak said.

"What did your family think when you suddenly showed up in Luxor, after all those years?" Charles asked.

"My mother is known across Egypt for her calmness and good humor," Farak answered. "However, she went crazy when I arrived at the compound. First, she'd cry, then she'd laugh. That first night, I heard her yelling at my father, saying he should have never sent me away and that her boy was stolen from her. From the moment I arrived at the Tarabin compound, I was never alone. My mother followed me around like a little puppy. It felt a little bit strange."

"Yeah, that would feel a little bit strange," Charles said.

"When the housemaid announced that I had a phone call, my mother was right there beside me. It was from Subira. Subira told me you were at a secret location, a location not to be revealed to me or to others. She told me where I was to meet my guides and informed me we'd be traveling on camel. Subira asked me if it was possible to bring the pyramid relic on our journey, the real relic. I told her only my grandfather knew where this relic was kept. However, if I asked him for the pyramid, he would insist on coming with me. In fact, I was sure that there would be no less than fifty Tarabin men on camels accompanying me."

"That would be quite a caravan, wouldn't it?" Charles responded dreamily.

"I went to my room to get ready. When I came out, my mother said she was ready, too. She had heard the conversation, and declared she was coming with me. There was nothing I could do to stop her. I told her we would be traveling by camel at night. Mother said she would not want to travel any other way."

"Your mother is amazing!" Charles exclaimed.

"As it turned out, my mother is a much better camel rider than I am, due to my many years at the Château du Mont. It took me a little while to relearn the way of it. You know, following the rocking gait of the camel."

"Yeah, it took me some time to learn how to ride, too," Charles interjected.

"We left the compound early in the morning. It was still dark. The night sky was breathtaking. As we traveled, my mother rode by my side, keeping up a steady conversation. She told me she was born in the Eye Tribe. I didn't know that. She told me her father was the Sheikh of the Eye Tribe."

"Wow! You're like a double prince," Charles said with awe.

"I hadn't thought of it that way," Farak said. "My mother told me about her tribe. Like many Bedouins, they travel at night. The planets, the moon, and the stars in their constellations are their guides. As we rode through the night, my mother pointed out the constellations above us. I have much to learn about constellations and how to follow them."

"Me, too," agreed the younger boy. "Maybe we can study them together."

"That's a good idea," Farak said. "After our informal astronomy lesson, my mother told me that when I left for the Château du Mont, it was the darkest, saddest moment of her life. She thought about flying straight to France, picking me up from the Château and running away with me. However, she did not know where we could go."

"I always planned to run away and join a circus. I was just waiting until I got better on the trapeze," Charles said. "Now, I'm starting to think I'd make a better cameleer."

"The only cameleer in Paris," Farak said, laughing. He grew serious again.

"I was a kid when I arrived at the Château du Mont. I never imagined that my mother was even sadder than I was when I was sent away. How could I know? Her letters never sounded sad; they were filled with stories, news, and advice."

"How often did she write you?" Charles asked.

"Every two weeks. She always wrote in Arabic so that I wouldn't forget my language."

"I wish my mother wrote me every two weeks," Charles said wistfully. "I'd especially like it if she wrote me in Arabic, but neither of us know Arabic. I plan to learn your native language as soon as I get back to the Château du Mont. When you go away to Brown University, do you think you could write me in Arabic?"

"Yes, my brother. I will write you. For now, let me finish my story. As my mother and I were riding our camels, side-by-side, she sang an old Bedouin song from her people, the Eyes. I had never heard her sing before. My mother told me she'd never been happier than last night riding in the desert at night with her jewel. She calls me her jewel. What can I do about it?"

Charles had to laugh at that. "That's worse than my nickname. My mom just calls me Chucky."

"I promise not to call you Chucky, if you don't refer to me as a jewel," Farak said with a grin. "Anyhow, what she did next was the most surprising part of the night. My mother showed me something. I couldn't believe it."

"What did she show you?" Charles asked

"She held up a bag, which sparkled in the moonlight. I asked her what was in the bag. She laughed and said it was the pyramid relic the woman had asked me to bring."

"Mother! How did you get possession of the pyramid relic?" I demanded. "You could be in so much trouble for stealing it from my grandfather."

"The pyramid relic is here?" Charles marveled.

"Yes, I told my mother she should not have taken it from the compound. I told her she could be in grave trouble, but she just started singing again."

As Farak finished the story, his mother entered the room. She was wearing a white gallabiyah and a long white headscarf draped over her still-damp hair.

"I gather you visited the pool of the Son of Sobek, Mother," Farak said with a smile.

Farak's mother laughed heartily. She then launched into a story in Arabic, which Farak translated.

When I was a little girl, my mother took me to a temple dedicated to Sobek. My mother loved all temples, no matter who they were dedicated to. But she thought I would love to see the Son of Sobek, a real crocodile. The temple my mother took me to was in Crocodileopolis. I do not believe this was the temple, though, as I remember entering through wide doors and it being light inside. The priest brought out meat and cakes to entice the Son of Sobek out of his pond. He was nearly twenty feet long, and he had lots of teeth.

Charles thrilled at the image. For some reason, he hadn't imagined the Son of Sobek being quite so large. Farak continued translating his mother's tale.

The priests had gilded the crocodile's entire body with real gold. He wore a crown and bracelets covered in jewels in all the colors of the rainbow. As a child, I thought this Son of Sobek was both beautiful and horrible.

"I thought the same thing when I walked into the room with paintings of Sobek and his cosort," Charles said. "I was fascinated and horrified, especially when I understood I was to enter the Son of Sobek's pool."

Farak continued translating, turning his mother's story of the Temple of Sobek into English.

The priest said a little prayer connecting me to Sobek. He predicted that I would be a powerful leader, and that Sobek would always be my protector. My mother paid the priest some money. Then the Son of Sobek flipped his long body around and returned to the dark pond.

"Wow! I wish I could have seen the Son of Sobek," Charles said, imagining the enormous reptile covered in gold and jewels.

Farak listened for a moment as his mother concluded her story.

"Mother says she had nightmares about falling into Sobek's pond for many years. She never dreamed that one day she would walk willingly into the waters of the Pond of Sobek. "

As Farak finished telling her story, his mother began laughing again. It was the strongest laugh Charles had ever heard. He thought her laughter must have filled the entire temple-tomb. It was contagious, too. Soon the two serious boys joined her, as they remembered their own story of stepping into the dark, sacred Pond of Sobek, the god said to bring order out of chaos. As the trio laughed together, Charles felt a lightness he'd been missing, maybe his entire life. He actually felt safe, as though he were with family. Unfortunately, this sensation didn't last long.

The High Priestess came into the room and asked the Faruks if they had brought the real pyramid relic with them. Farak's mother held up a cloth bag covered with embroidery and sequins.

"I would like you and Farak to follow me," the High Priestess said abruptly. "Charles, we will return for you very soon."

But they didn't return for him soon. Hours passed, and Charles' newly-found lightness and feeling of family and safety were covered with darkness and resentment. They didn't need him anymore. They had what they wanted: the real pyramid relic. What could they be talking about? What was so important about this relic? What was its message? Why didn't his mother write to him every two weeks like Farak's mother did? Why should he go back to the Château du Mont? And why was he alone again?

CHAPTER 52

THE GHOST AND MR. SMITH

How long had he been in this room alone? Charles began to feel like he couldn't breathe. He had to get out of this temple or tomb or whatever it was. He needed sunlight and oxygen. He picked up the lantern and tried to remember his way back to the entrance of the Temple of Sobek. He walked up a steep ramp. At the top of the ramp, there were two ways to go. Should he go right, or should he go left? Charles felt like there was a hard ball in the pit of his stomach. He had been very careless; he should have paid more attention to his surroundings.

Returning to his room, Charles sat on the bed. Unable to sleep, he got up and reread his "Poem to Sobek," then paced the chamber. Lying down on the bed, he finally fell asleep. When he awoke, Charles thought he heard something. He looked out the curtained doorway and called out in the dark, "Hello?"

There was no response, but Charles did hear something that sounded like breathing. Whoever was there was standing just beyond the light cast by the lantern on the desk. Charles dashed over, picked up the lantern by its wire handle, and held it up as he stared out in the darkened hallway.

"Hello?" he called out again.

This time, he saw something about ten feet from the doorway. It was a tiny form, no taller than four feet, dressed in white from head to toe.

"Are you a ghost?" he whispered.

"No," the figure replied. "Are you a ghost?"

"Obviously, I'm not a ghost," Charles said.

"Who or what are you then?" the voice asked peevishly.

"I am Charles Dayton Stratton III."

"Oh," the vision in white said, moving one step closer to his lantern. The soft, flickering light made the figure look even more eerie.

"Are you sure you're not a ghost?" Charles asked.

The figure, which Charles now recognized as that of a young girl, sounded annoyed.

"Do you start every conversation like this? No, I'm not a ghost. The High Priestess sent me here. She wants to apologize for leaving you here for so long by yourself. Why'd you ask if I was a ghost?"

"Because you looked kind of like a ghost I once knew," Charles answered.

"You can't know a ghost," the girl said.

"Yes, I can," Charles said emphatically. "And that ghost looked quite a bit like you."

The girl shook her head. "I guess you've gone just a little bit crazy. The High Priestess said you'd be hungry, and that we should have lunch together."

"Why didn't you say so in the first place, instead of standing there like a ghost-girl?" Charles demanded.

"You certainly are grumpy," the girl said, walking a little closer.

"You'd be grumpy, too, if someone said they'd come and get you soon, and you sat in a dark little room for who knows how long," Charles retorted.

The man who'd guided Charles into the Temple of Sobek came up from behind the girl. He was carrying a large tray. Smiling up at the man, the girl said, "Askurut, Saki." Charles recognized that *askurut* was the Arabic word for thank you.

The man handed Charles the tray. The girl shined her flashlight down the corridor, gesturing for Charles to follow her. "Wait!" he said. He returned the lantern to the desk in his sleeping room. The tray was so heavy, he couldn't carry both the lantern and the tray.

Back in the corridor, he asked, "Where are we going?"

"Outside, of course," the girl answered.

"We can do that?" Charles asked, trying to keep up with the girl carrying the lantern while he was balancing a heavy tray.

"This isn't prison, you know," she said flippantly.

"I'm not so sure," Charles responded. "I tried to leave, but I couldn't find my way out."

"It's a labyrinth," the girl said. "Have you heard of one? It's good for secrecy and has meditative purposes. My mother said it trains your mind."

"Yes, I've heard of a labyrinth," Charles said. He thought back to how he'd walked the labyrinth with his mother at Chartres Cathedral. The difference was that in the cathedral, the labyrinth was just composed of different-colored tiles on the floor. Here, the labyrinth was the pathway itself.

Thinking about a labyrinth led him to remember his mother's only visit to the Château du Mont. It was Christmas. Mrs. Stratton came without warning, saying she wanted to take him to Chartres. She wanted them to walk the labyrinth together. Afterward, his mother directed him to a taxi. Jacques, for some strange reason, was in that taxi. His mother left in another taxi. Charles had been so mad, he tried to jump out of the moving cab. If his mother had stayed with him longer, he might have told her about earning $500 for his article "The Ghost of the Jangling Keys," published in

461

Ghost Stories Magazine. But she only stayed a few hours. Why didn't she stay longer?

The non-ghost girl spoke, jarring him out of his thoughts. "Labyrinths can be tricky, but once you learn the key, it's easy to find your way out."

"This path feels more like a maze than a labyrinth to me. You don't need instructions to get out of a labyrinth. Exactly what are you doing here, anyway?" Charles asked defiantly.

"I'm here with my mother. What are you doing here?" the girl asked as she made another turn, this time walking to the right.

"I was brought here by Subira and Rehima," Charles answered. "What's your name?"

"My name is Meriaten," the girl said.

"Akhenaten's first daughter?" Charles asked incredulously.

"That's silly. She died over three thousand years ago! I'm just named after the daughter of Akhenaten and Nefertiti."

"I meant that, and you know it," Charles said crossly. "Is your mother the High Priestess?"

"No, silly," the girl said.

Charles didn't like being called silly. He thought the girl was abrupt and rude, but then he remembered that he'd been rude, too. "I'm sorry if I sounded mad earlier. It's just that I spent hours in that room. I come from the United States, but I go to school in France. Why do you speak English?"

"I speak English because my father, Count William Martin, is from England," the girl explained. "My mother is, of course, Egyptian. I speak both Arabic and English, and I'm learning other languages."

"So, you live here?" Charles asked.

"No, my dad is teaching at the Cairo University this summer," Meriaten told him. "My mother comes here several times a year, but this is the first time she's allowed me to come with her."

"You wanted to come here?" Charles asked in surprise.

"Yes, I begged her to let me come here," the girl replied.

Charles looked at the reliefs on the walls as they walked past the Pond of Sobek. Charles watched as Meriaten skipped up the seven steps, while he struggled up the stairs, as the tray felt like it was getting heavier. Meriaten pushed the stone door open with ease.

Once outside the temple, the children were nearly blinded by the midday sun. Charles put the tray on a large flat boulder and waited until his eyes adjusted. When they did, he looked at the girl standing beside him. Her skin was the color of dark tea with cream in it. Her eyes were what Charles' art teacher called hazel. Hazel eyes change color. Sometimes hazel eyes look bluish, sometimes greenish, sometimes goldish, sometimes light brown and sometimes, even reddish. Mademoiselle Fleuret hadn't mentioned how or why hazel eyes change color. Charles thought it would be interesting to have eyes that change color; his were always deep blue. Here in the desert sun, the girl's eyes were the color of greenish-gold hay, like he'd seen in the donkey carts in the green zone between the Nile and the desert. A strand of curly brown hair had slipped out of her headscarf. Her expression looked like she was taking everything in at once. When the girl looked towards Charles, he looked away.

"Let's sit under the stone bridge," the girl said, pointing to the two boulders that leaned against each other, shading the pathway underneath them. "We'll have some shade, but from there we can see everything. I'm starved, aren't you? My mother says I must be growing because I'm starved all the time."

"How old are you?"

"I am twelve-and-a-half years old," the girl answered.

"Really?" Charles asked, appraising the small girl beside him.

"Well, no. I just turned twelve, but I will be twelve-and-a-half soon."

"Me, too," Charles answered.

Meriaten handed Charles a package wrapped in tin foil.

Unwrapping the tin foil, Charles found a sandwich. He took a bite, then exclaimed, "Peanut butter and jelly!"

"Yes. For some reason, it's my favorite food right now. My mother packs it whenever we go on a trip."

"It's delicious," Charles mumbled with his mouth full. "I haven't had a peanut butter and jelly sandwich since I left my home in America. They don't serve peanut butter and jelly sandwiches at my school in France, the Château du Mont."

"Is that where your parents live?" the girl asked.

"No, we have a place in the United States. My parents are generally on trips. That's why they sent me away to school."

"Oh," the girl in white said, handing Charles another sandwich. "Now tell me, what are you doing here?"

Charles reached into the bag he'd tossed over his shoulder as he left his room. He pulled out the pyramid replica wrapped in its red cloth and gave it to Meriaten. She carefully unwrapped the cloth and held up the pyramid. The sun shined down on its capstone and sent out golden rays in all directions.

Meriaten said with shock in her voice, "You have a pyramid? Do you know what this place is called?"

"I've heard it called the Temple of Sobek and the Tomb of a Thousand Names."

"Well, I have another name for you. We call it the Tomb of the Pyramid Seekers. My mother is a leader of the Pyramid Seekers. It's kind of a school to prepare us for world change. We study ancient Egyptian knowledge and also new knowledge, including technology like computers. I love computers."

"I don't have a computer. I'm going to ask my parents for one when I get home. Madame Constance believes we should learn the basics of education before adding any of what she calls 'newfangled' technology."

"Newfangled," the girl said, laughing. "That's a funny word."

"So, what is a Pyramid Seeker?"

"All I know is that it's a small group, mostly women, who are seeking some ancient pyramids like this one. My mother taught me a little poem about it."

One little pyramid stands alone
Searching for a brother of its very own.
When there are two, the third comes home.
The fourth can be found at Aten's throne.
Translate, you, on all the sides:
One, two, three, four, and five,
Messages concealed in poetry.
The pyramids together are the key
To solve Queen Tye's great mystery.
And with this the future will be
Forever, forever, changed.

"I memorized it, but I don't know what it means."

"It's a riddle, Meriaten," Charles said, a gleam in his eye. "We need to solve it!"

"Where'd you get this pyramid?" the girl asked, looking at all of its sides: one, two, three, four, and five.

"I have to tell you that this isn't the real pyramid. It's a replica of an heirloom relic that belongs to the Tarabin Tribe," Charles explained. "I was given this pyramid by Farak, a student at the Château du Mont. Farak is a Bedouin prince. But here is the amazing thing: The real pyramid is here. Farak and his mother arrived with it today. Rehima and Subira asked them to come."

"That makes two pyramids because the High Priestess has one," Meriaten said, then added, *'One little pyramid stands alone'*—that must be the High Priestess' pyramid. The Pyramids Seekers are searching for a brother of its very own. Now, there are two relic pyramids."

"It all makes sense now. I showed this pyramid to the people of the City of the Dead. Subira and Rehima were there, along with another woman. They thought it was the real pyramid. They put their hands like this."

Charles showed Meriaten the signal, putting his two pointer fingers and two thumbs together.

"If they hadn't made this signal, I would have never followed Subira and Rehima. Anyway, that is how I got here."

"This pyramid looks like the High Priestess' pyramid. How can you tell the difference from a real pyramid and a replica pyramid?" Meriaten asked as she held the pyramid up to the sun.

"Farak told me that the replica pyramid is like the relic pyramid, except for the writing on the bottom. Other than that, all I know is the Tarabin Tribe has passed down the pyramid and instructions from leader to leader for thousands of years. No one in their tribe has been able to read the language engraved on the pyramid, but Jacques and I suspect it is Cuneiform."

"Who is Jacques?"

"I guess you would call him my chaperone. He works at my school, and my parents asked him to bring me to Egypt for my birthday. I believe I turned twelve a few days ago. I lost track of time."

"You look older than twelve," Meriaten said.

"I feel older," Charles said, taking another bite of his peanut butter and jelly sandwich.

"I should have recognized this writing. I have actually begun studying Cuneiform. I'm not very good at reading it yet. It still looks like many lines going this way and that to me, but I keep trying. Neither my mother nor the High Priestess can read the lines on pyramid number one."

"I met a man, Dr. McAllister, who's an expert in Cuneiform. He even wrote a book on it called '*Cuneiform.*' I bought the book. I haven't had time to study the writing yet. Tell me the beginning of the riddle again, Meriaten."

"Okay," she said. *'One little pyramid stands alone, searching for a brother of its very own. When there are two, the third comes home.'*

"Where do you think home is?" Charles asked the girl.

"I don't know."

A large lizard came between Charles and the girl. She tossed the lizard a breadcrumb. The lizard stuck out its tongue and flicked it into his mouth.

"I guess it likes peanut butter, too," Charles said with a laugh.

"I'm training him," Meriaten said.

"You can train a lizard?" Charles asked.

"Yes, you can, but you have to be careful. Some lizards are venomous and aggressive. I wish that wasn't true, because my father says they are very intelligent and can even be taught to count."

"Really?" Charles said. "I don't believe you."

"Look it up. I did," Meriaten said, as she began eating a second sandwich.

Charles looked towards the small oasis at the base of the boulders, wondering where the camels were that Farak and his mother had ridden to the temple. He lifted his eyes towards the steep path where he'd traveled with Subira and Rehima. The hair stood up on his arms, and he blinked his eyes several times to make sure that he wasn't imagining things. No, he was sure that there was movement on top of the ridge.

Charles could hear Subira in his mind, saying that no one came to the Tomb of Sobek except at night. There were definitely riders on the ridge, and it was not night. As they moved further down the path, he could see that there were two riders and three camels.

Charles whispered to Meriaten, "Get down behind those boulders and keep quiet."

"What? Why? What's going on?" Meriaten asked in a whisper.

"Can you see those figures coming down the path?"

"Yes, I see three camels and two riders."

"I recognize one of the riders. It's Mr. Smith. I met him on the plane from Paris to Cairo. We've seen him several times since then. I believed he was after me for some reason, but now I'm sure of it. We have to get inside. As soon as the riders disappear in the next twist in the path—run."

Charles handed Meriaten the rest of the food and wrappings that were on the tray.

"Now, run Meriaten," Charles whispered. He followed with the tray, but he wasn't carrying it. Instead, he was dragging it on the ground, erasing their footsteps.

"That was good thinking, Charles, erasing our footsteps," Meriaten whispered as they walked back into the stone entrance of the Temple of Sobek.

"Can you guide me to my room? I have to get out of here fast. If I'm not here, then they won't bother trying to break into the Temple of Sobek."

"Charles Stratton, you're not going out there alone. I will get the High Priestess," Meriaten said.

The girl who was definitely not a ghost led him to his room. Then she dashed off. Charles found the clothes Farak had given him. They had been washed and folded. He put on his gallabiyah, then scanned the room to make sure he left nothing behind. The High Priestess rushed into the room, waving a note.

"You are correct, Charles. Subira writes that there was a man in the market across from the museum offering a lot of money to anyone who would help him find his beloved nephew, who was lost in the Western Desert. He left the marketplace with a Bedouin with a notorious reputation. We must hide you. Meriaten has agreed to stay with you."

The girl came into the room. She was wearing a tan gallabiyah and head-scarf.

"Saki will guide us to where you will have to go," Meriaten said in a whisper.

"Where are we going?" Charles asked.

"The Tomb of a Thousand Names," the High Priestess answered.

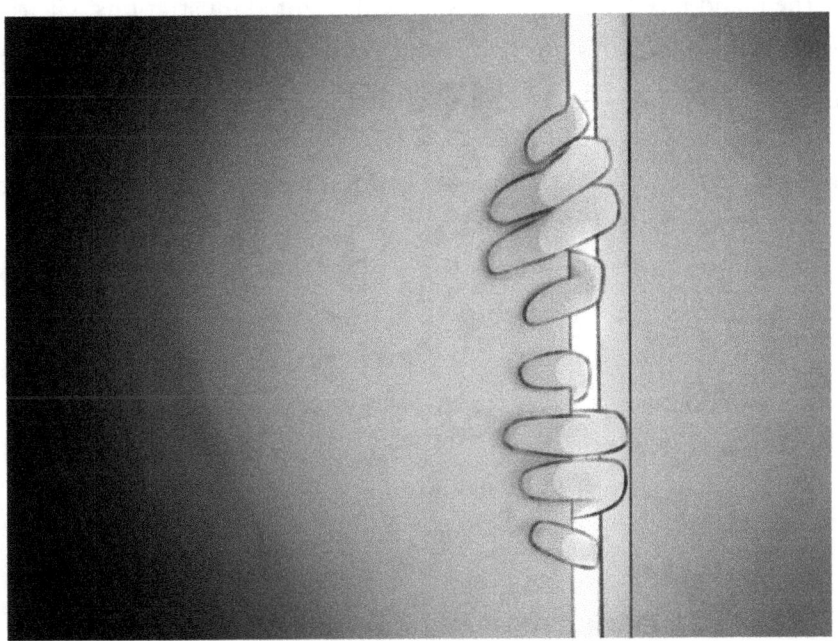

CHAPTER 53

IMMUREMENT

The caretaker, Saki, was carrying a lantern. He led the children through a tangle of interconnecting pathways. They walked up and down, turned right, then left, then left. Or was it right? Charles couldn't remember. He realized this wasn't a meditative labyrinth. It was a maze. He'd looked up the difference between the two kinds of paths after walking the labyrinth at Chartres Cathedral with his mother. The labyrinth is a single snaking path, winding around and around and around. There is only one route and one destination. Stay on the labyrinth and you'll eventually get through. The maze, however, has many different paths, doors, and dead ends. The destination is always unsure and sometimes unrealized.

After what seemed like hours of walking, the three travelers entered a small room with doors on two of the four walls. Charles reminded himself to pay attention to the door they had entered. But Saki stopped walking, turned, and faced a solid stone wall with painted illustrations. Charles recognized the figures on the reliefs as gods of the underworld: Osiris, god of death, and his wife Isis, goddess of the underworld; Anubis, the jackal-headed god of funerals and mummification; and, at the very bottom of the wall, Nephthys, the goddess whose task was to comfort the newly dead.

"Is this the entrance to the Tomb of a Thousand Names?" Charles asked, his voice echoing off the wall in front of them.

Saki nodded. Charles gave Meriaten an anxious look, then said, "You don't have to go in with me if you don't want to."

"You're scared, aren't you?" the girl retorted.

"No, not exactly. It's just that Mr. Smith is my problem, not yours."

"For me, this is not a problem. This is a destination," she answered with excitement in her voice.

Their guide gave a little laugh. Evidently, Saki, like many Egyptians, understood English, but preferred not to speak the language.

"I've never been in this part of the temple before, though I know of its existence. How do we get in, Saki?" Meriaten whispered.

The caretaker placed his lantern on the floor and pointed to a carved pyramid a few inches up from the stone floor, which neither Charles nor Meriaten had noticed. The light from Saki's lantern lit up its small gold capstone. Charles gasped.

"Look, Meriaten! It's just like the pyramid Farak gave me. It even has Cuneiform writing on it. Let me see if I can remove it from the wall. Maybe this is the home of the third pyramid in your riddle."

Charles pulled on the pyramid relief, but it didn't budge. Saki gestured for him to push on the pyramid instead. As he did, a lever appeared a foot to the left of the pyramid. Charles pushed on the stone handle, but it didn't move. Saki pointed to his right foot. Charles stood up and, placing his foot on the lever, gave it a couple of strong pumps. As he did, a small crack appeared near the corner of the wall. The caretaker placed his well-worn fingers into the crack and, with effort, pulled open a gap large enough for the girl and boy to pass through in single-file.

"Wait," Charles said, as he walked back to the pyramid. Again, he pulled on it with his fingers, but it was stuck tight. "I guess this isn't a real pyramid, Meriaten."

Charles turned back to where the girl was standing, slightly behind Saki. The old Egyptian held up his lantern, its soft light revealing a small room. The guide motioned for Charles to enter. Immediately, Charles heard the sound of stone on stone. Everything went black, completely, and utterly black. Charles couldn't breathe. He'd been locked in a small room, a room he recognized, a room all too familiar. He'd just finished reading Edgar Allan Poe's story, *The Cask of Amontillado*. From this story, he'd learned the word immurement. It was a form of imprisonment where a person is enclosed in a space with no exit, often resulting in death. Charles had made a mistake. He wanted out of this room right now.

Why hadn't he just asked Mr. Smith what he was doing in the desert with an extra camel? Maybe Jacques had befriended Mr. Smith and asked him to come out and find Charles, because Jacques didn't like to ride camels. Now he was here in the Tomb of a Thousand Names without light and without air. Charles placed his hands on the stone wall, feeling for anything: a lever, a handle, a knob, a button, a grip. He pounded on the stone wall with his fist. His chest ached. He felt dizzy. He knew for sure he was about to pass out. Finally, Charles realized he was holding his own breath. He opened his mouth and gulped in air mixed with the smell of old dirt. Then he placed his back against the stone wall and slid to the floor. He heard a click. A beam of light illuminated the wall above him, then dropped down and hit him straight in the face.

"What are you doing down there?" asked the girl behind the flashlight.

"I'm sitting. Why didn't you tell me you had a flashlight?"

"You didn't ask."

"Where'd you get it?"

"From Saki."

The air Charles was breathing was easing the pain in his chest. Slowly, his head began to clear.

"My mother said it's called the Road to the Light."

"The Road to the Light? Really?" Charles said in disbelief. "It looks completely black to me. There's no light, at least until you turned on your flashlight."

"There are several meanings to the phrase Road to the Light," Meriaten said. "My mother said it can mean the path of illumination."

"You mean like the Path of Knowledge? So this can't be a room. It must be a path. It means there's a way out of here," Charles said, relieved. "It means we're not going to die of dehydration or suffocation."

"That's ridiculous," Meriaten scoffed.

"Evidently, you haven't read Edgar Allen Poe."

"Who?"

"Never mind. Let's get out of here. Which way do we go?"

"My mother told me to give you this message," Meriaten said. "Turn to the right, to go straight to the light. But if you seek Aten's rays, then you must choose the other way."

"Doesn't anybody just say things outright around here? It sounds like another riddle," Charles said, trying to see Meriaten behind the beam of her flashlight.

"My mother told me you must be the one to choose."

"But what does the riddle mean?" Charles asked.

"I don't know," said the voice from behind the flashlight.

'Turn to the right to go straight to the light,' Charles intoned. "That must mean going to the right is the fastest way out of here."

Charles moved on to the next part of the rhyme: 'If you seek Aten's rays, then you must choose the other way.'

"Aten's rays must mean the rays radiating from behind the sun," he mused. "This means that to find Aten, or to find out more about Aten, one must choose the left-hand path."

"That's a good guess, Charles, and that is much longer and perhaps more dangerous," Meriaten said, her flashlight beam roving around the square room. "I think I see paths on both sides of the room. Which way do we go, Charles?"

"One minute ago, I would have chosen the right-hand path in a heartbeat. But now I don't know," Charles admitted. "One thing is certain, when I get out of here, the American Embassy will ship me straight back to my school in France. My time in Egypt will be over."

Charles felt a lump in his throat as he thought about the dream-trip he had expected for his stay in Egypt.

"I won't have taken the cruise down the Nile River. I won't have explored the famous temples, built thousands of years ago along what the Egyptians called the River of Light. I won't get to see King Tut's tomb in the Valley of the Kings."

"That's too bad," Meriaten said.

"The advantage to the right-hand path is that we'll be out in the light sooner. But I want to learn more about ancient Egypt. Would it be okay with you, Meriaten, if we take the longer way out—the left-hand path?"

"I knew you would choose the Path of Knowledge, which is another name for the Tomb of a Thousand Names. Let's go, Charles."

Charles moved forward but Meriaten didn't. He felt a strong jolt as his head bumped into hers. Everything went black.

"Ouch!" Meriaten cried.

"What happened?" Charles called out.

"You bumped into my head, making me drop the flashlight."

"You stay still and let me feel around for the flashlight," Charles said, dropping down on his hands and knees. "Okay, I found it, but the batteries have fallen out."

"I'll help you find them," Meriaten said.

Feeling the top of Charles' head, she knelt next to him.

"Hold these," Charles said, feeling for the girl's hand and placing two batteries in her palm.

"There are three batteries, C batteries. You need to find another one," Meriaten directed Charles.

"Here's the third battery. Now, if I can just put them in the right direction."

"Feel for the little buttons on top of the batteries," Meriaten instructed. "I believe they should face towards the top of the flashlight."

"I know that. I have them in, but the flashlight is still not working."

"Did you push the button, Charles?" Meriaten asked.

"Of course, I pushed the button," Charles responded irritably. "Let me try to put them in the other way. No, that didn't work either."

"Let me try," Meriaten said, feeling in the dark for the flashlight.

"Oh, no," Charles said.

"What?" Meriaten responded.

"I just felt the top of the flashlight case. The glass is broken, and the bulb is, too."

"What are we going to do?" the girl asked anxiously.

"We could start screaming," Charles suggested. He yelled out, "Help! Help! Can anybody hear me?"

"Charles, I am so sorry I dropped the flashlight. I guess we'll have to stay here until someone comes and lets us out."

"Did your mother or the High Priestess tell you any more about the left-hand path or even the right-hand path?" Charles asked.

"Yes, they gave me a map!" Meriaten said

"Great!" Charles exclaimed. "We have a map, but no light to read it by. We shouldn't have come in here alone. They shouldn't have let us. Why did they let us enter the Tomb of a Thousand Names by ourselves? Didn't they understand that we're kids, and we might drop the flashlight, or the battery might run out or something?" Charles was trembling by this time.

"I can't believe my ill-fortune," he lamented. "I must have been given the Pharaoh's Curse when I climbed inside the sarcophagus in the King's Chamber of the Great Pyramid. Ever since I entered that stone box with people chanting around me, things have gone terribly wrong."

"I don't believe in curses," Meriaten said. "However, everything was just fine here at the Temple of Sobek—until I met you, Charles. Maybe you're the curse."

"If your mom had just given me the flashlight and the map, I could have found my way out without any help from you. I'm experienced in map reading, and I know how to keep hold of a flashlight."

Charles heard a sob from the girl kneeling not too far from him. He actually felt like sobbing himself. They were alone in the Tomb of a Thousand Names, and it was dark, dark as a tomb.

CHAPTER 54

JACQUES AND THE RAVEN

**Let my heart be still a moment and this mystery explore;—
'Tis the wind and nothing more!**
Edgar Allan Poe

J acques watched as the red tail ilghts of the yellow taxi disappeared in the blackness of the night, tires screeching in its rush to get out of the parking lot of the City of the Dead. He pulled up the sleeve of his gallabiyah and felt for the button on his watch. The tiny light revealed that it was 11:11 p.m., nearly midnight, and way past his bedtime. Nonetheless, here he was, absolutely alone and about to enter the Western Cemetery of the City of the Dead. Just an hour ago, at the meeting in the Pizza Hut, they'd all been looking for clues in the photographs Albert had taken that morning, in this exact spot. The most alarming image captured what looked like a black-robed arm, pointing to a partial shadow of a fedora hat. Jacques had encountered a similar view at the Cairo Museum, where he thought he had spotted a man in a gangster hat lurking. He seemed to be crouching behind an Egyptian statue of the cow goddess, Hathor.

The other significant photograph was taken in an undeveloped area just outside of the Western Cemetery. While Fran pointed out that there were piles of camel poop all around, Jacques noticed footprints that looked like a child's shoe. Feeling like Mrs. Montgomery, Jacques thought about where the clues might lead. His first thought was that Charles was likely to be followed by Mr. Smith. His second thought was that someone wanted to get help for Charles, evidenced by the robed arm pointing to Mr. Smith. His third thought was that Charles left the area by camel.

Where Charles was going, and why, Jacques could not figure out. Whatever the reasons, however, looking at these photographs stunned him. He became like a marionette, a stringed puppet, with someone else holding the controls. He found himself walking out of the Pizza Hut door. He turned left to the Khemitology Guest House, entered the small entryway, walked up the narrow wooden stairs, and entered the third-story room he shared with Mr. Montgomery.

Once in the room, without completely understanding where he was going, Jacques began to pack. In a cloth shoulder bag, he placed a flashlight, batteries, a scarf, and the gold compass Charles had given him the previous Christmas. He walked to the small closet tucked in the back of the room and pulled out the tan gallabiyah Dr. Awyan had given him. Up until now, he'd never worn it or even tried it on. But tonight, Jacques remembered Charles' admonition that sometimes you need to blend in, to not look like a tourist. At the moment, that's what he wanted to do. Blend in.

The gallabiyah Dr. Awyan had given him was large enough that Jacques just slipped it over his clothes. It wasn't until then that he understood he had to go back to the City of the Dead, and that it had to be now, tonight. Maybe Dr. Bernstein was right about this unseen connection, this quantum entanglement, this ability to communicate in non-traditional ways. At this moment, Jacques believed that finding Charles was his undertaking, his responsibility. As the man in the beige gallabiyah walked out the door, he didn't look in the mirror. If he had, he would have discovered a changed man.

Once downstairs, Jacques went into the kitchen and tossed sandwiches, cookies, and a canteen of water into his cloth bag. Walking out into the night, he found the temperature was neither hot nor cold. The nearly full moon cast its light on the Sphinx, giving it a pale silvery glow. Jacques could almost see its half-opened eyes peering at him, perhaps creating riddles for boys like Charles to solve.

Behind the Sphinx, Jacques could see the shadowy forms of the three Giza pyramids. The star-filled sky loomed over his head, seemingly endless. The three bright stars of Orion's belt hovered over the three pyramids, in an almost exact pattern. Dr. Awyan had told Charles and Jacques that the position of these stars, combined with the ancient position of the constellation of Leo, held the key to the true function of the pyramids. They were not built by the Pharaoh Khufu as future tombs for himself and his royal family. In fact, they were not built by Khufu at all. The Khemitologists believed they had evidence that the pyramids and Sphinx were built thousands of years before Khufu set foot on the earth.

Tonight, as Jacques gazed at Orion's belt, he wasn't thinking of the functions or age of the pyramids, but of the constellation itself. He was thinking of Orion, the hunter god in Greek mythology. To Jacques, it symbolized his quest. The constellation signaled to him that the waiting was over. He was the hunter, and he had to find Charles. As Jacques walked quietly away from the Khemitology Guest House, he'd spotted a lone taxi parked in front of the Sphinx. It was hours after the Giza Plateau had been closed to tourists. Was the cab driver's unexpected presence a coincidence or fate?

Jacques walked across the road, his gallabiyah swinging around his legs. The driver opened the back door of his vehicle and Jacques stepped in. He told the driver he wanted to go to the the City of the Dead. The driver looked unnerved. He said something in Arabic that sounded like a warning to Jacques.

"I want to get to the City of the Dead," Jacques repeated, adding that his specific destination was the Western Cemetery.

The taxi driver made a U-turn, then drove slowly past the cheery lights of the Pizza Hut. Maybe he should have left a note telling Mr. Montgomery where he was going, but it was too late now. The taxi driver drove out of the archeological zone and into the little town of Giza. Turning east he entered the freeway, then exited at a sign indicating the City of the Dead. The taxi turned again at the sign identifying the Western Cemetery. The yellow cab pulled into the parking lot and Jacques paid the driver, watching as he sped off.

So here he was, standing alone in the parking lot. That afternoon, the City of the Dead had been filled with life: women hanging clothes on ropes strung between the tops of old headstones, children playing, babies crying, old people sitting in metal chairs in the tomb doorways, watching. Now all this life was hidden beneath an inky blackness that erased everything. The few lights that twinkled here and there turned out to be the last gasps of burners, small stoves placed outside the tomb-homes to cool.

Following the narrow beam of light shining from his red plastic flashlight, Jacques walked up the stairs and turned to the right. He was headed for the Wasims' residence. Their tomb-home was on the first of many rows of tombs that had been built in this part of the necropolis. The Wasims lived about half a mile down an unpaved path made of sand and small rock, punctuated with broken pieces of cement and tile. It was a precarious walk in the daytime, and even more so at night. As Jacques walked down the corridor, he asked himself what his plan was. He answered, to retrace the path Charles must have taken the night of his second disappearance.

As Jacques walked, he became aware that he was not alone. Behind him, he heard *crunch–crunch–crunch-crunch*. Someone was following him on this sandy path. Without turning around, Jacques picked up his pace. The steps behind him sped up as well. Jacques spun around, pointing his flashlight behind him. Six feet away was a large shadowy white form.

It gave out a low "ohhhm,"sound.

Raising the beam of the light, Jacques discovered two luminous black eyes staring at him. They belonged to a cow, a very large, white cow. Jacques wondered what a cow was doing in the City of the Dead, then quickly realized the answer. It was to provide milk to the many babies, toddlers, and children who lived in these ancestral tombs. Even so, Jacques thought, he didn't need to be followed by a cow, not at night, nearly midnight.

"Shoo!" Jacques said. The cow must have been lonely, because it didn't move. It just stared back at him

"Go away! Go back to wherever you came from," Jacques commanded, waving his hands wildly in the air. The cow responded by moving closer to Jacques, who jumped away.

A great laugh came from the doorway of a moderate-sized tomb-home on the right-hand and side of the pathway. The laugh came from a small, hunched figure squatting in the doorway. The shadowy form was outlined by a halo of golden light, cast by a kerosene lamp.

"Excuse me, I am sorry to disturb you," Jacques said quietly, with a slight bow. The cow moved closer and nibbled at Jacques' hand. He gave out a yell and almost lost his footing trying to escape the cool touch of this insistent cow's snout.

The figure in the doorway laughed even louder—loud enough to wake the dead. Pointed in the direction of the laughing figure, the flashlight's beam made the toothless old man appear like some kind of gruesome, grinning monster. Jacques couldn't help but wonder if this was all a dream. The man in the doorway stood up and signaled for Jacques to wait, then walked back inside the tomb. Returning, he placed something in Jacques' hand. Shining his light on it, Jacques discovered an amulet made of beautiful silver lines backed by a gleaming piece of abalone shell, shimmering pink, blue and white in the beam of his flashlight.

It might have been the same man who'd given Fran a necklace that afternoon. Jacques smiled at the man, then reached into his bag to give him some money. Before Jacques could pull out his wallet, the old man walked back into the tomb. He shut the heavy wooden door, leaving only a fine line of gold at the bottom, the only sign that someone was living inside this tomb. With the door closed, it was pitch-dark again. Jacques slid the necklace over his head. It fell heavily against his chest. The cow mooed, nudging Jacques with her soft white nose. He pointed the flashlight down the path in front of him. The cow and man walked side-by-side. Jacques didn't have much experience with farm animals, actually none at all. He'd glimpsed cows standing in knee-high grass in the fields of France, but that was about all. Still, as the two walked silently together, Jacques began to find the cow's presence comforting.

"Do you know what Mrs. Montgomery told me today before we picked up Bernadette at the airport?" Jacques asked. The cow softly butted her head against Jacques' shoulder.

"She said there was a time in her life when she thought she was looking for comfort, for safety. Then, it crossed her mind that if she didn't listen to her fears, she'd have a chance of making a positive difference in her life, and possibly in the lives of others."

"If, on the other hand, she clung to security above all things," Jacques continued, "there was a huge chance she would make no impact on the world at all. Mrs. Montgomery suggested I might benefit from having a similar talk with myself."

Looking at the beast plodding by his side, Jacques suddenly remembered his visit to the Cairo Museum. He'd addressed a large statue of the ancient Egyptians' bovine fertility goddess. Now he was conversing with a real-life cow, one that was strangely nocturnal. Life, Jacques realized, was strange and getting stranger.

"You know, your ears look a lot like those of the goddess Hathor."

The cow brushed against him, seemingly pleased by the compliment. Jacques continued speaking to the cow like the best friend he never had, as he and the cow walked down the path.

"I always felt that life had dealt me a very bad hand. My parents were murdered. I was just a baby at the time. They were working in the Resistance against the Nazis, who'd taken hold in France."

"After their death, my grandparents took care of me," he confided. "At the end of the war, my grandmother was also killed. She, too, had been working for the Resistance. Then my grandfather became ill and was unable to care for me. He placed me at the Château du Mont, a boarding school for boys. I was five years old."

"I was separated from the other kids, placed on the third floor in the same room Charles and David now share," Jacques said. "I don't know if I was placed there for safety or because I was different from the other students. Whatever the reason was, I got used to being alone."

Jacques stopped talking and the pair moved quietly along the path. The cow gave Jacques a sympathetic moo, then nudged him as if to remind him she was still there, listening.

"So, you want more of my story?" Jacques said.

Talking aloud, even to a cow, made Jacques feel less alone and confounded. It was also a relief to speak about his difficult past, to a creature who wouldn't go around repeating it.

"My grandfather left me enough money to go to college. I chose Cambridge Regional College in the United Kingdom, noted for its strong vocational and music programs. It was there I learned to care for and repair many things: cars, radios, heaters, coolers, plumbing, organs. I discovered I loved working with my hands and knowing I could fix things. After college, I couldn't decide what to do, so I went back to the Château du Mont. Madame Constance had just become the headmistress. I offered to help maintain the ancient mansion. She was glad for my help, and I felt comfortable and safe. Now my room at the Château du Mont is in a round tower attached to the main building. It feels very much like one of these tomb-homes, minus the coffin. It has one small window, about eight feet from the floor. In the afternoon, the light streams in, making everything look sparkly, magical. In my room I have felt almost like Merlin the magician. I have my piano, my violin, and my potbelly stove, where I cook soup, tea, and cookies."

"I've been content, contented as a cow," Jacques said, laughing, surprised at remembering this old saying. "However, things changed when Charles and David came to my room asking me to interpret something for them. It turned out to be a journal they had discovered buried in the stone wall around the school. I began to question things and to feel less comfortable. Then, last December, Bernadette showed up. She was hired as a replacement for the kitchen workers for the holidays. Bernadette was nice, and a great cook, but for some reason around her I began to question things, to become less content. I was almost glad when she left."

Jacques stopped speaking. The cow was no longer beside him. She wasn't behind him either. He'd been abandoned by his companion. Maybe his story hadn't been exciting enough to keep the cow's attention. He should have told her the part about the ghosts and the treasure Charles and David discovered. But the cow was gone, and Jacques felt more alone than he had before. He reached a place where, instead of tombs, about fifty individual graves marked by pillars of varying heights were scattered along both sides of the path. Some of the pillars were only four feet high, while others towered high above Jacques' head. The gravestones were made of crumbling cement or ornately-carved white marble. Jacques remembered passing this place on the way to the Wasims' tomb-home. This was also where the young people played soccer, kicking their old and battered ball deftly around the stone markers.

As Jacques directed the beam of light around the gravestones, he heard a flutter of wings from the top of a tall pillar directly above his head. He flashed the beam of light into two beady eyes that were staring down at him. The eyes belonged to a huge raven, which was cocking its head this way and that.

Jacques couldn't help but think of Edgar Allan Poe's poem, "The Raven." He'd loved this poem as a boy, and had memorized every word.

"Would you like to hear a poem about a raven?" he asked the bird. "I think I still remember it."

Once upon a midnight dreary,
While I pondered, weak and weary,
Over many a quaint and curious volume of forgotten lore,
While I nodded, nearly napping, suddenly there came a tapping,
As of someone gently rapping, rapping at my chamber door.
'Tis some visitor,' I muttered, 'tapping at my chamber door—Only this,
and nothing more.'

"What do you think, Raven?" Jacques asked. The raven gave out a sharp caw.

"Here is the last stanza."

And the raven, never flitting,
still is sitting, still is sitting,
On the pallid bust of Pallas
just above my chamber door.
And his eyes have all the seeming
of a demon's that is dreaming,
And the lamplight o'er him streaming
throws his shadow on the floor;
And my soul from out that shadow that lies floating on
the floor
Shall be lifted—nevermore!

The great raven flapped its large wings in appreciation. Jacques loved the sound of this poem, but what did it mean? One of his professors said that it expressed Poe's belief that poetry was "a mournful and never-ending remembrance." Jacques had believed this professor's theory, thinking it was like his own life, a mournful and never-ending remembrance. Charles, however, had made him question his instructor's interpretation of Poe's poem.

"Raven," Jacques said, "it seems I have taken to talking to animals here in the City of the Dead. Shall I tell you my idea of what Poe might have meant by the refrain 'Nevermore'? I think it is the past that is nevermore; it is the past that must cease to exist. Those who refuse to let it go find themselves forever mournful, living as Poe had, so that he concluded that the past lay like a shadow floating, floating on the floor, and it shall be lifted—nevermore."

Why was he thinking these strange thoughts? Jacques guessed that was what happened when it was nearly midnight and you were in a cemetery. The raven jumped off the pillar, beating its wings against an invisible force, and then, rising up, disappearing into the night.

Jacques took a deep breath and kept walking. About twenty minutes later, the narrow corridor opened up into a more spacious area. Jacques recognized this as the place where the young translator, Aamen, had related the story of Charles being put off the train by the conductor, blocked from the train station by a policeman, and hit over the head by a falling box.

Looking towards the largest and most ornate tomb in the Western Cemetery, Jacques wasn't surprised to find the raven waiting for him.

"Hello, Raven," he said to the bird, then turned to the large space in front of him and called out, "Where are you, Charles?"

From deep within the shadows of a nearby tomb came a voice asking, "Are you Jacques?"

He was shocked, but answered, "Yes, I am Jacques Gerard. Do you know where Charles is?"

At this question, the raven flew away, as if his job was finished. The noise of Jacques' heart almost blocked out the answer to his question.

"We thought that you would come tonight," said the voice. "And yes, we know where Charles is. Are you ready?"

"Ready for what?" Jacques asked, pointing the beam of his flashlight in the direction of the voice.

Two women dressed in black robes, heads covered by long, black headscarves, walked towards him. Aamen had told the group at the Khemitology Guest House that there were three women in black robes with black headscarves standing at the very back of the crowd the night Charles disappeared. Aamen had added that it was not unusual for women in the City of the Dead to wear black, but now two of the three women were here at near-midnight. They must be the women Charles had followed.

"Where are we going?" Jacques called out to the women, who had moved down the path. They didn't answer. Jacques hesitated, then ran to catch up. If there was any chance that they might help him find Charles, he had to follow them. When he passed the Wasims' tomb-home, he wondered if he should call out to them, tell them he was here—tell them he was following two women who knew his name and where Charles might be. But there was no time for that. The women were already far ahead of him, and Jacques was afraid he would lose sight of them, as they seemed to fade in and out of the light. Nearly half an hour later, the women reached the cemetery's western edge. No longer in the tombs' shadows, the full moon created what is called a white night, a night almost as bright as day.

Jacques put his flashlight into his shoulder bag. He knew where he was, the desert area where Alfred's photos showed footprints. Looking north, Jacques saw the famous rocky cliff jutting strangely out of the flat desert. To the east was the dark form of a robed man and three camels. He appeared to be waiting for the women, and possibly for Jacques. It crossed his mind that he might be disappearing, just like Charles had disappeared several days ago. Why hadn't he left a note at the guest house telling his friends he was going to the City of the Dead to find Charles? At least they would know that much.

"Where are we going?" Jacques yelled out again to the women nearly half a block away. His voice startled the night and Jacques himself. He broke into a run, afraid the women might leave without him, or at least without telling him where Charles could be found. The two women in black reached the man with the three camels. The cameleer pulled one of the camels down on his knees, then helped the taller of the two women onto the camel's humped back. The camel jumped up from its front knees to its front feet, then jumped from its back knees to its back feet. This reminded Jacques that he'd promised

487

himself he'd never ride a camel again. The second camel knelt, and the second woman was up.

The two women in black looked down at Jacques from their eight-foot perches. Despite his vow, it became apparent Jacques was about to take another camel ride. He was now face-to-face with the cameleer. The bright moon revealed a man who'd spent his life in the desert. His dark face was map-like with its many lines and crevices. Though he wasn't smiling, there was a look of kindness in his eyes. He pulled the reins of the riderless camel, and it knelt down in front of Jacques.

Jacques reviewed in his mind the advice Charles had given him about mounting a camel, the first of which was to relax. He had warned, "Don't lean back like you think you should when the camel is jumping from its front knees to its front feet; hold your knees tightly to its side instead and sit straight. Then, don't lean forward as the camel jumps from its back knees to its back feet like you'd feel like doing. End the process with a smile."

That's what Jacques did, mainly by ignoring his natural intuition. When the camel was up on its feet, it occurred to Jacques that he was proud of himself. Apparently, he just needed prompting—to be introduced to something and become acquainted with it—before he was ready to jump into new and unexpected things. He began to feel as though he were finally out of a box he'd been hiding in, a box of his own construction. Instead of a box, he was now inside some other shape, but what kind? Of course, he realized. It was a pyramid.

When the camel was standing on its feet, Jacques smiled down at the cameleer. Sitting on this camel, dressed in a gallabiyah, Jacques felt a little like T.E. Lawrence, as portrayed in the movie "Lawrence of Arabia," Charles' favorite movie. Now he was ready to ride out into the desert to find the boy he was responsible for, to find the missing Charles Dayton Stratton III.

CHAPTER 55

THE FOLLOWER

All men dream; but not equally. —T. E. Lawrence

A few moments earlier, Jacques had felt like Peter O'Toole in the movie
"Lawrence of Arabia": proud, tall, maybe even dashing. However, the
minute his camel took its first speedy steps, Jacques reached for the edge of
the cloth saddle. Grasping it with both hands he pulled himself forward,
crouching down, bottom facing the star-filled sky, knees digging into his
chest. He looked like a terrified jockey. And he was breathing so hard, he
sounded like a chugging steam train. Jacques no longer felt like Lawrence
of Arabia. The previous time he'd ridden a camel—when he had sworn he'd

never ride a camel again—Yousef Awyan was holding his dromedary's reins. He'd been leisurely leading Jacques on the sandy, well-worn path between the Great Pyramid and the Sphinx; and it was broad daylight. This time it was midnight in the desert on the edge of the City of the Dead, with no observable path, and his dromedary's pace was anything but leisurely.

His one-humped beast was probably trying to catch up to the two women in black. The two women on camels were about a city block in front of him. Jacques only suspected this because his eyes were glued straight down towards the rocky sand on the desert floor, eight feet below him. He was wondering again if he should jump off the camel. Then he wondered again, why he hadn't left a note about his intention to go to the City of the Dead. Then, he wondered who these women were, and why Charles had followed them. And finally, he wondered what he was doing in Egypt in the first place. At the end of all his wonderings, Jacques remembered a quote by T.E. Lawrence: *'All men dream; but not equally.'*

When he'd first read the words, Jacques had pondered what the author meant. Lawrence didn't appear to be referring to the act of dreaming, but more to having dreams. Traveling to Egypt wasn't Jacques' dream; it was Charles' dream. What was Jacques' dream? He wasn't sure. One thing was certain. If he had a dream, it wasn't equal to Charles' dream.

Since he could do nothing else in his present jockey position, Jacques ruminated further on T.E. Lawrence's words. He concluded that he should make up his own quote: 'If you do not have a dream; borrow one.' That's what he had done. He'd borrowed or, rather, stepped into Charles' dream. Now all he knew was that he'd brought Charles to Egypt, and the boy was his responsibility. Jacques had to find Charles, even if it meant riding a camel in the desert in the middle of the night, following two strange women dressed all in black, leading him towards an unknown destination.

Jacques was startled by a voice next to his right ear.

"Mr. Jacques Gerard," the voice said, "my people, the Bedouins, after several thousands years of experimentation, have concluded that the most efficient way to ride a camel—is not the one you have chosen."

Jacques was aware that the Egyptian woman was laughing at him.

"May I suggest you use your stomach muscles to sit up?" she advised. "Then ride while keeping your back straight, yet relaxed. Also, it would be advantageous for you to lower your legs, letting them fall gracefully down the sides of your camel. And here is the key to successful camel riding: imagine yourself not as a separate being but asone with your camel."

Jacques grumbled inwardly. It was easy for her to say; she'd been riding camels since birth. He couldn't see in his current position, however, and it wasn't that comfortable. His camel had slowed down, making it easier for him to sit up.

"Very good, and I should tell you one more thing," the woman said. "I believe you are holding your camel's reins a bit too firmly, which is confusing him. He cannot decide if you want him to stop or if you want to go."

Jacques allowed his reins to slacken.

"The name of your camel is Alttabie, the Follower. He has been trained to follow other camels; he never takes the lead. The only reason one needs reins at all for this camel is that he occasionally gets confused as to which camel he is supposed to be following. At that time, he might need a little guidance."

I am sitting on a confused camel, Jacques thought with consternation.

"Now, Mr. Jacques, as we must cross the Nile before dawn, you must hurry."

The woman in black leaned forward, making a hooting sound. Her camel sped off into the night, causing her black headscarf to flap like a raven's wing in a windstorm.

"Excuse me," Jacques said aloud to his camel, "but aren't you supposed to be following her camel?"

Jacques' camel moved slightly faster, perhaps because Jacques was no longer tightly gripping his reins. Still, he seemed to prefer following the other camels at a steady pace. It had been a long day for Jacques. There'd been the visit to the City of the Dead, the retrieval of Bernadette and Mademoiselle Fleuret at the Cairo Airport, and the Chinese dinner. There'd been the meeting in the Pizza Hut, the midnight trek through the City of the Dead, and now this camel ride. Jacques pressed the button on his watch and saw that it was now two-thirty a.m. He could barely keep his eyes open. There seemed to be only one solution, he'd have to talk to the camel.

"Excuse me," Jacques said. "It seems I have taken to speaking with animals lately. At near midnight, in City of the Dead, I conversed with a large white cow. When she tromped off, I had a conversation with a huge black raven. Perhaps if you and I were to have a conversation, it might help both of us stay awake."

The camel didn't reply.

"So, we are going to cross the Nile. We are east of the river. To get to the west we must either use a boat, which is unlikely, or cross at a bridge."

The camel gave a gravelly snort, which Jacques took as a yes. Jacques looked forward and found the two camels and their riders were quite far ahead. He shivered, becoming aware that the temperature had drastically dropped. He reached into his cloth bag and pulled out his jacket. He awkwardly put his jacket on over the galabeya, one arm and then the other, as the camel moved up and down like a carousel horse.

He continued addressing the dromedary. "I must apologize, Monsieur Camel, but I cannot remember what Subira called you—something about the Follower. Do you mind if I call you Caboose? It is an English word, often applied to the car at the end of a train, but it means one who follows. Isn't that appropriate? Caboose, do you like the name?"

The camel snorted. The silver-white moon, now far above the horizon, had taken on a smaller appearance. Things looked more shadowy; the women and camels ahead of Jacques and his mount appeared as silhouettes.

"Caboose, I believe those two women are waiting for us. Perhaps we could speed up a bit."

Caboose didn't like being rushed. Jacques, still shivering, fumbled for the headscarf—Egyptians called it a keffiyeh—also in his shoulder bag. Tucking the reins into the front of his saddle, he used both hands to arrange the keffiyeh over his hair, then tied it on with a black band. Jacques might not have known this but, with his gallibyah, his headscarf, his dark eyes, and his newfound prowess at camel riding, he could now pass as a Bedouin man.

"Caboose, we are lucky to have the moon to light our way tonight," Jacques said. "I wonder what Bedouins do when there is no moon. For my part, I brought a flashlight. Maybe the Bedouins carried lanterns or torches. What do you think?"

Caboose chose not to answer. He was trotting forward to join the other camels.

The women in black had moved their camels off the sand and onto the pavement of a two-lane road. They had traveled south of the City of the Dead. As Caboose moved to join the group, the taller of the two women, the one who didn't speak English, made a clicking sound. At this signal, her camel knelt. She jumped off her mount and returned to the desert sand. She turned her back to them and, in the fading moonlight, began swishing and swirling, and dipping and twirling, moving from one section of the desert to the other. Was it a dance of celebration, a ritual of some kind, perhaps a prayer? Whatever it was, considering Subira's insistence that they were in a hurry, Jacques thought it quite strange. When the woman turned around, he saw that she was holding a straw broom.

"Rehima is removing the footprints of our camels, so we cannot be followed," Subira said in a soft voice.

"Oh, you are worried that we are being followed? By whom? Why?" Jacques asked.

"We do not have time to speak of these things now. We must cross the Nile before dawn or the traffic will be so heavy, hours will be added to our travel."

"Exactly where are we going?" Jacques asked Subira.

The woman and her camel were already moving down the road. If she answered, he couldn't hear it, as Rehima's camel was bleating loudly in protest of being left behind.

The woman dragging her broom returned to her agitated camel. She stroked him on his soft nose and replaced her broom in its holder at the rear of the cloth saddle. Then, grabbing the front of the saddle, Rehima nimbly pulled herself up to a sitting position, situated slightly forward on the camel's hump.

As Jacques watched, he couldn't help but think that a two-humped camel would make for a more comfortable and secure ride. Unfortunately, in an article he had read after his first camel ride, the two-humped camels, the Bactrian camels, were native to Asia, not Africa.

Once Rehima was settled, her camel made some other sound and jumped from its front knees to its front feet, and then from his back knees to his back feet, causing him to dip forward and then backwards at 45-degree angles. Rehima looked like she was being held up by strings. She probably was telling herself to be one with her camel, like Charles had instructed him so long ago.

The woman started down the road to join Subira. Jacques called her back. Rehima, who Jacques now thought of as the sweet smiling one, turned her camel around and rode up to his side. He handed her two sandwiches wrapped in aluminum foil, two oranges and two cookies.

"Shukraan," Rehima said, the smile on her face just visible in the fading moonlight.

She and her camel pulled ahead. Jacques could see the two women unwrapping the cheese and lamb sandwiches he had grabbed back at the Khemitology Guest House. It was a good thing he had, because he was starving. He unwrapped his sandwich. With a full mouth, he apologized to Caboose for not bringing anything for him to eat. He figured that Caboose would forgive him as he read that camels can go without food for a month or more.

The three camels and their riders arrived at the bridge; a sign indicated that this was the Boulaq Bridge. He'd read about this bridge in his tour book. It is a drawbridge that crosses the Nile on the east bank to an island called—he forgot what the island was called—but then you crossed over the island to the other side of the Nile, the West Bank. The moon had just set, leaving only a few pale planets to light their way. Jacques was grateful for the lights lining the bridge that reflected on the dark river, making it look like a star-filled sky.

He looked straight down many feet below to the boats and ships waiting impatiently for the bridge to rise. He became aware that, from his uneasy perch atop his camel, he could easily fall into the precipice, never to be seen again. The thought made him dizzy. He decided he should dismount and walk his camel across the bridge.

"Down," he called out to Caboose.

Caboose evidently didn't understand English, as he continued forward. Jacques then imitated the clicking sound Rehima had made when she commanded her camel to kneel. Just as he did this, a camel led by a woman in a blue gallabayah walked the other way, back towards the eastern end of the bridge. True to his reputation as a confused camel, Caboose turned around, and quite happily followed the white camel.

Jacques waved his arms and called out to Subira and Rehima, but the sound of ships' engines, waiting to be set free, drowned his calls. Jacques kicked his heels against the camel's side while explaining that they were headed in the wrong direction. Nothing dissuaded his camel from his chosen path. Jacques and Caboose were on their way back to the City of the Dead.

CHAPTER 56

THE BRIDGE AND THE PLAN

Jacques looked up at the eastern sky. It looked like a child's drawing
with rich crayon-colored stripes of purple, pink, orange, gold, and
yellow, but he was not supposed to be looking at the sunrise. It was his
stupid camel's fault. He and Caboose were safely on the bridge heading
west when a small white dromedary carrying a load of yellow straw tied
with blue rope walked by them traveling east. Caboose turned around
and followed the white camel. The white camel was led by a woman in a
beige gallibyah, walking ever so slowly, like she had no place to go, and
had all the time in the world.

"Caboose!" Jacques yelled at the top of his lungs, "turn around right
now. We need to go west, not east!"

Caboose ignored him. Jacques pulled on his reins, kicked his camel's ribs firmly, and cried out, "Caboose, you are a follower. And followers don't get to choose who they follow. We have to go the other way."

Jacques pointed behind him. Caboose paid no attention to his rider.

"No wonder camels have such bad reputations. We should have taken a Jeep. I think Jeeps can travel in the desert, can they not?" Jacques called out in a loud voice.

Men, women, children, and even babies looked up in amazement at a grown man on a camel, dressed in a gallibyah, yelling at the top of his lungs seemingly to no one, and in a foreign language.

"All these people think that I am a madman," Jacques hollered, pulling hard on Caboose's reins. "But I am not a madman You are a mad, and very bad, camel. When you let me off, I am never going to ride a camel again."

Jacques looked back toward the bridge. He could see Subira and Rehima. They were halfway across the bridge, both unaware that Jacques and his camel had stepped off the bridge, going the wrong direction.

"Stop, Caboose!" Jacques ordered.

Miraculously, Caboose stopped, but only to bend down his head to nibble on a green weed that had pushed through a crack in the road. After finishing his plant snack, Caboose picked up his pace, until he was happily and ever so slowly walking behind the white camel.

Twisting his head around, Jacques saw that more pedestrians and vehicles of all kinds had moved onto the bridge. Then he saw a woman in black coming towards him, weaving her way around vehicles and pedestrians. It was Subira riding like the wind, her black headscarf whipping behind her like wings, her knees beating out a rhythm on her camel's sides. She and her dromedary sped forward, then stepped off the bridge. When Subira reached Jacques and his wayward camel, she reached down and grabbed Caboose's reins.

"Hello, Subira, sorry about Caboose," Jacques called out.

Subira gave him a quick smile, and dodged a tiny gray donkey pulling a cart piled high with bright green palm branches. Then she made an amazing

U-turn in the middle of traffic, heading towards the bridge. Going west once again with Caboose in tow, Subira weaved in and out of lines of trucks, buses, cars, auto-rickshaws, animal carts, pedestrians, and soldiers on camels. She and her camel did not slow down until they were were firmly on the other side of the drawbridge.

A few seconds later, Jacques heard a loud alarm, "Wonk! Wonk! Wonk!" Men, women, and children ran to get onto the bridge before the guard gates lowered. The sound of the alarm combined with a cacophony of clinks, wails, thuds, honks, screams, brays, and the nuzzling, bellowing, and grunting of camels, adding to the excitement. At the last moment, two men in gallabiyah threw themselves under the divider. They just missed being flattened by steel bars. If you hadn't crossed to one side of the gate, you would have to wait for the rising bridge to allow the tall boats and ships to pass, then lower in place again.

Subira kept up a swift pace. Jacques kept his eyes away from the edge of the bridge. Although he was not ready to confess this yet, he knew he was at least partially responsible for Caboose's following the white camel. As he and Caboose stepped onto the bridge, he looked down at the Nile and suddenly became dizzy. He thought, what if he fell off the camel, and tumbled a hundred feet into the river? His tour book had warned that Nile crocodiles were responsible for hundreds of death each year. He had no desire to be a crocodile's morning meal. At this thought, Jacques decided that he preferred to walk across the bridge. He tugged on Caboose's reins to get him to stop, which somehow made his camel aware of a little white camel going the other way. And that was how Jacques ended up going east, instead of west, over the bridge.

Subira continued to hold onto Caboose's reins as she weaved in and out of pedestrians and vehicles. There was nothing for Jacques to do but hold on tightly to the edge of the cloth saddle. After exiting the drawbridge, the three travelers turned west and then north on a paved street. Rehima dismounted from her camel, and dashed into an ornate old building. She rushed back and mounted her camel, shouting something in Arabic to Surbira.

"Where are we? Is this the Temple of Sobek?" Jacques asked.

"No, but we just learned that we must make a quick stop at the Town Square."

"Isn't that back the other way?" Jacques asked.

"Yes, we shall have to hurry. It is getting late," Subira said, urging her camel forward at a faster pace.

Jacques was about to complain, but then remembered the Egyptian Museum was also in the Town Square. Maybe he could get a message to the searchers back at the guest house. He would have to do this clandestinely as Subira evidently wanted to keep their destination secret. Jacques didn't have to tell his friends about the Temple of Sobek, but he did feel he should tell them was going to find Charles.

It was 6:30 a.m., and the museum would not be open for a couple of hours. How could he get the message to Dr. Awyan? Then, almost like a movie in his head, Jacques remembered the lunch he and Charles had with Dr. McAllister at the vendor across the street from the museum. It was there that Dr. McAllister had recited Akhenaten's poem. The vendor had been highly recommended by Samy. He and Charles had eaten at this vender's booth several times. He might remember them. He could ask the vender to get a message to Dr. McAllister, requesting that the tour guide get a message to Dr. Awyan.

In the lead, Rehima rode east. Jacques recognized the two huge stone lions guarding the entrance to the bridge. Charles and he had passed over the bridge several times with Samy. The Qasr el Ni Bridge is a swinging bridge, higher and longer than the drawbridge. Rehima twisted around and grabbed Caboose's reins just as a tour bus passed, going west. Twenty tourists leaned out their widows to snap photos of Jacques and his camel being led by a woman in a black robe and headscarf.

With my luck, thought Jacques, one of these photographs will end up on the front page of some French news magazine. Maybe this was a dream or nightmare, but there was nothing to do but continue the drama. Jacques went back to thinking about the message he needed to send to the people at the guest house.

When the riders arrived at the other end of the bridge, Rehima helped Jacques off his camel. Caboose sniffed the air and looked towards the various food vendors at the outdoor market. Loud beeps announced the bridge access was closing. The Egyptian police herded vehicles and pedestrians off of the bridge. The steel bridge's midsection began to rise, allowing the ships and boats to pass.

Fortunately, they were on the correct side, near the front of the Cairo Museum. On its right side was a cement building. It was a public toilet. Subira said she would hold Caboose's reins as Jacques went inside. Before entering, he glanced in the direction of the food vendor where he and Charles had eaten lunch with Dr. McAllister. There was the same man standing beside his barbecue, joking with customers. His robust body jiggled up and down as he laughed. Yes! The vendor was there. His visit to the men's room would allow him to write a message outside the notice of his two guides.

Joining the line of men washing their hands at a long steel sink, Jacques looked up and was startled by a man staring at him from behind the sink. Upon seeing this man, Jacques tugged at at his chin. The man behind the sink also tugged his chin. Could this be me, he wondered? His black hair, which he always controlled with a layer of hair oil, was tousled. His face, usually clean shaven, now had a swarthy five o'clock shadow. The man in the mirror had dark circles under his eyes, indicating he needed sleep. The most curious thing about the man staring back at him was a strange directness in his gaze that he had never seen before. Jacques wondered, if Charles came into this restroom, would the boy even recognize him?

Jacques pulled out the map he had placed in his shoulder bag and wrote a note on the map. He did not mention their destination, the Tomb of Sobek. Furthermore, he asked those reading his message to refrain from calling the police or the embassies until he contacted them. He had kept his promise to Subira. Pulling out several Egyptian pound notes, he placed them on top of the map. Emerging from the cement building, he found Rehima holding the reins of the three camels. Jacques pointed to the food stand across the street from the restroom and museum. Rehima nodded. He weaved his way through the traffic to the food vendor's booth. He ordered three sweet pastries. He passed the vendor the map with the money on top.

In a quiet voice, Jacques said, "Please give this to Dr. McAllister, Dr. McAllister at the Cairo Museum."

The man smiled, nodded, and pointed to the museum. Jacques nodded back and said yes. He had done all he could; now his focus was on finding Charles Dayton Stratton III. Unfortunately, Jacques thought, this required him getting back on Caboose, a ridiculous excuse for a camel.

CHAPTER 57

SINGING IN THE WESTERN DESERT

Ten miles of walking through the jewel-like colors of the green belt ended abruptly at the desert's edge. As Caboose reached the sand, he took a hesitant step, turned, and looked longingly at the road behind him. Jacques did, too. It looked like someone had drawn a straight boundary line precisely at this spot, where camel and man stood.

On one side was life: green plants, blue water, homes, roads, bridges, schools, shops, goats, donkeys, cows, men, women, children, and all the noise that came with them. On the other side was unending desert—pale gold in color—barren, waterless, lifeless, soundless.

Jacques wondered why people would choose to live in the great deserts. But they did. For hundreds of years, Bedouins and other nomadic tribes had called these barren regions home. They didn't build houses. They didn't claim the desert land. They borrowed it. Stopping at an oasis, they set up their tents for a few weeks to rest, celebrate their holidays, and sell their livestock to neighboring townspeople.

Then, almost inexplicably, they dismantled their camp and moved on, guided by their forefathers' oral history and great knowledge of stars and planets. Nomads didn't go off to work. Their very lives were their work. The desert was their friend and benefactor. The desert allowed them to be free, to rule themselves, to maintain their own culture, and to cultivate their own values.

As Jacques thought about the desert and the people who lived there, he began to feel the heat of an unshielded sun beat down on him. He rearranged his headscarf so the cloth would prevent sweat from dripping into his eyes. He reached for a bag tied to Caboose's cloth saddle and unscrewed the lid. Jacques took a swig of the warm water. It tasted like canvas but felt like life. He looked far ahead. He could see the two women, two camels, and their shadows, dark against the horizon.

"I hate to mention this, Caboose," Jacques said, "but you are falling behind again."

The camel said nothing. Jacques pulled up the sleeve of his gallabiyah and looked at his wristwatch. It was 10:30 a.m. "I hope that you are not as tired as I am. I cannot even remember when I slept last. Do you know where we are going, by any chance?" he asked his camel.

Caboose just kept plodding forward, one foot in front of the other, his furry body rocking back and forth, back and forth, back and forth. He found himself slipping into a dream. David, Charles, and Jacques were having tea and cookies in his magical turret room at the Château du Mont.

Jacques woke up just in time to keep himself from falling from his nine-foot perch. He straightened his back, pulling his body towards the sky until he was again sitting erect on the camel's single hump. The temperature was rising, and he was getting sleepier. He wondered what he could do to keep himself awake.

Answering himself, he said, "I could sing. Sing to you, Caboose. Sing to keep myself company. Sing to forget that it is blisteringly hot. Sing to try and keep my eyes open. Sing to keep from falling off your rather laughable saddle. Haven't you ever heard of the more practical, not to mention more comfortable, western saddle?"

"No? Okay. Now, Caboose, what do you want to hear?" Jacques asked his four-footed companion. "I am afraid we are in a bit of trouble. I can play many songs without words on piano or violin, but I only know the lyrics to a few songs. My repertoire consists of the French national anthem 'Le Marseillaise', a few Christmas carols, and 'Frère Jacques.' As a young child, I loved 'Frère Jacques,' believing it had been written just for me. I'll sing it for you in French and then in English."

Frère Jacques, Frère Jacques,
Dormez-vous? Dormez-vous?
Sonnez les matines! Sonnez les matines!
Ding, dang, dong! Ding, dang, dong!
Are you sleeping? Are you sleeping,
Brother John? Brother John?
Morning bells are ringing, morning bells are ringing,
Ding, ding, dong! Ding, ding, dong!

Caboose brayed discordantly. Jacques wasn't sure if Caboose was calling to the other camels or adding his part to a song usually sung as a round. Ahead, Subira and Rehima on their camels looked like tiny dark figures wading through a shimmering, shadowy, purple-blue lake.

Jacques felt sure this wasn't actually a lake, but instead a mirage. He'd studied this phenomenon in preparation for his trip to the Egyptian desert. If the ground is hot and the air above is cool, the hot ground warms the cool air's lower part. When the light moves through the cold air and into the layer of hot air, the air is refracted, making it look like water, a puddle on a path, a stream on a street or, as in this case, a shimmering lake in a scorching desert.

Then, ahead of the women and their camels appeared a strange rock protrusion bursting straight up from the flat landscape. Its height and base area were similar to that of the Sphinx. However, instead of spreading out, the formation tapered up like a tower, peak, or chimney. Jacques stared at it in amazement, forgetting to blink. Everything got blurry, and his eyes closed.

Shaking himself awake, Jacques said in a slurry voice, "I am sorry, Caboose, but I have to get off. I can't ride one second longer. I must sleep."

As he said this, the women and camels who had been in front of him disappeared. "Caboose, did you see that?" Jacques asked. "Where did they go? I cannot make sense of what I am seeing. I may be suffering from heatstroke. I read this can happen in the desert."

The sun was directly overhead. Jacques didn't have to check his watch to know it was high noon, and things were about to get hotter. A tiny form appeared. It looked like it was standing in the middle of a pale purplish-blue lake. Its arms were waving, beckoning him forth.

"Where did the other woman and their camels go?" Jacques asked Caboose.

His camel didn't say anything, just lumbered forward, never changing his pace. The figure disappeared. Now there was nothing ahead of Jacques but the lake, the desert sand, and the large rock protruding from the flat desert.

"I may be hallucinating, Caboose," Jacques said, feeling the rhythmic movement of his mount going back and forth, back and forth, back and forth, back and forth. He gently closed his eyes. Caboose stumbled over a rock. Jacques jerked himself awake.

He spoke sleepily to his dromedary. "What can I do, Caboose? I have already run through my repertoire of songs, and I just can't stay awake anymore."

There was one subject that could awaken every part of Jacques, from his feet to his brain. That one subject he hadn't allowed himself to think about. That one subject he'd picked up at the airport, less than twenty-four hours before. That one subject who wore a dress the color of the afternoon sun, and had a smile he believed outshone it.

The more Jacques thought about this subject, the wider awake he became. He could still hear her words when Mrs. Montgomery asked Bernadette if

Jacques was her friend. She'd announced to everyone in the Pizza Hut that both Charles and Jacques were her friends.

But what kind of friend was he? Here in the burning desert, a snowy Christmas loomed large in his mind. Everyone at the Château du Mont had gone home for the holidays except Charles, Farak, Bernadette, and Jacques. Bernadette had been hired as a substitute cook for the holidays, allowing the kitchen staff to be home with their families. Over the holidays, Bernadette became much more than a cook. The four of them decorated cookies, and made up baskets for the children of the local orphanage. At the orphanage, Bernadette talked easily with the parentless children. After visiting the orphanage, the four of them slid down Snowman's Hill on a red sled. They talked, laughed, and ate together. Jacques had never felt like that in his entire life—like he belonged.

When school was about to begin, Bernadette came to his tower room to say goodbye. She gave him a piece of paper with her address and phone number. She was returning to the American College in Paris where she was finishing her master's degree in English. He'd never called her, he'd never written her, but he'd never forgotten her.

Why hadn't he contacted her? That was a question he didn't want to ask himself. Instead, he asked himself another. Why would this beautiful, warm, fun-loving, intelligent woman want to be his friend? Thinking this led Jacques to wonder about all the people gathered in Cairo, Egypt, intent on finding Charles Dayton Stratton III. Mrs. Montgomery, the mystery writer, appeared to be interested in introducing Jacques to the man he could be. Fran had slipped his small hand into his as they walked through the City of the Dead. Mr. Montgomery, a shipping magnate, was his roommate at the guest house. He treated Jacques like an equal. Mademoiselle Fleuret gently teased Jacques for his lack of communication skills. In other words, they treated him like family, like the family he'd never had. And what had he done to deserve it?

"Caboose, we have to change," Jacques concluded. "I have to become a better man, and you have to become a better camel. Subira told me that you were trained to be a follower, and thus would never be a leader. Do you believe this? I think you can be a leader. I think the reason you keep falling behind is that you don't feel good about yourself. You lack confidence, and you haven't had enough people believing in you. However, Caboose, I believe in you."

CHAPTER 58

THE SECRET OASIS

Now, Caboose trotted forward towards the granite tower at a rapid pace. Jacques reached out and petted his dromedary, praising him for his speed, determination, fortitude, and transformation.

"You know," Jacques said, "I think I should name you something else besides Caboose. What should it be? Hmm. What if I call you Sadat, after the Egyptian President Anwar Sadat?"

The camel made a kissing sound with his big lips, and it was settled. The man with the sunburned face, five o'clock shadow, and dusty gallibyah had no idea how different he looked, how transformed he was. He no longer looked like that reluctant French tourist who declared he would never ride a camel again. Here, sitting on Sadat, Jacques Gerard could be mistaken for a Bedouin wanderer.

As man and camel approached the base of the stone tower, Jacques wasn't surprised the lake had disappeared, for the sun had heated the desert air and the conditions for a mirage no longer existed. However, he was surprised there was no one there to greet him.

"If you don't mind, Sadat, I'd better get down and have a look around."

Jacques attempted to imitate the sound Rehima made to get her camel to kneel. Sadat paid absolutely no attention to him. At this, Jacques grabbed the reins, gave them a sharp shake, dug his heels against Sadat's sides, and made a sucking sound against his teeth, "Pfheet." Caboose immediately jumped down on his front knees and onto his back knees. Jacques slipped off the red cloth saddle, landing on his feet.

"Now you have earned the name Sadat," Jacques told his camel, petting his floppy nose.

There were footprints of camels and humans all around the tower, but where did the two women in black go? Jacques stared at the pinnacle of the sixty-foot stone tower. He thought about climbing to the top, where he could get a panoramic view of the entire area, but there were no foot or hand holds to help him ascend its steep vertical sides.

Raising both hands to the sides of his mouth, Jacques called out, "Where are you?"

There was no reply. Jacques was about to call out again when Sadat began to bellow and roar. At this flamboyant commotion, Subira emerged seemingly from nowhere.

"Oh, here you are, Jacques Gerard," she said. "I thought it might take you a little longer to get to our oasis, or I else I would have been here to greet you."

"Sadat, which is what I named my trusty camel, decided to change his ways," Jacques said proudly. "He no longer wants to be a plodder, a follower. He is more like a guide."

Jacques patted his camel's neck. The camel gently nibbled his hand with his floppy lips. "Where are we? Is this where Charles is to meet us?" Jacques asked, looking around.

"No, we are at what we call the Secret Oasis," Subira said, pointing to the great rock protruding from the desert sand.

Jacques looked around for the oasis, but saw nothing but sand. Subira turned and walked straight towards the tall rock, pushed on a section of its gray stone, and a doorway magically opened. It was large enough for a camel to walk through. How had she accomplished this? Jacques figured the stone door must weigh a ton, maybe more. Subira had either used the fairy-tale phrase, *Open Sesame,* from "Ali Baba and the Forty Thieves, or else someone had invented a hinge or track to help open such a heavy stone door.

Sadat walked through the arched opening as though he had done this many times before. Jacques followed the camel, then turned to watch. Subira easily slid the rock door closed, its edges disappearing into its stone frame. Jacques had expected it to be dark inside the rock tower; surprisingly, it was brightly lit.

Looking up, Jacques saw a great gap at the top of the granite rock, undetectable from the outside. The nearly circular break was at least twenty feet in diameter. The sun shined down on two palm trees partially shading a well lined in stone. Subira's and Rehima's camels were drinking from its bluish water. Sadat ambled over, snorted a greeting to his fellow camels, then bent down to drink.

Jacques looked around for Rehima, but she was nowhere to be seen. Subira pulled a wooden mallet from her black robe. Walking to a particular section on the east side of the large corral, she hit the rock wall with the wooden mallet. It made a high-pitched sound: *ping, ping, ping...ping, ping, ping...ping, ping...ping*. At the last sound *ping* sound, Jacques heard a scraping noise of rock on rock. Someone on the inside of the stone wall pushed open the slab of rock. It was an elfin-sized door, somewhere between two and three feet high.

Subira bent down and entered the doorway. Jacques followed her on his hands and knees. As soon as he passed through the small door, he found himself in a large, cave-like room with a domed ceiling. Rehima, illuminated by the light of the opening door, greeted Jacques with the phrase,

'As-salaam-alykum,' meaning "Peace be with you." Jacques crossed his hands on his chest and bowed his head, repeating the greeting to her as best he could.

Subira pulled the stone door closed, shutting out the brilliant sunlight. Jacques looked around the now gloomy room, lit only by an oil lamp in the middle of the chamber. The cave-like room was large enough to hold at least a dozen people. Around the edge of the chambers were six straw pallets. As soon as Jacques saw them, he could see nothing else. He was exhausted beyond exhaustion, sleepy beyond sleepy.

Rehima handed him a cup of water. He drained it, returned the cup to Rehima, and pointed to one of the pallets furthest from the entrance. She nodded yes. Jacques walked to the edge of the cave and unceremoniously dropped onto the straw-stuffed bed. He was immediately in a deep and profound sleep.

The next thing he knew, he was back in the desert. This time he was completely alone—no camel, no rock tower, just waves of sand and a glaring sun in a gray-blue sky. He was tired. He was thirsty. He was questioning if he could survive much longer in this land hostile to plants and animals.

He took one more step forward and, suddenly, a trap door opened. He felt himself fall into a deep pit, about fifteen feet down to a stone slab. Sand from the desert floor followed him like a shower of hail. It kept raining down until he was nearly waist-deep in the pale gold sand. Sand was in his hair, in his ears, in his mouth. Jacques screamed a terrible scream.

Miraculously, a rope dropped down into the tomb-like room from above. Jacques grabbed it and struggled to pull himself out of the sand and the tomb. He was only three feet from the top of the stone enclosure, but he had no strength to pull himself up. A hand was offered, a hand covered in dirty white bandages. Jacques hesitated, grimaced, and reached for the bandaged hand, shocked by its bony grip.

With a jerk, Jacques was up to the desert floor. He lay for a while, face down. Then, turning over, he stared at glinting black eyes peering out from slits in a face swathed in white cotton. A thin, grim line in the bandages marked its mouth. Jacques felt like screaming, but this figure had saved him. "Thank you," *he said. "Hmmm," the figure answered in a low growl.*

Just then, Jacques heard the sound of the striking of a match, and smelled the sharp odor of sulfur dioxide. The vapor, combined with oxygen, caused an explosion that lit up the wooden matchstick's tip. A blue-and-yellow flame erupted, lighting the wick of an oil-filled lamp. Immediately, strange dark shadows danced on the cave room walls, bringing Jacques out of his dream.

As Jacques lay on the straw bed, he heard a sound: ping, ping, ping...ping, ping, ping...ping...ping. It was the sound of the secret signal. Rehima leaned over and pulled open the small stone door. Someone handed several large packages to Subira and Rehima. A hunched black form walked into the cave. Now, more shadows were dancing on the walls.

"*Ya'teek el' afye,*" the voice said as Subira shut the stone door.

The lamplight dimly revealed a woman a head shorter than the others. Her headscarf was pulled up over her face. Like the other women, she was wearing a floor-length black robe.

"Three women in black robes," Jacques whispered,

This woman in black might be the third woman Aamen said was standing with the other two in the back row of the City of the Dead the night Charles disappeared.

"Jacques," a voice called out.

Jacques jumped, hitting his head on the lower curve of the dome ceiling. Rubbing the bump on top of his head, he moved towards the center of the room where the three women were sitting. Suddenly, the cave was filled with the delicious aroma of flatbread, cheese, and tomato sauce. It smelled just like the Pizza Hut. He was famished. Jacques moved to where the women were sitting around the pale light of an oil lamp. He looked down at the new arrival and immediately felt he knew her.

"Mandisa, is that you?" he asked, shocked.

The woman removed the scarf covering her mouth and broke into her sunshine smile that had filled up the Pizza Hut, just as much as the smells of her great cooking.

"You?" he asked. "You are the third woman in black?"

Mandisa laughed her jolly laugh. Jacques was both confused and comforted. Mandisa was on his side, of this, he was sure. Still, there were questions to be answered.

"I do not understand," Jacques said, staring at the women.

"We will answer some of your questions after we have had our meal," Subira said, handing him a plate filled with Egyptian pizza, mango, figs, dates, melons, and the ruby red seeds of a pomegranate.

"Do you speak English, Mandisa?" he asked.

Mandisa shook her head no, then nodded yes. Subira explained that she spoke enough English to run the Pizza Hut, but understood more English than she could speak. As Jacques took a bite of pizza, he thought about the gatherings at the Pizza Hut. They'd all believed Mandisa could speak functional English, just enough to take orders, but didn't guess she understood what everyone was saying. No wonder Mandisa felt like she was one of the guest house members.

The women spoke among themselves for a moment, then laughed heartily.

"Mandisa was just telling us about the woman in yellow," Subira translated. "She said Mrs. Montgomery gave her a piece of paper, something about a fortune. The woman in yellow began yelling that you were thoughtless, and that she didn't know why she had come to Egypt. Mandisa thinks she loves you."

Jacques was stunned, amazed, confused, confounded, bewildered, perplexed, and mystified. He would have fallen to the ground if he weren't already sitting

"I do not think so," Jacques answered. "We barely know each other."

Mandisa said something to Subira. Rehima pointed to the now-open little stone door. Jacques got on his hands and knees, ready to exit. Subira said, "Mandisa wants to know, have you not heard of love at first sight?"

The three women in black laughed.

CHAPTER 59

THE THREE MUSKETEERS

He who has felt the deepest grief is best able to experience supreme happiness—Alexandre Dumas

Jacques crawled out of the diminutive cave door. As he did, he was startled to find himself face-to-face with a caramel-colored camel, who might have kissed him on the lips had he not turned his head away. "Back up, Sadat," Jacques said firmly.

Surprisingly, that's exactly what the camel did. He stood beside Jacques as the man tipped his head back and examined the large crater-like opening at the top of the sheer, sixty-foot rock. The roof opening made the secret oasis appear like an old volcano, hopefully an extinct volcano, Jacques thought. The sun was no longer visible through the window to the sky, having slowly moved east for its nightly nap. With no direct sun, the giant rock cast shadows across the stone corral, dulling the desert's heat. Three camels stood by two large palm trees. One after another, these ships of the desert sipped water from the large, stone-lined well. Sadat did not join his companions, preferring to stay by Jacques' side.

"This is a perfect hideout and a perfect place to rest," Jacques whispered to Sadat. "How do you think this secret oasis was created? Where did the water come from? Who invented the secret doors? Who carved out the little cave room?"

Jacques looked at Sadat but decided the camel wouldn't answer his questions, even if he knew the answers.

Subira ducked out of the low cave door. Seeing Jacques, she said, "Mandisa brings news that a man, a foreigner, is looking for a lost boy, claiming to be the boy's uncle. Mandisa believes the boy he seeks is Charles. The man, dressed all in gray, was flashing around a handful of money, saying he would pay for information and for a guide who would help him find his dear nephew."

"Mr. Smith is not related to Charles," Jacques growled. "I cannot think of why he would be after the boy, unless he plans to kidnap him for ransom or something like that."

"Mandisa heard that Mr. Smith hired an unscrupulous Bedouin, with a bad reputation and a good knowledge of the Western Desert," Subira said. "The Bedouin, with a rifle over his lap, and Mr. Smith, holding a gray umbrella over his head, left on camels around noon today. The Bedouin held the reins of a third, riderless camel."

"Do you think they know where Charles is?" Jacques asked.

"They are either following our foot tracks or they have somehow heard Charles is at the Tomb of Sobek," Subira answered.

"We should not have stopped to rest," Jacques said, as much to himself as to Subira.

"We could not have gone any farther without sleep, and it will be slow-going for this Mr. Smith and his gray umbrella. Umbrellas are not effective in the Western Desert," Subira explained. "The sun heats up the metal prongs and melts the cloth, and sudden winds pull umbrellas out of one's hands. Unfortunately for them, there is no known oasis between the greenbelt and the Temple of Sobek, so they will have no place to rest."

"We should get going then," Jacques said, adding a quick smile.

Subira noted that Jacques had transformed from a severe and careful fellow—who meted out smiles like they were jewels to be hoarded—into a handsome, bronze-faced man with a five-o'clock shadow and a grin that could charm even a middle-aged Bedouin woman. Subira smiled to herself behind the headscarf she'd fastened over her nose and mouth. Isn't it wonderful how people can change, she thought as she headed over to the camels, who were still drinking from the well.

Rehima emerged from the cave door and grabbed three rolled packages tied with rope. They had been tossed out from the cave door. She handed one of the packages to Jacques and carried the other two to the well. Jacques watched as the women lowered their camels and fastened the rolls to the rear of their saddles. He signaled for Sadat to kneel. Sadat immediately jumped down on his knees. Jacques petted his camel between two floppy ears and then, imitating the women, tied the package onto the rear of the saddle. The women led the three camels out of the stone door to the outside. Jacques and Sadat followed.

Once outside, they waited for Mandisa. She emerged from the secret oasis, black robe billowing behind her as a strange wind blew along the desert floor, rattling small rocks and sending up wisps of sand. Jacques couldn't help but think Mandisa looked like the bird he'd met at the City of the Dead, who loved the poem "The Raven."

Subira explained that Mandisa was to return to the Giza Plateau and that she'd suggested the others take the old way to the Temple of Sobek.

"It is a narrow path, only wide enough for one camel at a time," Subira cautioned. "On each side of this path is deep, soft sand, difficult to walk through, even for camels. It will be particularly hard to navigate in the dark, but it is the shortest way. Hopefully, we will reach our destination long before Mr. Smith and his companion do. We have about twenty more miles before we reach the old path. The moon will be setting, making things more challenging."

Mandisa pushed the great stone door. The door, when closed, blended seamlessly into its rock frame. Jacques thought that only those who'd been whispered the secret of entry would notice the fine metal wire that could begin the process of opening the door of the Secret Oasis.

Jacques approached Mandisa. He said, "When you get back to the Pizza Hut, could you tell the people from the guest house that I could not stay in the harbor anymore?"

At that, Mandisa pulled a small paper from a pocket in her galliabyah. It was Jacques' fortune from last night's Chinese dinner. It read, '*Ships in a harbor are safe, but that is not what ships are built for.*'

"That fortune was, indeed, my inspiration for this journey," Jacques said. "Also, would you tell Bernadette that, ah, I will be back soon, and she and I will talk?"

Mandisa looked up into Jacques' eyes, smiling her wonderful broad and toothy smile. Then, hiding all but her dark eyes behind her black headscarf, she turned towards her camel. Subira helped the woman up on the saddle, and Mandisa waved as she headed east.

Sitting astride their camels, the two remaining women rode towards the western horizon. Sadat sped up to a trot and was soon beside the other two camels. Jacques could not help but think of his favorite boyhood book, *The Three Musketeers* by Alexandre Dumas. That's how he felt. In a horizontal line, they were three people on camels, riding off to conquer evil and defend good.

As the three rode their camels side-by-side, Jacques kept thinking about the story of the Three Musketeers: Athos, Porthos, and Aramis. They were lifelong friends, but there was a fourth character, D'Artagnan. He was not a musketeer but dreamed of becoming one—of living, laughing, and working together with friends as they fought against evil.

That was Jacques as a boy. He dreamed of this kind of friendship and loyalty, and of becoming a hero. However, he'd never found his Athos, Porthos, and Aramis. He'd led a solitary life and had never become a hero. He'd blamed his isolation and dissatisfaction on losing his family at such a young age. But it was he that turned down Bernadette's friendship. How many other offers had he missed to find friendship or become a hero?

Jacques began to think about Sadat and his amazing transformation. The camel had been a follower, plodding reluctantly through the sandy desert, his heart back at the green zone. He'd refused to respond to Jacques' pleas, his soft but firm kicks on the ribcage, or his determined waggling of the camel's reins. Now, he appeared to be a loyal companion. Had Sadat changed? Or did he sense a change in his rider, in Jacques? And what about these women? They were taking him to find Charles, perhaps riding towards danger. Yet they treated him kindly and like a confidante.

At this thought, Jacques called out into the desert, '*And now gentleman, all for one and one for all!*'

Subira and Rehima stared at the fellow beside them, wondering what he meant by this. Even now, Jacques didn't recognize that he was on a hero's journey and that his own life had become a page-turner.

CHAPTER 60

THE RAIN OF KNIVES

T he travelers were no longer the Three Musketeers. Rehima had taken the lead, Jacques followed, and Subira brought up the rear. Jacques was aware that soon they would arrive at the Tomb of Sobek. He would get Charlesand they would fly back to the Château du Mont, their adventure over. Sadat seemed satisfied being the middle camel. He kept a distance of about seven feet behind Rehima's camel and was walking steadily and calmly. There was nothing for Jacques to do except think. But what should he think about?

Jacques looked at the surrounding landscape. Except for the sand, small rocks, and a few hardy tendrils of plant-life, the desert was empty. However, according to Dr. Bernstein, quantum physicists was beginning to question the concept of empty space. She said some physicists were even questioning the very existence of matter. What was this empty space all around him? Empty space that might allow things things to move faster than the speed of light, or empty space that was filled with packets of information? It crossed Jacques' mind that things were simpler before he met Dr. Bernstein.

Looking up, Jacques saw that Mercury, Venus, and Saturn had pushed through the dark gray of dusk, and were shining down on the three travelers and their camels. As Jacques felt the magic of nightfall, he understood why most scientists felt more comfortable studying classical physics, macroscopic things. Who would rather focus on the invisible, the non-tangible? People like Dr. Bernstein, that's who, Jacques said to himself.

If Jacques decided to become a physicist, he'd prefer to pursue classical physics. He'd love to spend time looking through telescopes at the stars, planets, moons, asteroids, comets, and spirals. He didn't even want to think about quantum physics. However, he couldn't ignore what Dr. Bernstein had said to him the day before, as they watched the sun rise over the Sphinx. She'd said that he, Jacques Gerard, would make an excellent study for her Research and Experiments in Quantum Physics class.

"Why me?" Jacques had asked.

"According to Mrs. Montgomery's notes," Dr. Bernstein answered, "you initially made one call to the Château du Mont and paid one visit to the American Embassy. Yet from these two contacts, many people ended up in Egypt to help you find Charles. In my mind, there is a possibility that you made a desperate plea, in a non-physical manner, to someone, anyone, who could help locate the boy for whom you were responsible."

He had disagreed. First, Jacques told Dr. Bernstein, all those people had come to Egypt because they knew Charles and wanted to help him. Second, he didn't believe in mind-reading or other kinds of magic. However, Dr. Bernstein insisted her hunch had merit.

"What kind of sense would it make that all these people, who'd never been to Egypt—who didn't know the language, culture or geography—would each get on a plane and fly to Cairo?" she'd asked. "What convinced nine people that they could somehow find a missing boy, when the police, the American and French embassies, not to mention you, could not?"

"Wouldn't Charles be a better subject for your classes?" Jacques had suggested.

"No," the physicist had countered, "because Charles did not have an overriding desire to be found. There was something more important to Charles than being found, or he'd never have left the City of the Dead to follow the three women in black. My hypothesis remains that you called out for help, and the universe brought these people together to support you."

Sadat stopped suddenly, almost tossing Jacques over his head. "What's the matter?" he asked his camel.

Sadat was braying and whipping his head and long neck around, attempting to return from where they had come. Jacques looked around. Rehima was already off her camel. Subira kicked the sides of her reluctant camel, attempting to move him westward to where Rehima was standing.

Subira yelled to Jacques, "Get off your camel immediately!"

Jacques patted Sadat on the head and then signaled for him to kneel. "What is it?" he asked.

Subira didn't answer. Instead, she joined Rehima, who was shading her eyes with her right hand and staring west. Jacques dismounted and walked up beside the two women. Even he noticed the change. The sun, which moments ago had been a brilliant amber sphere, was now veiled behind a thick layer of dust. Strange rolling clouds, taking the forms of mythical monsters, were hanging above the now almost invisible sun. The clouds, colored a mixture of slate and black, appeared to be sucking up the sand from the desert floor. Inside the dark clouds, bright white shards of lightning danced in every direction, with no pause between the strikes.

"What is it, a dust storm?" Jacques asked.

"Worse," Subira called out through the increasing noise of the wind. "Rehima tells me it is the Rain of Knives. We must prepare. We must hurry."

By now, all three camels were agitated and bawling loudly. Rehima was off her camel and untying a package she'd placed behind her saddle at the Secret

Oasis. Jacques did the same. Unrolling his pouch, he found a thick blanket and a long scarf. Jacques wondered what they needed these for, and what on earth was the Rain of Knives?

Jacques turned to look at Subira. She was unrolling her blanket, so intent on her preparations that she didn't notice what was happening just inches away. Subira's camel had a snake in his mouth, a long, light-colored snake with horns. The camel was whipping it around like a cowboy's lasso. The snake's head came very close to Subira's left cheek.

"Snake!" Jacques yelled out.

Subira jumped a couple feet away from the camel and the snake. A moment later, her camel dropped the viper to the ground and stomped on its four-foot-long body with his right front hoof. Jacques watched in horror as the camel leaned its head down to the sandy desert floor, and picked up the writhing snake with its thick floppy lips. This time, the dromedary slurped the snake down, like a big piece of lasagna.

"What should I do?" Jacques asked, running up to Subira.

"There is nothing you can do," she answered. "Go back to Sadat."

Jacques was shivering from head to toe. He couldn't tell if it was from the cold of the desert night, the vision of a camel eating a snake, the thought of the Rain of Knives, or the sound of thunder rumbling almost constantly now as the strange storm moved closer. The wind filled Rehima's and Subira's gallibyah with so much air, Jacques worried they might be carried off into the sky like balloons that had broken their tethers. Was it just a few minutes ago that he'd felt as though he belonged in the desert? Now, he wanted to wake up from this terrible nightmare.

Fighting the wind, Rehima returned to her camel. She pawed through her pack until she found a container of some kind. She carried it back to Subira's camel, which was dropping huge teardrops from each eye. Rehima placed what Jacques could now see was a dark green glass jar under the dromedary's lower eyelids, catching its teardrops as they fell. When the camel stopped crying, Rehima returned the jar to the saddlebag on her camel.

Subira led her camel over to where Sadat was kneeling and commanded him to get down on his knees. The two camels were head-to-head, bodies forming a V-shape. Rehima joined them, signaling for her camel to kneel. The three camels made a tight triangle.

"What about the snake? What is happening?" Jacques screamed, for the wind had increased in velocity and volume.

"We will talk about the snake later. The Rain of Knives is nigh."

"The Rain of Knives is nigh?" Jacques repeated.

Looking at the rapidly approaching storm, Rehima spoke in Arabic.

"Rehima says we must sit inside the triangle and keep our heads below the camels' humps," Subira translated. "We must hurry. She says we do not have much time."

Subira gestured to Rehima, who was tying a scarf around her camel's eyes. "Although I have never experienced the Rain of Knives myself, she has. Some of her family lost their eyesight. This kind of storm almost never happens, but Rehima says that after experiencing the Rain of Knives, she has never again traveled unprepared."

Subira explained the Rain of Knives to Jacques while helping him tie a fluttering scarf over Sadat's eyes. "It is created by a combination of clouds filled with icy rain and a strong wind that blows the sand high into the air and into the ice-cold clouds. The combination of sand, wind and ice create a knife-shaped hail that can blind humans or beasts, and ruin property."

As Subira said this, a blinding flash of lightning hit the ground several hundred feet from the travelers; the thunder that followed was deafening.

"It also creates lighting. Get inside the triangle," Subira ordered as she slipped into the space made by the camels. "Pull the blanket over your head and sit on the ends. Keep your eyes closed, and don't open them until the storm has passed."

Jacques watched as Rehima leaned against her camel, tucking the blanket under her until she looked like the chrysalis of a caterpillar. Subira followed suit. Jacques felt the pain of the first drop from the cloud and hurried to tuck his blanket around him. He leaned back against Sadat, who was bawling and trembling. The thunder shook the ground, and lightning filled the air with the smells of ozone and nitrogen dioxide.

So much for the silence and emptiness of the desert, Jacques thought. Even with his eyes tightly closed, he could see lightning strikes dancing around him. He could also feel the sting of the Rain of Knives through the blanket. How long would this storm last? Jacques wished he'd asked Subira. It was too late to ask now. The roaring wind and clashing thunder made communication impossible.

As Jacques sat under the blanket, looking and feeling like a human cocoon, he wondered if he'd ceased to be a good subject for Dr. Bernstein's physics classes. She said Charles didn't have an overwhelming desire to be found. Now, Jacques wondered if he had an overwhelming desire to find Charles, or even return to the Château du Mont. He should never have come on this trip. Then again, if he hadn't traveled to Egypt, he would never have met the people at the guest house. He wouldn't have learned to ride a camel. He would not have met the women in black, or seen the inside of the Secret Oasis.

Would he choose to go back to the man he was, content to fix cars, run errands, mow lawns, play a little music, and make tea on his wood stove? Well, having a cup of tea right now sounded good, but of the other things he was unsure. Jacques was facing questions as old as the first thinkers. What is the meaning of life? Do you live life, or do you choose life? Had he chosen his life? Jacques had always felt that he'd been dealt a bad hand. Yet he'd done nothing to change it. If he decided to change his life now, what would it look like? Could he ever go back to his old self?

Would he be like the physicists Dr. Bernstein described, who preferred not to examine things they didn't understand, like her example of a soccer ball? If you kick a soccer ball, it may go in any direction. But you don't expect it to disappear and then reappear as a beachball or a phantom basketball. While things like this happened in the quantum world, less adventurous physicists just wanted to keep their eyes closed. Did Jacques want to keep his eyes closed? And why had he not written or called Bernadette after the

Christmas holidays? He could still see her in his mind's eye. She'd come to his tower room dressed in that green cape. He'd opened the door but hadn't invited her in. Why not? She'd handed him a paper with her address and phone number, but he'd never used them.

The stinging pain of the Rain of Knives had come to an end, but the lightning storm lasted for hours, accompanied by rain. Jacques found himself falling in and out of sleep. Finally, Subira broke into his dream of fighting off monsters, asking, "Are you alright, Jacques?" He wanted to say that he was physically alright, but he wasn't sure he was mentally alright. Instead, he just said, "I'm fine. Are you alright?"

"We are alright," Subira answered.

The storm had passed, and the sun had set. It was now officially night. The full moon was just rising above the eastern horizon. Rehima brought out an oil lamp, lit the wick, and placed it between the three of them. She took the scarves off the camels' eyes, but the trio of travelers kept sitting in the space between the three beasts. Subira reached into another pack and brought out the leftovers from Mandisa's feast. The pizza tasted even better than it had in the oasis, and the water tasted like the best French bottled water. They ate and drank without talking.

Subira broke the silence. "While we were in the storm, I wondered why we had to face the Rain of Knives. Why now? Why us? It is such a rare occurrence."

"Did you get an answer?" Jacques asked.

"Yes, I think I did," she answered. "It is because you were with us."

"I caused it?" Jacques asked, surprise in his voice.

"Well, not exactly you, but all of us together," Subira said.

Rehima, clearly following the conversation, said something in Arabic. Subira translated her words into English. "Akhenaten and Nefertiti told their key-keepers that when certain signs came together, change would be upon the world, and the time for the veil of secrecy would come to an end."

"Are you trying to tell me that what happened tonight was predicted more than three thousand years ago?" Jacques asked.

"Time may not be as it appears," Subira said, her gentle smile illuminated by the lamp.

At times like this, Jacques wished he had Dr. Bernstein beside him. Subira's camel was rising up off its knees, reminding him of the earlier incident. "What about the camel and the snake?" he demanded. "What were you doing with that jar and the teardrops?"

"Although I cannot explain why a camel would choose to consume a desert horned viper, one of the deadliest snakes in the world, I will tell you a great secret," Subira said, lowering her voice, though there was no one else around. "Nearly two thousand years ago, the desert people discovered that when a camel eats a viper, it will soon begin dropping huge teardrops. If these tears are collected, they provide an effective remedy for anyone unfortunate enough to be bitten by this terrible reptile. We, therefore, consider this eating of the snake a great gift of Aten, and perhaps a sign."

"I have so many questions for you two. First, how did you know that I would come to the City of the Dead last night?" Jacques asked.

"Rehima said that she heard you calling us," Subira answered.

So Dr. Bernstein might be right, Jacques said to himself, watching the women mount their camels. "Wait, I have a couple more questions," he called out.

But the women had turned south, and were soon well ahead of Jacques and Sadat. Jacques gently kicked the side of his mount to catch up. It was no longer pitch-black. The moon, gold in color, had risen fully in the east. Stars burst out from behind clouds, filling the sky with patterns, animals, gods, goddesses, and heroes. These were the maps of the desert people, the sailors, the ancient explores. Now they were guiding Jacques—to where, he wasn't sure.

CHAPTER 61

JACQUES IN THE TEMPLE OF SOBEK

T he moon cast long shadows of camels and riders on the desert floor, but as it disappeared, allowing the stars and planets to take center-stage, the travelers could barely see the path in front of them. Rehima dismounted, found a lantern in her saddle bag, and lit it. Jacques, in the rear, turned on his flashlight. It sent out a pale, narrow beam, reaching only three or four feet in front of him and Sadat.

Jacques chided himself for not listening to the salesman at the travel store, who'd urged him to buy a flashlight that could be seen from a mile away. Doubting he'd need such a powerful and expensive flashlight, Jacques had purchased a cheap red plastic flashlight instead. He was sure if Mrs. Montgomery were by his side, she'd have a perfect quote for this occasion, something like, '*A cheap red flashlight is only good if you don't want to see where you are going.*'

How he got here, riding a camel in the desert in the middle of the night, he didn't know. For some reason, however, at this moment Jacques felt this was where he was supposed to be. After several hours of travel Subira stopped, ordered her camel to its knees, and slid off its side.

"It seems the Rain of Knives has covered the old path with sand, making it very difficult to see," she cautioned Jacques. "Mandisa urged us to use this ancient path because it is more direct, though extremely narrow. Throughout the centuries, it has been used only by small groups of travelers. If things had gone as planned, we would have arrived at the Temple of Sobek ahead of your mysterious Mr. Smith. Now, I am afraid we have lost hours."

"What are we going to do?" Jacques asked.

"That is a good question, Jacques," Subira said.

Rehima located her broom, which she'd tucked behind her camel's saddle. Handing Subira her lantern, she began sweeping this way and that, the sleeves of her dark gallabiyah flying through the air like swooping bats. Charles watched in fascination. "What is Rehima doing?" he asked.

"We know that the path is around here somewhere, but it is now covered with sand. We just have to find it," Subira said, lighting Rehima's sweeping with the lantern.

Finally, Jacques saw Rehima draw lines in the sand, marking the beginning of a path and its two edges. Jacques guessed it was five feet wide at most. The camels would have to keep within the boundaries for, as Subira made clear, the soft, deep sand on each side could make even a camel unsteady.

"I am afraid that we will have to walk our camels," Subira called out to Jacques. He was glad to get a chance to walk for a while.

"Keep as close as possible and follow Rehima," Subira said, grabbing the reins of her camel. Between steps on the nearly invisible path, Jacques grabbed glimpses of the glittering sky. After about an hour's walk, he was cold and exhausted. He reminded himself that he was on the trail to meet Charles, but his body wasn't listening.

Subira stopped and turned to Jacques. "I believe we should take a rest," she said, her voice betraying exhaustion. "The sun will be rising soon, and we will make faster progress."

Leaving the camels on the path, they stepped off into the desert. Jacques' leather street shoes were immediately buried, filled with sand and small rocks, causing him to pitch forward. He landed on his hands and knees. Lifting his head, he found himself eye-to-eye with the sitting Rehima and Subira, who were stifling laughter.

Jacques was in no mood for mirth. He said with irritation, "I have traveled for days, with little sleep and little water. I almost died of heatstroke. I have felt the pain of the Rain of Knives and watched a camel eat a poisonous snake, and for what? I don't even know what I am doing here. I do not know what Charles is doing here. He is just a boy, an American boy, a twelve-year-old boy."

Jacques' voice increased in volume. "And what about all the secrets you keep talking about: the Secret Oasis, the Temple of Sobek, the Tomb of a Thousand Names, the Key Holders, the Daughters of Aten? What does that have to do with Charles and me? And why did I not go to the police when we were in front of the museum? Nothing makes sense to me."

Jacques was listening to himself. He'd always been proud of being labeled even-tempered, tranquil, steady, calm, composed, imperturbable, controlled, dependable—a quiet man. Here he was in the Western Desert, yelling like a madman. Jacques sat on his bottom, pulled his feet out of the sand, and removed his shoes. Subira and Rehima were staring at him.

"We are sorry, Jacques," Subira said. "We know this has been difficult for you."

Her reply to Jacques' tirade did what can be called "taking the wind out of his sails." He liked these women. He liked his camel. He liked the desert night. Subira and Rehima had gone through everything he had, and yet all he'd thought about was himself.

Filled with remorse, Jacques apologized to the women sitting in the sand. "I am sorry. I am grateful to both of you for leading me to Charles."

Subira sought to encourage him. "When the sun comes up, you will see a little jagged mountain in front of us. From the top of this small mountain, you will be able to see an area of huge boulders, leaning this way and that. Hidden in these boulders is the secret entrance to the Temple of Sobek. In front of the boulders is a tiny oasis with a couple of palm trees reflected in its water."

"Until the sun rises, Jacques, why not take a little rest?" Subira suggested. "Just a little hint for walking in deep sand: if possible, you should walk with your shoes off."

Jacques smiled wryly. "Thank you for this belated information."

Subira continued with her advice. "And when you walk, walk flat-footed. The larger the surface area of your feet, the less likely you are to sink into the deep sand. Also, if possible, crawling on all fours is easier than walking upright."

"Got it," Jacques said as he removed his socks and tucked them into his shoes. He tied his shoes together by their laces, tossed them over his shoulder, and crawled on all fours to where Sadat was kneeling. He leaned against his camel's warm and furry, if somewhat malodorous, body. Sadat gave out a soft purring sound. Soon, both Sadat and Jacques were fast asleep.

After a storybook sunrise, in which the yellow rays of the sun shot through a pink and purple sky, the three travelers wound up a mountain path. Arriving at the top of the ridge, Rehima signaled for them to stop. She dismounted and crawled like a black widow spider to where she could look down on the Temple of Sobek. Returning to her camel, she said something to Subira in Arabic.

Jacques heard the name Mr. Smith. His stomach did a flip. Mr. Smith and the man with the gun must be at the Temple of Sobek. Subira turned to Jacques and spoke, confirming his suspicions. "Rehima saw Mr. Smith, his companion, and a camel without a rider. They were traveling south, beyond the entrance of the temple. We will wait until they are out of sight before we descend."

Twenty minutes later, they moved to the edge of the mountain trail. Jacques could not see Mr. Smith and his companion. He did see palm trees and the blue water of a tiny oasis. He also saw a steep, narrow path twisting like a snake down the mountain. On the right side was a sheer drop-off. Just looking at this path made Jacques dizzy. He had a strong urge to take the jockey position again, but he didn't want to be laughed at by Subira.

Holding his mouth in a tight line, he determined to keep his eyes away from the right side of the earthen path. The ride down seemed to take a lifetime. In actuality, it took little more than a half-hour. Reaching the flat desert, Jacques had a strong desire to jump off Sadat, kiss his camel, then kiss the ground, but he thought better of it.

As soon as the three dismounted from their dromedaries, the camels stood up and trotted towards the water, which was illuminated by dancing flames from a small fire pit surrounded by stones. The camels bent long and shaggy necks down to drink. Rehima disappeared behind a tall boulder about sixteen feet high. Jacques had studied his tour book, but no place looked like this area. What on earth was Charles doing here?

Rehima emerged holding a platter of food. Subira prepared a plate for Jacques and, handing it to him, announced that she and Rehima were going into the Temple of Sobek and would return within the hour.

Jacques called after the two women in dark gallabiyah. "Have you seen Charles?"

They must not have heard him, as they didn't reply. Jacques was famished. He sat on a rock, savoring the lamb, rice and flatbread while admiring the little oasis and thinking about the boulders around him. Where had these tall boulders come from? It looked like some giant had picked up these enormous stones and leaned them against each other. It was still early morning. The sun was behind the mountain. The temperature was pleasant; there was even a slight breeze. He would soon be with his young charge. Jacques felt fortunate.

Thirty minutes later—Jacques knew because he checked his watch—a man in a white gallabiyah emerged from behind the boulders. He signaled for Jacques to follow him. He followed the stranger as he wound his way up through the boulders. The man opened a secret stone door. Subira and Rehima were just inside the archway. They were both wearing white gallabiyah and matching long, white headscarves. Their dark hair, which peeked out of their headscarves, was damp.

Taking Jacques' plate, Subira said quietly, "Before you enter this temple, we ask that you bathe in the Pond of Sobek. Then you will be given a white gallabiyah like ours."

In a high-pitched voice, Jacques asked, "Do I get a headscarf, too?" Subira and Rehima looked at each other and burst out laughing.

"Jacques, you are a very surprising young man. I had no idea you were a comedian," Subira said. "We take this dip in Sobek's pond to help keep the temple clean and as a symbol to all visitors that this is a sacred place. Now, let me introduce you to Mr. Hamand. "

Despite the man's reserved expression, Jacques greeted him with a friendly smile. "Hello, Mr. Hamand," he said with a slight bow. Mr. Hamand gave Jacques a slight bow in return.

The Egyptian man, short in stature but strong in form, guided Jacques into a great room. There were more than fifty large candles flickering around a dark pool, illuminating hundreds of Egyptian reliefs. The dominant theme of these reliefs was, of course, the Egyptian god Sobek, the crocodile god with a man's body and a crocodile head. There were also etchings or reliefs of real crocodiles.

In some reliefs Sobek stood next to a figure with a woman's body and the head of a snake, wearing a golden crown. Jacques thought to himself, they were not the most attractive couple he'd seen.

Mr. Hamand, who had disappeared for a moment, returned with towels and a white gallabiyah. Jacques stepped to the side of the pool and peered down into the murky water. It wouldn't make sense, having real crocodiles in a pool where people were required to bathe. Still, Jacques kept staring into the water. Mr. Hamand kept staring at him.

Finally, giving his Egyptian guide a small smile that lacked confidence, Jacques stepped into the pool's tepid water. Instantly, he turned from being hesitant to wondering how long he would be allowed to stay in the Pond of Sobek. After about fifteen minutes, Jacques felt the eyes of Mr. Hamand boring into him. He reached for a folded towel on the pond's edge. His guide handed him a white gallabiyah. He was dressed and ready to meet Charles.

Rehima and Subira were waiting for him in a small side room. Rehima handed him a cup of water. "It appears that Mr. Smith and his nefarious companion were able to find the entrance to this temple," Subira said.

"What! Where is Charles? Is he alright?" Jacques asked.

"Yes, he is alright," Subira said. "Mr. Hamand told us that Charles was outside having lunch when he saw Mr. Smith coming down the mountain path. He told the young lady he was dining with about his suspicion that Mr. Smith might be trying to kidnap him. The girl told her mother and the High Priestess."

"The High Priestess requested that Mr. Hamand shut the stone door between the great room and the rest of the rooms of this temple," Subira continued. "This ability to shut off rooms transforms the Temple of Sobek into a kind of fortress. Then, she asked him to hide Charles and the girl in the Tomb of a Thousand Names. The Tomb of a Thousand Names runs underground south for five miles—if you take the right path."

"What happens if you take the wrong path?" Jacques asked, drawing laughter from Subira and Rehima.

"I should have said, if you take the right-hand path," Subira said. "The left-hand path is, well, more complicated. Back to the story of Mr. Smith. We were surprised that he was able to discover the entrance to the Temple of Sobek since its location has been a long-held secret, but money can buy many things. Mr. Smith, with the Bedouin man behind him, walked right into the entrance of the great room. He announced that he had come to pick up his dear nephew."

"Charles is definitely not his nephew," Jacques growled. "Charles never saw this man before our plane ride from France to Egypt. Waiting in the line for the restroom, a man in a gray suit—with a gray hat and a gray complexion—struck up a conversation with Charles. Charles immediately became suspicious. I guess his instinct was right."

"Yes, we know this," Subira said impatiently. "Charles told us about his meeting and how the Gray Man appeared to turn up in several other places. To continue, Mr. Hamand told his Bedouin guide there was no boy in the temple. He was telling the truth, as Charles and the girl Meriaten were in an area we call the Tomb of a Thousand Names."

"Mr. Hamand told the two men the rules of bathing in Sobek's pond and donning white gallibyah. The Egyptian man, who had a large scar on his face, took one look at the dark pond and began backing out of the temple," Subira said, chuckling at the thought. "Mr. Smith ordered his companion to come back, but the man refused. The Gray Man looked around the temple. Failing to see any other rooms, he left."

"There is a possibility that Mr. Smith and his friend might return," Subira continued. "We have decided it would be best for you to join Charles and Meriaten in the Tomb of a Thousand Names."

Rehima handed Jacques his shoulder bag, giving him a pat on the back.

"Thank you, Subira. Thank you, Rehima, for everything," he said sincerely.

Subira bowed her head slightly. "Mr. Saki Hamand will lead you to Charles. We hope to see you again before you leave Cairo."

The two women dressed in white left Jacques standing in the middle of a small stone room. He felt great sadness; he might never see these two women again. He hadn't even been able to say goodbye to Caboose, his camel, his friend. Jacques straightened his shoulders, reminding himself that the important thing was he'd soon be with Charles, the boy he'd lost.

And, just as Subira had reminded him, they'd soon be leaving Cairo for the Château du Mont. All he and Charles had left to do was find their way out of the Tomb of a Thousand Names.

CHAPTER 62

THE CHOICE

Jacques followed his guide through corridors that went up and down, sometimes to the left, sometimes to the right. At times, there were two paths to choose from, at others, three. The entire Temple of Sobek was like a giant maze. Jacques silently followed Mr. Hamand. The Egyptian made a sharp right, placed his lantern on the stone floor, and stood facing a wall. Jacques stared down at the lantern. He was dazzled by the golden glow of a capstone on top of a pyramid that had been carved into the wall.

"Charles' pyramid!" Jacques exclaimed.

The pyramid relief, about seven inches above the floor, looked exactly like a two-dimensional form of the pyramid Charles had shown Jacques at the Mena House. It even had Cuneiform writing on the visible side. What did it mean? Jacques had an uneasy feeling in the pit of his stomach. Could all this mystery and intrigue have just been a trap to get Charles' pyramid? If so, why? Charles said it wasn't even the real pyramid, that Farak's family had the real pyramid. Now, Farak was supposed to be here at the Temple of Sobek. Were they trying to get Farak's pyramid?

Mr. Hamand gestured for Jacques to lean down and push on the pyramid with his hand. When he did, a lever emerged from the wall, about ten inches to the right of the pyramid. The old Egyptian placed his foot on the lever and pushed down several times. A tiny gap appeared in the middle of the wall. Jacques guessed he was about to enter the Tomb of a Thousand Names. His guide pumped the lever until the gap was wide enough for his fingers. Then he reached into what turned out to be a stone door, pulling it aside until there was just enough room for Jacques to enter. The Egyptian indicated that Jacques should go through the door.

Jacques stepped inside and the door slid shut behind him. Immediately, Jacques was surrounded by the blackest black he had ever seen. It was as if all light had been consumed. He swallowed a scream, then whispered in a shaky voice, "Is anyone here?" The next thing he knew, he felt two arms around his waist.

"Jacques! Jacques, I knew you would come," Charles said emotionally.

"Meriaten," Charles called to an unseen companion. "This is Jacques, the man who brought me here to Egypt."

"Why are you in the dark?" Jacques asked as he fumbled in his bag for the cheap red flashlight, hands still trembling.

"We had a flashlight, but we dropped it and it broke," Charles answered.

Jacques turned on his flashlight and shined it on Charles, who was right next to him. "Light or dark, I am so glad to see you, Charles!" he said, patting the boy on the back.

"I was afraid you might have gone back to the Château du Mont," Charles confessed.

"I don't leave things behind when I travel, Charles," Jacques said. "Are you alright?"

"Yes, I'm alright," he answered. "I'm not alone. Meriaten is with me."

Jacques pointed the beam of his flashlight behind Charles. It landed on a small girl wearing a gallabiyah, a head cloth, and a smile.

"Hello, Jacques. Charles told me about you. I am glad to meet you," Meriaten said.

"I am glad to meet you, too, but what are you doing here?" Jacques inquired.

"I'm here with my mother," Meriaten replied.

Jacques, Charles, and Meriaten heard the sound of stone on stone. Someone else was coming. Could it be Mr. Smith? The trio moved behind the back wall, where there was a nearly invisible entry leading to a narrow pathway. All eyes were trained in the direction of the opening door. Jacques turned off his flashlight and he, Charles and Meriaten, hid behind the partition, holding their breath.

They heard the stone door open, then close. The three forms saw the soft yellow light of a lantern. Charles peeked around the corner. "Oh, hello, Farak," he said. "Guess who's here? It's Jacques."

"Hello, Jacques," Farak said. "This is an interesting place to meet, is it not?"

"How did you get here?" Jacques asked wonderingly.

"A woman named Subira telephoned my parents," the Egyptian boy answered. "She said she knew where Charles was, and wondered if I would trust her enough to be guided here. I told her yes, but my mother was eavesdropping and insisted on coming with me. We rode all night on camels. I have never seen my mother so happy. Would you believe that she has adopted Charles into our tribe, the Tarabin Tribe?"

"Yes, Jacques, I'm now an official Bedouin," Charles said. "Isn't that great?"

"Okay, I am positive that I am dreaming—that I am not here, and you are not a Bedouin. In fact, things have felt unreal for some time," the Château du Mont's all-around man said.

Jacques reached out to touch the stone wall behind him. It felt strangely cool and solid. "Alright then," he said. "I will pretend this is all true, and that we must get out of here. Does anyone know how to open the door from the inside?"

Meriaten shook her head. "No, I don't think we should try to go out that door," she said resolutely. "Mr. Smith and that other man may have returned. And anyway, my mother told me there is a right-hand path and a left-hand path out of here, and which one to take was Charles' decision."

Charles stood with his shoulders straight and a determined look in his deep blue eyes. "I have already chosen the left-hand path, the path of the initiate, the Path of Knowledge," he said.

"Exactly what is the path of the initiate?" Jacques asked.

"I can tell you," Meriaten said. "My mother told me this path is for the training of the New Key Holders, the Wisdom Keepers, the Daughters of Aten."

"You may notice, Miss Meriaten, that three of us cannot be Daughters of Aten," Jacques said.

Meriaten continued without responding. "My mother told me that all initiates must pass through the left-hand path before they are accepted into the order."

"What order?" Jacques asked.

"The Wisdom Keepers, the Holders of the Future," the girl explained. "My mother told me that up until this very time, only women who had no children or whose children were grown up could become Daughters of Aten. She says things are changing, and that I'm lucky to be allowed to take the path of the initiate, even though I'm only twelve. And probably you are all lucky to be the first males to be accepted into the Tomb of a Thousand Names, to take the Path of Knowledge and become the Truth Holders who will help form the new world."

"This all sounds a bit overwhelming," Jacques said, pointing his flashlight at the girl. "Personally, I think there are three ways out of here: right, left, and back. I think we should go back."

"My mother said they will meet us on the other side of the path, so I think we should start moving right now," Meriaten declared. "We must choose the right-hand path, the shortest route, or the left-hand path, the more complicated route."

"I vote for the right-hand path. The quicker we get out of here, the better for us all," Jacques said firmly.

Meriaten's mouth was set stubbornly. "Charles already picked the path of the initiate, and my mother said he was the one to choose."

Jacques was becoming exasperated. "First of all, Charles and I are not initiates," he said. "I don't even know what an initiate is. Second, I say we get out of this Tomb of a Thousand Names as fast we can. There is Mr. Smith to think about."

"Jacques, we're going home soon," Charles said. "Our trip will be over, and we won't have sailed on the Nile or visited Tel el Armana. I want to learn all I can in the little time we have left, so I choose the left-hand path. Do you agree, Farak?"

"Yes, Charles," the Bedouin boy said. "I agree."

"Charles Dayton Stratton III!" Jacques roared. "Have you any idea what I have gone through these past two weeks? I am responsible for you. I am responsible to your parents."

"Yeah, my parents," Charles scoffed. "They don't even know that I've been missing, do they?"

"We've been unable to get in touch with them," Jacques admitted. "However, I agreed to accompany you to Egypt. Your parents arranged for this trip, and it is my task to get you safely back to school."

"My parents were just trying to make up for not being with me on my twelfth birthday," Charles said defiantly.

"Please stop interrupting," Jacques said. "I have a responsibility to you and to Madame Constance. So far, I have failed miserably in my duty to protect you. Now, we must get back to the Château du Mont as fast as possible."

"It wasn't your fault, and it wasn't mine," Charles said. "We didn't know the conductor would put me off the train, or that the police would remove me from the train station, or that I would get a concussion and end up in the City of the Dead."

Jacques sighed, then said, "We are not laying blame here. I am your guardian, and I say we are taking the right-hand path so as to escape this Tomb of a Thousand Names the fastest way possible."

Farak held up the lantern, illuminating the man in front of him. "Jacques, Sir, is this what you really want?" he asked. "Do you hope to go back home and pretend this trip to Egypt never happened—back to your old life of running errands and repairing cars?"

Jacques stood with his arms crossed over his chest, mouth in a tight line. Behind him loomed his own large shadow. He thought about grabbing Charles and dragging him down the right-hand path, but he didn't move. Farak's question had pierced his protective armor and entered his heart like a sword.

Jacques said in a controlled voice, "This has nothing to do with how I feel. It has to do with Charles' safety."

"Do you think he is in danger now, with the three of us around him?" Farak posed. "Will Charles be more or less in danger if we take the left-hand path, the Path of Knowledge? As for me, I do not choose to go back to the old me, the lone boy who spent years feeling sorry for himself, isolated from others, not having the nerve to stand up to his family and demand a visit home."

"If this is the Path of Knowledge, I want this knowledge. And," the handsome Egyptian boy concluded, "if you will excuse me, Sir, I believe you need this knowledge, too."

Jacques stood like a statue for what seemed like a long time. He finally said, "Alright, the left-hand passage it will be. However, we had better be quick about it. How do we get out of here?"

"My mother gave me a map," Meriaten said. "Charles and I haven't had time to look at it."

Jacques examined the map. "It appears that behind this wall is a passageway that can be entered from either side. Here is the right-hand path, straight down with an indication of five miles. Here is the left-hand path, wandering all over the place and requiring choices."

"Before we go, let's have a vote," he suggested, already knowing the outcome. "How many of us would like to see the sun shining down on us in a blue, blue sky?" Jacques looked at the young people in front of him. No one raised their hand or voice. "Okay, let's begin," he said, resolved.

"Meriaten, your mother gave me this lantern for you," Farak said, handing the girl the oil lamp with the yellowish-gold light.

The four travelers walked behind the panel and headed down a corridor with smooth walls and a rough ceiling about ten feet above their heads. "Stop!" Meriaten said. "Did my mother send me any matches?"

"Oh, yes, she gave me a package of wooden matches," Farak said, passing them to Meriaten.

"We don't know how long we'll be here in the Tomb of a Thousand Names," the girl said. "I suggest we use Jacques' flashlight and save the lantern for later."

It was a good idea, Charles and Farak agreed. Jacques turned on his flashlight. Meriaten twisted a knob on her lantern and the flame died out. The flashlight produced less than half the light of the lantern; all it did was cast scary shadows on the stone walls, barely illuminating the ceiling. Jacques' thoughts returned to his made-up quote in the Western Desert: *Only buy a cheap, red plastic flashlight if you do not want to see where you are going.*

The explorers moved forward, undaunted. They hadn't yet reached the section where they were to choose their path. Jacques hoped the decrease in light might lead to a change of heart in the young people. When they reached the division, he stopped.

"This way," Meriaten said.

"Last chance," Jacques said in a cheery voice, pointing the other way.

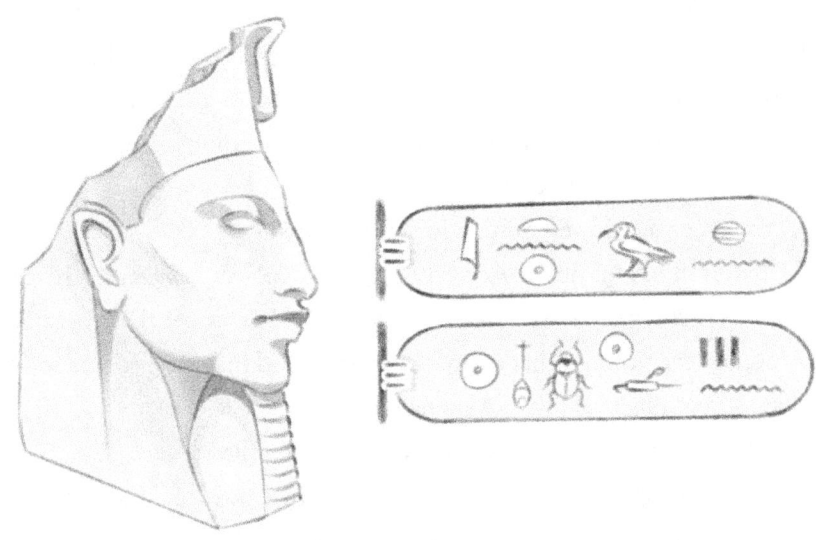

CHAPTER 63

AKHENATEN'S CHRONICLE

Farak was in the lead carrying the red flashlight, with Meriaten, Charles, and Jacques following. The four travelers walked swiftly through the tunnel-like corridor of the left-hand path. Jacques asked Meriaten if he could take a look at the map. Examining it, he said, "If this map is to scale, which I sincerely hope it is, we should reach the first room about now."

Farak moved to Jacques' side and peered at the small map. "I just noticed something," he said. "See this tiny writing near these rooms? The words appear to be labels written in Arabic."

Farak pointed to the first room on the map, saying, "It is labeled *Akhenaten's Chronicle*. The next is *Nefertiti's Story*. There might be a couple other rooms without labels, but the third room is the *Chamber of Secrets*, and the last is the *Room of Destruction*."

"Sounds promising," Jacques said.

"Isn't it strange that we're in the Tomb of a Thousand Names, under the Temple of Sobek, but the tomb appears to be dedicated to the period when Akhenaten was pharaoh?" Charles said. "It's particularly interesting because one of my main reasons for coming to Egypt was to go to Tel el Armana."

"Yes," Meriaten agreed. "Charles says there's supposed to be a ghost somewhere at Tel el Armana."

"You mean a mummy, don't you?" Farak asked.

Charles shook his head. "According to *Ghost Stories Magazine*, there's a ghost at Tel el Amarna in Tomb 11. I thought I'd never get there because I got lost and everything. That's why I think it's weird that these rooms appear to have something to do with Akhenaten."

"Life is filled with coincidences," Jacques said offhandedly.

But that wasn't what he was thinking. Jacques was thinking about Dr. Bernstein and her classes on the physics of entanglement, the non-local connection of all elements in the universe. Could Charles be calling to people who knew about Akhenaten, even from three thousand years ago, dragging all of them along with him on this adventure? Or was this all just a dream? Why, though, would he have such a strange and detailed dream? All Jacques could think of doing was to play his part and see where things went.

"I see something on the wall!" Farak exclaimed. "It is hard to make out using such a dim light. This thing is really more a toy than a tool." He drew closer, using the flashlight's beam to illuminate a section of the wall six feet from the floor.

"It's a cartouche, and an image of Akhenaten," Charles whispered.

"What is a cartouche?" Jacques asked.

"Cartouches are oblong groups of hieroglyphics representing the names of rulers or major cities in ancient Egypt," Charles explained. "In this case, these figures represent Akhenaten's name."

Farak continued moving Jacques' flashlight along the wall. "There is supposed to be a room here, but I cannot see a door," he said.

Jacques had the flashlight. He shined the beam along the floor. There, he noticed a fine metal wire. Jacques had seen this kind of wire before at the

Secret Oasis. Mandisa had used it to close the large stone door. Jacques had been impressed, thinking no one would ever notice the mechanism if they weren't looking for it. Even if someone spotted the wire, they might never guess that a thin silver thread could open and close a massive stone door.

Jacques quickly picked up the wire. Holding his arms straight up, palms open, he dramatically called out, "*Open Sesame.*" He gave a tug on the wire, hoping it would do its work. A section of the stone wall slid open, revealing a narrow doorway.

"Jacques!" Charles exclaimed. "How did you do that?"

"Magicians never reveal their secrets," Jacques answered with an enigmatic smile.

Meriaten broke in, saying, "Over there are some candles. We can use them and save the flashlight batteries and lantern fuel."

Each candle was sitting on an ornately-carved holder. There was a box of wooden matches in front of them. Meriaten struck a match on the floor and touched the wick with the flame. Using the burning candle, she lit the other candles, placing them around the room. Their flickering flames illuminated hundreds of colorful hieroglyphics.

"It's like a kaleidoscope in here," Charles said, slowly turning around and around the ten-by-twelve-foot room.

"I can't make heads or tails out of all these symbols," Jacques murmured, also turning.

Meriaten, putting on a teacher's persona, pointed to the wall with the most symbols and said, "Ancient Egyptian hieroglyphics can appear quite complex. They can be written and read right to left, left to right, up to down, down to up, and sometimes with no order at all."

"That complicates things a bit," Jacques responded.

"However," Meriaten continued, "the ancient scribes usually gave clues for reading the hieroglyphics. These clues are called *determinates*. One common determinate was a duck. If the duck faces right, you read right to left. If the duck faces left, you read left to right, and the same can apply to column writing."

"I like that, determinates, good to know," Jacques said, smiling at the girl with hundreds and hundreds of hieroglyphics behind her.

Charles was watching, too, wishing he hadn't left his Leica camera behind on the train. What a great photograph this would make—Meriaten, in her beige gallabiyah and headscarf, with all these colorful symbols around her. Unaware of his thoughts, the girl continued her lecture.

royal daughter   royal son

"Another example of a determinate is in this illustration," she said. "The characters for royal children look similar. The determinate here is a half-circle, meaning daughter. I think even you will be able to figure out some of these hieroglyphics, Jacques, as it is basically a picture language."

"So you, Charles, and Farak can all read hieroglyphics?" Jacques asked.

"I am still learning," the girl answered. "My mother says there is no complete dictionary or explanation of the ancient Egyptian hieroglyphics, so sometimes you just have to guess. That can be challenging. You can't always tell if the symbols are used to express something, or to show pronunciations."

"Very interesting, Miss Meriaten. Thank you. I will keep this in mind," Jacques said, bowing his head slightly in respect.

Charles, finding an uncomfortable place on the floor, sat down. He began fishing around in his shoulder bag. He brought out a pen and some paper. "Do you want to begin the translation?" he asked his Egyptian schoolmate. "I think it will be faster if I write down what you decipher."

Jacques was still turning around and around, staring at the four walls. "How would you know where to start?" he asked.

"If this is Akhenaten's story, it's likely it will begin when he was a child," Charles said. "Look there on the west wall behind Meriaten. There is a figure of a small person with a finger in his mouth. This is the symbol for baby, toddler, or small child. I'm guessing it is a male child, because there is no half-circle near the figure. Anyway, my suggestion is that we begin the story on the top of the west wall. Ready, Farak?"

"Ready," the Egyptian boy replied.

My name is Akhenaten, meaning servant of Aten, the one god. I was not born with this name. My father was Amenhotep III. I was named Amenhotep IV, which was odd since I was the second son. My brother, Thutmose, was my father's first-born. As the first-born son, he was destined to be pharaoh. Thutmose was trained to be a soldier and charioteer. He went with my father on the day of judgment and learned how to settle disputes. He was invited to festivals, he sang, and he danced. He was given a baby lion. Everyone knew my brother's name.

I was a sad child. I stayed in the temple with my mother, Tiye. She was not Egyptian; she was Nubian. While my brother played, danced, sang, and learned to be a soldier, I stayed in the temple, learning to write hieroglyphics and...

Farak hesitated, not knowing the meaning of the lines going in various directions.

"That's Cuneiform," Jacques interjected. "I recognize it from Dr. McAllister's book of the same name."

"You're right," Charles said, smiling up at his guardian.

Farak continued his translation.

From my mother, I learned reading, writing, mathematics, music, and the healing arts. I also learned something called making your heart blank.

"I believe making your heart blank means meditation," Farak said. "The ancient Egyptians didn't recognize the importance of the brain. During the mummification process, they even tossed the brain out, not preserving it like the other valued organs. I believe they thought the heart functioned in the way we consider the brain's function in modern times."

Farak returned to his translation, with Charles hurriedly scrawling his words onto paper.

I would sit on the floor and become very still, and I would hear voices or have dreams. But what boy wants to dream when they could be riding horses, or driving chariots, or learning to shoot the archer's bow? I was invisible. No one knew my name. My name was nowhere spoken in the palace or our city.

One day, my brother died. Everyone was sad. I was crying the hardest. I loved Thutmose more.

My father called me to his throne. He told me I would become pharaoh of both Upper and Lower Egypt.

"Jacques," Farak asked,"what do you think this figure is saying?"

Jacques looked at the image of a man standing, both arms bent at his waist, palms up.

"I think it means that he does not know how he can become a ruler," Jacques answered.

"That seems like a good guess, Jacques," Farak said. "Soon you will be reading hieroglyphics like the rest of us. Back to the translation. Amenhotep IV had just said that he didn't know how he could be a pharaoh."

'God will help you,' my father said to me. 'Which god?' I asked. He answered, 'Aten, the one true God.'

I asked my father if he believed in Aten. My mother had taught me about the one true God, but she said it was a great secret, that it was dangerous to talk about Aten.

Farak gestured toward the section of hieroglyphics he was reading.

"Here is the sign for danger from the priests," he said. "See? The priests are holding knives."

"Yes, and there is also a snake, a horned viper," Jacques added, shuddering at the memory of Rehima's camel eating the same kind of serpent. "That must mean danger, too. I can see that reading hieroglyphics is something like deciphering a puzzle. Now you may continue, Farak."

I said to my father, 'You are Pharaoh. How can you be challenged by priests?'

My father said that for many years, he believed in all the Egyptian gods and that the priests had the ability to speak to these gods for him. He said he paid these priests many coins to give him protection and success in battle. But he was not a happy pharaoh. When he met Tiye, she told him about the great loving God, who cares for all creation. This God says that anyone can speak to him directly, whether a farmer, a fisherman, a mother or a pharaoh. No one needed to pay the priests for this service. My father said that he became a believer in Aten and that this transformed his life. He was no longer a warrior, but a protector and kind leader of his people. However, my father knew the danger of declaring his allegiance to the one God. He told me, even though we believed in Aten, it had to be a great secret.

Farak pointed to an illustration of a finger over a symbol of a mouth, saying, "This symbol mean silence or secret." He continued translating the story composed by Akhenaten.

I became co-regent with my father, meaning we ruled together. My father was training me to become pharaoh. I discovered that I preferred life in the temple with my mother, Tiye. When I became older, however, a great gift came into my life. Her name was Nefertiti. We were both twelve years old.

"Twelve! That's the same age I am," Meriaten exclaimed.

Charles didn't say anything.

When we were older, we had a daughter. We wanted to name her Meriaten, meaning she who is beloved by Aten—but we knew there was danger in this. The priests would then have proof that Pharaoh no longer believed in many gods and all the services conducted by the priests.

To be sure naming our baby Meriaten was the right decision, I decided to make my heart blank, like my mother had taught me. I became silent and focused on the left side of my chest, where my heart is. I then heard Aten's commanding voice say, 'It is time to speak the words: Aten is the one God, the power behind the sun and all there is.'

I, Pharaoh, replied, 'If I declare Aten as the one God, my family will be in grave danger.'

Aten's voice, which I could hear speaking from my heart, became stronger. Aten declared that I, Pharaoh, was to build a new capital city, far away from the priests and their paid followers.

I traveled up the Nile searching for the location of a new capital city. We stopped in a deserted site, halfway between my two most important cities, Memphis and Thebes. The next morning, I looked toward the low cliffs on the East Bank. As I did, I saw the sun rise from a crevice in the cliff. I knew this was the location of my new capital city. I called it Akhenaten, meaning in service of

Aten. From Thebes and Memphis, I selected the best craftsmen to build this new city, the capital of Egypt. I instructed each workman who came to Akhenaten that we were building the most beautiful city ever created, a city dedicated to Aten, the one God. When our palaces were complete, my family slipped out of Thebes.

In the next three years, we brought nearly fifty-thousand citizens from Thebes and Cairo: carpenters, metal workers, farmers, fishermen, weavers, bakers, beer-makers, artists, musicians, teachers, and the holy ones dedicated to Aten. Together, we built schools, temples, the women's palace, government buildings, and homes for the workers. Never was there such a beautiful city.

"I wish I could have seen this city," Meriaten said breathlessly.

"It would be amazing to see a place like that, Meriaten," Charles agreed, looking up from his writing.

Farak continued.

When it was nearly complete, Aten gave me a message. I was to change my name from Amenhotep III to Akhenaten and give my city another name.

Charles said, "I was confused, but now I understand why the city and the Pharaoh seem to have the same name. Akhenaten means in service of Aten. But a city can't be in service. So Aten told the Pharaoh to take the name Akhenaten and to rename his capitol city, Tel el Armana."

Farak continued.

We made a call for volunteers to become citizens of Tel el Armana. However, some of the volunteers were secret followers of the priests of Thebes. Our hope was that, with time, our city, a place of peace and joy, would change all Egyptians' minds. My dreams, however, warned me that the priests planned to remove me from office and steal the treasures of Aten, hidden in mazes built under the palaces. Aten warned that great wealth is a corrupter of souls, and that it can cause even good people to do bad things. I have seen great battles in all the Mediterranean countries and territories. My dreams told me that the treasury room would be discovered, and this must not be allowed.

"What happened to the treasure?" Jacques asked.

"No one knows for sure," Charles said. "The books I've read say most of Amenhotep III's treasure disappeared after Akhenaten's time."

"That is the end of Akhenaten's story," Farak said.

Charles looked at the hieroglyphics and illustrations. Near the stone floor on the east wall, he discovered four tiny reliefs of pyramids. They each had miniature gold capstones and were covered in Cuneiform writing. They looked just like the relic pyramid belonging to Farak's family, only smaller.

"I wonder why they carved these four pyramids here?" Charles said. "Didn't you mention in your riddle poem, Meriaten, that four relic pyramids would be discovered?"

"That is what the poem says," Meriaten replied, touching each of the small pyramids.

"And Farak, didn't you tell me that when four pyramids come together, something great is supposed to happen?"

"Yes, that is the story my grandfather told me," Farak said.

"Wow, it may be that the pyramids have something to do with treasure," Jacques said dreamily.

Farak, ignoring Jacques' comment, said, "So far, we have two relic pyramids here at the Temple of Sobek, one belonging to my family and one belonging to the High Priestess. We have to find two more pyramids. I suggest we keep a sharp eye out for anything that might point our way to them."

"I guess we should move on," Jacques suggested.

Meriaten blew out the candles, then followed Farak out the door. As Jacques exited, he surreptitiously bent down and swooped up the silver wire. Holding his arms forward, palms down, he ordered the door to shut.

CHAPTER 64

MERIATEN'S STORY

Jacques took the lead, pointing the dim beam of his red plastic flashlight down the corridor. The next room on the map was *The Story of Nefertiti*. They were looking for her room and almost passed up a message carved into the corridor wall, very close to Akhenaten's room.

"Wait!" Farak called out. "I see Meriaten's cartouche on the wall, and there are more hieroglyphics."

"I'll light my lantern," Meriaten said with great excitement.

Charles pulled pen and paper from his shoulder bag. Farak pointed out that under Meriaten's cartouche was a small oblong circle, with a line at the bottom and symbols inside. It was the cartouche of the Pharaoh.

"Ready, Charles?" Farak asked.

"I'm ready."

"I'm ready, too," Meriaten said. "I am so excited to learn more about my namesake."

Farak began translating.

No one knows the greatness of our first daughter, Meriaten. I need to tell her story for, without Meriaten, we would not have enjoyed so many happy years in Tel el Armana.

When Meriaten was born, we lived in the palace in Thebes. At that time, I was still Amenhotep IV, co-Pharaoh with my father Amenhotep III. When naming our daughter, our firstborn, Nefertiti and I thought long and hard. Together, we took a bold and dangerous step. We called her Meriaten, meaning beloved by Aten.

There was already suspicion that the rulers, including my father and mother, were practicing a new religion—not worshiping the many gods of Egypt, but worshiping the one God, Aten. Naming our child Meriaten, confirmed the suspicion. All eyes were on our family, especially those of the wealthy and powerful high priests.

From the moment our daughter was born, we knew she was a special child. By six months, she was speaking many words. Every night, she would come to her mother and me, begging for stories. The stories she loved most were about Aten, who fashioned the stars, planets, mountains, oceans, rivers, lakes, streams, deserts, and our black land. We told her Aten was happy with what he had created but a little lonely. He decided to created life: trees, plants, animals and, most beloved of all, human beings. Meriaten learned the names of all the animals. She learned about the different lands, and the people who inhabited them.

Her favorite story was that one day we would move to a beautiful, rainbow-colored city filled with light, dedicated to Aten, the one God, the power behind the sun and all there is. In her baby voice, she declared that she loved Aten with all her heart.

"That is so cute," Meriaten said.

We did not tell her that we were moving to this city because our lives were in danger, and that this was partially because of her name.

One day, a high priest came to my throne room and asked me directly if I believed in the one God, Aten. I looked him straight in the eyes and realized I could not lie. I answered yes. He immediately left the room. I knew we must leave the palace in Thebes that very night. Nefertiti told Meriaten, who was now four, that we were going on a secret adventure, and we would leave in the middle of the night. We told her she should tell no one, not even her nursemaid. Meriaten was so excited, she went skipping around the palace. Her grandmother, Tiye, came into her room, kissed her, and told her she would join us on this great adventure soon.

"This is so exciting! I feel like skipping around this corridor," Meriaten said.

We slipped out of the palace at midnight and hid under a blanket in a donkey cart. Meriaten kept peeking out from the blanket we threw over us to hide from spying eyes. We drove ten miles north to the secondary port, where we boarded a small felucca. The stars and planets smiled down at us from an indigo sky.

Meriaten refused to sleep and refused to stop talking. At dawn, I saw our royal barge with its large square sails and its decorative hull and deck. I carried Meriaten to her sleeping pallet. Nefertiti and I felt safe for the first time since we left Thebes. The felucca returned to Thebes.

For us, this was a new beginning. To look at this little girl with her huge black eyes, inherited from her Nubian grandmother, and her lovely brown hair, one would not guess that she would be instrumental in helping form the new capital city of Tel el Armana.

"What did she do, Farak?" Meriaten asked.

"We are getting there, Meri," Farak answered.

I had already moved more than thirty-five thousand citizens from Thebes to Tel el Armana. I ensured we had all the trades necessary to create and maintain a functioning city: artists, architects, builders, bakers, brewers, farmers, fishermen, mathematicians, metallurgists, musicians, road builders, weavers, and more. I gave my people nice homes and good working conditions.

Although Tel el Amarna was dedicated to the one God, Aten, many of my citizens secretly held on to their belief in multiple gods and goddesses. They were afraid these gods would punish them if they failed to go to the priests and pay them to intercede. Nefertiti and I had weekly assemblies to teach our people about the loving God, Aten. Still, I received requests for priests to conduct their rituals, especially mummification for the deceased. This, Nefertiti and I would not allow.

Meriaten heard her mother and me talking about this. That is when things started. At seven years old, Meriaten took it upon herself to teach the residents of Tel el Amarna about Aten. On the first day, the children's nurse came to Nefertiti to report that Meriaten had run away from the palace. When our daughter returned in a dusty robe, brown curls escaping from her head cloth, her mother told the girl it was too dangerous for the daughter of Pharaoh to be out in the city alone.

The very next day, the nurse reported that Meriaten had run away again. Her mother asked Meriaten where she was going when she ran away from her nurse. She said she went to the water to tell the fisherman that Aten had created the fish for their families to eat and sell to others, allowing them to purchase the goods they needed. She finished by saying, 'That is how much Aten loves you.'

Meriaten told the fishermen that it hurt Aten's feelings for them to worship gods that were half-animal and half-human, when it was Aten who did all the work. Nefertiti admonished our daughter for putting herself in danger and making her caretakers worry. However, in the following days, she could be found in the field with the farmers, or in the orchard, the bakeries, the workshops of the stone and metal workers, or the stables.

Finally, her frantic nurse came to me. She told me all that Meriaten was doing. It was all I could do to keep from laughing out loud. However, I agreed that it was dangerous for the child of Pharaoh to be out in the city alone. I called Meriaten into the place of judgment. She was unafraid. She stood before me, a firm look on her face. I told her about the danger.

She said, 'Pharaoh, my father, you do not have time to talk to your people, but I have nothing to do but play and primp. You must allow me to do what you *and mother cannot. You must allow me to bring the words of Aten to the people of Tel el Armana.'*

I knew I could not punish her and that I could not stop her. In truth, I believed she was protected by Aten. As Meriaten grew older, the crowds around her grew larger. They were amazed at her storytelling. She told about Aten's creation of the sky, the stars, and the planets, and how Aten controlled their movement. She told them about the earth, the oceans, rivers, streams, and oases. This young girl told our people about all the animals, trees, plants, insects, and birds, saying Aten had created these for the enjoyment of his greatest creation of all, men, women, and children.

She added that it was not just the Egyptian people he loved and created this world for. He made it for all people. She spoke about all the principles that came from these stories. She asked her audiences to put away their old beliefs of the animal-headed gods and goddesses that demanded sacrifices and mummification. Could they not see that killing animals—not to nourish their bodies but to gain good fortune—would displease a loving God? Many people listened and believed.

"Oh!" Meriaten exclaimed. "I wish my parents were with me now to hear this wonderful story about the girl they named me after."

"You're lucky to have such a wonderful name," the boy just her age said. "Mine is just Charles."

"No, it is not just Charles," Farak said, "for my mother adopted you into the Tarabin Tribe. Your new name is Charles Tarabin Stratton, a name that contains the great history of the Bedouin people."

"Thank you for reminding me, Farak," Charles said solemnly.

"I wonder what happened to Meriaten when Tel el Amarna was destroyed?" present-day Meriaten mused. "I hope Akhenaten was right, that Aten protected her." With that, the girl blew out the lantern.

No one spoke as they moved down the corridor, their minds filled with the story they had just heard.

Not only the thirsty seek the water,

the water as well seeks the thirsty.
—Rumi

CHAPTER 65

RUMI AND PEANUT BUTTER COOKIES

Jacques took the lead with his red flashlight. The tunnel opened out to a large, cavernous room. Charles' chaperone placed his bag on the floor with a groan. What was in that thing? He pointed the beam into his cloth shoulder bag and gave a loud whoop.

"What is it, Jacques?" Charles asked.

"I think it is...yes, some kind soul put sandwiches in my bag," he said. "It smells like flatbread and peanut butter."

"My mother must have put the food in your bag before you entered the Tomb of a Thousand Names," Meriaten said. "I'm starving."

Jacques put on his best Dracula voice. "Vell, ve vill have to thank your mother if ve ever get out of here alive. Vhy are ve in such a dark, dark place?"

"Jacques, you are scaring Meri," Farak said accusingly.

"I'm not scared," Meriaten said. "I'm happy we're on the left-hand path. Oh, I loved how Akhenaten admired his daughter."

Charles agreed. "I've found out so much more about Akhenaten than I ever could have learned through books. I believe he was a great man."

"I can't wait to tell my parents the story of Akhenaten and Meriaten," the girl said excitedly. "Did you write all that down, Charles?"

"I did the best I could," Charles replied.

The four travelers were indeed hungry. Jacques distributed out the repast: folded flatbread filled with ground beef, onions, peppers, and spices, or peanut butter. All that was missing was something to drink. Jacques returned to his shoulder bag. "Guess what I found? Four empty copper cups, but no water," he said, holding up the metal vessels.

"I think I hear running water," Charles said. "Don't you?"

Everyone stopped talking. Meriaten said. "Let me have the flashlight, Jacques. Come on, Charles. Let's look around."

"And leave us in the dark?" Jacques asked with his mouth full.

Meriaten and Charles followed the sound of water. The source was at the far-right side of the large, rounded room. It was a small waterfall tumbling over the rocky side of the cavern wall, ending in a stone bowl. "Come on, Jacques and Farak," Meriaten called. "We found water."

"That was convenient," Jacques said. "I was thirsty, and water appeared. Hocus pocus, alakazam."

"Why do you keep acting like you're a magician?" Charles wondered.

"Because nothing has made sense since I first set foot in Cairo. The only explanation is that I am in a magical dreamland, and thus I must be magical or a magician."

"I see a sign to the right of the fountain," Charles said. "It appears to be written in Arabic. What does it say, Meriaten?"

Meriaten translated the inscription. "It says, *'Not only the thirsty seek the water, the water as well seeks the thirsty.'* The quote is attributed to Rumi."

"My point exactly," Jacques said. "Nothing on this journey makes sense. How can the water seek the thirsty? And furthermore, why is someone quoting an 8th century Persian poet in an ancient Egyptian tomb? Why can it not say something simple such as, 'Drink me,' like the label on the bottle in *Alice in Wonderland*—something short and to the point."

"I love *Alice in Wonderland!*" Meriaten exclaimed. "My mother read me Lewis Carroll's story so many times."

"Yes, it is quite the story," Jacques said. "Here, however, we are not faced with a children's tale. Instead, the words are like everything we have encountered: a puzzle we must solve, like the riddle of the Sphinx."

"I think the message is this," Farak said. "If you are really searching for something, you are likely to find it, for that thing will be searching for you also."

"I like that, Farak," Charles said. "I'm going to quote you in my notes, right alongside Rumi."

Jacques didn't pursue the subject further, but for some reason he thought again of Dr. Bernstein. It crossed his mind that the message on the fountain was meant for him. After all, he'd gone on a quest to find one small boy in a large country, and somehow people everywhere had converged to help him. Jacques still felt a rush of relief every time he saw Charles, knowing that whatever happened, his young charge was by his side.

For a long-dead poet to speak directly to him, Jacques thought, everyone would have to be non-locally connected to everything in the universe. Time, by necessity, would be non-linear. Jacques shook his head, trying to wake himself. He was thinking such ridiculous things, he truly must have fallen down a rabbit hole. What was it about the Tomb of a Thousand Names that made anything seem possible? It must be the dark, Jacques concluded. Being so far down, in a place where day and night ran together, had disoriented him. That was it.

While Jacques pondered this idea, Meriaten reached for the dipper that had been placed on one of the stones around the pond. She filled her copper cup and started to take a drink.

"Wait, I'll go first," Jacques said, taking the cup from the girl's hand before it could reach her lips.

"Hmmm! Delicious," Jacques said. "It is much better than the canvas-flavored water Rehima gave me. I guess it is safe, but where does this water come from?"

"Maybe it's connected with the oasis outside," Charles suggested. "It didn't dawn on me before, but there must be a good water source here. How else would the priests be able to fill the pond for the Son of Sobek?"

"Good thinking, Charles. I never questioned why the Temple of Sobek was so far away from everything," Meriaten said, filling her cup with tepid water.

"There must be an underground river or lake around here," Farak said. "That would certainly answer a lot of questions."

With their thirst quenched, the travelers were ready to continue to the next room. Jacques went to his shoulder bag to return the copper cups. While making space for the cups, he gave out another whoop. His three companions found Jacques pulling more paper-wrapped packages from his bag.

"What is it?" Meriaten asked.

"Cookies!" Jacques exclaimed. "From the smell, I dare say they are peanut butter cookies."

"Mom knows I love peanut butter cookies," Meriaten said, taking one of the paper-wrapped packages.

"Just what we need to buoy ourselves up, for we have decisions to make," Jacques said. "I see seven doors ahead, shooting off from this main cavern. We have to choose which is our path. By taking the left-hand path so far, we have enjoyed a nice introduction to Akhenaten, not to mention Meriaten—I mean the first Meriaten."

Their Meriaten, who had just polished off a cookie, smiled at this.

"Having gained some important knowledge, we could probably still find the right-hand path and be out of the Tomb of a Thousand Names in an hour. We can have the best of both worlds," Jacques said persuasively. "What do you think, my young friends?"

He shined his flashlight on Charles, then Farak, then Meriaten. They all stood with their arms crossed in front of them, wearing stubborn looks on their faces.

"Let's look at the map," Charles said. "Jacques is right about the possibility of finding the right-hand path. But where do the other paths lead?"

Jacques illuminated the map Farak had just rolled out and they all gathered around it.

"I think the seven doors are another way of keeping people from finding the true Path of Knowledge," Charles said. "One door leads to the right-hand path. Five lead to deadly dead-end paths. One door, however, leads to the left-hand path. Since we believe in democracy, let's vote. How many people wish to take the right-hand path with the hopes we might be back here somehow, at some later time?"

Jacques flicked his beam from one young person to another. No one raised their hand. "Just what I thought," he said wryly. "We are in unanimous agreement."

Taking a bite of a peanut butter cookie, Jacques led the way through the fifth doorway.

CHAPTER 66

WHISTLING IN THE DARK

In one drop of water
are found all the secrets of all the oceans;
in one aspect of you
are found all the aspects of existence.
—Khalil Gibran

The four travelers, led by the dim beam of Jacques' red flashlight, emerged from the golden room of *Nefertiti's Story*. Turning left, they traveled single-file down the narrow corridor, whose walls seemed to be closing in on them.

"I'm looking at Meri's map," Farak called out from the back of the line. "It indicates that the *Chamber of Secrets* is about three thousand meters from *Nefertiti's Story*. Depending on the condition of the pathway, we could be at the chamber in about an hour."

"What does chamber mean?" Meriaten asked, looking back at the tall, shadowy form behind her.

"As I recall, chamber has several meanings. It can mean a secret compartment or hiding place, a boardroom—I guess we can eliminate that one—or a sleeping room," Jacques elucidated.

"What kind of sleeping room?" Meriaten wondered.

"A more important question vould be, who might be sleeping inside this *Chamber of Secrets*," Jacques said, in his best Dracula voice. "And how long has he, she, or it been sleeping there?"

"So, Jacques," Farak said, "You think we are heading for a tomb?"

"Judging by our steep descent, the smell of stale air, and the sudden drop in temperature, it is a definite possibility," the man in the shadows said.

"Let's check the map," Farak suggested. Charles and Meriaten squeezed in beside the Bedouin boy as he unrolled the map, which was covered in maze-like lines.

"The straight line at the bottom is the right-hand path," Charles said, pointing. "See, it goes from the room where we started straight to the exit of the Tomb of a Thousand Names."

"We chose to avoid this simple path, for reasons that are still unclear to me," Jacques said.

"We can't be sure why we've taken the left-hand path until we've completed it," Meriaten said.

"That sounds rather vague and mysterious," Jacques said, staring at the young girl.

"The left-hand path, the Path of Knowledge, is mysterious," Charles said in a dramatic voice. "It's a tangle of twisted routes, some terminating in dead-ends. Without this map, we could be lost in this Tomb of a Thousand

Names for eternity." As he said this, the flashlight beam went off, casting the party in total and absolute darkness.

"Charles! Turn the light back on. That's not funny," Meriaten gasped.

"I didn't turn it off," Charles replied. "The batteries must have died."

"Okay, don't worry," Meriaten said in a calmer voice. "I'll light my lantern. Now, where did I put the matches?"

"You lost the matches?" Farak asked sharply.

"No, they're here somewhere," she said.

"It feels like the dark has eaten all the lights in the universe, like we've just been dragged into a black hole," Charles said theatrically. "Meriaten, let me hold your lantern while you look for the matches."

Feeling for Charles' hand, the girl handed him the wire handle of the oil lantern.

"Never fear," Jacques said. "The flashlight's batteries may have failed, but I have not. I put extra batteries in my shoulder bag the night I left the Khemitology Guest House. How long ago was that? I seem to have lost all sense of time."

Jacques, rummaging through his backpack, exclaimed, "I found one of the C batteries!"

"One C battery?" Charles scoffed. "What can we do with one battery?"

There was a rustling sound as Jacques fumbled through his shoulder bag. "I know I have the other one in here someplace," he said. "Here are the copper cups, my shaving kit, some plastic bags, a towel, and a pen. Okay, I found it. Here is the other battery. Now, who has the flashlight?"

"I do," Charles said, reaching toward Jacques' voice and bumping into the person next to him. "Sorry, Meriaten," he said. "First, let me give the old batteries to Farak, so we don't mix them up with the new ones."

"Where are you?" Jacques asked.

"Here I am," Farak said, reaching in front of him. "Is this you, Jacques?"

"Yes," their chaperone answered.

"Okay, Charles," Jacques said. "Hand me the flashlight."

"I think the little buttons on the end of the batteries go first, towards the light bulb," Charles instructed.

"I know where the batteries go, Charles," Jacques said irritably.

"I've never liked the dark," Meriaten said. "I still have to sleep with a nightlight. My mother said I will outgrow my fear of the dark when I am thirteen. Hey, I found the matches! They were in the pocket of my gallibyah."

"We won't need them," Jacques said. He turned on the flashlight, shining the beam first on Meriaten, then Charles, and then Farak. "As I suspected, we are all here. I suggest we conserve the fuel in Meriaten's lantern until we are closer to the exit. I seem to remember the salesperson in the hardware store informing me that batteries do not last long in cheap flashlights such as this one."

"Why'd you buy a cheap flashlight?" Charles questioned.

"I assumed our tour guides would provide us with light," Jacques said defensively. "Is that not their job? And, I might mention, the more expensive flashlights required three or four D batteries, making them quite heavy. Even so, I must admit I have my regrets."

"Let's look at the map again," Farak said.

"The map indicates that the *Chamber of Secrets* consists of several little rooms around a larger circular room," Jacques noted.

"I hear water," Charles said, moving ahead of the group.

"I hear water, too!" Meriaten confirmed.

Farak was still studying the map. "See? We failed to notice it before, but there is a second narrow path that leads north off this corridor to another circular room," he said. "It looks similar to the last circular room, the one with the water fountain. It also has seven doorways shooting out in different directions. How did we miss it?"

"Because on the map it is drawn in a fainter hue," Jacques said. "It is very confusing. I wish I had saved some breadcrumbs from our sandwiches."

"Why?" Farak asked.

"I know what you're referring to. It's the fairy tale of *Hansel and Gretel*, isn't it?" Meriaten said.

"I am unfamiliar with this story," Farak said, looking up from the map towards Meriaten.

"The short version is," Meri began, "once upon a time, during a terrible famine, there were two children, Hansel and Gretel. Their mother died, and there was hardly anything to eat. Their father was persuaded by his hateful second wife to take the children deep into the woods and leave them there. Hansel was suspicious and marked the path with breadcrumbs so he and his sister could find their way home. But the birds ate the breadcrumbs."

"What happened to the children?" Farak asked.

"They ended up at a witch's house made of gingerbread and candy. The horrible witch caught the children eating pieces of her house and put Hansel and Gretel into cages. She planned to eat them. The children tricked the witch into climbing into an oven, burned her alive, and then escaped and went back to their father. He was remorseful and had thrown out the evil stepmother."

"That is a terrible story," Farak said. "Surely, it was not designed for children."

"When I was younger, I thought it was the most frightening fairy tale ever," Meriaten agreed. "Do you think we might get lost down here, Jacques?"

"Too bad Jacques didn't save any breadcrumbs. If he had, at least we wouldn't have to worry about birds eating them," Charles joked.

"True," Jacques said. "However, through my extensive research of tombs—my primary source being the many mummy movies I have watched over the years—I can say with confidence that hungry scarabs are as bad as birds or worse about eating breadcrumbs, and anything else in their path."

"Have you ever seen a hungry scarab, Meri?" Charles asked.

"No, my mother wouldn't let me see those mummy movies," Meriaten answered. "She said they're stupid."

"Did she now? Did she see the 1932 movie 'The Mummy,' starring the great Boris Karloff?" Jacques demanded. "Has she seen 'The Mummy's Hand,' a gripping 1944 film starring Lon Chaney Jr.? Has she viewed my favorite, the 1955 comedic masterpiece, 'Abbott & Costello Meet the Mummy.' Pray tell?"

"I don't think she saw any of those," Meriaten answered.

"Then neither you nor your mother know anything about hungry scarabs. I rest my case," Jacques declared.

"I meant have you seen real scarabs, Meriaten, not movie scarabs," Charles clarified.

"Not yet," the girl answered. "I have seen bats, though. Maybe they eat breadcrumbs."

"I don't think so; bats mostly eat bugs," Charles said.

"What's the best way to hold a bat?" Jacques asked.

"What is the best way to hold a bat?" Meriaten repeated, confused.

"By its handle," Jacques guffawed.

"Really, I never thought of you as being funny, Jacques," Charles said.

"Oh, I can do better than that," their chaperone boasted. "What do you call an Egyptian doctor?"

"What?" Meriaten asked.

"A Cairo-practor." Jacques continued showing off his comedic repertoire. "What does the mummy say when the Pharaoh tells a joke?"

"What?" Meriaten asked.

"Nothing, he just groans. Ooaah! Ooah!" Jacques moaned.

Meriaten laughed. Charles shook his head, saying, "I'm afraid my chaperone has gone batty."

"Oh, gone batty, I get it!" Meriaten said.

"I don't think so, Charles. I have gone sane," Jacques said, making a manic expression with wide eyes and a too-wide smile.

"See, Jacques is in deNile," Charles quipped. "Get it? Denial? The Nile?"

With that, the explorers' laughter echoed off the stone walls, deep down under the Temple of Sobek and throughout the Tomb of a Thousand Names.

"When did you get so funny, Jacques?" Charles inquired.

"I can tell you exactly when and where," the Chateau's all-around man said. "I was in the Pizza Hut, across the street from the Sphinx, when I was cornered by a redheaded eight-year-old who insisted on bombarding me with Egyptian jokes."

"Fran is here?" Charles asked in surprise.

"Yes, with his mother, Dr. Bernstein. Allow me to share Fran's favorite joke," Jacques said. "A sphinx was guarding a road when a traveler walked by. The sphinx told the man he could pass, but only if he answered this riddle: 'What is wider than an ocean, heavier than a mountain, and unbound by the laws of physics? The man thought for a moment, then he smiled and said, 'I know. It's imagination.' The sphinx told the traveler he was wrong. The answer to the riddle, he said, is Fran's mother, Dr. Bernstein."

"I don't understand," Meriaten said.

"Dr. Bernstein is a quantum physicist," Charles explained. "She questions all the laws of traditional physics."

"I still don't think it's very funny," Meri said.

Charles looked at the once-serious man who'd brought him to Egypt.

"Jacques, why are you telling jokes down here?" Charles asked. "Oh, wait, I think I know. There's a phrase in the book *A Wrinkle in Time*."

"I love *A Wrinkle in Time*. Madeleine L'Engle is a wonderful writer," Meriaten said. "What's the phrase, Charles?"

"Whistling in the dark," he answered. "It means to act unconcerned in the face of danger."

"You may be right, Charles," Jacques said. "More to the point, psychologist Sigmund Freud believed, '*Laughter allows people to let off steam or release pent-up nervous energy.*' And from the moment I met my camel Caboose, I have found a strong need to let off steam, combined with great nervousness. So, I suppose I am whistling in the dark, as Charles says, as we move inevitably toward the *Room of Destruction*. Unless..."

Meriaten interrupted him. "I have a surprise, Jacques. While I was looking for matches, I discovered my mother had placed several neatly-wrapped packages in my shoulder bag. Just as I guessed, my mom packed more peanut butter cookies!"

"Good fortune has smiled down upon us," Jacques said as he took a bite of a peanut butter cookie. He called out, "Do not forget to save the crumbs."

CHAPTER 67

NEFERTITI'S STORY

J acques felt strangely lighthearted as he walked, eating his second peanut butter cookie. "Your mom is a fine baker, Meriaten," he said.

Farak held up the map, illuminating it with the flashlight. "It looks like *Nefertiti's Room* is about a thousand feet from here."

"Look!" Meriaten said. "There are hieroglyphics right here." Meriaten translated, as Farak shined Jacques' flashlight on the wall. "It reads, '*Beautiful are the Beauties of Aten*,' followed by '*The Beautiful One has Come*.' That long oval contains Nefertiti's cartouche."

Charles looked up and said, "That's strange."

"What's strange?" the girl asked.

"Remember, Jacques, that inside the long oval is a name or a city's name. This cartouche should be Nefertiti's name. Usually, a queen's name is symbolized by the illustration of a queen with a flower," Charles explained. "But in this cartouche of Nefertiti, the queen is accompanied by the symbol of a vultureVulture stands for the letter. It can mean sacred and protected by Pharaoh. It is known as the Pharaoh's chicken."

Meriaten laughed. "The Pharaoh's chicken? That's funny, Charles."

"It's not that funny," Charles said. "I read that anyone who dared to kill an Egyptian vulture was sentenced to immediate death. I guess it was Akhenaten's threat that if anyone did anything to Nefertiti, they wouldn't live to see another day."

"Oh, that is interesting. Now, how do we get into *Nefertiti's Room*?" Jacques asked. He hit the wall with his fist, making a thudding sound.

"You're the magician, Jacques," Charles answered.

Farak and Charles pushed on different sections of the wall. Nothing happened. They pushed on various hieroglyphics. Still, nothing happened. Meriaten stood back watching the boys, tipping her head this way and that. Then, she said, "I have an idea. Why don't you push on the cartouche?"

"Now, why did I not think of that?" Jacques asked.

Farak pushed in the middle of the cartouche. Nothing happened. "Try pushing just on the oval around the cartouche, Farak," Meriaten suggested.

That was the trick. The four explorers saw a lever pop out from the edge of the wall on the left-hand side of the corridor, about six feet from the cartouche. Farak dashed over to the side and pumped up and down on the lever. There was the sound of stone on stone. The doorway to *Nefertiti's Room* opened.

"Perhaps we should call it the Tomb of the Secret Doors," Jacques said. "What do you know about this place, Meriaten?"

"I don't know much of anything, except it's under the Temple of Sobek and is called the Tomb of a Thousand Names," Meriaten answered.

Jacques spoke to Farak, who was examining the map. "Is there anything on the map about a tomb? Maybe we are heading for Nefertiti's tomb," he said in a scary whisper.

"Stop that, Jacques," Farak demanded. "You are scaring Meri."

"I am not afraid. I have been in a lot of tombs," the girl said defiantly.

"Un-excavated tombs?" Charles asked.

"No, but I am still unafraid," Meriaten declared.

"Does anyone want to know my feelings?" Jacques wondered.

"What are your feelings?" Meriaten asked.

"Now that you ask, I am unsure what my feelings are," Jacques answered truthfully. He could almost hear Bernadette's voice saying, "That is an extreme understatement."

"We're wasting time," Meriaten complained, grabbing the flashlight and entering the stone door. She located six candles on ornate holders. She struck a match and lit one candle; from its flame, she lit the other five. The entire room shimmered gold.

"Wow!" Charles whispered in wonder. "I believe we have found Aten and Akhenaten's treasure. It was Nefertiti."

"I have never seen, or dreamed of, a room like this," Meriaten exclaimed, placing her small hands over her heart.

The room was larger than Akhenaten's. Each of the four walls was covered with hieroglyphics and illustrations, beautifully painted and accented in gold. There was a small stone bench in the middle of the room. Jacques lay down on it lengthwise, knees dangling comically over the edge. "Look at that ceiling," he said.

Meriaten, Farak, and Charles tipped their heads back and were astounded by thousands of stars in a cobalt sky. Some of these painted stars were connected by gold lines, forming constellations. There were animals and gods, many looking as though they were engaged in battle. On the south end of the ceiling was a rendering of five suns, clearly representing the sun's movement throughout the day.

"According to Dr. Awyan," Charles said, "the movement of the sun through the day and night, and through seasons, illustrates the ancient Egyptians' belief that time is a repeating cyclical pattern. Like the sun rising and setting, rising and setting, time is a repetition of birth and death, rebirth and death."

"That is funny," Jacques said. "I always thought the placement of the sun indicated when I should get up, when I should take a nap, and when I should go to bed." He ended his comment by snoring loudly from his place on the bench.

"Jacques!" Charles called out with disgust.

"My mother said we should take our travels through the Path of Knowledge seriously," Meriaten admonished their chaperone

"I am serious. I am seriously tired. You have no idea what I have been through," Jacques said. "Now, who is going to do the interpreting?"

"I will," Meriaten said, moving closer to the wall. "Here is an explanation that this message was originally written in Cuneiform by Nefertiti, then translated by a woman called Seshat into hieroglyphics. And then these hieroglyphics were carved and painted onto this wall by an artist. Alright, are you ready, Charles?"

I was twelve when I learned I was to marry the newly-crowned Pharaoh Amenhotep IV.

"See, the heel bone means ten and the two lines make it twelve. Nefertiti was the same age as I am now. Who would want to get married at twelve?" Meriaten asked emphatically. "Not Nefertiti, I guess, because it says she was sad. See, here is an eye with many tears. She didn't want to leave her mother but, as a royal daughter, she had no choice."

Meriaten gestured to the wall and said, "This series of small paintings shows Nefertiti being prepared to be taken to Pharaoh. She is dressed in a long gown covered in gold thread and colorful jewels. Her mother is putting a gold necklace around her neck. The next painting shows a handmaiden combing Nefertiti's black hair into an elaborate hairstyle. This illustration here shows two handmaidens, one painting dark kohl around Nefertiti's eyes, and the other preparing to put red on her lips."

"They carried her in a litter to..." Meriaten trailed off, uncertain.

"To Thebes," Farak said. "That is the cartouche for the ancient city Thebes, now called Luxor. That is where my family lives."

Meriaten nodded and continued her translation.

We went to the palace in Thebes. I walked into the throne room. There was no one there except one shy boy. He didn't look at me. 'Who is to be my husband?' I called out, but no one answered. A royal woman came into the throne room. She looked and looked at me.

"See, there are two sets of eyes," Meriaten explained. "This means double: looked and looked, or stared and stared."

'I am Queen Tiye, wife of Amenhotep III, and mother of Amenhotep IV,' the royal woman said, pointing to the boy sitting on the floor near a throne. He still didn't look at me. Queen Tiye called me to her side. I was frightened. A woman brought her a bowl filled with water and pink flower petals. With a cloth, the queen softly wiped off the black kohl around my eyes and the red from my lips, saying, 'You are too young for all this, don't you think?' I nodded my head in agreement. The beautiful queen gave me a robe of white linen. She took down my hair, removing the gold and jeweled ornaments. I was no longer afraid. I liked this kind woman.

Amenhotep IV was my age. He told me his brother was supposed to be Pharaoh but he died. He said it made him very sad. We had an elaborate marriage ceremony; both of us were dressed up like grown-ups. That first year, we saw very little of each other. Amenhotep IV was learning from his father, Amenhotep III, how to be Pharaoh. Meanwhile, Queen Tiye became my teacher.

"Am I going too fast, Charles?" Meriaten asked.

"I'm almost there," Charles said, scribbling. "Alright, go."

I learned to read and write, add and subtract, play the lyre, sing, and dance. My favorite subject was healing with voice and instruments. Queen Tiye told me that sound could cure disease and eliminate pain. I'd never heard this before. She also taught me about her God, Aten. She said he was the one God, the power behind the sun and all there is, and that there were no other true gods or goddesses.

My Pharaoh was taught to drive chariots. To my amazement, Amenhotep IV taught me how to drive a chariot, too. Some people did not like this; they didn't think girls should drive chariots.

"I can just picture it!" Meriaten interjected. "There are still men and boys today who complain about women driving cars."

"You have happened upon a great truth, young lady," Jacques said. "There is a proverb in the Bible, '*There is nothing new under the sun,*' about how things never really change."

"There is nothing new under the sun," Charles repeated. "If that's true, it explains why this story feels so fresh, like it was written today. Please continue, Meriaten."

Oh, how I loved driving my chariot, holding the reins of my beautiful white horse. He could gallop so fast! I felt free, freer than anything, freer than at any time in my entire life.

"Here is an illustration of Nefertiti driving her chariot," Meriaten said. "See these birds flying around her? They signify her feeling of freedom."

My Pharaoh became my friend; we were growing up together. I had my first daughter, Meriaten, a beautiful baby. Pharaoh and I loved this girl-child. We were filled with joy.

"You are a very good interpreter of hieroglyphics, Meriaten," Jacques said. "It almost makes me want to study the subject. Maybe I will when we get back to the Château du Mont."

"I wish I had my Leica with me," Charles said mournfully. "It's impossible to capture this room—all these colors, the stories in hieroglyphics, and all these beautiful illustrations and reliefs—without a camera. All I have available to me is words."

"This might be true, Charles, but you have a gift for painting pictures with words," Jacques said, glancing at the boy's writing.

"Thank you, Jacques," Charles said, still writing furiously. "But it would be a lot easier with a camera."

"Are you ready, Charles?" Meriaten asked.

"One minute. Okay, I'm ready, Meriaten," the boy answered. The girl continued translating the hieroglyphics.

One day, Queen Tiye spoke to me. She said that Pharaoh Amenhotep IV, my husband, would soon declare to his people that there were not many gods and goddesses but only one God, Aten. He would tell his people that Aten created all men, women, animals, fish, birds, insects, trees, plants, water, earth, air, and sky. He would also proclaim that all humankind could pray or speak directly to Aten. Amenhotep IV would tell his people there was no need to pay priests to pray for them or to perform rituals in order for the deceased to have a happy afterlife.

"That sounds dangerous," Farak said. "Those words would have been considered sacrilege, and an attack on the priesthood."

"You're right, Farak," Meriaten agreed. "The hieroglyphics talk about that."

Holding my hands in hers, Queen Tiye told me this would anger the high priests and that many of our people would be reluctant to change their religious beliefs. My husband said he would ask his people to think, to use their hearts, to question what kind of priests would tell them that mummifying a raven, a monkey, an ibis, or a person was a requirement for obtaining a happy afterlife, and charge them for this strange service.

Pharaoh decided to build a new capital city he called Akhenaten, meaning of great use to Aten. However, when the city was nearly complete, Pharaoh took the name Akhenaten himself and named the capital Tel el Armana. Akhenaten and I began to design the new city together. Pharaoh brought builders to make our visions come true. Everyone who came to Tel el Amarna declared it the most beautiful city ever built. The structures were bathed in light, and all the walls and entrances were painted in rainbow colors or decorated with beautiful murals of nature and strange animals.

"I can almost see this city in my mind's eye," Meriaten said, stopping her translation.

Jacques looked at the three youths, Charles on the bench writing and Meriaten and Farak standing together at the west wall reading Nefertiti's story. How had he come to be here with these three young people, each able to interpret ancient hieroglyphics? It seemed like some kind of miracle. He really needed to have a serious talk with Dr. Bernstein about spooky particles at a distance.

Charles finished writing what Meriaten had interpreted, then announced he was ready for the next section.

When we were in our palace in Thebes, Akhenaten rushed into my room and announced that we, Meriaten, Akhenaten and I, must leave immediately. I asked him why. Pharaoh said there were spies in the palace who had told the priests that we rejected the gods and goddess. One of Akhenaten's servants told him they were coming in the morning. We escaped that night, hiding in the back of a donkey cart. We went to the river and boarded a felucca, and finally after traveling for days we boarded our royal barge. Meriaten and I agreed that it was a grand adventure.

Not long after we moved to Tel el Armana, Akhenaten told me I was to be crowned co-Pharaoh. I was to become his twin Pharaoh. I told him no, our people would not accept a woman as Pharaoh, not even our own citizens of Tel el Armana. Akhenaten insisted, saying Aten had given him a message. He was to help free women, declaring them equal in the eyes of Aten, and thus equal in the eyes of all people. I will admit that I was fearful. Akhenaten set the date for a great festival.

No one knew what was to happen. We stood on a balcony together, looking out over thousands and thousands of our people. Akhenaten delivered Aten's message, then placed the crown of Upper and Lower Egypt on my head. Afterwards, we handed out many gifts to our people; there were games, music, and dancing. It was one of the proudest moments of my life. At the end of the festival, I drove my golden chariot down the King's Road, waving at all the people of our beautiful city.

"I wish I could have gone to that festival," Meriaten said wistfully.

Charles looked up from his writing, frowning. "You might think twice if you knew what would happen to this capital city."

"We can learn about that in *The Room of Destruction*," Farak said. "Let us for now enjoy this description of a happy time."

"I agree," Jacques said. "In fact, since we already have a good idea what happened, why not skip the room of sad stories altogether, and be free of this maze a little faster?"

Jacques' suggestion was, of course, ignored.

"Do you want to continue, Meriaten?" Farak asked.

"Yes, I am ready," she said solemnly.

In Tel el Armana, I had five more daughters. Along with Meriaten, this made six girls. After each child's birth, I would lay the baby in a basket at Akhenaten's feet and walk away. I was afraid he'd be angry that I had not given him a son. However, each time, he would call me back to the throne room, saying God does not make mistakes. He loved his daughters. Akhenaten was a caring and joyful father.

As the girls grew older, Pharaoh took them to visit the people in their workplaces. He taught the girls about irrigation, planting, baking, animal-rearing, metallurgy, stone-carving, engineering, carpentry, pottery, glass-making, and all the arts. Akhenaten built schools and invited all who sought education to attend. Some people did not think girls, or the workers' children, should be allowed to go to school. Akhenaten, however, believed that an educated populace makes a great city, a great country.

One day, I told Akhenaten that his daughters were growing up and that rulers were already asking him to send his daughters to marry their sons. His greatest gift to me was a promise. He vowed he would never send our daughters to marry leaders or their sons for political or economic reasons. He said he wanted them to marry only for love. Akhenaten was breaking a tradition, which made some of the rulers of adjacent kingdoms very angry.

"I like Akhenaten. He seems like such a nice father, like my own dad," Meriaten said.

"I like him, too," Farak agreed.

"It's strange," Charles said, "that even today, some so-called Egyptologists call Akhenaten the Nefarious Pharaoh, as if he were evil. These Egyptologists, anthropologists, and historians say he was self-centered and believed that he, Pharaoh, alone, was Aten's son."

"They seem to be ignorant of his great qualities," Charles continued. "Dr. McAllister, who works at the Cairo Museum, says it's because these scholars are too lazy to learn how to read Akhenaten's words directly. If they had, they'd never doubt his goodness. Go on, Meriaten."

"Oh, no! Something terrible happened," the girl said, pointing to an eye with many tears falling from it.

Our daughter, Meketaten, became ill. I could not help her. She died. She was only twelve years old.

"She died at my age," Meriaten said, her face scrunched up, eyes brimming with tears. "Nefertiti says many people expected a long and elaborate funeral for the princess, involving mummification. However, Aten did not believe in such a ritual."

A small royal tomb was built for Meketaten in the hills above the city. We had a simple ceremony. Some people did not like this. In front of Meketaten's tomb, we found carved stone figures of animal-headed gods and goddesses. This reminded us that not all of our citizens accepted Aten as the one God. Meriaten gave me great comfort by continuing to go among our people, describing how Aten loved them.

After Meketaten's death, I was distraught, unable to move or think. Then I remembered Tiye's teaching of sound healing. It was too late to heal Meketaten, but maybe we could save someone else's child, or mother, grandmother, or husband. I asked Akhenaten to build me a healing center, not a hospital but a temple, a place to experiment with various healing techniques.

With Tiye's help, Akhenaten designed the healing temple using the same principles employed in the pyramids and temples noted for healing. We had running water under the rooms. We controlled the direction of its flow by levers. We had rooms of different sizes, lined with different mineral stones, or painted in different colors. We had lyres and sistrums, and we chanted the sacred vowels. We kept records of people who came with various illnesses, making note of their various responses to the different rooms and techniques.

"This illustration shows women holding various staffs with lines coming out of them; I don't know what it means," Meriaten said, pointing to a large relief.

"I believe the lines mean something like electricity, or maybe electromagnetic force, or even gravity," Farak guessed.

"That would be what Dr. Awyan would say," Charles agreed. "When we were in the Great Pyramid with Dr. Awyan, there was a woman who led vowel chants inside the King's Chamber. I was the first to go into what some people call the sarcophagus, which is not really a sarcophagus but a large rectangular box with no lid."

"I could feel these different sounds bouncing off the pink limestone wall and going through my body," Charles continued. "I felt like I was outside of time and space, kind of like in a dream. This woman said that different frequencies have different effects on the body, and that she's experimenting using different frequencies in healing."

Jacques shook his head, remembering. "I do not know why I refused to take a turn climbing into that rectangular box to listen to the different frequencies. I would do it now. Sometimes, I think I am becoming another person."

"I know what you mean, Jacques," Farak said. "That is how I felt when I realized I was becoming accustomed to life in France. What else does it say, Meri?"

"Nefertiti writes that although she still had a broken heart from the loss of her daughter Meketaten, she found happiness in the healing temple, in helping others. See," Meriaten said, pointing. "In this picture, people are lined up, waiting to come into the healing temple. Nefertiti says she believes this healing work to be among the most important legacies of Tel el Armana. Here, she says all the notes from the experiments and their results are in the Palace of Records."

"Where do you think the Palace of Records might be?" Charles asked.

"I don't know. Maybe we'll find it somewhere here in this Tomb of a Thousand Names," Meriaten said, then continued her interpreting.

Whenever I have a few hours, I go over these notes. I dream that I could have saved my beautiful daughter, as we seemed to save others. Then, I remember Aten declared that there is no death, and that life and death are part of a cycle.

I don't quite understand this, but last night I dreamed I held my daughter in my arms again.

Meriaten was crying.

"I believe that is enough," Jacques said. "It is very tragic, perhaps too tragic for a child to think about. And, if we hope to ever get out of this tomb, which seems to be as much a book as a place, we had better move on."

Jacques handed Meriaten the flashlight. Farak carried her lantern, and Jacques placed the candles back where they'd found them. He blew them out, one by one.

"It almost feels like we are closing up Nefertiti's tomb," Charles said somberly as he slid the stone door shut.

Jacques patted Meriaten on the back. She was still weeping.

CHAPTER 68

THE SECRET OF TUTANKHAMUN

The four travelers were energized by water and the cookies baked by Meriaten's mother. Using the map, they found themselves back on the left-hand path on their way to the *Chamber of Secrets*.

"I usually love secrets, but I'm feeling a little unsure as to where these secrets might lead," Charles said, walking a little slower than the rest of his party.

"I don't think you should worry about the *Room of Secrets*," Meriaten said. "The place you should worry about is our next stop, the *Room of Destruction*."

"Thanks for reminding us, Meriaten," Jacques said with a ring of sarcasm.

Meriaten pointed. "Here it is. It's probably a secret entrance. I believe we should look for a symbol meaning secret. Of course, there are several ways of expressing the concept of secret in hieroglyphics."

"I found it," Jacques said. "Here is a figure with a finger across his mouth. I will just push it." A small crack appeared in the wall about five feet away.

"I guess we are all becoming experts at opening secret passageways. I wonder what we will do with this knowledge when we return to the Château du Mont," Jacques said, leading his group into the next room.

"Here is where we start," the Egyptian teen said, gesturing at the western wall. "The hieroglyphics begin with the same explanation that preceded the other stories: the writing was translated from Cuneiform by Seshat. This one ends in this small cartouche of Nefertiti, meaning the story is probably told in her voice."

"Turn around and look behind you, Farak!" Charles exclaimed. "It's a life-sized replica of Tutankhamun's throne. Jacques and I saw the real throne in King Tut's Room in the Cairo Museum. Remember, Jacques?"

"I am not sure anyone could forget seeing such a wonderful room full of treasure," his chaperone said.

"Jacques became hypnotized, staring at all that gold," Charles related. "Meanwhile, I was hypnotized by the photography documenting the excavation of King Tut's tomb. Staring at the black-and-white images, I missed an important piece of information."

"What did you miss, Charles?" Meriaten asked.

"It's this," Charles explained, motioning to the backrest of the golden throne. "Everything I've read about the young pharaoh, Tutankhamun, declares that the boy-king reinstated the religion of multiple gods and goddesses. He denounced the views of his predecessor Pharaoh Akhenaten who, as we know, believed there was only one god."

Charles continued his line of inquiry. "So why would Tutankhamun rule from a throne with an image of Aten on its backrest, not to mention pictures of two people who just happen to be Akhenaten and Nefertiti? You can tell it's them because the symbol for Aten, the rays ending with little hands, is reaching towards the pharaoh and his queen."

"You are right, Charles. I never heard about this before. Why didn't the historians and Egyptologists mention this?" asked Farak.

"That is an excellent question," Jacques mused, examining the throne carved in the wall. "Another question is, why are the chairs in my tower room so plain? Do you think I should paint them gold, Charles?"

"Jacques, what's happened to you?" Charles asked. "You're not acting normal."

"Another excellent question," his chaperone answered. "As we edge towards the *Room of Destruction*, it has dawned on me that someone has to bring a little levity into our group."

"As far as your chairs go, this is not a chair," Charles retorted. "It's a throne. And Tutankhamun was Pharaoh while you, my honored chaperone, are not."

"The lion sitting at the foot of King Tut's throne looks so real," Meriaten said. "I feel like it could jump off the wall and into my arms. And, I still can't get over the fact that not one of my books on the discovery of Tutankhamun's tomb mentioned that his throne had this beautiful image of Akhenaten and Nefertiti carved into the backrest."

"That is what I have been trying to telling you. Nothing seems to make sense," Jacques said. "It is like that quote from Alice in Wonderland: *I know who I was when I got up this morning, but I've changed several times since then.* Given our circumstances, the words of Lewis Carroll resonate with me. Spending all this time underground is as disorienting as going down a rabbit hole."

"It's time we find what is at the bottom of this particular rabbit hole," Farak said, then began interpreting.

Akhenaten and I had a seventh child, a boy-child. As with our other infants, I placed the baby in a basket and set it at the foot of Pharaoh Akhenaten's throne. I quietly left the room. A few moments later, Akhenaten called me back into his throne room. He had picked up the baby and unwrapped his blanket. He was holding our son on his lap. The baby was beautiful, except one of his legs did not look as strong as the other, and there was a slight imperfection on his upper lip. Akhenaten looked very serious, except when he looked at our baby. Gazing down at the boy-child, Pharaoh gave him the sweetest smile and bounced him up and down on his lap. The baby stared back at Pharaoh, smiling a toothless smile.

Akhenaten asked me to bring our daughters and trusted personal servants into the throne room. Re-entering the throne room, the first thing I saw was Akhenaten holding the sleeping baby in his arms. Akhenaten said, 'See this boy? One of his legs is not like the other. We may not understand the reason for this. However, we know Aten does not make mistakes. This boy, who I call Tutankhaten, meaning the living image of Aten, is perfect in Aten's eyes, and in Nefertiti's and my eyes.'

"Akhenaten and Nefertiti were Tutankhamun's parents? How then, can it be true that King Tut rejected the God his parents so loved? This is definitely a mystery," Charles said.

"I never heard about the parentage of Tutankhamun either," Farak concurred.

"How could they not know who King Tut's parents were?" Meriaten asked.

"Because the priests didn't want anyone to know. That's why they destroyed Tel el Armana," Charles answered.

"But why did Tutankhamun allow them to change his name?" Meriaten asked.

"May I kindly ask that Farak continue reading? Then, perhaps we will discover the answer," Jacques suggested.

Akhenaten said, 'I proclaim this boy heir to the throne. We vow to love him and to see him as perfect. However, I fear people will question a god that would give Pharaoh a son with an imperfect leg. This thought may cause some of our people to turn back to their old beliefs, bringing power to the high priests. For now, we must keep the birth of our son, Tutankhaten, a secret.'

"It makes me mad when I hear so many people calling Akhenaten nefarious, when he was such a nice man," Meriaten said, her lips in a tight line.

"Meriaten, Akhenaten was not just a nice man. He was a brave man, a courageous man, a man willing to stand up for his beliefs. Few people do this," Jacques said fervently.

Charles looked at Jacques. Ever since his guardian had arrived at the Temple of Sobek, you could never tell what would come out of his mouth. "Let's keep going," Charles said to Farak, who returned to his translation.

When Tutankhaten was three years old, Akhenaten brought him a present. It was a lion cub. This fuzzy lion was so tiny, I could hold him in the palms of my hands. Akhenaten told us the cub's mother had been killed, and he would need a great deal of attention to survive. My daughters and I fed the baby lion cow's milk from a jar. We called the baby lion Asoon.

"I would love to have a lion," Charles said with great feeling. "I have never even had a dog."

"As you can see," Meriaten said, "here is an illustration of the prince as a toddler. He is holding onto the lion's mane. Asoon is helping Tutankhaten learn to walk. Later, down here, Tutankhaten begins using a stick to help him walk. It is a beautifully-carved stick with some kind of crystal on top."

"Carry on, Farak. What does Nefertiti say?" Charles asked, pen in hand.

I used to love looking out of my sleeping room window early in the morning and watching Tutankhaten and Asoon walking together, the best of friends. I felt sad in my heart that Tutankhaten could not go to festivals or ceremonies or visit the worksites as his sisters did. However, at this time, we all felt this secrecy was necessary.

When Tutankhaten turned four, Akhenaten and I began taking our son on river trips aboard our royal barge. Tutankhaten and I traveled from our palace to the Nile in a covered litter carried by four trusted servants. The litter had several layers of curtains. We could see out, but no one could see in. The litter carriers would walk us aboard the royal barge and then lay the litter down on the beautiful wooden floor. Tutankhaten would jump out of the curtains with a great whoop. No one noticed the boy in the plain, beige robe running around the deck of our barge, laughing, singing, dancing—free.

When Tutankhaten turned five, Akhenaten asked a craftsman to design a throne for our son, an adult-sized throne he could use even when he was a grown man. There were two lion's heads on the front of the throne's arms, and four lion's feet on the throne's legs. The lion theme on his throne was a tribute to Tutankhaten's friend Asoon.

On the front of the backrest was a relief. Even I was surprised at how much the carving looked like Akhenaten and me. We told Tutankhaten that we called his royal seat the Throne of Remembrance. It was to remind him of how much his parents cared for him. Tutankhaten loved his throne. He would climb upon it and order his sisters, servants, and even Asoon to bring him food or toys. We began calling Tutankhaten 'King Tut.'

For King Tut's sixth birthday, he begged me to allow Asoon to come on the barge with him. I told my son, 'I can hide you beside me in the litter, but I could not hide a nearly-grown lion.' He asked me, 'Why must I hide, Mother?' I did not know what to tell my son. I was fortunate for, on this day, his sixteen-year-old sister Meriaten was sitting beside Tutankhaten. She told him he was born to be Pharaoh, the ruler of all Egypt, a very large country.

She put her arms around Tutankhaten's thin shoulders and said that, in some ways, being Pharaoh is a great privilege, and in others, a terrible burden. No child born to the pharaohs is allowed to be free, unlike the workers' children whose only concern is for their own family. Everything we do is observed and often judged by our people. While the workers' children only have to think about their families, we must always think about every person from Aswan to the Mediterranean Sea. She reminded her brother how fortunate he was to travel up and down the Nile with his parents to see all the beauty of nature: the birds, the fish, the animals. She reminded him that Aten was smiling down upon us for all the sacrifices we made. I love my beautiful and wise Meriaten. Strangely, Tutankhaten did not ask this question again.

Everyone who knew Tutankhaten loved him. He was a good student, made everyone laugh, and had the most wonderful singing voice. As he grew older, women from the healing temple came to the children's room to instruct our King Tut in chanting and singing the vowels. I often thought he would make a powerful healer, if he were not destined to be Pharaoh. When he was seven, Tutankhaten and I would go out on the barge at night, and he would sing to the stars as we floated over the dark waters. This is something a mother could never forget.

I needed joyful memories, because Akhenaten and I were aware of the danger that lurked around the throne of Pharaoh. Rumors reached our ears that more and more traitors were infiltrating our city. The priests' men told our people they would be punished for forgetting the old gods and goddesses. Many believed them. I worried about what would happen to my son and his sisters. Akhenaten told me that Aten believes we must find joy in our lives, celebrating all that is good. He said it is important to be aware of the future, to prepare for what might come, but that worrying about the future will not change it.

One night, after one of these talks, Akhenaten took me out on the barge at night, just the two of us. It was a new moon; the stars sparkled in an ebony sky. Pharaoh held me in his arms. I told him I was very fortunate to have so much love around me and would not change my life for anything.

"I wish I didn't know what happened to this family," Meriaten said solemnly. "I feel like I know these people, and Meriaten is so wise and kind. I hope I will grow to be like her."

"My opinion, should anyone want to hear it, is that you are already very much like your namesake," Jacques said. "If we've reached the end, Farak, I suggest we move on. For some reason, this room feels even smaller than it did when we first entered. I guess it is filled with too many memories."

Farak looked at his map. "It says we should go to the next room to the right."

"I could eat another of your mother's peanut butter cookies, Meriaten," Jacques said. "Traveling back in time makes me hungry and tired." He looked into his shoulder bag again. "No cookies. *Quel dommage!* Let's go."

CHAPTER 69

GODS AND GODDESSES

The four travelers left *Tutankhaten's Room* behind. They followed the
map and turned right into a short passageway that led to the next
room. Meriaten lit the candles, revealing a long, narrow room, six feet wide
and ten feet long. On one wall were hieroglyphics. On the other three were
large, colorful paintings of the many Egyptian gods and goddesses.

"This room doesn't make sense!" Farak exclaimed. "As you can see, the
story is written by Nefertiti, who didn't believe in multiple gods."

Charles was facing the rear wall, writing down the names of the deities in
front of him and mumbling again about leaving his camera behind.

"I agree with you, Farak. It's confusing to see all these gods on the Path of
Knowledge," Charles said. "I must admit, I've loved studying the stories of
the old Egyptian gods and goddesses. But traveling the Tomb of a Thousand
Names makes me wonder if I'll have to give up the gods and goddesses and
their stories, trading them for the one God, Aten. I can understand how

Egyptologists might not like Akhenaten, how they might call him nefarious for removing references of the old gods and goddesses from his temple."

"Can't we believe in both?" Meriaten asked, twirling slowly around the room, admiring scenes of gods and goddesses.

"I'm not sure, Meriaten," Charles answered. "Akhenaten didn't think so. Okay, Farak, I'm ready for you to translate."

"This is Nefertiti writing," Farak reminded everyone.

Akhenaten entered my coral-and-turquoise hall wearing a white robe that fell just above his knees. On his chest was fastened a gold breastplate decorated with jewels that sparkled in the rays of the morning sun, which danced in from my open balcony.

Pharaoh only wore this breastplate on special occasions. He was not wearing his headdress, either. He walked swiftly to stand before me. He bowed deeply. I have told Akhenaten many times that he should not bow to me, as I am his wife. However, Akhenaten said he will always bow before Pharaoh and, since I am Pharaoh, his co-ruler, he will always bow to me. I stood up, smiled, and bowed to him.

'You look serious, my Lord. What has happened?'

Akhenaten asked me to walk with him to my balcony. We looked down on our orchard. All the fruit trees were covered with riotous pink-and-white blossoms. Beyond the orchard, I could see the healing temple Akhenaten built for me after the death of our daughter. My husband placed his arm around my shoulder and spoke to me gently.

'Together we have created this beautiful city dedicated to Aten. We have been happy here.'

I agreed that, for the most part, we had been happy. Then Akhenaten told me the priests in Thebes were forming a large army, and intended to invade Tel el Armana.

'What should we do? What can we do?' I asked Pharaoh.

'We cannot stop them,' he answered. 'Tel el Amarna is a city of peace. We do not have the weapons or the soldiers to defeat even a small army, certainly not the large army the priests are forming. It has been reported that the priests in

Thebes have ordered our names and images to be erased from every temple and government building. Some of the priests' men have infiltrated our city. They are telling our citizens that they will be punished for having forgotten the old gods and goddesses.'

'What can we do?' I repeated.

'When this invasion occurs, and it will occur within two years, you must convince the invaders that I alone forced you and the children and all the people of Tel El Amarna to denounce the old gods and goddesses.'

'That would be a lie! I will not do this, Akenaten,' I said, tears welling in my eyes and pain piercing my heart.

My husband looked over the railing of my balcony. He smiled at all he saw before him.

Then Akhenaten said, 'Nefertiti, you must tell the priests that even though I ordered my family to worship the one God, Aten, you secretly helped our children remember the old gods and goddesses, the true gods and goddesses. And with the help of my mother, Tiye, you taught the children all the rituals necessary to practice their true religion.'

I told Akhenaten that I could not do this. He asked what I would do to save the lives of our children. I thought of our daughters and Tutankhaten. I saw their beautiful, trusting faces. Answering his question, I said that I would give my life for my children.

Pharaoh kissed my forehead and said, 'I knew you would say this, for you are not only beautiful but a courageous, fearless, and loving mother.'

He said he believed these evil priests would need to erase his name and all that it stands for. He said he was not afraid of death, because Aten says there is no death. However, Akhenaten said that I must protect myself and our children. Pharaoh said I needed to do this, not only because of my great love of family but because our children are the Holders of the Future, the Keepers of the Name of Aten.

What could I say or do? My heart was broken into many pieces.

Pharaoh told me he was going to send a teacher tomorrow.

'So soon?' I asked.

He said the teacher would instruct our children and me about the various gods and goddesses. Without this knowledge, the story about following the religion of the priests would not be believed.

I asked Akhenaten how we could accept this teaching when we love and believe only in Aten. He told me that the gods and goddesses have always been part of the sacred teachings and spiritual initiation. Pharaoh said that while the old gods and goddesses are not creator gods, their attributes and skills, expressed through their interwoven stories, stand as symbols of the qualities we need to live successfully in communities—in families, towns, cities, kingdoms, and countries.

He said knowledge of these gods and their stories can assist spiritual and political leaders in assessing their communities. These gods or goddesses or neters can help leaders determine whether things are in balance, and what needs to be strengthened, controlled, or eliminated. He said that these gods, these neters, are neither good nor bad. They are just knowledge, but the priests took ownership of these symbolic beings. They began charging even the poorest of the poor for religious services. For hundreds of years, even the kings and pharaohs fell under the sway of these high priests.

As Akhenaten explained, even he accepted the need for the priests to pray to the gods for his success, and that he must prepare for his death by building a tomb, paying in advance for the mummification process.

"I hate mummification," Meriaten said. "It's stupid to think that mummifying an animal or a human would ensure you a good afterlife."

"I agree wholeheartedly, Meriaten," Jacques said. "I remember feeling almost ill the day Samy, our taxi driver, took us to the Step Pyramid at Saqqara. He told us we were walking over millions of mummified ravens, ibises, monkeys, cats, and human beings. I found it gruesome."

"Shall I continue? Farak said. "Where was I?"

"The gods and goddess are not true gods, but their stories have the power to teach humans how they can better live together in community," Charles repeated.

"Before you go on, Farak, I have a confession," Charles added. "I loved learning about all the gods and goddesses and their characteristics. I loved studying all their stories, ceremonies, and every detail of the mummification process. It wasn't until I met Dr. Awyan and real Egyptian people that I understood how the process was abused. Still, I understand how many Egyptologists do not want to give up on all the complexities of the ancient gods, all their stories, their interesting forms, and their characteristics."

"I guess my parents, who are Egyptologists, must have been attracted by the stories and tombs and all the art that goes with these gods and goddesses," Meriaten said. "I had never thought about this before. I think Akhenaten must have understood this too. He seems like such a wise and caring person. Will you continue, Farak?"

Akhenaten told me, 'The priests are not out to destroy us. Their aim is to destroy Aten, whom they consider a threat to their wealth and power. I believed building a new capital city, far away from Thebes and Memphis, would stop them. But it has not.'

'Now you must teach our children about the Egyptian gods and goddesses, not only to save their lives but to preserve the memory of Aten until such a time as the world is ready to embrace the one true and loving God.'

I asked Akhenaten why Aten would allow terrible things to happen, like the impending invasion of his capital city. Pharaoh told me that through meditation he began to understand that Aten lives out of space, matter, and time; thus, humans cannot know what Aten knows. Akhenaten admitted that he, too, had questioned Aten. Why had he allowed our daughter, Meketaten, to die so young? Akhenaten told me he though Aten had forsaken him.

However, he said, 'Through my work in the healing temple, Pharaoh was reminded that although we may not always understand Aten, we must never forget that Aten is all good and all love.

***

The teacher arrived at the family palace the next day. She turned out to be Queen Tiye, Akhenaten's mother, my greatest teacher and the children's grandmother. As I predicted, when I told my daughters they were to study the ancient religion of Egyptian gods and goddesses, they rebelled, especially Meriaten, now a young woman of seventeen. I told them we should at least listen to what their grandmother, Queen Tiye, had to teach us.

Tiye brought with her a container of tiny copper figures. They were miniature replicas of Egyptian gods and goddesses; many had animal heads and human bodies. My daughters did not like them, saying they were ugly and fearsome. However six-year-old Tutankhaten began playing with the little copper figures, asking each of them their names and making them move around the floor in front of his throne.

'Hello, what is your name?' our King Tut would ask.

Queen Tiye replied in a sweet, soft voice, 'My name is Hathor. I create and maintain all life on earth. I am the cow goddess representing the mother, the caretaker. I also represent humanity's ability to create and share that which is joyful: love, poetry, singing, dance, and the appreciation of beauty.'

'What is your name?' Tutankhaten asked, holding up a figure of a jackal.

In a low voice, Queen Tiye said, 'I am Anubis. I help judge souls after their death. I weigh the heart of the deceased against Ma'at or truth, represented by a feather. If the person's heart is lighter than the feather, I allow them to ascend to a heavenly existence. If not, well, I shall not tell you of his or her terrible fate.'

Tutankhaten laughed at this and wanted to continue his game. Queen Tiye came out of her character as the jackal to say that Anubis was not evil, that by requiring a standard of truth and ethical behavior, he kept evil out of Egypt. Having a conscience, and the ability to determine good from bad is necessary for people living in a community. If there is corruption among the people, civilization will eventually fall.

Tiye identified the gods and goddesses, and explained that most Egyptian deities are related. Some are related directly as husbands, wives, sons, or daughters. However, no matter who they are, almost all are related by one continuous story: the death and resurrection of Osiris.

"When I was a child," Charles said, "I memorized all the major gods and goddesses, their qualities, and their role in the Osiris tale."

"Exactly how old were you when you were a child, Charles?" Jacques asked with a smile.

"I was seven or eight," he replied. "My mother bought me every book on ancient Egypt she could find. I read them all. Of course, this was before she and my father sent me away to the Château du Mont."

"How old were you when you got sent away to school, Charles?" Meriaten asked.

"I was ten years old. I guess I was luckier than Farak; he was only seven," Charles added, looking at the young man studying the wall of hieroglyphics before him.

"I'm the one who is lucky," Meriaten said. "My parents mostly take me with them where they travel. I didn't realize how fortunate I was until I met you, Charles, and you, Farak."

Jacques didn't say anything about his childhood, about the death of his mother, father, and grandmother when he was a toddler. He didn't mention that when he was four years old, his grandfather became too sick to care for him and sent young Jacques to the Château du Mont. At the time, the headmaster of the Château du Mont was Monsieur Boucher. The headmaster's intimidating last name—Boucher was the French word for "butcher"—suited him perfectly.

As a child, Jacques was terrified of this overly-strict headmaster, the rule-keeper. Monsieur Boucher took no notice of the sad little boy facing the world alone in his third-floor room, the same room David and Charles now shared. Jacques hid his loneliness and fear from everyone, especially from himself. Because of this, a part of this sad little boy stayed with him, even as he grew older.

However, deep in the Tomb of a Thousand Names, in the *Chamber of Secrets,* in the room of the gods and goddesses, he was no longer that abandoned child. He was the adult, the chaperone of three brave and intelligent young people.

On the one hand, this knowledge made Jacques think he should find the fastest way to the right-hand path and drag these young people straight out of the tomb of sad stories and into the sunlight. On the other hand, he felt he had a purpose here, a role yet unfolding. Exactly what this purpose was he didn't know, but he felt it strongly. At this moment, he realized he was not just an observer. He was not a reluctant traveler, a bystander, a spectator, or even just a chaperone. He was supposed to be here. Even though he couldn't read hieroglyphics, he had a part to play in all this. Jacques felt this strongly.

Waking from his deep thought, Jacques asked Farak to continue.

Queen Tiye told the children, 'Going back to Hathor, the goddess with bovine features, you can see that her cow form makes sense, for the cow helps people survive, especially children. Her center of worship is the temple at Dendera. Her male equivalent is Bes. Bes is widely worshiped as a deity of music, merriment, and childbirth. He is a protector of children and is associated with medical practices. Can you see how these deities are connected with qualities or powers people need for a society to thrive?'

Tutankhaten picked up another figure, a strange-looking combination of animals, with giraffe horns and a horse-like face.

Tutankhaten asked gruffly, 'What is your name?'

Queen Tiye answered in a slow, gravelly voice. 'My name is Set. I am the god of the desert, storms, disorder, and violence.'

King Tut picked up this figure and chased the other gods and goddesses around the floor, making them scream in terror. Queen Tiye again came out of character to say Set is believed to be evil by many; his necessary element is as a destroyer. His ultimate role is to destroy the old so something new can take its place.

Tutankhaten picked up a goddess with wings. He brought Set face-to-face with this winged goddess, saying, 'I am Set, and I will destroy you.'

His grandmother said, 'Tutankhaten, you have picked up Isis, the most powerful of the goddesses and the greatest healer. Isis is the wife of Osiris, whom Set killed. Isis brought Osiris back to life.'

'That is all for now.' she concluded. 'I will be back tomorrow and we will continue our lessons.'

Nefertiti says that through Tiye, she learned that many gods and goddesses have something to do with healing and health. Looking at these gods as characteristics or powers people need to live successfully in communities made sense to her.

The next day, they learned about Thoth, master of knowledge and teacher of all languages, mathematics, science, and sacred texts—patron of scribes. He is depicted as an ibis bird or a baboon. Ma'at has wings, like Isis. They learned Ma'at is the goddess of truth, justice, balance, and order. I had to agree that one would not want a city without the force of Ma'at. Ptah, depicted as a blue or green man, is the patron of craftspeople and architects and is credited with inventing masonry. Without him, there would be no pyramids or temples. Sekhmet is depicted with the body of a woman and the head of a lion. She is the protector of Pharaoh and, when necessary, leads his people in warfare.

Tutankhaten asked his grandmother to give him the tiny figure of Sekhmet, because he loved his lion so much. I told my children I had no idea there were that many gods and goddesses in the Egyptian pantheon, but I was stunned by how many of these gods were directly related to the health and happiness of Aten's children.

In the end, my daughters could not help but be captivated by Tiye's teachings. I am not saying that they abandoned their beloved Aten, but their grandmother's lessons helped them understand why people might call on a specific god or goddess to help them in times of trouble. To tell the truth, after learning about the powers of the goddess Sekhmet, I felt like calling on the lion goddess to help protect our city from invasion by the priests and their army.

"That is the end of Nefertiti's message regarding gods and goddesses," Charles said.

"What happened to Nefertiti?" Jacques asked.

"I only know that Tutankhaten and his sisters survived. Tutankhaten's name was changed to Tutankhamun. He was crowned Pharaoh at eight or nine years old," Charles related. "He died at eighteen or nineteen.

"That is quite young," Jacques said.

"Maybe that's why he's such a mystery," Charles speculated.

"According to Egyptologists, the boy-king Tutankhamun rejected the idea of the one god, and everything fell back to the old ways. But I don't believe it, not for a moment," Charles said. "That's why he kept the throne his father crafted for him when he was just five years old."

Jacques helped Charles gather up his papers, and the four travelers went to the next room.

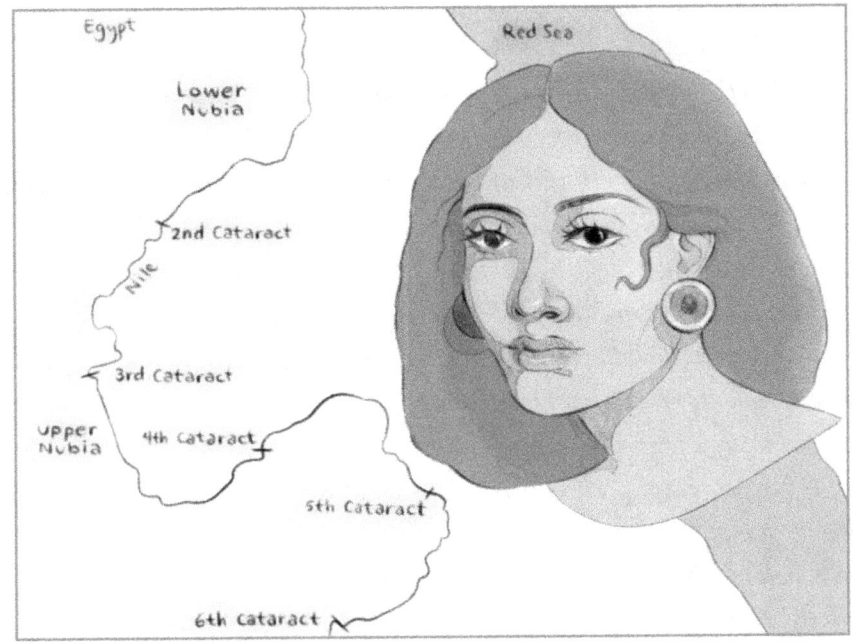

CHAPTER 70

QUEEN TIYE'S CHALLENGE

Holding the red flashlight, Farak led the explorers into the next room. Meriaten lit the the candles. Looking around the room, they could see its simplicity: no gold, no elaborate illustrations, just a beautiful carving of a young girl.

"It's a girl, but it's not Meriaten or Nefertiti. It says Tiye. That is, of course, Akhenaten's mother. Shall I translate, Charles?" Meriaten asked.

"Yes, especially since this wall has a relief of a girl about your age," Charles replied from his spot on the stone floor.

"At the beginning of the writing, like in the other rooms, there is a reference to the translator, Seshat. I think most of these stories in the Tomb of a Thousand names were written after the destruction of Tel el Armana," Charles said, pen in hand. "Go, Meriaten."

I am Queen Tiye, wife of Amenhotep III and mother of Akhenaten.

Charles said, "I know a little about Queen Tiye. She was one of the most powerful queens in ancient Egypt."

Here is the story of my early days with Amenhotep III, and my greatest challenge. Six years ago, the city of Tel el Amarna was a dream or a commandment by Aten. Now, with its multicolored buildings completed, it looked like a colossal flowerbed surrounded by a deep blue sky.

One spring morning, Akhenaten asked me to walk with him in his beautiful orchard. The fruit trees were in bloom and we were surrounded by thousands of pink-and-white blossoms and their sweet fragrance. A yellowish-orange sun peeked out from its bed in the rocky cliffs, east of the city. Akhenaten and I stopped to say a prayer of gratefulness to Aten.

After our prayer, Akhenaten said, 'Mother, could you tell me again about your first meeting with my father?'

I had told him the story many times, but I said nothing about it. In truth, I loved telling this story, so full of romance and the beginning of a great, if tumultuous, life with Amenhotep III.

'As you know, I was born during the reign of Amenhotep III, but I was not Egyptian. I was born in Nubia, in the kingdom called Kush. Like Egypt, Nubia runs along the Nile River which, as in Egypt, provides a fertile strip of land that makes life possible in the desert. However, nature played a great trick on the people of Egypt. It placed six cataracts along the river, making travel by water from Upper Egypt to Nubia and onto Central Africa impossible.

Explorers, traders, and invaders face great challenges. They must travel around the six cataracts, then cross the rocky and waterless Nubian desert. Or, they can travel east, sailing the Red Sea south, and still face crossing our desert lands.

The difficulty of travel would not have been an issue for the Egyptians if they did not desire what Nubia had: gold, minerals, gemstones and, just as importantly, access to the goods of Southeast Africa. These include dates, incense, crafts and ebony, a hard and sleek dark wood much coveted by rulers and wealthy citizens of Egypt.

Sometimes, the Egyptians bartered grains, vegetables, oils, wine, beer, linen, and other goods with Nubia. Other times, the Egyptians just took what they wanted, relocating to Nubia to become its rulers. Eventually, however, they would miss Egypt, with its kinder waters and deserts. They would leave Nubia, preferring to trade with our country rather than live in our challenging land.

I was born during a time of peace. My mother Tjuyu was a High Priestess and primary adviser to the Queen of Upper and Lower Nubia. My father, Yuya, was the Master of the Horses of the Royal Court. His main responsibility was to keep the trade routes open to Africa.

Due to my parents' high positions, I was raised in the palace. The palace was the tallest building in all of Nubia. From its tower, I could see the ribbon of blue, the Nile River, rushing towards Egypt. Looking down from the tower, I could watch the working people rushing here and there.

Few people wanted to climb the 253 steep steps to the top of the tower. The tower seemed like my own private hiding place. There, I dreamed of traveling far away from this palace, which often felt to me like a prison. I wanted to be free, free to go anywhere I wanted.

"I have those kinds of dreams, too," Meriaten said. "How are you doing, Charles?"

"I'm almost caught up, Meriaten. I know very little about Nubia, so this is interesting to me. You can continue now," Charles said, pen poised over his paper.

From the earliest age, I was recognized as having the gift of languages. I was just born that way. When I heard a new word, I remembered it, no matter what dialect or language. When I was twelve, a great Sumerian teacher, Urhammu— meaning rays of light—was brought to the palace to teach me to speak the language of Mesopotamia, and to write Cuneiform and Egyptian hieroglyphics. Whenever foreigners came to the palace, the queen asked me to join her. I would have preferred to go to my rooftop hide-out or visit the horses in the stable. Still, I admit these visitors from faraway places helped extend my vocabulary and improve my pronunciation.

One day, when I was fourteen, the queen received a message that Amenhotep III and his soldiers were coming to the palace. In the past, Nubia had been invaded by other Egyptian pharaohs, but at this time we were living in peace, trading our goods for the goods of Egypt. Everyone knew that Amenhotep III had a reputation for invading cities, stealing treasure, and even kidnapping men, women, and children to become Egyptian slaves.

I was frightened by this pharaoh and his soldiers. I wanted to hide in my room but when he arrived, the queen called me into her Great Hall. She said, 'I want you and your mother to be with me when Pharaoh Amenhotep comes before me.'

'Why me?' I asked.

She reminded me that she did not speak Egyptian and needed me to translate for her. I said I did not deserve such an honor. I did not mention that I was terrified of this man. Queen Abu smiled and said I was ready for the commission. Further, she insisted I was the only person who could secure peace between Egypt and Nubia. I wanted to ask what she meant, but one of her guards came to speak to Her Majesty.

I was sitting in my chamber when a woman brought me a red dress with golden thread running through it. She said it was a gift from the queen. I had never owned such a grown-up dress before. My mother entered wearing a gown the lavender color of the flower called Lily of the Nile. I wondered why we should all dress up for this man with a bad reputation.

My mother was carrying an elaborately-carved wooden box. She opened it slowly. Inside the box was a necklace and matching bracelet. They were made of gold and sprinkled with colorful gemstones that sparkled in the sunlight that came through my chamber's windows. My mother told me the jewelry was a gift to the queen from Amenhotep II, Amenhotep III's father. She said the queen wanted me to wear the necklace and bracelet when Pharaoh came to meet her in the Great Hall.

Mother told me it was to honor Pharaoh. I told her I did not want to honor Pharaoh. Mother told me that as you grow up, you must do many things you don't want to do. That made me frown. I could see the downward pull of my mouth in the mirror as the necklace was fastened around my neck. Mother told me it was a great honor for someone so young to be Queen Abu's translator, and then she gave me some instructions.

Mother and I walked together to the Great Hall. Queen Abu sat on her throne, which was raised up on a dais with five golden steps. She was wearing a gown of gold and a headpiece with many strands of beads made of carnelian and lapis lazuli. I had not seen her dress this way before. I wondered who this Amenhotep III was, and why he had come?

One of the Queen's guards entered the Great Hall, proclaiming, 'Amenhotep III, Pharaoh of Upper and Lower Egypt, requests to enter the hall.' The Queen nodded her permission. The Pharaoh of Egypt entered. He wore a short white tunic with sporrans hanging around his waist. Around his neck, he wore a wide wesekh made of beads of lapis lazuli, carnelian, and gold. In the center of the wesekh was a falcon, signifying the god Horus, representing superhuman strength.

I thought he looked very strong, probably because he was in so many battles. On his head, he wore a tall red-and-white crown. My mother told me the crown had two sides, signifying that Amenhotep III was Pharaoh of Upper and Lower Egypt.

Pharaoh bowed to the queen, then smiled at my mother, but I could see that he could not keep his eyes off the girl in the red dress, me. Pharaoh asked to speak to the king and his vizier. Through my translation from Nubian into Egyptian, the queen informed Pharaoh that the king was in Upper Nubia. Translating from Nubian to Egyptian, I told Amenhotep that when the king was away, the queen was head of state for both Upper and Lower Nubia.

At a sign from the queen, I brought a chair for Amenhotep III and placed it between my mother and me. The three of us looked up at our beautiful queen. Queen Abu asked me to tell Pharaoh his reputation had preceded him, and that there was a fear among the Nubians that he had come to steal our treasure. His face showed surprise at such bluntness. I could tell he did not know whether to look at the queen, look at me since I was the interpreter, or leave the room *altogether. I smiled at Amenhotep and he smiled back. It was at this time I realized how clever the queen was.*

Queen Abu had me tell Pharaoh that she would give him all the gold in Kush's treasury. However, if he wished for Aten to smile down upon him as he took our treasure, Amenhotep should exchange this gold for grains and vegetables. Amenhotep asked how many grains and vegetables he would need to exchange for such blessings. Translating for Queen Abu, I told him that it should be equal in weight to the gold he planned to take.

Amenhotep laughed and laughed, then asked, 'Am I to be out-negotiated by this young girl?' I insisted that I was just translating for my queen, and that my words had nothing to do with me or what I thought. He just laughed. The queen invited Pharaoh and his men to a great feast to be held the next evening. She said she was sure he would enjoy the cuisine and the eminent Nubian musicians, singers, and dancers. Amenhotep accepted.

I was sitting in my room when a woman brought me a new dress. This one was white, embroidered with gold thread. Sitting on top of the dress was a small gold crown. I read a note from the queen. She asked that my mother and I enter the feasting hall with her.

When I entered the dining hall, I saw Amenhotep III sitting in an elaborately-carved ebony chair in back of a long table. He was surrounded by thirty of his men. Behind Pharaoh and his delegation were many servants holding large wooden trays filled with meats, vegetables, fruit, and sweets. The servers stood motionless, waiting for directions from the queen.

My mother and I walked behind Queen Abu as she moved to a small table off to the right side of the room. Once we were seated, the queen gave me a nod. I was frightened, but I walked right in front of Amenhotep III. There was only a table between us. Everyone stopped talking. All eyes were upon me. I took a deep breath, then raised my voice and spoke in Egyptian.

'We welcome you as family, Pharaoh from Egypt. We have learned from our god, Aten, that all men and women are created by him; that all men and women are his children. Aten taught us that he loves all his human creations, no matter where they live, no matter what language they speak, and no matter

what gods they worship, for he knows he is the one god, the creator of all. Amenhotep, we welcome you and send blessings to you from Aten in the form of this great feast we are about to enjoy.'

Amenhotep and his men were silent after I spoke. Then, Amenhotep stood up and thanked the queen for her gracious invitation. I returned to the small table where Queen Abu and my mother sat. The Queen smiled at me and said I had done well. The servers placed the food on the tables, and wine and beer were poured.

"I cannot tell you how much I wish I could be at that banquet at this very moment," Jacques said. "I am famished."

"You're interrupting the story," Meriaten said accusingly before returning to her translation.

After dinner, our most talented singers, musicians, and dancers entertained the guests. Pharaoh's men laughed, clapped, and toasted each performance, enjoying the wine and beer, but Amenhotep sat quietly. I felt his eyes fall upon me, then shift to the dancers, then back to me.

At a signal from Queen Abu, I walked up to Pharaoh; the table was still between us. I asked if he would like to see the city from the tower. He nodded and followed me without speaking. We wound our way up the steep stairs to the rooftop. We looked up at a dark sky glittering with stars and planets. Then, we stared down at the lanterns and cooking fires below us. The many flames looked like a reflection of the night sky. It was beautiful.

Amenhotep asked me, 'Do you believe in this one god you speak of?' When I said yes, Pharaoh asked if I would teach him about Aten. I said, 'Yes, I will teach you.' In a very quiet voice, a kind voice, he asked if I would be his queen. I looked him straight in the eyes. I knew this had been the Queen's plan, but I felt that it was my life's mission. I agreed to be his queen and teach him about Aten.

Then Pharaoh asked me, what was the first thing I would teach him? I told him that the first lesson was gold could not be eaten, or drunk. I told him that gold might be beautiful, but it is only an ornament. And yet, it has caused good men to do very bad things. I told him Aten believes the great lesson his children must discover is what is worth fighting for and what is not. Amenhotep said nothing, but I felt he heard me. I left for Thebes within a week. It was difficult to leave my friends and family, but it was also what I had dreamed of from my rooftop perch since I was young.

I finished my story and looked at my son, Amenhotep IV, now Akhenaten. I said, 'Your father was my greatest student, and you are my greatest gift to Aten.'

Akhenaten took my hand and said, 'Thank you, Mother, for telling this story again. The first lesson you taught father is what I wish to talk to you about. Aten has spoken. The priests are preparing to destroy Tel el Amarna. It is my understanding that their preparations may take several years, but they are coming. We cannot allow them to get their hands on Aten's treasure. As you told my father, gold is nothing but an ornament, but it can corrupt the hearts of men and women. If the high priests steal Aten's treasure, they will attempt to take over all of Egypt and all the neighboring countries, perhaps even Mesopotamia. They will cause wars among the kingdoms. Many people will die, and more will suffer. We cannot allow this.'

I told Akhenaten I understood; the treasure must be moved from Tel el Armana. My son told me I was the only one who could do it. 'But how can I do this?' I asked my son.

"I need a minute to catch up," Charles interrupted. Farak stood beside Meriaten, while Jacques and Charles sat on the floor. No one spoke as Charles wrote this part of the story of Akhenaten and Tiye.

"Okay, Meriaten. I'm caught up," Charles said.

"This is almost like a movie, isn't it?" Meriaten asked.

"I sort of feel like it's more than a movie, like I'm actually there, in ancient Egypt," Charles whispered. "Okay, Meriaten, I'm ready. Akhenaten has asked his mother to help him hide the treasure to keep it away from the high priests."

'However you decide to do this, Mother, it must be kept secret. It must be kept secret not only from our friends, our loyal servants, and our children, but from Nefertiti and, most of all, from me.'

'You? Keep it a secret from you? How can I do this?' I asked my son.

'You must, Mother, because torture can reveal any secret.'

My heart was broken, but I knew he was right. The high priests must not gain more power by stealing my husband's, now Akhenaten's, treasure.

"Do you think Queen Tiye might have placed the treasure down here, in the Tomb of a Thousand Names?" Jacques asked, jumping up to peek out the door.

"Jacques, I saw it in your eyes when we were in King Tutankhamen's room at the museum. You seemed hypnotized, mesmerized, almost mummy-like. I just want to remind you, Jacques, that Akhenaten says that gold is a corrupter of souls," Charles said.

"What you saw in me, young Charles, was strictly academic admiration for Egyptian art—Egyptian art that just happened to be covered with 18-carat gold," Jacques insisted.

"Right," Charles said, with all the sarcasm a twelve-year-old could muster.

Jacques asked, "Do you think the treasure Akhenaten is talking about ended up in King Tutankhamun's tomb?"

"From what I have read, the treasure in King Tut's tomb would have been a drop in the bucket compared to the gold, silver, minerals, jewels, and important documents that once belonged to Amenhotep III."

"Where did it go?" Meriaten asked.

"As far as I know, the treasure has yet to be discovered," Farak said. "I see Meriaten has reached the end of Tiye's story. We have found no hints as to where the treasure could have gone. We have one more room in this *Chamber of Secrets*."

"Maybe we will get a hint about the location of the treasure in that room," Jacques said, leading the group out of the second *Room of Secrets*. Meriaten blew out the candles.

CHAPTER 71

AKHENATEN'S TREASURE

Meriaten pointed towards some symbols on the outside of an arched doorway. "This must be the next room in this *Chamber of Secrets*," the girl whispered."The symbol is followed by the letters '*dj,*' probably adjo."

"I've seen this word before," Farak said, placing his finger on the letters. "It means wealth. Next to it is the symbol of an *ankh*, which may also mean wealth. Underneath the ankh are the symbols for gold and silver."

"I'll lead. I think we have discovered Akhenaten's treasure!" Jacques said exuberantly. As they entered the next room, however, they found no gold, silver, or jewels. There was just one carved illustration of a woman leading a donkey, and on the other walls were hieroglyphics.

"Like the other stories, it begins with the translator, Seshat," Farak said, gesturing to the hieroglyphics. "She's telling the story of a friend of Tiye named Yuba. Shall I begin translating, Charles?"

"Yes, I'm ready," Charles called from his seat on the floor, back resting on the eastern wall.

In the middle of the night, I heard a knock at my door. It was Tiye. She said, 'I need help and you are the only person who can help me, Yuba.' I asked, 'What is it, my lady?' She said, 'We must remove the treasure from the treasuries and hide it somewhere, and this must be done in complete secrecy.'

I thought I must be dreaming. I told Queen Tiye this was impossible. She said, 'Yuba, you and I have been friends for many years. There is nothing you and I cannot do, especially if it must be done.' This was not my plan, nor is it my story. Still, I have played my part, and Tiye has asked me to relate the tale of how we kept Akhenaten's treasure out of the hands of the evil priests. I cannot do this without telling you a little about Queen Tiye and our long friendship.

My name is Yuba, born in the city of Kush in the country of Nubia. Tiye, who lived in the palace, loved horses. I was a stable boy. When she was nine, she began coming to the stable, helping me feed, brush, and exercise the Royal Horses. She and I were the same age. Tiye became my friend. It did not matter to her that she lived in the palace and I lived in a room in the stables. She was allowed to come because her father was Commander of the Royal Horses but, in truth, he was seldom at the stables. Tiye and I would ride the horses to keep them fit and strong. She would bring me food from the Queen's table. For me, it was the best childhood anyone could imagine.

When Tiye was fourteen, Pharaoh Amenhotep III came to Kush. Tiye agreed to become his queen. I felt very sad. As she prepared to leave for Thebes, Tiye asked Queen Abu if I could come with her to care for her horses. The queen agreed. When I first moved to Thebes, I cared for the royal horses. Tiye, however, had other plans for me. I was trained as an architect and builder. I met and married an Egyptian woman, Tani, who was very kind and funny. We had five sons. They all became architects and builders like me. My sons and I had plenty of work around Thebes, building temples and government houses. Life was full, and we were happy.

One evening, I received a visit from Tiye. She told me Amenhotep IV had changed his name to Akhenaten and planned on building a new capital city.

Tiye wanted my sons and me to work with her son and Queen Nefertiti to build a city of light dedicated to our god, Aten. She told me the location was to be 250 miles north of Thebes. It was barren land. My sons and I went to look at the site. There were no rock quarries nearby. I wondered how we were to build such a city out of nothing. Together, Akhenaten, my sons, and I invented a different kind of building material we named talatats: hard clay bricks. These smaller bricks allowed great freedom in design, making it faster to build.

One of our tasks was to protect Akhenaten's great treasure. We designed secret doors and complicated mazes that would block anyone from entering the treasury rooms. Once built, it took many months and many men to transfer Pharaoh's treasure from its hidden place near Thebes to to Tel el Armana. Only my sons and I, along with a few trusted followers of Akhenaten, knew where this treasure was hidden.

I had heard rumors the priests were building an army to raid our capital city, so I was not surprised by Tiye's news of their intention to invade Tel el Armana. I asked Tiye what Akhenaten's plans were. She said that when Amenhotep III stepped down from his position as Pharaoh, he gave all his treasure—said to be the largest treasury in history—to Akhenaten. Akhenaten immediately gave this treasure to Aten, meaning it could only be used for purposes that would please Aten. No part of this wealth could be used to buy power or royal friendships, and it could not be used to wage war against other kingdoms. Akhenaten declared Tel el Amarna a City of Peace.

The night Tiye came to my door, I offered her a chair. She sat on it, straight and tall, like she did on the throne we built for her. As she told me of the priests' plan, I asked her, 'What does this mean?' She said that the city of Tel el Amarna would most likely be taken over by the priests and their men. Akhenaten wanted us to prepare for such an event. 'My son,' she confided, 'has asked me to devise a plan to take Aten's treasure away from Tel el Armana, to hide it where it cannot be found by the priests and their soldiers.'

I told Tiye I did not believe this was possible. 'Aten has warned Akhenaten that if the priests gain control of this great treasure, they will believe themselves to be all-powerful.' she responded. 'They will take over other kingships; there will be war throughout our region. So much suffering and death will come, and for what? For mere decoration: gold and silver.'

I reminded my Queen, 'Under the temple and palaces we have built mazes, doors that go nowhere, secret passageways and entrances; the invaders will not be able to enter the treasuries.' Tiye disagreed, saying even our cleverest tricks would provide little protection. 'Akhenaten insists they will tear down every talatat from every building in Tel el Armana. The high priests and their army will not stop until all the treasure is discovered.'

'What should we do? What can we do?' I asked my queen, heart pounding at the dreadful news. Tiye said Akhenaten believed it would take the priests several years to build a large, strong army. They must also convince the people of Egypt that Akhenaten must be removed from his position as Pharaoh. 'So,' Tiye said, 'we have a little time, maybe two years, to remove Aten's treasure before the invasion.'

I told my Queen I would begin organizing citizens immediately to move Aten's treasure to another place. She stopped me, holding up her hand, then placing her finger to her lips. Tiye told me Akhenaten had decreed the plan must be carried out in complete secrecy. No one in his family, none of their servants, none of Pharaoh's associates, not Nefertiti, and especially not Akhenaten himself, must know when the treasure was moved, and where it was hidden.

'I have prayed for a solution,' Tiye said, 'and I have a plan. Yesterday, I called upon the Daughters of Aten, just as the sun set on the horizon, to come quietly to my great hall. I told them to walk in twos and threes, and to tell no one where they were going.'

Tiye had formed the Daughters of Aten by mobilizing women whose children had grown and therefore had no employment. She had watched these women sitting on doorsteps or gossiping with others like themselves as they walked through the city streets and markets. She saw they had lost their passion, and felt they had no purpose. Tiye said Aten teaches that everyone who takes life must have a purpose. She gathered these women like flowers, and they blossomed. Some became healers, like my wife; others became caretakers, helping families facing great suffering. Tiye told me that two hundred women gathered in her great hall.'

I asked, 'Do you plan on turning the Daughters of Aten into soldiers, to fight the priests and their men?'

Queen Tiye laughed heartily at my suggestion. Then she answered seriously; this was not her plan. She had asked for volunteers to do something more difficult than fighting off priests and their soldiers, a task far more challenging and requiring even greater courage. 'So what is it you ask of the Daughters of Aten?' I asked.

Tiye said, 'I asked them to help me move Aten's treasure to a place where the priests could not find it.' Queen Tiye told me her plan was for several women to leave on donkeys or camels with small loads of Aten's treasure packed under their supplies. They would need to travel far to locate safe places in which to hide their load of Akhenaten's treasury.

Those who volunteered would leave their homes at night, telling no one. They couldn't say goodbye to their children or grandchildren or their sisters or brothers, not even their husbands. They must leave without a guarantee that they would ever return to Tel el Amarna. They would leave without a map, a guide, or even a plan of where they might find a safe place to hide their fragments of Aten's treasure.

Tiye warned that those who volunteered would walk under the burning sun and stumble through desert sands. Once their quantity of treasure had been hidden, they must record the site and assure this location got to the record keepers. Finally, she said, those who volunteered must find and initiate others like themselves, vowing to keep Aten's treasure and Aten's teachings a secret until the world was ready.'

'Of the two hundred women gathered before me,' Tiye said, 'one hundred and fifty agreed to leave Tel el Armana, and the rest agreed to help.' I asked her what she wanted of me. 'Our travelers must have water, shade, and rest,' she explained. 'I request that you and your sons locate or build such places. Someone passing, even nearby, must not be aware of these secret places. They must be like secret oases.'

619

"I have been to one of these secret oases," Jacques said, his voice raised in amazement.

"You have? When? How?" Charles asked.

"Subira and Rehima took me to one on our way to the Temple of Sobek," Jacques said. "It was a delightful surprise. No one would have recognized that it was an oasis from the outside."

"Where is it?" Charles asked. "I'd love to see it."

"Charlie, my boy, it is called a secret oasis because it is a secret. I do not have the approval to reveal such a secret, even to you," Jacques said. "I am sure this Tomb of a Thousand Names must have been designed and built by Yuba and his sons. It fits the description of a safe place that Tiye described to Yuba."

"You'll have to tell us more about this secret oasis, Jacques. You seem to always have something up your sleeve," Charles said. "But right now, there's just a little bit more to translate."

Farak said, "Are you ready, Charles?"

"I am ready," Charles said, and picked up his pen.

Yuba and his sons had the key and the map to the treasuries. They would place some of Aten's treasure underneath the Daughters of Aten's camping equipment, clothing, and food. At first, it was very discouraging. It seemed such a cumbersome and slow way to carry out this immense amount of treasure. However, he writes here that he had underestimated the Daughters of Aten. Within several weeks they had made a new plan, a relay plan.

A few women would go to the first oasis, where they joined the earlier group of Daughters of Aten and their pack animals. They would put new supplies in the oasis, then return to Tel el Amarna with unburdened animals. The women at the secret oasis would then transfer the treasure to the rested animals and move to various lands purchased by Yuba and his sons.

They purchased lands from Aswan to the Mediterranean Sea. These places became way stations for the Daughters of Aten, each carrying a bit of Aten's Treasure. The women who ran the way stations integrated into the nearby community. They became trusted citizens. Many of these women were trained in the healing arts. Their ability to heal was greatly appreciated by their neighbors. It was a wonderful plan, much faster and safer than the original idea. Within six months, many properties had been purchased. No one wondered about these simple women who came to visit their healer friends.

At the end of two years, there was just a token amount of treasure remaining in each of the treasuries in Tel el Armana.

"That was so clever of them," Meriaten said in amazement.

"Look at this wall on the south side of the room," Farak said, gesturing. "It's written in hieroglyphics. It seems to be calendar dates and names. Some of the names have another number, possibly a return date."

"Does it mention where any of the treasure was hidden?" Jacques asked.

"No, it doesn't. That is strange, isn't it? They had to keep a record of where these women hid their part of the treasure, but it's not on this wall. Where could it be?" Farak asked his companions.

"No answer? Since there is no information as to the whereabouts of Aten's treasure, let us leave this *Chamber of Secrets* and head for the light at the end of the tunnel," Jacques suggested.

Meriaten lit her lantern. Jacques put the red flashlight into his shoulder bag. Farak closed the door to the *Chamber of Secrets* and led the reluctant group towards the *Room of Destruction*.

CHAPTER 72

EGYPTIAN II'S AND THE PYRAMID RELIC

W ith Charles in the lead, they walked out of the *Chamber of Secrets.* Jacques pushed the hieroglyphic for secret, a finger over a mouth, and the door shut. Now, they were headed for the *Room of Destruction.* Jacques didn't want to see Meriaten cry again or end this Path of Knowledge with such sadness.

As Jacques shut the door of the *Chamber of Secrets,* he was almost positive Yuba and his sons had designed the secret doors and rooms in this Tomb of a Thousand Names. He would have liked to have met Yuba, but he wouldn't choose to go back such a terrible time in history.

As the troop turned left on the left-hand path, the corridor widened and the ceiling rose. There was a feeling that the end was coming.

"Lady and gentlemen, I do not think we should go to the *Room of Destruction* today," Jacques said.

"We have to go," Meriaten said with determination.

"I am with Meri," Farak added. "We must bravely face what happened to Tel el Armana. And if not today, when?"

Jacques had no answer.

"I have been reading an author named Joseph Campbell," Farak continued. "He would call our journey through this Tomb of a Thousand Names the Hero's Journey or, in Meriaten's case, the Heroine's Journey."

"I read Joseph Campbell in my anthropology class this year," Charles added. "He believes a hero is hidden in each of us. Campbell said, '*A Hero's Journey is a journey to depths in which dark resistances are overcome and long-forgotten powers resurrected.*' I love that description."

"Really, Charles, I don't think you are supposed to read about the Hero's Journey until you are more my age," Jacques said.

Ignoring his chaperone, Charles expounded further on the subject. "On the Hero's Journey, long-forgotten powers will be found and brought back to life."

"That is it exactly. Because of this, I feel strongly that we should avoid this last room," Jacques cautioned. "The whole brought-back-to-life thing sounds too much like the mummy movies I have seen."

"On a Hero's Journey, you must face the wondrous and the terrifying," Farak said.

"Can't you guys read something light, like comic books or something?" Jacques quipped. "How far are we from the *Room of Destruction?*"

"It doesn't look that far, maybe a thousand feet," Farak answered.

They were speeding towards the end of their journey when Charles stopped in front of a large and colorful engraving of Nefertiti driving her chariot down the King's Road. Shining down on her was the symbol of Aten, the sun's beams reaching towards her, each ray ending in a tiny little hand. Around Nefertiti, there were farmers, soldiers, and people praying. There was nothing else on the corridor's walls, just this striking relief.

"I wish I could drive her chariot with that beautiful horse," Meriaten sighed.

"I would love to stay longer, admiring this amazing art, but it's getting late," Farak said. "Since there is nothing to translate, we had better move on. I'm beginning to feel like we have been in the *Tomb of a Thousand Names* for years."

"Moving on sounds like a great idea," Jacques agreed, "unless you want to consider the strange fact that there is a surprising number of upside-down U's and 1's hidden in this work of art. In other words, there are a lot of hieroglyphs of the number eleven."

"You're right, Jacques!" Charles said, staring in amazement at the illustration. "It's so obvious. Why didn't I notice it?"

Meriaten moved closer to the etching and began touching the ancient Egyptian hieroglyphics for eleven. "There are more elevens in this painting than you would first think. They're hidden throughout this illustration."

"As you know, the 1 symbol can be on either side of the hieroglyphic number for ten, the upside down U," Meriaten continued. "The one turns the ten into the hieroglyphic 11. Whoever carved and painted this illustration was quite clever. But what do all these elevens mean?"

"Hmm, good question," Jacques said, looking at Charles. "What does 11 mean?"

"The only thing I can think of is Tomb 11," Charles answered. "Jacques, do you think it's a coincidence, or a sign that we need to go to Tomb 11?"

"I am not sure I am qualified to answer your question, Charles," Jacques answered. "However, I have heard you mention Tomb 11 to Dr. McAllister, and we did make plans to visit Tel el Amarna together. I just assumed we would be looking for this Tomb 11."

"What is inside Tomb 11?" Farak asked.

"A ghost," Charles said matter-of-factly.

"A ghost of what, or who?" Farak inquired.

"I don't know who the ghost is," Charles responded.

"Okay, how did you find out about this ghost?" Farak asked.

"It's a long story. The short story is, after accepting my account of the child-ghosts from the French Revolution haunting the Château du Mont,

Ghost Stories Magazine sent me something," Charles said. "They gave me a list of one thousand haunted places, and asked me to submit another story. Near the top of the list was The Ghost of Tomb 11, Tel el Amarna, Egypt. Since I've always loved Egypt, I thought that 'The Ghost of Tomb 11' would be a perfect next story."

"You knew about this, Jacques?" Farak asked.

"I don't think I quite understood that we came to Egypt to become ghost hunters," Jacques said wryly.

"What is a ghost, Charles?" Meriaten asked.

"According to *Ghost Stories Magazine,* a ghost is a spirit who has unfinished business," Charles explained. "When their business is finished, they go where everyone else goes when they die. I'd hoped to find out what unfinished business this Ghost of Tomb 11 might have."

Meriaten was busy counting the symbols of eleven on the large relief of Nefertiti. "Hey!" she exclaimed. "When I touched the eleven here on the wheel of Nefertiti's chariot, it felt like a button. Should I push it?"

"Let Jacques push it, Meri; he is the one who noticed all the elevens," Farak said.

As Jacques pushed the 11 in the center of the chariot wheel, they heard a scraping sound near the floor. A box slid out from the wall. "What's in it?" Meriaten asked.

"The only way to find out is to open it," Jacques said, pulling the stone box out of the wall with his fingertips. The box was about eight-by-eight inches square. Jacques searched for a way to open the beautiful container, covered in hieroglyphics. Charles, Farak and Meriaten gathered around him. Meriaten was jumping up and down in anticipation. As the top of the box slid open, they saw a flash of gold glimmering in the lantern light.

"It's a pyramid," Farak whispered. "You found another pyramid, Jacques."

Jacques took the pyramid out of the box and handed it to Farak, who meticulously examined all five sides. He finally declared that it was not a replica but a true pyramid relic. Meriaten chanted her rhyme.

One little pyramid stands alone,

Searching for a brother of its very own.

When there are two, the third comes home.

The fourth can be found at Aten's throne.

"Aten's throne. That must be in Tel el Amarna," Charles interjected.

Translate you, on all the sides,

One, two, three, four, and five,

Messages concealed in poetry.

The pyramids together are the key

To solve Queen Tye's great mystery.

And with this all will be

Forever, forever, changed.

"Do you believe finding this pyramid was luck?" Farak asked.

The Egyptian teen's question prompted Jacques to think about Dr. Bernstein and the classes she planned to teach at the university in Paris, where she would encourage students to create experiments regarding entanglement. He also recalled that Dr. Bernstein had said Jacques would make a good subject. Why, he hadn't the slightest idea. But how had they managed to find the pyramid in this Tomb of a Thousand Names?

Farak said, "Look on this box."

"It's got nice carvings," Charles said.

"Yes, but it has something else. It is written in Arabic. It is the symbols for the Eye Tribe and the Tarabin Tribe. Why is there a reference to my mother and father's tribes on this box that held the pyramid?" Farak asked, looking puzzled.

"Why?" Meriaten echoed.

"The only thing I can think of is that successors of the Daughters of Aten made connections with the Bedouin tribes," Farak conjectured.

"I remember a story my mother told me when I was a child. She said some women visited the Eye Tribe's camp hundreds and hundreds of years ago," Meriaten related. "They asked if they could ride with Bedouins. In exchange, they said they would teach the women of the tribe the healing arts. I think several of the pyramids are connected to the Bedouins through the Daughters of Aten."

"But what does this have to do with today?" Jacques asked.

"It means that the time is near. Change is coming, and we're all playing a part," Meriaten said, excitement in her voice. "All we have to do is find the fourth pyramid."

"That shouldn't be too difficult," Jacques said with exaggerated confidence. "It is somewhere between Upper and Lower Egypt."

"You know it's in Tomb 11, Jacques," Charles said. "We just have to find a way to get there."

CHAPTER 73

THE ROOM OF DESTRUCTION

T he thirsty travelers ascended several thousand feet, up through the
tunnel-like corridor. Jacques kept calling for a rest, claiming the
walk was steeper than the pathway to the King's Chamber in the Great
Pyramid. They were ready to step out into the light, but there was one
more destination: the *Room of Destruction*. What would they find? The
people of ancient Tel el Amarna were no longer simply names in dry and
inaccurate history books. The explorers felt they knew these people, even
though they'd lived more than three thousand years ago.

Jacques couldn't help but remember Dr. Bernstein's hypothesis that
everything and everyone was connected in time and space. At the moment,
however, he was exhausted and didn't want to ponder connections. Instead,

he said, "When I get out of here, I will find a cool, shady place under a boulder and take a nice, long nap."

"What if there's a horned viper under your boulder?" Charles asked.

"Charles, could you keep your imagination out of my fantasy?" Jacques admonished his charge.

"If you'd stop fantasizing, you wouldn't walk so slow," Charles grumbled.

"I'm with Jacques. I do not know when I slept last," Farak said, yawning. "I will locate my own shade, maybe under a palm tree, trailing my fingers in the blue, blue water of an oasis."

Jacques stopped to catch his breath from the demanding climb, then asked Farak what his map said. "My map is not talking right now," the Egyptian boy answered, also breathing hard.

Meriaten—who was in the lead—turned around, putting the lantern on the floor and her hands on her hips. "This isn't funny. I get the feeling you're all dragging your feet. We're never going to get out of here if you don't speed up. Now let's go."

"You're right, Meri," Farak said. "Here's the map, and here is the *Room of Destruction*. It should be around here somewhere."

Jacques took the lead, shining his red plastic flashlight this way and that. Charles, having grabbed the lantern, was behind Jacques. Meriaten and Farak walked as close to Charles as possible while they struggled up the steep stone slab.

"Here it is," Jacques said, shining the beam of his light on a relief carved into the rock wall. "You do not need to study hieroglyphics to interpret this sign. Here is a man who looks like a priest with a cloud over his head. Several men with weapons are following him. Next, there are two men with sledgehammers tearing down a wall or building, and a man with a rake smoothing out the land. *Le voilà!* We have reached the *Room of Destruction*."

"Where's the entrance?" Meriaten asked.

"I thought that was your area of expertise," Farak said, smiling at the girl.

The four explorers stared at the wall. "Maybe if we touched the cloud?" Meriaten suggested.

Nothing happened. Charles and Farak began pounding here and there on the stone wall. Jacques looked down towards the floor. Seeing the glint of a fine wire, he scooped up the line and gave it a tug. A small gap appeared between two sections of the stone wall. Jacques pushed on the wall and the door opened.

"You forgot to say *Open Sesame,*" Charles pointed out.

"Do you think it is too late? *Open Sesame,*" Jacques pronounced dramatically.

"I found out your secret, Jacques. I saw the wire this time," Charles said. "It's amazing that such a thin wire could open a stone door. What kind of material is it made from?"

"I do not know. What do you think?" Jacques replied.

"My father told me that in ancient Egypt they had only copper, silver and gold," Meriaten answered. "Each of these is a very soft metal. That's why most Egyptologists think all the temples and pyramids were made from stone tools. This idea of stone-on-stone construction is hard to believe, though."

"I recently read in *National Geographic* that they found a knife made of iron in Tutankhamun's tomb," Farak said. "The article said it was made from metal found at the crash site of a meteorite."

"Wow! That's interesting," Charles said. "So there's a possibility the wire is made from off-planet material."

"Off-planet material? You have the strangest way of saying things, Charles," Jacques remarked. "However, we know Tiye's friend Yuba was an inventor. He mentioned designing mazes and secret entrances. It is clear to me that, with the help of his sons, he designed and built this Tomb of a Thousand Names."

"It's hard to believe Yuba was once just a stable boy in Nubia. How did Tiye recognize his talents?" Farak wondered.

"Maybe he was so talented because Tiye believed in him," Meriaten said. "My father says there's a lot of power in believing in someone."

The girl lit the candle she found on the floor of the west wall and proceeded to light five more candles. Farak told her they didn't need candles. They could now use her lantern, since they were almost to the exit. Meriaten, however, insisted everything looked more ancient, more sacred, by candlelight.

Charles sat on a bench in the middle of the room and arranged his papers and pen. Jacques looked at the boy with whom he'd come to Egypt; he appeared exhausted. There were dark circles under his eyes and slight wrinkles on his forehead. Charles had gone through things an adult would barely survive. Jacques knew this for a fact, because he'd questioned his own survival as he and Caboose traversed the Western Desert.

Jacques reached down and patted Charles on his back, saying, "Before we start, I want to tell you how much I appreciate your writing down all these stories, without even one word of complaint."

Following Jacques' lead, Meriaten moved to pat Charles on the back. "Thank you," she said, bowing her head slightly. "Without you, Charles, I might never have learned more about the girl I'm named after. I will remember this day for the rest of my life."

"Charles, if you hadn't been pushed off the train, I wouldn't have returned to Egypt," Farak said. "And without you, no one would be able to remember all the details of this amazing journey through the Tomb of a Thousand Names."

"Thank you all, but I couldn't have written these stories without you, especially without Jacques' red plastic flashlight," Charles said, laughing. His three companions joined Charles and their laughter spilled out into the dark corridors of the Tomb of Secrets, the Tomb of Sad Stories, the Tomb of a Thousand Names, making everything lighter.

"Are you ready, Charles?" Farak asked.

"Pen at the ready," Charles responded.

"Here is the introduction by the scribe Seshat, explaining how the writing was in Cuneiform, then translated into hieroglyphics," Farak said. "This story is by Yuba."

On that fateful morning, Akhenaten arose to greet the sun on the balcony at the east side of his palace. He then moved to a west window and stared down at the city of Tel el Armana. Just then, without knocking, one of his guards entered

Pharaoh's hall. He announced the city gates had been breached. Akhenaten didn't have to be told; he could see what was happening in Aten's city through the large window facing the blue Nile.

As Pharaoh had instructed, the residents of Tel el Amarna gathered peacefully in the streets, carrying their possessions on their backs. They were being directed to the Nile, where many boats gathered to begin the transfer of citizens from Tel el Amarna to Thebes. As the soldiers came nearer the palaces, some of Akhenaten's guards refused to surrender, fighting against unbelievable odds.

The Daughters of Aten who were still in Tel el Amarna had already been evacuated under Pharaoh's order, as had my family and I. We were hiding in secret tombs on the cliffs of Tel el Armana. We had filled these tombs with supplies. We watched with horror as Tiye, the princesses, and Tutankhaten were taken from their palace. We did not see what happened to Nefertiti or Akhenaten. Tiye told me Akhenaten had foreseen his own death.

Meriaten sat down on the stone floor, tears streaming down her face. Jacques patted her on her head-cloth. Farak continued his translation.

After capturing the city, thousands of enslaved people and soldiers came with hammers and rakes. They searched for supplies, food, beer, and jewelry. Foremost in the priests' minds, however, was Akhenaten's treasure. In their search, they flattened every building, home, temple, palace, orchard, and garden. Everything was destroyed. There was nothing we could do but watch in solemn sorrow.

Maybe I was to blame for this destruction, for it was I who invented the talatat, the mud-brick we used to build Tel el Armana. These bricks made the city easy to construct, but even easier to tear down. We should have used stone, but little was available near this desert location. Maybe I could have found another building technique, but I did not guess what destruction lay ahead. Our small group remained hidden for several weeks, watching as everything was leveled to the ground, buried. In the end, we watched as the priests' soldiers raked the sand, until it looked like the day Akhenaten had first discovered it.

"I knew about the destruction of Tel el Armana, but somehow it's sadder in the words of Yuba," Charles said.

When all the ships had sailed, and all the soldiers had gone, we left our tombs to meet the Daughters of Aten and other allies who had gathered under the Temple of Sobek in the Tomb of a Thousand Names.

There were many tears, but we were comforted by the knowledge that we had prevented the high priests from finding Aten's treasure. We all took an oath to keep Tiye's secret until the world was ready for such wealth. Then, we devised a plan to capture the stories of Akhenaten, Nefertiti, and Tiye, presenting them in such a way that they will never be forgotten. This is how the Tomb of a Thousand Names became the Tomb of a Thousand Stories.

"This is the end of the writing on the western wall, but there is more on the southern wall," Farak announced. "If you are ready, Charles, this writing is called *The Destruction of the Great Pyramid of Giza.* It was also written in Yuba's voice."

While Tel el Amarna was being built, Akhenaten traveled to Giza, near the city of Memphis. Pharaoh looked at the Great Pyramid, shining white in the afternoon sun. Akhenaten said he had received a message. Aten wanted to use the pyramid to communicate important messages to all people, not just Egyptians. He asked Akhenaten to place four messages on the smooth limestone covering of the Great Pyramid, which could be seen from far away and read by people from many lands.

Akhenaten sent for his most talented and courageous scribes, carvers, and artists to travel north to the Giza plateau. One of these was my oldest son. A great scaffolding was built to carve and paint the messages on each sloping side of the Great Pyramid. The messages were in Cuneiform.

"I'm not sure I want to hear about what comes next, but go on," Charles said.

When Tel el Amarna was destroyed, the high priests sent their soldiers to remove the messages on the Great Pyramid.

"Why'd they do that?" Meriaten asked.

"It's because they wanted to erase all references to Akhenaten and Aten," Charles said, looking back down at his writing. "Okay, Farak, go."

The high priests thought they could sand off the messages on the Great Pyramid. In fact, the Cuneiform writing had been carved deeply into the limestone covering of the pyramid. Meanwhile, the tar-like paint, which made the messages visible from far away, was thick and hard. After many unsuccessful attempts, the high priests ordered the polished limestone that covered the Great Pyramid to be completely removed.

"That's terrible," Meriaten said mournfully.

"I've never heard this theory, but it makes sense, doesn't it?" Charles asked. "Many Egyptologists believe poor people removed the limestone covering on the great pyramid to use as flooring for their homes or temples. They believe these people climbed up the pyramid's steep, smooth sides and chipped off every bit of the outer casing, and they did this without damaging the pyramid's essential structure."

"It was always unbelievable to me," Charles continued. "If the people wanted a stone floor, it would be much easier, not to mention safer, to go to one of the stone quarries near Memphis."

"What about the gold capstone?" Jacques asked.

"It says here that it was Akhenaten who ordered the capstone to be covered in solid gold," Farak said. "The capstone was estimated to be twenty-two feet high on each side, and it says the gold was three to four inches thick."

"That is a lot of gold," Jacques said, shaking his head in astonishment.

Meriaten was glowering, her arms crossed and tucked under her armpits. "They ruined the Great Pyramid, and that makes me so mad!" she exclaimed. "They did it just because they didn't like its messages. Exactly what did the messages say?"

Farak translated the hieroglyphics.

Side 1

All people are related through Aten's creation.
Relatives should not kill or injure each other.
Therefore, there should be no wars.
Peace be with you.

"I don't believe in war either," Meriaten said, anger still smoldering in her voice.

Side 2

Freedom and joy are Aten's gifts.
They cannot be taken away,
But they can be given away.
Wear freedom and joy on your sleeves for all to see.

Side 3

All humans are created in Aten's image.
All have the power to manifest anything and everything.
To exercise this power requires only recognition and practice.

Side 4

Aten listens to all prayers.
No representative is needed.
No sacrifice or mummification is required.
A happy afterlife is guaranteed to all.

"These seems like great messages to me," Meriaten said.

"Yes, but don't you see?" Charles replied. "The priests couldn't allow anyone to read these messages, especially the words on the fourth side. If people thought they could speak directly to God, that priests weren't necessary, the priests would be out of a job and out of money."

"I can see how they wouldn't have liked that one bit," the Egyptian girl said.

"Is there anything about what was written on the pyramid's base, Farak?" Charles asked.

"No, that's all it says," the Egyptian boy answered.

As Charles bent to pick up his papers, he called to Meriaten to blow out the candles. "Yes, Meriaten, blow out the candles," Farak repeated, adding, "It's time for us to leave this Room of Sad Stories."

"Wait! We cannot leave this room yet," Jacques called out.

"Why not?" Charles asked his guardian.

"Because we are not here to feel sad," he said.

"How should we feel?" Meriaten asked, looking up at Jacques.

"I will tell you how I feel!" Jacques exclaimed. "I feel inspired. I feel grateful. I feel connected to these people who lived so long ago, who faced great challenges, who saw such horrors, and did so with courage, bravery, and selflessness. I feel indebted to these people who, instead of feeling sorry for themselves, were determined to bring about a better world—a world they would never even see."

"For me, I rename this room," Jacques continued, raising his hands in the air, "*The Room of Transformation*. Shall we go?"

CHAPTER 74

SESHAT AND THE TEMPLE OF HEALING

"According to the map, we should be out of the Tomb of a Thousand Names in twenty minutes or so," Farak said.

"In some ways, I'm sad this is going to be over," Meriaten said. "It's been tiring and tragic, but interesting, exciting, and fun."

"Jacques and I will soon be on our way to the Château du Mont, and this will all just seem like a dream," Charles said. "And I might never see you again, Meriaten."

For a few seconds, no one said anything. Then Jacques broke the silence. "Now look here, my dear friends. People on sad journeys are not allowed to be sad," he declared, wondering what on earth he meant by his words.

"Look!" exclaimed Farak, who was in the lead holding the lantern. "There are two tunnel-like pathways ahead of us. This division was not on the map. I wonder why?"

The four exhausted travelers stared at the two almost identical pathways, one veering right, the other left. They were about four feet wide and seven feet tall. Jacques asked Farak for the map.

"Farak is correct," he concluded. "There is nothing on the map that shows there are two paths to the exit. What should we do?"

Meriaten asked for Jacques' red flashlight. Walking slowly forward, she shined the light around the entrance to the two paths. "I don't see anything. Wait! Here is some faded writing."

"What does it say?" Charles asked, moving beside Meriaten. She said it was a quote in Arabic, which she proceeded to translate.

If you come to a division in the road,
and do not know which way to go,
ask the paths, for one will know.
—Rumi

"It sounds more like a riddle from *Alice in Wonderland* than a quote from a 13th century Persian poet," Jacques mumbled. "How can a path know anything? It is just a path. I do not know for sure, but it appears the main message of this Tomb of a Thousand Names is that too much time in complete darkness make one go crazy."

Holding his arms straight in front of him, hands up, Jacques spoke in a commanding voice. "Pathways, which way should we go?"

"Really, Jacques," Charles said with a slight frown.

"Well, it was an idea. An idea, I might remind you, put forth by Rumi, considered the greatest mystic poet of Islam," Charles' guardian said with a slight smile.

"There must be a clue here somewhere," Farak said.

The Egyptian teen reached for the flashlight and inspected the walls and ceilings. Finally, pointing the flashlight's beam towards the stone floor, he said, "There appears to be one major difference in the paths. The right-hand path is much smoother than the left-hand path."

"Good observation, Farak. Now let's go," Jacques said brightly, headed for the right-hand path.

"I think we should take the path less traveled," Charles suggested.

"The path less traveled," Jacques repeated. "Doesn't that sound like a poem or something?" he quipped, referring to Robert Frost's famous poem *The Road Not Taken*.

"Charles Dayton Stratton III," Jacques called in exasperation, "for thousands of years, travelers on the Path of Knowledge apparently went right, making the path smooth. And yet you want us to go left?"

"I understand what you're saying, Jacques, but I have a feeling we should take the path less traveled, the left-hand path," the American boy in the tan gallibyah said.

"My mother said it's Charles' decision to make," Meriaten reminded her companions.

"Alright, Charles, you lead, but it doesn't make sense to me," Jacques said.

The troop moved forth on the rougher path. Farak, in the lead with the flashlight, aimed its beam from one side of the narrow pathway to the other. After about a hundred steps, he announced, "Look! Here's another quote. It says, '*I know you are tired, but come this way.*' It's by Rumi again."

"How did he know I was tired?" Jacques mused.

"Jacques, anyone who travels the left-hand path is going to be tired," Charles explained.

"I understand, but Rumi is a Persian poet. How did he know we would be here, and that we would be tired and hungry, not to mention thirsty and a little lost?" Jacques asked.

"I found another quote. It's carved on the pathway floor. Meri, light your lantern and bring it here. The writing is so faint," Farak said, kneeling on the rough stone floor.

"What does it say, Farak?" Charles asked, pen and paper in hand.

'A drop of water is beautiful, but drops combined is music.'

"What do you think it means?" Meriaten asked.

Jacques said nothing, but it occurred to him that before traveling to Egypt, he'd lived his life like a lone drop of water. He played the violin and organ, but he was beginning to understand that in order to truly make music, he needed others to merge with. He'd have to think about it later, especially since the walls of the pathway were closing in on them. Jacques, Farak and Charles had to duck their heads, as the ceiling was now only five feet high and the width of the path had shrunk from three to two feet.

"I am beginning to think we should go back and take the right-hand path," Jacques called out.

"Listen!" Meriaten said. "I think I hear water."

"I do, too," Farak agreed. "It sounds like it's coming from behind this wall."

The Egyptian teen touched the wall on the left-hand side of the corridor. Seeing no illustrations or hieroglyphics Farak, along with Charles and Jacques, began pounding on different places on the wall. Meriaten watched for a moment. Then, holding her hand in front of her, she said in a commanding voice, "*Open Sesame,*" and the door cracked open.

"How'd you do that, Meriaten?" Charles cried out in surprise.

"As a noted person once said, 'A magician never reveals their secrets.' Besides," Meriaten said with a mischievous smile, "I saw Jacques pull on a silver cord to open one of the secret doorways."

"Jacques, you've been holding out on me!" Charles admonished him.

"Huh?" Jacques shrugged innocently.

Together, Farak and Charles pried open the secret stone door, making a gap large enough for their party to slip through. Walking toward the sound of water, the explorers discovered a large, ornately-carved pink stone fountain. Water dripped down from a stone pipe originating in the ceiling. It then trickled down over the edge of the bowl, falling gently into a small shimmering stream that disappeared in the shadows. Without saying anything, Jacques passed out the copper cups. After they had drunk their fill, Jacques gathered the cups.

Meriaten lit her lantern and called out, "Oh my!" Jacques immediately moved beside the girl, ready to defend her. The two boys followed. Ten feet in front of them, lit up by the shadowy light of the lantern, was a life-sized leopard. Standing beside the leopard was a young woman dressed in leopard skin. On her head, she wore a crown of seven leaves. The leopard and the woman looked so lifelike, it took the four travelers a few seconds to realize they were staring at statues.

"Its Seshat!" Meriaten said. She walked towards the leopard, then reached out and gave it a pat on its head.

"Hello, Seshat," Jacques said, bowing to the beautiful statue. "May I ask if it was you who translated all the stories from Cuneiform into hieroglyphics?"

"No, Jacques, this is the original Seshat. My mother told me about her. She's from the pre-dynastic era of Egypt, before the pharaohs, before written history, actually," Meriaten replied.

"I've never even heard of Seshat. Is she a goddess?" Charles asked, retrieving pen and paper from his shoulder bag.

"No, she is not a goddess. She was called a divine being," Meriaten replied. "According to Mother, Seshat was created by God, with the charge to discover and invent methods and tools that would help people live successfully in large communities. Mother says when people were living as hunter-gatherers in small tribes, they had little need for farming tools. They didn't need methods for distributing goods and services, or to design large buildings. Seshat was the first scientist as well as the first mathematician.

"And you," Meriaten said, indicating Charles, "might be interested to know she was the creator of written language and the first poet."

"Funny, I always heard it was Djehuty or Thoth who did all this," Charles said, sitting down on the floor in front of the statues, pen and paper in hand.

Meriaten shook her head. "According to my mother, it was Seshat. After inventing all these tools, she told God she didn't want to teach what she'd created to the people on earth. The Creator gave Djehuty, meaning he who is like the Ibis, the task of teaching all Seshat had invented and developed."

"Sehsat didn't even want to take credit for what she accomplished. Since Djehuty was the teacher of all knowledge, people naturally believed he was the creator," Meriaten continued. "Many believe Seshat was the daughter of Thoth or his consort. Mother says that's because the later Egyptians refused to believe that Egypt was originally a matriarchal society."

"That's interesting, Meriaten. Dr. Awyan, the Key Holder who lives across the road from the Sphinx, also believes Egypt was originally matriarchal," Charles said.

Meriaten picked up two candles and a box of matches she discovered behind the statues. She gave one candle to Charles and one to Farak.

"See these pots on the pillars beside the statues of Seshat and her leopard? They are fire bowls," she whispered. "The high priestess has one in her temple. Did you know that all high priestesses of the Tomb of a Thousand Names go by the name Seshat? When our high priestess takes on her form, she lights her fire bowl."

Mother says that inside the bowl is something called *naphtha*," Meriaten continued. "It's a kind of fuel. The high priestess just brings the candles close to the edge of the bowl, and the flame ignites the fumes." Meriaten lit the candles held by Farak and Charles. "Both of you do this at the same time for effect," she instructed the boys. "Just wait until I count to three.

Jacques heard Meriaten and, attempting to stop the boys from what he viewed as a dangerous deed, called out "Wait!" But it was too late. Farak and Charles brought their candles near the large fire bowls. There was a loud whoosh. The flames from the fire bowls lit up their entire surroundings. Behind Seshat and her leopard were eight great pillars, nearly sixteen feet tall. Each perimeter was nearly three feet in circumference.

Each column was covered with hundreds, maybe thousands, of hieroglyphics and pictographs. The pillars held up a ceiling painted a deep blue, covered in white stars. Dark lines connected some of these stars. Farak identified them as forming ancient Egyptian constellations.

To the right of the pillars was a multicolored building made from talatat, the bricks invented by Akhenaten and Yuba that the builder and his sons and his sons used to construct the Pharaoh's new capital city, Tel el Armana.

Carrying her lantern, Meriaten ran up the seven steps leading to the arched entrance of the coral-colored building, the others following in her wake. Off a main hallway were small rooms, five on each side, making ten in all. In each room was stone, three feet high and long enough for a person to lie on.

Jacques looked into the first room, which was painted a dark blue. He thought about taking a short nap but instead followed the others. Each succeeding room was a different color: coral, turquoise, yellow, green, dark blue, and white. The hallway ended in one large room with alabaster jars, many with lids shaped like animals, lining the walls.

"I wonder what's in these jars?" Charles mused, breaking the silence.

"Probably oils," Meriaten replied, picking up something from the floor. "This is a sistrum, a healing instrument used by the ancient Egyptians. It's still used by some modern Egyptian healers."

On the top part of the sistrum's handle was a woman's head with cow ears. "This, of course, is Hathor, goddess of music, dance, love and family," Meriaten noted.

Above the handle were three layers of thick copper wires set in a long, oval copper frame. Strung on each wire were seven copper coins. Meriaten shook the instrument. It made a drum-like, jangling sound. Jacques leaned over and picked up a small harp. He ran his fingers across the strings and they emitted a soft, melodious sound.

"That's a lyre, Jacques," Meriaten informed him.

"Really? It looks like a truth-teller to me." Jacques chuckled at his own joke.

"This is serious, Jacques. This is a sacred space. I'm sure this is a replica of Nefertiti's healing temple, the one Akhenaten built for her after the death of their daughter," Meriaten said, shaking the sistrum several times.

"Meriaten is right, Jacques," Charles agreed. "This place feels sacred."

"I will apologize to Seshat on the way out, which I think should be soon," Jacques said.

But Farak had found and lit several candles in ornate candle holders made of alabaster, like the jars around the room. The candles and Meriaten's lantern revealed hieroglyphics on the western wall.

"These hieroglyphics are written by Seshat," Farak observed. "Charles, are you ready?"

"Yes, I'm ready," he said.

As the Bedouin teen began interpreting the hieroglyphics, Jacques softly strummed the strings of the lyre. Meanwhile, Meriaten shook the sistrum.

I am Seshat.

Holding a pen in my right hand and an ink pot in my left,
I bring the past into the present,
And the present into the future.
They call me the inventor of the written word, the record keeper.
I am Seshat, Lady of the Seven Stars,
Watcher of the skies.
I recognized the patterns and movement of the stars and planets,
And named the constellations, allowing for the creation of the first map
So travelers could find their way through the the cool nights of the desert.
It was I who first observed the movements of the sun and the moon,
And from this devised a calendar, the friend of farmers,
Harbinger of the coming floods and reminder of the celebration of the
sacred days.
I am Seshat. I have been called the first architect,
Creator of the scale and other tools of measurement,
Allowing for the perception of time and space itself
And the refinement of geometry, allowing for the construction
Of cities, palaces, pyramids, and temples.

I am the revealer of the sacred mathematics
Found in music, art, and dance.

I have been called the curer of diseases, restorer of health,
Discoverer of the magic of sound and medicinal plants.
And I am Seshat, the great storyteller,
For it is through story that all I have discovered or developed
Is passed on to the people of Egypt and beyond.
And now, you who are reading this
Inside the healing temple of Nefertiti
Must also become storytellers.

"Is she talking to us?" Jacques asked, eyes wide.

"It appears so, Jacques," Charles replied with a laugh.

"Seshat's words sounded so beautiful with you playing the lyre behind them," Meriaten said. "When did you learn to play the lyre, Jacques?"

"Oh, Jacques can play any instrument. He graduated from college with a degree in music," Charles said, sounding proud of his guardian's talent.

"Graduating from college with a music degree does not mean you can play every instrument, Charles," Jacques insisted. "However, when I strummed the lyre, I recognized that its strings were tuned to the key of C. Any stringed instrument tuned to C can be strummed or plucked, and the result will inevitably be harmonious."

As Jacques returned the lyre to its place on the floor, he noticed something shiny next to a pot with a lid shaped like a baboon. Picking it up, he was shocked to see it was a pendant like the one he was wearing, given to him by the old man in the City of the Dead. What was it doing here in Seshat's temple? He was about to go down the rabbit hole again, but then Jacques reminded himself they had to find the exit to this Tomb of a Thousand Names. He'd have to think about the meaning of the pendant later. To serve as a reminder, he pulled his own pendant out from under his gallabiyah. It glittered in the candlelight.

As the four reached the statues, Jacques bowed to Seshat, saying, "Thank you, Mademoiselle Seshat, for this lovely experience. Or is this a dream? I am not sure. *Pardonnez-moi.* I apologize if I failed to treat this sacred experience with the proper regard."

"I realize you might have more to say," Jacques continued. "However, as the leader of this intrepid group, I know we must leave, returning to the light so we can begin our mission of telling stories and transforming the world."

Jacques placed the pendant he'd just discovered inside the healing temple at the foot of the statue of Seshat. Charles wondered if Jacques was serious or being overly dramatic.

The travelers headed towards the door, but before they reached it, Charles called out, "Wait!" He was standing in front of some more writing. This time, it was in English. "I don't believe it," Charles said.

"What don't you believe?" Meriaten asked.

"We are in the Tomb of a Thousand Names, in Egypt, and on the wall is a poem by Percy Bysshe Shelley," Charles answered. "You're right, Jacques. This must be a dream."

"Why is it any stranger than anything else we've found here?" Meriaten asked.

"Because before my trip to Egypt, my mother sent me a book of poetry by Percy Bysshe Shelley," Charles replied. "My mother wrote in a letter that when she read his poetry, she thought of me. She said she believes I will someday be a great writer like Shelley."

"Your mother is right," Farak said. "Of that, I am certain."

"Here is why it's so coincidental," Charles continued. "Aside from the copy of *The Egyptian Book of the Dead* my father gave me, I brought one other book to Egypt: *The Poetical Works of Percy Bysshe Shelley*. Then somehow, out of all the writers in the world, a part of one of Shelley's poems appears in English on the wall of the Tomb of a Thousand Names. This is what it says:

'A man, to be greatly good, must imagine intensely and comprehensively; he must put himself in the place of another and many others; the pains and pleasures of his species must become his own. The great instrument of moral good is the imagination.'

"I agree. I love imagination," Jacques said, "Right now, I am imaging emerging from this Tomb of a Thousand Names and seeing sunlight again."

"And I am imagining seeing my mother again," Meriaten said, skipping out the sliding door of Seshat's temple.

As Charles started to follow Meriaten, he tripped over Jacques' foot, causing him to drop all the papers on which he'd written throughout this long trck through the Tomb of a Thousand Names. His papers flew everywhere. Farak and Jacques stopped to help Charles gather his writing.

Suddenly, they heard a scream.

CHAPTER 75

MR. SMITH AND THE RESCUE

"I t's Meri," Farak said, rushing towards the end of the Tomb of a Thousand Names.

Charles grabbed the last of his scattered papers and ran after Jacques, who was several yards behind Farak. There was a dramatic turn to the right; then they spilled out into a room. The southern end was covered with large boulders, casting the exit in dark and menacing shadows. Only a few shards of light, spilling through the cracks in the rocks, hinted that the Path of Knowledge had come to an end.

Before Jacques and Charles reached the boulders, Farak turned to face them. He held a finger in front of his mouth, his right hand raised in warning. They could hear voices from the other side of the boulders.

"Ask the girl what she is doing here," a gruff male voice commanded.

Charles, Farak, and Jacques knew it was Mr. Smith speaking. Another male voice repeated Mr. Smith's question, this time in Arabic. Meriaten answered in Arabic.

"What did she say?" Mr. Smith demanded.

"She asked what we are doing here," the man translated.

"Ask her if she is alone," Mr. Smith instructed.

The three remaining travelers exchanged worried glances. It was all they could do to keep from jumping out of the tunnel, saying, "No, she is not alone! She is very much under our protection." But Farak signaled that they should wait.

The second man spoke in Arabic, then in English to Mr. Smith. "The girl says she is here with her mother. She claims she has a stomachache. Her mother has gone a short distance away to pick some herbs."

Mr. Smith leaned over the side of his camel and addressed Meriaten directly. "Have you seen a boy about your age?"

Meriaten waited until the translator spoke in Arabic before answering. The second man relayed her response. "She says she has seen plenty of boys her age."

"She is being evasive," Mr. Smith grumbled.

"What does that mean?" the other voice asked.

"Never mind!" Mr. Smith retorted. "Tell her I am looking for my nephew who is about twelve. He speaks English. Ask her if she has seen him."

The bilingual henchman questioned Meriaten again. "She says she has not seen your nephew," he translated.

"I am getting tired of this. Grab the girl," Mr. Smith demanded.

"Wait," his companion said. "The girl says her father is Holder of the Sword of the Quarter Moon. She says he is a Sheikh, that everyone knows him, and that he has a bad temper and a terrible reputation."

"Well, I don't see anybody around here," Mr. Smith shouted.

Meriaten said some words in Arabic that shook the translator's confidence. "She said that since I am a Bedouin, I should know her father. I told her I might have heard of him," the man said with fear in his voice.

"I don't believe her. Get off your camel and get that girl," Mr. Smith commanded.

Meriaten spoke again to Mr. Smith's accomplice. "The girl says if we try to take her, she doesn't want to think what will happen to us," he relayed.

"Tell her to come here," Mr. Smith ordered.

Meanwhile, Jacques, Farak, and Charles gathered rocks the size of baseballs, ready to rescue Meriaten. The three began to wind their way between boulders. As Farak emerged, he saw a great storm coming from the west side of the exit to the Tomb of a Thousand Names. At the same time, he heard a high-pitched undulating vocal sound. Jacques believed the scream could terrify a ghost.

Mr. Smith called out to his companion. "Where are you going? Come back!"

"It is the Holder of the Sword of the Quarter Moon. I will not stay." The Bedouin kicked the sides of his camel and headed east up the sandy path.

Seeing the dust coming from behind the boulders, Mr. Smith called after the Bedouin. "Hey, wait! Wait for me!"

Farak watched as Mr. Smith galloped up the sandy path, following his nefarious companion. The Egyptian teen looked back towards the dust storm. Emerging from a cloud of yellowish sand was a woman, her long salt-and-pepper hair streaming wildly behind her. She was traveling on a camel, full speed, which is forty miles an hour. She reached the bottom of the sandy path where the two men had disappeared. She pulled on the reins and her camel slowed.

"Mother!" Farak called out.

"That is your mother?" Jacques asked in amazement.

"I have never heard you use the *zaghrouta*," Farak said in wonder.

"I don't know what the zaghrouta is, but it certainly scared those men away," Charles remarked.

"It scared me, too," Jacques claimed. "How does one make that sound?"

"You make the sound of a zaghrouta by rapidly moving your tongue back and forth in your mouth, combined with a high-pitched scream. In English, it's called ululating," Meriaten explained. "My mother is teaching me how to make this sound, but I had no idea how useful it could be if you want to scare someone away."

"It was also helpful that my mother was carrying a sword," Farak said, then asked, "Why do you have the royal sword, Mother?"

Farak's mother answered him in Arabic, then spoke briefly with Meriaten. Translating for Jacques and Charles, the girl told them, "Farak's mother says they'll have to discuss the Sword of the Quarter Moon later." With that, the Mother of the Tarabin Tribe rode off in pursuit of Mr. Smith.

"Thank heavens your mother arrived when she did, Farak," Charles said breathlessly.

"I have to admit, I was a little afraid I might be kidnapped," the girl in the dusty galabeyha said.

Farak turned to Meriaten, saying, "You were a true heroine. I do not know what would have happened to us had you not been here."

"I knew you were behind me, or I wouldn't have been so courageous," Meriaten replied, blushing slightly.

The travelers and Farak's mother watched as a caravan of camels stopped in front of the exit to the Tomb of a Thousand Names. Rehima and Subira were in the lead, followed by Meriaten's mother. Saki, the temple guide, was riding Stubborn Sahara.

"Sahara is being uncooperative. Why am I not surprised?" Charles asked, shaking his head.

"And look, there is Caboose. That poor man holding his reins is trying to get him to speed up. *Bonne chance*!" Jacques called out with a laugh, wishing the rider good luck in French.

"That poor man is my father," Meriaten informed him.

Jacques corrected himself. "I meant that impressive, dignified man."

Meriaten's mother ordered her camel to kneel for her to dismount. She ran over to her daughter and hugged her, asking in Arabic if all were safe.

"We're all safe, Mother," Meriaten answered in English.

Astride her camel, Farak's mother returned from following the two men to the top of the sandy ridge.

"Mother!" he said, baffled by the spectacle his mother had made.

"Now that I know you are all secure, I can make a confession," the Mother of the Tarabin Tribe said. "That was the most fun I have ever had in my entire life."

"You're the best camel-rider I ever met," Charles said with admiration.

"Thank you, Charles Tarabin Stratton," Farak's mother said with a broad smile. "Now I must go and help prepare dinner."

Charles turned to the girl standing beside him and said, "One minute she's chasing a criminal, the next minute she's fixing dinner. What a mother! Meriaten, when did you meet the Holder of the Sword of the Quarter Moon?"

"Never. I totally made him up!" Meriaten answered.

"You made him up, and the Bedouin believed you?" Farak said, impressed.

"Didn't Charles' poet, Percy Shelley, say that the best tool for good was the imagination?" Meriaten asked slyly.

"When you grow up, Meri, I don't know whether you are going to be a great writer like Charles, or a great actress. Whatever occupation you choose, I am sure it is going to have the word great in front of it," the Egyptian teen said.

A man from among the caravan come near, reached out and hugged Meriaten. He was grinning from ear to ear.

"Father, let me introduce you to my companions," she said, grinning back. "We traveled the Path of Knowledge together through the Tomb of a Thousand Names. I think I might be the luckiest girl in the world to travel with such brave and wonderful initiates."

Charles thought Meriaten was laying the praise on a little thick, but he didn't say so.

Meriaten said, "We didn't expect you, Father. How did you get here?"

"It's rather complicated. I have a student named Tiye. She informed me that her mother, Mandisa, told her a man named Mr. Smith was chasing a boy named Charles," he explained. "She said that this Mr. Smith was accompanied by a nefarious Bedouin, and that they were on their way to the Temple of Sobek. I knew that you and your mother were here."

"I called the captain of the Egyptian police and told him about Mr. Smith. I said that he was somewhere in the Western Desert, but I couldn't tell him the exact location," he continued. "I asked them to be prepared to pick up Mr. Smith and his henchman when they reached the green belt. I had no idea my daughter would frighten this Mr. Smith off before I could rescue her."

With that, he gave the girl another hug. Meriaten's mother walked toward her husband and daughter.

"Mom, this is Jacques Gerard," Meriaten said. "He loves your peanut butter cookies."

"That is true," Jacques said, bowing slightly. "Without your cookies, I doubt I would have survived our adventure through the Tomb of a Thousand Names."

"Oh, here comes the High Priestess. Let me introduce you. This is Jacques," the girl said. "You should hear him play the lyre."

"Come on," Meriaten's mother said, "Let's help Farak's mother with dinner."

The High Priestess turned to Jacques and said, "I would love to hear you play the lyre, Mr. Gerard."

"I told Meriaten that anyone can play the lyre if the strings have been tuned correctly," Jacques replied humbly.

"Can I learn to play a lyre?" Charles asked his chaperone.

"I would be happy to teach you," Jacques said, looking not at Charles but straight into the dark eyes of the High Priestess or, as she was sometimes called, Seshat.

"You are wondering how old I am," the High Priestess observed.

"No. Yes. I mean, you do not look very old," Jacques said, fumbling for the right words. "It is just that you feel old." He corrected himself. "That's not right. What I mean is, it feels like you are the ancient personification of knowledge. Does that make any sense to you?"

"Yes, Jacques, it does make sense," the dark-eyed woman said. "Seshat is the record-keeper, but she is also the discoverer and developer of all humans' need to live in cooperation with each other. The Daughters of Seshat follow in her footsteps. Seshat is the coordinator of the Daughters of Aten and other initiates."

"We took the path of the initiates. Does this mean you're now our leader?" Charles asked.

"Up to this time, we have not accepted children or men into our order," she replied. "However, things are changing. It is up to the High Priestess—up to Seshat, in this case, up to me—to decide who shall be asked to take the pledge of allegiance."

"Allegiance to what?" Jacques asked.

"To the Earth and all living things," the High Priestess replied. "It is up to Seshat to decide the time and the steps that must be taken, but we are given signs."

"It's the pyramids, isn't it?" Charles said. "It's the pyramids coming together."

"We do not often review the journeys of those who take the Path of Knowledge," the High Priestess said. "However, Meriaten told me you discovered a third pyramid."

Charles said solemnly, "I know you have a pyramid, Farak's family has a pyramid, and Jacques has one in his shoulder bag. I have a pyramid, but it's a replica. In other words, it's a fake."

"There is no such thing as a fake pyramid, Charles," the High Priestess assured him. "It was your replica pyramid that brought the other three together."

"Wow! I didn't think of it that way," Charles said. "That makes sense. The pyramids are the sign."

"So we have three out of four pyramids. If the fourth is found, what is it signaling?" Jacques asked.

"That is something we will have to figure out, right, Jacques?" Seshat answered with a bell-like laugh.

Jacques wondered why everyone kept asking him things he knew nothing about. "Charles and I must return to the Château du Mont in France," he said. "He has classes, and I must return to work."

"You know, Jacques," the High Priestess advised, "you do not have to live in a tomb or a temple to be an initiate, to be of service to the future."

Just then, Meriaten came running, yelling, "Charles, did you hear? We are going to camp out tonight, and tomorrow we're going to Tel el Armana!"

"Tel el Armana? Tomorrow?" Charles yelled back at the girl.

The High Priestess spoke to the boy beside her. "I heard from Meriaten that there was something you needed to do in Tel el Armana."

"There is something," Charles said breathlessly. "I have to talk to the Ghost of Tomb 11. Well, I don't have to, but I want to. It's one of the reasons I came to Egypt. This is a wish come true. Is that alright with you, Jacques?" Before his guardian could answer, Charles ran to join Meriaten.

The High Priestess addressed Jacques. "Meriaten told me you discovered many hieroglyphics of the number 11 in Nefertiti's relief."

"For some reason," Jacques replied, "when I stared at the painting the upside down U's and 1's—which, of course, means 11—jumped out at me.

The High Priestess laughed at the thought of the French man teaching her about Egyptian math. "It is strange, Jacques Gerard, that no other initiate has mentioned the Egyptian elevens in this painting. What do you think it means?" she asked.

"I think it means there is a fourth pyramid in Tomb 11, Tel el Armana," he answered.

"I agree," the High Priestess told Jacques. "That is why you will join this caravan leaving tomorrow for Tel el Armana."

Jacques felt like yelling to his camel, "We are going to Tel el Armana tomorrow, Caboose Sadat. Get ready!" But he didn't.

"Meriaten knows the riddle of the four pyramids," the High Priestess noted. "Maybe it is time to bring them all together. Here is the third relic pyramid."

The High Priestess handed Jacques a beautiful padded black velvet bag covered with gold beads and jewels. He didn't need to open the bag; he could feel the pyramid shape through the cloth.

"We will have dinner soon. You would all benefit from an early bedtime," the High Priestess suggested. "Your caravan leaves before dawn."

"You are not coming?" Jacques asked.

"No, I am staying here," Seshat answered.

"I hope I will see you again," Jacques said.

"I always keep in touch with those who have traveled the Path of Knowledge," the High Priestess said. She waved as she walked back to her camel.

Jacques found himself alone. He looked at the people around him. They were making dinner, putting up tents, unpacking camels. He was too tired to move or think. Suddenly, something bumped his back, hard. He turned around and found himself face-to-face with a camel.

"Oh, it is you, Caboose," the Château du Mont's all-around man said. "Did you miss me?" Caboose snorted.

"I missed you, too, but I notice that you have gone back to your old ways. You made it quite difficult for Meriaten's father," Jacques chided his camel. Reaching up and patting him under his furry neck, Jacques asked Caboose if he would like to go to Tel el Amarna the next day. The camel brayed loudly, which Jacques took to mean yes.

"About your name. Do you mind if I call you Caboose Sadat? That way, you can be both a follower and leader; maybe that can apply to all of us," Jacques said, laughing at his own cleverness.

The last light of the sun disappeared in the west. The moon had yet to rise. The sky was like black velvet. Little tents had been raised. Beside each tent was a glowing lantern. From where Jacques stood, it looked like the night sky reflected on the desert floor.

"Come on, Jacques!" Charles called. "Dinner is ready."

After dinner, the boy and his guardian walked together to their tent. Charles looked up at a star-filled sky. He asked, "Can you see the Milky Way, and do you see those three stars in a row?"

"I do, Charles," Jacques said.

"That's Orion's belt," Charles said, pointing. "Dr. Awyan says those three stars have something to do with the placement of the Pyramids of Giza."

As man and boy looked up at the Milky Way, a large shooting star streaked across the sky, traveling from west to east.

"I think that meteor is pointing the way to Tel el Armana," Charles said. "You know, Jacques, this trip to Egypt didn't turn out the way I thought it would, but I wouldn't change it for anything."

"Me neither, Charles. Me neither," Jacques said.

CHAPTER 76

SAMY AND THE SCARAB RING

Everyone in the Pizza Hut was buzzing with the news that Jacques and Charles had been reported found and safe, and that Mr. Smith and his henchman had been detained by the Egyptian police.

Dr. Awyan came in the blue door and tossed a package to Fran and another to David. Fran immediately tore open the brown paper package and pulled out a periwinkle-blue turban. He plopped it on his head, saying, "It just fits, Dr. Awyan. Now I can really blend in, just like Charles."

David carefully unwrapped his package. It was a tan gallabiyah. He put it over his clothes. It fit perfectly.

"Cool!" Fran exclaimed. "Now you have a gallabiyah just like me, and you have a kaffiyeh. We can both blend in."

"I have one more surprise for you all," Dr. Awyan announced with his toothy grin. "We have heard Fran suggest several times that we just needed to get on camels and go out and find Charles and Jacques. Well, that is what you are going to do today."

"Whoopee!" Fran said, falling to the floor.

"Where are we going?" David asked.

"Tel el Armana, the ruins of Akhenaten's capital city," the old Egyptian answered.

"Tel el Armana!" David repeated in amazement.

Dr. Awyan looked around the room, then announced, "I suggest you all dress for a camel ride."

With a wave of his hand, the founder of the School of Khemitology walked out of the pizza parlor. Dr. Stratton, Alfred, Bernadette, and Mademoiselle Fleuret followed as though the elderly Egyptologist were the Pied Piper. They each greeted Samy as he entered the Pizza Hut.

"Where is everybody going?" the taxi driver asked Fran.

"They are getting dressed appropriately," Fran answered.

"Appropriately for what?" asked the man in the blue Hawaiian shirt imprinted with red surfboards and red woody station wagons.

"It's just like I have been saying from the beginning," Fran said. "We all need to get on camels and go find Charles and Jacques. David has a gallabiyah, and I have a turban."

"I can see that," Samy said, smiling at the boy in the blue turban.

"Come on, Fran," David said. "Let's get ready. I know where to look for Charles."

"Where?" asked the ginger-haired boy.

"It's a secret," David answered in a whisper.

Samy walked to where Mrs. Montgomery was packing up her large purple bag. He needed to get the straight story.

"We are going on a tour bus to the archaeological site of Tel el Armana," Mrs. Montgomery explained. "Once we have arrived, Farak's father has arranged for everyone to take a camel ride from the Nile River outside the city of Tel el Amarna to the King's Road."

"I guess you don't need the tour bus of the Grateful Dead today," Samy said, pointing to the vehicle parked in front of the Pizza Hut.

"Not today, but we do need you, Samy," the mystery writer said. "You can ride in the tour bus with us. I hear it has great air conditioning."

Mandisa gave Samy a plate of food. Twenty minutes later, the guest house adventurers began streaming back into the Pizza Hut. Dr. Stratton and Alfred were in matching safari outfits, perfectly pressed. Dr. Bernstein had on her usual white long-sleeved shirt and tan pants. Mademoiselle Fleuret swished into the room wearing her full circle-floral skirt, pink tights peeking out from its hem. Her outfit was completed by her blue artist's smock, pink tennis shoes with yellow laces, and a scarf that tastefully matched her shoes. Sparkling at her neck was the stunning necklace Farak's family had given her.

Bernadette, walking in behind the art teacher, was wearing jeans and a long-sleeved yellow jacket. She carried a straw hat in her hand. Fran, David and Charles wore their tan gallabiyah. David wore a matching headscarf, and Fran had on his sky-blue turban. They all looked ready to jump on camels to find Charles and Jacques.

The excited conversation stopped when a man wearing a flowing tan gallabiyah walked in the door.

"Hello, Dr. McAllister. Thank you for picking up Aamen," Mrs. Montgomery said.

"How did you know who he was, Grandmother?" David asked.

"Simple deduction, David," she answered. "He walked into the Pizza Hut like he belonged here, and he was the only person I have never seen before."

"That makes sense," her grandson said.

"I believe it was the novelist Richard Yates who wrote, '*I've come to believe that only a very, very few matters in the world can ever be trusted to make sense.*' To me, that makes sense, given that nothing has made sense since we set foot on Egyptian soil or sand," Mr. Montgomery said.

David and his grandmother laughed at Mr. Montgomery's attempt to imitate his wife.

"Scientists are always looking for the laws behind something that appears senseless," Dr. Bernstein said.

"Yes, Dr. Bernstein. With you and my wife around, things seem to be jumping in and of out of these laws. People disappearing. People gathering. People riding camels. Mothers and grandmothers becoming mystery writers," George said, picking up one of his wife's sugar cookies from a plate on the table.

"If it looks like there is no sense, no meaning, we have to strive to find it. It's a requirement if we are going to find any sense of purpose in our lives," Mrs. Montgomery said, summing up the conversation.

"Well said. I particularly like the part about finding a sense of purpose," Dr. Bernstein remarked.

"I hate to interrupt this interesting conversation, but there is a woman outside by the bus of the Grateful Dead," Alfred said. "She looks confused. Maybe she's lost."

"It's Madame Constance!" Fran exclaimed. "And she's dressed just like you and Dr. Stratton."

"I expected her," Dr. Bernstein said, "and she is just in time, too."

"She told you she was coming?" Mademoiselle Fleuret asked.

"No, I just had a hunch," the physicist answered.

David and Fran ran out the door. The guest house group watched through the plate-glass window as the boys pointed to the Sphinx, which looked quite jolly this morning, and then toward the Pizza Hut.

When the older woman in a safari outfit walked in the door, Mrs. Montgomery said, "Welcome, Madame Constance," and everyone in the Pizza Hut applauded. "You are just in time. The tour bus is here. Grab your lunch sacks."

"Wait!" Fran said. "I thought we were riding camels to go find Charles."

"It is a five-hour bus ride to Tel el Armana. Who knows how long a camel ride that might be?" Mrs. Montgomery said. "Farak's father and grandfather are arranging camel rides for all of us from the Nile outside the city of Tel el Amarna to the King's Road. Let's go."

Mrs. Montgomery was standing by the bus driver inside the bus, with a clipboard in one hand and a microphone with a curly black cord in the other.

She said into the mic, "We don't want to lose anyone. When I call out your name, say here or present."

"Mr. George Montgomery."

"You know I am here, Dorothy. I am sitting by you, here in the front seat," her husband said.

"David Montgomery.

"Here."

"Dr. Bernstein."

"Here."

"Fran Bernstein."

"I'm here, Mrs. Montgomery."

"Mademoiselle Fleuret."

"Present."

"Bernadette."

"*Je suis là.*"

"Dr. Stratton."

"I am definitely here, Mrs. Montgomery," the professor answered.

"Alfred P. Hart."

"Here."

"Dr. McAllister."

"Present, Madam Montgomery."

"Aamen Halabi."

"I am here, Mrs. Montgomery."

Samy entered the bus carrying a portable tape player. Mrs. Montgomery added his name to the list, then called out, "Samy, the man without a last name, are you here or present?"

"Here," Samy called out as he moved to the middle of the bus and sat in a seat in front of Mademoiselle Fleuret.

He said to her, "I brought music."

Three more people stood outside the bus.

"Hello, Yousef Awyan; thank you so much for coming. And who is behind you? Oh, Mandisa and Tiye, welcome."

Mrs. Montgomery looked out the bus door and noted a closed sign on the door of the Pizza Hut.

"You have to say here or present," Fran called out from the back seat of the bus.

"You are right, Fran," Mrs. Montgomery said.

"Yousef Awyan."

"Here."

"Mandisa."

"She's here," Fran confirmed. "Mandisa, do you and Tiye want to sit back here with me and David?"

"Tiye."

"*Huna*, Arabic for here," the girl in a white headscarf said, moving back towards the boys in the rear of the bus.

"Okay, we have sixteen people, not counting our bus driver Mohamed Salah. He asks that we call him Mohamed. As you heard, it is a five-hour drive. Mohamed claims his bus has the best air conditioning in Cairo, so we will be very comfortable. Alright, Mohamed, we are ready."

Samy was sitting in an aisle seat across from Bernadette. He took out a small box from his shirt pocket and opened it. It glittered gold.

"What do you have there, Samy?" Bernadette asked as she leaned across the aisle to take a closer look.

"It's a gift for Jacques," Samy said with a smile. "I got it from my cousin at a good price."

"It's a ring with a scarab on it," Bernadette said.

Samy gave her the ring for a closer examination.

"It is lovely," Bernadette said.

"Yes, it even has a tasteful bit of lapis lazuli embedded in the wings of the scarab. It is believed that lapis lazuli represents strength, wisdom, loyalty, royalty, intellect, and truth. Jacques tried this ring on in my cousin's store but reluctantly he gave it back to my cousin, trading it for three silver bookmarks with Bastet the cat goddess engraved on them."

"Mademoiselle Fleuret and I found two bookmarks that match this description in our room yesterday," Bernadette said. "We didn't know where these bookmarks came from. Mrs. Montgomery said that she also found a bookmark with a cat on it in her room. Do you think they were from Jacques?"

"Yes, Jacques must have secretly given you all a present. On the bookmark is Bastet, the daughter of the sun god Ra. Bastet is associated with protection. I guess Jacques wanted to protect his women," Samy said with a laugh. "Considering all Jacques must have gone through on his search for Charles, I thought he would appreciate this little trinket as a memento of his trip to Egypt."

"That is very considerate of you, Samy. Jacques could certainly use some of the qualities of lapis lazuli," Bernadette said, turning to stare out the window.

"It's real gold, 18 karat. Jacques often speaks of gold and of scarabs. He seemed to have quite an attraction to both," Samy said with a mischievous smile.

Bernadette handed the ring back to Samy, thinking that Jacques was a very mysterious fellow.

The girl in the yellow jacket watched as Madame Constance walked unsteadily from the front of the bus to where Dr. Bernstein was sitting.

Madame Constance asked Fran's mother if she could sit with her for a moment.

"Of course, I would be happy to have company," Dr. Bernstein said to the woman dressed like she was heading for a safari.

"Fran told me that you knew I was coming. Did Dr. Awyan tell you?" the headmistress of the Château du Mont inquired.

"No, he did not tell me. And I didn't say I knew you were coming, but that I had a feeling, a hunch, an intuition, or you could call it a guess."

"In the classes you are to teach this summer, you plan on exploring the idea that there is a science, a physics, behind these feelings, hunches, or whatever they are?"

"Yes," Dr. Bernstein said. "We are exploring the structure of *spacetime* and the idea that we live in a web of information, that we are all connected, entangled, as we say. We will be studying Einstein-Podolsky-Rosen's paradox, using field equations, and also the concepts of black holes and wormholes. In my classes, we will attempt to show, through mathematics and thought experiments, that there is a scientific explanation behind such esoteric subjects as remote viewing, distance communication, distance healing and, perhaps, time travel. Maybe it is black holes and wormholes that connect us and allow for the development of a web of information."

"It sounds complicated. But why I am asking is, well—you see—I heard your voice in my head," Madame Constance said. "It said you wanted me to come, that you were encouraging me to come, and that you were sure I could find a way. I called my sister, and it popped out of my mouth that I needed her to run the school for a week or so. She has done this before. She lives in Italy. She said she would come immediately."

"Then, it seemed like my ticket to Cairo appeared magically, well, not magically. Actually, I just picked up the phone and ordered a ticket. However, everything went so smoothly. The next thing I knew, I was on a plane bound for Cairo. What I want to know is, did you somehow summon me, put it in my head that I must come to Egypt?"

Dr. Bernstein smiled and reached over and hugged Madame Constance.

She said, "Yes, yes, I did, and you came right on time, Madame Constance, and dressed appropriately."

"You know, I have always dreamed of taking a camel ride in the desert," Madame Constance mused.

"Yes, I know," Dr. Bernstein said with a smile.

Mademoiselle Fleuret and Samy sang surfer tunes as they passed scenes of the working people of Egypt and the sparkle of the Nile River.

The bus pulled into a parking lot filled with horse trailers and livestock trucks. David was ready to find his roommate. Fran was ready to find his camel. Dr. Stratton was wondering what he would say to his grandson. There was excitement in the desert air.

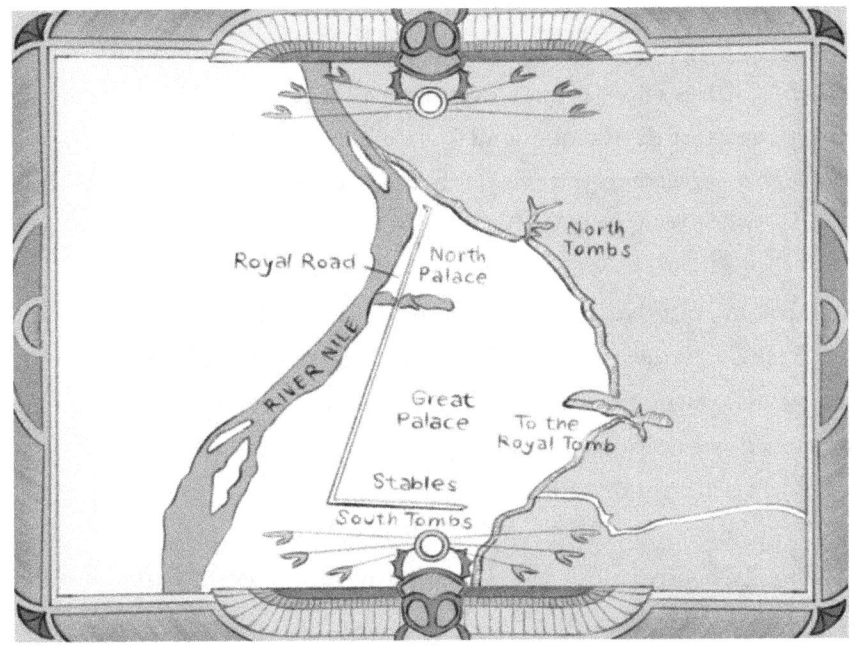

CHAPTER 77

THE CARAVAN TO TEL EL ARMANA

Peeking out the flap of the tiny tent, Charles saw that the thousands of stars that had filled the night sky had faded into the slate color of early morning. He could hear the grumbling of camels and the soft sounds of people breaking camp. Between him and the oasis was a large campfire, with flames of orange and yellow wildly dancing here and there. Shadowy forms moved around the blazing fire. This was it, the day Charles had been waiting for. They would be going to Tel el Armana, Egypt. He glanced back inside the tent. In the pale lamplight, he could see Jacques zipped up in a mummy bag, sleeping like the living dead.

Ducking out of the tent, Charles was greeted by the chill of the early-morning desert. He jogged towards the fire and was silently greeted by

Meriaten and Farak. The girl poured him a cup of hot tea, adding milk and sugar. The cup felt warm in his cold hands.

"I was thinking how strange it is that we're going to Tel el Amarna today," Charles said. "You see, even after all that's happened, it turns out this is the exact day Jacques and I planned to tour Tel el Armana—the day before we were to leave for France. I guess it could be a coincidence, but doesn't it seem strange?"

"It appears we have all experienced a number of coincidences," Farak said, passing out flatbread with mango jelly spread on top.

"Yeah," Charles agreed. "It's almost felt like someone has been writing a story, purposely adding in extraordinary twists of fate. If I hadn't written down a lot of what happened over these last sixteen days, I wouldn't believe it myself."

"Oh, I have something for you, Charles," Meriaten said.

The girl handed him a rolled-up piece of parchment. Charles unrolled it and leaned closer to the fire to see what was on the paper. It was a hand-drawn map entitled the *City of the Sun's Disk*. "Wow, a map of Tel el Armana! Where did you get this?" Charles asked Meriaten.

"Last night, I asked my father to draw you this map," she replied. "Of course, he knows Tel el Amarna like the back of his hand. Remember, that's where my parents met. They were both working at the same archaeological dig. They fell in love and got married, just like in a fairy tale."

"This is a great map. Where's your father?" Charles asked, looking around the camp. "I need to thank him."

"You can't thank him now, because he has already left for Cairo," Meriaten said. "Father is teaching classes today. Mother is going to stay with the High Priestess, but I get to go with you to Tel el Armana. Isn't that great? Malika told Mother she'll keep an eye on me."

"Who's Malika?" Charles asked.

"Malika is the name of Farak's mother. It means princess or empress, doesn't it, Farak?" Without waiting for an answer, Meriaten added, "Malika says she seldom uses her given name, but she didn't want me calling her Farak's mother all the time."

"I wonder what I should call her?" Charles mused, picking up a piece of flatbread warmed by the fire.

"Just don't call her Your Majesty," Farak said with a laugh. "She does not like that. I used to her tease her with that name when I was young, and she would get so mad."

Jacques joined them, still wrapped in his mummy bag. Meriaten poured the sleepy-looking man a cup of tea from a large, blackened pot sitting on a grill near the fire. Subira and Rehima came from the oasis and joined the fireside group.

"I am glad you are up," Subira said. "The camels are saddled and ready to go. We will be leaving soon."

"You're coming, too?" Charles asked.

"Yes, Rehima and I are coming with you," Subira said with a smile.

"I'm so happy!" Charles exclaimed. "I'm not ready to say goodbye to you, and tomorrow Jacques and I will be leaving for France. I don't know how I'm going to thank you. Both of you have been so amazing, introducing me to the family in the desert and everything."

Rehima reached out and gave Charles a hug. Within a few minutes, the party was mounted on camels, ready to leave the Tomb of a Thousand Names beneath the Temple of Sobek for the capital city of Tel el Armana. It was a merry morning ride. Farak's mother and Meriaten took the lead. Jacques followed on Caboose. Charles was next on Sahara. Behind them were six cameleers.

"Who cares if I never got to take a boat ride on the Nile?" Charles thought as he rode through the desert, surrounded by camels and riders. He couldn't believe that he, Charles Dayton Stratton III, was in a real caravan headed for Tomb 11, Tel el Armana, Egypt.

The sun was still low in the eastern sky when the camels stepped out of the sandy desert into the green zone. A half-hour later, the camels clipped-clopped over a one-lane bridge that spanned the Nile River at one of its narrowest points. On the other side of the bridge, the caravan was greeted by several livestock trucks, a medium-sized bus, and a large lunch.

Subira informed the caravan that in order to save several hours of traveling on camels under the burning sun, the bus and trucks would transport them to Akhenaten's capital city. Charles boarded the bus and sat on the right side so he could better view the Nile that ran beside the road. The bus driver dodged donkey carts piled high with hay, drove past great ibises swooping over deep blue irrigation canals, and sped past small farms where men, women, and children picked fruit from mango trees or worked, bent over, in lush fields.

Charles again lamented not having his camera. But the scenery whooshed by so fast, he probably wouldn't have been able to capture the Egyptian countryside anyway. He told himself to just take photographs in his mind. After a pleasant few hours, the bus driver pulled into a gravel parking lot. The bus was followed by the trucks transporting the camels. Emerging from the bus, Charles unrolled the map Meriaten had given him. Jacques, Farak, Malika, and Meri gathered around him.

"See, we are here. This parking lot appears to be about 10 kilometers from the actual city of Tel el Amarna. I estimate it will take only a half-hour's camel ride to reach the main road," Charles said. "There are two Royal Tomb areas. The map indicates that Tomb 11 is in the Southern Royal Tomb area. Meriaten's father marked Tomb 11 with a red X, and next to the X is the hieroglyphic symbol for scribe. Her father wrote what I believe is the scribe's name, Paatenemheb."

"You're correct, Charles," Meriaten said. "Last night, my father told me Paatenemheb had been the military adviser for Akhenaten's father, Amenhotep III. Since Akhenaten had declared Tel el Amarna a city of peace, he no longer needed a military adviser. Instead, he made Paatenemheb his personal scribe. As such, Paatenemhep was given the position for communications between Pharaoh and the leaders of other kingdoms, from Nubia to Syria."

Caboose, tied to one of the trucks outside, interrupted Meriaten with loud continual grunting.

"Sorry, everyone. I believe my camel is calling me," Jacques said, pointing towards the tawny, long-legged beast. Rehima led the noisy dromedary to Jacques. Caboose greeted him with a strong knock on his shoulder.

"Caboose, be careful!" he exclaimed with a frown. Jacques made the pffing noise, and Caboose immediately moved to his knees. Grabbing a handful of the cloth saddle, Jacques easily pulled himself up on the camel's single hump. Charles looked up at his guardian, looming nine feet above him. With his wrinkled gallabiyah, unkempt hair, and unshaven face, he could have easily been an extra in the movie "Lawrence of Arabia." Charles turned to examine Farak, his mother, and Meriaten. Yes, he thought, all of them could be extras in his favorite movie of all time.

"We have some people we must meet, so we are going to stay back with the trucks and the bus," Subira announced.

Charles, Farak, Meriaten, and Jacques were too excited about riding to Akhenaten's capital city to ask who Rehima and Subira were waiting for. The troop took off, Malika in the lead. Farak rode up beside Charles. He said, "Look at my mother. She's riding that camel as though she were a queen."

Hearing him, Meriaten said, "She is a queen, Farak. Queen Malika. I guess that makes you a prince, Prince Farak."

"I don't feel like a prince," Farak said.

"To tell the truth, you don't look like a prince," Charles said with a laugh.

"You don't look any better, Charles," Jacques said, pulling a wrinkled headscarf from his backpack and patting it down over his own wild hair.

As the five riders arrived at the edge of Tel el Armana, Charles was no longer excited. He'd been warned the city had been razed to the ground, but he hadn't expected to see such devastation. Before him stretched a flat, barren wasteland covered with rocky sand, with nothing green, not even a weed. "This is sad," Meriaten said in a broken voice. "We read that beautiful description of this city by Nefertiti, and saw the replica of the healing temple. Now it looks like this, like nothing."

Charles looked up at the eastern ridge, pointing to the niche where Akhenaten could watch the sun rise in the morning. At this time of day, however, the sun was high in the sky, beating down on the heads of the travelers. How on earth had Akhenaten selected this desolate place for his new capital city? "The map indicates we should turn right on the Royal Road," Charles said. "We'll recognize the road because it's mostly straight, and it's wide enough for several trucks to drive side-by-side."

"I remember Nefertiti's description of driving her chariot down the Royal Road the day she was crowned co-Pharaoh of Upper and Lower Egypt by Akhenaten," Meriaten said. "Queen Nefertiti's story made me feel like I was really there. I felt like I was her daughter Meriaten, and I was watching her drive her chariot behind a beautiful horse, her hair streaming behind her, a smile on her face. She said that was the happiest day of her life."

"Hearing you describe the scene makes me feel like I'm there watching her, too," Farak told Meri.

Jacques joined the young people and asked where they should go next. "We turn right on the Royal Road," Charles said, consulting the map. "After a mile, we need to turn left on Stable Road."

The small caravan turned left towards the Archaeological Zone, then right on the wide Royal Road. Meriaten imagined driving a chariot rather than riding her camel. It was more than a mile before they turned onto a narrower road. It was marked by a sign in English reading, 'To the stable and upper Southern Royal Tomb area.' A quarter-mile later they encountered another sign with the words, 'To the stable.'

"I don't see anything down this road," Meriaten said, frowning.

"I think I see some kind of excavation. However, you are right, Meriaten," Farak agreed. "There is nothing to indicate there was ever a stable down this road. If you want, we can stop here on the way back from visiting the Royal Tomb area."

"I don't need to see it. I will never forget Tiye and Yuba's story, and how they both loved horses from childhood," Meriaten said, eyes shining. "Their shared love of horses led to a lifelong friendship, even though Yuba was an orphaned stable boy and Tiye was the wife of Amenhotep III, mother of Akhenaten. It was such a beautiful story."

"Tiye was an amazing woman. I think you are amazing as well, Meriaten. You certainly live up to your namesake," Farak said, speeding up his camel to pass the girl.

As they approached the low-lying rocky ridge, Charles was surprised to find the Royal Tomb had been carved into the middle of the cliff, rather than further up off on top of the cliff. When Charles expressed his surprise, Meriaten said, "Maybe Akhenaten directed the tombs to be built so close to the city to make it easier for Nefertiti and Pharaoh to visit the tomb of their daughter who died so young."

"Maybe, Meriaten," Charles said.

The five riders reached the bottom of the rocky crag.

"This is it," Charles announced. "According to this map, there are steps leading up to the Royal Tomb area."

The troop dismounted their camels and led them to a shady cliff area. Charles ran up to the stairs, which made a soft curve to the south. He stopped abruptly. He ran back down a couple of stairs and whispered, "There are two soldiers and a metal gate blocking our way up to the Royal Tomb area, and the soldiers have rifles."

Farak said, "You stay here and I will talk to them."

The Egyptian teen talked to the soldiers in Arabic. Charles didn't need a translator to understand that, for some reason, entry to the Royal Tomb archaeological area was closed. He couldn't believe it. He'd come all the way from France, almost died in Cairo, traveled through the Tomb of a Thousand Names, and now he wouldn't be allowed to go up to Tomb 11!

Malika caught up with Charles, Jacques, Farak, and Meriaten. Farak told his mother the area was closed. She smiled sweetly, then walked boldly up to the two soldiers. A few minutes later, the soldiers placed their rifles against two red plastic chairs. Both gave Malika a deep bow.

"I don't know what Mother said to them, but we have permission to pass," Farak said. "Mother claims the stairs are much too steep for her. She insists she would prefer to stay down and talk to the nice young soldiers. I don't believe her for a minute."

"You're right," Jacques said, "but without her, we would not be able to go up to the Royal Tombs."

"Yeah. Your mother is amazing," Charles agreed.

"I must admit, I may have underestimated her, even when I was living in Luxor or when I was reading all the letters she sent me at the Château du Mont. I should have written her better letters, but I didn't," Farak said remorsefully.

Charles wondered if he had underestimated his own mother. Had he taken her for granted? Was that why she sent him away to a boarding school? Maybe everything was his fault. While Charles was ruminating, Meriaten took the lead.

"Look," the girl in the beige gallibeyah said, pointing to a faint symbol carved in stone above a stone doorway. "It's hard to read, but I recognize the hieroglyphics. It says Royal Scribe."

Charles unrolled the map and said, "See, Jacques? Meriaten's father wrote the scribe's name in English and in hieroglyphics. His name, Paatenemheb, contains the word Aten."

"What do those other symbols say?" Jacques asked.

Charles sat down on the ground and retrieved pen and paper from his shoulder bag. He began writing, saying what he was writing aloud: *'His name shall not be among the living.'*

"This is the tomb of Paatenemheb, the Royal Scribe!" Charles exclaimed. "I can't believe it! We found Tomb 11 in Tel el Armana, Egypt."

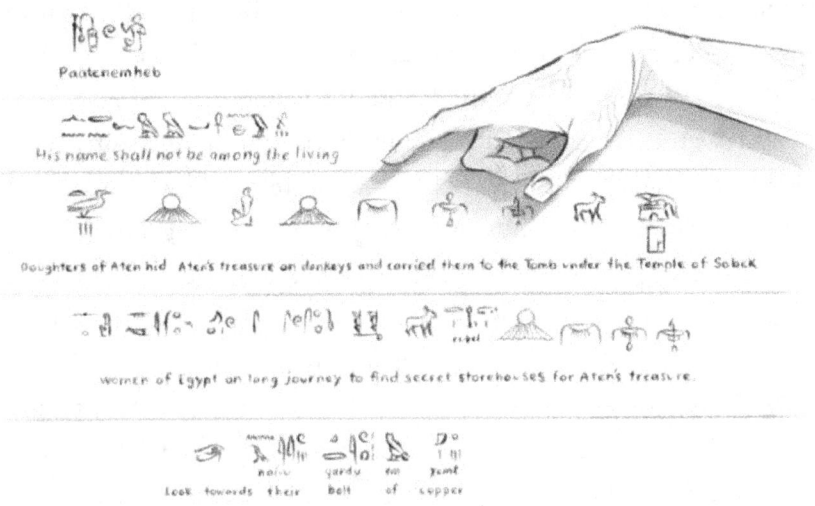

Paatenemheb

His name shall not be among the living

Daughters of Aten hid Aten's treasure on donkeys and carried them to the Tomb under the Temple of Sobek

women of Egypt on long journey to find secret storehouses for Aten's treasure.

Look towards their belt of copper

CHAPTER 78

THE GHOST OF TOMB 11

T he four adventurers stood outside the small stone entrance of Tomb 11. "What are we looking for?" Farak asked the American boy, who looked like a bedraggled Bedouin.

"I think it's a ghost," Meriaten answered. "Charles believes he can see ghosts. He even thought I was a ghost when we first met."

"A ghost? You thought Meriaten was a ghost? Are we looking for a ghost, Charles?" the Egyptian boy asked.

"To answer your last question, Farak, I don't know what we're looking for. *Ghost Story Magazine* published my first story, 'The Ghost of the Jangling Keys.' The publisher sent me a list of one thousand haunted places, inviting me to submit another story," Charles explained.

"The Ghost of Tomb 11, Tel el Armana, Egypt was at the top of the list. David and I decided that since I loved Egypt so much, the Ghost of Tomb 11 should be my next story," Charles continued. "But then, David's parents wouldn't let him come with Jacques and me to Egypt. They thought he was too young. My parents didn't think I was too young."

"Excuse me, Farak and Charles, but this is quite a long story, and you might notice the sun is rising, as is the temperature. Maybe we can discuss this further inside Paatenemheb's tomb," Jacques said, ducking into the narrow, five-foot-high stone entrance. Charles, David and Meriaten followed. There appeared to be a fake door just beyond the entrance. Walking to the right of this stone door, which blocked the light of day, it was nearly pitch-black.

"It definitely looks like a tomb. I guess I had better get out my trusty red flashlight," Jacques said. There was a click as he turned on the light. Jacques flashed the narrow beam around the eight-by-ten-foot stone chamber. "This tomb appears unfinished. I wonder why?"

"Maybe because it wasn't meant for him. He just borrowed it," Meriaten ventured. "Mom and dad told me that was a common practice in ancient Egypt."

"It's also a common practice in modern Egypt, in the City of the Dead," Charles said.

"If it is the wrong tomb," Jacques said, still training the beam of his flashlight around the small enclosure, "maybe there will be no ghost and no treasure."

"You're right about the tomb being unfinished, and maybe there is no ghost, but you're wrong about the treasure, Jacques," Charles said.

"Where is it?" Meriaten and Jacques asked in harmony.

"Look!" Charles exclaimed. "See this wall? It's covered in Cuneiform. I wish I hadn't left my Cuneiform book on the train. You didn't bring it, did you, Jacques?"

"No, I forgot to bring it," Jacques said with a tone of sarcasm in his voice.

Meriaten traced her fingers over the wedge-like symbols carved into the stone on the west wall. "Even with a Cuneiform book, it would take you a long time to learn the writing system. I should know. I've been trying to learn Cuneiform for a month, and I can't read one word of this."

"If only Dr. McAllister were here. He could read it; he could translate it," Charles said gloomily from his place on the floor.

"Maybe we could ask the Ghost of Tomb 11 to translate this message. Are you here, Mr. Scribe?" Jacques called out, arms held up, waving his hands in the air.

"Jacques, that isn't how you call a ghost," Charles scolded his guardian.

"Really? I believe I have called a ghost or two before, young Mr. Stratton," Jacques retorted.

"Not an Egyptian scribe," Charles replied firmly.

"Could you two be quiet for one minute?" Meriaten demanded, stamping her foot on the stone floor. "I think I hear something."

Charles and Jacques stopped talking. "I don't hear anything, Meriaten," Charles said after a few seconds.

"Well, I thought I heard someone calling your name, Charles," the girl said.

Jacques turned off his flashlight. There was just a faint, shadowy light coming from the entrance of the tomb.

"Maybe I heard something, too," Farak whispered. "Do you think it is a ghost?"

"Are you in here, Charles?" a voice called from outside the tomb.

Charles stood up. "David! It's David, my roommate at the Château du Mont," he said in disbelief. "How could David be here? Am I dreaming?"

A shadowy form entered the tomb and sped towards Charles' voice. However, coming from the bright sunlight into the dark tomb, David couldn't see a thing. He bumped into Charles, knocking him to the ground. Jacques flipped on the flashlight. Charles was lying flat on tomb's floor.

"Are you all right, Charles?" Meriaten asked.

"I think so," he replied.

David reached down to help his roommate up. "I'm sorry, Charles. It's just that I thought you might be dead. But you're not. You're alive! You're in a tomb but you're alive, Charles."

"It's Tomb 11, David. We're inside Tomb 11, just like we dreamed we would be," Charles said. "How did you get here? And how did you get past the soldiers?"

"I came with Dr. McAllister," David answered. "He's an Egyptologist. He has a pass to go anywhere he wants in the Archaeological Zones, so the soldiers let us in."

"Jacques and I know Dr. McAllister, but where is he?" Charles asked.

"I am here," the tour guide from the Cairo Museum said, ducking into the tomb. Jacques aimed his flashlight towards the tall man wearing a blue gallabiyah and matching keffiyeh, topped off with a flowing, cream-colored scarf.

"We've been waiting for you," Charles said in salutation.

"Waiting for me?" the tour guide said with a laugh.

"Well, at least wishing for you," Charles clarified. "Let me introduce you to my friends. This is Farak. He is the grandson of the leader of the Tarabin Tribe."

"I am pleased to meet you, Farak," Dr. McAllister said. "I believe I met your mother entertaining the soldiers at the entrance of the Southern Royal Tomb area."

"And this is Meriaten," Charles said, indicating the girl.

"Ah, Meriaten, the firstborn daughter of Akhenaten and Nefertiti," Dr. McAllister said with a low bow.

"Yes, but this Meriaten is the daughter of two Egyptologists," Charles replied. "Her parents actually met here in Tel el Armana. They were working at the same excavation and then they got married."

"Pleased to meet you, young lady," Dr. McAllister said.

"You already met David. But how did you get here, Dr. McAllister?" Charles asked.

"I rode up here with the gang on a bus," he answered. "It's quite an eclectic group, if you ask me. I only know everyone is going to be relieved to discover both you and Jacques are still among the living. Now, I gather you want me to translate the Cuneiform on the wall."

"Yes, we do," Charles said, sitting back down on the floor, pen in hand and papers on his lap.

"Are you ready, Charles?" Dr. McAllister asked. Charles answered in the affirmative.

"The writing begins over here," Dr. McAllister said. "Paatenemheb makes it clear that these are not his words but those of the Pharaoh Akhenaten." The author and tour guide opened his arms wide, then raised them slightly towards the tomb's ceiling. Jacques kept his flashlight beam on the writing.

Aten is on my head like a crown, and I shall never be without Him.

For I should not have known how to love Aten,

If He had not continuously loved me.

Who is able to distinguish love, except him who is loved?

"That is very beautiful," Meriaten said, moving closer to Dr. McAllister.

The sky pays homage to you.

Law and Truth embrace you at morning and evening.

You have given to us Your fellowship,

Not that You were in need of us,

But that we are always in need of You.

"Are you getting this all down?" Jacques asked Charles.

"Yes, I'm almost ready. Okay, continue, Dr. McAllister."

He who delights in Life will become living.

Indeed, he who is joined to Him

Who is immortal,

Truly shall be immortal.

"Akhenaten was a great poet, don't you agree, Dr. McAllister?" Charles asked.

"Yes, I do agree. I believe that he was the first true poet of ancient Egypt," the translator answered.

Oh, Shepherd, Oh, Lord, Oh, Self-Existent One,
Creator of all things,
You make the tongues of all the spirit beings.
You have made all that spring forth from the waters,
And You shoot up from them over the land of the pools of the Divine Lake.
How many are the things which you have made!
You created the land by your will.
You alone created peoples, herds, and flocks,
Everything on the face of the earth that walks on its feet,
Everything in the air that flies with its wings.
You give to everyone his place.
You frame their lives.
Your variegated lights and colors cannot be numbered
And cannot be comprehended.
Aten of the day,
Revered by every distant land,
You make their life.
You placed a Nile in the heaven that it may rain upon them,
That it may make waters upon the hills like the great sea,
Irrigating their fields among their cities.
How excellent are your ways!

Dr. McAllister stopped reading and said, "I have read the writing inside this tomb a number of times, but each time it touches me deeply."

"It touches me deeply, too," the girl standing next to Dr. McAllister said.

"Wait a minute!" the translator exclaimed. "I see some tiny symbols on the wall near the floor where Charles is sitting. I have never noticed them before. Jacques, come a little closer with your light. I'll try to translate what it says. This writing is no longer in the voice of Akhenaten but in the voice of the scribe Paatenemheb."

My Lord appointed me the officer in charge of the great city of God, and all its monuments and treasures. But I could not stop the terrible destruction. When it was done, Akhenaten came to me one night in my dream. Pharaoh commanded that I deliver this message to the seekers: 'Your radiance is in your hands, and is as fair as bright copper metal.'

"What does it mean?" Charles asked Dr. McAllister.

"I think it means Paatenemheb took responsibility for Tel el Armana's destruction," the man in the blue gallabiyah said, his voice bouncing off the stone walls of Tomb 11. "But as for the final line, *'Your radiance is in your hands, and is as fair as bright copper metal,'* I do not know."

Turning towards Meriaten, Dr. McAllister said, "Well, young lady, I think you should introduce me to Farak's mother. On the way down, you can tell me about your parents' work here in Tel el Armana."

When they left, Jacques said, "Somehow I ended up carrying the three relic pyramids that have been discovered: the Tarabin Pyramid, the High Priestess' Pyramid and the one we found near the illustration of Nefertiti driving her chariot—the one with all the elevens in it. I have a strong feeling we should place them on the floor near Paatenemheb's writing."

"Charles, do you notice the drop in temperature?" David asked. "The same thing happened when we met the Ghosts of the Jangling Keys."

"What does a drop in temperature mean?" Farak asked with a nervous laugh.

"Well, it could mean that a ghost is nigh," Jacques answered, using the same word Subira had employed when the Rain of Knives was nearly upon them, adding a little more mystery to the moment.

"I think I see something," Farak observed. "It's like a shimmering pool of light."

"That's it!" Charles exclaimed. "That's how I first saw the ghosts: a translucent, shimmering pool of light."

"Welcome, Paatenemheb, honorable scribe of Akhenaten," Jacques said, attempting to imitate Dr. McAllister.

"I don't think he can understand or speak English or French, Jacques. I don't think he could even understand Arabic. I read ancient Egyptian is more like the Coptic language. But I have an idea. As Royal Scribe, Paatenemheb would naturally understand hieroglyphics as well as Cuneiform. We can try to communicate with him through hieroglyphics," Charles suggested. "What do you think I should say, Jacques?"

"I think you should tell Paatenemheb that we have taken the Path of Knowledge in the Tomb of a Thousand Names," Jacques answered. "Tell him that through stories, we have learned a great deal about Akhenaten, the great Pharaoh, and we've mastered a valuable lesson."

"Which lesson?" Charles asked. Jacques gazed at the boy whom he'd lost and found. "Some things are worth standing up for," he said. Charles looked up at his guardian. He thought, you could never tell what would come out of Jacques' mouth next. The all-around man of the Château du Mont had become unpredictable.

"That is what we learned," Farak agreed.

At that moment, a ghostly disembodied hand emerged from the shimmering, translucent pool of light. "This is something I didn't expect," Farak said, moving closer to Jacques, who pointed his flashlight's narrow beam towards the pyramids and the ghostly hand.

"The hand is gesturing to something. It's pointing to some specific symbols, symbols that were not written in Cuneiform," Charles said. "It's pointing to the symbols for Kush, Elephantine Island, the Red Sea, and Syria. And the strange thing is, the symbols are the only ones that have been painted the color of copper."

Farak squatted next to Charles. "Look. The hand is pointing to the three relic pyramids, then to that very tiny pyramid, which is also copper-colored. Charles, I think he's telling you to push on the little copper pyramid. Maybe it is one of Yuba's buttons!"

Charles reached over and pushed the symbol of a tiny copper-colored pyramid. "I hear something. It sounds like another drawer opened," Farak said, moving to the stone drawer that had just slid out of the wall.

"How did you do that?" David asked

"We will talk about this later, David. What do you see?" Jacques asked, pointing his light toward Farak. The Bedouin boy carefully removed something from the drawer.

"It is the fourth relic pyramid!" the Egyptian boy exclaimed.

Charles began chanting Meriaten's poem.

One little pyramid stands alone,

"That was the high priestess' pyramid," Charles said.

Searching for a brother of its very own.

"That is your relic pyramid, Farak."

When there are two, the third comes home.

"That's the pyramid we found in the Tomb of a Thousand Names."

The fourth can be found at Aten's throne,

"This must be it, here in Tel el Armana!" Charlies exclaimed. "This is Aten's throne."

Translate, you, on all the sides,

One, two, three, four, and five,

Messages concealed in poetry.

The pyramids together reveal the key

That solves Queen Tye's great mystery.

And with this all will be

Forever, forever, changed.

"We have discovered all four relic pyramids. As Jacques says, change is nigh," Charles declared.

"What's on the bottom of the pyramid, Farak?" Jacques asked.

The teen turned over the pyramid and examined the bottom or fifth side. "There is nothing but a layer of copper."

"Why are we being directed to copper?" Charles wondered aloud.

"The hand is fading. I think the ghost is leaving. Can you feel how the temperature is no longer as cold?" David asked. "It's just like it happened before with the Ghosts of the Jangling Keys."

Before the hand could completely disappear, Charles called out to the scribe, "Thank you, Paatenemheb."

Jacques said, "Paatenemheb, we will give the four pyramids to the High Priestess. She will know what to do with them. And Charles Dayton Stratton III will tell the true story of Akhenaten and Tel el Armana, establishing that

Akhenaten was not nefarious, but instead a man who loved his family, his people, and the one God, Aten."

"The temperature is normal again. The scribe must be gone," David said.

"Now, let's go down and thank my mother for occupying those soldiers, thus allowing us to stay up here so long," Farak suggested.

"And we have to ask Dr. McAllister if he knows anything about ancient copper," Jacques said, wrapping up the pyramids and placing them in his shoulder bag.

"What do you think will happen to Paatenemheb?" David asked Jacques.

"I have a feeling he will go to where he was meant to go, something like the Ghosts of the Jangling Keys. I feel his assignment or responsibility is over. But I have another feeling that Charles' assignment might have just begun."

"Where do all these feelings come from, Jacques?" Charles asked.

"I do not know, but I am opening myself up to the mysteries of the new physics," Jacques responded. "You will have to talk to Fran's mother to better understand."

"Fran's mother?"

"She's here in Egypt," David said. "She came to find you, Charles; a lot of people did."

"Who? Who are they?" Charles asked.

"Let's go down to the King's Road and you can find out for yourself," his roommate said.

David and Charles ran down the stone steps, saluting the two soldiers as they passed the gate. Farak and Jacques followed. Meriaten, Malika, and Dr. McAllister were standing in the shade by the camels. Meriaten handed the newcomers sweet cakes wrapped in leaves. Farak's mother passed around a canvas canteen filled with water.

"I suggest we move along, as it appears to be getting hotter," Dr. McAllister said, dramatically wiping his forehead with his sleeve.

"I need to ask you a question," Charles said. "Do you know anything about copper in the ancient days, maybe three thousand years ago?"

"Yes, I know something about ancient copper," Dr. McAllister said, his enthusiasm for archaeology palpable. "On March 14, 1952, in Cave 3 near the Dead Sea, a copper scroll was discovered. The scroll was eight feet in length and about a foot in width. Because of its age and deterioration, it took many years to prepare the scroll for translation.

"What they found mystified the archaeological world." Dr. McAllister continued dramatically, "The copper scroll turned out to be a list of various locations where treasure could be found. For each location, there was a detailed description of the gold, silver, jewelry, art, and documents that had been hidden away."

"Did they find the treasure?" Jacques asked with interest.

"No, they didn't. None of the treasure has been discovered. Some believe the locations are under various temples in Israel. However, they can't be sure because the names of the locations on the scrolls have long since been changed."

"Do they know where the treasures came from?" Jacques asked.

"No, nobody knows exactly where the treasure came from," Dr. McAllister answered. "Why are you asking about the copper scroll?"

"We are not asking about the scrolls, just about ancient copper," Jacques answered. "It appears you are right, Dr. McAllister. It is getting even hotter out here. I suggest we head back to our air-conditioned bus."

Dr. McAllister, Malika, Subira and Rehima rode off towards the King's Road. Jacques helped David and Meriaten get on their camels, Farak, Charles and Jacques mounted their camels.

"Did I miss anything?" Meriaten asked. "I should have stayed with you."

"You can read Charles' journal when we are back on the bus, Meri," the Bedouin teen assured her. And the Five Musketeers rode off side-by-side.

CHAPTER 79

RIDING THE WIND

Rehima arrived on a camel and addressed Malika in Arabic. Charles asked Farak what she was saying.

"She says my grandfather and father are on the Royal Road," Farak explained. "They, and the highest officials, are wearing traditional military dress and riding the royal horses. Behind them are many people on camels."

"Why does your mother look worried?" Meriaten asked.

"She knows my grandfather and father are going to be angry," Farak answered. "I let my mother leave the compound without telling anyone where she was going. In their minds, I endangered their *Sheikha*, their empress. I feel like running away, but I'm too old for that."

"You can be too old to run away?" Charles asked his schoolmate.

"Yes," the Egyptian teen replied, "because as you get older, it's like running away from yourself." Farak gave his camel a slight kick and headed down the Stable Road.

"I'll go with you," Meriaten cried, urging her camel to catch up with Farak.

"Me, too," Dr. McAllister said, following the youths.

Malika passed all of them. Charles thought to himself, the day of reckoning has come. Several thousand feet ahead, two people on camels rode towards them. One wore a colorful floral skirt, a blue artist's smock, and a pink headscarf.

"It's my art professor from the Château du Mont!" Charles exclaimed in disbelief. He called out, "What are you doing here, Mademoiselle Fleuret?"

"According to Fran, we are here to rescue you, but we may be too late," she replied. "It looks like you have already been rescued. Let me introduce you to Alfred P. Hart."

"Greetings, Charles," Mr. Hart said. "I brought your father's Leica M3 1954—I mean your Leica, the one you left on the train."

He handed Charles the silver camera his father had given him the previous Christmas. Charles could see it had a fresh load of black-and-white film and was ready to go.

"Thank you," Charles said. "I'll never be parted from my Leica again, Mr. Hart. Who did you say you are?"

"I am a friend of your grandfather, Dr. Stratton," Alfred said. "When your father turned twelve, Dr. Stratton gave Charlie this Leica. He loved taking photos. He and I went on many photo shoots together."

Charles couldn't imagine people calling his father Charlie. Charles Dayton Stratton II fit him better. His father was always so controlled, so disciplined, so orderly and, much of the time, missing in action. Thinking about his father, it dawned on Charles that during his time in the desert, he'd unceremoniously moved from eleven to twelve years old. It was an age his mother claimed was quite auspicious.

"So you know my grandfather?" Charles asked Alfred P. Hart.

Mademoiselle Fleuret answered for him. "Alfred is your grandfather's butler, although your grandfather denies this and insists instead that Mr. Hart is his great friend. I know you are going to love the eldest Mr. Stratton, everybody does. You gave us quite a scare, Charles. I hope you have a story that is worth all the trouble you have caused."

She laughed a laugh that seemed to fill the destroyed city of Tel el Armana. "Now that I know you are safe and you, too, Jacques, I have to admit this is the experience of a lifetime," Mademoiselle Fleuret said. She lifted her camera and snapped a closeup of Jacques in his dusty, wrinkled gallabiyah. Then, pointing her camera toward Charles, she pushed the shutter button down.

"Charles, could you take a photo of Alfred and me with my camera?" she asked. "I have color film. Get closer to me, Alfred." Once Charles had captured the moment, Mademoiselle Fleuret said, "Okay, Mr. Hart, let's you and I go back."

Charles took a photo of his teacher and the man in the safari outfit leaving the scene. As the two camel riders set off for the Royal Road, another camel appeared.

"Charles, we're here to save you!" a voice called out.

"That looks like Bernadette, but it sounds like Francis Bacon Bernstein," Charles said to David.

"Fran is riding behind Bernadette. His mother didn't want him riding a camel alone," David said.

"Fran, what are you doing here, and Bernadette, too?" Charles asked, his thoughts getting hazier.

"I forgot to mention that everyone in the world has come to Cairo to find you," Jacques said. "Well, almost everyone."

"Hello, Charles," the young woman in the yellow jacket and straw hat said. "I am so happy to see that you are safe and none the worse for your wild journey."

"What about Jacques?" Fran asked. "Are you happy to see him safe?"

"No, not very. He is a foolish man and whatever happened to him, he deserved," Bernadette said, turning her camel around.

"How did you do that?" Jacques asked the young woman.

"Do what?" Bernadette asked coldly.

"How did you get your camel to turn around?" Jacques answered. "That is why I did not return after I went to the City of the Dead. My camel here simply would not turn around. He is what is called a follower, and not a good follower either."

"He walked so slowly behind Rehima and Subira, I nearly died of heatstroke," Jacques continued. "I named him Caboose, because he is always at the end of the train. And I am sorry, Bernadette. I have behaved badly, like my camel."

As if in answer, Caboose gave a loud, grumbling roar.

"Believe me, Jacques," the boy in the blue turban said, "Bernadette was plenty upset the night you disappeared. Weren't you, Miss Bernadette?"

"Fran!" the young woman exclaimed, lightly admonishing the boy before kicking her camel's side and leaving the scene.

"That boy is so funny," Meriaten said with a giggle.

"He is funny, and he is a mathematical genius," Charles said. "He will no doubt be very famous someday."

As the small caravan turned onto the Royal Road, they met Farak, his mother, Dr. McAllister, and Rehima. They were watching as a parade of horses and riders advanced towards them. "I have not seen true royal Arabian horses like these, even at the best horse shows," Dr. McAllister said in amazement. "Who are these people?"

"At the head of this procession is my grandfather, Sultan of the Tarabin Tribe, and beside him is my father," Farak said.

"They came to find us?" Charles asked.

Farak shook his head. "They are not here to find you, Charles. They're here to find me, and I don't think it is going to be good."

"Why?" Mrs. Montgomery asked.

"They believe I put my mother, the Sultana, in danger by causing her to secretly leave the compound," the Egyptian teen explained.

"That wasn't your fault, Farak," Meriaten declared. "You tried to convince your mother not to come with you."

"They won't see it that way," Farak said. "Firstly, my mother should have been my highest responsibility. She is not only my mother, but the mother of all Bedouins of the Tarabin Tribe. Secondly, they are going to accuse me of stealing the relic pyramid, the pyramid the Tarabin Tribe has guarded for hundreds and hundreds of years."

"What do you think they'll do to you?" Charles asked.

"At the very least, they'll send me immediately to Brown University in the United States," Farak answered. "If they're angry enough, I could be unrecognized by the Tarabin Tribe."

"Unrecognized," Charles echoed. "Does that mean you could be kicked out of your own tribe?"

"It is a possibility," Farak answered. "These are serious crimes."

Malika rode up next to her son, speaking to him in Arabic. Charles asked Meriaten what she was saying.

"She says Farak cannot be in trouble for stealing the pyramid, because the pyramid belongs to her," Meriaten related. "She says it has always belonged to her. Her mother gave it to her, and her grandmother gave it to her mother. It has belonged to the royal Bedouin women in her lineage for hundreds and hundreds of years. Now, though, she says she's going to give her relic pyramid to the High Priestess. And she is going to join the Daughters of Aten."

"Who are the Daughters of Aten?" Dr. McAllister asked.

"It's an organization over three thousand years old," Charles informed the museum guide. "It was organized by Tiye, Akhenaten's mother."

"That's extraordinary! Where did you learn all this, Charles?" Dr. McAllister wondered.

"We learned it on the Path of Knowledge," the boy answered.

"Where is this Path of Knowledge?" the Egyptologist inquired.

"I believe that is a topic for another place and another time," Jacques suggested, turning towards the conversation between mother and son.

"Mother, I am going with you to talk to Grandfather and Father, and that is final," Farak said.

The two Bedouins rode towards the lines of horses led by Farak's grandfather. As they approached, the Sultan's horse reared up on his hind legs, front legs clawing the air menacingly. There was a stern look on the Sultan's face. In his hand, he held up the Sword of the Quarter Moon.

"He is just trying to intimidate Farak," Meriaten said angrily. "I am going up there to tell that Sultan how lucky he is to have such a wonderful grandson, and that he should not go around scaring people."

"Meriaten," Jacques said, "I think we had better let Farak handle this."

Farak dismounted and stood before the leader of the Tarabin Tribe. Farak's mother also dismounted and stood before her husband's horse. She was waving her arms wildly in the air, occasionally pointing towards Charles and his tiny caravan. Farak's grandfather pointed his sword towards his grandson.

"If he even thinks of touching one hair on Farak's head, he will have to deal with me," Jacques said.

Charles stared at his guardian. One thing was for sure, this wasn't the man he'd come to Egypt with. That man wouldn't think of taking on a Sultan with a sword. Jacques urged Caboose a little closer to the line of horses.

From behind the first line of horses, a Bedouin stepped forward. Holding the reins of a pure white Arabian horse, he handed them to Farak's grandfather. Charles could see the horse's large eyes and large dark nostrils from where he stood, hundreds of feet away. The Arabian horse held its white tail high above his body; from there, it flowed like a mountain stream, almost to the ground.

"I have never seen a horse as beautiful as this one," Dr. McAllister exclaimed. "Its lineage must have come directly from the royal line of Bedouin horses."

To Charles, the horse looked familiar. It was almost identical to the horse that pulled Nefertiti's two-wheeled chariot down the Royal Road the day she was crowned Co-Pharaoh of Upper and Lower Egypt. But this horse wasn't pulling a chariot. Instead, it looked ready for battle. It wore a saddle, horse blanket, bridle, and breastplate of metallic gold and royal blue. As the horse moved forward, it didn't walk. It pranced, lifting its forelegs high above the ground with each step.

The man with the sword slid off his horse. He was given the reins of the white horse. He signaled Farak to come forward.

"I don't think the Sultan is going to punish Farak," Charles said. "I believe he is going to give him that beautiful horse."

Malika came and stood by Farak. Someone from the second row of horses came up to Farak's mother and handed her a flowing royal-blue tob. She helped her son put the robe over his wrinkled gallabiyah, turning him from a scruffy-looking teenager into a Bedouin prince.

"This is like a fairytale!" Meriaten exclaimed. "Farak looks so handsome and valiant."

Charles captured this transformation in black-and-white, almost wishing he had color film. Jacques looked relieved. He said, "I gather this ceremony means Farak will not be kicked out of the Tarabin Tribe."

The young prince mounted the white stallion and then, leaning forward, rode around all the people in the Bedouin caravan. Completing this, Farak rode back towards the small caravan of his friends. As he got closer, Farak called out, "Charles, get off your camel and come here."

Rehima helped Charles off Sahara. Stopping in front of the small caravan, Farak proclaimed, "This is the horse I have dreamed about all my life. I have named him Alriho, meaning the Wind. Come aboard, Charles, for without you this moment would never have happened."

With a helping hand from Farak, Charles climbed up on the saddle behind his friend. Moving from a trot to a canter, Farak guided the white horse south on the Royal Road, until they reached the Stable Road. He wheeled his horse about and Farak and Charles flew like the wind back towards the large caravan. People were cheering, applauding, and making joyful zaghrouta sounds.

When the small caravan approached the parade of horses, Farak's mother emerged from the second row. She was riding a beautiful brown Arabian horse with a long black mane and tail. Her tob was a deep maroon with gold trim. Never judge a book by its cover, Jacques thought as they drew closer to the Sultana. He watched as a Bedouin man helped Charles off Alriho. Charles was guided to stand by Farak's father.

Farak's mother called out something in Arabic, which Meriaten translated for Charles: "I have informed my father-in-law, the Sultan, that I have adopted Charles Taraban Stratton III into our tribe. He wishes to speak to you, Charles."

Farak's father spoke in English. He translated for the Sultan. "My grandson tells me that you love Egypt," he said.

"Yes, I have loved Egypt since I was a child," Charles answered seriously.

Farak's father turned and said something to the Sultan; they both laughed. Farak's father called out in a commanding voice. "Charles Tarabin Dayton Stratton III is now Bedouin. He is always welcome in our encampments and is entitled to our protection forevermore."

The Sultan placed a chain with a large emblem on it over Charles' head. Charles recognized it from Farak's story of when, as a seven-year-old, he held council with his grandfather in the Room of Swords. It was a smaller version of what the Sultan wore that day, a royal white eagle that was the symbol of the Sit Shahena.

Charles wondered what position Malika really held in this Bedouin tribe. Dr. Awyan said many Egyptologists didn't understand that ancient Egypt was matriarchal, not patriarchal. If the pyramid really belonged to Farak's mother, and she was really able to adopt Charles into the tribe, perhaps she was as powerful as the Sultan himself. Charles thought all this, but he just made a slight bow and said, "Thank you."

"Let me translate what the Sultan is saying now," Meriaten said.

'Mademoiselle Fleuret came to our compound to speak to Farak's father and me. She asserted that we had used a young boy for our own personal ends. Mademoiselle Fleuret told us that even if we thought it was a good end, if it was without the boy's clear consent, we were taking away his personal power, his will. This, she said, was not good. We have thought about what Mademoiselle Fleuret told us. We agree this was not ethical. Farak Faruk, we give you back your will.'

Rehima helped Charles back up onto Stubborn Sahara. The horses, riders, and camels turned around and faced the other way on the Royal Road, making the end of the caravan the beginning.

CHAPTER 80

A WILD WAVE IS IMMINENT

J acques watch athe woman riding towards him on a tall, tawny-colored camel. As she drew closer, he called out in surprise, "Madame Constance, you look—you look radiant."

"Really, Jacques," the headmistress of the Château du Mont said, patting her long gray locks, which had escaped her usual tight bun and were now cascading beyond her shoulders.

Madame Constance was, indeed, completely transformed. She wore a tan safari jacket and tan pants tucked into high leather boots. The outfit was topped off by a pith helmet with a strangely-familiar sprig of lavender tucked into the headband.

"Yes, you look radiant. But what are you doing here?" the man wearing a wrinkled gallabiyah and a confused smile asked.

"That is a good question. However, Jacques, a better question might be why did I not come sooner. It has been a terrible ordeal, you and Charles lost, and me feeling helpless. Then, I thought I heard Dr. Bernstein's voice say, 'Helplessness or action, Madam Constance: which do you choose?' The next thing I knew, I was on a 747 headed for Cairo."

"I arrived this very morning, just in time to come on this grand adventure to find you and Charles. And here I am, riding on a camel. Honestly, I feel like I was born to ride a camel. You can see so much more from this perspective, do you not agree, Jacques? And you are safe, both you and Charles are safe," Madam Constance concluded emotionally.

"Yes, we are safe. Let me introduce you to Stubborn Sahara, my camel," Charles said.

"Hello, Stubborn Sahara. You look like quite a character," the headmistress said.

"That's an understatement, Madame Constance," Charles said laughing. "She might just be the reason Jacques and I became lost."

"Oh my. I will have to hear your story, Charles."

The headmistress gestured to the ribbon of blue running along the Archaeological Zone of Tel el Armana. "I still remember when I first learned about the Nile River. I was twelve. From that moment, I dreamed of traveling its dark blue waters, filled with crocodiles and hippopotamuses. And look at this desert! Yes, there is something to be said about the cool days and tall, shady trees of France. But here in the desert—with its wide expanse, its emptiness, its silence—one can really think. Do you not agree, Jacques?"

"I concur," Jacques agreed.

"Oh, yes, and I hope you do not mind but we are not going straight back to the Château du Mont," the headmistress announced.

"Really?" the two amazed listeners chimed in unison.

"Dr. Awyan—a dear man—and I have arranged for a five-day journey up the Nile River. There will be quite a group of us. I thought that since we have been unable to contact your parents, Charles, they would not mind if we extended your vacation a bit," Madame Constance said blithely.

"Am to stay in Egypt, too?" Jacques asked.

"Yes, of course. Without you, Jacques, I do not know if we..." the headmistress was too emotional to continue.

Charles lifted his Leica and carefully aimed the lens of his camera towards the headmistress of the Château du Mont. He hoped he'd managed to capture the change he instinctively felt in her.

"Charles," Madame Constance said, "I wish to speak to Jacques alone for just a moment."

Charles turned his camel and camera towards Meriaten. She was on her camel talking to Rehima and Subira, also on camels. He rode over to join them.

After a brief conversation with Madame Constance, Jacques scanned the parking lot for the girl in the bright yellow jacket. He found her looking east, framed by the archaeological site of Tel el Amarna with its low, shadowy cliffs cradling the royal tombs. Jacques gently kicked Caboose's sides and rode up beside the woman. Ignoring the man beside her, she turned her head to admire the Nile.

"Madame Constance has just informed me that she would be honored if I would become her co-Pharaoh at the Château du Mont," Jacques told Bernadette.

"Co-Pharaoh?" Bernadette said with a snort.

"Well, actually co-principal," Jacques clarified. "She said it was time to make some changes at the school. I have agreed. My first act is to ask if you would consider becoming one of the English teachers at the Château du Mont."

Bernadette surveyed the man on the funny-looking camel next to her. He was wearing a wrinkled, cream-colored gallabiyah, a dusty headscarf, and a five o'clock shadow. She'd liked the Jacques she had met last Christmas, but this man was new. This man was a stranger to her.

Her cheeks turned red as she felt Jacques staring at her intently. Then she answered formally, "I would be honored, Mr. Gerard."

"Thank you," Jacques said. "Just one question: Are you going on the Nile cruise?"

Bernadette affirmed that she would be joining the excursion. "Good," Jacques said as the girl in the yellow jacket rode away on her camel.

Mademoiselle Fleuret took Bernadette's place beside Jacques. She was riding a white camel with a purple velvet saddle. The camel was decorated with a matching headdress and bridle, both embellished with brass bells that jingled as the dromedary walked.

"Have you seen Charles?" Mademoiselle Fleuret asked. "I think it is time he meets his grandfather, and that his grandfather meets him."

"Charles is behind you," Jacques responded.

"Oh, hello, Charles," the Chateau's art teacher said. "Have you met your grandfather yet?"

"No," Charles replied, suddenly feeling shy.

"I will introduce you," Mademoiselle Fleuret said. Turning her camel in the other direction, she gestured to a stout man leaning over a petite brown camel. A cameleer was holding its reins. The rider clutched the edge of his camel's green-and-red plaid saddle. His stance made him look something like a jockey.

"Dr. Charles Stratton, this is Charles Dayton Stratton III," Mademoiselle Fleuret said with a flourish.

Charles inspected his new acquaintance. The man with the red face holding onto the cloth saddle didn't look like his father. "Do you know my parents?" he demanded.

"Charles, this is not the way to greet a man who came from the United States to find you," Mademoiselle Fleuret said as she turned her camel to-wards Bernadette.

"Thank you for coming to find me," Charles said to the man with whom he shared a name.

"To answer the question about your parents, I do not know your mother. Of course, I knew—I mean know—your father, my son, Charles Dayton Stratton II."

"Why didn't you ever come to our house?" Charles responded accusingly.

"That, young man, is a long story best not told in this pitiless heat," Dr. Stratton replied. "Just know I came to Egypt to find you, and here you are."

"We have quite a bit to figure out, don't we?" Charles said.

"Yes, Grandson. Yes, we do," the man replied, dabbing his eyes with one hand and clutching the camel's cloth saddle with the other.

"Are you coming on the Nile trip?" Charles asked.

"I am indeed. I hope we can make a good start on getting to know one another," Dr. Stratton said.

The cameleer indicated it was time for Dr. Stratton to dismount. Charles walked Sahara over to one of the livestock trucks. There was no one else around, just Sahara and him. Charles signaled for Stubborn Sahara to kneel, and she did. Once down, Sahara knocked his shoulder with her soft snout.

He realized this was the last time he would see his camel, the one he bought for a gold coin. That night seemed so long ago, practically a lifetime. Charles put his arms around Sahara's neck. His camel let out a long and mournful cry.

"Goodbye, Sahara. I will never forget you." Charles didn't cry as loud as Stubborn Sahara, but he wept just as mournfully. Rehima walked up and, giving Charles a sympathetic glance, took Sahara away. Charles heard Fran calling him and quickly wiped away his tears.

"Charles!" the younger boy exclaimed. "Now that I—I mean we—have rescued you, here's the plan. We're all going back to the School of Khemitology. My mom is traveling to Paris to teach, but I get to go on the Nile trip with you and David. Madame Constance has agreed to keep an eye on me."

"We're going to return to Cairo, pack our clothes and take a night train to Luxor," Fran continued. "Then we'll get on a ship and head up the Nile River." The younger boy grinned, revealing his jack o'lantern teeth.

"Francis Bacon, come here and get on this bus, immediately," Dr. Bernstein called to her son. Then, noticing Charles, she greeted him enthusiastically. "I am happy to see you," she said. "You look well."

Aamen walked over to the livestock truck. He grabbed Charles' right hand. Pumping it up and down, he said, "Your honorable grandfather is arranging for me to receive full tuition at Cairo University. I never expected such a thing. He has also arranged for me to receive room and board, so I do not have to travel so far every day to attend classes."

"Furthermore," the interpreter continued, "one of the agents at the American Embassy has invited me to intern there for the rest of the summer. Meeting you has been an amazing privilege, Mr. Stratton." The young Egyptian ended his speech with a deep bow.

Charles tried to explain that all he did was get lost but before he could say anything, Aamen ran off to talk to Alfred. Charles walked over to where Samy and Jacques were talking. Just as he got there, Samy reached into his pants pocket and pulled out a blue velvet box, handing it to the Château's new co-principal.

"What is this?" Jacques asked as he opened the box.

"It's your ring," Charles said exuberantly. "It's the gold ring with the scarab on it, the one you wanted so badly."

"Thank you, Samy," Jacques said, placing the scarab ring on his finger.

"You know, the scarab is the symbol of rebirth," the taxi driver said with a smile.

"And all this time, I thought these little creatures were something to fear," Jacques said. "Rebirth? Well, Samy, it feels appropriate for this moment in time. I want to thank you for..."

Before Jacques could finish his sentence, Samy slipped away. A black car with tinted windows had just pulled into the small parking lot. Two men jumped out of the car. They wore black suits, white shirts, narrow black ties, and dark sunglasses. They asked to speak to Mr. Gerard. Hearing this, Mrs. Montgomery went to find Jacques.

Finding him by Sadat, she said, "Excuse me, Jacques, but I believe the CIA wishes to speak to us."

"The CIA wants to speak to us?" Jacques echoed. "Is it about Mr. Smith?"

Mrs. Montgomery shook her head. "No, I asked them about Mr. Smith. They said they just need to ask us a few questions about Charles' parents."

"Charles' parents?" Jacques repeated in wonderment.

Turning to Jacques, David's grandmother asked, "Just out of curiosity, Jacques, did Samy ever mention his last name?"

"No, he said he just goes by Samy," Jacques replied. "Why?"

"Because a man in a Hawaiian shirt happens to be standing behind the bus we came in," she said. "He is just near enough to hear anything the Men in Black have to say."

Jacques looked over at the bus. Behind the double rear tires, he could see a pair of vibrant green flip-flops. Taking the lead, Mrs. Montgomery walked to the men standing by their car. She introduced Jacques. "This is Jacques Gerard, the guardian of Charles Dayton Stratton III while he is in Egypt."

"Good, we wanted to talk to Mr. Gerard," the taller of the two men said.

Mrs. Montgomery held up a hand. "Before you answer, Jacques, I would like to ask these gentlemen why the CIA is interested in Charles' parents."

"We didn't say we were CIA," the younger of the two men said.

"You didn't have to," said the woman in the safari hat with a stem of lavender tucked into its band.

The two Men in Black looked at each other. The older one shrugged his shoulders. The younger one said, "All we know thus far is that Mr. and Mrs. Stratton were in the area of Belize. Their boat has been found, but they have not."

"Can you tell us why the CIA would be interested in a couple on vacation in Belize?" Mrs. Montgomery inquired with an innocent smile.

"We just need to know when you last heard from the Strattons, and when you are due to hear from them," the older man said with a smile that matched that of Mrs. Montgomery.

Jacques answered, "I heard from Mr. Stratton just before we left, three-and-a-half weeks ago. We talked about this trip to Egypt. He told me that he and his wife would be out of touch for a little more than a month. The month isn't over yet."

"Do you know a Mr. Smith?" the younger man asked.

"Excuse me, gentlemen. Do you have any identification on you?" Mrs. Montgomery asked.

Jacques looked at David's grandmother and decided she was even more suspicious than Charles.

"Just one last thing. Where can we get in touch with you, should we have any more questions?" the younger agent asked.

"As professional CIA agents, I believe you know perfectly well how to get in touch with us, at least with Jacques Gerard. Goodbye, gentlemen."

"I do not understand you, Mrs. Montgomery," Jacques whispered as they walked away from the agents. "These men gave us terrible news about Charles' parents, announcing that they might be missing in Belize, and you sounded uncooperative."

"Jacques, I don't like this one bit," she said, shaking her head. "Belize is not at all a safe place, especially for a twelve-year-old boy, a professor of philosophy, a co-principal, and a mysterious taxi driver."

"What about a mystery writer?" Jacques asked, squinting as he looked directly at Mrs. Montgomery.

"As a writer, I generally concoct my own mysteries. I sincerely hope that my involvement in this real-life mystery will not become a trend," she declared. "Jacques, I am sure the Strattons will be in contact with you and Charles soon, but we shall keep our bags packed, just in case."

Samy walked by Mrs. Montgomery and Jacques in his neon-green flip-flops and rolled-up pants He gave them the shaka sign.

"What does Samy mean by that gesture, Jacques?" Mrs. Montgomery asked.

"Samy said it is the surfer greeting. It might be encouraging someone to 'just hang loose'—or it might mean a wild wave is imminent."

ABOUT THE AUTHOR

Penelope Torribio

Penelope Torribio is an Author, Educator, Teacher-trainer, Behavior Transformation Specialist, Singer-songwriter, and Family Entertainer.

She is the visionary founder of 1 World Education and the innovative originator of the Connected Classroom. Her leadership has brought students together to develop habits of creative thinking, particularly thinking like writers. She is a teacher-trainer and a noted presenter for her interactive shows teaching THINK LIKE A WRITER from the stage in the United States and in India, Thailand, Indonesia, and Myanmar.

She is the author of ArtSmart, superior learning in the inclusive Classroom
Future in Our Hands, what everyone should know about education
Directive Drawing for Diagnosis, Intervention and Development

Never Get Too Close to a Fish, a book about the death of a pet
Einstein in My Garden, photos and reflections on bugs
The Magic in You, from vacant lot to community garden

Penelope has recently come out with a new novel series she calls Edu-tain-ment Novels where she teaches concepts in THINK LIKE A WRITER through her exciting adventure stories, *The Ghost of the Jangling Keys* and *The Ghost of Tomb 11, Tel el Amarna, Egypt.*

www.ingramcontent.com/pod-product-compliance
Lightning Source LLC
Chambersburg PA
CBHW071328020726
47502CB00001B/6